The

Book

Of

Phoebe

✝

J. Fez

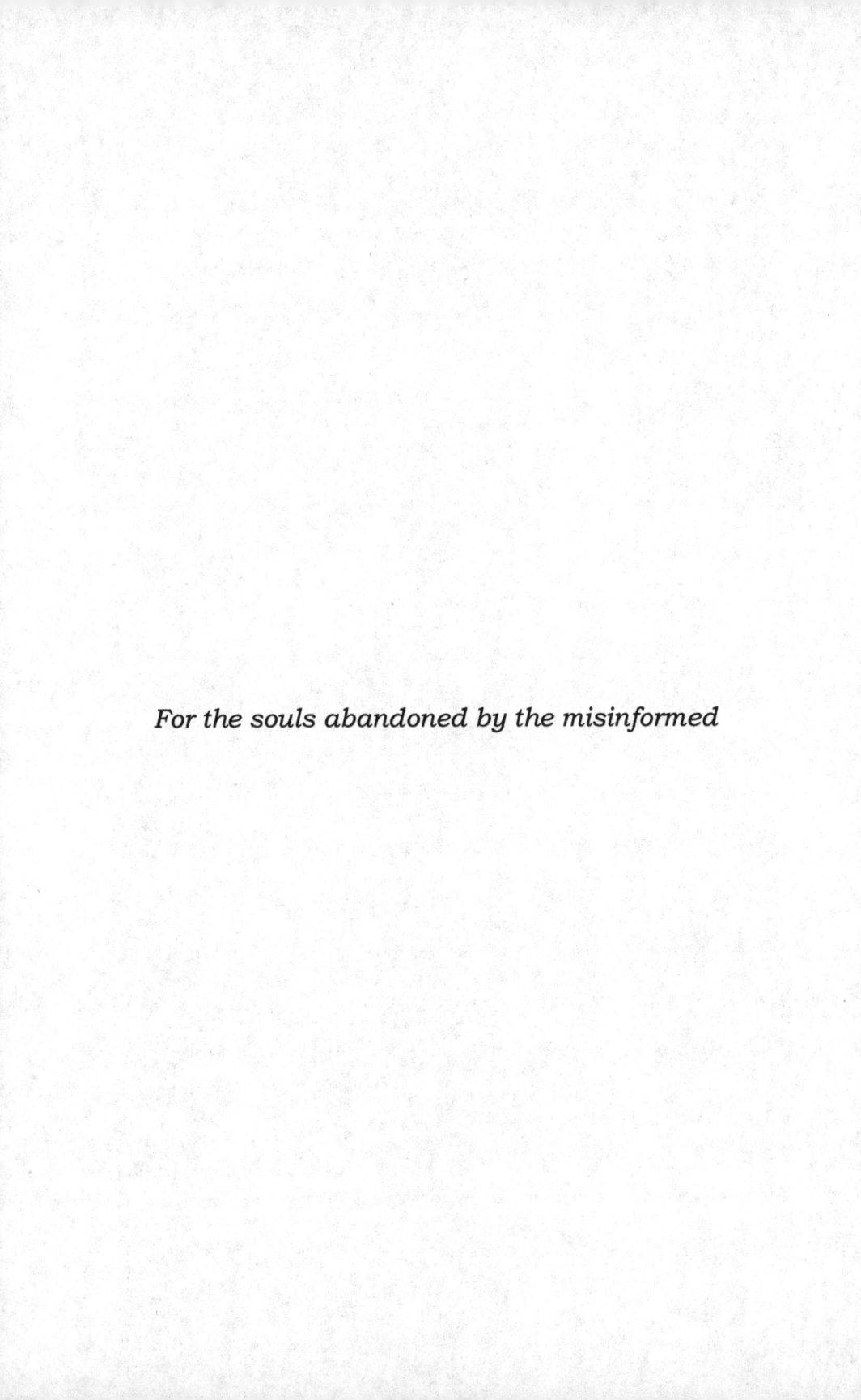

For the souls abandoned by the misinformed

"We are born to love before we're taught to hate."

Author's Note

I am not a religious expert by any stretch of the imagination. While I am spiritual, this book was written as a way for my Midwestern upbringing to finally come to terms with my sexuality. The small towns surrounding my development rejected my presence within religious sanctums and perceived my interest in faith as inconceivable. The prejudice within one of these very towns had led to some rather traumatic instances within my upbringing. Like most, I was made to hate myself.

All the biblical information referenced within this novel was given to me by various members of an All-Inclusive Church. After numerous coffees and dinners with pastors and members, I chose the topics I felt needed to be addressed. I was also advised to view The Good Book differently. If man was to put each passage under a microscope, we could then begin to notice the Bible is simply a compilation of letters in which the writer was recollecting on their journey through faith. This is why we see an overexuberance of contradictions. One man's journey will never be the same as another's. Each individual lived through God in their own unique way. The world was rough with so much still left to discover. Through faith, man was able to struggle yet still survive and persevere. This in turn led to the various extremes we see within The Holy Bible. As we see, these primitive contradictions still plague mankind today due to various groups viewing these written letters as binding Dogma rather than stories of lessons and faith.

Many heterosexual "womb to tomb" Christians were eager to clarify religious teachings when I'd sought help in understanding the most vexing passages. People who often hadn't even known a queer person but knew they loved everyone regardless of who they fell in love with.

Practicing faith deeply and openly often comes across as off-putting to the queer community due to the stigma surrounding organized religion. An innumerable amount of people long for a sense of belonging yet refuse to look toward religion as a result of trauma surrounding this same stigma. Christianity is often associated with hate and prejudice because a person less informed told them their existence was shameful. A vast majority of the people who use Bible quotes in attempts to spread hate, seemingly know very little about the teachings of Jesus Christ. Often acting similarly to the ones who spat on Him during His crucifixion. Who abandoned Him in His hour of need.

The damage misinformed "people of God" cause to innocent lives is insurmountable. They hide behind religious pretense as an excuse to be terrible to others. It's inexcusable no matter how hard they try to blame God for their wrongdoings. This story was written with the intention of shedding light on all the misinformation and quell the anger and hurt the misinformed may have caused. However, I can't stress enough that this is nothing more than a group of Christians' interpretation on what the Bible is trying to say.

No official religious denomination is given on purpose. Regardless of references to specific denominations, it is merely a platform in which you, the reader, can see your own past traumas and hopefully charter a journey through them. A journey toward setting aside the misplaced anger a prejudiced person gifted you.

While this story is a work of fiction, it is meant to affirm the plethora of people who believe they are not allowed to be who they are and still maintain a relationship with God. I take full responsibility for any inaccuracies and deeply apologize for whom it may offend. Certain topics within this book may be troubling for some readers. Regardless of this being a romance with a HEA, much like real life, the journey is often gritty and disconcerting. Take care of your mental health and read the content warnings on my Instagram *@JFezAuthor* before deciding to read this story.

Also, please continue to the end for the playlist associated with this novel and bonus material, including an exclusive look into the second book within the Mystic Harbor Series.

For those who choose to proceed, I hope Phoebe and Blake's journey elicits a (hopefully positive) response within you by the end. Enjoy!

Chapter 1
Phoebe

The things we do for family.

I was cleaning my apartment a week ago, when I heard a knock at my door. And there was my mother with this…thing. The dress has long sleeves and is made of velvet. VELVET! With a column of sequins down the middle. It reminds me of a very tacky Christmas dress. Yet, of course, my mother insisted I wear it. "Doris made it for you! We don't want her to think we don't like it, Phoebe."

Sometimes, I wish I could be someone else. Don't get me wrong, I love my life. I love my job; I love my parents, best friends, and even my boyfriend. What I don't love is this dress. I tried to tell my mother it was hideous when she'd given it to me.

"But I actually *don't* like it," I'd whined.

My mother shot me her infamous glare. The one that says *don't-make-me-and-your-father-look-bad-in-front-of-the-congregation.* Ever since I can remember, she'd been putting my sister and me in matching outfits, forcing us to smile in every picture. Her hallmark phrase when we were young was, "Children are meant to be seen, not heard."

At least it'll keep me warm during the service, I think. The Nave is always a crisp sixty-five, so this might be a blessing in disguise. The dress is floor length and covers every inch of skin I have, which I find enjoyable. Maybe not in the warm spring weather we've been having lately, but nonetheless. It clings to my body in a way that almost gives the impression I exercise. Realistically, I'm thin, but I've never been toned. I have the female version of a "dad bod" for a twenty-six-year-old woman, but this dress is fitting to my body in a way that's almost making me confident.

With this new resolution, I give myself another once over in the mirror, wrinkling my nose and making a disgusted face. *Not working. Just keep getting ready.* I tame my wavy black hair, which is always worsened by sleep, with my straightener. There is no reason anyone in the congregation should ever see it like this. What would everyone say if they didn't always see me at my best?

My mother's lessons sit on my shoulders like a permanent backpack I can reach into before making any decisions or conducting myself around other people.

Now it's time for the makeup, which isn't anything flashy. I typically go with nude palettes. Red is the color of a harlot and Lord knows I'm anything but; given I'm voluntarily saving all of myself for marriage. After setting my foundation, I highlight my cheekbones, add a neutral eye shadow and lip gloss. A little bit of mascara, and I'm done.

I like knowing where everything is. Being able to reach for my brush without looking is a comfort I can't describe. I'm not well with change or things deviating from structure. My soul thrives on it.

I always look, though.

When reaching for something, I mean. I need to. To be sure. I like the idea of knowing I don't have to, but I could never trust something solely on faith. I need to see it and touch it. Double, triple, quadruple check it. My mantra is 'everything has a home,' and all things need to find their way back to their home when we are finished with them. My life is very meticulously put together with structure. If one thing were to be out of place, I would come apart at the seams. Call it perfectionism. I call it peace.

Before leaving my apartment, I clean the few dishes in the sink. One of the perks of living alone—I only have my own messes to clean. I grab the trash in the bin, replace the bag, and head out the door, doing a quick once-over before locking it. I can't stand coming home to a messy house. Heaven forbid something is out of place when I return.

✝

Easter was two weeks ago, and the flowers are finally blooming, eliciting a wondrous spirit of rebirth within the crisp, fresh air. Leaves are returning to the trees, and with it, a beautiful mix of pink and white petals flow in the breeze along the street as I stroll. The sweet, citrusy scent of the magnolia trees is light and clean and fill my lungs with an eagerness for adventure.

How can people not believe in the beauty of God's creations? You can literally feel His presence in the air! He made all of this, and people pass by it, not even giving it a second glance. My church isn't far from my apartment, and I refuse to ignore His message. It's too nice of a day not to walk.

Cool wind swishes through my hair as I walk past a few of the old historic houses while taking in the fresh pine of the trees. The gentle breeze is making me grateful I decided not to drive. It's the perfect temperature.

Mystic Harbor's population of twenty or so thousand is divided into predominantly two districts: The regular and the Seedy Side. There's also the rich resort district but the general population are generally determined on whether they're Seedy or regular. It has one hospital, one high school, and two middle and elementary schools. There are more churches than banks on my side of town which some of the members of my church associate to why it's safe to live here.

Regardless of the number of churches, there's only one worth mentioning. The best church in town—the Evangelical Church of Mystic Harbor—but everyone calls it EC for short. Okay, I might be a little biased since it's the church I grew up in, but my friends and family are here, and most of the older members watched me grow. The community has done everything for me. From teaching me to ride a bike in the parking lot, to helping me with grants and scholarships for college. It isn't always easy keeping up impressions, but obviously, the juice is worth the squeeze in the long run.

"Hey, Phoebe!" Jaime, the barista at Blessed Beans, greets me as I enter. "Cutting it close!"

"Yeah, but I need my coffee!" I sway up to the register where she's already ringing me up.

"Bet you're grateful Lent is over." She turns to make my drink.

"You have no idea." This year, I'd given up coffee. Which was fine…except I never start my day without a steaming cup to wake the senses. But I did it and learned what it meant to sacrifice and show self-discipline. Longest forty days of my life. "It's beautiful out there!"

"It is!" she agrees, already starting on my drink. "I'll have to be sure to pay close attention to God's presence while I'm walking to service!"

"Oh, you'll definitely feel Him today!" I say, fighting a smirk crawling up one side of my face, watching her make my hazelnut flat white with an extra shot. I wave goodbye. "See you at service!" Then I continue my journey.

✝

My congregation is small in comparison to some of the others in the area, but what EC lacks in numbers, it more than makes up for with the community. This church is one of the only churches left from when the town was first colonized by pilgrims, making it the small, old chapel style with the pointed roof and white paneling. A bell housed in a small opening at the very top rings out three times, reminding people service will be starting soon.

The members of EC are quite the judgy and opinionated bunch—with good reason, I'm sure. We're taught the correct way the Bible was meant to be interpreted. But let's say you were seen hanging out on the Seedy Side without a good explanation. You'd be labeled an unkempt individual. I don't think I'll ever understand this one. It doesn't seem very Christian in my opinion.

Reformation teaches you to question everything. I refuse to believe something without first doing my own research. To this day, my father says my curiosity is an amazing gift. Not everyone dares to find their own answers. Over three-fourths of my congregation believe things exclusively because the pastor says it. Which is great because our pastor would never lead us astray, but when you've known him your entire life, it'd stand to reason you'd love him the way I do.

As I walk up to EC, there's all the usual faces, yet my eyes seem to focus on a face I've never seen before. She has a short jaw-length bob with the sides slightly shorter, chin length. Which isn't normally a hairstyle women who attend this church fashion. Long hair down or in a bun is really more their style. Young or old, the hair is the same.

Making matters worse, her hair is black, showing random highlights of blue underneath as the sun shines down on it. The church isn't much for dyed hair, that's for sure. Her clothes are also interesting. Her gray slacks are clearly from the men's section of Target. While she is lanky and tall, there's a very slight mound of breasts clinging to her very fitting black button-up. Which is the only way I can tell she is, in fact, a woman. I, as well as everyone here, know she's not from this side of town. Something about her seems familiar, though.

"Hey, honey! I see you're wearing my dress!" Doris greets me with the exuberance of a child, bracing her hands on my arms before squeezing. She is wearing a sundress with blue and yellow flowers on it. She's a short and stout woman. Like a teapot.

Oh right. I forgot I'm still in this ugly dress. I feel stupid. *The things we do for family,* I remind myself. This isn't my style at all. Sundress, sure. Maxi, sign me up. But this? I feel like I am wearing a trash bag made out of velvet. "Hey, Mrs. Doris, hi!" I pull her in for a hug. "Oh, I just love the dress!" I paste on my best smile and pray I'm convincing enough for her to believe I thoroughly enjoy it.

"Oh honey, you mean it?" *Yup, she bought it.* "It only took me three hours." *I can tell.* "Just cut the pattern and threw it together!"

I imagine her buying the hideous fabric and deciding *this* would make a cute dress. "Oh, you have the eye of a beautiful seamstress, Mrs. Doris!" I say instead.

"I was thinking about making you another one!" She practically jumps, which, at her age, I'd rather she didn't.

Panic fills my mind at the thought of being forced to wear her next monstrosity. I don't want to picture it.

"Oh no, there are plenty of less fortunate who deserve your abilities more." I place a calming hand on her bicep. "Allow me to stay humble. I'm not as deserving as those in need, Mrs. Doris. You could even clothe the children with these abilities!"

"Phoebe, you are such a sweet soul," she says flatly. "Truly, God has blessed your parents with an angel. Speaking of which, where are your parents?" she asks, scanning the crowd on the lawn.

"I'm not sure, but when I see them, I'll send them your way," I say, squeezing her arm before walking toward my friends and boyfriend. I don't want her to keep me here any longer.

I can't explain why, but I find myself glancing back again at the new guest of the church. She seems to be extremely nervous, judging by her demeanor. Is she thinking about leaving? I don't want her to think this isn't a place for her. No one in search of God should ever feel as though they aren't allowed to seek refuge within any church, especially not ours. I hold up a finger to my friends and boyfriend, who stare at me in confusion as I change my course, walking over to this mystery.

As I walk up, a million thoughts swim through my mind. What if she doesn't want anyone talking to her? What if she *is* wanting to leave? What if she's rude? But as I'm about to turn back, she makes eye contact, noticing my approach. *Oh crud. No turning back now.* I try to plaster on my most welcoming persona.

I'm about to open my mouth when I'm met with the most radiating blue eyes known to man. They aren't icy blue. No…they're deeper. Like an ocean washing away my next words. *What did I come over here for?* I think, breaking eye contact almost immediately finding the ground instead.

"Let me guess?" she asks. Her voice is an octave higher than I'd imagined. I was expecting low or raspy, but rather it's a nice alto that could probably sing some soprano if she tried. "I need to leave?"

"No!" I respond a little too hastily.

Peering up from the grass, I settle for the advice my etiquette teacher had once taught me. *"If you're ever nervous to meet someone's gaze, simply look at the center of their forehead. Where their nose meets their eyebrows."*

I do just so. "I was going to ask if you were new here."

"You could say that, yeah." She rubs the back of her neck, shifting her gaze around the yard. For reasons that make no sense to me, I'm moved to ease her anxiety. *God is giving you a job, Phoebe.* I think. *Don't back out.* There honestly is no reason to be uncomfortable here.

"It's a really great place. Don't worry," I tell her, still fixed between her eyebrows. No unibrow. Not a single hair out of place. Did she get them professionally done, or was she miraculously born with perfect eyebrows? I'm kind of envious, honestly. Even though I know better than to be jealous. "The pastor does an amazing sermon. If you stay, you can see for yourself."

I really want her to stay, and I don't know why. *No, Phoebe, God wants her to stay, and He's called upon you. He must believe you to be the best person for this task. Don't question His message. Besides,* I try to remind myself. *New members are a good thing for the church. Of course, you want her here.*

She shoots a slight smirk at me, which causes my eyes to divert from the top of her nose back to her eyes. My stomach swoops like I'm going down a hill. "Don't worry, I'm staying."

I try my best to smirk back and find myself yet again glancing at the ground. The air between us feels thicker than I like, and I can't figure out why. All I know is I need to leave. "Okay, have a good service," I mutter hastily, turning on my heels before she can respond and keep me planted there for any longer. I try not to walk too quickly, but the further I get away from that woman, the more I can seemingly breathe again.

"What was that about?" Eve asks when I finally reach my two best friends and boyfriend at the front steps of the chapel. Eve has been in my life since she moved here in the sixth grade. She can be quite pushy at the best of times and always surrounds herself with others, soaking up as much of the energy in the room as possible.

"Why does it matter?" Zoe responds.

Zoe is a light-skinned woman with long, tight, curly hair. Eve is exactly the opposite with her milky skin, freckles, and chest length dark red hair. I've known Zoe since we were born. Our parents are lifelong friends, and our mothers deliberately planned for children at the same time. We're only three months apart in age. There are even pictures of us bathing together as toddlers. Our family albums are practically interchangeable.

"Maybe she was just introducing herself to a newcomer." She waves her arm passively. "It's not a sin, Eve."

Eve's face scrunches with clear disgust. "Umm, have you seen her? The girl *screams* sins." I hope the woman can't hear this.

"Honestly, Zo, I have to agree with Eve," Ethan, my boyfriend of a year and a half, chimes in, resting his arms on the railing of the steps. A white collar is folded over the neckline of his tight maroon sweater vest, accentuating his broad shoulders before descending to his well-defined core. "What would possess someone to think they could show up to church looking like that?"

As I'm about to explain, my mother crunches through the grass behind me. Swinging one arm around my back—not to genuinely show affection but to mumble, barely moving her mouth, "Did you see her?"

"The girl?" I respond, peering over to where the enigmatic woman is scrolling intently on her phone.

"Of course, the girl. Who else?" My mother shifts her scrutiny around the entire group. What would the congregation think if she were talking poorly about someone else? "She has no business here."

"Well, hang on, Mrs. A." Zoe's face scrunches incredulously. "She has just as much business seeking God as we do."

"No amount of praying can fix her predisposition," my mother scorns the new visitor, raking her brown eyes up and down our guest's men's apparel.

Eve and Ethan cover their mouths, snickering.

"She has a point." Ethan's voice is all gravel as he pushes out his chest, lifting his nose high up in the air. I have a sudden urge to slap that look off his face. "No saving a queer."

"How do you know she's…*queer?*" I whisper the word "queer," almost embarrassed. It feels like I'm saying a curse word.

"Baby, look at her! Would you wear that?"

"Do you see what I'm wearing?" I reference the dress and watch as my mother turns away, waving me off.

One of the sun's rays beam down on me like a spotlight. My skin sticks to the velvet material of this horrid dress as people who call themselves my family ignore my discomfort. I try to remember whether I put on deodorant before I left the house today. I can't decide which is worse: checking if I smell, or pretending I don't.

After a moment, Eve sighs, holds out her hand and tilts her head in my direction. "Yeah, but you had to wear that for Mrs. Doris. Miss Boy Clothes decided to look like a guy all on her own." She waves her hand up and down in the direction of the newcomer. "And none of it is from the ladies' sections."

Seven-year-old Nora shrieks from behind me as little Eli tags her. "You're it!" he shouts, pushing through my group of friends. We laugh as Vanessa Arlington admonishes him, making her son apologize and say 'excuse me.' Which he does hastily before continuing his wild antics.

"So, wearing guys' clothes makes you…that word?" I can't say it. I don't like it. Honestly, this entire conversation is making me even more uncomfortable than this stupid dress. I pray for God to blow a cool breeze through the old maple tree behind us, said to be older than EC itself.

"It's not the only thing, but it helps. Trust me, babe, that woman is a dyke."

My head snaps up in disbelief at his words, but my mother grabs his wrist before I can slap him. "Language!" she says low. Her eyes burning a warning as he cowers with embarrassment. *Good.* My mother shifts her focus back on me. "Did I see you talking to her?"

Oh, finally I get to answer the initial question so I can go inside. Away from these people and out of the scorching radiation, causing sweat to settle on my lower back. I shift my weight to the other foot. "Yeah, to say hi. Introduce myself. She's new. I figured the more, the merrier."

My mother's eyes practically bulge out of her head. I wish she'd blink. "Honey, we don't need her kind at this church. We're trying to expand the congregation, sure," she tilts her head, "but with one comes many. Older members would leave in search of a different church. Your father could even lose his job." She drops her hand on my shoulder, squeezing the muscle there. "It's best to keep them away."

"I guess that makes sense," I respond, even though it really doesn't. I peek at Zoe, who has her arms crossed, shaking her head.

"Maybe Pastor Pete will have a sermon that scares her off." Ethan lifts his shoulders. "One that explains this is a place for the truly righteous."

"Maybe drop a hint or two that this sermon is tailored made for her to get out?" Eve supplies, wrapping her arm around Ethan's. I hate it when she does this. Flirting with him, feigning amusement at the pretentious stuff he says as if I'm not even here.

I join nervously in their mirth because I'm not sure what to say or do. "Well, I'm gonna go in. You know I hate if I'm not in the center pew."

"Typical Phoebe. I'll join you." Zoe's light hazel eyes look almost piercing as she glares at the group before looping her arm through mine and walking me into the narthex. "They annoy me sometimes," she says when the door finally booms shut behind us.

"Yeah, church should be for everyone," I say.

"And what if she's seeking repentance?" Zoe adds. "Is she not allowed to because she doesn't enjoy the feel of women's clothing?"

"Right now, *I'm* not even enjoying the feel of women's clothing," I mutter.

"Yeah, seriously, Phoebz. It's hideous." Zoe wrinkles her nose.

"I feel like Christmas. I can't wait to get out of this thing," I whisper as the door creaks open, and Mrs. Doris walks inside. "Oops." I share a stifled snicker with Zoe.

"It's okay," she whispers, wiping away a tear of amusement. "I don't think she heard us."

✝

"...In the book of Matthew, Chapter 28, Verses 19 and 20, it is written, 'Therefore go and make disciples of all nations, baptizing them in the name of the Father and of the Son and of the Holy Spirit, and teaching them to obey everything I have commanded you. And surely I am with you always, to the very end of the age.' And isn't it our duty to spread the good news of God's love? That is, in fact, what evangelical means, of course, the spreading of good news. Why, then, would we keep God for ourselves?" my father speaks, but I can't help but glance over at where the new person is sitting.

She's on the wall farthest from me, also nearing the center, but two pews closer to the front. She is looking intently at the pastor, as if truly trying to take in as much of it as possible. Her posture is very straight and rigid. I wonder if I helped at all when I tried to make her feel at ease. It doesn't seem like it. She is biting her nails as she listens.

"...and we are called to follow Jesus!" My father does his impactful pause, glancing around the congregation, positively radiating. "Amen."

"Amen," we all respond and rise to sing the psalm while they prepare for the communion.

My mind is flooded with a million thoughts as I find myself yet again glancing in her direction as she rises to sing from the book of psalms. I've gotten used to these songs. I swear I know all of them. Okay, maybe not *all* of them, but most.

It's funny, though, watching her slip on the words but still trying to seem like she knows how to read music. At least she's participating. Some of the new folks don't even bother standing when we're asked to. It makes me wonder why they even cared to visit in the first place?

Why is she here? She had to have known she'd be gawked at. Is she seeking repentance, like Zoe said? I know it's not my place to wonder what she could've done. That's between her and God, but I can't stop my brain from being vexed by everything about her. It's just odd. In all my years, no one like her has ever dreamed of stepping foot into EC. Not that I have any issues with it. I worry I'm starting to sound like Eve, Ethan, and my mother. Matthew 7:1 clearly states, "Do not judge, so that you may not be judged." I don't want to be a hypocrite.

"Share this love with your neighbors!" my father shouts, ripping me out of my thoughts. I shake a few hands and am pulled into a few hugs from the older ladies saying, "Peace be with you," to everyone I come in contact with. Some people hate this part of the service, but I find it to be my favorite. Allowing us to join together and share our love for one another.

I glance over. Barely anyone is accepting a handshake from the woman. Which makes me sad, but she is too far away for me to offer her peace. She meets my eye from across the room, and before even thinking it through, I form my hands into a peace sign and mouth the word "peace" to her as well. She beams. I can't help but mirror the expression. I realize I've been grinning for an unreasonable amount of time, so I try to cover it up before anyone notices and asks questions. Wait, why am I hiding my smile in the first place?

We sit back down in our seats, and my mind again begins to wander. Does she know she's being judged? I wonder if it happens often and she's used to that. Does it hurt? Seeing as how she's still here, it must not hurt too bad, right? I decide she must be used to it.

When it's time for communion, I notice she also comes forth to receive the offering. Either she's lying, or she truly has gone through communion. I know for sure this church does not allow an open table. This means only members can receive the sacrament. I wonder, with how judgy everyone has become, if they'll give her the body and blood of Christ. I'd be embarrassed if they didn't. I know my mother doesn't think this strange new guest belongs here, but I don't understand why. Isn't she just as worthy as any of God's other children? Surely she wouldn't be lying about receiving this feast.

Thankfully, she is given both the blood and body. I knew EC wasn't that bad. Not everyone shares the same views as some of the other members. It's a great relief to me. Yet, I still can't seem to figure out why my eyes keep finding their way to her throughout the rest of the service.

✝

By the time I make it out the door after the service, she's gone. It's not like I expected her to wait around and chat with people who clearly don't like her. Even if she did, I was stopped repeatedly by other members of the church to talk about this and that. It's very hard to get away sometimes. Usually, they'll go on and on while I'm desperately coming up with polite ways to excuse myself. The second I do manage to escape one conversation, however, I'm roped into another one.

When I make it to the yard, my mother is already up my butt to find my father. "I'm pretty sure he's still inside, Mom."

She lets out a sigh. "Well, tell him I'll meet him at the house." She turns and walks down the street before making a sharp right around the building.

I walk back into the church and head to the office. It's there I find my father talking to Zoe. Hushed voices halt at my approach. I wonder why. Could this have something to do with our new guest?

"Hey, Dad," I say, slumping down on the second sofa. "Beautiful sermon today."

"I'll talk to you later, Pastor Pete," Zoe says before giving my father a hug and walking out of the room.

"What were you guys talking about?" I ask, but I already know what he's going to say.

"That is between us and God, Phoebe. Is everything okay?" he asks calmly. My father has a voice so low and calm, it'd always soothe me to sleep, and as a result, I've always felt closer to him than my mother. Priscilla Appleton has always been about appearances, whereas my father is surprisingly more easygoing. "Let kids be kids," he used to tell my mother when she was getting out of control with impressions. "People expect them to be kids. Not robots."

"Yeah, Mom wanted me to let you know she left. 'Meet you at home,' she said."

"I figured as much," he responds, stretching as he stands up. "I'll give her a call and let her know I'll be late. I have counseling scheduled with the Melvin's at noon."

"Okay," I say, standing on my tiptoes to give him a kiss on the cheek. My father is a tall man, but not lanky. He used to have muscles when he was younger, but in his old age, it has turned into a serious dad bod. Probably where I get mine from. "Well, I've done about as much 'Peopling' as I can do today. If you need me, I'll be at my apartment."

"Alright, Peep, be careful walking home."

I spin on my toes cheerily to face him once more. "Always!" I say. "It's a beautiful day."

Chapter 2

Phoebe

I'm not sure why my mind is reeling right now, but I can't stop thinking about the woman at church this morning. Her eyes were kind and familiar. It's hard for me to believe she would be a bad person. Thoughts of her have me standing in my closet after changing out of that god awful dress, running my fingers along the thin fabric of the same black hoodie I've had since high school. I can't explain why, but it reminds me of the woman at the church. The actual owner of this tattered garment, however, is nowhere near the same. But a faint siren is blaring at the base of my skull, drawing them together somehow.

I haven't run into another Seedy Sider since Dakota. Not to mention EC's behavior toward today's unexpected visitor isn't much different from my high school's reaction to Dakota. Both outcasts, trying to exist in a world they sense they'll never fit into. Why is that? This question has plagued me since I was fourteen years old. Some days, I wonder if I'll ever get my answer.

Regardless of the reasoning, holding this hoodie makes me wonder what happened to the ghost from my freshman year.

> It was the first day of high school. As I entered the cafeteria, I couldn't help but notice a table inhabiting a lone girl. I'm not surprised she's wearing a frown, given she's by herself. I decided this simply would not do. I walked past my friends, who seemed very confused, as I headed toward the table where the girl was seated, peering down at her tray while she pushed some corn around with her fork. Her hair was the lightest blonde and hung down right below her collarbone. It was almost white and very straight. Yet her eyebrows were a dark brown.

"This seat taken?" I asked, placing my tray down on the table opposite her, anyway.

"Does it look taken?" she mumbled without glancing up from the corn.

"Phoebe," I said, swinging my foot around the bench.

She finally looked up only briefly to tell me her name. "Dakota." She nodded before allowing her head to fall back to her tray.

I learned she went to Washington Middle School, which is on the Seedy Side. Mystic only had one high school, however, so Seedy Siders tended to enroll in the neighboring town, Cypress's, high school. Her stepfather forced her to attend Mystic, much to her chagrin.

"Look around you, Phoebe. I don't belong here."

I didn't understand.

"You belong wherever you'd like," I said. "No one should be allowed to tell you where you can and can't go."

"Thanks for the vote of confidence, but I don't need your pity."

"It's not pity." I shook my head, flustered.

"It's adorable you think the world accepts everyone so easily," Dakota said as the bell rang for the end of lunch.

"Well," I said, looking up. My body grew warm and cold as I met her gaze. Those eyes. Deep and blue. I divert my gaze to my tray, unable to continue looking. "Maybe we can have lunch again?"

"I mean, I'm surprised you survived this one, but sure." She smirked. "Shouldn't you be sitting with your friends, though?" She gestured toward Eve and Zoe, sitting a few tables down.

Glancing back, Eve mouthed the words "What the f—?" at me as she was getting up from her seat, grabbing her book bag.

"How did you—?"

"The redheaded one has been glaring at me since you walked over. For a second there, I thought she might actually vomit."

"Oh right, Eve. Don't worry, I'm half convinced that's just her face at this point." I rolled my eyes, much to Dakota's amusement.

"What the hell?" Eve asked as I set my bag on the floor in chemistry class, grabbing out a notebook and pencil.

"What?"

"Umm, lunch? You hanging out with Miss Edward Scissorhands."

I try to hide my discomfort by saying, "She doesn't look anything like that."

"Okay, the grudge then." She waved me off. "Whatever. Why were you hanging out with her instead of us? Did we make you mad or something?"

"You're starting to," I mumbled. "She was by herself. I felt bad. I figured she could use a friend. Is that okay?"

"Live your life, Phoebz. But don't come crying to me when everyone is staring at you the same way they look at her."

"And how do they look at her? They don't even know her." I tapped my pencil on my notebook, wishing class would start so Eve would drop it.

"She looks like trouble. Dark clothes? Yeah, people in our circles think that's what devil worshippers wear."

I brushed her off. "No, they don't."

Eve threw her arm around my shoulder. "Just wait, Phoebz. One day you'll be hanging out with her, the next you'll be chained to a table being sacrificed to Beelzebub." Eve winked, letting me know she wasn't serious. She was only worried for me. But Dakota seemed harmless and the people in our circles didn't know anything.

I lay on my couch, staring up at the ceiling. Why does it seem like this is a trending thing? It happened to Dakota and now it's happening to this woman at church. It isn't right. My actions back then weren't much better, but I refuse to accept I am like Eve or my mother. I won't judge a book by its cover. If I see this girl again, I have a moral obligation as a Christian to make it right. I have to make it right for Dakota. Odd doesn't mean bad, and a good Christian would open their heart and accept all of God's children in.

✝

Awaking to the vibration of my phone in my pocket, I push the black hoodie off of my body and sit up. The clock on the wall lets me know it's 3:47 PM. I can't believe I fell asleep on my couch. I'm not much of a napper, but I guess my spiraling brain was enough to wear me out.

My phone is still vibrating as I pull it from my pocket. "ETHAN," the screen says.

"Hello," I answer, voice still heavy with sleep.

"Baby? Did I wake you?" He sounds confused and also like he's driving. I swear he's always driving when he calls me. "I can call back if now's not a good time."

I narrowly avoid telling him it's never a good time. "No, it's okay," I say, clearing my throat, sitting up on the couch. I put him on speaker before tossing my phone on the coffee table. I rub my eyes. "I wasn't planning on falling asleep. I just got to laying down, and it all hit me. What's up?"

"Well…I was wondering if you were doing anything tonight? We haven't gone on a date in a while. Did you want to catch dinner?" he asks bashfully.

He knows I'll say yes. I can't really recall a time I've told him no unless it came to sex. "Depends," I joke. "Where you taking me?"

I stand, zipping up the hoodie, heading to the closet in my room.

"Well, that depends…where do you want to go?"

I roll my eyes, putting the jacket on a hanger. "Are we sitting down or going for something fast?"

"Your wish is my command, m'lady."

I hate when he does this. The pet names and not knowing what he wants. Always pressing it on to me. He thinks it's cute and I'm sure someone out there somewhere might think it is. I'm not that kind of girl, though. Then again, I'm not even sure I know what kind of girl I am. I just know it isn't that.

I place the hanger back on the rack and rub the frayed fabric of the sleeve between my fingers.

"Pick me up at 7:00," I sigh. "I'm sure I'll make a decision by then."

✝

At the very edge of my side of Mystic Harbor, overlooking the ocean is a beautiful Harrison & Hayes Resort. Only the most well to do people can afford a room within this luxury utopia. The rich and powerful who vacation at H&H seldom step foot outside of the resort. Can't really see a reason why they'd want to, given the private beaches, various activities, and multiple five-star restaurants. The Dock is a floating restaurant within walking distance of the resort. It's my favorite restaurant and more crowded than I had anticipated when I'd suggested it. Luckily, they bring us through the low lighting to a candlelit table next to a window overlooking the ocean outside. Perks of being my father's daughter: optimal seating and no waiting lists. The Harrison's have been members of EC's congregation long before partnering with Hayes to create the world-renowned resort. Hence the perks.

"Do you know what today is?" Ethan asks as he closes his menu, pushing his elbows up on the rich, dark maple of the table to get closer to me.

"Sunday?" I say, pretending to no avail to care while peering out the window at the pinks and oranges of sun beginning to set.

Ethan's great. He really is, but sometimes I feel as though, besides attending the same church, we have nothing in common. He didn't even attend EC when I first met him. He only started going to get closer to me after. Even back then, I found almost everything he did to be slightly annoying. It's hard to put on a face the more annoying he is.

I have no real reason to end things, though. He's a great guy…even if the mere sound of his voice grates on my nerves. He has some off-putting qualities, but his one redeeming quality is his ability to compromise. When he realizes he's done something that bothers me, he encourages me to talk about it. *"Communication is the foundation to any relationship."* What can you expect from a child psychologist?

After I express my feelings, he always works on the issue. It's irritating. How can you break up with someone when you'd be the bad guy for ending it? The church would side with him, and my mother would kill me for appearing bad in front of the congregation.

"Well," he lifts a shoulder in contemplation, "yes…we had church. Besides that." His lips part nervously to expose a few perfectly straight teeth while running a hand through his short surfer hair.

"No?" I respond, hoping I'm decently masking my irritation. He could probably do all this boyfriend stuff without me in all honesty. "Should I?" Like I said, when he notices something's bothering me, he encourages me to talk and works to solve the issue. It just takes him forever to realize I'm upset and I hate being an imposition with my feelings.

"Two years ago," he checks the deep blue screen of his silver Montblanc watch, "at…wait for it…"

I wait, but the moment seems to drag for an hour. I'm tempted to scream *WILL YOU GET TO THE POINT ALREADY?!* But I don't. Instead, I grow jealous of the seagulls outside this window and their ability to fly off to anywhere they want, whenever they feel like it. *Would he even notice if I slipped into a coma right now? Or would he just keep counting down the seconds on his expensive watch?*

"…this very moment we met at the skating rink!" His chin lifts high in the air as if I'm supposed to reward him for remembering such a random detail. I have to admit it is kind of impressive, though I refuse to feed his already swollen ego.

My eyes widen in disbelief. "Gosh, you remember the time? Why?"

"Because! I had made plans with Reese to play poker at 8:00 that night. I remember walking to the concessions counter and staring up at the clock, and it said 7:27. Then I turned my head, and I couldn't look away. The prettiest girl in the skating rink was ordering a hot dog. I thought, 'So she likes hot dogs.'" He winks. I fight the urge to throw up. Comments like that are the reason it took me six months to finally agree to date him. Well, and the fact he'd joined my church and started following me around like a lost puppy.

"I remember," I say through gritted teeth, bunching up a ball of my dress with my hand under the table. "Because you said it." I adorn my most mocking tone, "'So you like hot dogs, huh?'" Then, rolling my eyes, I add, "And then you laughed for five minutes solid."

"It wasn't five minutes." He sweeps me off, choosing yet again to take my comment as playfulness. "But hey I've learned a lot since then." He lifts his head confidently.

"Have you?" I deadpan.

He holds his hands up. "Hey! I don't make sexual jokes anymore! I also didn't know your dad was the pastor of the most influential church in Mystic. Even if I had…most PKs are wild."

"Yup." I swirl my straw around my glass. "I'm just boring."

"Not boring! I never said boring. I…" He pauses, eyes searching…is he beginning to realize I'm upset? He shakes off whatever fleeting thought had entered his mind. "I got you this."

Nope. The lights are on, but apparently nobody's home.

He reaches into his satchel and pulls out a crushed rose. Why did he put it in his bag? As he hands it to me, a few of the red petals fall onto the table.

"Thanks?" I say, tilting my head, trying to smell the flower to let him know I appreciate the gesture. Only the scent of expensive cologne he'd gotten for Christmas inhabits the petals. How long has this flower been in his bag?

"You don't like it." He says it as a statement, not a question, as his shoulders slump in defeat.

I frown, searching his hurt brown eyes. "No, Ethan, it's just—"

"—How we doing?" a young, overexuberant waiter interrupts. "You guys about ready to order? Or do you need some more time?"

"We'll need—"

"—I'll have the chicken alfredo," I interrupt. The sooner we can get this over with, the sooner I can go back to…well, I don't really have anything else, but honestly, anything is better than whatever this is. "Is it possible to get extra chicken?"

"Of course." The waiter scribbles down my order before turning to Ethan. "And for you?"

Ethan shrinks a little in his seat before finally ordering the steak, rare. Which is disgusting. Like, it's not even cooked. But judge not lest ye be judged. If he wants to get E. Coli, I won't stop him.

After the waiter leaves, Ethan peers around the restaurant. His favorite thing to do is people watch which I'm also not into. It doesn't matter how many times I tell him, either. It's his go-to conversation starter.

"Can you believe church today?" he whispers.

I glance up from my straw. *When did I start swirling again?* "What do you mean?"

"The gay chick," he supplies. "What on earth would possess her to think church was okay? Especially *our* church."

"I don't see why she wouldn't be allowed to repent for her sins." Heat rises to my cheeks. Why am I getting this angry? "Besides, do you actually know if she's…that?"

"Gay? No," he shakes his head disbelievingly, "but like your mom said, she could corrupt the church. She could bring us all down."

"How can you say that if you don't even know her?" I ask. "For all we know, she could be a mother or searching for a husband. Maybe she has a boyfriend. How can you judge her without knowing anything about her?"

"It's her type. Were we not looking at the same person?" he asks, his body growing more rigid by the second. He's pulling at the cuffs of his dress shirt.

"I don't know." I stand my ground, leaning back in my chair, crossing my arms. "I don't know her."

It'd be ridiculous for him to get upset after judging someone unjustly. What? I'm supposed to go along with it? He can be as mad as he wants with me because I'll never stoop to his level. You'd think he'd know me better after two years…as of today, apparently.

"Are you pissed off at me or something?" It comes out as a whisper as he scans around the restaurant, clearly hoping no one is watching us.

The million-dollar question! Finally. And the skies have parted. Praise Jesus! Those wheels have started turning. Someone give this man an award!

"Language," I say flatly. He knows I hate swearing, but that doesn't stop him from letting out a disdainful breath, anyway. "I don't like you casting judgment on others. I've told you this. Yet you always seem to think that one day, I'll join you in the hazing."

He beams at me sympathetically. "I'm looking out for your father's church, Phoebe." He reaches for my hand across the table, but I pull away.

"Don't," I hiss, making sure no one is witnessing me making a scene.

His eyes search mine, desperately trying to make amends. "If your father loses the congregation, what then? If he allows sin to fill every nook and cranny of the church, what happens then, Phoebe? Does your dad retire? Because no God-respecting church will ever allow him to spread the word of God again. Not knowing what they know."

I examine my lap, fidgeting with my fingers. We both know we've reached an impasse. Neither one of us is going to get through to the other, instead sitting here as a long silence settles between us until our food arrives. *Finally!* I think and begin eating. I'm eating entirely too fast. I hope I don't get a stomachache, but Lord, I need this to end already.

✝

After dinner, we park outside my apartment in Ethan's new Chevy Silverado. Not like he or I know the first thing about cars, though. He even pays to have someone install new wiper blades. After a moment of silence, I go to reach for the door handle, but he grabs my other hand and pulls me toward him. "Listen, I'm sorry. I can do better." He gives me his best bashful expression. Lifting the armrest between us while shifting to face me. "I know that you care about all of God's creations, but I worry one day you might end up in trouble for it. I know I'm an asshole—"

"Language," I say dully because he doesn't ever watch his mouth, and I know he isn't going to start today.

"But I've gotten better!" he presses on, placing my hands to his chest, gently forcing me to turn my body more toward him. "I love you, Phoebe." He sounds sincere, and I can't devastate him without a response.

"Love you too." I'm looking everywhere but at him when I say it, though. Shifting my weight from one hip to the other in the seat. "I don't like the judgment. I don't like the hatred. And I especially didn't appreciate when you said the word you said this morning before service."

He tilts his head, narrowing his eyes. "What word?" His hand tenses over mine.

"You know…The one that starts with 'D?' My mom had to tell you to watch your mouth."

"Dyke?" I am suddenly irritated all over. This time, he notices instantly.

He drops one hand from mine at his chest and gently strokes a thumb over my cheek. "I'm sorry. No, that's not okay. It won't happen again." He uses the hand massaging my cheek to carefully push my chin up until I meet his gaze. "I promise." He pulls me in delicately and places a kiss on my forehead. After a moment, his mouth trails to my nose, kissing it softly before pulling away. He then places a third kiss on my mouth. It takes a second for my body to register and respond. After what feels like a pause—Ethan doesn't even seem to notice—my mouth begins to open and close mechanically, as it should during kissing. I hate this part. Kissing isn't my thing.

It doesn't take long for his body to shift closer to mine as his hands find my hips. I hear his breathing increase as he slides his tongue into my mouth. Too wet. Too wide. I'm getting spit all over my face. But isn't this how kissing is? Rough and rugged. Filled with passion and desire to devour your partner? All of the romance novels in my mother's bookshelf—she thinks I don't know about, but I've secretly read every one—say it is. Steamy and lustful. I analyzed them growing up, trying to figure out what I was meant to do when the time arose. And one of those moments is seemingly now. A flip switches on in my brain, reminding me it's time to take action.

I wrap my arms around his neck and move my legs to brace him between them. One hand finds its way to my breast over my clothes. He is squeezing uncomfortably hard. I'm halfway afraid he might tear it off. It's like he's turning a radio dial. Seriously? What is happening? Do I tell him to stop? What if I upset him?

His kissing makes me nauseous as I push down the thought of drinking spit. Grabbing some of his hair, I cant my head to the side, pulling his mouth to kiss my neck instead. This seems to entice him more. His kisses are sloppy: all tongue, no suction. I'm struggling to believe anyone could find pleasure from this. Has anyone ever told him any of this is good before? How does he have so much saliva?

Finally, the hand on my breast stops, and I hear the zipper of his pants. Before I know what's happening, he's grabbing my hand from his hair and trying to get me to touch him. This is where I draw the line. I don't want to touch it! And besides, I am a woman of God! Women of God do not touch those things.

"Ethan," I grunt as I try to get his hand to release my wrist. "Stop. Slow down a second."

He does. Ethan is more than a gentleman and has been waiting very patiently for a year and a half for me to be ready. But he knows the rules.

"I know, I know." He sighs into my neck, which now feels cold and drippy. I need a shower ASAP. "Marriage."

"Marriage," I repeat. When we first got together, Ethan used to try to push this. Coming up with little loopholes. *"It's not sex if you just touch it," "It's not sex if I touch you,"* et cetera, et cetera. But about eight months in, I think it really started to settle in for him. No ring, no hanky panky.

Once, after things were intimate, and I told him we needed to stop, he actually tried to propose to me right there in the cab of his truck. And I doubled over in unrestrained amusement. "You're joking," I said. "You think I'm saying yes like this?"

He seemed pretty embarrassed, which caused me to apologize and explain, "No, I only mean, when my future children ask me how Daddy proposed, I don't want it to be 'well, Daddy was trying to *get it on,* and Mommy said no. So right there in his truck, he popped the question. No ring or nothing. And, of course, I said yes.'"

"You don't have to be rude," he'd responded.

And the only logical thing I could think to say in response was, "Well, I'm sorry, but this isn't the right time."

Thing is, I don't even know if I want to have kids. The idea of carrying them is terrifying. I've always found adopting a better option. There's never short supply of children in the world. Why do I have to make another? Why can't I help one already in need of a home? An older, housebroken one.

Realistically, though, I like my peace and quiet. I like my space, and I like my house not trashed every single day. You clean it, they trash it. It sounds like madness. Would I even be a good mother? I worry I wouldn't.

After placing a very short but sweet—preventing him from sticking his tongue into my intestines again—kiss, I tell Ethan goodnight and watch him drive off.

I need a drink. Where'd that come from? I don't drink. I've never been a drinker. Not that it's against what I believe. Even Job took to his wine during times of struggle. Alcohol in moderation isn't a sin. But I've never needed a drink like I need one right now. I peek at my phone. It's 10:30. Way too late to buy a bottle from a liquor store.

Honestly, I'm worried someone from the church might notice me in there and tell my mother I was buying alcohol. My mind doesn't seem to want to go to a liquor store, anyway. A little voice inside of me is telling me to go to a bar. But any bar poses the same dilemma.

Unless...

I hop in my car, grabbing a fast-food napkin from the center console, wiping my neck before pulling out my phone. After a second of scrolling, I hit start on the directions and find myself finally heading to a bar...

...On the Seedy Side of town.

Chapter 3

Phoebe

I'm tired of playing by my mother's rules. Piper would be impressed. My older sister always did enjoy going against my mother's wishes. It was almost a guarantee if my mother told her not to do something, she'd do it. Completely out of spite.

She'd love to see me over here. Maybe not alone. She'd prefer to go with me, but whose fault is it she's not here? She left. Decided the city was a billion times better than being here with me. Just like Zoe and Eve in high school. Just like Dakota. I'd spent an exuberant amount of hours convincing myself I was fine on my own. Tonight comes as no surprise to me.

Doesn't matter that I don't really travel further than a few blocks from my apartment. Everything is right down the road. I never need to go further for any reason.

Tonight, my body, mind, and soul crave adventure. I haven't felt this urge since high school. The adventures of Dakota were some of the best of my life. The Seedy Side never caused any issues for me back then. Why would it now? Dakota wasn't my Seedy bodyguard. I don't need her or anyone else to go to a bar.

The Siren's Song is a small bar right on the edge of the Seedy Side. Right as you're leaving my section of town and entering the unknown. By definition, I'm not even fully on the Seedy Side. I'm…dipping my toe in.

The parking lot is well paved, with freshly painted lines for each parking space. I guess I figured this side of town would be gravel with potholes that took out your front end if you weren't paying attention, but everything seems very well established. It's almost as if this place is freshly opened, but there are positive reviews online dating back at least two years.

When I enter the bar, it's dimly lit, and it takes my eyes a second to adjust. There're eight pool tables to the left of the entrance with blue table tops that seem to be new. Or maybe they're well taken care of. Either way, I've never played the game, always wanted to learn, though. Unfortunately, the only places you can find a pool table are places I've never been able to be seen in. What would the congregation think if they saw me frequenting a place like this?

There's a big light illuminating a quote behind the bar spanning the entire back wall. The quote reads, "Give me your tired, your poor, your huddled masses yearning to breathe free, the wretched refuse of your teeming shore. Send these, the homeless, tempest-tossed to me, I lift my lamp beside the golden door!"

I remember this! It's part of the poem lying at the feet beneath the Statue of Liberty. Thank you, high school history. I was worried I'd never use you.

But here I am, a degenerate at a bar on the outskirts of town, hoping not to get recognized as the pastor's kid, drinking swill beside these "huddled masses." Feeling like a jerk for walking on the still damp, freshly mopped floor. The smell strangely reminds me of EC, though. It's the same cleaner we use. The smell of chemical with a faint hint of lemon calms my nerves as I find an empty seat at the bar.

Which isn't exactly a challenge given the building is empty. What a perfect place for self-reflection. Maybe answer some of the pestering questions darkening my usually sunny disposition. Why am I upset? How has today gotten away from me? Why am I even here right now?

Am I being more sensitive, or does the world around me actually seem uglier than usual? Ethan cursing before church, for example. He just figured it was okay. He didn't even seem to care about judging and insulting one of God's children right outside of His house of worship. That can't be in my head. Was this the reason I didn't enjoy our little make-out session in his truck?

Actually, no. I've never enjoyed that, but life is no fairytale. I know that for sure. The butterflies and the spark? It's made up. Life is no Disney movie, either. No one just sweeps someone off their feet. I've always been a levelheaded person, with my feet firmly planted on the ground. To believe one day, I'd experience some fake feelings made up by the candy and hallmark company is sheer gullibility.

Life is black and white. Plain and simple. Magic isn't real. Miracles only happen in the Bible by saints. Those gifted with the ability to present the common man with proof God truly was speaking to them. Those who see in shades of gray are lying to themselves. I've known the world was ugly and unfair since being forced to watch the injustices of Dakota. Why am I becoming sensitive to it now after everything I witnessed as a teenager?

> I was walking through the halls in between classes, trying to shake off a weird discomfort growing within me from the quiet desolation of the school. All the students were already in class as I wandered to the

bathroom. I noticed the word "DYKE" was spray-painted on one of the lockers as I walked by it. I tried to ignore the sinking in my gut, knowing whose locker it was.

Just make it to the bathroom, Appleton, I thought as I directed my gaze to the ground and kept walking. *It's not your locker, it's not your problem.*

When I made it to the bathroom, I heard a loud CLAP coming from the other side of the door, followed by a slight whimper. "I bet this faggot wants to touch us too." They chuckled. I couldn't listen.

Part of me wanted to turn around. Wanted to find another place to alleviate my bladder. My hand was resting on the door while a part of me mustered up the courage to push it open. "Please," I heard her familiar voice rasp out in desperation. "It wasn't like that. I can explain. Please let m—"

I heard another CLAP. "Shut up, dyke!" Gosh, I still hate that word.

Before I knew what I was doing, my body was pushing its way into the room, where I was met with three girls. One of which had Dakota pressed against the wall by her throat. The second girl watched and cackled as Dakota squirmed in the first person's grip, begging for release. The two bullies' sneers quickly faltered at my entrance.

For a moment, my eyes met Dakota's red from tears, pleading for me to do something, say something. I couldn't. I had nothing. She'd told me to leave her alone. My vision stayed fixed on the floor, finding a stall. I sat in there, fighting my own tears, as I listened to them whisper, "If your faggot ass so much as looks in another girl's direction in this school, we'll find you. Clear?"

I heard a thud before a release of air, followed by footsteps exiting the bathroom. I peeked below the metal divider to find Dakota on the ground, coughing. She sniffled, letting out a slight grunt as she staggered to her feet. For a moment, I sat silently, wiping at the tears flowing freely down my cheeks. I wanted to go out there. I wanted to hold her and tell her everything would be okay. I wanted to find those girls and beat them senseless with my trig book. Instead, I did nothing. *Just go,* I thought. *I can't help you...You told me to stay away.*

I held my mouth to stop a sob from escaping my lips. Her face will forever be burned into my mind: the trail of tears streaming down both sides of her brightly reddened cheeks, her short, blonde hair made up into two pigtails, in tatters from the altercation, those eyes—pleading, begging for help.

Please, I stifled another whimper with my hand. *I can't help you...*

"Hey!" an over-enthusiastic voice snaps me back into reality. "Can I get you anything?" I glance up from the bar I've, apparently, been rubbing my nail across, scraping off the imaginary dirt, to be met with the same type of deep blue eyes I remembered from all those years ago. *God, what are you working at?* I ask Him. *Am I not burdened enough?*

"Oh," I say wearily. "I didn't know you worked here."

Judging by the frown taking over her expression while quickly grabbing a glass to dry with a bar towel, I don't think she's buying my smile. "You doing okay?" she asks, setting the cup down before propping her elbows up on the bar. She leans, moving in closer.

"Fine," I lie.

She isn't buying it. "Suit yourself," she says, pushing herself off the counter. "Thirsty?"

"Umm…" I say nervously, scanning the bottles behind her. "What is there?" It didn't occur to me—never having drank—I would have no idea how or what to order. I mean, sure, I've had reds and whites. This place doesn't appear to have a wine cellar hiding underneath the floorboards, though, that's for sure.

"It's a bar." She giggles lightly. "You tell me."

"Tell you what?" I'm so confused. This was a bad idea. And now, someone here recognizes me. If she goes to church next Sunday, she'll probably tell everyone. This is embarrassing. "I should go."

"Wait!" She grabs my arm, instantly freezing me in place as a jolt of electricity shoots down my spine. "Don't go," she pleads and then, as if reading my mind, adds, "You're safe here. No one's going to say they saw you. Bar rule." She points to a sign behind her. **"WHAT HAPPENS AT SIREN'S, STAYS AT SIREN'S."**

"How do I know that no one will?" Seems kind of ridiculous to think everyone in this bar has some kind of honor system. It's a seedy bar on the Seedy Side. Seedy people aren't exactly known for being...well...not seedy.

"Have you ever heard about this place?" She extends her arms, gesturing to the pristine pool tables and sparkly black counter.

My bottom lip juts out as I tilt my head side to side before shaking it.

"See?" Her lips curl upward, exposing a crooked front canine. "I take it you've never drunk, huh?"

"What makes you think that? I-I drink." The song changes on the jukebox. The volume is too low to determine whether I've ever heard it before.

"Oh yeah, princess?" Her brows raise in interest when she notices the irritation her little "nickname" elicited. "Then what're you havin'?"

I narrow my eyes and move in closer, popping my elbows up onto the bar. "A drink."

She mimics the gesture, flattening her palms on the surface. "What kind?"

Pushing myself back until I hit the back of the barstool, my voice comes out as more of a whine. "The kind that gets you drunk!" She's making me feel stupid, but I refuse to back down.

"They all do that. Which one?" Her eyebrow arches.

"Umm..." Bottles line the wall behind her, lit up by hidden spotlights, illuminating the glass shelving they rest on. I haven't the slightest clue what any of these are, so I randomly point. "That one."

"Oh, yeah?" she says, grabbing the bottle I'm pointing at. She holds it up in front of me. "This one?" The look on this enigmatic woman's face seems genuinely intrigued. "Okay, well," her shoulders lift as she inspects every angle of the little glass bottle, "...how do you want it?"

I smack my palm on the bar. "What do you mean 'how do I want it?'" I shriek. Why am I acting like this right now? "In a glass, of course."

"You want this." The woman points to the small red bottle, sucking in her lips to hide a smirk. "In a glass?"

"Well...isn't that how you drink it?" I shake my head, the temperature in the room rising at least twenty degrees since I first walked in.

She sets the bottle down on a rubber mat beside us. "Can I see some ID?"

"Why do you need my ID?"

She glances around at the low lights hanging above each pool table. "Because you're in a bar?" She doesn't say it. She asks it. Like it's a question. Like she's not sure why I'm asking. And *I'm* not sure why I'm even here. "Are you even old enough to drink this?" She furrows her brow playfully.

I lick my lips slowly, sucking in a chemical lemon filled breath in through my nose. "Is twenty-six old enough?"

"Is that what your ID says?"

I lean my whole body onto the bar once more. "Would I be in here if it didn't?" Why am I meeting her questions with questions? I'm not sure. For some reason, even though I'm slightly irritated, this frustration isn't the same as it is with Ethan. My stomach doesn't do backflips when I'm angry at him. I don't feel an instinctual pull to match eye contact with Ethan like I am in this moment, either. I always crave punching him in his smug, annoying face, but this is entirely different. No, I just feel a pull to be closer to her. To continue the playfulness she's giving me, even though we both know I don't belong here.

She leans into my space on the bar. "Then prove it," she growls, her voice barely above a whisper as she looks down at the bar before returning her gaze to mine. "ID."

Words escape my brain, falling short on my tongue. That whisper, in combination with her gesture, took the wind completely out of my lungs. I'm holding my breath as I concede, pulling my wallet from my bag. Handing her the ID, her eyes crinkle victoriously, baring her crooked canine once more.

"Phoebe, huh?"

My brows furrow. "I'm sorry?"

"I'm not sure I have a way to ring this up, Phoebe."

"What?" I'm shocked. How could she not have a way of ringing it up after dragging this out? "Why is it even on the shelf, then?"

"Because this is a syrup." She snorts. "It's grenadine." I think she can sense how stupid I feel because she quickly responds, "I'll tell you what? How about I make you a drink, and you tell me what you think?"

I lift a playful brow. "And if I don't like it?"

"Then don't drink it." She waves me off. "I'll make you a new one." The woman then shovels ice into a metal cup. "We'll find out what you like together, okay?" She winks at me. Heat instantly fills my cheeks.

"Okay." Something about her eases me. She's magnetic. "So, what'd you think of EC?"

She tilts her head to the side, weighing out her next words. "Meh. The sermon was nice."

"Pastor Pete has a way with words." I watch as she pours some liquids into the cup.

She lifts one eyebrow, not raising her head, while placing another cup upside down on top of the first one before shaking. "I bet." I watch as she uses the strainer on the lid to pour the contents into a fresh, empty glass, leaving the ice behind. She adds a slight amount of what I now know is "grenadine" on the top of the drink, causing the blue mixture to turn purple at the top. She drops a cherry and straw in before sliding it to me. "Try this."

I do as I'm told, and to my amazement, it actually tastes good! Nothing like communion wine, that's for sure. It kind of reminds me of a melted purple popsicle. "This has alcohol in it?" I take two more big gulps. Gosh, it's like Kool-aid!

"You bet your ass it does." She throws her head back. I debate on asking her not to cuss, but can I do that here? I'm at a bar. What do I expect? People to recite the gospel? I'm out of my depth. "We call that dangerous."

"Dangerous?" I stare at my glass. "Why?"

"Just...go easy on it, okay?"

My body feels incredibly light. Kind of shaky, but not shaky. It's hard to describe. Like a cold chill washing over every joint in my body. I know this isn't drunk. I've seen drunk people on TV, and they can't keep their balance to save their lives. I've read in books you become dizzy. I'm not dizzy. My body's...relaxed. I wonder why I'm feeling this way.

"I didn't catch your name," I say, trying to steer my attention away from my body.

She lifts my glass and puts a square card underneath it. "Blake." She blushes shyly, avoiding eye contact.

"Well, hello, Blake. I'm Phoebe."

"I know," she titters.

"You know? Oh right! My ID. Because I don't look twenty-one."

"You do look twenty-one." She tamps down her amusement while wiping the bar in front of me. "I was just enjoying myself."

I quirk an eyebrow as a flutter settles low in my belly. "Enjoying *what*, exactly?"

"You're adorable when you're upset." She's still not looking at me.

A sudden wave rolls through my shoulders. "I'm not adorable." I take another big swig of my drink. Is half of it seriously already gone? "I'm firm."

"I'll take your word for it." She nods at the counter.

"What's that supposed to mean?" I sit up straight, allowing my legs to swing freely under the bar stool. I feel fidgety and light. "I can be quite assertive; I'll have you know. So...watch out."

"I guess I'll have to see for myself." She gazes to her left toward a guy standing by a door leading to the back. "Hang on a second," she says, gesturing to him before disappearing through a side door with the man. I finish off my drink. I don't know what to do with myself now as I wait. She comes back a few minutes later, carrying two cases of beer. I watch as she stocks them in a fridge on the wall in front of me.

"Want another?" she asks.

I shake my head, realizing everything is kind of in slow motion. Is this drunk? What happens if I stand and can't? Should I be driving? I didn't think of what I'd do after drinking. I can't get a DUI. *Stupid.*

"Are you okay? Want me to call you a cab?" she offers.

"I...I need my car tomorrow...Blake...?" I turn and glance at her, slightly embarrassed.

"Well, there were like four shots in that drink you just downed, Phoebe. You want me to call someone—"

"—You can't!" I bury my head in my arm on the bar. If anyone were to find out about this, they'd kill me. Especially Zoe and Eve. "I'm stupid." My chest sinks. "I'm not sure why I decided to do this...I don't drink."

"Then why did you?" The question seems genuine. She isn't following it up with an I-Told-You-So or I-Thought-You-Said-You-Did. No, she's worried. "Look, I know you don't think you can trust me, but..." She pauses, randomly rinsing out my glass in the sink below the bar.

"But what?"

"You're in a safe space, okay? If you need to stay here and sober up, I'll wait with you. If you need a cab, I'll call you one. Okay?" She meets my eyes, and I find myself falling into them. My vision trails down to the curve of her mouth. A light pink, full bottom lip. A perfect cupid's bow at the top. I bet they're soft. They seem soft. Why would it even matter if they were soft?

My face flushes as I find my way back to her eyes. "Phoebe," she says gently. "Are you okay? For real." She grabs the towel again, this time drying her hands.

"I...I don't know what I am," I admit, grateful the bar is empty. No one has to witness this slight existential crisis after only one drink.

She sighs, peering up at the ceiling, before dropping the towel and walking around the bar to my seat. She extends out her hand. "Come on."

Without thinking, I take her outstretched hand. She leads me outside, locking the front doors behind her. "You have keys? That's so cool," I say.

Her face floods with mirth. "Yeah. Keys are cool. They come with the bar."

"Wait! You *own* this place? How old are you?"

Blake's tongue juts out to lick at her lips. "Same age as you, Phoebe. Which one's yours?"

"Mine? My car?" I look around. There are only four cars in the parking lot, but they all seem a little smudgy. "The white civic. But Blake...I-I can't drive like this."

She nudges my shoulder and holds out her palm. "Keys," she demands gently. Sober Phoebe wouldn't trust anyone with her keys. She wouldn't allow anyone to drive her brand-new Honda Civic Type-R—not even Zoe, and she's been begging—but I have work tomorrow. I need my car. There's also something very comforting about Blake. She's not threatening in the slightest.

"But…How will you get home?"

"I have my ways," she hisses, narrowing her eyebrows. "I'm just fucking with you. I'll call my friend."

"The guy you went to the back with?"

Blake nods. "Delaney. He's good people. Let me take you home."

Call it stupid, call it intuition, but I feel like I can trust her. I feel safe. So, I hand over my keys with little physical restraint. My mouth is a different matter, though. "Don't wreck my baby."

"Your baby, huh? You gonna marry her?" She snickers, unlocking the doors.

"Nope, I'll never marry," I admit, sliding into the passenger seat. *Why am I tired all of a sudden?* "But don't tell Ethan that."

"Ethan? Who's Ethan?" she asks, pressing the brake and ignition button simultaneously. As the dash illuminates and does its flashy greeting on the screen, she growls, "Hot damn, this is sexy as fuck."

I blush. "Ethan is my boyfriend. For a year and a half now, he's been trying to get in my pants. But no marriage, no booty! And I mean NO marriage!" I hide my face in my lap as I giggle hysterically. Everything is spinny when I move my head, yet I can't resist moving it in every direction, regardless. It's fun.

"I'm glad I cut you off when I did," she jests, putting the car in drive. "Guide me, Phoebe." As she creeps the car forward, I instinctually put my hand in her lap for some unexplainable reason.

Blake immediately slams on the brake. Pinning both hands on the wheel, her head slowly drops to her lap. "What are you doing?" she scrapes out.

I, too, look down. "I…" What *am* I doing? I jerk my hand back. "I don't know. Oh God! I mean, oh gosh. Lord, what's happening to me?" I start laughing, but wait…am I crying? I'm crying. I need to get out of this car. "Can you just call me a cab? I…I—"

"Stop," she says softly. Putting the car in park, she grabs my hand. I freeze. "Phoebe." Meeting her gaze causes another rush of adrenaline to course through my bloodstream. "I'm taking you home, okay? I'll keep my hands on the wheel, and you keep yours," she puts my hand on my lap, "there, okay? Last thing I want is for you to do something you'll regret tomorrow. Sound good?"

I wipe my face on my shoulder without removing my hands from my lap. "Okay." I sniffle. *I'm so stupid.*

"Why are you crying?" she asks, thumbing away a tear from my cheek. Her hand is remarkably soft and warm.

"I don't know." The abrupt admission makes more tears fall.

She sighs. Turning her whole body toward me, grabbing me by the shoulders, she pulls my face into her chest. The feeling of warmth and comfort makes me sob even harder. Why am I *blubbering*? Is this what alcohol does? "Shh…" She threads her fingers through my hair. "It's okay. Let it out."

And I do. I let out the embarrassment of what I just did, the way I felt earlier when Ethan was touching me. He insulted this amazing woman, who is now driving me home, letting me put snot and tears all over her shirt. She smells of cedar cologne and liquor she must've spilled on herself. I sob over Dakota and the abandonment that always comes when I think of her. The girl on the floor, pleading for me to help her and I didn't. I wanted her to leave. Just go, so I wouldn't have to witness the hell Mystic High put her through. And she did. One day, she was gone. No goodbyes. No words spoken. I never saw her again. I never told her I was sorry. I'll never be able to make it right, and that's my cross to bear.

"Shh…" she says again. I wrap my arms around her and squeeze deeply.

I don't cry often. I typically don't find there's a reason to. But I'm crying now, and all the tears I've held back for the last twelve years are being pushed out like open floodgates. The despair and emptiness surrounding my life has finally consumed me. I realize how lonely I am, even with all of my family and friends around.

The steady thrum of her heart against my ear centers my thoughts. Some people have it worse. "I-I can't imagine what it'd be like to have been you this morning," I finally muster.

Blake's lungs expand as she draws a breath. "What do you mean?" Her soporific voice is passive, almost distracted, as she holds me in her arms.

I close my eyes, letting the blue light of the dashboard dissolve as I focus on the sensation of her wrapping a tendril of my hair around her finger. Blake allows the strand to unspool before tracing that same finger along the top of my shoulder. "The way they treated you. The way they looked at you. You…You tried to share with your neighbors, and they rejected you."

"You didn't reject me." Her soothing voice carries a certain hopeful charm. As if reminding herself of the good that still exists within the world.

I question whether there really is good outside of the remoteness of this car. "Yet everyone else did! Why would they do that?" If my presence is meant to set an example for my family, why, then, do people think treating others abrasively is somehow justifiable in the eyes of our Lord?

"That's people." She lifts one shoulder. "They'll always try to fix what they don't understand. I'm used to it," she groans.

I pull away, blinking at her a few times. "You shouldn't have to be."

"I'm a lesbian." She rolls her head upward to the fabric headliner above us. "Full of sin." She mocks quotations with her fingers. "It's okay. I went there searching for something."

"Did you find it? I can help you. Were you searching for repentance?" I want to go back to hugging, already missing the scent of her, but the moment has passed. The absence of Blake's warmth makes me cognizant of the chill resonating deep within my spine, frosting my nervous system as I turn on the heat.

Blake arches her brow. A mischievous grin peaking at one corner of her mouth. "Acceptance, actually."

"Acceptance?" I ask. Acceptance for the way she dresses? Surely, she can't mean acceptance for being a sinner. For turning away from a woman's destiny. For choosing a homosexual lifestyle.

"I lost someone," she confesses as tears form in her eyes, threatening to fall at any moment. "Someone who meant a lot to me. I was angry. I was lost. We had a plan, and with him gone, I just…I couldn't figure out a solid way to go on. Until my feet led me to the Holy Side. They led me to EC."

"You should talk to my dad." I wipe my nose on my sleeve.

"Meet your parents? Thanks, Phoebe, but we just met," she jokes.

"No," I say, pushing her shoulder playfully. "He's the pastor. If you're searching for answers over loss, he'd be able to help."

She puts the car in drive. "Ready?" she asks. Is she changing the subject?

"Yes, turn left onto the street." If she is, I have to accept it. I can't force her to do anything. I just really, really wish she would.

"Okay, hands," she teases, but I put them on my lap, anyway. I don't know what came over me, but I'm much more sober now. "I'll think about it," she finally says after a long pause.

"Turn left on Monroe. And don't think, Blake. Please." I give her my best pouty face.

"And what do I get if I face those Jesus Fucks again?" she asks, signaling before making the turn. "They truly are sacks of shit, Phoebe."

"Resolution?" I try.

She sucks her teeth. "Tempting, but…try again."

"Guidance?"

A smile quirks up her mouth as she moves her hair out of her face, tucking it behind her ear. "Keep going."

"To see me again?" Her eyes meet mine only briefly before returning to the road.

"That, I'd go for." I notice her cheeks flushing when the light from oncoming traffic illuminates her face. There goes my stomach doing the flippy stuff again.

"Well, I never miss a service, so…" My face warms too. "Turn here." I point right, and she complies.

The rest of the car ride is quiet, but not awkward. She eventually turns my radio to a rock station, lowering the volume to still hear my directions while mouthing the words to the songs. I have my hand out my window, riding the waves of the wind.

Blake is nice. How people can judge someone before realizing how beautiful they truly are baffles me.

"This is me," I say, directing her where to park. She hops out of the car, locking it up behind her.

"Can I trust you to get yourself inside?" she asks, handing me my keys hesitantly.

"Yes," I mumble, eyes finding the grass. "I'm sorry. I'm a mess."

"No." She takes a step into my space. "You're beautiful." Focusing intently as she tucks a strand of my hair behind my ear, she adds, "And flawed. Which is nice."

"Nice?" I cover my face. "I 'flawed' all over your shirt."

"Washable." She moves my hands, deep blues finding their way into my soul, burying deep into my spine, causing the hairs on the back of my neck to rise. "I came to the church to find acceptance, but finding you was worth the trip. The impression of you will last a lifetime." Why can't I seem to pull my eyes from hers now? They're like whirlpools, dragging me in deeper and deeper. "But I'll see you again?" she asks, interrupting the moment. I'm now realizing we're just staring into each other's eyes.

"Yes." My eyebrows twitch upward. "Sunday?"

"Or sooner," she teases.

✝

Twenty minutes later, as I lay down to sleep, I find myself smiling. Today didn't end up that bad after all. I thank God for bringing Blake into my life.

Chapter 4

Blake

"Honestly, it was fine," I say to Delaney as he taps the keg under the counter.

"Mhmm," he responds sardonically. After a moment, he sighs. "Jude wanted you guys to start outreach, sure, but it's only been two months, Blake. I know you. And I know Jude. He'd never have agreed to let you go to EC by yourself." He starts walking away, and I follow. "Just quit bullshitting me."

"How am I bullshitting you?" I ask, playing coy. "I knew if I told you, you would've kept me from doing it, and I'm a grown-ass woman. I don't need bubble wrap around me, Doe-Boy, and I don't need to answer or check in with you, either."

"You went there secretly hoping they'd fuck you up. Don't act like this was some healthy thing to extend your and Jude's plan for the city, B. You wanted someone to tell you off or start something. Give you a reason. Anything to feel something again."

"No, I didn't," I say, hoping my tone is believable. "It was for the sole purpose of getting the plan in motion. He wanted outreach. It's been two years. What are we waiting for? Siren's is in the black. It's starting to gain some traction on this side of town. No point wasting even more years. Life is short. Or have you not noticed?" I jab, hoping the reminder will make him drop it.

It doesn't.

"I already watched them put one of you in the ground, B! I'm not doing it again." He shakes his head. Burning holes into the side of my face, I grab a cutting board and knife. "I could've gone with you. Why didn't you tell me?"

Because you would've stopped me or, worse, tried to join me. Because everything you're saying is right, I think. A part of me really did crave an outlet for how unfair the universe is being right now. The old me would've fought someone who deserved a good ass beating. Who better than a bigot abusing the gospel for personal gain? "You think a queen like yourself and a butch like me showing up wouldn't have caused even more issues than one of us? It was fine."

I lift a shoulder, grabbing a lemon, chopping it into wedges. "I mean, the people were as shitty as you'd expect. Super rude. Judgy." Which we knew. You don't go to EC to find the salt of the Earth. They're horrible. I wasn't there for the adults. I was there for the next generations. The kids who would grow up and run EC in the next ten years. The ones who decide in a few years to go to seminary and preach the gospel.

I let the silence linger while I cut up a few more lemons, tossing them into a clear container. "The world is changing, Doe-Boy. It's time Mystic caught up. One inconspicuous new visitor from the other side of town isn't a sign of war like two or more would be." I stare at him blankly. "You know one queer is enough to have old lady Myrna clutching her pearls…but two is enough to demand our swift exit. Double the sin."

I put the lid on the container, reaching for the date/time labels above my head.

"So…" he sighs, finally done admonishing me. He opens the fridge, pulls out a box of limes, and places it on the table next to me. "What happened?"

I tsk, tilting my head from side to side. "Not quite an olive branch, but I'll take it." I bump his shoulder with mine, reaching for a lime. "I thought you'd never ask."

"Yeah, well," he says, grabbing his own cutting board and bowl. "You came back. You're in one piece. I still think you're full of shit. You went there itching for a fight. Obviously, you didn't find one, though, so…"

"Nope." I shrug. He doesn't need to know I ran into Phoebe Appleton. Matter of fact, I'm pretty sure if he found out, he'd make sure I never went back. And I need to go back. For Jude. "I even signed up to help them with some flowerbeds around the church this weekend."

"You're not fucking serious." Delaney cuts into his lime with so much aggression I worry he's going to cut off a finger. "Helping the enemy spruce up the place in order to invite more bigots in?" He crosses his arms.

"More people to educate. They recently did a total reno of the Nave. Doubled it in size. Obviously, they're trying to expand the congregation." After finishing another container of limes and labeling them, I turn to grab the jar of cherries on an overhead shelf. "So, I help them draw in more victims—"

"And educate them," he finishes.

"Saving them from growing up ashamed, homeless, or worse…like their parents." I twist the metal lid for the cherries, but it's screwed on pretty tight. "My first service was all judgment, but the more active I become in their community, the more heads I'll turn." I grab a towel and try loosening the lid again with the towel for grip. "Heads with questions—fuck, this is really on there."

Delaney sets down the knife before walking over to me. "Questions you have answers to."

I nod as he twists off the lid with very little effort before handing it back to me. "Yeah, whatever, show off. I loosened it for you."

"Anyone we know?" he asks, causing the cherries to splash against the container. Droplets of sweet juice landing on my face and mouth.

My tongue drags along my bottom lip, licking up the sugary syrup as I reach for a napkin to wipe at the rest of the mess on my forehead and cheeks. "A few people I knew from High School. Everyone you'd expect."

Except Phoebe, I think.

I really hadn't expected her to be there. The Phoebe Dakota knew wasn't judgmental or opinionated. Dakota glorified her for being sweet. To find out Phoebe's father is the pastor of EC came as a *big* surprise. It's impossible for me to believe she's the same person Dakota knew once I discovered Phoebe grew up in that church.

I feel incomprehensibly bad for Phoebe. How can she accept herself when her world doesn't accept anything? EC is very much an Old Testament kind of crowd.

It's the most well-known church on the Holy Side. Not only are they the most influential, they're also the most prejudiced. They're responsible for some of the biggest charities in our community. Homeless, battered women, and low-income families, to name a few. Everyone on the Holy Side knows of EC. Respects EC. *Fears* EC. One false step, and they'll destroy you. Everyone knows it's best to stay far away from them if you're of an "unsavory" type.

The oldest, most powerful names in Mystic are upstanding members. Judges, bankers, you name it. But not the mayor. Conroy Adams has always been a neutral party hoping to expand the population. That's where Jude and I came in.

"I think you're finally ready," Jude had said.

"Ready for what?" I asked.

"I have a business proposition for you." Jude stacked up the wooden Jenga blocks we'd been playing with, putting them back in their box.

"Business proposition?" I'd asked. "You want to go into business with me?" The idea my brother, a respected genius in our Podunk little town, would be naïve enough to entrust me, the fuck up, with any version of responsibility was baffling.

Jude walked to his bedroom, returning with a portfolio, pulling out a printed paper with a building for sale and handing it to me.

My eyes widened. "You want a recovering addict to work at a bar? Are you insane? Are you trying to get me to relapse?"

"Just…hear me out, okay?" He laid another paper full of numbers and percentages on top of the first. "I've been working with the city. Did you know eighty-seven percent of Mystic's population is connected to some religious affiliation?"

"I'm not surprised," I said, scratching my nose.

"Of that eighty-seven percent, forty-four percent attend discriminative congregations. Roughly half the town!" he said with a combination of disgust and fascination. "Worse yet, a quarter of that forty-four percent are religious extremists. That's somewhere in the vicinity of two thousand aggressively hateful people on the Holy Side who attend churches like the Evangelical Church of Mystic Harbor."

"That place isn't a church. It's a fucking cult," I spat out.

He nodded, holding up his hands. "No argument here." He points to more of the numbers. "Of these estimated two thousand people, less than half are children, born into this toxic way of thinking. Molded or manipulated through fear mongering in the form of religious pretense. Scared of being disowned or abused like—" He stopped abruptly.

"Like me…" I finished for him.

He nodded sympathetically. "They either become the abusers or live to be abused. The population of this town is slowly decreasing each year. Younger generations are moving the second they turn eighteen. Soon, Mystic will be nothing more than a ghost town."

"So, the bigots are destroying this town?" I chuckled. "I doubt that. EC has some of the best funded charities within city limits."

"That isn't going to matter soon," he said, exasperated with great Moxy. "With Mystic's conservative—bordering on violent—predisposition, people don't care to be here. Those charities may help the city's population, but without people to offer assistance to, they won't last long."

"What does this have to do with a bar?" I attempted to steer the conversation back on track.

"What if we offered people like you an out?" He slid the paper for the bar on top of the sheet of stats and points to it. "A safe haven. No more wandering to another city to find safety from bigotry and prejudice. No more seeking the comfort of substances and warm bodies for approval. What if there would've been a place you could have gone, outside of the church, when you ran away? We could offer people like you shelter." He shook his head, searching his large brain for the right word. "Advocacy."

"Well," Delaney huffs, popping a top on the limes, pulling me back to reality. "Let's hope you didn't lead any of the nut jobs here."

"No one asked any questions." I keep my gaze fixed on the silver prep table. "I think they were more pissed off the pastor allowed me to partake in communion."

Delaney almost drops the container of limes before staring at me with wide eyes. "What?! I thought they were closed table?"

"They are, dude," I say, feigning indifference.

"Then why did you even go up there?" He puts his hand on his hip. "You really were trying to start shit!"

I hold my forefinger and thumb an inch apart. "Okay, maybe that was slightly me making waves." I sneer. "I honestly have no fucking clue why he allowed me to partake, but you could see Edna in the first row about to have a whole ass stroke. Priceless." I throw a cashew into my mouth.

"Dammit, Blake!" Delaney shouts.

✝

Siren's is dead. Typically is on Sundays, but at least we get to catch up on some deep cleaning and maintenance before the health inspectors come in for the hundredth time. They always try to shut us down but can never find anything on us. We keep the bar so far above code, not a single thing can stick to us. Jude insisted on this from day one. He had a sense the Holy Side would be waiting like vultures for the day we'd slip up.

They can try all they want. Honestly, it's more enjoyable that way. As if to say we're here, and there isn't a single thing you can do about it. I love it. I'd worked a few days at random fast-food restaurants, and not a single one got a perfect score like we do. Jude was very particular about who he hired, and he made sure everyone was properly vetted before being employed. They understand the mission and want to be a part of it.

I restock the paper towels in the bathroom before returning up front. And there she is. I'd know her silhouette sitting on that barstool anywhere. Phoebe Appleton—the daughter of the pastor in the most influential church in Mystic Harbor—is sitting at my bar. No fucking way. I had to double-take. I genuinely can't believe it! Not only is she here, but she's by herself. Just like every other time I've ever seen her.

Play it cool, I remind myself, walking back behind the bar. My eyes lock on her, scratching at the counter. Her head is propped in one hand, lost in thought.

"Hey!" *So much for cool.* "Can I get you anything?"

She beams up, her vision joining reality. I wonder what she was thinking about. Clearly, she's troubled if she's here. Maybe she knows about what Siren's stands for. No. No way. I need to be doing something. Quickly, I grab a glass and the towel next to it and start drying.

"Oh." She feigns elation, but I'm not convinced it's genuine. *Yup, definitely troubled.* "I didn't know you worked here." Panic flushes her face, and I can't help but be sorry for her. I can't imagine living in a world where you have to be scared of who's going to see you.

"You doing okay?" I ask, hoping she'll let me be her therapist. That is, after all, what us bartenders are best at. I lean forward with my elbows on the counter.

"Fine." She's lying, still keeping up appearances. I want to tear down those walls. Show her there's no reason to hide here. It's the whole reason Siren's exists.

"Suit yourself. Thirsty?"

"Umm…What is there?"

✝

"I'm not adorable," she says, ten minutes of closet flirting and half a drink later. "I'm firm," she practically growls.

I'm sure you are. I'm shaking. "I'll take your word for it."

"What's that supposed to mean?" She straightens her back, swinging her legs. Okay, yeah, four shots in one drink might've been too many. I might have gotten Phoebe drunk. Whoops. "I can be quite assertive; I'll have you know. So…watch out."

"I guess I'll have to see for myself." And man, do I want to. I imagine her bossing me around would be sexy as fuck.

I peer over her shoulder to find Delaney with his arms crossed, pissed. *Shit.* "Hang on a second."

I excuse myself and follow him as he storms to the supply closet, knowing I'll follow.

"Are you fucking kidding me, Blake?" he all but shouts as I close the door.

"Shh! She'll hear you!" I whisper.

"Is that who I fucking think it is?"

"Who?"

"I will fuck you up," he says, tone flat.

"I'd like to see you try." I straighten, making myself appear taller than I am. Delaney and I are about the same height, but he knows without a doubt he'd lose that fight. He came from a life of money and class. His chiseled abs are a combination of CrossFit and Pilates. My strength and endurance came from the streets, forced to run from danger or hold my own. I've been a fighter since I was twelve years old. We are not the same. Not to mention the billion hardships I've dealt with while he sat comfortably in his family's money, never having to get his hands dirty.

I decide to break the tension. "Listen." This isn't a pissing contest, and there's no point lying. Phoebe Appleton is in our bar after he'd just said he didn't want any drama here. "Yes, it's Phoebe," I say before quickly adding, "But she's not here to start issues!"

Delaney lets out an incredulous laugh. "Not here to start issues? Are you fucking serious, Blake? Does she know about Dakota? Is she here to ask questions?"

"Don't fucking bring Dakota into this!" Dakota's dead and he knows how sensitive the topic of her is for me. Yet he still insists on picking the scab of this inherently tender wound.

"That doesn't answer my question, B. Does she know?"

"No." I throw my hands up. "But…" I hesitate before adding, "…her dad is the pastor of EC."

His body slumps as he lets out a massive sigh. "Why the fuck is she here, Blake?"

"I don't know. Why don't you go ask her?"

"Not a fucking shot in hell that I'm talking to her! Is that why you went to EC? To search for Phoebe?" He shifts his weight to the other leg, anger burning hot in his eyes.

"No!" I exclaim. "I had no idea she was a major figurehead in that shitty church! I swear!" Before I can fully think it through, I add, "But she's the only person who greeted me there. She's not like them."

"Well, hooray for you!" he needles. "You must be so fucking happy but hear me when I say this," he points an accusatory finger at me, "this is on you."

"Jude would want—"

"Don't!" he hisses. "Jude would be just as pissed, and you know it!"

I disagree. Jude wanted us to bridge the gap between the Holy Side. He'd be more understanding when I explained running into her was a happy accident. Maybe less "happy" and completely accidental, but he wouldn't be attacking me in a supply closet like Delaney right now.

"No, he wouldn't," is all I can think to say.

Tears well in his eyes before he rubs them away. "Whatever, Blake. I'm leaving. I trust you can close up shop without any issue. Just handle this."

"I will." I grab two cases of beer from a shelf before returning to Phoebe at the bar. I stock the fridge closest to us, looking at the clock. Two more hours before closing time. I can do this.

†

"Can I trust you to get yourself inside?" I ask as I hand her back her keys, hoping she doesn't invite me in. I like to think I've behaved very well so far. I can't keep pushing my luck.

"Yes," she says, looking at the ground. "I'm sorry. I'm a mess."

"No." I take a step closer to her. "You're beautiful." I find a stray strand of her hair, tucking it gently behind her ear. God, even her fucking ears are perfect. It's ridiculous. "And flawed. Which is nice."

"Nice?" Her brows furrow derisively. "I 'flawed' all over your shirt."

"Washable." Our eyes meet again, and if I don't leave, I'm going to kiss her and then hate myself for the next six months. "I came to the church to find acceptance. But finding you was worth the trip." *Step away, Blake. Step the fuck back.* "The impression of you will last a lifetime." I sink into the emerald palace of her eyes, glinting slightly in the streetlight. I need to break this fucking spell, and NOW. "But I'll see you again?" I ask, breaking the trance.

"Yes." She bats her lashes shyly, which sends a surge of electricity down my spine. "Sunday?"

"Or sooner." I'm seriously counting on her being at the flowerbed shit her church has planned Saturday.

I watch to make sure she makes it safely inside before skipping down the street and walking the two miles back to my house in the chilly night air. Calling Delaney would only ruin this high I'm riding from experiencing a world of Phoebe. It's easy to understand what Dakota saw in her all those years ago.

It's also just as terrifying.

Chapter 5

Phoebe

"The impression of you will last a lifetime," Blake says in a soft whisper as she moves my hair behind my ear. Stepping closer, I place my hands on her waist, glancing down. Her breathing increases upon approaching. Peering up into her eyes, I see the ocean. The sound of seagulls and waves crashing on the shore envelop my senses. The taste of salt in the air.

She pulls in her perfect, full bottom lip to nibble on it nervously. "Don't be nervous," I say, my body rushing with something unrecognizable. Confusion takes over as I watch her mouth take in air.

"The impression of you." Still ringing in my head as my body instinctually pulls her closer. Our bodies now touching. Her breath on my face becomes entangled with the breeze coming off the ocean until they are indecipherable from each other.

This feeling. The way my body is moving is uncontrollable. It's like trying to will your heart to beat, it does it involuntarily without conscience. My breath like the gentle ebb and flow of waves, drawing back and pushing out. Like something other than me is pulling the strings. I'm a marionette, insouciant to consequences as my mouth gently meets hers. My heartbeat rings in my ears like a fire alarm. Beep, beep, beep. Over and over again.

"Blake." My voice is airy and full of desire. My hands find her hair, gripping for more as I open my mouth wider, inviting her in.

Beep, beep, beep...

...BEEP! BEEP! BEEP!

My alarm jerks me into consciousness. What the heck was that? My eyes dart around the room. I snap upright abruptly as my bedroom takes form, and I try to comprehend my reality. What?

It was a dream. I was dreaming. It wasn't real. Couldn't be. I would never! That's…but why? Never in my life would I have such a sinful dream. It doesn't make sense.

I squint at my alarm clock. 5:45 AM. My mind is completely scattered, but I have no time to worry about that now. I have to be at work in forty-five minutes to prep the surgery suite for our first operation. I'll need coffee. Lots of coffee. I hop in a quick shower before throwing my still-wet hair up into the fastest bun.

Normally, I shower the night before, straighten it before I put it in a pony. Today, however, I guess I'm just throwing caution to the wind. Then again, I guess it'd be more accurate to say the "caution throwing" occurred last night when I went out, knowing I had to work in the morning. To a bar. I honestly can't even believe I went *out*. And drank! Alcohol. On the Seedy Side. Who am I?

I don't even glance behind me to make sure the house is in order before slamming the door shut and locking it. I race to my perfectly parked car in its space. As if no one ever drove it last night. When I get in, I'm hit with a faint smell of cedar and am instantly reminded.

> *"I'll keep my hands on the wheel, and you keep yours…there. Okay?"*

I smack my forehead. *Stupid,* I think as I start the car. No time for my usual five-minute warm-up. Mama's late! I put her in reverse and head to work.

✝

"You look like shit, Phoebz," Zoe says as I enter the vet clinic two minutes late with the largest flat white Jaime could give me with four extra shots of espresso. She'd regarded me strangely when I'd ordered it. "You good?"

"Language," I mumble and start washing my hands. "And I'm fine. Can a girl not be tired?"

"I mean, a girl can, yes, but that's never been you. Miss 'I go to bed every night at the same time after finishing my fifteen-step nighty night checklist.'" She grabs the jacket I'd carelessly thrown on the chair, hanging it on the rack in the closet. "You're always so 'done up.' Usually, you make me look like a sack of potatoes. Rough night?"

"I look fine," I say, drying my hands and putting on some gloves. "First Jaime, now you. Why is everyone making such a big deal? So, I didn't dry my hair. I don't always come to work perfect." I roll my eyes and start wiping down surfaces.

"You're not wearing makeup either," she points out.

"Who are you?" I throw my hands down to my sides and let out a sigh as I turn around to face her. "My keeper?"

"What's going on with you?" she asks, now washing her hands while simultaneously growing defensive. "Phoebz, seriously, I'm just asking if you're okay. You seem…" She peers around, trying to find the right word. "…Off." Her expression appears genuinely hurt by my behavior.

I let out a sigh and hand her some gloves. "I'm sorry. I didn't sleep well."

"Something keeping you up?" She lays the operating tools out on the table.

"No." I say it almost too quickly. She doesn't seem to notice. "Had a bad dream."

"Wanna talk about it?" I'm met with raised eyebrows, genuinely intrigued. This is the first time I think I've ever mentioned a dream to anyone. I don't normally care about my dreams. Typically, I'll wake up and think, *that was weird…huh…oh well,* and then continue about my day.

But this dream. This one won't seem to go away. Like an earworm sitting at the back of my mind. I can still hear seagulls. Why the heck do I still hear stupid seagulls?

Great. And now I'm irritated again. For no reason. I want to go home. I'm entirely too uncomfortable to be around people right now. I'm already reaching my social limit, and it's only 6:42 in the morning.

"No…" I respond. "I really don't." If just thinking about my dream is causing frustration, I need to find a way to push this down until I have a safe place to process it, and right now, animals depend on me, Dr. Auburn, and even my best friend Dr. Zoe Weatherly, depend on me even more, I can't unearth this here.

And even if I did unearth this with Zoe, what would I say? What even *is* there to say? Regardless of what came out, it would all imply things I *know* aren't true, and they most certainly aren't me. I'm *not* gay! What if she thinks having this weird dream means I'll soon be trying to touch her or, worse, force myself on her? I just got her back. She's been gone for the last two years, living in the city, in order to get her DVM. Upon graduating, she moved back to Mystic Harbor, which was only five months ago in December.

The dream meant nothing. Stupid brain doesn't know how to compartmentalize while I'm sleeping. It meshed boyfriend emotions and sympathy for an outcast into one solid blob until I was on a beach of sin and seagulls.

And with a woman, brain? Seriously? Next thing I know, you'll have me dreaming I'm making out with a sandwich because I went to Subway for lunch while talking to Ethan on the phone or something.

"Suit yourself." Zoe raises one brow. "But know when you *are* ready, I'll be here. I've known you since birth, Phoebz. There isn't a single struggle I wouldn't hold your hand and walk through with you."

Doubtful, I think, but settle for a thank you and continue setting up before Dr. Auburn walks in. Today is going to be a long one.

✝

"…and one day, Phoebz, I'm not playing. I *will* punch her." Zoe is going on about Eve again. This has always been her favorite topic. They argue so much, I seriously can't believe they aren't sisters. "These hands are rated 'E' for 'Everyone,' and I hope she has a glove."

I put Lucky in his designated kennel before petting him under the chin. He licks my hand, causing the corner of my mouth to rise. "A glove?"

"Yeah, to catch these hands." She fake punches the air before smiling exuberantly.

I smack her arm playfully. "Stop, she's not that bad. She just has opinions."

"Stupid opinions. About bigoted stuff." She follows me down the hall and out to my car, where we both get in. By golly, it's hot! I turn on the engine, setting the AC to the second fan setting. "Acting like that girl isn't allowed to worship. Who does she think she is? The pope?"

"We all have a right to our opinions, Zo," I say, even though I agree with her.

"She has *no* right casting judgment, is what I'm saying." She opens her window as I start driving. "Not if your opinion hurts innocent people."

"But…I think her heart is in the right place. Her approach is just off." I switch off the AC. No sense wasting gas when Zoe's plan is more logical. I roll down my window instead.

"What's that supposed to mean?" Zoe turns her entire body toward me in the car. There's no way if we got in an accident, she'd survive. You're meant to face straight ahead in case the airbag goes off.

"Homosexuality is a sin, Zoe. You know it as well as I do." I wave my hand carelessly. "Love thy neighbor and all that *is* important, and I agree, Eve was in the wrong there, but she's simply trying, in the best way she knows how, to show this girl the error of her ways. Like a fire alarm. It's painful and deafening, but it could save your life."

"Bullshit." She slaps her hand on her lap.

"Language."

"You really believe that? You don't honestly believe new girl's actions are worse than Eve's behavior toward her?"

I'm not sure why she's getting mad.

"I never said it was *worse*. I think it's apples to apples. The Bible has *clear* intentions of how we should carry ourselves. We are all flawed. Children of Adam. Without repentance, our souls would remain in sin and fester. Neither sin can be absolved without first seeking forgiveness, and since neither one is asking for it, neither one is right. I don't have issues with either one of them, and you know I love Eve."

"So, you're taking her side?"

"I'm not taking anyone's side. I'm simply stating it is not our place to judge which sin is higher on God's 'smite' list." I rotate my palm upward, pulling into the drive-thru at Arby's. "Now what do you want? On me."

✝

We sit outside at a picnic table behind the vet clinic, eating our lunch. Eve must've really set Zoe off because this is turning into an all-day event. If I wasn't burned out on people before I'd even arrived to work this morning, I sure am now. She has now decided to make a list of why Eve is pure evil, as if this will cause me to overlook the sins of Blake. I've been trying my best to be an ear for her to vent, nodding when needed and adding the occasional "I know, right?" or "That's fair." But I keep fantasizing my life is a cartoon where I can rip my ears off and set them down for her and walk away from this conversation and go about my life. Maybe take a bath. I love baths. The silence would be amazing. Peaceful even.

"—And Ethan," she says, pulling me from my revery, forcing me to rejoin the conversation.

I clear my throat, blinking repeatedly. "What about him?" When had she started talking bad about him?

"The way she flirts with him like you're not even there? It's not very Christian of her to covet another woman's man." She crosses her arms adorning an expression that says I should know all of this already. It does bother me, admittedly less than it should, but my skin does crawl at the belief Eve would solicit this type of conduct toward her friends. I can't come up with a single reason to excuse it, either. Women should be helping each other.

I prop one elbow on the picnic table, resting my head in my palm, tracing my fingertip along the weathered grains of the wood. "Pretty sure that's only a thing for men in the Bible, but yeah," I say, kicking some dirt with my foot beneath me. I like to believe times have changed. Women are capable of much more now, no longer oppressed. "I'm not sure what that's all about."

Zoe speaks around a mouthful of food. "She's a bitch, Phoebz—"

"Language." Sitting up, I place the rest of my sandwich back in the bag, no longer hungry. This day long conversation has officially worn me down.

"That's what it's about. Haven't you been listening to anything I've been trying to say?" She swallows audibly, then takes another large bite.

How could I not?

"Zo, all I hear is you continuously bad-mouthing our best friend." I drop my head, burying it in my arms on the table before groaning. "How is any of this better than her actions? She thinks you're her friend."

"What if I don't want to be her friend?" This has my attention, causing me to lift up and blink at her. She balls up the foil paper to her sandwich, throwing it in the bag. "What if I *never* wanted to be her friend in the first place?"

Her hazel eyes darken with indignation. This isn't the first time in our history she has said something harshly in the moment, only to recant it later, once she's calmed down. Zoe is quite known for her impulsivity. The amount of times she's said someone was dead to her, only to forgive them a month later, is innumerable. "You don't mean that." I blink rapidly.

"Phoebe, I only tolerate her for you. But I don't understand why you still do. The two years I didn't have to be around her got me thinking." She puts her hand on my arm, her firm fingers squeezing gently. "We had a good thing going before she came along. Everything was simpler. I came back hoping she would've grown up, and here she is still treating you like shit."

"Language," I say dully, too lost in thought to care.

"She judges literally everyone for everything." She paces as she counts the reasons on her hand. "She's hurtful. She hasn't hung out with us more than once in the entire five months since I moved back. Even then, it was only for, what, thirty minutes before she had to go for some bullshit reason. She's hateful—"

"I hear you." I stand and face her, grabbing her shoulders to halt her movements. I can't keep listening to this. "She does text me regularly, though."

Zoe shakes her head, pushing out of my grip, ignoring all sense of reasoning.

"Look, I don't know what Eve did to make you this upset, Zo, but she's your friend. You should tell her what's bothering you because I remember a time when you guys hung out more with each other than me."

Glancing over her shoulder, she drops exasperatedly onto the bench. "How many times do I have to tell you I'm sorry about high school, Phoebe? Eve and I haven't seen eye to eye on extremely important topics since we graduated."

I hold up my hand. "We have history together, Zoe. Good and bad. We've argued and disagreed so many times. It doesn't mean we don't get over them. You love her."

She bites the inside of her cheek. "Some things can't be mended, Phoebe. We disagree on major core values. There's no forgiving that. Not to mention, even if there was a way to forgo our beliefs, she hasn't hung out with us in forever. She's practically removing *herself* from our friend group."

"We are all busy being adults. You were gone for *two years*."

Zoe shakes her head. "I had to, Phoebe. That's not fair. If Mystic offered med school, I would've done my clinicals here, and you know that."

Nodding, I say, "And I understand that, Zo. What I'm saying is, in a week, you're going to eat these words, and I think deep down, you know it. So can we *please* stop raising pitchforks at one of our *best friends* and talk about something else?"

Silence fills the space. The sound of chirping birds and passing cars surrounds the wordlessness. I can finally breathe. Peace at last.

"I'll talk about something else." Her voice cuts through the tranquil sounds of our urban jungle. "But before I move on, I need you to know. Eve is one of *your* best friends. Friend, as she may be, you're my only best. There." She holds her hands up like she's on trial. "I'm done. I've said all I need to say." Then she acts like she's wiping dirt off her hands, and we head inside.

Lord almighty, help her.

✝

I grab myself a glass of water from the fridge and sit down at the counter bar. "Home at last," I say to my empty house. The quiet's interrupted by the buzzing hum of the fridge as it kicks on. I can hear my sink dripping water. And the neighbor upstairs vacuuming.

The quiet doesn't bother me. It offers me time to reflect, which I enjoy. More often than not, my mind is a crowded room where everyone is talking over one another. It's very easy for me to become overstimulated and anxiety-ridden even in the quiet of this kitchen. Placing all the noises into their own respective places can be quite the fete, and without moments like these, I'd probably have been put in a padded room years ago.

Eve *is* my friend, but Zoe does have merit in asking why. Why would I allow her to treat me the way she frequently does? Why do I allow her to be hateful to others? The answer isn't a simple one. It barely makes sense to me. Like something on the tip of your tongue. You have enough of the puzzle to understand it, but no one else around you can fathom what you see. You can't even *explain* it. It just makes sense.

> The summer before sixth grade, I'd made a mistake.
> I wouldn't consider it a big mistake, but I guess that's determined in the eye of the beholder. Zoe and Piper were at summer camp. I had mono and had to stay home. Well, by the grace of God, I managed to

recover a week after they'd left, but without Zoe there to hang out, I was forced to go on solo adventures.

Mostly, I'd climb trees and hang out up there. One day, another girl asked if she could join, and we pretended she was a princess trapped at the top of a burning tree.

When I made it to the top, she'd asked, "However will I repay you?"

"No need. Just pay it forward. You'll save the next one!" I said, waving her off before I turned to make my journey back down the limbs of the old walnut tree. Before I could even think, though, she grabbed my hand and turned me around, laying a fat kiss on my cheek.

"Thank you, sweet prince!" she said and climbed down, leaving my mind reeling.

I was no prince. I hadn't even been pretending to be one. We're both girls, I thought. I didn't even know we could play games this way. *Okay, I guess I'm a prince.* I plucked a tulip off a bush in someone's yard. "For you, my princess." I bowed with the flower extended and my other hand behind my back.

We were in stitches as her older sister came up. She'd seen the entire bow and didn't appear half as entertained. "Melissa, Mom wants you inside," she said, shooting me the ugliest glare.

"It was fun meeting you," I said as she left.

I heard her sister yelling at her but couldn't make out why she was in trouble. I watched as the older girl took the flower from Melissa and threw it on the ground. Maybe her parents don't like her bringing in flowers? I thought.

I never saw Melissa again after that.

But I did see her sister on the first day of school. She stood a good six inches taller when she came up behind me, shoving my tiny frame to the ground.

"Hey, queer," she said.

I turned around slowly, peering up at the taller girl. "Me? No, I'm not—" but before I could finish, she kicked sand into my face. Tiny rocks got into my eyes and mouth as I started coughing, unable to see or breathe. "Stop!" I pleaded, panic settling into my bloodstream. That's when a loud whoosh came from beside me, directly followed by a loud smack.

I tried to open my eyes but couldn't really make out anything through the watery, bright mess.

"Let's get you to the nurse," I heard a girl say as she pulled me up by my elbow. My nose was running, and I kept crying, trying to rub my eyes. "Don't rub them," she said, wrapping her arms around mine and guiding me quickly into the school.

"It burns so bad," I cried.

"I know. Almost there." Her voice was gentle yet urgent.

When my vision finally returned, her copper hair was the first thing to take form.

She leaned down and placed her hand on my shoulder. "Hey, you okay?"

"Better now," I said, blinking rapidly. My eyes still burned from irritation and embarrassment. "I don't know why she came at me like that."

"Well, I hope she knows why I broke her nose." Her nose scrunched as her mouth curled upward, causing her gunmetal blue eyes to twinkle slightly. "Eve." She extended out her freckled hand for me to shake.

"You…You broke her nose?" I asked as I shook her hand.

Her shoulders rose. "Judging by the amount of blood, I'd say so. I don't fight like a girl. I have three older brothers. Kicking rocks in someone's face is pathetic." She stated it passively. Like breaking people's nose is a common, everyday thing to do. "She's lucky she only has a broken nose to remember me by."

"I'm sorry. I'm Phoebe. I didn't say that earlier."

"Well, listen here, Phoebe." She ran her thumb along my bicep. "I got your back, okay? Let me know if she comes back." She winked at me.

Melissa's sister never bothered me again after that. And no one ever found out why she'd attacked me in the first place, which was a relief. Best of all, Eve always had my back. No questions asked.

Yeah, she's stubborn and has a temper, but Eve saved my life that day, and she didn't even know me or what happened. She saw injustice taking place and acted impulsively. I know there's a good person in there, even if her outside seems very much like a cactus.

What bothers me is how people tend to fixate on what they're observing, while refusing to question what their eyes *aren't* seeing. They perceive half of a situation—or sometimes even less—and somehow decide it's enough to form viable facts upon. No rhyme or reason will ever change their mind. What's worse is the aggressive aspect. I got rocks thrown in my face for playing pretend—which wasn't even my idea in the first place—and somehow, that warranted the ill manner of their intent.

I'm curious by nature. I have to find out for myself. I have to hear both sides of a story before I can draw an accurate conclusion. This isn't even a Reformation thing. It's true in science, too. Believe what you want, but believe it because you've investigated every angle of it. Pick it apart until there's nothing left to analyze. Try to put yourself in other people's positions before resorting to aggression.

Eve is probably the way she is toward people like Blake because she was raised similar to me.

I must've been about five, playing in my room with my dolls. I couldn't find my Ken, so I decided to use two Barbies instead. Shortly after making them kiss, my mother walked in.

"What are you doing, Peep?" she asked, scanning my room. "Where's Ken?"

"I couldn't find him," I replied. "But it's okay, Barbie loves her."

"Peep." She grabbed one of the dolls out of my hand. "That is NOT how you play," she said sternly, but not yelling. "Barbie doesn't kiss Barbie."

"Why not?" I remember being so confused. My five-year-old brain didn't know the difference. Didn't understand what could possibly be wrong.

"Because, sweetie, God doesn't like that." She pulled me in, kissing the top of my head.

She stood up and walked to my door, one of my dolls still in her hand. "Now find Ken and make Barbie a woman of God, okay?"

I understand Zoe's frustrations. Eve had it harder than both of us. Her parents were very big into corporal punishment. Acting out of turn would get her smacked. After her father died, when she was sixteen and we were fifteen, her three older brothers began battling for the title of Man of the House. This often meant they'd insult and hit her before shoving her in small, confined places as punishment when she misbehaved. Her family had extremely high expectations she had no choice but to fulfill.

Zoe's parents were the exact opposite. They're good people, spiritual, always encouraging Zoe to do anything she desires. Zoe calls it "child-led" parenting. Which never made sense to me.

Regardless, Zoe turned out to be a smart, successful, beautiful individual who is just as inquisitive as I am. I understand how someone like Eve would be frustrating to someone raised completely different.

The older we got, the more vocal Eve became with her opinions. Eve and Zoe are seemingly night and day. Fire and Ice. Oil and water. Sitting in between their stubbornness has always been easier than picking a side because I appreciate them both in different ways. Certain things I need Zoe's understanding and compassion for, while other things definitely require some of Eve's abrasive, blunt reality.

When I became friends with Dakota, I promised her I wasn't going to let her be alone. Ultimately, this led to Eve stating her disapproval. And when Eve began throwing her opinions around, she was relentless. Something her entire family has in common.

After a while, Dakota found another friend named Sam. She was a very sweet girl. Eve used to joke she looked like me, but I never saw it. Her hair was enviously straight, without straightening, thin, and dark brown. Mine is thick and black. Her gait was different, and her clothing style was also nothing like mine. Yeah, we were the same height—five-four—but that's about all I could tell was the same.

When Dakota told me to leave her alone, I was devastated but respectfully rejoined my place between Eve and Zoe at our table, and all was right in the universe again.

I wonder if Blake has friends. I mean, the man she works with, she had mentioned, was a friend. But is he a true friend or just a work friend? Is he her only friend?

If she has more than him, does she also have to sit and listen to them bicker and argue or is that something exclusively attuned to my friend group?

Does she have siblings? And if she does, do they live in Mystic? I wonder if her family packed up and ditched her to move three hours into the city like mine did. Or maybe they'd be like Eve's brothers, whom she doesn't talk to unless she's forced.

Does Blake sit at home alone every night, unable to talk to her friends and family about her loss? She said her heart led her to EC. If I lost someone regardless of religion, I'd confide in my friends. Even if sometimes there's no getting through to either one of them. She didn't, though.

What if the person Blake lost was the only one who really understood her? Sometimes I feel like I lost that person when Dakota disappeared. I make a mental note to ask Blake if she shows up on Sunday. I'll be her friend if she needs one.

Chapter 6

Phoebe

Sometimes, my mother drives me insane. She's always making decisions on my behalf without consulting me first. While I was at work, she had come in. Couldn't even shoot me a text or call when I was off. No. Of course not. She just shows up at my place of work unannounced, causing my body to stiffen.

When I walk into the lobby, there she is. You'd think she owns every room she walks into by the way her nose points highly in the air. I've convinced myself it's because she's pompous enough to think she's "holier" than everyone around her.

Oftentimes, I've wondered how she and my father even got together. They are polar opposites. Where her heart is cold, his is full of warmth. Where she shuts people out, my father opens the door to everyone. There was even a period when I was younger when I thought their marriage was some kind of arrangement contrived out of convenience.

My mother is shorter and stalkier than my sister and me who take after my dad in almost every single way. Honestly, we don't look much like my mother at all. If you saw us together and didn't know us, I don't believe you'd think we were related. Today, I wish that were true.

"Hey, Peep." She smiles, but it doesn't reach her brown eyes. This is how most of her smiles are. All for show. I immediately know I'm not going to enjoy anything she's about to say. Why else would she visit me in a public setting? She knows I wouldn't tarnish our family's image in front of witnesses.

"Everything okay?" I ask, giving her a hug because if other people don't see us hug, they may think we aren't close. Not being close means whispers in the church. Whispers in the church mean my mother will remind me how much of a disappointment I am to our family.

"Of course." She feigns amusement as she brushes her long, light brown hair over her shoulder, shifting her gaze to the lobby of people holding their pets. "I wanted to remind you about Saturday!"

"Saturday?" What is she talking about? I genuinely haven't the slightest clue. I smooth out my already straightened scrubs in anticipation of her answer.

"Don't fidget." Her perfectly manicured hands hover over my wrists as she darts her gaze between the multiple people and their pets. I drop my hands to my sides immediately. Growing up, my mother would always say, "A lady never fidgets." After realizing she wasn't getting through to Piper and me, she'd hired the etiquette teacher. Mrs. Tipton was mean. Smacking our hands with a ruler like a nun in Catholic school. Until Piper spit in her face for pulling her hair after Piper refused to let her braid it. She quit after that. The lessons she taught us still stuck with me, though. In all honesty, most days I wonder why I still bother. It's pointless. No matter the lengths I go to bend over backward to keep up my mother's image, she never fails to remind me of how I could be better.

"I'm so glad I came to remind you. I figured you'd forget," she continues. "We're doing the flowerbeds around the church. You signed up."

Except I didn't. "Oh, right!" I say nervously, glancing over at a man who's letting his puppy smell a woman's golden retriever. "Can't believe I almost spaced. What time was that again?"

"First light! 7:00 AM." She curls her upper lip at a woman who has a bearded dragon on her shoulder rather than having it in the carrier she's set down on the floor beside her. I can practically hear her complaining about disease carrying 'lizards' in your home. She pulls a bottle of hand sanitizer from her purse and, as she's rubbing it into her palms, says, "There're so many flowers, and only four people signed up. I figure your father and the only other man will grab the flowers from the truck and dig the holes while us girls plant them."

"Sounds good." I sigh, sinking a little before catching myself and straightening my shoulders. 7:00 AM on a Saturday was not my plan at all. Guess I won't be sleeping in. This will totally throw off my relax-urday routine. As a matter of fact, it's going to throw relaxing completely in the trash. It's the only day I don't have to paste on a face and pretend to be perfect. Usually, I don't even get out of my jammies. I sleep until noon and give my hair a break by doing a deep conditioner. I even slather on a mud mask to add moisture to my face. I spend most of the day doing puzzles and binging on one of my many streaming subscriptions. It's my vacation from being anyone but myself. I like to dedicate one day a week to no one but me. So much for that dream.

"I'll see you tomorrow at the market," she says. Not asks. Great. I always love the subtle reminders my life is not mine. It's the community's.

I nod as she kisses my cheek and walks out. Letting out a deep breath, I watch her turning right down the street with a clueless grimace on her face.

I jump as my phone chimes.

Mother (9:47 AM)
Don't forget your sunblock!! Wouldn't want a repeat of last month :)

I roll my eyes.

Zoe meets me in the back to ask, "What did she want?"

"No one signed up to help plant the flowers around EC this Saturday. So, I guess I'm helping." I shake my head.

Zoe sighs. "Do you want my help?"

I drop my shoulders, defeated. "It doesn't matter."

"I can take a day out of my non-existent personal life to help my best friend." She nudges my arm with her elbow. "Besides, it's your relax-urday! The more people we can rally together, the faster the shit gets done. I'll call Eve and see if she wants to help too. What time?"

This is why Zoe is my best friend. With the exception of the two years she was gone in the city, she's never left me to handle my mother on my own. Admittedly, the four years of high school were rough, with her always seeming to have a test to study for when I needed her most. This slowly dwindled as college hit. Since we both wanted to be vet techs, we'd attended the same community college in Cypress. She decided to continue her education, however, which eventually led to her going to med school in the same city Piper lives in.

I was perfectly fine settling at vet tech. She promised when she eventually opens her own clinic, though, I'll be her first employee. I'm a simple person, very frugal in my expenses. I don't really require much and save predominantly all of my paychecks after bills.

Okay, fine, I spend quite a bit on streaming services, but what else am I supposed to do with my free time? Eve is always busy doing lord knows what, and Zoe spends predominantly every waking second at work. I learned halfway through my freshman year of high school the characters in movies and shows were there for me more than anyone else.

"7:00 AM."

✝

That night, I draw myself a bath. *Mama needs a bath*, I think as I turn the knob for the hot water. After what feels like an eternity, the tub is finally filled to the perfect temperature, and I strip down, dipping my toes in first, allowing my body to adjust to the soothing warmth before sinking down into the water completely.

Exhaling the tension in my shoulders, my phone rings. Leave it to the forces of pure evil to not let me find peace in these bubbles. I even lit candles! Nope. My phone just *has* to ring. And it just *has* to be my sister.

"Hey, Pipez," I say, placing my cell on the ledge of the bath. I love my sister, don't get me wrong, but mentally I'm excruciatingly drained, and it's only Tuesday. Something tells me I may actually die by my next relax-urday.

"What's wrong with you?" Not even a hello. Her enigmatic ability to read me is downright ridiculous from a hundred and ninety miles away.

I roll back, bending my knees to fully submerge my body into the hot, blissful, milky solution. "How do you do that?"

"Do what?" An image of her palm on her chest as she feigns ignorance emerges from the fog of my subconscious.

I play along anyway. "Know that something's wrong."

She laughs in amusement. "Hate to break it to you, but I know you better than you know yourself, sis."

Huffing out a breath, I push a few of the bubbles away from my chin. "Doubtful."

"Give it time." She always says this, and then when I do anything at all out of my norm, she says, 'I knew it.' Honestly, I think she likes taking credit for any form of chaos she can.

That's the thing about Piper. She has always been known to stir the pot. Not really with my father, but definitely with my mother. Sometimes, this behavior would put my father in a rough spot with the congregation. No one could control my sister's free spirit, which drove a control freak like my mother insane. Embarrassed by my sister, she eventually allowed her to stay home on Sundays.

This used to make me jealous. I wondered what it would be like to not have to go. I'm well aware it's important to be reminded we are not alone in our faith, but even understanding the significance didn't stop my resentment toward never being allotted a free second for myself. My life has always been about polishing the tarnish Piper caused to the Appleton name.

The Appleton namesake has never meant much to Piper, however, given she's agnostic. She believes there's something out there, but believes the Bible is just a book. *"Any book that gives you a set of rules declaring how you're meant to conduct your life was written by a control freak like Mom,"* she says. *"No creator would give you hormones and reproductive organs but force you to wait until marriage to have sex. He wouldn't create women only to treat them as poorly as what's written in the Bible."*

"Are you in a bath?" she asks, the sound of her guitar gently playing in the background. I used to lay awake staring at my ceiling listening to the sound of her gentle strumming bleed through the shared wall of our childhood bedrooms. To say she's attached to her guitar is an understatement. It's been her practical security blanket since she was twelve years old. Where she goes, the guitar is sure to follow.

"Yes." I inhale the cherry blossom aroma of the bubble bath before letting out a languorous sigh. "Is that an issue?"

"No. I just miss my baby sister. You sound exhausted."

Steam rises from the rippling surface of my water, circling around the coolness of the room before transforming into droplets of moisture on the fogged up mirror above the sink. "I am. This week has been draining."

"It's only Tuesday, Peep."

I squeeze my eyes closed. "Don't remind me."

"Is Mom riding your ass too hard?"

I open my mouth.

"And if you say 'Language,' I will reach through the phone and slap you."

Narrowing my eyes, I press my lips together firmly.

"I haven't burst into flames yet, making your idea people shouldn't cuss completely comical."

Pinching the bridge of my nose, I slowly open the lid to the emotions I've been bottling. "Tomorrow is my monthly turn to run the EC Charities booth at the farmer's market." There's no use arguing with my sister. She can be quite relentless at the best of times, and it's too early in the week to exhaust myself with pointless corrections she'll never even consider. I need all of my energy to survive until next Saturday, when I'll finally get to decompress. "And she came to my work today to remind me I volunteered to plant flowers around EC this Saturday."

"You're fucking joking," she gasps. "Relax-urday?!"

"Mhmm." I submerge my ears, drowning out my sister's usual tirade into nothing more than an inaudible muffle. I comb my fingers through my locks, dampening them. I stay like this longer than necessary, drawing my focus to the steady inspiration and expiration of my breathing, lulling me into a state of serenity.

When I decidedly lift my head from the immersion of peace, I'm met with a frustrated sigh. "Why did you volunteer your one day of solace?"

"I'll give you one guess," I huff. She knows how our mother is. I would never sacrifice a Saturday unless I was forced.

"When are you going to tell Mom to fuck off?" Piper grits out.

"When she's wrong." I grab the shampoo, glob a good amount into my hand, and start lathering it into my strands. As annoyed as I am to relinquish my personal day, I've already processed why she'd do it. She wouldn't have volunteered me if there were enough bodies already participating. We need the church to look pristine if we're going to expand the congregation, and my family can't do it alone.

"She's always wrong. You deserve at least one day a week where Mom doesn't own you."

Piper thinks my mother is double hard on me to compensate for not being able to control her. "She runs you too hard, Peep. No self-respecting person should be required to be at their mother's beck and call in their mid-twenties."

"I know, but it helps Dad, and he deserves it."

"He doesn't ask for that. It's not necessary, and he knows it. Mom is a fucking Nazi with a dollhouse. And heaven forbid her precious dolls don't make her look good by keeping up appearances."

"I know." I roll my eyes. Sometimes Piper can be such a broken record. Most days I can listen to her complain for hours. Not today, however. I was already frustrated before she interrupted my desperate attempt at hydro hypnosis. Moisture meditation? Whatever. I'm unable to foster my usual platitudes as I'm sure I'll be dispensing them at great excess throughout the week. In other words, I have none to spare in attempts to placate my sister's ire toward our mother. "You remind me why you left literally every time we talk."

"Because, Peep!" she says, practically whining in desperation. "You need to, too! The person she expects you to be is NOT who you are." A dissonant boom from the strings of her guitar is quickly halted by her palm. Silence lingers on the line as Piper levels her unexpected indignation. "And I'm worried for you."

"Worried for me?" I furrow my brows. Sitting up, I deposit body wash onto my loofah. "I know who I am, Pipez. Thank you, but I'm an adult. Mom isn't controlling *who I am,* just what I do."

"One day, Peep, you're going to wake up and crave the woman you *really* are. And that woman will mean more to you than any woman Mom forces you to be. It happened to me, and I promise it'll happen to you."

"Hilarious," I deadpan, scrubbing my arms. It's frustrating that she assumes she knows me. She left the second she turned eighteen. The only time I ever see her is on holidays, and usually, she's only here for a few hours before she heads back to the city three hours away. We haven't been around each other for more than four hours, twice a year, in about ten years.

"Laugh all you want, Phoebe, but just know, when it happens—because it *will* happen—your world is going to fall apart."

The loofah falls from my fingers. "Geez! You're so dramatic. This has always been your issue." I'm vibrating with anger now. My face burning for reasons beyond my scalding bathing preferences. "You left! You don't know me anymore."

"I've offered for you to stay with me. To visit me! You refuse to leave that stupid fucking town and that piece of shit church!" I flinch at her words. "And I need you to know you'll always have me. No matter how much you strive to please them, THOSE PEOPLE will still turn on you. Call me the enemy for leaving, but I love you, and I always will. I didn't leave *you,* Phoebe." She takes in a deep breath. "I left *them.* "

So much for a peaceful bath.

Chapter 7

Phoebe

I hate this. It's so early. I'm standing outside the church and absolutely no one is here. I glance down at my phone. 7:05. My mother *did* say 7:00, didn't she? Whatever. I need coffee. Blessed Beans is only a few minutes from here. She can get mad all she wants, but if I don't get some coffee in me, I think everyone is about to be upset. Especially since they've decided not to show up on time.

"Phoebe?" Her soft, alto voice rings out from behind me. My stomach dips. I turn around, and standing there in a ripped pair of jeans and form-fitting white tank top, is Blake.

My mind jumps back to the last time we saw each other. How stupid I was in the car. Actually, I'm just going to say the entire night. From the grenadine to not thinking about a DD to my hand in her lap. Everything. I'm so ashamed. Maybe she's gullible enough to believe one drink could have made me forget the whole night. Doesn't alcohol make you do and then forget stupid stuff? I just won't bring it up.

She is lanky and a good four inches taller than me, but her arms definitely indicate she works out. And like her lips, her skin seems soft. My body fights a random urge to reach out and find out if I'm right. I shouldn't.

"Blake?" I walk toward her. "What are you doing here?"

"Flower beds, right?" She scans the barren church yard, eyes landing on the desolate playground on the side. "Am I early?"

"I mean, I was told 7:00, but since no one is here, I'm getting coffee. It's too early for this," I grumble. The sun is climbing higher in the sky and bringing with it an undesirable warmth. I'm already dreading what mid-morning and afternoon will feel like. I collect my hair, piling it into a messy bun to prevent the irritating stickiness already beginning on my neck. The later my family is, the hotter it's going to get.

"Mm, coffee sounds so good. Can I join you?"

A sudden hot/cold settles down my entire body, and my eyes can't seem to meet hers. "If you want to," I say. *Relax, Appleton,* I think, and turn abruptly, beginning my journey to Blessed Beans. I'm not sure she's following, but I'm hoping.

"Slow down," she says, fast walking toward me. "You need coffee desperately enough to run to it?"

"I'm not running," I say, continuing my hasty march. "You just walk slow."

She jogs out in front of me, turning. We lock eyes as she jogs backward. "We've been 'walking' for less than two seconds, and my calves burn."

"Maybe you should exercise more," I tease.

"I run five days a week." The thought of her running fills my mind. Sweating. Breathing heavily as she maintains her pace. Suddenly, I'm reminded of my dream. My hands in her hair as her lips slide against mine— "You, okay?" She lifts her knees while continuing to jog backwards.

I shake my head, attempting to rid my intrusive thoughts. "Yeah, why wouldn't I be?"

"I'm not sure." She smirks, grabbing my arms and forcing me to stop unless I want to crash into her. "Look, are you embarrassed?"

My stomach drops. "Wh-why would I be embarrassed?"

She shoots me an *I'm-not-stupid* look.

I shake my head again, acting clueless. "You're gonna make me say it?" she asks, her voice dripping with discomfort.

"You didn't even have to bring it up," I argue, heat rising to my cheeks.

"So, you are embarrassed." She grins in amusement. Gosh, even her smile is captivating. Her teeth are perfectly white and straight, except one of her canines is crooked.

"Can we just talk about something else?" I say, tapping my foot and looking everywhere but at her full bottom lip.

She drops her hands from my arms. "Yeah, sure. I'm sorry. What do you want to talk about?"

We continue to walk side by side. "So, you own a bar?" I ask.

Blake nods, considering the question. "Yeah, with my brother, Jude," she says, rubbing the back of her neck.

"Oh, you have a brother?" My hand accidentally brushes hers as we walk, causing my body to shift slightly away from her. "Older or younger?"

"Younger. Not by much." She seems slightly uncomfortable as she talks. "We're eleven months apart. It was his idea to open the bar. He let me choose the name, though."

"Oh, that guy was your brother?"

"Delaney?" She waves her hand. "No. My brother doesn't work there anymore."

Is he another person who she can't speak to about her loss? The more I try to get to know her, the lonelier she seems to be. "Why not?"

We approach the coffee shop, and she moves in front of me to open the door. The smell of coffee soothes my sense as it wafts toward me. "Umm, well..." She gestures me inside. "Because he passed away two months ago."

My stomach sinks. "He...I'm so sorry." I feel bad for asking. I wanted to change the topic to stop the awkwardness, and now I've tripped and fallen into something more awkward than my stupid bar scene. *Good job me.* "Is he the reason you came to EC?"

"Yes." We find a table, and once we're seated across from each other, her chin lifts to peer at the menu behind the counter. "What's good here?"

"I usually get a hazelnut flat white with an extra shot," I say. "You needed to find acceptance for his death?"

"Hang on," she says, rising to her feet. "Let me order our drinks."

She takes off to the counter, where Jaime takes her order. I can't believe I'm asking these questions. I would totally understand if she changed the topic. I can't even imagine how hard it would be to go to work every day at a place that reminded me of Piper. Let alone spout on about her to a person I barely know a mere two months after her death. Piper may drive me insane, but knowing she'd never annoy me again would be devastating. I'm not sure I'd even want to talk about it with people I do know, and we haven't created something together like a bar I'm left to tend to without her.

"Sorry," she says as she sits back down.

"Don't be. How much do I owe you for the coffee?"

She waves her hand, avoiding eye contact. "My treat."

"I have money," I say before realizing how rude it sounds. I didn't mean for it to come out quite that abrasive. I should be the one paying, though. She was over here answering my questions about a topic I deemed as still rather fresh *and* paying for my coffee?

"You'll get the next one." She says it as if she's confident we'll ever have coffee together again. I want to know where this confidence comes from. Unless she's just trying to move on from the topic. I take the hint.

"Sorry, you said he was the reason you showed up at EC?" What was I doing? I could've used the moment to change the topic, but instead, I went straight back to it.

She lets out a sigh. "Oh, yeah. Okay, so—"

"Chapel! Two flat whites," Jaime calls.

"One sec." She runs and grabs the cups before placing one in front of me and sitting back down.

"Okay, Siren's Song was Jude's idea. I was living with him a few months before he asked me to help him with a business idea." I can't help but notice her long, slender fingers wrapping around her cup as she briefly blows on her coffee before taking a sip. "This *is* good coffee."

"It really is." I bow my head shyly.

"'A place for everyone,' he said." Her face lights up as she reminisces about her late brother. "He'd noticed a vacant building for sale right in the middle of town, and it gave him the idea."

"Everyone? Isn't that every bar?" I take a sip of my drink, which burns my tongue, but I try to play it off.

"Not the LGBT-Plus."

"Like…" I pause because I don't know if the next words out of my mouth will offend her, but I decide to say it anyway, "…the homosexuals?"

"'Homosexuals.'" Her eyes light with mirth as she imitates me. I'm not sure what's funny. I'm just trying to understand. Did I go to a gay bar by accident? "Not just gay people, Phoebe, but yeah, them, too."

"Is…Siren's Song a…gay bar?"

"No!" she says quickly, probably sensing my nervousness. "It's just a bar. A safe haven. I came up with the name because Siren's are known for causing destruction, causing ships to crash, and many people to lose their lives, but they're actually just lonely and misunderstood. They call out their song to those lost in the ocean. Sailors would hear their song and follow in search of refuge. That's what the bar is for. It's for all of those 'lost at sea.' Just trying to find a home.

"Jude saw a lot of misery in our community. Too many lost souls searching for a place to belong. He'd *begged* me to move back to Mystic. *Begged* me to start this. I'd promised myself I would never come back here. Certain parts of Mystic Harbor are quite ugly. You know?"

Right, the Seedy Side, for example. "You lived here?" I asked. I've never seen her around. "Did you go to Cypress?"

"Yeah," she says. "I would've continued to live there too, but after my mom and new stepdad moved to Texas, they left us the house. Jude was living there alone."

"He didn't have a wife? Or girlfriend?"

"No. Jude was Ace."

"Ace? What? Like awesome?"

The corners of her mouth tip up to bare her crooked canine. "Asexual. He didn't date. He wasn't interested in girls."

"Boys?"

"Nope. No one." She covers her mouth to hide her amusement. "Fuck, it surprises me how little you know about this stuff." She smiles, pressing her cup to her bottom lip. Which causes me to lick mine. "It's honestly adorable."

My face flushes, and I fidget in my seat. "I'm sorry," I say, kind of nervous, wishing I knew more. Was there a way I could learn to shut off my romantic interests? Was it that simple? I'd never thought to try and turn off my attraction completely. I was beginning to realize there was this entire world out there I never knew existed. God made us to like the opposite gender. Like puzzle pieces made to fit together. Mesh into one. I never knew he gave some people the choice to not like anyone at all.

"Don't be, point is, you get to learn it now. And I can teach you." She raises one eyebrow nervously. "If you want me to, of course?"

"I have been known to be quite inquisitive. I'd probably annoy you with all of my questions."

"Never." She meets my gaze. Light reflects off her dark blue eyes—so incredibly perfect it makes my whole body tremble. Her knee brushes against mine under the table and my stomach does backflips for absolutely no comprehensible reason.

"So," my voice croaks. I clear my throat and move my knee away. Not touching makes things easier. Don't want her to think it was on purpose. Not after the car incident. "Sorry, so you agreed to move back in to help him with this bar?"

"Yeah, I couldn't let him live alone. But the bar is only Step One." She shifts in her seat, and now her foot is touching mine.

My body freezes.

Maybe she wants it to be on purpose. My gaze drops to the table, envisioning our feet below, and then back up at her before scanning around to make sure no one is witnessing this. Given the place is empty and Jaime is in the back means no. We are on our own little island, and no one would notice but us. Even if Jaime did reappear, the angle of the seats would still obstruct her view, unless she came out from behind the bar. Which she never does. Would it be wrong to not move? I bite my lip as I contemplate. I should...right? Then why don't I want to? My body wills my other foot forward instead, boxing hers in.

"Step One?" I can't meet her eyes, but hear her inhale deeply.

"Yeah," she says softer, sliding her leg forward until her calf is pressing against mine. My legs tighten, and my head feels hazy. "Step One."

My heart is pounding in my ears, and I can't seem to catch my breath. I clear my throat. "Wh-what's Step Two?"

Her eyes glance down at my mouth. I feel dizzy. My legs are too shaky to stand up.

"Step Two," she says as she moves her leg up mine and leans in, placing her arms on the table, "is educating girls like you."

"Girls like me?" I ask, but my voice can't seem to rise above a whisper. "Like me, how?" I fight the urge to lean in too.

I watch my hand gently grab Blake's wrist on the table. Her other hand moves closer to mine, and she trails the back of my wrist with her finger. Heat pools below my belly button, and now my mind can't seem to focus on anything but kissing her. How her lips would feel on mine. If it'd be sloppy like Ethan's. I can't—*shouldn't*—be thinking about this. Why am I? Where is all of this coming from? How did I go from getting to know a perfect stranger to touching her like this?

DING!

The door chimes as three teenagers walk in. I jump and separate in such a haste my head spins. "We should head back," I suggest. The fog surrounding my brain slowly begins to dissipate as I force myself to remember where we are.

She remains still for a moment, a crease forming in her forehead, probably trying to comprehend why I'm jumpy. "Yeah," she agrees, clearing her throat, before rising from her seat, seemingly unphased by our light touches. So why am I a total fumbling mess as I stagger to my unexpectedly wobbly feet?

As we're walking back, I try to break the awkward silence. "How did your brother pass, if you don't mind me asking?"

"Sudden Cardiac Death. It's genetic. Short answer is his heart muscles randomly thickened, which made it harder for his heart to pump blood. One minute, he was dancing in our living room—he was a goof like that—and the next, he was gone…" Her eyes begin to water. She wipes them away, quickly changing the subject. "But enough heavy." Her mood instantly shifts, her eyes still red. "Ready to plant some flowers?"

"There you are!" my mother yells from beside Eve, Zoe, and my father. Her eyes quickly pan to Blake with disgust. "We're just waiting on a," she glimpses at the sign-up list, "Blake Chapel, so he can help your dad get the flowers off the truck and start digging the holes."

"That's me." Blake raises her hand confidently and walks to where my father is standing. She claps her hands together, ignoring the fact my mother misgendered her. Guess she's used to it with a name like 'Blake.' "Where're the flowers?"

"Of course, that's Blake," my mother huffs under her breath and rolls her eyes. "Why would a parent give their daughter a boy's name?"

"Because it's cool?" Zoe says, arms crossed, at my mother. Does she want to punch her too? She's been incomprehensibly confrontational lately.

"For a boy," Eve supplies.

"You know I've had about en—"

"Can we plant some flowers?" I interject, voice laced with irritation.

"Whatever. I'm going to help Pastor Pete and Blake." I watch Zoe walk over to where Blake is now in the bed of the truck, passing off the pots of flowers to my father on the ground. Her tank is riding up, and I definitely don't notice her hip bone and how it meets the waistband of her pants. Why is my mouth dry?

"Zoe is becoming a problem," my mother says. "She better learn to respect her elders or—"

"Or what, Mother?" I snap. "You'll tell me I'm not allowed to see her anymore? Why do you have to act terribly?"

"Phoebe!" Eve chimes in, prying herself between us. "What's gotten into you?"

My mother gasps. "Did you forget who you were talking to?"

I can't deal with either one of them right now. The judgment is too much. I can only take so much hate and disgust before shutting down. I storm off before saying something I know I'll regret. "Did everyone wake up on the wrong side of the bed this morning?" she yells as I'm walking away.

I sit on a park bench and watch my father and Zoe talking to Blake. They seem to all be getting along. Why can't my mother get on board? If the pastor is fine with her, what's the problem?

I wonder what they're talking about. Whatever it is, they're being very quiet while they dig. *Is this what it looks like,* I think, *when the devil tempts you?* Surely, my father isn't that naïve. She may be able to pull the wool over Zoe's eyes, but surely not my father, too. The pastor? I've heard of people of faith being conned by the devil. Being dragged down and made to believe their acts are objective in the name of the Lord when, in reality, it's all a smoke screen orchestrated by the devil to poison and corrupt the flock. Is this how it starts?

Occasionally, Blake beams in my direction. It causes my stomach to flutter. I feel sick. She's so pretty. She could have any guy she wants. She could be happy with any guy if she wasn't obsessed with sin.

I peer over at my mother and Eve, who are digging holes in a flower garden on the opposite side of the church from my father. Judging by their faces, I know they're talking bad about her.

My mother does have a point, though: we cannot condone sin. She's only doing her moral obligation as a Christian to cast out Blake's wrongdoings, and how is she rewarded? She's separated herself from my father and Zoe planting flowers with the only other person not swayed by corruption.

It's my father's job to love the sinner and show them the way. That responsibility doesn't fall on my mother. She calls it like it is. Always has. I walk back over to where she is on her chosen side of the church opposite them. Her back is turned to the group, not even wanting to see what they could be doing with Blake.

"I'm sorry, Mom," I say. "I know you're only trying to protect us from falling victim to sin."

My mother grabs my hand, pulling me down into a hug. My chin rests on her shoulder, watching Blake drop a flower bush into a hole. She looks over at me, frowning slightly. I close my eyes and think about the strength I'll need to pull myself away from her. I shouldn't see her anymore. Today is evidence enough. I fell victim to her magnetism. I gave in to temptation. Only slightly, but I still did. It's hard not being near her, and I have no clue why.

We finish planting all of the flowers around 3:00, my body so sore and dirty I'm ready to sleep a thousand hours. As I walk up to where my father's little group is, their voices quiet. "All finished over there, Peep?"

Blake giggles. "Peep?"

I roll my eyes. "Yeah, I'm going home." I turn to walk off.

"Wait." Blake grabs my arm gently. I stop and turn, staring at her hand on my arm, wishing she'd let go. Everyone is watching this interaction, and I can't breathe. "I'll see you tomorrow, right?"

I move my arm out of her clutch.

"Right." I feign happiness. I'm guessing my smile isn't genuine enough however because hers drains from her face completely. I don't know what she's expecting. She's not a boy. I have a boyfriend. She may have managed to find a vulnerable spot in the coffee shop, but it won't happen again. I will not be tricked twice. I will show God no level of temptation will make me fall from His grace.

For He is my shepherd. Nice try, Satan. You really had me going.

†

If a person chooses sin, is it possible to change their mind? Does Blake even know the consequences of her choices? Maybe if she would've known Dakota. If we would've gone to the same school. Is it too late for her?

> I had finished grabbing my tray of food and was heading to the table when I noticed Dakota sitting alone. I'd promised she'd never sit alone, so I headed over to her table but was stopped by a hand, grabbing me forcefully and pulling me down to sit.
>
> "Stay here today," Zoe said, a concerned look on her face.
>
> "Wh-why?" I asked.
>
> "Trust us, just stay here."

I peered over at Dakota, who was extremely devastated.

"No, look at her. She's upset. I promised her she'd never sit alone. Where's Sam?" I stood again, only to be pulled down once more by Zoe.

"With any luck, Sam isn't anywhere near that disgusting freak. I hope she learned her lesson." Eve scoffed.

"Phoebz, listen to me. You can NOT go over there right now."

"Lesson? What lesson?" I preemptively grew furious, my skin hot as I trembled. "I can't abandon her! What the heck is going on?!"

"She molested her, Phoebz." Eve rolled her eyes as if I was supposed to know.

"Who? Molested...what?!" Tears formed in my eyes. I still couldn't take my eyes off Dakota. Her elbow was on the table with her head in her hands, fingers in her blonde hair, when someone approached her. She sat upright to look at them, and they dumped the entire contents of their tray on her lap, causing her to immediately stand in shock, now covered in gravy, potatoes, and mystery rib.

"Dyke!" the guy yelled.

"Your little Queer Edward Scissorhands over there molested Sam. Sam confessed everything," Eve responded, gesturing to Dakota, now crying and running toward the bathroom.

"She would never! I have to go talk to her." I moved but got pushed back down.

"What, and get raped in a bathroom? I think not, Phoebe. Sit your ass back down." Eve took a bite out of an apple. Then, while still chewing, said, "Even if she didn't touch you. It doesn't matter. Being seen with her will only rope you in as a dyke too."

I glanced at Zoe, fighting back tears. "She's right, Phoebz. You can't help her."

I can't help you. Ringing in my ears. *Just go...*

I knew what was right and wrong. I should've ignored everyone trying to keep us apart, even if it was Dakota herself. I should've been there for her when no one else was. Defended her. Fought the bullies beside her. What if God is sending me Blake as a second chance to do what's right?

I have to help Blake. I have to try at least. I can't abandon her like I abandoned Dakota. I have to do something. I *have* to see her again! I have to save her. For Dakota.

Chapter 8

Phoebe

Sunday, I arrive at church and instantly find myself searching for Blake. I decided to wear my favorite dress, a hunter-green maxi. It hugs my chest and middle perfectly before flowing freely to the floor below my waist. This brings out my eyes and exposes my shoulders—my best features.

Blake's not here yet. I honestly have no idea how I'm going to ask if I can save her, anyway. If I approach this incorrectly, it could lead to hostility, and that's the last thing I want. I need to figure out a way to tackle this from a place of love. Something that says I care and want to help them with their lifestyle choices.

She truly *does* seem like an amazing person. Anyone willing to close their bar early and drive someone home only to find their own way home can't be too terrible. I'd hate for her to burn because of one immoral transgression.

I mean, maybe she has more transgressions. I can't be sure, given I don't know her that well. But if there's one thing church has taught me, it's that no one is inherently evil. Everyone has a heart. It's just a matter of figuring out how to reach their heart without judging them.

How do I go about asking if she'd like to be saved without coming off as if I'm judging her? I tell myself I'll figure it out once I see her. But where is she?

As I'm scanning the crowd, someone's arm grabs my waist from behind. "Hey, babe," Ethan says as I turn. He places both of his hands on my hips and kisses my cheek. "I can't wait for today's service."

"Yeah?" I ask, kind of confused how today would be different from any other Sunday. I mean, my father is an amazing pastor. It'd be naïve of me to think his sermons don't touch other's spirits as much as they touch mine.

"Yeah," he preens. "Your dad is letting me read today!"

I'm still scanning around, not fully listening. Then...

...There she is.

I notice the ram bar on the front of her matte black old Dodge truck first. I watch as she jumps out, smoothing her long-sleeved button-up as she approaches the church. This one is maroon against her black slacks. Her hair is pulled into a high ponytail. It's so short, it barely fits into the elastic. My stomach fills with excitement as I start to go over what I'm going to say.

But what if she doesn't stick around after the service long enough for me to ask her? I should probably ask her now.

"At least," Ethan runs his hand through his hair, drawing my attention back to his uninteresting ramble, "it inspired *me*."

"I'm sure it'll be very uplifting! I can't wait to hear it. You're going to do great!" I squeeze his bicep, trying to stave off what seems to be nervousness.

He'll do fine. He's read passages for the service before. He doesn't stammer or misread. I'm not sure why he's nervous this time, but I have every faith his arrogance will carry him through. Like it always does. "Excuse me, Ethan," I say.

I watch her face light up with my approach. The tips of her ears get red as her crooked canine enters my periphery.

I can't explain why I'm smiling too. It's as if she's contagious, and I'm catching her merriment.

"Hey," I say, walking up, unable to meet her gaze. I've settled for the ground again. It truly is nice grass. My father hired a very good landscaper, who offered him a discount on behalf of also being a member of the church. Looking at it now, I think my father should pay him more.

"Hi," she says, rubbing the back of her neck, her lips curling upward. "I'm really glad you're here."

"You thought I wouldn't be?" My stomach bottoms out as I search the ground for stability.

"No. I knew you would, but…" she shifts her weight from foot to foot. "You just seemed upset yesterday. Did…" Now she's the one observing the grass. "Did I do something?"

I know she's talking about the coffee shop. I'm not sure what to say. If I talk about it, would I be giving it power? Would that be counterintuitive? Would not addressing it be rude?

"I'm fine," I decide. Addressing it may help inspire her to be more susceptible to what I'm going to ask. "I just had a lot to think about."

"Oh, yeah?" Her eyes widen in interest, finding my face again. "Any resolutions? Epiphanies?"

"Yes, actually." I lift my chin. *Confidence is key, Appleton. Confidence is key.* If I can stay poised and positive, maybe it'll show her what's necessary. "Could we talk more about it after the service?" *Please say yes, please say yes, please say yes.*

"I'd love that." She smirks.

"Okay!" I'm more overjoyed than I probably should be, but my body feels like icy hot around her. My arms are weak. I want to sit down. I have no idea how she does that. "Don't go anywhere. I tend to get stopped a lot, and I'd hate for you to feel like I'm not trying to get to you. I am, I promise. It's just…everyone knows me, and they all want to tell me things, and when I leave one person, another one is right there and—"

"Phoebe!" She stops me. "I'll wait for you, okay?" Her eyes meet mine, and I can't seem to pull away; it's causing a swoop low in my belly. Why is breathing always a task around her? "I promise."

Oof. The way she promises sends another flush of heat through me. I glance down at her arms and am reminded of what they look like under her sleeves. The muscles, how flat her stomach is. I wonder if her stomach has muscle tone, too. Decipherable marks? Does she have freckles? What I've seen so far seems flawless, and I know God couldn't possibly have made her flawless.

Well, he didn't, did he? She has one massive flaw. I hope she lets me help her. I need to be able to spend more time with her.

"Okay, sorry."

A single brow shoots up. "For what?" she asks.

"Rambling. I ramble. I didn't mean to. My dad says sometimes I talk in circles. I don't mean to. I just can't seem to find the words, and then I talk and talk, and I can't seem to find the words so—"

"You're rambling again."

"Right! After the service…" I bite my tongue. Why am I being like this?

"I'll see you then."

I start to walk away but stop and turn. "Sit near me, okay?"

She grins. "Okay."

✝

I could kill Ethan. Seriously. I've now been drawn into such a predicament I'm not sure I'll ever be able to pull myself out. The service is now over, and everyone's smiling, laughing, and *congratulating* me! I feel sick. So sick. I want to go home. I want to shroud myself in darkness. I need to be alone. How do I backpedal this?

We were all sitting down after singing a psalm, and Ethan, with a dance in his feet, jumped up the step to the pulpit and placed his paper down. The congregation seemed to enjoy his goofiness. He cleared his throat with too much enthusiasm— practically saying the word 'ahem.' "This reading is from Deuteronomy Chapter 31, Verses 6-8: 'Be strong and courageous. Do not be afraid or terrified because of them, for the Lord your God goes with you; he will never leave you nor forsake you. Then Moses summoned Joshua and said to him in the presence of all

Israel, 'Be strong and courageous, for you must go with this people into the land that the Lord swore to their ancestors to give them, and you must divide it among them as their inheritance. The Lord himself goes before you and will be with you; he will never leave you nor forsake you. Do not be afraid; do not be discouraged.' Beautiful. Absolutely beautiful passage. 'Be strong and courageous.' Umm…Phoebe…" All the pews creaked as bodies turned to face me. I peered up from my pamphlet.

What is he doing?

"I'd like to say a few words," he continued. "You've been with me, helping me become a better man and a better Christian."

Please sit down. The reading is over. SIT DOWN! my mind screamed. I hate when the attention is on me. There were too many eyes. I glanced over at Blake, who was looking at me with a very confused expression. I glowered back at Ethan.

"I know it's not the easiest thing to do. I'm a difficult person at the best of times." He smirked while the crowd let out a quiet laugh. His lowered his head still meeting my eye. *Can he even do this? This isn't the right time to give your own speeches. It's a time for worship and praise! It's God's time!* "I've been thinking a lot, trying to come up with the right words to tell you how I feel." He gripped his paper tightly, pressing his body against the pulpit. *Great. Tell me later. When it isn't God's hour.*

I peered at Zoe, who was mouthing the words, "What is happening?"

"I have no idea," I mouthed back, starting to panic. *Why isn't anyone stopping this?* I've never been made the center of the congregation before. This is why I never joined the choir. He continued talking, but I couldn't hear him.

Everyone was staring at me and it reminded me of a time in kindergarten, when they made me the main event at a stupid school program. I was in a mask and was told to dance around, but when I saw all the people, I froze. They were all staring at me. I was so embarrassed. So overwhelmed, I started crying. And not some tiny cry. I broke down, sobbing like a baby on stage while everyone glared at me. The music was blaring. I could dance around like I was supposed to. I was frozen. Like now. Worst childhood memory ever. Thinking about it still causes my eyes to tear up.

Needless to say, my mother was *not* pleased with me that night. I'd made a mockery of our family. She had everything but kind words for me when we got to the car. I remember sobbing while she attacked everything not perfect about me.

Is that going to happen now? I shifted my gaze toward my mother, staring longingly at Ethan as he hopped down the step to the pulpit. She hung on to every syllable while gently holding the chain of her necklace. *Oh no.*

Ethan took a big breath. "Phoebe Appleton."

Jesus! When had he ended up beside me?

He knelt down and pulled a box from his coat pocket before opening it to reveal a diamond ring bigger than I'd ever pick for myself. Then again, we'd never talked about rings. Because we are nowhere near that point in our relationship!

"Will you marry me?"

I glanced around. Eve was sinking in her seat, clearly jealous the attention wasn't on her. All eyes were on me. I wanted to cry. If I said no, what would it say about my family? My father gazed intently, waiting on my response. I could tell he hadn't prepared for this, but he needed to finish the service. He was checking his watch.

But *marry Ethan?* I didn't have a choice. I found Blake, grinning. It wasn't the same joyous expression everyone else was adorning. It almost looked like she was tamping down amusement at my predicament. And that's when it hit me.

"I'll never marry. But don't tell Ethan that."

Oh, God—no—gosh. I meant, oh gosh. My brain was scrambling.

"No marriage, no booty! And I mean NO marriage!"

Did she seriously think it was funny? She probably expected me to say no. And given the information, I should've said no. Our relationship was nowhere near marriage. It would've made sense and been completely fair for me to have respectfully declined the proposal and then do what I probably should've done forever ago and break up with him.

Why haven't I broken up with him? Lord knows I wouldn't have been sitting there with somewhere around fifty-five pairs of eyes on me, expecting the fairytale ending that comes at the end of every one of my mother's romance novels. Seriously, not a single person in this church *wasn't staring* at me. And with the exception of Blake giggling like a child, my father growing impatient, and Zoe pressing me to say something, everyone had whale eyes.

I couldn't say no. It would've destroyed Ethan…and then my mother would've destroyed me…because I destroyed the church's view of our family. I still want to throw up. Nope. Can't throw up. "Yes, Ethan Fenech." My lips twisted into something I prayed resembled excitement. Blake's eyes darted between me and Ethan as I let out a disingenuous flutter of mirth for good measure. Tears of embarrassment still burn my eyes. "Okay."

"Yeah?" he'd asked, rising to his feet.

"Yes," I said again, more to myself than to him. He slid the ring on my left ring finger and pulled me into the aisle to wrap his arms around me, for a kiss.

I've never kissed anyone in church before. I haven't deemed it appropriate until I said, 'I do.' Right? Even my parents don't kiss in church. None of the other members do either. It felt wrong. This whole thing feels so wrong. When he pulled away, my eyes went straight to Blake, who stared down at her lap practically the rest of the service, excluding the times we would rise.

How do I fix it? I can't get *married!* This is not how I saw my life going. I mean, sure, one day, but…to Ethan? I'll have to sleep with him now. I'm not ready to *have sex* with him! I'm not ready to do that with *anyone!* Is that even me? I can't breathe.

I make my way through the crowd, almost unable to focus on all of the "*Congratulations, Phoebe's*" and "*So proud of you's.*" Then there's my personal favorite. "*How soon until children?*" I'm trying desperately to hold up this fake expression of excitement, being sure to tack on a thank you with every interaction, but if I don't escape soon, I'm going to puke.

Finally, I make it out the door. I close my eyes and look up at the sky. Fresh air. I take a deep breath in, then let it out. It's okay. Finally, I can breathe.

Chapter 9

Blake

I kick my tire outside the church. I feel stupid. My body is pulsing with quite an assortment of emotions, all fighting to captain the ship. Confusion, anger, sadness, even a splash of elation being overtaken by jealousy. Why am I jealous? She's not mine…

…But she *is* queer! This isn't her. She can't marry this…this douchebag. High-jacking a church service? Who does he think he is, stealing the show like that? Jesus? I really don't like this guy.

Then, having to watch him kiss her. It didn't look natural at all. How did no one else see it? I want to punch him. Tell him to get his grubby dick beaters off her. What the fuck is wrong with me? I may assume I know her, but I know nothing about Phoebe. Dakota knew her, what? Ten years ago? I know *of* her. No way the girl I drove home the other night would've said yes to his proposal.

Grief and confusion fight for consumption in my head at the realization she's stuck. She can't marry him. She can't—

The door bursts open and she's practically clawing her way out of the chapel. She's alone, hyperventilating, and I don't know how to make her smile. Sadness doesn't suit her.

"Congrats, Appleton," I call out to her from my truck. No one is around as she approaches me. "Or should I say, 'Future Mrs. Fenech.'"

She's almost to me when she rolls her eyes and shifts her body slightly to walk past me instead. I reach forward and grab her wrist, letting go when her body stills. "Hold on, just wait a second," I beg.

"I can't do this right now, Blake," she groans despairingly. "I need to go home. Just…" I watch as her eyes fill with tears. "Just let me go home." She again motions to leave.

"Let me take you," I plead. "Please."

Phoebe stops abruptly deciding whether to take me up on the offer. Eventually walking to the passenger side and getting in. She's quiet as I start the engine.

"What is going on? You're getting married! Shouldn't you be happy?" I force excitement, knowing damn well why she's not, but I need to hear her say it. I need to know this isn't what she wants. Why did she even say yes?

"Don't act like you care," she bites back.

I move back, eyes widening. "What?" I'm not sure why she's taking her decision to get married out on me. My grip tightens on the wheel as I try to keep my words as level as possible. "Phoebe, I do care." This is ridiculous. Her bitterness stings and before I can hold it back, I hear myself adding, "What the hell?"

She throws her hand up, gesturing toward the church out her window. "You were laughing at me in there!" Oh…that. Makes sense she'd be upset, but she said she'd never get married. I was expecting her to stick it to him. Tell him where he could shove that ring. Hearing her accept the proposal was a massive knife to my chest. "'Ha-ha,' laugh it up," she says, gesturing her hands for me to keep the insults coming. "Bring up what I said in the car about not marrying. I know, okay? I know what I said."

I frown, letting out a breath. "I wasn't going to." Being made the object of her sour mood wasn't exactly what I had planned for my Sunday. I'm not used to biting my tongue when someone is yelling at me.

"No, it's fine. It's funny. It's hilarious! I'm marrying Ethan. I'm a hypocrite, and soon, I'll be a full-blown Christian stereotype. Married and pregnant. Sunday school and soccer practice. Livin' the dream!" she spits out.

Then why did you say yes?! I want to shout as I pull up in front of her apartment. I allow the sound of me shifting my truck in park to be the only sound between us as I wipe my palms on my slacks.

I grind my molars and press my thumb and index finger into the corner of my eyes, fighting back the migraine forming there. "I take it you don't want to talk about it?"

"No." She sniffles, causing me to shift my focus back to her.

"Okay." I tap my fingers on the wheel, letting the silence linger between us. If she doesn't want to talk, I'll just be here, then. Sitting with her in this clearly overwhelming moment. Her thoughts are so loud I swear I can hear the roaring static of her brain swallowing up all of the empty spaces in the cab of my old Dodge.

Her head falls into her lap as she takes a few deep breaths, trying to sort through this mess. "I can't be here. It won't be long until Zoe or Eve or someone else shows up. I need to be alone." Her breathing shudders through her panic attack. I rub her back.

"Where do you want to go?"

"Anywhere," she hiccups. "Away from this life. I can't do this."

I put my truck in reverse and back out of the spot. Before I can think about it, I'm taking her the two miles across town to my house, listening to the sound of her gentle sobs filling the empty spaces between us.

When we're parked in my driveway, she finally lifts her head from her lap. "Where are we?"

Her face is red and soaked, and I find my thumb wiping her cheek before I can tell myself to stop. "My house."

"Your house?"

I tilt my head. "You said you wanted to escape your life. What better place than somewhere not on the Holy Side?"

Her eyes meet mine before scrunching up again, throwing her face into my chest. "What am I doing?" she whines.

I run my hand through her hair, taking in the scent of her passionflower shampoo. "Do you want some coffee?" I ask. I learned from her coffee order that she seems to really like coffee. Her entire demeanor had changed after the first sip.

Phoebe laughs through her tears. "Coffee would be so nice."

"Good!" I say, bouncing slightly as she sits up in her seat. "I can do that!" I run around to her side and open the door, extending my hand. When she takes it, my body amps up even more, and I all but drag her inside, gesturing for her to have a seat on my couch.

"You wanted to talk to me after the service?" I ask, powering on the espresso machine. As it grinds up the beans, I grab a mug and fill it with milk.

"Right, yeah, I know, but…can it wait until later? I'm not sure I can word it right now."

"Well," I say softly, steaming the milk. "Can you try?"

"I wanted to do something for you, but I'm not sure how to put it into words," she sighs.

She wants to do something for me? "Oh!" Is she questioning her sexuality? Surely, she wasn't going to ask me to experiment with her before getting completely derailed by a marriage proposal from a douche canoe. I clear my throat. "Phoebe, you, you don't have to, uhh…do anything for me." *You have a fiancé.* Even before the fiancé, he was still her boyfriend. Was she going to break up with him? No. No way.

I pour the shot of espresso into the mug of steamed milk, then add some hazelnut syrup from the cabinet. "I-I know you aren't the most experienced person, and I don't want you to feel any pressure to do anything for me."

I place the cup down in front of her on the coffee table. I watch her grow offensive as I sit down beside her.

"What do you mean?" she protests. "I'm totally experienced! I know more about this than most! Heck, I like to think I know more than most due to being curious by nature."

Wait a second. Have I misread the situation? I only assumed Phoebe had never been with a woman. Could it be she has? Regardless, I can't be a part of it now. Even if she did correct the situation by talking to her boyfriend—sorry, "fiancé"—and refused to marry him, it still wouldn't change the fact her father is the figurehead of the most prejudiced church in Mystic Harbor. The whole situation has "complicated" written all over it.

"Phoebe, I...Your dad's a pastor and—"

"I mean, if you'd feel more comfortable, I'm sure I could ask him if he'd join."

What the fuck is happening? "J—?! No! No! I'm good!" What kind of flipper family does she live in? Fuck no.

"Well, I haven't even asked you yet." Her tone raises slightly in frustration. "How can you not at least think it over if you don't even know what I'm going to ask?" She crosses her arms, pinning me with an irate gaze.

I hesitate, rewinding the tape in my brain and realizing we probably aren't talking about the same thing. My face ignites with embarrassment. "I'm sorry. You're right. What's your question?"

She mulls over something in her mind for a while before finally beginning. "It must be hard."

Being such an idiot? Believe me, I know, I think before deciding not to fill in any more blanks. "What must be hard?" I ask.

"Wait...Is this a hazelnut flat white?" She scooches closer, pointing at the mug, a smile peaking onto her cheeks.

I nod, worried if I speak, I'll make an even bigger ass out of myself. I reposition myself due to nervousness when my shoe taps into hers. She isn't moving away, though. I'm overthinking this. Why am I overthinking everything? It's fine.

"Umm...your life," she begins again. "Like...the way you live." I'm beginning to realize it's not just me. She seems distracted now, too. Something is clearly charging up between us. She has to be feeling it, as well.

"The way I live?" I'm trying my hardest to not read into anything, though. I drop my hands, hoping the feeling of the couch's fabric will help keep me rooted in reality. I didn't even realize her hand was there. My fingers brush against hers, but moving it will only raise suspicion. This isn't a big deal unless I make it one. Why can't I seem to concentrate on what she's trying to say? Where is she even going with this?

"Yeah, like…" Heat settles in my belly as her pinky runs along mine before hooking them together. *It's not a big deal,* I think, refusing to draw attention to it. "Umm…"

My face flushes as my blood warms. Finding her eyes, I notice redness forming on her cheeks as well. I can't figure out what to do with my hands. I'm frozen. I can't move them. I try to focus on regulating my breathing, but my entire body wants to react—especially when her eyes gravitate to my lips. She's biting her bottom one. Just barely, but the bottom of her front teeth pull the left corner in. What would it be like to be the one biting that lip?

"I'm—I'm sorry." She shakes her head. "I can't remember what I was saying." The nervous breath she releases hits my face. When did we get this close? I fight back the smirk trying to invade my expression.

God, the combination of her eyes and her biting her lip is giving me chills. So close.

Her attention falls to my mouth again, which creates an entirely new shockwave to course through my extremities. The air is unexpectedly thick, but I try to will my lungs to continue breathing normally. But now that I'm thinking about it, I can't *stop* thinking about it.

"The way I live my life is hard," I whisper, enjoying our body's reactions to each other. Why am I whispering? No. It's only logical. There's no point shouting when she's only about three inches from my face now. Wouldn't wanna startle anybody.

I have a sudden desire to pull her in, feel that bottom lip for myself. It's been over six years since I've even thought about kissing someone. This urge is almost too strong. This isn't real. Can't be. Then why is it taking everything in me not to stop moving toward her? It's me, right? I'm moving closer? It's not her. I'm the problem here.

"Right," she rasps, clearing her throat.

She's magnetic. It's the only explanation as to why my body follows hers as she leans back on the couch, my other hand taking residence on her hip.

I'm invading her space. She moved back. A sign to stop. But her body is giving me a totally different response. Her breath caught at my decision to follow her, pupils blown with arousal. Seemingly monitoring the rapid beating of my heart, her palm is flat on my sternum. The other is resting on my forearm as my thumb strokes her hip gently. Her neck has decided to join the pinkening of her cheeks as she eyes my mouth once more.

"I'm sorry. I don't know what I'm doing," I confess softly, darting down to gaze at her mouth, then back to her darkened eyes. I pull back when her grip on my forearm tightens.

"Stay," she breathes. I shouldn't. I know we need to stop, yet I'm frozen again. I don't want this feeling to end. *She's engaged. She's in the closet, and I refuse to be her experiment.* It can't happen like this.

Her head is moving even closer now. Good to know I'm not the only problem in this scenario. If I don't stop this, I know I'll lose control. We're going to do something we'll both come to regret. But *fuck,* this stupid fucking gravity is too strong! It's pulling me in, soaking my boxers from the cartwheels currently taking place in my stomach.

SHE'S GETTING FUCKING MARRIED!

I watch her mouth until her lips gently graze mine.

She'll probably be celebrating her engagement tonight with her friends, Blake!

My mind flashes back to their kiss during today's service, which sealed the reality of their future nuptials.

Her phone chimes. The fog around my brain dissipates. Now's my chance!

"The way I live my life is hard!" I shout as I jump backward. Stumbling only a little over my own feet as I attempt to stand.

I moved so quickly, I'm wondering if it happened at all. But the sudden throbbing between my legs lets me know it definitely did.

"Yes!" She clears her throat, sitting up. "Can you come over tomorrow for dinner?"

What is it about her that keeps drawing me in, makes me flirtatious, makes me a total idiot who doesn't have any manners? Is it the lack of sex? Six years is a long time, but it's never been an issue until now. No. Sex may have been a thing I thought I needed before, but I know better now. It'll only get me hurt. I can behave myself. A friendship with Phoebe Appleton is good enough.

"I'd love that." I beam through my lashes. "What time?"

She bounces in her seat with excitement. "Five?" Then tries a little too hard to play it cool. "But if five is too early, it can be later—or sooner. Whatever. What time do you eat dinner? I eat dinner around five, so I figured that'd be fine, but if you eat earlier or later, that's fine t—"

"Five is fine." I smile big enough to hurt my cheeks. It's too fucking cute when she rambles.

"Yeah?" She looks like a puppy wagging its tail. "Okay. Five. I'll see you at five."

She's stuck in a loop. It's the most adorable thing. "Just to make sure—you said five, right?"

Her cheeks flush in embarrassment. I give her a wink. "Kidding."

Her shoulders deflate as she exhales for probably the first time since I sat down.

"Do you need to get that?" I gesture to her ringing phone. She can't seem to pull her gaze away from mine, though. She shakes her head and glances down at the screen. She closes her eyes, pinching the bridge of her nose.

After debating for a few more rings, she sighs. "Yeah, I really should." She stands and answers it, walking out the front door.

I try to calm my beating heart while collapsing back onto the couch. After a minute or two, she returns. "I'm sorry…I have to go."

As saddened as I am by her leaving, I know it's the right thing to do. I'm not recognizing myself around her right now. You'd think I was a horny high schooler. "I'll get my keys."

Chapter 10

Phoebe

When I return to my apartment, Zoe is already waiting for me by the door. I open it, and she follows me inside. When the door is completely shut, she starts complaining. "Sorry, Eve isn't showing up...Heaven forbid she has to celebrate someone other than herself." Her gaze shoots to the ceiling in frustration.

"It's whatever," I say as I throw my keys in their designated bowl on the table by the door. *The fewer people I have to be around, the better.*

"Umm. No?" she says, as if telling me how to feel is going to matter. Eve is Eve. I'm used to Eve being absent for the big moments since adulthood. Usually, it's her waitressing job that takes up most of her time but when she is free, she's dead to the world.

And then it dawns on me. I never actually asked Blake if she'd let me save her soul. *Stupid*, I think. Hopefully, the air will be different tomorrow, and I can ask her before she even has the opportunity to make my head do stupid stuff by sitting next to me. What even was that back there?

Closing my eyes and exhaling, I say, "It's typical Eve. What were you expecting?"

I'm hoping she won't press it. I really don't know how to articulate right now. Not well enough to talk about that can of worms. I'm unexpectedly very exhausted. Probably because I didn't have my routine relax-urday. It's going to be a long week, and I just don't have the ambition to try and pick at the scab that is my entire brain right now.

Zoe looks like she's going to ask, anyway. She decides against it, however. "Girl, talk to me about church," she decides instead and then spends the next forty-five minutes listening to me completely freak out.

"You have to tell him you made a mistake, Phoebe. You can't go into a marriage for the wrong reasons."

"I know," I whine, sinking back on the couch, clutching a pillow to my face and screaming into it. "But how? My mother will kill me. The church will find out. What if Ethan hates me?"

"Who cares what anyone else thinks? It's not their life, Phoebz. Where is he, anyway? I thought you were with him when I called."

Panic fills me. Do I tell her I was with Blake? Would she think I was doing things with her? No way. Zoe knows me better than that. I'm not gay. I can't exactly lie to her, but turns out I don't have to because my phone rings.

"It's Ethan," I tell her, swiping the screen to answer.

"Hey, babe," he says. It sounds like he's driving. I swear it's like he only ever calls me when he's in his car.

"Hey," I say. "Are you driving somewhere?"

"Yeah. I'm heading to the city." He seems distracted. Probably by traffic. "I have to tell my parents the good news!"

"Why didn't he take you?" Zoe whispers, only loud enough for me to hear.

I raise my shoulders slightly.

"Oh, okay." I chuckle nervously.

"Tell him!" she mouths, and I shake my head. She slaps my knee before grabbing a notepad off my coffee table and writing something down.

"I wanted to call because I couldn't find you after the service. Your mom wants us to have dinner with them on Friday to hammer out the details."

I glance over at Zoe as she flips up the notepad. It says, "Bitch, tell him!"

I push the phone away from my face. "Not on the phone," I grind out, snatching the notepad from her greedy palms before tossing it and narrowly missing her face.

With a "hmph," she sucks in her lips and crosses her arms.

"What's that, babe?" Ethan asks as I hear the annoying ticking of his blinker.

"Oh, I said, 'When will you be home?'"

"Oh, sorry, service is cutting out. I'll be back tomorrow." I hear the faint sound of a voice.

"Is someone with you?" I tilt my head, hoping it'll improve my hearing. Zoe's head perks up and she sits on the arm of the couch beside me, trying to also hear.

"Hmm?" He pauses as I listen more intently to the white noise of the car in motion on his end. "No, the radio, but I better get off here before I lose you, babe. I love you."

"Love—" beep beep beep. I glimpse at the screen. Call ended. "—you too, I guess."

"Very romantic," Zoe says, rubbing my back while letting out an exasperated breath. "Don't even spend the day of your engagement with your fiancé. Just go on a road trip. Don't even offer to invite said fiancé to go with you. Honestly, that boy makes absolutely no sense. Why didn't you tell him?! He's about to tell his family, Phoebe!"

"A conversation like that is going to take some time." I rub my burning eyes, the lids heavy. "Don't you think it should be done in person? Not while he's losing service."

"Right, so make it more awkward when he has to break it to his family that this trip was for nothing. 'Just kidding, Mom and Dad.'"

"I know! I really wish he would've told me before he decided to go. Not when he was on the road already. Can we talk about something else for a while? My brain hurts."

And this is why I love Zoe; unlike Eve, she showed up for me. She didn't ask me to leave the comfort of my space, either. She even stayed an extra five hours—not talking about it—helping me instead with dinner. Then joining me to eat it while watching a couple of movies.

✝

That night, my mind had decided to take it upon itself to finish what started on Blake's couch...

...Our lips press together as my breathing increases. One of my hands pulls the hair tie from her pony, causing the tendrils of black to fall freely into her face before I grab a handful, pulling her closer, tracing kisses down her jaw and onto her neck. I suck in her flesh and bite down sharply, listening to the sweet sounds of a stinging hiss followed by heavy pants in my ear.

My tongue trails up her neck to the shell of her ear. "Is this okay?" I whisper, but my voice doesn't sound like mine. It's hers, laced in elation. The words she'd said now loaded with emotion. Somehow, we've traded places. I'm her, but more confident. I'm not pulling away like she had.

She nods as my hand on her hip slowly trails lower down the center of her body until it finds the zipper to her slacks. I press my eager hand between the crevice of her thighs. A moan escapes Blake's parted lips, loud enough to rattle the ground beneath us as I flick my fingertip over the sensitive bud of her—

BEEP, BEEP, BEEP...

My eyes snap open immediately. It takes a second for me to realize I'm sweating. Why is there throbbing between my legs? No. No! I push down the screaming in my brain. The desperate cries to reach into my soft silk shorts and chase the feelings my dream had been eliciting. I never have and I never will give in to arousal. Eventually, this urge will go away. It always does.

Regardless, this isn't good. How am I supposed to help her shy away from sin when I can't seem to pull my mind away from sinning *with* her? Pressing my hands together and closing my eyes, I begin to pray. "Lord, please grant me wisdom to make peace with my troubled thoughts. Give me the strength and guidance to help Blake see the error of her ways and turn back to you. Amen." I cross myself and jump out of bed.

Time to get ready for the day.

✝

Work seemed to drag on, but mainly because I was trying to go over what I was going to say when Blake showed up at my apartment later.

I decided against the straightforward approach. "Hey, can I save your soul from burning in hell?" I felt it might come on too strong and blindside her.

Then I played around with the idea of beginning with a catchy kick starter, like, "You know what I hate? Fire and brimstone! Speaking of which, have you given any thought to where your soul might be headed?" But I figured that sounded too "culty."

Maybe a joke? "Hell might be too warm. Wanna come to heaven with me?" But I wasn't sure she'd find it funny.

How does one articulate this?

I'm still thinking about it when I hear the knock on my door. *Guess I'm gonna wing it.* I put down the knife I'm using to cut vegetables and grab the towel on the counter beside me, wiping my hands as I answer the door.

Her outfit is very simple but still nice: baggy jeans, a zipped-up gray hoodie, and a white baseball hat. A paper bag is nestled comfortably in one of her arms. "Hi," she beams.

I'm not sure why my cheeks warm, but they do. *Is this okay?* My mind recalled. Butterflies fill my stomach. My dream resurfaces, as I envision my hand between her thighs. *Uh, oh.*

"Hi," I say, quickly turning on my heels. I can't look at her right now. I might actually explode. Turn into a full liquid and make a mess all over her and the floor. Pretty sure the embarrassment is catching up with me. That's why I feel funny. I'm not sure why I nodded my approval when she all but climbed onto my lap yesterday. I should've pushed her away. Why didn't I push her away?

Instead, I invited her over to my house.

No. I did that to help her see the error of her ways. What happened yesterday had no weight on why she's here now. I walk back to the kitchen. "You didn't have to bring anything."

I decide to focus on the veggies. "Well, I figured if you were making dinner, the least I could do was bring dessert," she says, joining me in the kitchen. She comes up beside me and places the bag down on the counter, pulling out a chocolate cake. Her arm brushes mine as she asks, "Can I put this in your fridge?" The sudden closeness makes my body shiver as I nod, continuing to stare at the cutting board. *Stupid small kitchen.*

She puts the cake away, remaining beside me. Standing over my shoulder. My neck and face flush with an insurmountable amount of heat. "Can I congratulate you yet?"

This makes me turn my head in her direction. The endless blue of her eyes forces my gaze to deviate rapidly as I forget how to breathe. "I'd rather you didn't."

Her eyebrows pinch together as she tilts her head, which is a perfectly justifiable response. Most people who'd agreed to marry their boyfriend would be over the moon. They'd want to show off the ring, find annoying ways to fit it into every conversation. But the girls who said yes would've been ready to marry their boyfriends. They'd have gotten a ring they truly wanted because they'd have had conversations about it. Women who said yes would've said yes because they wanted to, not because they felt pressured to.

"You're not wearing your ring," Blake says, gently stroking the pad of her middle finger over my naked one.

I grab a bell pepper. "It was too big," I lie, beginning to chop, the sweet, spicy smell surrounding the area immediately.

Standing behind me, she positions her hand on the counter beside me. I close my eyes, trying desperately to control my heart pounding violently in my throat. "It fit fine when he slid it on your finger." The low timbre of her voice only inches from my ear isn't helping my nerves.

"Yeah, well, I didn't want to wear it while I was cutting vegetables, okay?" my voice croaks.

Blake grabs a piece of pepper off my cutting board and tosses it in her mouth. "Bullshit."

I set down the knife politely and turn to face her. "Language."

She narrows her eyes mischievously. "Where in the Bible does it say you can't cuss?"

I straighten out my shirt, lifting my chin. "Ephesians 4:29 'Do not let any unwholesome talk come out of your mouths, but only what is helpful for building others up according to their needs, that it may benefit those who listen.'"

"Hmm…" she rubs her chin. "Sounds to me like it's advising against saying hurtful or negative things to anyone. Not necessarily to refrain from saying 'fuck' or 'shit.'"

I return to my work on the cutting board. "Perhaps, but I'd rather not take any chances." The veggies sizzle the moment they hit the pan.

"So, when do you plan on having children?" she presses on, peaking into one of my cabinets.

I wrinkle my nose, watching her in disbelief. *Sure, just make yourself at home.* "I-I haven't given it much thought. What exactly are you doing?"

She pauses to peer at me, her hand resting on a new cabinet to snoop through. "Looking for a glass."

I point to the correct cabinet and then the pantry. "And ice is in the freezer."

"You want one?" she asks, reaching for a glass. I shake my head, reaching for my own drink. "Do you want children?"

My breath catches right at the same time I'm sipping. Coughing violently, she moves closer to pat my back. I step away, shaking my head. I finally manage to scrape out, "I-I'm not sure."

She shoots me a very puzzled glare. "Isn't that the point of marriage in the eyes of God? To 'be fruitful and multiply' or whatever?"

"I suppose so."

Her forehead creases. "Well, if you don't want any kids, are you on birth control?"

"No, I mean, I guess if we were doing that, I would, but..." This conversation is further reminding me why I need to break things off with Ethan. I'm not ready to have sex. The thought of his sloppy kisses and grunting body on top of mine is making me sick. "...it wouldn't be right away, anyway." My face flushes. This is embarrassing.

Ice clatters against glass as she deposits them into her cup. The thermal stress of the water being poured over the cubes causes them to crackle and squeak. "Wouldn't be right away? Don't people usually do that on their honeymoon?"

"I mean, if I'm not ready, I'm not ready." I don't even see why we're talking about this. Sex is entirely too personal and definitely none of her business.

"Wait..." She abandons the empty bottle on the counter in front of her, raising her glass to her lips. "So, you've *really* never..."

"Nope. Never." *And don't intend to.*

"I seriously thought you were joking!" She takes a sip, chewing on a piece of ice. "Not with anyone?"

"No." I shift from foot to foot, reaching for an onion. My eyes sting after only a few chops.

Why can't she drop it? Is she getting a kick out of making me uncomfortable?

She lowers her head before beaming up at me through her lashes. "So, you're a..."

My shoulders slump on an exhale. "Yes," I confess exasperatedly. *Is that a problem?*

"Not even—"

"Nothing!" I slam the knife down. I'm not trying to be rude, but I don't think I want to hear what she was going to say next.

"God." Shaking her head incredulously, she walks to the other side of the counter, plopping down onto one of my barstools. "That must be hard. I can't imagine never having done *anything* at twenty-six years old. I'd go insane. Is it too forward if I ask if you at least…you know…"

"If I what?" I'm not sure how many questions there could be on this topic. I figured 'nothing' kind of summed it up.

"Take care of yourself? You know…sexually?" Blake winks seductively, sending a flutter to my chest. Through heavy lids, I watch her tongue jut out, slowly wetting her lips.

"Like, do I…?" Apparently, my thermostat broke because the room is now at least thirty degrees hotter and my entire body is burning up. Is she asking me if I touch myself? Does she somehow know about my dream? The thought makes me wonder if she does. Oh, great, now my mind is venturing to an image of her lithe fingers delicately skimming along smooth alabaster skin. Her thumb grazing over her navel before descending even lower, eventually arriving at its destination between her legs. Biting her lip as she—

"I forgot to ask if you have any allergies," I redirect, clearing my throat, dropping the onions in the pan to join the peppers. "Is there anything you don't like?" I need to get off this topic.

She arches an eyebrow. Of course, I don't do that. *Does she think I do that?*

"Nope. I'm sure whatever you're making is fine." Blake is scanning my apartment and I can't tell if she's enjoying what she's seeing or if she's judging it. Or is she simply trying to avoid eye contact with me as well? She leans over the counter, grabbing a baby carrot from a bowl of veggies next on my chopping block. "So, what did you want to talk about yesterday?"

Maybe I could save her soul without actually *asking*. Maybe I could present her with the facts, and she'd come to it on her own. I figure this is probably the best approach. "I was wondering if you'd want to maybe have Bible sessions with me on Mondays."

Tilting her head, she says, "Like…Bible study?"

"Yeah. You know, because you're attending EC, I figured maybe you'd want to learn a little bit about it. I don't know how much you know already."

She crosses her arms as all of her playfulness evaporates. "I know enough." Then she's reaching for a paper towel off the spool beside her and meticulously folding it into a square slightly larger than her glass, which she sets on top of it.

"Can you ever really know *enough*?" I say, refusing to lift my head from the pan I'm stirring. Why is meeting her gaze such a challenge right now?

"I don't know," she says, then asks, "Do you?"

"Do I what?"

"Know enough about the Bible to make a definitive statement on it?"

Her tone is challenging and her crossed arms are coming off slightly confrontational. I definitely refuse to look at her now. I wonder if she can see my hand shaking as I stir the veggies around the pan. Can she somehow see right through my plan?

"I like to think I do."

"Oh, yeah?" She sways side to side on the stool as she speaks. "Why's that?"

"Because…I've been learning the teachings since birth."

"From the same church, though," she deadpans, holding her water to her lips. "Meaning, you've learned one church's beliefs. Do you know any other variations of the same book?"

"Why would I need to?" I shake my head. "It all comes from the same book."

"Well." She narrows her eyes. "There's the New Testament. The Old Testament. New Revised Standard Version, New International Version—"

"What's your point?"

"Each one is translated slightly different, isn't it? Couldn't changing one word change the whole construct?"

"Certain passages say the same thing in all the versions. If you want, after dinner I could show you?" *Please say yes.*

"Fine, but just know." She raises one corner of her mouth. "I can be quite inquisitive as well."

"That's okay. I'm here to answer anything. It's best to ask questions to better form your own conclusions."

"How very Lutheran of you," she jokes.

"So, I'm told," I say, beaming.

✝

After putting our dishes in the sink, I grab the two tiny plates I prepared—a slice of cake and a fork on each—and bring them out to the living room. My mind debates sitting next to her, but I conclude the opposite end of the couch from her is safer.

"Alright!" She stretches as I try not to notice her shirt lifting slightly, exposing some skin on her stomach, a V-cut on either side of her hips leading into her pants. I reach for my Bible. This would have been better if I had told her to bring hers. Does she even own a Bible? "Let's do this."

I clear my throat and open to the page I bookmarked for our first reading. Obviously, I had to choose the most popular selection on the topic of homosexuality. Blake scoots next to me on the couch to be able to read over my shoulder. My whole body ignites at the press of her arm and hip on mine. "Genesis

19." Blake's shoulders sink, body very still. Staring forward, now seeming rigid. She lets out a sigh.

"Really?" Is she mad? She's biting her cheek and shaking her head while gazing at the ceiling, a frustrated breath escaping her mouth.

"Do you know it?" I pretend to be clueless as I gauge the situation.

"Phoebe." Blake rubs her eyes. "What are you doing?"

"You said you wanted a Bible chapter that's the same in every version." I rotate my palms upward, feigning indifference.

"Ah, yes…" she says, the muscles in her jaw tense as she taps a finger on her lap. "Sodom and fucking Gomorrah." She runs a hand through her hair before shaking her head, deciding to rise to her feet. "You know what? Never mind."

"Wait, what are you doing?" My heart plunges into my stomach, but I can't will myself to stand. She can't leave. She just got here. I have to find my legs and follow her.

I push myself up off the couch, trailing behind her as she heads to the door.

"Leaving. Keep the cake," she says, heading to the door, but I grab her by the wrist before she can. She freezes, anger in her eyes as she turns toward me.

"Don't go," I beg. The thought of her leaving and me sitting alone in this apartment is almost unbearable. I'm not sure why, but I hate the idea of her being mad at me.

"You really think you can 'turn me straight?'"

"Would it make sense if I explained why?"

She taps her leg, her fists balled up, but she's staying, which makes me assume she's giving me a chance. "This better be good."

"I…I care about you." I let go of her wrist. "I can't be around you if I don't figure out a way to lead you away from this sin."

"SIN?! Oh, that's rich!" She throws up her hands before finding the ceiling once more, grinding her teeth. "You really think loving who you love is a sin? Like what? I'm going to burn in hell because I eat pussy instead of sucking dick?"

"Language…" I say, sinking into myself, overwhelmingly uncomfortable. My heart is beating so fast it hurts. This was a stupid idea. Why did I think I could ever convince her to let me help? Maybe Ethan *was* right. *You can't fix a queer.* "In Matthew 22:39 Jesus said, 'Thou shalt love thy neighbor as thyself.' How can I do that without warning my neighbor when their sin is corrupting their soul?!"

"Fuck that! Where does it say you have to do anything for a sinner besides love them?"

I glare in defiance. "I'm glad you asked. Leviticus 19:17 'You shall not hate in your heart anyone of your kin; you shall reprove your neighbor, or you will incur guilt yourself.'"

She raises her eyebrows, unsure of what to say. I press on. "And also, Isaiah 58:1! 'Shout out; do not hold back! Lift up your voice like a trumpet! Announce to my people their rebellion, to the house of Jacob their sins.'"

"So, believing love is genderless is my transgression?" She tilts her head. "You sure you want to do this?"

When I nod insistently, her expression a mixture of irritation and amusement as she practically stomps past me and grabs the Bible before sitting back down on the couch, leaning into the coffee table. She practically slams the good book down, gesturing for me to sit. "Okay, hotshot. Give it your best. Show me where it says Sodom and Gomorrah were deduced to fire and brimstone on the sole premise of homosexuality."

I stare at her for a second before sitting back down. This has to be a trap, right? Am I walking into a trap? Because it feels like she's challenging me.

Only one way to find out.

I sit down beside her and turn to Genesis 19. I read the entire chapter before looking over at her. She's sitting silently with her elbows resting on her knees. Her right hand tapping her lip in contemplation.

"So," she finally speaks, "you think demanding they bring out their guests—who were not mere men but rather angels, mind you—to rape them is the entire subject matter of this chapter?"

"I mean...isn't it?" How can she think it's about anything else? "God sent the angels to see if the town was worth destroying, and first thing they see are these rapists. Who happen to be...you know."

"Say gay, Phoebe." She peers up at me through her lashes. "You won't burn in hell for saying gay."

I wrinkle my nose and smooth out my shirt. "No thank you."

She rolls her eyes. "First off." She grabs the book and skims before saying, "In Verse 8, Lot says, 'Look, I have two daughters who have not known a man; let me bring them out to you, and do to them as you please; only do nothing to these men, for they have come under the shelter of my roof.' You think pimping out your daughters in order to spare angels is somehow *better* than homosexuality?"

"Well, no, but—"

"Phoebe, I'm going to respectfully stop you because you should have done better research."

"Excuse me?" Heat rises to my face. She's not even letting me speak. She somehow thinks she knows the Bible better than me? I think not...Right? How could she? Before last week, she didn't even go to church.

"Do you understand the power an angel possesses?"

"Yes," I say through gritted teeth.

"Okay, good." She nods. "Because if you didn't, then you weren't paying attention as you read to me. Before the men could even touch the angels, they were blinded and trapped inside Lot's house. He didn't have to offer up his daughters. That was fucked up! Angels can hold their own. Turn men to powder just for looking at them wrong. They didn't, but they could've."

How does she know this much about the Bible? I watch as she flips through the pages. "Ah! Right here. Ezekiel 16:49 'This was the guilt of your sister Sodom: she and her daughters had pride, excess of food, and prosperous ease but did not aid the poor and needy.'" She looks me in the eye, hers darker than usual. "Now do you understand what this means?" Is she talking to me like I'm a child? Like I'm stupid?

I snatch the book from her hands and open to another passage I bookmarked for today. "Jude 1:7 'Likewise, Sodom and Gomorrah and the surrounding cities, which, in the same manner as they, indulged in sexual immorality and pursued unnatural lust, serve as an example by undergoing a punishment of eternal fire.'"

She leans in and points. "Jude 1:4 'For certain intruders have stolen in among you, people who long ago were designated for this condemnation as ungodly, who pervert the grace of our God into debauchery and deny our only Master and Lord, Jesus Christ.' Do you even know what it meant to be a man back then?" She says it calmly, but I can hear a slight annoyance in her tone. "It meant being strong. It meant being the penetrator. Any act of being penetrated meant you were less than a man. And we all know how they felt about women."

She rolls her eyes. "Those men weren't gay, Phoebe. They were trying to overpower anyone who threatened them. In Ezekial, the choice words were 'pride,' 'excess of food,' '*prosperous ease.*' Phoebe, they were greedy and power-hungry! And they knew the angels were sent to judge the town. It was disgusting and immoral to sleep with an angel, let alone emasculate one. Not sure why they ever thought they could get that far, but whatever.

"So yeah, what you read is correct, but only one part of why it was destroyed. Penetrating anyone without consent is immoral, not two consenting adults of the same gender making love." She takes another bite of her cake. "In my passage, it says they didn't help aid the poor and needy. They wanted to hit God where it hurt, and you know what?" She narrows her eyes. "They fucked around, and then they found out. It wasn't because they were gay, Phoebe." Blake's hand falls onto my thigh, right above my knee, for reassurance. I stop breathing as my body tenses. "It's because they tried to go up against their creator by disrespecting their neighbors."

It's nothing. Her hand is on my leg. Not a big deal. But an unexplainable silence has now taken over the room. The air has changed. A cold chill is charging up my entire body. Why? Zoe put her hand on my thigh a million times, but it's never felt as charged as Blake's slender fingers on the fabric of my jeans right now.

Focus, Appleton. Think of something else, but my mind can't seem to think about anything besides the shock waves her touch is sending to my stomach. "Blake," I whisper, biting my lip. I try to focus on my breathing. Her closeness has me trying to rationalize.

There was nothing wrong with reaching out and touching her hand in Blessed Beans last week. Today is no different. It'll show I appreciate the comfort. Even if it doesn't, there's no one here to judge the manner of intent my actions would convey. Surely touching a hand won't send me to hell. Right?

No, it's not okay. I have to tell her. I have to break this spell I seem to be under. "I shouldn't..." I trail off. I need to tell her to go. Tell her she can't try to kiss me again. What about Ethan? As of right now, I still have a fiance. I'm still getting married. I don't want to, but I agreed to it. I know adultery is sinful. The Bible has a pretty cut-and-paste definition about that one. Not to mention Blake is a girl! She may dress like a boy, but I *know* she isn't one, and so does God.

"M-make me leave." She shudders, her voice impossibly gentle. But even telling myself everything I already know doesn't stop my mind from wanting to know what life would be like with Blake. If God accepted that kind of thing, of course. I know what it'll be like with Ethan. Never being happy. Never getting to understand why my skin flushes while my body chills around her. I'm stuck with Ethan, but not of my volition.

I shake my head, looking up from her hand through my lashes, searching her eyes. My tongue juts out to wet my lower lip at the sight of her pinked cheeks and heavy lids. "I can't." It comes out quieter than I anticipated. I'm not even sure she heard it. If it wasn't for the sharp inhalation in reaction to my admittance, I'd still be left wondering. If we're being completely honest, my life has never been of my own accord. I was put on this earth to seemingly make everyone else happy. Blend in to make my family look good while simultaneously putting out Piper's fires, even if it meant being miserable. Why can't I, just once, have something for myself?

I put my fingers gently on her wrist, pushing down all of the alarms blaring in my ears, voices screaming for me to stop. I don't want to stop. This feeling is terrifying, but terrifying has never felt this good. My heart's pounding, blood's coursing, knees weakening, but the tingle between my legs is invigorating, and I don't want it to ever end.

The heat from her palm is soaking into the material as her thumb slowly starts making circles on my jeans. I know it's wrong. I know everything about this is wrong. I'm not stupid. Why then can't I seem to convince myself to make it stop?

Obviously, I have questions, and without allowing myself a sample—giving in just a little—I won't be able to understand why she makes me feel like this…My lips long for hers against mine so badly it's haunting my dreams.

"Phoebe…"

Wanting and needing are two completely different things, however. I don't need this, and I won't die without it. So why does it feel like I'll explode if I stop? I can't help her if I'm guilty of the same charges.

"Shh…" I swallow past the dryness in my throat. "Please."

Am I guilty? I need to know. Need to see Blake's expressions as my thumb gently strokes her bottom lip.

I turn and bend my leg under myself on the couch, keeping my hand on hers. I don't want her to think I'm moving to stop this; I want to be able to see her. Maybe peering into her eyes will help me understand what's happening. Maybe it's happening to her as well. My hand follows her fingertips as they slowly trail up the inside of my bent leg on the couch. The action causes me to take in a sharp breath. She does the same. Her eyes seem heavy, and her pupils are growing larger by the second.

What if there's a way for me to get my answers and move on? If I can save her later down the road, then we both win, but right now, my mind can't move on from the sudden need to know what her lips would feel like on mine. Her mouth parts slightly as my thumb glides against her bottom lip. *So soft.* The sight causes me to take my own between my teeth as I ponder my next course of action.

Who knows? Maybe it won't even be special. Kissing her will take the power out of it. Curiosity killing the cat and all that. She shifts her body until we are mirroring each other on the couch. Face to face as we both try to breathe normally.

"'The Lord is gracious and merciful, slow to anger and abounding in steadfast love,'" she says, before clearing her throat. *Keep talking.* Her voice is causing the hairs on the back of my neck to rise, and I'm addicted to this feeling. She swallows hard, moving closer. My eyes widen at her approach. "'The Lord is good to all, and his compassion is over all that he has made.'" A pleasant gust of her warm breath moves past my face as she speaks. My heart pounds in my ears as my thumb departs from her lip, only to find its way to her cheek. My whole body is thrumming as I force myself to stay frozen. *Don't. Don't do this.* "Psalm 145:8-9," she whispers, pausing mere inches from my face. She's waiting for me to close the gap. Her eyes fall to my mouth as her tongue juts out to lick her bottom lip slowly. Pieces of my resolve disintegrate at the sight, causing me to lick mine.

I'm struggling to hold back the desire taking me over. *The Lord is gracious.* I focus on my breathing as I force myself to remain still. *Don't do this, Phoebe.*

Merciful. An image flashes into my mind of what would happen if I did it. If I let go and removed the space between us. I'm acutely more present. My thoughts grow quiet until all I hear is Blake's breath and my heart pounding in my ears. Nothing but Blake, and this tingling in my stomach seems to exist.

Slow to anger. Her breath on my skin feels too good to stop. *Abounding in steadfast love.* I give in. I grab the back of her neck and close the gap between us, pressing my mouth to hers firmly. The ferocity of my action causes a small moan to escape from her mouth.

She grabs my shoulders, gently pulling me away before peering down at her lap. "I'm sorry. I should—" but the doors already open. I refuse to let her get away from me again. Impulsion and desire are in the front seat, and I can't hold myself back anymore. I'm entranced by cedar and this new discovery of the silkiness of her lips. The sweetness of chocolate on her mouth. It's too late for me to concentrate on anything other than the lust erupting deep inside my stomach, sending electrical signals into all of my extremities. I need more, and before I can think it through, I'm reaching, fisting her shirt with my hands, pulling her back in. Relief washes over my joints as her mouth opens, inviting me in for more.

One night to take the power out of my inquisitions. Give in just once. Get it out of my system. One day, we'll look back at this night on the couch and laugh at its foolishness. But I won't be able to save her soul until I've crossed everything off my list that's been plaguing me.

For the sake of research, I decide to take her bottom lip in between mine. I grab her hat and toss it aimlessly. She smiles against my mouth as the hat hits the floor, but I need my fingers in her hair. The hand she had on my thigh is now grabbing. Kneading my jeans with her palm and fingers, I long for her to bring her hand higher. To touch me where my legs meet my body.

The kneading stops before her other hand finds the rib below my breast, her thumb gently caressing the material of my shirt. Bolts of electricity shoot throughout my entire body. My mind keeps shifting from what is right to what is wrong, but the more she touches me, the quieter the wrong seems to get. Everything feels too good to be wrong. I'm hot as warm moisture settles in my underwear. My hips want to move aimlessly to relieve the tension. I wonder if her body feels the same.

Blake's hand inches its way up my thigh, and I notice my hips instinctually rocking to meet her fingers. Our kissing becomes more rapid, our breath doing the same. She starts panting, causing my thoughts to become erratic. I slide my hands under her shirt, gripping her pelvis. Her skin is so soft.

Blake's hand on my rib moves behind my back while the other one moves to grip my hip. Still kissing, she guides me backward on the couch until my head gently hits the armrest. She gets on top of me before breaking the kiss for only a second to ask, "Is this too far?"

"Uh-uh," I breathe, shaking my head frantically, a slight pant escaping my lips as she trails a path with her mouth to the pulse point on my neck. My face floods with heat as shivers run down my spine.

I let out a moan as she sucks and nibbles on the tender skin. My hips roll uncontrollably as her teeth graze my flesh. She puffs out a breath and repositions herself. Her hand on my hip is now making my body feel small against her palm. The grip of her long slender fingers is firm but gentle on my waist. She props her thigh in between mine. Her other hand finds its way to the side of my neck, bracing my face as she kisses a path up to the shell of my ear.

"Tell me when to stop," she whispers and presses her knee against my aching center.

My legs instinctually snap closed around the pressure of her knee on my sex. My lashes flutter from the sensation of her moving against me. "Oh, God," I whimper into her ear. Is this too much? Doesn't matter because it feels too good. I don't ever want this to end. "Blake…" I whimper.

"Thought you're not supposed to say His name in vain?" The corner of her mouth quirks up, exposing her crooked canine, clearly relishing the sudden collapse of my convictions. She's right. It just came out. My brain is fizzing and frothing over. I'm acting purely on impulse and instinct.

"Shh…" I whisper, trying and failing to cover her mouth with my shaky hand while simultaneously bucking my aching center harder down onto her knee. Pretty sure taking the Lord's name in vain isn't the worst thing happening right now, and I need her to stop talking. It'll only make me start thinking—and I'm done thinking.

Before I have time to argue, my breath is taken from my lungs. She's increased her thrusting and is kissing my collarbone with more suction and teeth. I grab her face, pulling her up. I need to kiss her while my hips move in time to her movements. Opening my mouth, I allow her tongue to find mine, and when they finally slide against each other, another tingle runs down my body, rushing to the place where her leg is pressed. Her hips gyrate as mine continue to chase her motions.

Kissing Ethan has never felt like this, but I decide I don't want to think about him right now, either. I don't want to think about anything honestly. Not Ethan, not sin. Just this.

I've fully dived off the deep end into a world of yearning, salaciousness, and Blake. I want her mouth, her hands, her body. I want to feel the rush of her breath falling onto my neck, hear her panting in my ear as she thrusts her pelvis just right into my center. The only thing my mind can focus on is how warm her hand is as she's pushing my hips into her leg.

"Does that feel good?" she whispers into my mouth. I drop my hands, hooking my thumbs into her waistband, pressing circles into either side of her V-cut.

"M-hmm," I stutter, struggling to do basic human things, like catch my breath or articulate. I close my eyes. "Don't...stop."

And she doesn't. She seems to be bathing in my mannerisms. Her cheeks flushed, finding the shell of my ear and nibbling on the lobe before joining her mouth to mine again.

"Yeah, baby?" she hisses. My skin is cold, but my interior ignites with heat from the pet name. My legs start to tense and tremble as something wells up inside of me, causing my back to arch against her with every thrust. I'm starting to find it harder to follow her movements.

"Yes, yes, yes," I growl with every press of her leg into my vagina. I can't focus on kissing anymore, resorting instead to throwing my head backward onto the armrest, trying to open my eyes, but they keep snapping closed. I don't know what it is, but it's like climbing a mountain, and I've almost reached the top. The air up here is thicker. It's almost as if I'm holding my breath.

Blake doesn't seem to mind that I'm unable to continue kissing. Her mouth ventures to a place on my neck right below my ear. Her teeth gently nip, causing a surge of butterflies in my stomach. I can't believe this is happening. It feels so good. How have I been denying myself something this insatiably pleasurable for twenty-six years?

"Yeah...God, yeah...don't stop," I moan quietly, eyes opening slowly to see Blake smirking as she sways her knee into my center over and over. My entire body begins to coil. "Blake, don't stop," I repeat. Begging, hands tensing into her waist. "Please, don't stop. Right there." I'm a broken record as my nails dig deeper. "Don't stop."

Without warning, my eyes screw shut, and I'm completely unable to follow her thrusts anymore. After pushing her knee into my vagina two, three more times, I'm sent over the edge as I'm hit with wave after wave of intense pleasure. "That's it, Phoebe," she whispers into my ear, smiling as my whole body surges and twitches repetitiously. "Come for me."

She continues thrusting as I convulse into her. This feeling is magnificent. With every wave, I find myself smiling, biting my lip, trying to prevent it, but it does nothing. I'm boiling over the top, a deep, uncontrollable moan escaping from within me, anyway. She doesn't let up rocking until my body stops trembling and my hands fall from her waist, too heavy and shaky to hold on to anything.

When I'm finally able to keep my eyes open for more than a split second, I'm met with hers, which are completely blown out and heavy, her hair a total mess on top of her head. Face flushed and chest heaving. Her body falls onto mine and her head rests gently in the crook of my shoulder. Her hot breath hits my neck. I wrap my arms around her body. Our breath mingles as the fog surrounding my brain clears. I'm staring at the ceiling as our breathing regains its regular rhythm.

Without warning, the ceiling becomes blurry. Tears fall from my face as a knot forms in my throat.

Why did I do that? What have I done?

Chapter 11

Phoebe

"Whoa, hey." Blake takes my face in her hand. "You okay?"

I swat her hands away, pressing my palms into my eyes as a million thoughts rush into my brain. I'm so stupid. I need to sit up. I need her to get off me. I can't believe I did that. Why did I do that?

"I need you to leave," I muster shakily. I can't look at her. Looking will only solidify the truth. It really happened. I did that.

"Phoebe…"

She sits up, and I follow. *Stop crying,* I think as I bring my knees to my chest and rest my chin on them. It's weird because I'm not sobbing. It's as if shock is still numbing my senses, but my soul is weeping. Tears fall heedlessly down my expressionless face.

My soul. What happens to my soul now?

"Blake." I meet her eyes, but only briefly. Why can't I look at her now? What did she do to me? "Please…" Her face is indescribable. A combination of hurt and shame. Panic and confusion. "Just go." I stare straight ahead as I wipe my nose on my knee. "I need you to go."

She wants to say more, but even she knows there are no words for this. Nothing can fix it.

She rises to her feet and stands for a second, staring, straightening her tousled hair. I shift my gaze to hers. She's about to cry, tears threatening to fall at any moment. Her head darts around aimlessly, trying to come up with something, anything, to make this right. One solitary tear rolls down her cheek, falling onto the cloth material of her jacket. "I'm sorry." Her voice cracks. Then she grabs her hat off the floor, and I listen as the door clicks closed behind her.

I walk over to my door and lock it before walking to the bathroom and starting the shower. I feel dirty. I need to purify myself. I need to get clean. Steam clouds the room as I strip down and step inside.

It's then I can finally exhale—I didn't even realize I'd been holding my breath—and with it comes a sob, unlike anything I've ever experienced. The water hits my hair and flows down my outline.

How could I do this? I was trying to help her. Obviously, I didn't, and I cheated on my fiancé in doing so. I gave in to temptation. *Good job.*

I need to wash this off of me. Wash Blake off of me. As I sob, I grab my loofah, depositing entirely too much body wash. I scrub until my skin is red and raw. Until my entire body burns.

But the water's not hot enough to disinfect me. I turn it up. I'm still dirty. I can still feel the press of her knee between my legs.

That's it, Phoebe. Come for me.

Unrestrained laughter escapes my lungs as tears continue to fall heedlessly down my face. I can't describe this. It's like elation and despair. There's a pit in my stomach and a flutter in my chest. *Did I have an orgasm? Is that what it feels like?* I can finally see why people choose to do it. And frequently.

It shouldn't have felt that good. Not with a girl. No, this isn't normal. This isn't okay. I press my back to the wall and slide down until I'm balled up on the floor, holding my knees, rocking back and forth.

Is this too far?

I can't breathe. The water trickles down my face, threatening to drown me as I gasp for air through the tears. I watch as the heat rolls over the top of the curtain, leaving deposits of condensation on the ceiling.

Uh-uh.

I remain this way until the water runs cold.

I'm finally done crying by the time I shut the water off and wrap a towel around myself. On my way to bed, I find myself stopping in front of the mirror and as I push the fog away, I'm met with myself. Same black hair, same green eyes, yet something's different. Who am I?

One day, Peep, you're going to wake up and crave the woman you really are.

Is this who I really am?
A sinner?

Chapter 12

Phoebe

"Hey, queer!" Melissa's sister's voice reverberates in my ears.

I'm standing in the middle of church, all eyes on me. The roar of laughter and obscenities fight for consumption of the Nave.

"Dyke!" It's Ethan. Grimacing. Eyes cold.

I turn to see my father standing at the pulpit and run toward the safety of his arms.

"Dad!" I cry. "It's not true." His face is expressionless, and staring straight ahead. "I-I can explain." Still no reaction. "LOOK AT ME!" I shout.

His head turns slowly toward me, locking with my gaze. "And I saw another mighty angel coming down from heaven, wrapped in a cloud, with a rainbow over his head."

"What? Dad? I-I don't understand," I say as he continues talking.

It's as if he isn't hearing me. Just speaking, never stopping. Eyes dead. "Setting his right foot on the sea and his left foot on the land, he gave a great shout, like a lion roaring. And when he shouted, the seven thunders sounded."

An unanticipated roar of thunder causes the ground beneath me to quake. It shakes so violently I lose my balance, collapsing to the ground. I grab at the floor and find myself at my father's feet. He still hasn't stopped his speech, his body now leaning down to me. Dead eyes burning, "Take it and eat; it will be bitter to your stomach but sweet as honey in your mouth."

I need to leave. I have to get out of this church before the ceiling comes down. "Dad, we have to go! The building is collapsing!"

I try to pull him, but he won't budge. It's then I realize he's chained to the pulpit. Why won't he stop talking?

"The first woe has passed. There are still two woes to come."

I find my balance and run down the aisle toward the door, shouting, "God save me!"

Throwing the door open, I'm met with Blake, who is sporting a malevolent grin. "God's not listening, Phoebe." She pulls me into a passionate kiss, refusing to let go as I thrash for release!

The crowd shouts, "Can't fix queer!" over and over.

"Stop!" I shout, prying my face away from hers. "Stop! Stop!"

"STOP!" I shout, sitting up in my bed. I'm drenched in sweat. Panting, heart racing. I glance at my phone. 4:27 in the morning. Great.

✝

As I wait for Ethan to pick me up, I'm pacing around my living room, biting my nails. I ignore the pain of ripping off an annoying hangnail on my thumb before heading to the kitchen sink to spit it out.

It's not that I don't want to see my family, but since the other night with Blake, I've been off, not sleeping, and when I do, it's not for long. These dreams are corrupting my mind. Taking over any semblance of peace residing within me.

It's resonating throughout the day as well. As different as I feel, no one seems to notice. Except Zoe, that is. I haven't been very talkative. Thoughts of Blake are living rent free in my head now. My hands on her hips. Her lips on mine. The warmth of her hand as they guided my hips into—

—come for me.

My stomach flutters and moisture pools low every time my brain relives it, and I can't seem to stop the intrusive thoughts before they start. I failed her.

Should I even keep trying? I think. *What if this compulsion consumes me again?* I smack my forehead over and over again, hoping I can dislodge it from my brain. *No. I'm not like Blake. She's the one with the corruption. She's simply clutching onto me as she descends into hell.* No, the question shouldn't be whether I should continue. It needs to be how I can stop myself from giving in.

A knock on my door pushes away all of my contemplation, only to fill me with a new dread. Facing Ethan for the first time since I cheated. I know I need to tell him. I'll add it to the list because telling him will only make him think I'm a…Well, I'm not, so there's no point in talking about it. I should focus more on finding the right time to tell him I can't marry him. I can still turn this around and fix it. I *have* to fix it. If I don't, I'll have to marry him. Have *sex* with him. The thought makes my stomach churn, and I think I may actually need to throw up.

I answer the door, and he wraps an arm around the small of my back, pulling me in until our body are pressed together. His mouth claims my bottom lip. "You look tired," he says as I gently push him away by the shoulders. His soft thumb drags across my cheek, investigating me. "You okay?"

"I'm fine," I mumble as I turn toward my coat hanging beside the door. "Just haven't really been sleeping well."

"Wanna talk about it?" he asks, coming up behind me, running his hands up and down my biceps. The contact causes me to freeze.

"I—" I bite my lip, trying to draw the courage to tell him I don't love him. An annoying discomfort washes over my shoulders as I grow tense with his touch. As if he didn't drop a massive bombshell on me in front of everyone. Marriage, when you have no choice, should be a pretty obvious explanation for this exhaustion. Blake notwithstanding. Of course, he wouldn't see it that way.

Sometimes, I wonder if he's worse than my mother when it comes to making himself look good. Bag yourself a pastor's daughter and put a ring on it. Then tell everyone without her even being there. Nothing strange there. Why would it? Impressions are everything. Everyone knows that.

I clear my throat. "Probably my mattress."

His fingers dig soothing circles into my neck and shoulders then. Why does he have to be sweet all the time? Why can't he be a jerk and make this easy for me?

Sometimes, I wish I would've been born not from a parent but rather the primordial ooze. No God to fear will smite me. No crowd to impress. No forced emotions. No dinners. No weddings. What I want when I want it. I know it's selfish. God forgive me, but I'm exhausted and wish my brain would take a night off. Just one night free of my father quoting revelations. One night not hearing the word "dyke" or "queer."

I'm not. Why won't my brain stop tormenting me with this? Has the devil presented himself as Blake? Am I playing with fire, trying to save her? Is this a fool's errand?

No. In Jonah and the Whale, God gave Jonah a mission he also thought was ridiculous. We all know what happened when Jonah tried to ignore the message. I can't ignore God, okay, but how the heck am I supposed to get it through to her when the temptation keeps overtaking me at every turn? I know they say God wouldn't give you hardships you couldn't handle, but…my prayers seem to be falling on deaf ears.

Where are you, God? I really need you. I know the intention is not to do it for me, but I'm lost in the dark and without something—anything—to guide me. I don't see how that's possible.

"If you want, you could stay the night on my mattress. I could rub your back until you fall asleep." The corner of his mouth rises. He moves my hair to one side, gently kissing my neck as he whispers into my ear. "My mattress is very expensive."

"I think I'd sleep less," I tease nervously, turning to face him. Nice try. He'd try all night to get in my pants. That's why I stopped inviting him over. "Can we just get this over with?" I gently push past him, and he watches as I lock the door.

The entire drive to my parents. He has his left hand on the steering wheel and the other on my thigh above the fabric of my dress. When his thumb starts rubbing circles, I'm instantly reminded of Blake's hand. I shiver.

Stop thinking about it.

✝

We finally arrive at my parent's house but the three minute drive felt like an eternity. My mother is so excited when we pull up, she waves from the porch. Well, not excited to see me. Never to see me.

"Ethan! Hi!" she says, dragging out the "Hi" in the most pretentious way imaginable as we approach. I stifle the urge to roll my eyes as my stomach twists in irritation.

Ethan brought a bottle of Sauvignon Blanc. Such a suck-up. He knows my mother can't resist her wines. He's grinning from ear to ear. *Maybe THEY should get married,* I think.

First thing I do when I get inside is find my father. I know exactly where he is, too. Ever since I was a kid, I knew I could find him in his home office, which was just a tiny room with bookshelves lining every wall and a desk with a computer and multiple piles of paperwork stacked neatly on top. His rolling chair barely has the chance to roll due to how cramped the space is. It really isn't much bigger than a closet, but this has always been his little paradise. An island away from my mother—a "man cave," if you will. Sometimes he'll be reading or playing a game. Other times he's working, sending out emails to guests of the church, or writing his sermons. No matter what he's doing, though, his expression always softens when I walk in.

I move a stack of papers on his desk to the side and sit down. "Hey, Dad. Whatcha doing?"

"Peep, you're early," he says, closing his book before peering at his desktop for the time.

"It's 5:12, Dad. We're actually late."

"Oh, but not by much," he says. "I guess I lost track of time reading this passage, trying to put together my next sermon." He shuffles through the pages. "What do you think about Phillip and the Ethiopian eunuch?"

This is one of my favorite passages, and he knows it. I can't help the upturn of my lips. "I love it, Dad, that's perfect!"

My father has always been an easygoing guy. Some people would freak out if you moved their meticulous stack of papers to sit on their desk. They'd expect you to stand. Not my father. You could be late—or early—as long as you arrived. If my father didn't like someone, you'd never know because he treats everyone equally. And much like Phillip, he would preach the gospel to anyone willing to listen. "I thought you would." He stands up and walks with me to the kitchen where we find my mother putting the last of the food on the table as Ethan sits there watching her slave away.

He can't even be bothered to offer her some help? Is this how my life will be? Me slaving over a hot stove while still being expected to clean the house and tend to our children?

Oof. Children.

My stomach roils at the thought. I know it's supposed to be the most magical time in a woman's life. Being connected to this tiny baby for a short amount of time. I've heard all the stories. Read all the books, trying to wrap my mind around what my body is made for. Still, no matter how much I try to accept my lease in life, nothing about it seems appealing.

Assuming I survive and don't drown after Ethan grunts on top of me for ten minutes if I'm lucky, I then have to carry this alien inside of me. Kicking the wind out of me, making me pee myself randomly. And then, I have to push it out. Well, it's also possible they'd slice open my entire stomach and pull it out, lion king style, holding it to the light, like Rafiki standing on Pride Rock. All the while, it's screaming, all covered in grossness. Not sure if that's better or worse than being cut from my vagina to my butt.

I know this is what life is. This is what I'm meant to do. It makes no sense to me why I'm not excited by this engagement. Did God make me defective?

"Ethan," my father says as we sit down at the table. "Would you like to lead us in Grace?"

"Of course, Pastor P."

We all join hands—my right hand in Ethan's and my left in my father's—before bowing my head.

"Heavenly Father, please bless this food we are about to eat. Thank you, Lord, for the amazing weather and this amazing family accepting me as their own. Please help the truly sinful and misguided find your presence in their heart." I kick him under the table. Really? Is he talking about Blake right now? Why's he obsessed with her? *I wonder what she's doing right now.* Wait…Why am I thinking that? "Please watch over us and help us to keep your love and your light in our spirits. In Jesus's name. Amen."

"Amen," we all say in unison as I cross myself. I notice my father lift his head and find his way from Ethan to me, then back to Ethan, then down to his plate.

"Let's eat," he says and digs in. He spends most of the dinner with his mouth full, not saying much. My mother, on the other hand, does the opposite.

"Mmm, Ethan, this wine is amazing!" Her rounded cheeks bunch as she gives him a tight lipped, smug smile.

"Thanks, Mrs. A. There's this beautiful vineyard right outside of Peachton. I noticed it on my way home from the city." He lifts his glass and gestures to her. "I saw this one and instantly thought you'd love it."

Gosh, he makes me sick. Any closer to her butt and his nose will be permanently stained brown. "Well." My mother hides a blush. Great. She's blushing. This is gross. "That's so sweet of you! I'm so glad my baby girl found you!" She takes another sip off her glass before adding, "Oh! Peep, I wanted to go over a few things."

My head lifts from my plate for the first time since we started eating. "Things?"

"Yeah, for the wedding, silly! Have you thought about the flowers?"

Honestly, Mom, I'm still trying to figure out how to tell all of you there won't be a wedding, I think, but decide to say, "No. I'm not really into flowers."

"You love it when I get you flowers," Ethan tries, giving me a wink.

Ah yes, the smashed flowers you stuff in your satchel. The epitome of romantic. I especially love how all of the petals fall off after two days and make a mess out of my counter. Not to mention how difficult it is to wash a skinny little vase. A dish I only use for a few days and then have to clean. Just for it to sit in my cabinet for four to five months before I need it again…for only a few days.

Why does anyone enjoy the concept of snuffing out one of nature's beautiful creations when they could nurture it, allow it to grow, and keep it for a lifetime?

"You know I do," I say through gritted teeth before noticing my father is looking at me. When we lock eyes, he goes back to staring at his plate.

"Well, sweetie, you have to have flowers at your wedding," my mother says in disbelief.

"Sounds good. I just don't know what I like, I guess."

"I'll help you!" she says, rising before walking to the living room to grab something off the table. When she returns, she hands me a two-inch thick three-ring binder. I grab my napkin from my lap and wipe off my mouth before grabbing it from her. I gently push my plate up, making room for the binder. When I open it, the color leaves my face.

It's a planner. For my wedding. "Shouldn't *I* be making this?" I ask.

"Well, have you?" she retorts, sinking back into her seat, one eyebrow raised.

"I mean, no…" I turn to see Ethan, excited and amazed. Like a puppy waiting for me to turn the page or throw a ball. Something tells me he'd chase it. "But I got engaged less than a week ago, Mom."

"There isn't much time, baby. I decided the wedding should be in the fall. Absolutely beautiful time! The leaves are changing colors."

Dying, the leaves are dying. Everything is dying. That's autumn. The death of beauty. I think.

"And the weather isn't all rainy."

You mean feeding the Earth and allowing it to grow, be born.

"I found this reasonably priced beautiful place. If we put money in for it now, they said they'd hold it for you!"

"Wait, what? What place?"

"Bear Ridge."

I hate Bear Ridge. We used to camp there every summer for the fourth of July. The water was too cold on the lake, there was trash everywhere, and there really aren't any beautiful landscapes. Not to mention the mosquitoes. One year Zoe counted thirty-eight bites on my legs and back. It genuinely is the worst, and to think I'm going to stand outside getting bitten to heck while I'm saying my "I do's" is sheer gullibility. I know why they're offering us a good price. No one in their right mind would get married there.

"Pass," I say. "I'm not getting eaten alive on my wedding day." I envision Ethan and me standing at the altar, hands joined, peering into each other's eyes, a dot on his forehead, him smacking his face constantly before rejoining our hands. I'd be wearing a veil, a full-length dress complete with sleeves! A perfectly tailored mosquito net! I bite my cheek to stave off the humor. That'd be priceless.

"Well, we could get citronella candles! And spray off and—"

I laugh incredulously. "Mom, do you hear yourself right now? There is nothing beautiful about spraying off on a wedding dress. Besides, I'm not even sure how much a dress would cost, but it won't be cheap. No way I'd have it paid off by fall."

"Already got that covered!" She leans over the table and flips the pages. "Doris gave me some designs. You just let her know and she'll only charge you the cost for fabric."

"DORIS?!" I shout, causing my father to chime in with a warning.

"Peep, lower your voice."

"Doris is NOT making me a wedding dress, Mom. I'm sorry. No." I shake my head and wave my hands.

"Well," Ethan chimes in with raised eyebrows, setting down his fork, "it'd save us money. I found the perfect groom's cake. It's totally me! It's got a fish with a hook in its mouth and a tackle box that says, 'Hooked for life.' Problem is, it's $737." I didn't even know he liked to fish. He's never even mentioned fishing with friends. Who is this guy?

"Seven—NO!" I close the book. "Just no. That's too expensive! That'd be more than the cake."

"Peep," my mother says, pushing my hand off the book and reopening it. "It's not that bad. A good wedding cake will be what's remembered most! You want it to be a cake people talk about twenty years down the road!"

I can't breathe. I bring my fingers to my temple to make sure I'm not sweating because it feels like I'm overheating. Forever is seeming a little bit too permanent for me right now. "Twenty years down the road? God—sorry, gosh, that's a long time!"

My father interjects. "Hang on, Priscilla, give Peep time to process."

Process? I can't process this. If I don't figure out a way to call off this wedding, I'll be drowning in debt and stressed for months! Fall? I'd be married in less than seven months! I figured I'd have longer. I'd have more time to find the right words before a penny got sunk into entertaining this idea. Besides, if I can't figure out how to call it off, and I'm forced to actually go through with this—because I'm spineless, shouldn't it be perfect? You only get one.

My mother doesn't listen to my father's suggestion. She keeps flipping through the pages until she hits the cake section. "Now these are some of the cheapest I could find from Ivana Grace. Now, I made some calls and talked to her assistant. She said Ivana would call me back within the next week and so I'll need to know by then what cake you're going with. Have you thought of a theme?"

"Football." Ethan raises his hand. He has to be joking. I've heard of men joking about this kind of stuff, but he can't possibly think any self-respecting woman would agree to that. But if the sparkle in his eye and his thrust out chest is anything to go off of, he's actually seriously suggesting it. Am I still in my nightmare, or did I wake up in the twilight zone?

"Theme?" I'm choking at the realization this is the man I'm expected to spend forever with. Football? Absolutely not. I stand. "Excuse me." I grab my napkin from my lap and place it gently on the pages in the binder. "I have to use the restroom."

I walk as calmly as my heart will allow down the hallway. Once I'm inside, I lock the door and sink down onto the closed toilet lid. Head in hands. Married in less than seven months? Forever. Eight months from now, I'll be trapped. I haven't even started living yet. At the rate this is going, I'll be barefoot and pregnant a year from now. I can't do this.

How do I fix this—because it's starting to seem like there's no way out. Unless I fake my own death. Fly to Canada. Change my name. Maybe Piper would help me. She lives for chaos. Shoot, she might even go with me. Keep me company until we can establish ourselves.

I pull out my phone to check my savings. Can I even afford to pull this off? Maybe I can sneak out the window right now. But as I'm logging in to my bank, a text comes through. I don't recognize the number, but there's no doubt in my mind who it is.

Unknown Number (6:07 PM)
Hey, I hope it's okay that I asked Zoe for your number

I don't respond. Why would Zoe do that? How did she have Zoe's number in the first place? Do they talk behind my back?

I'm now more annoyed at her than I am with Blake, and I didn't grind on Zoe until I had an orgasm while God watched in disgust. I glance at the time stamp and realize she can see I'm reading her messages.

Unknown Number (6:09 PM)
Please Phoebe. Would it be okay if I came to church on Sunday?

I think about typing something, but what would I say? I can't tell her not to come to church. It's not up to me. I finally respond.

Me (6:09 PM)
It's not my church. It's everyone's church

Unknown Number (6:10 PM)
I'm aware of how church works…That's not what I asked you

Me (6:11 PM)
Do whatever.

Unknown Number (6:11 PM)
Just say you don't want me to

Me (6:11 PM)
Didn't say that

Unknown Number (6:12 PM)
You're implying it

Me (6:12 PM)
No Blake I'm not. I can't tell you not to go to church

Unknown Number (6:14 PM)
Listen I know this is confusing for you.

Unknown Number (6:14 PM)
I'm sorry.

Unknown Number (6:14 PM)
Really sorry.

Unknown Number (6:14 PM)
You made some very good points

Unknown Number (6:15 PM)
and then I crossed a line.

But did she? I remember she tried to pull away. I lunged at her. I couldn't fight the urge. She really was trying. She even apologized. Am I acting unjustly toward her? Was she even in the wrong? I mean, we both were in the wrong. Right?

I rub the pad of my finger along the side of my phone in contemplation before finally responding.

Me (6:16 PM)
No...

Me (6:16 PM)
I'm sorry...

Unknown Number (6:17 PM)
You?

Unknown Number (6:17 PM)
For what?

Unknown Number (6:17 PM)
You didn't do anything.

Me (6:17 PM)
I did though...

Me (6:18 PM)
I started it and I'm sorry.

Unknown Number (6:18 PM)
Yeah...

Unknown Number (6:18 PM)
but I finished it. 😉

I hold my stomach, trying to quell the flutters as I will my mouth not to grin.

Me (6:18 PM)
Yes...

Me (6:18 PM)
I suppose you did.

Now I can't breathe for a different reason. I shift on the toilet seat as I bite my lip.

Me (6:19 PM)
The point is I'd love for us to keep trying to do these sessions

Me (6:19 PM)
Just...you have to keep your hands on your bible

Me (6:19 PM)
Also

Me (6:19 PM)
Bring your own bible

Unknown Number (6:20 PM)

Finally, a little calmer, I decide to head back out to the kitchen. My mother is putting food away. Ethan and my father have disappeared. "Where'd everybody go?" I ask, grabbing the plates off the table and bringing them to the sink.

"Your dad wanted to talk to Ethan. He's been being a baby about this whole engagement."

"Dad? Being a baby?" I ask as I take the washcloth from beside the sink and soak it in the dishwater my mother is washing the dishes with.

"Yeah. Apparently, Ethan didn't ask your father's permission." She rolls her eyes. "I guess it meant a lot to him."

"He didn't?" I can't believe he wouldn't ask the pastor before marrying his daughter. Isn't that kind of a stereotypical thing? Unless...could he maybe have thought my father wouldn't approve? I mean, I don't know why he wouldn't, but for someone obsessed with looking good, it amazes me Ethan would bypass such a key element.

"It's no big deal, but your father seems to think it is. Maybe he's not ready for his baby to grow up."

"I can't say I blame him. I'm not sure I'm ready anymore, either." I wipe down the kitchen table as I contemplate.

"What do you mean?" What did I mean? Getting married sounds so adult. I'm not childish by any means. I pay my own bills, bought my own car. Went to college. Pay my own taxes.

Marriage seems different somehow. Maybe it's the realization that the next step is becoming your parents. Raising your own children.

Before I can answer her question, she's answering it for me. "Oh Peep, is it your wedding night you're worried about?"

The idea of a very sweaty Ethan on top of me enters my internal thoughts. I scrunch my nose. "What?" I stop making circles with the towel on the table.

"It's safe to say you haven't been being impure, right?"

"Mom, I'm not trying to talk about this."

"No, honey, it's okay!" she says, walking over and pulling me into a hug. "I was nervous with your father the first time as well."

"Mom!" Why is the world bound and determined to make me nauseous lately?

"I know, I know." She pulls back from me and holds up her palms. "This isn't something you want to talk about, but if not your mother, who else?"

"Literally anyone else, Mom."

"Now it may not feel very good the first time." She ignores me. "But the key is to buy yourself something nice from that store Victoria's Secret. You want to really accentuate those hips, honey. They are perfect for childbearing."

"Mom, if you don't stop talking, I'm going to go," I threaten.

"And there's this numbing stuff you can buy if it hurts."

"ETHAN!" I shout across the house. "WE'RE GOING!" I walk to the hall closet and grab our jackets. She follows me, however, ignoring my discomfort.

"Okay, fine, I'll stop, but one last thing, okay?"

"What?" I say, stopping before the door.

"The numbing stuff can take away from you having a good time, so before you try that, I'll send you a text of some lubrication your father and I use. If you're anything like me, you could have allergies, so it's best to use the right kind to avoid breaking out." Yup, the small amount of dinner I did get to enjoy is about to come back up. I can feel it.

Would sticking my fingers in my ears and humming really loud be immature? Honestly, I'm almost to the point of not caring. I walk as fast as my legs will carry me without turning into a full-on sprint. When I'm outside, I bolt to Ethan's truck or a birdbath. Whatever comes first. "Who said we can't enjoy ourselves too?" she shouts from the doorstep.

Ethan comes up behind her and gives her a hug. I'm already in the cab with the door closed, begging to be home. *Find your happy place, Appleton.* I hum a song and disassociate until Ethan gets in, and we're pulling onto the street.

I should tell him. Right now. I can't take another day of my mother planning things out and possibly showing up at my house with lube and lingerie.

Yup. Right now.

"Eth—" But Ethan reaches for the nob, cranking up the volume on the Christian rock station so loud I can't even hear myself think. He sings along to Crowder, looking at me as if expecting me to sing along. I nod through raised eyebrows. Gosh, I'm over this.

When he finally puts his truck in park beside my car, he leans in closer, lifting the center console to remove any obstructions between us. "I know the wedding stuff seems like a lot. We don't need to rush it." He places his hand on my thigh.

I look at it and think about my life. I have to tell him I can't do this. Not now, not ever. I'm not ready.

Then I remember God wouldn't give me anything I can't handle. Maybe Ethan is exactly where I'm meant to be, and God has forced my hand as a reminder to stop being scared. A life of sin and stagnancy isn't where I'm meant to be. I'm meant to move forward, and Ethan has been patiently waiting.

It could be worse. He could be abusive. He could be forceful. I could be marrying him because I'm scared he'll hurt me if I don't. He truly is an all-around good man. Very respectful toward women. He has a good job as a child psychologist. Volunteers at the wildlife conservation on the weekends. Why do I shut him out?

He's also very attractive with his blond surfer hair that falls to about his chin, wavy and soft. The honey of his eyes are jaw-dropping and any children we have would be blessed to have those eyes. He takes very good care of himself, lifting weights four times a week. Most women would be lucky to run their hands along his washboard abs or feel his strong embrace. He knows how to have fun and be goofy. Mainly with his guy friends, drinking beer and watching or playing sports. He's incredibly active. I can tell he'd build a tree house and go camping with our boys. He'd even play tea party with our girls or let them do his hair and makeup.

I need to understand why the idea of him touching me makes me sick. It shouldn't. I should let this go. I move forward in the seat and watch his hand find the spot between my legs. I take a deep breath and bite my lip. *I can do this.*

"Sorry," he says, moving his hand back, but before he can fully lift it, I grab his wrist and push it further between my legs under my dress. I study him. "Are you sure?" he says.

"No." I let out a sigh, squeezing my eyes shut. "But maybe a little?"

He moves his leg up onto the seat to face me. His breath is steady, and his eyes are glistening off the streetlights. He slides his hand up slowly. I can't look at him. I need to look somewhere else. I decide to grab him and pull him onto me as I lay back in the seat. His mouth finds my pulse point.

As his lips hit my neck, a flash of Blake's crooked canine at Blessed Beans drinking her coffee enters my mind. *No, go away,* I think, shutting my eyes tightly. His left hand pulls the top hem of my dress down to expose my bra-clad breast. And as he slides his hand under my bra, he releases a heavy sigh into my neck. My hands find his hair and tug out of reflex as he pinches my nipple in between his thumb and forefinger.

The novels say my pelvis should be moving. I should be sighing really sexily. I should be digging my nails into his back and in his hair. But I chew my nails, meaning it'd just be my fingers, I suppose. Some of the books have suggested talking to him. Telling him what I want him to do, but I want him to stop, so I decide to stay quiet. My center moves mechanically up and down on his hand before he licks his fingers and slides my panties to the side, touching what would be dry, but we know he has more than enough saliva to make up for that. Why would my mother even suggest lube? This man drools like a stressed-out dog at a grooming salon at the first signs of anything sexual. Oh, life of bladder infections, here I come.

I close my eyes as he circles aimlessly. I hear the low, gentle hum of Blake's admiration, which thrusts me back into reality. *Stop.*

"Can I go inside?" he asks.

"No!" He doesn't. He respectfully continues moving his fingers up and down.

"Does that feel good?" he pants, moving down to take my nipple into his mouth.

"Yeah." I try to say it breathlessly and if it isn't authentic, Ethan doesn't seem to notice. *I can do this, dammit,* I think, squeezing my eyes shut tightly as he laps at my chest while holding the other one in his hand.

> *"We'll find out what you like together, okay?"*

That day she made me my first drink. That wink. Such a gorgeous wink. Her eyes. Deep, deep blue. The smell of cedar floods my nose and chills run down my spine. Things start to wake up between my legs.

Is it working? Am I actually allowing Ethan to please me? Maybe marriage won't be too bad after all. I grab his wrist to feel what he's doing to my center. "Oh yeah," I sigh, smirking in excitement as I close my eyes again. *It's working! I'm normal. I can be normal. Just focus. Focus.*

> Step Two...

I lick my lips,

> *...is educating girls like you.*

I buck my hips into Ethan's eager fingers. My eyebrows furrow as I concentrate.

> *Is this okay?*

"Mhmm...Right there." My body twists as I push myself to climax. "I'm close."

> *That's it, Phoebe.*

"Right."

> *Come for me.*

My back arches. "There!"

"Shit!" Ethan says as I release. It isn't nearly as exciting as the one with Blake, but maybe nothing can compare to your first time. He sits up and removes his hand as I'm shaking in the seat. I watch as he wipes his fingers on his shirt. I feel sick.

I press my palms into my eyes. *Don't cry. Don't cry. Why the fuck didn't I like that?*

"You okay?" Ethan asks after a while.

Why does everyone keep asking me that? Why does this keep happening after? What the *fuck* is wrong with me? I don't even care I said that. Something is wrong. Something is very wrong. I'm broken. I need to leave.

"I have to go," I say shamefully, pushing down my dress, avoiding eye contact.

"Phoebe, wait," he says, but I open the door and gently close it behind me. I need to be alone.

Ethan doesn't follow.

✝

When I make it inside, I'm crying and hyperventilating. My phone rings, and the screen reads Pipez. I can't right now. I hit ignore.

She calls again. I know her. She'll keep calling. A normal human would shut their phone off, but I can't. Which she also knows.

I wipe back my tears and try to steady my voice. "Hello." I wince at the sound of my involuntary croak.

"Well, I called to congratulate you," she says as I wish ill intent on whoever told her about my recent engagement. "But are you crying?"

Ugh…"Nope. Just sick," I lie, stripping off my dress and walking to my room. I feel disgusting and the stickiness of my apartment isn't helping.

Her voice bursts out of the speakerphone. "Is there a reason why you're lying to your only sister?"

Coming to a stop at my mirror, I set down my phone and lean in. "I'm not." I take in the quiver of my lip, trying to push down the sinking in my chest. My reflection begins to ripple and blur from the pooling of water on my lower lids.

Piper's voice is stern and commanding as she says, "Tell me. Now."

"Just leave it alone, Piper," I say, wiping away the collection of moisture with the back of my hand before it can trail the contours of my face, falling heedlessly into the basin beneath me. My jaw clenches and I sniffle, trying to force myself to stop this ridiculousness. Convince myself I'm overreacting, and these tears are useless.

"You know I never will." I squeeze my eyes shut, listening to the gentle strumming of Piper's guitar as I bend completely over the counter, pressing the heels of my palms into my eyes. I take a steadying breath, forcing my nose to register the stale minty-ness of my toothpaste.

"I'm just tired, okay?" I'm too exhausted to fight. Flooded with consternation, unable to summon the appropriate words to call off this wedding and still save face. Yet, I can't make myself want Ethan, either. I desperately need a hot shower…and then I need this day to be over. "I just want to go to bed. It's been a long week, and I need to crawl into a hole and shy away from the world tomorrow."

"Ah, relax-urday coming in clutch." I can hear her playfulness through the phone before her tone flattens once more into concern. "Now stop bullshitting me, Peep. What's going on?"

How does she do that? She literally always knows beyond a shadow of a doubt. She's ridiculously confident in her assumptions for someone who lives three hours away! It's not like we're twins with some connectivity. At least I don't have it.

"You're right, okay?" I finally cave. "Is that what you want to hear?" My knees have officially lost the battle with gravity. I find myself sitting down on the floor, throwing the battle of maintaining my voice to the wind as I rest my head in my hands. "I'm broken."

"Broken?" she all but screeches with dismay. Like she didn't see this coming. "Phoebe," she says firmly, "you're not broken. I never said that."

"Yes! Yes, you did!" I smack my forehead. "You said I'm too broken to be what Mom needs me to be."

"No," she says, her voice taut. "I said you're going to crave the woman you really are. Not that you're broken."

"But I am!" I shout. "I am broken! I'm calling out to God, and he's not listening because he thinks I'm a shitty human being. I know I am!"

"Umm…" Silence floods the space. "Should I say language?"

I scowl, even though she can't see it. "And the worst part is, I can't fix me. I can fix everyone else. I can fix members at EC. I can even fix Mom, but I can't fix me, and I can't fix Blake."

"Blake? Wait, Phoebe, who's Blake? Calm down for a minute," she insists, continuing to strum on her guitar. "Just breathe. Okay. In through your nose."

I do as she instructs, allowing the gentle harmony of chords to enter my ears. I recognize the song immediately. She used to play it for me when we were kids. Landslide by Fleetwood Mac.

"Out through your mouth. Good. Okay, again." She guides me a few more times before starting to hum. Finally, the sobbing stops. The quavering of my throat stops too. "Okay, from the top. Who's Blake?"

"She's just a girl at church." I wipe the tears from my reddened face, rising to my feet. "I've been trying to help her find God, but I can't. I want to. I really want to. God sent her to me. I know He did. So why can't I seem to find the right way to save her?"

"How can you be so sure God sent her to you?"

"You mean like maybe it was the devil?"

"Definitely not. Come on, Phoebe. Get your head out of your ass." She hits the hollow body of her instrument, her tone half amusement, half I-should-know-better. "You know who you're talking to."

A smile creeps up my face. This entire week, I've been nothing but serious—drowning in my thoughts—but leave it to my sister to help lighten my distress. It feels good to smile. "Not every person sent to you by God needs saving. Sometimes things just happen." She continues to strum, a song I've never heard filling my room. "Sometimes, they're lessons of personal growth. Have you ever stopped to think if God actually *is* real, He may be sending you a message? To focus on fixing yourself for once."

"Fix myself how?" I ask. How do I fix not wanting to be touched by Ethan? I'm going to end up marrying him, and this is something I truly need to figure out. If Piper has answers, she needs to tell me.

She stops strumming the strings before responding. "That I can't answer, Peep. I'm not the one who said you were broken. Because you're not. You're just not the Phoebe you're meant to be yet. She's on her way, though. I can feel it."

"Thanks for nothing." I roll my eyes. I love our dynamic. I can be upfront, and she knows not to take me too personally.

"Best I can say is if this whole Jesus thing is your cup of tea, then lean back onto God, Phoebe, and trust He'll move you in the right direction."

Chapter 13

Phoebe

In the eighth grade, Eve, Zoe, and I went to a friendly volleyball game at the Christian college. Eve and Zoe were arguing over two boys, and which one was more attractive. I guess I was a late bloomer because I still wasn't attracted to boys. Every time they swooned over them, I found myself trying desperately to fit in.

"Phoebe." Eve nudged my arm with hers. "Which one?"

"Phoebe, just say the brunette to shut her up," Zoe insisted, pointing to a man leaping forward to hit the ball before collapsing in the sand. "You know it's the brunette."

"They're both cute." I'm obviously trying to keep the peace, and they twig on it.

"You haven't even looked at them!" Eve shouted. "You've been staring at your nails pretty much the entire time. Also," she grabbed my hand and put it in my lap, "stop biting your damn fingernails!"

"Language."

She crosses her arms. "So clearly," she returned her attention to Zoe while I continued biting, "you haven't noticed his abs."

"I'm not really into muscles!" Zoe confessed. "How about you, Phoebe? Does your future man have to have muscles?"

"I mean no…" I wasn't sure what to say. I wasn't sure what my type was, but neither one of them seemed to fit it. "Could you imagine if we looked like her, though?" I pointed to a girl who was spiking the ball to the blond guy. She was wearing tight shorts that hugged low on her hips. Sweat was beading on her chest, falling into the crevice of her sports bra. Watching her chest rise and fall as she playfully pushed one of the other guys on her team was fascinating. I decided I liked her hair pulled back into a baseball cap and wondered if I could pull off the same look.

"I guess so," Eve replied, wrinkling her nose.

"I'd give anything for her tan," Zoe joked.

My eyes dipped to her butt.

"Did you just look at her ass?" Eve asked, face scrunched up in disgust.

"What?" I instantly became nervous. "So? Those shorts are cute," I defended. "When I get older, I'm thinking I should get a pair."

"You wouldn't make it past your front door." Eve chuckled.

"She'd never make it out of the store." Zoe joined in Eve's mirth.

I wring my hands in my lap. "I guess you're right."

Eve tried to veer the conversation back on track.

"Okay, but stop being a lesbo and answer the question."

"I'm not a…that," I said.

"Shut up, Eve," Zoe snapped. "Name a girl who doesn't look at another girl's butt?"

"A straight one," she countered. "Seriously, we ask her about guys, and she comments about the girl."

"She doesn't have to think either one is hot." Zoe blinked rapidly.

"Only one reason she wouldn't think they were attractive, Zo." She made a peace sign with her fingers and held it up to her mouth before sticking out her tongue.

"Eww." I laughed uncomfortably while Zoe punched her arm.

"Oww! You bitch!" she yowled before slapping Zoe's arm hard enough to leave a welt.

✝

"Lean back onto God, lean back onto God," I repeat as I ring the doorbell to the address Blake had texted me.

Blake Chapel (11:47 AM)
Since we had the last lesson at your apartment, can we have it at my house this time?

I agree because I can't think of a reason why not to.

✝

The sun is starting to set, leaving a beautiful pink and red on the horizon as I pull into the freshly paved driveway, being sure to park behind her old Dodge.

I can't help but admire the small one-story white panel ranch-style house as I walk up the stone pathway to the door, my Bible tucked tightly to my chest. The smell of fresh cut grass envelops my senses as I avoid the spray of the sprinkler system showering the perfect blemish-free yard. The porch is made of large gray stone railings and white pillars. Two wooden rocking chairs sit to the right of the wooden front door. It'd be a perfect place to sit and take in the smell of the neatly manicured pine bushes wrapping around the front of the porch. How peaceful it'd be to fill your lungs of petrichor meshed with balsam from the shrubs during a crisp rain. The steam rolling off a fresh mug of coffee.

I exhale right as Blake opens the door and I'm hit with the smell of cedar. Those gorgeous blue eyes as she displays her crooked canine cause my chest to tighten. She's wearing a loose black tank top with white trim and baggy dark blue jeans.

I haven't seen her since…since what happened, and without warning, I'm filled with a wave of anxiety. As she opens her mouth to probably say hi, I start rambling. "Do you have a landscaper? I just noticed your yard looks amazing. Is he a gardener? My dad wants to hire a gardener, but we have a landscaper. He actually gives my dad a discount. I mean, he goes to our church, and *offered* my dad a discount—" She rolls her eyes and grabs my hand, pulling me inside.

"You're rambling," she teases as she shuts the door.

"I'm sorry," I say, staring at my feet.

"Don't be." She turns and starts walking to the living room. Her walk is slightly feminine, and I can't help but notice the sway of her hips as she steps.

I'm not sure what to do, or if I'm meant to follow, so I stand in the doorway, watching as she sits down on the couch. Her house is an open concept, and while I'm standing at the door, I can see the entire kitchen to my left and the living room directly in front of me. To the right of the living room is a hallway with doors leading to what I'm assuming would be the bedrooms and bathroom.

"I hope you like—" She looks up from the bags she's opening on the coffee table to see me still standing at the door. "You can come in." She raises a sultry brow. "I won't bite."

A rush of warmth surges through my extremities. I walk over to the couch and sit beside her nervously, being sure to leave a good three feet of distance. She seems to find this funny.

"Phoebe." She lifts an amused brow. "You don't have to perform an exorcism." She gestures to my Bible, which I don't realize is still clutched to my chest. "You can unclench."

I release my breath and relax my shoulders. "Sorry."

"Stop apologizing." She sifts through the bags again. "I didn't know what you ate. So, I hope you like chicken enchiladas because I ordered a fuck-ton."

"Language." She sarcastically mouths the word with me, still unpacking the food. I sigh. "Yes."

"Yes, what?"

"Chicken enchiladas are fine." I nod.

She sorts out the food onto the plates and then grabs for her Bible. Which, of course, is on the side table closest to me, causing her to reach over my body. "Excuse me," she breathes as she does. "So," she bites her lip, "what's today's lesson?"

I clear my throat and open my book, which is now on my lap. "Umm…" My tongue is sticking to the roof of my mouth. "Do you have any water?"

Blake springs up instantly, and I watch as she grabs two glasses from a cabinet in the kitchen. "Do you want ice?"

I shake my head. She fills them up with water from the fridge and carries them back to the table, placing down two wooden coasters before handing me a glass and setting the other one down. Coasters, huh?

Her house is very clean. I wonder if she cleaned it specifically for me or if it's always like this. There isn't a single bit of dust anywhere. Underneath the smell of the food in front of us is a hint of lemon and clean laundry. The atmosphere is light, as if she opens the windows daily, forbidding the air from ever growing stale or stuffy.

When she sits back down, however, I notice she is now sitting closer to me. I take a swig of my glass, holding it to my chest for a second. I don't know what to say. I feel nervous, and I don't know why, but I need to get it together.

"What's on the roster for today, Professor Appleton?"

"Don't call me that," I say, face heating. Such a dorky comment, but it comforts me enough to focus on the passage I have planned. "Judges."

She seems intrigued. "Ooo, this one oughtta be good." She rubs her hands together mischievously before opening her Bible and finding the passages.

I roll my eyes and begin reading it aloud.

"A Levite and his concubine travel to Gibeah, where they are hosted by an old man—"

"Okay, prostitution is fine, but being gay isn't. Got it." I lift my head from the book and glare at her, nostrils flaring. She waves her hand. "Sorry, go on."

"Concubine doesn't mean prostitute. A concubine is an unmarried woman who lives with a man." It baffles me how people constantly get that wrong. "Which could range from servant to mistress."

"Still wrong," she grins. "Those with concubines were often met with family strife or other negative consequences for their actions."

I let out a huff and continue reading. When I'm finished, her face is full of worry. Is she finally seeing what I've been saying all along? I gesture for her to speak, hoping for some positivity that maybe this is working.

"Phoebe, this story is horrible."

"Isn't it?"

"But I don't see what it has to do with homosexuality." She licks her bottom lip.

"What?!" My jaw drops. "The men of the city demanded to rape the Levite!"

"Again, that was an emasculation tactic. It had nothing to do with the act of love." I watch as her lips wrap around her fork while she takes a bite, remembering how they felt on my neck. Tingles rush through my body. *Focus!* "And clearly, they didn't give a shit about 'loving thy neighbor' when they treated those women the way they did."

"Will you watch your mouth, please?" I ask, growing frustrated.

"Looks like you're watching it for me." She raises an eyebrow before smirking and taking another bite.

I freeze. "I-I am not. I'm just…"

"And he offered up his virgin daughter to be defiled and raped," she presses on, reaching for her water. "Fucking Father of the Year," she says into her glass before taking a sip.

I decide against asking her to stop cussing again.

"Clearly, you're missing the part where he had no choice. It was either that or allow them to rape those men!"

She nods in mock agreement. "So, raping a virgin is better than raping a man?"

I narrow my eyes, blinking repeatedly. What a ridiculous thing to say. "Well, no, but…"

"Because rape is nonconsensual sex. Which is what they mean when they say immoral sexual acts are a sin." She shuffles back to Genesis. "Right here!" She points. "It says, 'But they replied, 'Stand back!' And they said, 'This fellow came here as an alien, and he would play the judge! Now we will deal worse with you than with them.' They're trying to punish him by emasculating him because they think he's judging them! Which—I mean—they were…The things they were doing were truly heinous, but again, it's not a crime against loving the same gender." She sighs. "Listen, Phoebe, there isn't a single place in the ancient Hebrew translation of the Bible where the word homosexual is used."

"It's inferred! What about Leviticus 18:22? 'You shall not lie with a male as with a woman; it is an abomination.'" I lean in and grab my fork, taking a bite of my food.

"Whoa, whoa, whoa, missy!" Blake drops her fork and straightens herself out before again flipping the pages. "I knew you'd bring this one up again! I've been studying!" she preens. "You're skipping over the first part!" She skims the page. "Ah! Leviticus 18:3-4 'You shall not do as they do in the land of Egypt, where you lived, and you shall not do as they do in the land of Canaan, to which I am bringing you. You shall not follow their statutes. My ordinances you shall observe, and my statutes you shall keep, following them: I am the Lord your God.' And then they list all the things those people are doing, clearly while not walking with God." She smirks. "It's explaining that people within these areas have given into wickedness. They had no regard for the Lord. These particular Levites were sent to Canaan with the sole purpose of becoming priests. The expectation for them was much higher than an average man. As we learned from Sodom and Gomorrah, turning to a life of wickedness will only lead to being smited…or… smote? Fire and brimstone…and all that." She waves her hand.

Heat rises to my ears. She's completely wrong! I shuffle through my own Bible. "'But because of cases of sexual immorality, each man should have his own wife and each woman her own husband.' Corinthians 7:2."

"Because that's consensual sex! Sleeping with another man was never more than a tactic used to shame and overpower a 'lesser' man back then!" She grabs my book out of my hands, grinning. "'Now concerning the matters about which you wrote: "It is good for a man not to touch a woman."'" She raises her eyebrows, sucking in her lips to stifle her delight over 'one-upping' me. "Interesting," she states with a condescending tone before licking her finger to continue turning the pages. I fight back the memory of her hands on my skin. "John 4:8: 'Whoever does not love does not know God, for God is love.'"

"What does that have to do with homosexuals?"

"I'm getting' there! John 4:*16:* 'So we have known and believe the love that God has for us. God is love, and those who abide in love abide in God, and God abides in them.' So why can't a gay person live in love *and* live in God as long as it's consensual?"

"Because that's not love," I assert.

"It's not? You're telling me because I'm a woman, I can't love you?" Her mouth slams shut as she realizes what she said.

This throws any thought process I have to a screeching halt. *Love me?*

"I mean…not you per se…just…" She rubs the back of her neck. "Like anyone." She can't seem to look at me now, deciding to continue reading instead. "John 4:20-21, 'Those who say, 'I love God,' and hate a brother or sister are liars, for those who do not love a brother or sister, whom they have seen, cannot love God, whom they have not seen. The commandment we have from him is this: those who love God must love their brothers and sisters also.' Explain why your church thinks it's okay to hate me?"

I don't hate her. Love is a strong word, though. I love my sister and my mother, sure, but to love another woman romantically? I'm not even sure I can love *anyone* romantically. She didn't even say romantically. Why am I thinking it?

I rise to my feet and walk across the living room to the fireplace. Above it, on the mantel, is a series of pictures. One is of Blake standing next to a heavyset man about five inches taller than her. He isn't overweight. Just very strong. They're holding giant scissors together and cutting the ribbon for Siren's Song. Her expression is what catches my eye. I'm not sure I've ever seen her quite this radiant. Her eyes are bright and full of life. She's absolutely beautiful.

My eyes move to the picture next to it. One of her on the man's shoulders in water chest deep. Their arms are both over their heads, showing off their muscles. I trace the frame with my finger. The water is impossibly clear, and the background is gorgeous. Blake comes up behind my shoulder.

There's another picture of them in a tree. She's sitting on the branch with her body propped up on her arm, one leg stretched out while the other is dangling. He's down below it with his arms crossed, back leaning against the trunk. One foot propped up behind him.

"Is this Jude?" I ask.

"Yeah." She presses her body against mine while reaching past me to pick up the picture of them cutting the ribbon. One corner of her mouth arches.

My body warms and my heart rate quickens. "You seemed pretty close."

"He was my best friend." Her eyes begin to water. "He loved Siren's Song."

My back relaxes into her chest involuntarily. I feel secure against her. Safe. "So do you," I say, my voice barely above a whisper. I turn my head to meet her gaze over my shoulder. We're standing so close it's taking everything I have to breathe normally.

My eyes wander to her lips, remembering what it was like when they met on my couch. Soft. Warm.

She steps back and clears her throat. "Okay," she sighs. "I think we need to talk about it."

"About what?"

"Phoebe, if you make me say it, you're not going to like what comes out." She raises an eyebrow. I turn around to face her.

"No, there's nothing to talk about." I shake my head. *We shouldn't.* "I'm okay." Why is my throat so dang dry?

"You're not," she nearly whines, slumping her shoulders. "I'm sorry. I got carried away."

"It's okay." My gaze flies everywhere but at her. I knew we'd have to talk about this eventually, but I was kind of hoping maybe we could just…not. Pretend it never happened. Go back to the way things were. Forget how good it felt to climax against her body.

No. It was a temporary lapse of judgment.

"Is it? Because you look like you're scared I'm going to hurt you right now." Her body slumps as her brimming tears threaten to fall any moment. I don't want her to be upset. I'm not scared of her. I honestly don't know how to act now that we…I forced myself on her. I mean, sure, she touched my leg, but what female hasn't touched their friend's leg when talking? I gave into a curiosity I don't even fully understand. A curiosity I'm still trying to figure out.

"Fine," I concede, lifting my hands and dropping them at my sides. "I failed you, okay? Is that what you want to hear?"

"Failed me?" She shakes her head as her eyes narrow. How is she confused? I kissed her. "You didn't. Why would you even think that?"

It's almost as if she's completely forgotten we wouldn't have even been alone in the same room together if I hadn't been trying to turn her away from this immoral lust consuming her. Was she only humoring my efforts as a means to get closer to me? To turn me against God? I feel stupid. Tricked. Which causes a spark within me as my blood boils.

"Do you even want to be saved?" I shout, frustration seeping out with every word. I had been vulnerable. Had she pretended to want to be saved only to lure me into her trap?

"Do I have to be?" She crosses her arms. "Because nothing you have been saying has a leg to stand on! It boils down to the same thing over and over."

"And what's that? You'll never listen to reason?" My voice is louder than it should be.

"People were hurting God and their neighbors intentionally. I didn't choose this! People like you think I wake up every morning and make the elective decision to be gay. I decide every day to worship created people like some kind of sex addict over the one who created all of us. I haven't slept with a woman in over six years, and you can bet your ass when I had, it was consensual! Phoebe, thinking your way, is ignorant!" I stumble back slightly at her words. "It ignores the experience of millions of committed and faithful Christians who always have and always *will* follow God first. Even after realizing they were gay."

I walk past her to my water, taking a swig. I endure her words, allowing them to course through me like a trail of sparking gunpowder leading to a vat of gasoline. "As long as you aren't forcing yourself on others, being power hungry, or worshipping a person over God, it's not a sin to like another woman. People don't become homosexuals by deciding to abandon God like your church has tricked you into believing. They don't *become* gay. It's not a choice. It's who I am. I wasn't made in a warehouse. I was born to love like everyone else."

"But corruption of the mind is a sin!" I shout before thinking it through, setting down my glass on its designated coaster. At least I haven't lost *all* of my manners.

She scrunches her forehead. "Who am I corrupting?"

"Me!" I blurt before realizing the impact it'll have. "Ever since you…" I glance around at nothing, as if I'll find the words written on a wall. "You know…"

"Gave you an orgasm?" she insists, eyebrows raised.

"Yes!" I stomp. "You corrupted me. You've placed this perversion on my soul, and now I can't stop thinking about it. I want to do it again and again."

"What?!" She blinks repeatedly. "I didn't put anything but my leg on you. You literally said it was okay. I didn't pervert you, Phoebe. You came at me. I tried to stop you!" She's waving her arms frantically as her face grows more and more red. "The *'perversion'* you're speaking of," she points at the ground as she takes a step closer, her darkened eyes bore deep into my soul, "was always there. It's always been there. Don't fucking tell me you weren't thinking about it at the coffee shop. Or when you came over last week. Or when you put your hand on my leg when I drove you home from Siren's."

"No." I shake my head. "You did that. You're messing with my head!" I push away tears. "You broke me."

"Goddammit, Phoebe, you're not broken!" She throws her hands in the air. "You've always been like this. You know it, and I know it. Why won't you let me help you come to terms with that?" She gently places her hands on my forearms, but I step out of her orbit.

"I don't need help. I need to be saved. I *am* broken! You broke me with your violations!" I spit out, scanning her from bottom to top. "You've violated the parts of me I held most sacred!"

She falls silent at my admission, nodding and biting the inside of her cheek.

Why did I say that? It was so hurtful. Her body vibrates as she balls her fists at her sides. "Leave," she croaks, pointing to the door. Her voice is devoid of emotion as tears fall freely from her eyes. My body slumps as I watch her lip quiver violently. "GET. OUT!" I startle at the volume of her sudden shout.

It was my choice, after she pulled away, to keep going. She even asked if what she was doing was okay before progressing. *"Tell me when to stop."* But I didn't tell her to stop. I gave her permission. I literally didn't take no for an answer. Even after she pulled away from the kiss, I pulled her in again.

"I-I didn't mean that," I stammer. "Blake, can we just—"

"No. We fucking can't!" she spits out disbelievingly. "I violated you? I…what? Raped you?"

"I didn't say rape. I—"

"No, Phoebe, I get it. You think I'm a terrible person. I rape and violate people. You'll never see past this stupid fucking idea of me because I'm gay! I love women, so there's no possible way I could be a good fuckin' person. Is that what you believe?"

"No, I—"

"But you know what?" Her deep blue irises have turned light against her bloodshot eyes. Her body shakes as she stops her tears from falling. "I am a good person! I'm a million times better than the judgy pieces of shit you affiliate with, and if you can't see that, you can fuck off with the rest of them." She shoos me with her hand. "Please leave."

I grab her wrist, but she swings her arm violently to avoid my touch. "I'm a good person," she says again through gritted teeth, chin wobbling, straining not to cry again. "I'm a really good fucking person!" she shouts, pointing at the ground, causing her tears to fall heedlessly down her cheeks.

My body rushes forward to swing my arms around her. It works, but now she's thrashing in my arms. "Let go of me!"

I tighten my grip around her until she can no longer move. "No," I say gently into her ear. "I'm sorry."

"Phoebe, let go!" she shouts, still squirming.

"I'm not letting go, Blake. I didn't mean it."

"I'm a good person!" she reaffirms, growing weaker, the fight in her dissolving.

"You are. I'm sorry. I didn't mean that."

"I'm a really good person." Her face collapses into my shoulder, hands pressing tightly to my back. The fight in her completely dissipates as her body shudders. She's sobbing into me. "I wouldn't hurt anyone."

"I know you wouldn't. I'm so sorry." I kiss the top of her head as I relax my grip around her slightly. "You're an amazing person."

Lifting her head, blue/gray eyes meet mine, sparkling against the light, tears still collecting at the bottom. I decide to take her red, soaked face in both hands, using my thumbs to wipe her cheeks. "You're so beautiful," I huff.

I don't know why I said it. I mean, I'm thinking it, but I can't seem to keep it in as I'm holding her broken spirit in my arms. *I* broke it. I didn't mean to. I have to fix it. There's a scar on her forehead, and I'm tempted to ask how she got it. I settle for placing my lips there instead, kissing gently. She gasps in response.

I want to do it again. If every wound could be fixed by a kiss, I would do it gladly for Blake. But the damage I've caused is deeper than skin. Destroying her spirit will take more than placing loving intent upon her flesh. How do I go deeper? If only my hands had the ability to heal. To manifest a warmth that would radiate enough resolve to fix everything that's ever hurt her.

My nose glides down her temple. *Breathe normal. Relax,* I think before I place my mouth on her cheek, dragging out a slow, delicate kiss lasting a moment longer than needed. I exhale. *Why am I holding my breath?* My stomach flips as her fingertips brush gently against my ribs before resting on my hips. My body shivers. I can't seem to resist this urge. My mind has convinced itself with every kiss, I'm making it better.

I tilt my head, moving to the other side of her face, softly grazing her lips with mine as I pass before placing my own on a scar at the corner of her mouth. She lets out a steadying breath. Fighting this is pointless. I am weak. There's a scar on her bottom lip. I find it, taking it into my mouth tenderly. She stiffens.

Our kissing is slow at first. I inhale sharply as I guide her to the wall directly next to the mantle. Only then do things become more frantic. I'm groping and sliding my hands over every part of her body aimlessly.

I need to feel her skin. I need the energy rushing through my hands to pass to her, and clothing is hindering my inhibitions, so I lift her tank top and place my fingers on her ribs. Our breathing quickens as I lift her shirt higher and higher.

She raises her arms, and I pull it off, throwing it on the floor. A rush of blood warms my entire body at the sight of a tattoo—a cross on her left rib. It extends from the bottom of her breast to where her rib ends. I have a sudden desire to place my hand upon it. To use her body as a vessel to communicate with God himself. I'm drunk off the smell of cedar flooding my senses as I trail kisses down her cheek to her jaw—lower still—before latching onto her neck. Her hands find my butt gripping and guiding my hips into hers. She lets out a slight whimper, which only makes me want to chase the feeling more. I want to hear that soft whimper over and over. More importantly, I want to be the one who causes them.

"Fuck," she whispers, clearly overcome.

Heat pools below my belly button and drives something inside me to seek more. This isn't a want; I *need* more of her. I slide my hand underneath her sports bra and lift it over her small breasts before taking her already-raised nipple into my mouth, flicking my tongue, causing her hips to rock between my body and the wall.

"Phoebe," she says, beautiful and breathless, my stomach doing cartwheels. Soon, I notice her hands have left my butt and are trying to take off my shirt. I let them with only a mild amount of disdain at losing contact with her breast. I quickly return, and my thumbs press firmly into her hip bones, steadying their movement. The way her body sways for my touch is intoxicating.

All my life, I've tried to fix people. Fix issues not mine to repair. This is entirely different. I've been forced to please everyone, but this time, it isn't forced. I'm pleasing her because I want to, not because she's asking me to. I'd choose this forever because up until this moment I'd never thought I'd have a choice about whether I want to make someone happy or whether I do it because I have to. She's not making me do this. Honestly, she *told* me to leave, but I persistently stayed, and she let me. She's letting me seek atonement for my wrongdoings. Now, I have to show her I'm capable of making amends. She'd given me an out, but I chose her. If choosing her will always feel this good, I think I'd like to do it more.

Blake grabs either side of my head and lifts it to meet her mouth and as my torso presses into her despairingly, the press of warm skin on mine causes me to rotate my hips into hers. Her hands have become a distraction. I want to please her, but she's making me want her to replay last week. I refuse to let this be about my own selfish needs again. I grab her wrists and hold them over her head with my left hand firmly against the wall. She smiles into my mouth as my other hand tries to undo the button of her pants. I'm struggling. I've never had to do this before, but I'm determined. I have to know what she feels like. If her underwear feels as soaked as mine.

She lets out a delightful breath. "Let me help you," she says, but her voice isn't her usual recognizable alto. It's more airy, slightly higher in tone. My blood races at the sound. I let go of her wrists, allowing her to unbutton her jeans. Once they're undone, I grab them and pin them forcefully above her head again.

She mewls when my palm gently sinks down past the waistband and finds the collection of moisture settled in her boxers. I'm completely gone on the fact she wears men's boxers instead of panties. Her back bucks against the wall, sliding back and forth on my fingers. "Fuck." It flows out of her mouth in the most beautiful whisper.

But does this even *actually* feel good? Am I doing it right? I'm trying to please her, but I'm not one hundred percent sure I know what I'm doing. I've never even touched myself before. How am I supposed to please her? And if I don't know what I'm doing, how can I show her how sorry I am? I'm out of my depth.

She must sense it. "You're doing so good, baby," she moans. "Keep touching me. Just like that." Something ignites within me at the presence of that word again. *Baby.*

She's boosting my ego. Making me cocky. "Yeah?" I bite her bottom lip. "I'm your baby?"

"Yes," she gasps, her hips synchronizing with the sliding of my fingers along her saturated heat. "Yes, baby. Don't stop." She's pleading, begging, her eyes dark like sapphires.

"What if I do this?" I slide the hood slowly between the pads of my index and middle finger, repeatedly flicking up and down, causing a primal groan to escape her throat as her leg wraps around mine.

"Holy shit, yes," she whimpers, a flush creeping over her face and chest. Her expression has become desperate. "Faster, baby," she murmurs, her voice still an octave higher, pupils dilated and pleading.

Her knees shake as I increase the speed, stopping occasionally to slide my fingers lower, ghosting her entrance before returning to her now swollen hood. Even holding her wrists above her head isn't going to keep her legs in this position. I make a hasty decision to release her wrists and remove my fingers from her jeans. She whimpers at their absence before I guide her body down to the rug on her hardwood floor.

Once there, she beams at me with the most seductive gaze, sliding off her jeans. In only her boxers and bra pushed up on her chest, her face is captivating. All sexed up and hungry, causing even more moisture to collect in my underwear. I'm throbbing and slightly achy from the sight.

"You're so sexy," I say in disbelief, drinking up the image of her.

I'm surprised by the person I'm becoming around her. Not in a negative way. I love feeling like this. Intense and impulsive. It's hard to believe I'd ever be the type of person to use "sexy" when describing anyone. I'm not sure why I wouldn't. I don't think there are any Bible passages against complimenting your sexual partner. Then again, I'm not sure this is what God had in mind when he gave us sexual partners in the first place.

Nope.

Not thinking about that right now.

Right now, I'm making Blake feel as good as she made me feel on my couch. I'm finishing what I started. Given she has more of a track record pertaining to sexual conquest than I do, I don't think a knee over clothing will elicit the same response.

My hand slips back into the waistband of her boxers, zeroing in on my new favorite spot once more. Touching her is addictive, and now that I've felt this, I can't go without her silky wetness sliding against my fingertip. Her body trembles beneath my hand as I circle my finger between her legs. "Mmm…" She pouts her lip. "I missed your fingers."

I'm relieved we're in agreement. "I love touching you," I admit, my mouth finding her collarbone and beginning a path up to her ear with my tongue.

She throws her arm around my neck, burying her fist in my hair while the other one unbuttons my pants. Her unexpected hand sliding along my center causes a rush of warmth and tingles to course through my entire body. I let out an inaudible sound in her ear. It's incredibly sensational—the tips of my ears burn, my knees grow weak. It wasn't like this in Ethan's truck. Not even close. I'm engulfed in a pleasure I've never experienced, causing me to lose focus and bury my head in her neck. I'm gasping into her shoulder, hips trying desperately to follow her movements but failing completely.

"That feel good?" she preens. Cocky. She already knows the answer.

"Yeah," I choke out as I try to concentrate on my hand still on her center. "S-so good." I'm whimpering, lip quivering. This was supposed to be about her! I need to focus. I need to…*God,* I need to focus! I'm in a race against the clock now. I may have gotten a head start, but she clearly has a better understanding on the matter. I recklessly begin circling my fingertip over her hood, pressing slightly.

"Oh, God," she groans as her hips thrust upward, seeking more of me. "Fuck me," she groans into my ear. "Please."

What if I'm bad at it? I refuse to let her think I'm clueless. Without another thought, I watch her face soften as the warmth of her body closes around my middle finger. I gradually pull it out, only to sink it back in to the knuckle. Her breath catches along with mine.

Then her hand twitches on me, and my stomach flutters. I moan as I glance down at my hand, watching my finger slide in and out of her with grace, dancing with her pelvis as she pushes back against my palm. The sight causes my face to flush and my ears to burn. I almost don't realize her hand has stopped working me. If I can keep this up, maybe I can bring her to climax first.

"More," she begs, which causes me to join my index finger to my middle while gently sliding into her, gradually increasing speed. "Oh…yeah." She gasps, increasing the speed of her own hand between my legs. "That's perfect. Just like that." The image of her is intoxicating, causing my brain to froth. "Don't stop." I match the speed of her circles with the pumping of my fingers as her hips buck sporadically into my hand.

Soon, it becomes too much.

"Make me come," she whimpers as her hand in my hair slides to the back of my neck, gripping tightly. Her legs tense as I struggle to keep my focus. My hips twitch as well from her losing control. I'm leaning over her, knees threatening to buckle at any moment. But her hand is becoming erratic as well. Her body tightens around my fingers as I thrust them in with fervor, hooking my fingers upward inside her after noting the first time seemed to steal her breath.

It's anyone's guess who will tap out first. Obviously, both of us are determined to stand our ground. Soon, however, she's moaning louder and louder, hips shooting upward into my body. The hypnotizing sight causes my pelvis to convulse against her fingers.

The world is fuzzy, and I have tunnel vision. All I see is Blake, eyes closed tightly, chest heaving, until our bodies stop shaking. I collapse onto her chest, and she pulls my face into hers for a kiss. It's passionate but not as frantic as when we started.

"Don't go," she says, burying her face into my neck and wrapping her arms tightly around me. "Please."

"I won't," I whisper, shutting my eyes, focusing on the rise and fall of her chest as she breathes.

✝

Eventually, we move to her room. Her bed is soft, and the black pillows smell like her. We didn't bother to put our clothes back on, sliding under the blanket, needing to feel skin instead. Her head's buried in my neck as she holds me.

I'm in my own little paradise. Nothing seems to matter but Blake's arm around my stomach. It's hard to even believe God could find something as simplistic as her embrace wrong.

"Why are you fighting this so much?" she asks into my neck, giving me goosebumps.

"What do you mean?" I ask, staring up at the ceiling.

"This?" She kisses my neck. "How could it be wrong?"

"I...I don't know anymore." I shake my head.

"Then why do you feel you need to save me?"

"Dakota," I admit before thinking, realizing she has no idea who that is. Should I even be talking about another woman with her after the night we had?

Her head raises, looking at me. All of her previous exhaustion appears to have vanished from her expression. "Huh?"

"A girl I knew my freshman year." Her face softens but now I can't help but wonder if she knows her. I mean, it is a small town, it'd make sense. I didn't know of any other gay people, but Blake probably would. Maybe she came into Siren's. Right? Do gay people talk? When Dakota transferred, she had to transfer somewhere, right? Is it possible they went to the same school? Does she know what happened to her? I hope she turned out okay. I decide to go for it.

"Do...do you know her?"

"Umm…" She seems nervous, her body lifting slightly to search my eyes. "I used to…"

"Wait…Is she okay? I—I'm sorry, I'm not trying to make things weird, but…I just…I never got to help her…I watched her life fall apart, and instead of helping her…I—"

"She could handle herself, Phoebe. I'm sure she wouldn't have accepted your help even if you offered it," she says, practically shutting me down. "She's not struggling anymore. She's in a good place now."

"She is? But you said you used to know her. Not anymore? How did you know her?"

"Phoebe." Blake turns my head toward her before kissing me sincerely. "I'm tired." She lays her head back on my chest. "Can we talk about this tomorrow? I just want to keep this moment. I promise I'll tell you how I know her over breakfast."

She's right. Talking about the tragedy of Dakota was sure to spoil my mood. I can only assume by Blake's demeanor this story will only get worse.

Tonight isn't about the past or even the repercussions tomorrow holds. Tonight is about just this. Falling asleep to the warmth of Blake's embrace.

It can wait.

✝

I can't move away from it. Some of the best times of my life were with Dakota, and if she knows her or—knew her?—my body is too hyped up over the possibility of seeing her again. I can't sleep. She knows her. Blake knows Dakota.

Did she stumble into Siren's Song at some point? Is that how she met her? Would it be too much to ask if she could arrange a meeting? I'd love to apologize in person.

I spend another fifty minutes pondering how to ask Blake in the morning while I listen to the sweet sounds of her sleeping. She doesn't snore, but her breathing gets heavy. Occasionally she twitches, which is super adorable.

After a while, I need to use the restroom. Moving Blake aside, I try to figure out her house in the dark. Luckily, the dim lighting from a lamp in the living room guides my way.

"Water," I decide while I'm peeing. I always wake up thirsty. "I should get water." I walk to the kitchen and flip on the light. I remember where Blake keeps the glasses. I help myself, filling it at the fridge.

However, as I'm filling the cup, something catches my eye; a postcard hanging from a magnet on the fridge with "Italia" written in big blue letters. Pictures of Italy scattered on the front.

Photos of her and her brother on white sand beaches, forests, now Italy? I enjoy the fact that she travels. Would it be possible for us to visit Italy one day? France? Spain? I flip it over and almost drop the glass of water.

I shouldn't have been snooping. I know that now. I should've turned around and went back to bed. I could've gotten water in the morning. Asked Blake to get it for me.

> Dakota,
>
> If Jude were still alive, he wouldn't let you miss out on all the beauty that lay beyond Siren's. He always said you deserved to see the world beyond Mystic. Next time, no excuses. Do it for your brother.
>
> We miss you,
> Mom and Greg

I squint at the postcard, flipping it over to see if maybe there's more clues. This has to be a coincidence. It'd be sheer gullibility to think there was only ever one Dakota in Mystic. Besides. Mine vanished twelve years ago.

"Dakota?" I let out a small disbelieving laugh.

"Phoebe." Blake's voice floods the kitchen and pulls me out of my contemplation. She's standing in only her boxers and sports bra; her hands are up, palms out, as if trying to approach a wild animal. "Let me explain." She's pale and trembling. Why is she sweating?

It takes a second for my brain to register what's going on. Blake. Is she? They would be the same age but…But why would she?

The temperature of the room increases rapidly, igniting it in flame, as rage boils over from deep within me. Every inch of my body becomes unrecognizable, even to myself. How could I be this stupid?

"Fuck you!" I'm shouting it over and over, throwing the postcard at her—which drifts in the wind, not landing anywhere near her.

I make it to her in two quick strides and repeatedly shove my open palms into her chest as she tries to grab my hands. "Just listen, stop," she pleads. She has her feet planted, consternation written all over her face. She stops fighting back, then, allowing me to shove her, marking up her chest.

The fight isn't worth it anymore. I stomp to the living room, grab my shirt off the floor, and slide it over my head. My hair is in my eyes, so I grab the elastic off my wrist, throwing my hair into a bun because I'm inconceivably mad at that too now. I don't look back as I storm out the front door, slamming the screen behind me.

I miss the last step of the porch and catch myself with both hands on the side of her truck. The metal placard on the side reads "Dakota" and I feel even more stupid as my heart breaks at how ignorant I've been. I push tears back from my eyes as I fall to the ground, barely noticing the rocks digging into my knees as I stagger to reach my car. I slam my door when I slide in. I don't even remember turning the engine on before I'm peeling out of her driveway.

Chapter 14

Phoebe

The earthy aroma of autumn leaves pushed their way down my street, depositing at the base of my porch. It was the beginning of October, my freshman year, and some people already had their decorations out. Ghosts and spiderwebs covered porches and lawns, accentuating the changing colors of the trees.

On this particular morning, I was lying on my bed, staring at the ceiling. Zoe and Eve had gotten boyfriends and would rather spend their weekends going on dates and I was tired of being a fifth wheel. Making out wasn't exactly at the top of my To-Do List.

I rose from my bed when there was a knock on my door.

"Hey, Peep," my father said, soft eyes full of sadness. "Not hanging out with the girls?"

"No." I frowned and sat back on my bed, grabbing a book and presenting it to him. "Figured I'd read since they have plans."

"It's a beautiful day, Peep. You should go outside."

"There's nothing to do." I pointed at the book cover. I wasn't really feeling this particular book, but with nothing else to do, the completist in me felt like it was time to polish it off.

"I could drop you off at the harbor," he suggested.

"No, I'll just find a nice, quiet spot to read." I stood and threw on a light jacket. The weather was a nice seventy-five, so I really didn't need it, but in case I found a shaded area or needed something to lie on. I figured it could also make for a nice pillow. "What time do you need me home?"

"Curfew's eleven, and Peep."

I sprung to my tippy toes and kissed his cheek.

"Be careful, okay?"

I flash him my most positive expression. "Always. Love you, Dad." And on that note, I left. Really, I left because if I didn't, I'd have to tolerate my father's sad stares as if I was missing out on my youth.

A fresh cool breeze filled my nose with the smell of crisp leaves and soil as I lay down on the earth in the park. I closed my eyes, thinking maybe I could take a nap.

As the sound of birds lulled me into a sense of tranquility, I heard the crinkling of feet rustling through the leafy grass approach my outline. I turned my head and opened my eyes, blocking the sun.

I saw her shoes first. Black Adidas with three white stripes standing next to my face. I panned up to see ripped black overalls, a black light hoodie tied around her waist, a white T-shirt two sizes too big, her white hair in a low ponytail, and piercing blue eyes under dark eyebrows beaming down at me.

"I could've stepped on you." Dakota's lip curled up on one side.

I raised to my elbows, grinning. "Well, I'm glad you didn't."

"Taking a nap?" she asked, sitting down beside me in the grass before freezing. "I'm sorry. Is it okay if I sit next to you?" She glanced around. The park was empty, but even if it hadn't been, I'm not sure why I'd have cared. I pulled one of my knees up to my chest.

"Why wouldn't it be okay?"

Her shoulders slumped as she brushed some dirt off her pants. "I don't know. I'd hate to take up anyone's space."

I bumped my shoulder into hers. I loved spending time with her. It kind of hurt me to know people made her feel that way. "There will always be room for you in my spaces."

We looked out at a tree, quiet for a while, but it wasn't an uncomfortable silence. We both watched as a cat tried unsuccessfully to catch a squirrel. Eventually, she let out a sigh and turned to me. "Can I take you somewhere?"

I tugged on my earlobe curiously as I thought of the places she would take me. "Like where?" There weren't any places I haven't already traveled in this park, but a walk would be nice, regardless.

Dakota stood up and reached out her hand. "Do you like surprises?" She winked.

That wink. Blake at the bar. *"We'll find out what you like together, okay?"* echoes around my brain as I rock back and forth, knees tucked to my chest. I'd collapsed onto the floor right when I'd walked into my apartment.

I grabbed her outstretched hand and allowed her to pull me up. We walked side by side for a while, talking about music and school. I found out she really liked nineties rock and hated Spanish class.

Finally, she stopped in front of a car, and I watched as she pulled out keys. "Ready?"

"Wait." I chewed on my lip as I shifted my gaze around. "What?"

She scratched her nose, turned her head, giving me a side-longed glance. "Didn't you say I could take you somewhere?"

"Wait…you have a license?" I frowned. I knew the answer, given we were only fourteen.

She gave me a blank stare. "No."

"Dakota! Did you steal a car?"

"What the fuck, Phoebe. No!" She furrowed her brows playfully. A single, crooked, front tooth on full display as her lips part into a nervous grin.

I smack my tear-soaked forehead over and over. How could I possibly have forgotten about Dakota's crooked canine? I'm so stupid! Sure, it'd been twelve years, but how on earth could I have forgotten the most monumental thing in my memories of her?

"My mom lets me borrow it sometimes." She wiped a tear from her eye from the comedy of my question. Not sure why she found it so funny. I barely knew her. She was very content with being labeled a rebel, so how was I supposed to know where the stories ended and the real her began?

"She lets her fourteen-year-old daughter take the car?" I was finding it hard to believe. I was almost positive when I became street-legal, my parents still wouldn't allow me to do anything in their car.

"More like, she is going through a lot and doesn't really care what I do as long as I bring home food for her and my brother," she admitted.

I couldn't imagine having to grow up so fast. "So, we're going grocery shopping then?"

"No." Apparently, I was hilarious for whatever reason. "I mean, if you want to come with me later...I'm not sure when you have to be home."

"Not till eleven," I said, still deciding if I should trust her behind the wheel. If we got into an accident, I'd be screwed. My mother would kill me. And with someone from the Seedy Side? Worse if we were on the Seedy Side when it happened. "But you don't have a license." I took a step back.

"Live a little," she groaned.

I hesitated, wanting to, but the risk of having to face my mother was almost crippling.

Dakota walked around to my side and placed her hands on either side of my face. "Phoebe, I've been driving since my feet could reach the pedals. If I promise to keep you safe, will you trust me?"

I unfocused my gaze in contemplation. Trust. Such a big word. I trusted my parents. I trusted Zoe and Eve. So why wouldn't I trust her? She hadn't given me a reason not to. I bounced on my heel before swallowing my fear and pushing past her to jump into the car. I made sure to put on my seat belt, though. Just in case.

As the engine roared to life, rock music blasted through the speakers. "Sorry," she said bashfully, reaching for the dial.

"I've never heard this one," I said, placing my hand over hers, stopping her from turning it all the way off.

"The Strokes?" she asked, wrinkling her nose. "Really? Who hasn't heard of The Strokes? What do you listen to?"

"Usually the Christian station. My mom doesn't want me to fall into the 'perversion of music' or something." I tugged at the bottom of my ear.

"Oh, man." She rubbed the back of her neck.

Classic Blake. Rubbing the back of her neck in uncertainty.

"...Should've known." She drummed her long, slender fingers repetitiously against the steering wheel.

"Known what?" I wanted to grab her hand and stop the nerves but feared an accident. I regretted getting in the car because what if she thought the same thing everyone in my church did? Our sides of town shouldn't mesh.

"I'm on the Holy Side. Of course I'd have a Christian girl in my car." She chuckled.

"I mean." I searched my nails for one to chew on. "My dad is a pastor." But I refused to indulge any further.

"Shit," she said, and I wondered if she was having second thoughts. Should I have asked her to let me out before she made the mistake of bringing me across "enemy lines?" Somewhere we both knew I didn't belong. The unspoken knowledge hung between us, whether you voiced the concerns or not. I refused to say it then, but I needed to know what was beyond my neighborhood. Needed to know if the rumors were true. She asked me to trust her.

"Language." I was attempting to lighten the storm cloud of anxiety accumulating in the car as we traversed into the unknown.

She played along. "What?"

"You said a swear." I felt childish saying it.

"You're funny," she said before realizing I was serious. The color drained from her face. "Sorry." She cleared her throat and yet again we both became apparent of the storm stalking us down this quiet county road.

Leave it to me to bring back the tension. "It's okay. Everyone I know swears."

"So, why is it a big deal?"

Dakota goes back to tapping her fingers on the steering wheel and this time I do place my hand on hers. She switches to her left hand on the wheel.

I didn't know the answer then, but I would later go on to ask my mother why swearing was bad, and she quoted Ephesians 4:29. "I was just taught not to."

"And do you always do what your parents tell you?" she teased, patting my shoulder.

My body slumped in the seat as I grumbled, "Well, I'm in your car, so…"

"Fair point." She tsked. "So do you want to listen to The Strokes, or will your mommy be mad?" She flicked my thigh.

I sighed. Great, now she was making fun of me. I felt like I had a point to prove. Being the pastor's kid didn't mean I couldn't be a rebel like Piper. I raised an eyebrow at her. "Only if they find out. You plan on telling them?"

She seemed to like my answer as she turned up the music and drove toward the coast. She sang along, knowing every line pumping out of the stereo and she loved to sing along.

"Ready?" she asked, hopping out of the car after parking on the side of the road in the middle of nowhere. Where the heck was she leading me?

I followed blindly, hoping I wouldn't live to regret trusting her like this. We were at least ten miles out of town. "What are we doing?"

"You seem to like nature," she chirped.

"I do." I took in the green of the trees and the sound of the birds chirping. If we ventured further into this forestation, I could find myself falling asleep to the smell of fresh pine as the wind whistled through the branches.

"You ever want to just…" Kicking the dirt, she snaps a twig in her hand. "Escape it all?"

"Only every day," I admitted, my body growing warm at the idea. I was starting to realize maybe we weren't very dissimilar than people tried to play us out to be. Not sure why growing up in different neighborhoods would make us polar opposites in the first place.

"Okay." She started walking. I tripped over my foot when I began trailing after her. "Do it."

"I can't." I threw my hands down in defeat. "I have to go home eventually, and I have no idea where I am."

She grabbed my waist gently. "I know." Her voice was soft as she turned me until my back was to her, facing a trail. "But for now, you don't." She was still holding my hips. "Lead the way." Her breath on my ear made my eyes heavy with complacency as I found my feet taking slow steadying steps, growing even more confident than the one before it.

"I…Dakota, I don't know where I am. What if I get lost?"

"Phoebe, trust me. I've taken this trail a million times. Where you go, I go. I won't let you get lost." She grabbed my hand and interlocked our fingers, pulling me forward.

It took my body a few paces to finally calm down and enjoy the warmth of her palm against mine, the scent of moss and earth surrounding us, the cadence of insects creating a perfect harmony with the song of the birds. "So," I finally said after a moment's silence. "You come here to escape?"

"Yeah." She was still holding my hand, which felt strangely normal. I knew the second we separated, I'd lose my confidence. It felt as though I was stronger with her, and knowing this new truth made me regret when we'd be apart. "I escape a lot."

"Why?"

"It's a long story."

I could sense this place was where she went to escape from reality. It wasn't the place she wanted to talk about it. "Fair enough," I said rather than press it. It's her story. She wasn't required to tell me anything. It didn't escape me, however, that she'd brought me here for a reason. I don't think she had fully comprehended her ability to tell me why yet.

"I can give you the cliff notes," she offered, squeezing my hand, as if drawing strength from it like I had been. "If you want."

I enjoyed the inch she was giving me, deciding I'd take as many as she'd let me have. "Of course."

She sighed. "My dad died four years ago." She seemed almost numb to it. Distracting herself by grabbing a stick off the ground. "My mom didn't bounce back well. She spends most of her time…" she hesitated, trying to come up with the right words, "…sleeping. She's pretty sad most nights and can be forgetful. It just…I started to pick up the slack for her— which is fine! I'm not complaining," she insisted.

"Hence the driving."

She nodded, hitting a bush with the stick. "I mean, it's fine. I have the car most of the time and get to go on adventures whenever I want."

"I'm sorry about your dad." I pulled her to a stop facing me.

Dakota's eyes searched the ground. "I'm working through it, you know?"

I nodded, fighting back the urge to ask how he died, figuring this was as much as she was going to give me on this topic. Maybe I'd get the long version another day.

We continued to walk in silence until we arrived at a riverbed. I sat down in the dirt. She kicked off her shoes and socks, marching to the water's edge, extending her arms as if presenting it to me.

Dakota skipped stones along the water. There was a certain sense of comfortability to the silence we were experiencing being in each other's company. It's as if through nonverbal cues, we understood each other. I couldn't help but be impressed by her ability to skip stones at least five or six times before they'd sink into the water.

"You're pretty good at that," I called out to her.

The sun behind her traced her outline, and I was silenced by her visage. How happy she had looked, crooked canine fully exposed, not a care in the world, finally happy to have someone else to share this with is probably one of my favorite memories of her. It's her stock photo in my mind whenever I think of her.

Shortly after this memory, though, she was slipping her shoes back on over her wet feet and stuffing her socks in her pocket. "Come here." She grabbed my wrist and pulled me up a narrow-overgrown path in between the trees.

Eventually, we came across a big, old, two-story, abandoned plantation-style house. 15505 Stone's Throw Road. The roof was collapsing, and vines were overtaking the front and sides.

"Should we be here?" I asked as we walked around to the front of the gigantic, dilapidated house. She stopped on the porch to entertain my question. Her expression was amused as her mouth piqued into a sheepish grin, simultaneously pushing open the front door. A loud creaking squeal came from the old, rusted hinges.

"You worry too much." She chuckled, interlacing our fingers once more and pulling me through the double-door entrance. "I come here a lot." She spun around the run-down building, taking in every crack and cobweb with admiration. "One day, I'll fix it up." Her eyes were full of wonder as she released my hand and walked further into the space, envisioning something I didn't think I'd ever see.

To me, this place was beyond repair, but the way she beamed at the torn wallpaper and broken hardwood suggested she wasn't seeing what I was. "Look at this kitchen!" She began walking through the threshold. Her voice dripping with excitement and wonder. Meanwhile, I wasn't sure how she could possibly see more than what was clearly here.

There was a hole in the middle of the floor, exposing the basement down below, for heaven's sake. *Are the floors even sturdy enough to hold both of us?* I wondered, keeping my feet planted in the entrance. The cabinets gave a certain 1920s vibe, which I was sure was nice once upon a time. An old fridge was slightly pulled out from the wall, its doors open, missing the shelves. There was a nest of twigs and animal droppings inside. I pondered for a moment if mice had called this place home longer than any person had.

Yet her eyes were full of enchantment. She walked around the island and pointed to a vacant area to the left of a counter. There was a crunch as her feet treaded across broken glass strewn about the floor from busted-out windows. The wind was whistling through the holes in the broken panes. "Breakfast nook! I could see a bench table here!"

It was hard at first for me to imagine what it was she was seeing, but I wanted to feel the same beauty as she did. Stars literally shimmered from her dark blue eyes as she imagined herself in a room completely different from the one we were currently standing in. No, Dakota was standing in a room with sturdy floorboards. That didn't smell of rotted wood and rat droppings. She had no fear as she gallivanted around the room.

My feet, however, were still firmly planted in the doorway to the hall, afraid to step into a kitchen with a hole in the floor. Maybe her weight was fine, but I refused to believe it could support both of us at once.

Dakota then walked past me and grabbed my hand again, pulling me until I was completely turned around and walking into what appeared to have been a living room at one point, judging by the crooked couch exposing springs in the center of the room. Dirt collected on what was left of the fabric. Beside the furniture, there was an old fireplace along an entire brick wall.

She grabbed her phone and put on "Dreams" by The Cranberries. She threw it on an old coffee table covered in mold and leaves. As it blared through the speakers, she pulled my body into hers, swinging me as if we were in a ballroom. "Just imagine it, Phoebe! There's ten bedrooms! More if you fully finish the basement."

"What are you doing?" I said joyfully as she wrapped one arm around my waist.

"Dance with me!" she said, swaying her body energetically, causing mine to follow suit.

I couldn't help the elation spilling from my body as I clumsily followed her steps around the room, tripping over her feet on occasion, but she didn't seem to care. She just continued guiding me around the room. "When I fix this place up," she said more gently, our speed slowing down slightly. "I'll have my own mansion." Her mind was seemingly somewhere else as she envisioned her make-believe life. As if she needed the dream to keep going.

"You deserve that, Dakota. Can I help you fix it up?"

Our bodies had somehow pressed into each other as she snapped back to reality, peering deeply into me as if no one had ever offered her their help. "I'll let you have one of the rooms!" She lifted her arm, spinning me before placing her opposite hand on my hip.

I'd never danced with anyone before, but the sureness of her body seemed to instruct me. She was singing the words with so much enthusiasm.

My face hurt from smiling as she spun me again. I tripped on my way back into her body this time, which caused me to collapse against her chest. Her eyes met mine, her hands on my hips to brace me. She was positively beaming as she sang. For a moment, all I could hear was the sound of the drums from the music. Before I could register what my body was experiencing, she was pressing my middle to hers and moving us in circles again. She was such a good dancer. Maybe that's why, in this moment, I wasn't worried about anything. Not the floorboards. Not being caught hanging out with a Seedy Sider. Nothing. All I could feel was happiness. For the first time since I could remember, I wasn't worried about fitting in or acting normal. I didn't feel out of place or like I didn't belong. There was no reason to act like anyone other than myself. With Dakota, I could finally be myself.

Her eyes locked on to mine. A rush of blood pumped through my entire body, sending signals to my extremities. I felt a tingling in my toes and the tips of my fingers. I'd never felt this alive. The adrenaline was causing my knees to grow weak. Her hand in mine...

"Goddammit, Phoebe! You're not broken! You've always been like this! You know it, and I know it! Why won't you let me help you come to terms with that?"

She knew. She always knew. I've felt this before. This pull to be near Blake wasn't a call from God. It was my body recognizing the feelings I'd had—recognizing Dakota.

I rub my face with my hands before grabbing my phone and staring at the screen. Two unread messages.

Blake (11:42 PM)
Phoebe, I swear I can explain

Blake (11:47 PM)
Please...

She knows I'm seeing the messages now. Knows I'm ignoring her.

Blake (11:57 PM)
Please let me explain

Blake (11:58 PM)
Don't do this...I just got you back...don't leave me without letting me explain...

I toss my phone to the floor and bury my face in my palms.
I just got you back...

A week after visiting Stone's Throw Manor, I was sitting in my room reading poems by Emily Dickinson. I was hooked. Deciding to shut herself in and write poetry after losing the love of her life made sense to me. I, too, wasn't convinced I'd ever find love. I still wasn't into boys the same way Zoe and Eve were. I was starting to think I never would. Dying alone might not be too bad if I could express myself the way Emily did.

My room was quiet, with the exception of the soft music playing low in the background. *Clink.* Funny, the current song hadn't had drums. *Clink.* It couldn't be my music—clink—I stare at my speaker. The sound isn't coming from there. I search around in confusion—clink—what is going on? It took longer than I'm proud of to realize the sound was coming from my window.

I opened it to find Dakota on my front lawn. "What are you doing?" I scanned the darkness disbelievingly.

She didn't say anything but rather gestured for me to come down. Everyone was asleep, and the house was dark when I used the wall to navigate through the hallway. A light was on under Piper's door. As I walked past, I tripped over something, causing a loud rumbling. I prayed it wasn't as loud as I thought it was in the silence of the house.

Her door opened—dang it.

"What are you doing?" she whispered.

"I'm—" I glared down at my feet to find what had given me away. A shoebox my mother had told her to put in her room hours ago. I glared at the object of my frustration. "Why didn't you put this in your room?" I scowled.

"Are you mad about the box or that I caught you?" Piper raised one eyebrow and crossed her arms, knowing she had me beat.

I hate how good my sister is at reading me. Even when we were kids. "Please don't tell." I frowned.

"One condition." She wiggled one finger in front of my face. "What the fuck are you doing?"

"I'm um…" What was I doing? "Dakota is here."

"Cool." She put her hand on her hip. "Now who the fuck is Dakota?"

"A-a friend." I had always been able to be honest with Piper, and with her penchant for chaos, I knew I could tell her pretty much anything. Typically, my own stubbornness to not prove her right was the only reason I'd ever withheld details. "She's uhh…"

"She?" Her eyebrows raised with piqued interest, leaning back to get a better view of me.

"Yes, she's from the Seedy Side," I said slowly, pinching my eyebrows together.

Her grin was malevolent. "Seedy Side, eh? Is she dangerous?"

"Yes, Seedy Side, and no, she wouldn't hurt a fly. I promise." I held my hand up. "On God."

She waved nonchalantly. "Okay." She turned to walk back into her room. "I'll cover. Have fun." Then she closed her door.

This is why I love my sister. I made it downstairs and slipped on my shoes next to the door, meeting Dakota on the porch.

"Come with me."

Was she out of her mind? I couldn't go anywhere. What if my parents woke up? This was insane. Escaping outside was one thing, but leaving was a big ask. Then again, Piper had said she'd cover.

I headed toward her mom's car without another word.

"Really?" Dakota still hadn't moved from the porch.

I stopped and turned. "What?"

"I figured you'd fight me." She blinked rapidly, moving in my direction. "I had a whole speech planned. Phoebe Appleton, you never stop amazing me."

My cheeks flushed as we climbed into the car, and she began driving. "Park down the street next time. My parents' room is right there." I pointed to one of the front windows of the house before buckling my seatbelt. "Where are we going?" I had my hand out the window, riding the waves of the wind.

"Surprise." She drove another fifteen minutes, all the while singing along to Radiohead pouring out from the speakers.

I'm reminded of Blake singing along to the music on the radio in my car the night she drove me home. My hand out the window. Everything about her so familiar. So comfortable without need for explanation. How does one forget such finite details of her favorite memories? How much did Dakota remember? Did she know who I was all along or remember somewhere along the way?

"My feet led me to EC."

Was it really a coincidence like she'd suggested? How long has she been keeping up this lie?

We pulled up behind a movie theater, and she grabbed a bookbag from the backseat. I watched her strap it over her shoulders before climbing onto a dumpster. She jumped from the dumpster to the bottom rung of a ladder to a fire escape, pulling it down.

"Ladies first." She bowed and extended her hand chivalrously.

"Is this legal?" I scowled, backing away slowly.

She tilted her head playfully. "Depends whether we get caught."

I thought about refusing. I thought about what I would tell my parents. I decided, at this point, there wasn't anything I could say. I was beyond the point of weighing pros and cons. I'd have to take whatever punishment they gave me and move on. So I climbed the ladder, with Dakota in tow.

"I come up here a lot." She placed the bookbag on the ground and started pulling out random contents. She pulled out a blanket and laid it on the concrete next to where I was standing.

"You take all your friends up here?" I scanned my surroundings, running my fingers along a dusty industrial AC unit.

"What friends?" She lifted a brow.

I frowned, unable to figure out an appropriate response. She noticed and quickly changed the subject. "Today is the Orionid meteor shower. We should be getting twenty to thirty an hour!" She sat down on the blanket. Her excitement was enthralling.

"I've never seen a meteor shower." My body flooded with excitement and an indescribable admiration for her to consider me for this. Meteor showers don't happen every day and she's used to doing things by herself, yet she went out of her way to include me in this with her.

"Well, after tonight, you will." She grabbed my hand, pulling me down onto the blanket with her. "Lay back," she said, grabbing a second blanket from her bag and placing it gently over us. Then she grabbed her phone and threw on some low music before laying back, arm pressed against mine. Side by side.

We sat watching the sky, talking about literally everything that crossed our minds. I found out she liked working on cars, which is how her mom's car hadn't broken down yet.

"So, who taught you?" I asked.

"My dad taught me the basics before he died. Spark plugs and oil changes. My stepdad has taught me a little bit, but mainly, I look things up on the internet."

"Oh, that's right. I forgot you had a stepdad. He made you go to Mystic High instead of Cypress, right?"

"Yeah," she groaned out. "My mom decided to date a guy from the Holy Side. He's a douche."

I wanted to shake his hand and thank him for giving us the chance to meet, but something told me if Dakota disliked him, there was probably a very good reason. It wasn't my place to ask, though, so I left it alone. Dakota had a lot of things she didn't talk about.

She was an iceberg of a person, and I wanted nothing more than to be the person she finally opened up to.

A bright light flew across the sky. "There!" I said, clinging to her way more excited than I probably had the right to be.

The song changed on her phone as she slid her arm around me. I rested my head on her chest. The acoustics were peaceful. I opened my eyes to see her mouthing the words. And in that moment, I remember my chest filling with an exuberant amount of warmth at how beautiful she was under the night sky. The stars reflected in her pupils as she whispered the song softly.

"What's this song called?" I asked.

"Green eyes," she responded, turning her head toward me. "It's by Coldplay."

Her hand found mine resting on her chest under the blanket, and I felt a chill as it wrapped around mine. She was so beautiful in the glow of the moon as she continued the lyrics under her breath.

When we returned to my house that night, she kicked the dirt gently with her foot as she walked me to my door. "Hey, can I ask you something?"

"Of course." She could've asked me for anything, and I would've said or done it all for her.

"I..." She rubbed the back of her neck. "Never mind, it's kind of stupid."

"No!" I grabbed her hand and took it in mine. Dakota never asked me for anything. She didn't ask me to sit next to her. She hadn't tried to be my friend. She was the only person who gave me a choice. She was used to losing things. Used to change. Until that day in the park, she'd never approached anyone. Just me. She wouldn't have revealed tiny bits and pieces of herself by inviting someone into her world. Even if it wasn't the largest pieces of her life, I had a feeling no one else ever saw the places she went to escape.

While my friends were busy tossing me aside for newer and better things, Dakota, she came to me. This closeness between us happened fast, like flipping on a switch. "Tell me." I stepped into her space.

"I just…" She let out a sigh, looking up at the sky before grabbing my hands and placing them between our chests. "Listen, I'm not good at expressing myself, and I really enjoy your company. It got me thinking. I don't have any friends. I know it might be embarrassing being seen with me, but…could you…" She walked her finger along my mailbox trying to distract her gaze from mine. "If people gave you shit, would you leave me alone?"

"No? Dakota, I'm not embarrassed of you." I was surprised she'd ask. I think I needed her just as much, if not more, than she needed me. I turned her head toward mine. "How about I promise if I ever glance over and see you sitting by yourself, I'll sit next to you?"

If she wanted me to stay, why would she lie? She had a million reasons and just as many opportunities to tell me the truth.

I was swindled. I was conned. Did Blake—or I guess Dakota—lie to get her hand in my pants? Am I just a pawn in her plan to hurt God, to show Him she can corrupt His flock? Is this how Sam felt? Was Dakota's negative high school experience brought upon by herself? What happened to Sam?

So many questions, and not a single one I can answer myself, and I can't ask her. I'm afraid if I see her, I'll start shoving her again. I've never been a violent person before. Then again, I've never allowed myself to be so vulnerable with another person. I've never given in to the darkest temptations lying dormant beneath my skin. Temptations nesting in tiny crevices of my mind. Practically cloaked, inaudible whisperings that recently began taking shape, becoming full-fledged screams.

Chapter 15

Blake

I need her to respond.

"GODDAMMIT!" I scream, ripping up the postcard my mom had sent me. I'd been telling her for years now to stop calling me Dakota!

Dakota is dead! I'm not her anymore. I'm…I'm better now!

She's reading the messages!

So why isn't she fucking responding?! If I could explain…I know she'll understand. I just need her to give me a chance.

Dakota was sick. The worst kind of human. She was hurting and took her misery out on everyone. Why the fuck would Phoebe care about Dakota, anyway? I'm better than her! I need her to see it.

If she'd answer her fucking phone—

I swallow back the knot in my throat and type out one more pleading text.

If someone was happy, Dakota was a storm cloud—no! A hurricane—determined to rip apart their lives. It's miserable to admit she got *off* on other people's torments.

She didn't need anyone because every time she cared about someone, they'd hurt her. Physically or emotionally—sometimes both. While burying her pain with drugs, she'd managed to convince herself everyone would always leave eventually, so she cut them off early by refusing to care. It's no wonder no one stuck around.

Well, with the exception of Jude and Delaney.

The story only got worse when she dropped out of high school the second she turned eighteen—so close to graduating—but she was stupid.

"When are you going to stop sleeping with other people's wives, Kota?" Jude had asked her once when she'd come to visit him in his college dorm after sweet-talking Mary—another one of her tawdry fucks—into letting her borrow her car.

Mary was a sweet woman who deserved better than her piece of shit husband, who believed a woman's place was in the kitchen and a queer's was in the ground.

Not saying Dakota was any better. Mary would clean Dakota up when she'd stumble in drunk as fuck when the husband was out of town. And how did she repay her? By doing lines of coke off Mary's ass, then making sure she was thoroughly fucked in ways her husband never could before leaving, of course.

"When I'm done being angry over how they hurt me," she'd said passively.

I was done talking about her. Done pretending she existed at all. She'd taken up more than enough of my time, and in the beginning of my sobriety, it was nearly impossible to live in her shadow. My sponsor had suggested after my second relapse in the first six months, maybe I needed to create someone I could be proud of.

"Maybe growth and repair isn't for you, D," Dylan had said one morning when Dakota had staggered out of her guest bedroom after another bender. "Maybe a *rebirth* is more up your alley." She'd put a cup of coffee down in front of her.

Too embarrassed to talk after briefly remembering giving Dylan the fresh scratches on her face, she hung her head, peering at the mug in shame. Dylan had found her at some random trap house and had scooped her up before the people she was hanging out with could escalate the molesting to a full-blown rape situation. They'd drugged her. She'd gone there for cocaine, but the lines tasted off. Turns out it was GHB.

Now, a normal person knew not to touch Dakota unless they wanted to get hurt, she was by no stretch of the imagination, a tactile person. She'd throw punches at anyone so much as trying to *sympathize* with her. But Dylan wasn't a normal person. She was strong and fierce and ex-military. She was the perfect sponsor for someone like Dakota. Dylan was just as stubborn and had just as much fight, but she was calm. Devoting most of her spare time to mixed martial arts had taught her how to quell the rage brewing within her, and she was bound and determined to teach Dakota the same. No matter the cost.

"You said you thought the house on Stone's Throw was your mansion, right? You believed it was fixed and perfect? You were proud of it, weren't you?"

Dakota nodded.

"Your body is like that house. It needs fixed. So, tell me, is the person you are *right now* the person you're proud of?" she asked candidly, which earned her a brief head shake but still no eye contact.

Listen, I know I'm Dakota, and Dakota is me, okay? I just hate associating myself with her after what she did to Phoebe, but I'll try.

Who had "I" been proud of...?

I lay on my bed, reading yet another romance novel.
Lately, I'd been devouring them if only to escape into
a world far away from this bedroom. My music played

quietly on my desk. If only life could be like these books. Some kind of light at the end of this tunnel I called life. If only I could fall into the arms of a man and find comfort and safety in his strong embrace. "If only, if only, if only."

I'd realized pretty quickly dancing with Phoebe at Stone's Throw Manor had been a mistake. Somehow, my brain had confused the feelings I should have been having toward guys, with holding Phoebe instead. I wanted to hold her in my arms, yet I knew I wasn't a dude. I knew I needed to stop this stupid delusion. Problem was, I didn't know how to turn it off. Ever since that day, I couldn't seem to peel the image of her very rounded cheekbones and cheerful expression out of my head.

It crawled around like an earworm in my prefrontal cortex. She was in me. In my soul. I'm not sure even the jaws of life could've pried her sweet scent and soft skin from the deepest crevices of the grooves within my brain. The way her breathing sounded. The smell of her shampoo as the wind whipped through her hair while I spun her into my chest. The way her neck glistened with sweat as we hiked the short distance back from that old abandoned house. It kept replaying over and over in my mind.

Followed by random sprinkles of me pushing her up against a wall and kissing her until her body relaxed in my arms. Her legs wrapping around my middle as I lifted her, my arms firmly gripping the backs of her thighs as we kissed. Her hands fisting my hair.

The flutter forming in my stomach made me nauseous. How could this have happened? She was a pastor's daughter. A good girl—a Holy Sider! The chances of my thoughts becoming reality were next to never. I kept telling myself it wasn't going to happen, but my stupid brain kept clinging to the hope maybe one day…maybe she could love me. Maybe we could ride off into the sunset and put Mystic Harbor in our rearview. For once, I could get the "W."

"I fucking told you I'd be home when I felt like it!" I heard my stepfather shout from the living room.

"Okay," my mother's shaky voice responded. "I just wanted to know you were okay."

Furniture was tossed into a wall, followed by the gentle whimper of my mom. "Mind your fucking business, how about that?" he shouted. "Why can't a man just come home without problems? Why do you have to constantly be on my fucking dick all the time?!"

"Please, Austin," she pleaded. "The kids are slee—"

"Fuck those fucking ungrateful kids! They're half the reason I stay out so goddamn long! You got one who won't shut her fucking mouth and follow orders, and the other's halfway retarded!" The sound of glass shattering against the wall connected to my room came next. My stomach sank.

I knew better than to try to break this up. He'd set me straight pretty early in their relationship for getting in between them. It always baffled me why my mom didn't kick him out. Or, at least, stand up for us when he insulted us. Did she agree with him? There always seemed to be an excuse attached to staying. My personal favorite was when she blamed it on my dad's death. He'd left her with a mortgage and two kids. She'd never needed to work before, and given her mental state, she never started after he died, either. Who would watch us? Was always her response. Honestly, I took care of her and Jude more than she ever tended to us. She didn't know how.

Austin was her new sugar daddy. An "upstanding" criminal defense lawyer from the Holy Side. We should be grateful and respect him for keeping food in our stomachs and a roof over our heads. Blah fucking blah. No child should have to listen to this. She knew it. Hell, even someone fully brain-damaged could see the way he treated us wasn't right. We all knew he was out banging his secretary, Abby, anyway. It wasn't confirmed until six years later, though, when Jude and I finally saw him again after he stormed out on my mom. They had a child together who looked exactly like him. He was seven years old. I'm just glad he'd never gotten my mom pregnant.

The sound of him slapping her came next. It never got easier hearing her cries and pleas for him to stop.

A whisper came from the vent on my floor. "Kota."

I walked over, kneeling, placing my face close enough to respond quietly. "Headphones, Jude. Try to sleep. It'll be better tomorrow."

"I can't…" His voice was trembling.

"Window," I said, staggering to my feet, sliding the pane open quietly. Within a second, Jude had crawled out of his window and into mine.

"I hate this," he sobbed, falling into my already open arms. His face dampened my shirt within seconds.

"I know…" What else could I say? We were just kids. Jude only being thirteen and me fourteen. I was stubborn, though, refusing to show Austin any weakness. Always standing my ground. Jude would avoid these situations by hiding in his room. I'd stolen the noise-canceling headphones for his twelfth birthday, hoping it'd help. Sometimes, it did, but when the arguing was taking place in the living room rather than their bedroom on the other side of the house, it made things impossible.

"I can't listen, Kota. I can't listen anymore. He's right, I'm stupid, but I can't help it. I can't fix it." He sobbed into my chest as I cupped his ears tightly, guiding him under my bed in hopes of dampening the sound.

"Hey! You're not stupid, JudeBug. You're smarter than probably everyone in this town combined! He's the one that's stupid," I whispered, choking back my own tears, but they weren't tears of sadness. No. I was angry. I felt powerless. My blood boiled at the revelation I couldn't stop this man three times my body weight from hurting my mom and insulting my brother. I felt like nothing. "You're working hard and still taking those summer classes again this year, right?"

"Yeah." He sniffled into my chest.

"Okay, good. You're almost graduated." I swallowed back the knot growing in my chest. "You get that scholarship, and you get the fuck out of here, okay? Promise me."

"What if Mom doesn't sign off?" he grumbled into my chest. "What if Austin makes me stay?"

My eyes stung as I stared up at the springs underneath my mattress. I had already planned to strong-arm my spineless mom. She was drunk most of the time anyway, but the second we were alone, she'd get a piece of my mind. No way she was going to hold Jude back. He deserved it, and I would die to make that happen. "She will. It's going to be okay. I promise."

With one hand pressing Jude's ears to my body, I used the other to grab my blanket from the top of my bed, wrapping us up. "Just listen to my breathing, okay?" I said evenly. "Try to follow it."

I let my chest rise as I took in a long, steadying breath before releasing slowly. "Breathe like me, Jude." I continued the motions until I felt his body soften against me. I hummed his favorite song by Adele, "Make You Feel My Love," until he fell asleep in my arms.

When the fighting in the living room finally stopped, I slid out from under the bed, pulling the blanket over my little brother. I placed a pillow under his head before putting on the Adele album, hoping it was loud enough to drown out any more noise, but not too loud to have Austin in here screaming.

I needed to leave. The situation was too much, and if I didn't find something—anything—to help me escape, I'd have a breakdown, kill Austin in his sleep for touching my mom and calling Jude mentally disabled.

The anger inside of me boiled so furiously I'd even felt it toward my mother for doing this to Jude. Never once choosing us. I could handle myself, but she knew

Jude was special. She knew he was a literal genius with a heart of glass. He couldn't decipher regular human interactions, either. He didn't understand what he'd done to deserve the "Punishments of Austin."

When Austin forced me to go to high school at Mystic, I was angry I had to leave Jude in that middle school unprotected. People thought because he spent more time with his head in the clouds or his nose in a book, he was more likely to shoot up a school or kill someone. In reality, he was the most peaceful person on the planet. He once cried because a spider was in his room. I remember having to go in there, catch it in a cup, and release it a block away from the house because he wouldn't let me kill it.

Incessant bullying taught me at a very young age. The world was a cruel place, full of people who cast out what they didn't understand before they'd ever waste time trying to comprehend it.

I climbed out my window and grabbed my bike. I had no idea where I was going. I just remembered telling myself the harder I peddled, the further I'd be from my problems. The more exhausted I became, the less I thought about how fucked my head was.

Until images of her shot like a lightning bolt down my spine as I peddled even harder, trying to rid myself of these stupid thoughts—because they were stupid.

Finally, I stopped to catch my breath. My chest heaving, I squinted up at the street sign to figure out where my troubled mind had taken me. Honestly…it wasn't a surprise that it led me straight to her house. I glanced at my watch: 9:45. I shouldn't be here, but where else would I have gone? Stone's Throw Manor was ten miles from my house, too far to peddle at night, and it's not like I had any other friends. So, I walked beside my bike, hiding it in the bushes beside her house, before grabbing a few pebbles and, for the third time this week, prepared my body to launch them at her window.

However, something stopped me. Lately, her light would turn off after the second pebble hit the pane. My cue to meet her on the porch. She didn't want to risk waking the prudent Appletons. Tonight, I hadn't brought my mom's car, though. We couldn't go anywhere. So, I took a risk. I shimmied the rope of a swing tied around a tree budded up against the side of her house. Once I pulled myself up onto the branch, I sidled my way to the roof and tip-toed gently to her window. Using my nail, I quietly tapped in quick succession on the glass. Soon, I saw the light of her bedside lamp, casting shadows on the pink paint and purple trim of her bedroom.

I hid on the side of the window, knowing she'd startle when she saw me. I had to somehow do this without waking everyone in her house. When I heard her window slide along the track, I waited until her head was fully out before cupping my hands over her mouth and the back of her neck. She inhaled quickly, letting out a tiny shriek.

"It's me!" I whispered. "Don't freak out."

Her eyes shifted onto me before I felt her relax into my hands. I let go of her soft face, pushing away the thoughts of her lips against my palm.

"What the heck, Dakota?" she hissed, punching my arm. "I almost peed myself!" Even angry, she still made my body flood with heat.

I rubbed my arm. "I know. I'm so sorry. My mom has the car," I lied, "so I rode my bike. I just—" Just what? I can't tell her what happened. If I did, she'd probably think she could save me by telling her parents. I'd lose my mom. They'd throw Jude and me into the system and probably split us up. Any person would be lucky to have my genius brother, but a stubborn kid with nothing to offer? Yeah, I'd get thrown back a billion times until my eighteenth birthday. I couldn't have that. Couldn't see Jude ripped out of my life. He needed to go to college. Needed a fighting chance at a good life. I decided on, "I was bored."

"You were bored?" she deadpanned. "So, you decided, 'Why not go scare the pants off Phoebe on Halloween?'"

"Is that what day it is?" I had genuinely forgotten the holiday. Growing up, we couldn't afford costumes, and my mom was too drunk before the sun even set to take us trick-or-treating. Austin never gave anything he wasn't legally required to, so ever since my dad died, Jude and I stayed home. I'd completely forgotten it was a day to be spooky. "Why aren't you out trick or treating or whatever?" I needled playfully.

"Why aren't you?" She raised an eyebrow.

"That shit's for kids," I responded as she smacked my arm again.

"Language, Dakota."

"English."

She rolled her eyes, taking a step back. Waiting. After a moment's confusion, she finally said, "Well?"

"Well, what?" I asked. Honestly, I hadn't really thought any further than this. I just needed to see her face like a junkie getting a fix. Overthrow my bad feelings with good ones.

"Are you going to come in?"

"Wait—can I?"

"No." She chuckled softly. "But you're already here, so…"

I rubbed the back of my neck. "You don't want to sit out here and look at the stars?"

"Umm…It's kind of like thirty-four degrees out here," she responded, rubbing her sleeveless arms. The camisole she wore was incredibly nice, though.

"So? You don't own blankets?"

"I own something even better." She pulled my shirt. "An insulated house with heat."

Before I could argue, I was climbing in. I figured I'd already come this far, so what's four extra feet through her window?

I definitely didn't belong in her room. It felt weird. Where my house had walls with holes and patches missing in the cigarette-burned carpets, hers was the opposite. Very neat and clean. Books on shelves weren't blanketed in ash and dust. I rather enjoyed the absence of water rings on her furniture—the severe compulsion to prevent them had developed in these years. You could say in this moment, as I'd studied her room, taking in the fresh scent devoid of cigarettes, was when I'd decided I would never bring her to my home or even tell her where I lived. I wanted to live this life. Thus, my incessant need for everything to be spotless and perfect was born.

Her lavender comforter and pink pillowcases complimented the walls and trim. I knew the chances of me amounting to anything substantial enough to afford a nice house with matching aesthetics were next to nil, but I wanted so badly to fit into this world. A world smelling of clean laundry and a hint of flower petals. The scent I smelled on her when we were dancing in Stone's Throw. A scent I never wanted to go without.

Phoebe pulled out the chair from her desk and gestured for me to sit. I tried to calm my nerves as I sat. Her family home felt stuffy; I didn't belong here. The eyes of God were just waiting to smite me. The picture of Jesus in a frame on her desk and the cross hanging above her door definitely weren't helping. I tried everything within me to relax.

Without preamble, my back grew rigid and I felt like bolting out of this room that was so far removed from the one I grew up in. Who was I trying to fool? A person like me doesn't befriend a person like Phoebe. Depraved thoughts of corrupting her pure, innocent mind on this lavender comforter circled around my mind like buzzards circled prey. I was the visage of evil in her world. *Just keep your hands to yourself,* I reminded.

I could be like her. With her by my side, I might even be able to amount to something worthy of existing in the far corners of this universe she called home. I wanted more than anything to fit beside her.

"You aren't hanging out with your friends today?" I asked, clearing my throat, trying hard not to fidget as she plopped herself down on her stomach on the bed adjacent to me.

She sighed. "Nope. They went to a party with their boyfriends."

"They didn't invite you?" It made no sense to me, given they seemed pretty close. I had surmised they'd grown up together and figured they were inseparable.

"They did." She rubbed a stray thread of fabric between her fingers before smoothing it out with her palms. "It's just not really my thing. Sometimes I worry we have completely different interests."

"Like what?" I asked, gliding closer to her in the chair.

"Boys, for one." She shook her head. "I must be a late bloomer or something because I haven't really found anyone that piques my interest. I tried hanging out with them anyway, but honestly, they kind of ignore me when their boyfriends are around." She chuckled lightly. "I guess it takes a lot of energy to be involved with someone. I'm old news."

"No, you're not," I said, gently placing my hand on the wrist she had resting on the blanket. "You're the best news." My stomach dropped at this confession. I shouldn't have said it. I removed my hand from hers, scooching back. I needed to control myself. She had no idea how much impact her presence had on me. The only decent thing going on in my life back then was having her around, and if I ruined it by making her uncomfortable, I'm not sure what I would've done.

She met my eyes briefly before dropping them back to her blanket. "That's because I'm new news to you. When we were kids, you couldn't separate us. Heck, Zoe is practically my sister. Our parents planned us around the same time. We've known each other since birth. Eve came later but fit in perfectly. The three musketeers." I could sense the devastation in her tone by expressing this. "But we all have to grow up sometime. I guess I'm late to the party." She sat up and crossed her legs. "I don't think I'll ever be a partier, though."

"Bull—" I slapped my hand over my mouth. Her eyes darted to me as mine darted to the cross above the door behind her. "Sorry...I mean...that's not true. Just—your definition of party is entirely different. Like..." I searched her room before tugging the blanket out from under her. "Uppies," I said playfully, watching her eye light as she stood.

She beamed. "What are you doing?"

"You'll see!" I said, throwing her comforter over the chair and bed. I tossed a few of her pillows in the space below and ensured the structure wouldn't collapse before poking my head out. "The password's Worcestershire!" Then I disappeared inside once more.

"A fort? How old are you?" She giggled but went along with my effort anyway by poking her head in. "It's too dark," she said, climbing out and leaving the room. When she returned, she switched off the light, walling the room in inky blackness. I heard the sound of a lighter clicking multiple times as light flashed through the seams of the blanket before she returned with a three-wick candle and a flashlight. "That oughtta do it. Okay, wash-worses—whatever, I'm in here already," she grunted, centering the candle in the middle of our base.

I grabbed the flashlight and held it under my chin, allowing the light to cast shadows under my eyes. "Do you want to hear a scary story?" I rasped.

"I'm a chicken," she admitted shyly, sitting beside me. "Maybe that's why Eve and Zoe didn't fight me to go to the party after I declined. They'd have felt obligated to keep everything PG. I don't know..."

For a moment, everything fell silent. I wasn't sure what to say, but I'd have taken her problems over mine any day of the week. If all I'd had to worry about was not hanging out with my friends, my life would've been simple. What I wouldn't have given to have friends in general.

"I like you just the way you are," I said.

"I'm grateful God moved me to introduce myself that first day." She scooched to sit beside me, our thighs pressed together. "It's like He knew you'd get me."

I was grateful for her as well. I wanted to tell her I'd always be there if being near her meant forgetting about my issues, even for a minute. I'd be a better person if it meant I could stay inside this bubble, away from the real world, with her forever.

"Phoebe?" I began nervously, hoping my next comment wouldn't come off too weird, but I needed it. More than I think I'd ever needed anything at that point.

"Hmm?"

"Can I—" I tried to remain calm as I forced out a request I'd never been able to ask since my dad died. "Can I hug you?"

Normal people hug. Girls hug girls all the time. I hug my brother when he needs it. It wasn't weird unless I made it weird. Hugging wasn't going to make me burn in hell for all eternity. I convinced myself there was nothing wrong with it. I just really needed it after the night I was having, and I could sense she needed one, too.

Before I knew what was happening, she had moved the candle to the side and was crashing her body into mine. Holding me close and wrapping her arms around me so tight I didn't even care that I couldn't breathe. I felt safe. I'd missed this reassuring embrace. An embrace I made sure to give Jude whenever and wherever he needed it, because I knew what it was like to go without it. No one, since my dad, ever held me like this. Everyone just assumed I was too strong emotionally to desire things like comfort. In reality, I was dying on the inside, behind a mask of nothingness.

The thing about Phoebe and I was we were very opposite people, but our core loneliness was the same. Besides my brother, I hadn't received physical touch of any kind since my dad died. He had always been the comforting one. The one to wrestle and play or hold you while he read bedtime stories. Not to say my mom didn't ever hold me, but it'd been years since she had even invited herself into mine or Jude's personal space. I'm not sure she knew what to do with herself or how to confront the loss our family shared.

The afternoon my dad's heart gave out, my mom changed. We'd become a burden too strong—a demand to fill shoes too big. He was the playful one who put us above himself, regardless of the cost. She struggled with alcoholism and depression our entire lives, so having to raise two kids alone was unbearable. After his death, she'd started drinking more.

I killed him. It was my fault. If only I hadn't begged him to push me on that stupid swing, he wouldn't have gotten his heart rate up. He was tired. He'd just gotten home from work and wanted to sit down. "Five minutes," he'd conceded. "I'll push you for five minutes, and then I'm going to sit down."

If it wasn't me exactly, it was my brother and me. His selflessness for us kids was what killed him. If we were never born, he might've gotten his heart checked. The doctors could've caught it and been able to save him before my ten-year-old self was holding his lifeless body on the lawn, screaming for Jude to get Mom as the swing came back and smacked me in the face, causing the scar on the bridge of my nose. It's funny how I didn't even notice the blood pouring out of me until the EMTs requested I go in as well. I couldn't even look at myself in the mirror without the memory replaying over and over again. I knew how to push myself on the swings. I just refused to grow up around my dad. I wanted to be his little girl forever. I was so fucking stupid.

I buried my face in Phoebe's shoulder, wiping a stray tear with my hand, pretending to scratch my nose. If she knew I was crying, she might let go. Who knew when this moment would come again? "You're not alone," I whispered, trying to steady my voice, praying she didn't notice the tears.

"Neither are you," she whispered back. "I promise."

Instinctually, I kissed her shoulder, immediately regretting it as her arms tightened around me, our bodies freezing. Her sharp inhale was the only sound between us, but if this gesture bothered her, she didn't express it. She even blew out the candle and sunk us into a laying position, my chest resting in the crook of her shoulder as her arm wrapped around my waist.

Being held by Phoebe—my middle pressing tightly to her side—felt so natural. And I wondered why we couldn't stay like this forever. In our own world underneath the blanket, reading a book together with only the glow of a flashlight. Sleep had never come easier than it had in her arms that night.

"Wake up, Phoebe, it's time for sch—" Our bodies startled awake as her mom threw open her door, before realizing a blanket fort was constructed in the center of her room. "And take that down. You have a bed for a reason," she instructed before moving to the next door down the hall.

I could hear the rapid beat of Phoebe's heart as we both lay stock-still, listening to her mom bang abruptly on the door next to Phoebe's. "Pip! Up! Now!" she yelled before we heard her footsteps stomp down the stairs.

Phoebe shot up and practically crawled to the door, shouting down to her mom, "I'm up! Getting dressed!" She gently closed the door, tearing apart the fort as I surveyed my surroundings.

"I'm sor—" She leaped over and covered my mouth, moving in close to my ear.

"My sister will hear you!" she hissed. Her breath on my neck sent a shiver down my spine. She gestured toward the window, opening it and all but shoving me out the way I came last night. "We'll talk later, okay?"

And on that note, she closed the window, and I tip-toed around the side of the roof, sliding down the rope.

I retrieved my bike and sprinted the two miles back to my house.

Strangely, I managed to slide back into bed before anyone even noticed I had left. I dangled my arm off the side of my bed so Jude could see it from underneath. My alarm buzzed two minutes later, finally waking him.

Near disaster, but no damage done.

Thank God.

For everything…

Dakota—*I*—wished I was more like Phoebe.

Wished I'd had the nice house and perfect family. I'd wished for so much more than the hand I was dealt.

"It's time to put all of Dakota's hurt and pain into a box and set her aside like she's set everyone else aside," Dylan had said, ending her spiel and seeing it was working. "Really think about who you want to be. Dakota's dead. We'll throw her a funeral. I'll make sure—I'm sorry, I didn't catch your name?"

"Blake," I said, clearing my throat. "I'm Blake."

"Nice to meet you, Blake. I'll make sure to send you an invitation to the funeral. Everyone who's ever been hurt by her will get an invite to the after party too, and boy, you deserve to be a VIP after everything she's done to you."

…Then she did. Dylan actually set up a funeral. Jude bought the casket. She sent out invitations. Very few showed up, but Delaney and my mom were there. I made amends and became the woman I was meant to be. Eating right, exercising. It was amazing.

I even bought my first truck. My 1987 Dodge Dakota is a memory of who I carry with me everywhere I go. She's old, but I can fix her when she breaks. She'll take me on whatever journey is next.

Phoebe.

Sweet, caring, understanding Phoebe.

The only person who'd made Dakota open up. The only person who had ever shown Dakota kindness without judgment.

She'd taken Phoebe to Stone's Throw Manor and had told her about her dreams to fix it up. No one else knew about it. For reasons she couldn't seem to justify, she'd needed to give Phoebe freedom for once. She had to let her live— just once—by allowing her to make decisions for herself. At 15505 Stone's Throw Road, Dakota made the rules. She wanted to give that to Phoebe, too. She'd softened for her after learning Phoebe was stuck in a world of obligations.

She craved to watch that part of Phoebe flourish because it would've been the most beautiful thing Dakota could've ever done. It was her only redeeming quality.

They were so different, but equally alone. In a world filled with so much loneliness, they'd found each other. If that isn't one of God's miracles, I don't know what is because Phoebe's hold on Dakota's heart reminded her to have faith in God every day—through everything.

But she was also the person who had hurt Phoebe, not me. I'm not ready to go there. I tried, okay. I just can't. I've admitted as much as I can to myself today.

Quite frankly, talking about Dakota, dredging up the past, is exhausting. I know I should've told Phoebe. I know omitting the fact I was once Dakota is wrong, but I haven't associated myself with her anguish in years, and I guess a part of me thought if Phoebe didn't know who Dakota really was, maybe it'd never come up. I'd hoped maybe Phoebe didn't even remember her at all. It was twelve years ago, after all.

No, I fucked up. I should've told her. The time Phoebe and Dakota spent together was incredible. If it had left a lasting impression on me, I should've known. It would've done the same for Phoebe. If she doesn't ever want to talk to me again, I have to respect it.

…But if, by some fucking grace of God, her inquisitive nature leads her back to me, I will try my absolute best to lay everything down for her. I'll show her all of it. I have to. I'll give her every. Single. Disgusting corner of my life, if it means I get to keep her this time.

Blake (12:45 AM)
I understand you have a lot to process...When you're ready, you know where to find me...

Chapter 16

Phoebe

After crying myself to sleep, I wake just as devastated. I abandoned God for nothing but a smokescreen. I feel stupid. A true person of God would've been able to refrain from temptation. I can't believe I knowingly abandoned my faith, and for what? Lies. Deception. I'd wanted to find Dakota again. Just not like this. Never in a million years would I have thought she could've hurt me worse than when I lost her.

My body is on autopilot the rest of the day. People are talking—*Zoe* is talking—but I can't concentrate. Halfway through, Dr. Auburn asks me to go home.

"Do you need anything?" Zoe asks.

"No," I say, not even caring I was sent home. I don't care about anything. I'm an empty shell. Is this what it's like flying too close to the sun? I guess I'll ask Icarus when I ultimately reach the same unfortunate demise. It feels as though I've already died. Or perhaps the organ responsible for producing a spring of positive emotion has been poisoned and since dried up, leaving an empty hollow deep within me.

Less than twenty-four hours ago, I'd been happier than I ever have in my entire existence. Yet today, I feel nothing at all. I decide against going home. There is one place I need to go more.

†

There were only two cars in the parking lot when I pulled up to EC. One of them being my father's. As I'm pushing open the heavy door and walking inside, I'm instantly overwhelmed with guilt. *Please forgive me, Lord,* I think as I dip my finger in the Holy water and cross myself before entering the Nave.

I duck into a pew and bow my head, interlocking my fingers in prayer. "Lord, forgive me, for I have sinned before you. Wash away my sin, purify me, and help me to turn from this sin," I whisper. I can't feel His presence anymore. Has God abandoned me? Was my prayer not worthy enough for his grace?

I try another. "Have mercy on me, oh God, according to your unfailing love; according to your great compassion, blot out my transgressions." Tears fall onto my interlocked fingers resting on my lap. "Wash away all my iniquity and cleanse me from my sin. For I know my transgressions and my sin is always before me."

God's not listening, Phoebe.

My dream reverberates and rattles around my skull.

"Make me come."

I squeeze my eyes closed and press my thumb and index finger into the corners. All I see when I close my eyes is her. Swinging me around as we danced in Stone's Throw Manor. Smiling while she was drying a glass at the bar. The way her eyes twinkled in the moonlight, mouthing the words to Coldplay under the stars. My shoulders heave as I sob uncontrollably, struggling to stifle the sound.

Why am I without His love? I made a mistake, but doesn't everyone? Why isn't he listening anymore? Why has he forsaken me? I try again, more desperate. "Lord Jesus, you chose to be called the friend of sinners." I sniffle. "Free me from my sins and bring forth a harvest of love, holiness, and truth."

"Peep?" my father's voice rings out behind me. He pushes his hip into my body, commanding me to slide over so he can sit next to me in the pew. "What's going on, baby?" He's enveloping me in his embrace as I cry into his shirt uncontrollably. The smell of his Stetson cologne reminds me of waking to the scent of him getting ready every morning when I was young.

"I'm not worthy!" I say a little too loud. "He doesn't love me! He's abandoned me, Dad. I can't feel Him anymore."

"Whoa, wait, wait." He runs his hand through my hair, his low, soothing voice lulling me into what I can only perceive to be a false sense of tranquility. If he knew…if I told him…"Why on Earth would you think that?"

I cry even harder. No. I can't tell my father. I was so stupid. I should be ashamed. So how do I word my transgressions without him seeing me differently? I don't know what I'd do if I lost my dignity, father, and God all in one day.

"I…" I hesitate, searching for a way to articulate the innermost turmoil stirring up my usually calm water. "I accepted evil into my home. Allowed corruption to disturb my good intentions. I thought I could be strong enough to help shine a light on the wrongdoings and bring them back to the Lord, but I'm weak." I hiccup as I bury my face in his shoulder. Feeling his embrace for what might be the last time. "I'm so weak. I can't save them. I can't even save myself."

"Who, Phoebe? Who is evil?"

I can't hide from him. Nor can I allow myself to lie to him. While my mother would attack my imperfections and attempt to shame them out of me, my father held me in them. Taught me how to embrace the uncontrollable. Accept it. He's the one person who has always provided me with a safe space to seek atonement for my misdoings. "Blake," I scrape out shamefully. "I wanted to save her."

"Phoebe, what would make you think Blake is evil?"

I push away from the comfort of his chest to search his face incredulously. "She's a sinner, Dad."

His eyebrows pinch together. "Because she's gay?"

I nod.

My father isn't a man to assume, which leads me to believe he has learned this information firsthand. I wonder when he would have spoken to her. Did she admit her sexuality to him the day of the flowerbeds? When she drove me home from Siren's, she had mentioned her disposition so carelessly, but is it a stretch to believe she'd speak it so outwardly to a pastor she'd just met?

"Honey, immoral sin doesn't manifest as love. It manifests as power or control. What makes you believe her love for another would be sinful?" A crease forms in his forehead as his eyes widen in concern. "Has she overpowered you?" His hand tenses on my shoulder.

"No," I say, shaking my head, "but...she lied to me."

His head falls as the color leaves his face. "What is it you've discovered?"

My stomach sinks. *That orgasms feel better when this complete stranger was causing them.* My stomach sinks. "She wasn't who she said she was. A wolf in sheep's clothing."

A small sense of relief washes over him. It's almost as if he's not saying something. As if we're talking about two separate things. Does he know about her attempts to use EC as a vessel to create outreach for the queer community? "And has she expressed the manner of her intent?"

"No." I sniffle, wiping my tears.

His strong hand gently squeezes my bicep. "I think you need to talk to her, Peep." He moves my hair out of my face, tucking it behind my ear. "Sometimes, things may be the opposite of their initial perception. I may not know her very well, but from what I *have* learned about her character, her intentions seem pure." He rubs my back in reassurance as I gaze at the kaleidoscopic beam peeking through the stained-glass windows, sparkling as it unifies with the dustiness of the Nave. "Proverbs 25:2 reminds us it is the glory of God to conceal things, but the glory of kings is to search things out. Promise me, you'll give her a proper trial before condemning her completely, Peep." My father stands and extends his hand to help me rise as well.

I know he's right in his urging. I'm just unsure of how to look Blake in the eye after committing the pleasurable acts leading to this discovery. If only I could resist the compulsion to hear those sweet moans in my ear once more. If only I knew how to tamp down the rush of being the cause of those heady sounds. I simply don't have the strength or confidence to face her again and not continue committing shameful acts. Whether it be by punching her for lying to me or slamming my mouth into hers in a bruising kiss full of lust and desire. Neither one will aid in finding answers.

Yet I can't resist my impulses around her.

"And Peep?" my father calls as I'm about to push open the heavy wooden door. "God never stops listening. Often, our minds just become too loud to hear Him clearly."

✝

Blake (12:45 AM)
I understand you have a lot to process...When you're ready, you know where to find me...

Yeah. I know where to find you, but I'm still not sure I can handle seeing you without wanting to hit you. She and I both know I will seek answers. Eventually. We also know the only one who has those answers is her. The curiosity within me always leads me back to understanding. What I do with that information after it's revealed is another matter. I can't, however, remain neutral long enough to seek resolution if I punch her in her crooked canine the second she opens her mouth. So, I need to stay away.

It's 4:00 in the afternoon by the time I push through the door of my apartment, ready to take a bath. I stopped off at the liquor store, deciding I'd have a glass of wine while I soaked.

The bath would have to wait, however, because when I entered the living room, I was greeted by my sister sitting on my couch watching TV. "You don't have Hulu?"

I sigh, throwing my keys in the bowl by the door. "You know that key is for emergencies only."

Her brows knit together. "And this isn't one?" she asks, turning off the TV and throwing the remote onto the coffee table creating a loud clatter in the now silent room. "Hmm...three hours is kind of far for someone bleeding out. Not sure why you'd even give me a key then."

"How long have you been here, Piper?" If she'd have shown up at my house on any other day, I'd be ecstatic, but today I really don't want to deal with anyone.

"About fifteen minutes."

"Cool, cool. But why?"

She pats the seat, gesturing for me to sit down next to her. "Zoe called me."

"Gosh." I decline the invitation to sit. Opting, rather, for the kitchen to grab two glasses. I need a drink, and I'm sure Piper would, too. "Sometimes it feels like Zoe is more your best friend than mine!" I mutter through gritted teeth. Honestly, first Zoe gives my number to Blake and now she's calling my sister when I have an off day? She's been out of my life for the past two years, only to come back and destroy it. Filling it with so much turmoil, I'll eventually disintegrate until I am one with the Earth once more. Ashes to ashes. We are dust, and to dust we shall return.

"She's all yours, Peep. I would never take your best friend." She holds up her hands.

"It was just a bad day. I'm not sure why she'd call you."

"Let's not get hung up on the details here, Peep. The fact is, she did." Her eyebrows raise as she walks around the couch to my kitchen.

After a long pause, she begins again. "So, clearly, we're doing this the hard way."

I hand her the second glass. "Hard way? What are you talking about?"

"Peep, you know I'm not one to beat around the bush." She pauses to take a sip, making a face. "Ugh! Is this Sangiovese?"

"No one said you had to drink it. Just figured I'd offer since I'm having one."

She ponders it for a second before saying, "Meh, I prefer my whiskey, but 'when in Rome,' I guess." After taking two more big swigs—which makes me wonder if she's an alcoholic in the city because who drinks wine like that—she continues. "And no one else is going to be as upfront as I am."

"Up front about what?" I have one hand on the counter while the other pulls my glass up to my lips. It's horrible. If I'm going to be a lady who drinks, I really need to learn my alcoholic beverages. My body takes on the same light feeling it felt the night I was at Siren's Song, though, which was the goal, so I continue.

"What did Blake do?" Her blue eyes flash at me mischievously as panic floods my system. She notices my eyes grow wide before adding, "And don't say it's not about Blake or whatever bullshit you're thinking of spewing right now. Save me some time." She takes another sip before making a face and setting the glass down. "And buy liquor like a big girl, Peep. This shit is horrible."

I walk over to my couch as she swivels around on the barstool, keeping eye contact with me the entire time.

"Does Zoe know?" I ask, looking down.

I'm not sure why that's my first question. There's no sense in lying to Piper because she knows my tells. Not to mention, she clearly already knows something is up. If Zoe contacted her after my weird behavior today, I believe it's a safe question to ask. I'm not sure how Zoe would even know, though. She couldn't possibly know Blake and I had been hanging out.

"Know what?" There goes her devious smirk again. Her black hair falls into her face as she pushes it behind her ear.

"What do you want me to say, Piper?"

She scoffs. "If I knew that, I wouldn't have driven three fucking hours to ask." She throws her arms up. "I'd be skipping to the advice part already."

"It's nothing. Really." I shake my head. "I—she—" I blink rapidly. Honestly, how do I even say this? Being truthful would involve understanding what's been happening, and I can't explain what I've done. My brain can't seem to process it. Tears form in my eyes. "I honestly don't know how to make sense of anything enough to explain it."

She signals she understands with a nod and an expression of concern before taking one last big swig, finishing off her glass, and seating herself next to me on the couch. "From the top. How did it start?"

So, I tell her about the day Blake came to church and my intentions to make her comfortable enough to stay. Next, I explained that night at the bar.

Her eyes widen as her shoulders push back, taking in my complete outline. Running a hand through her hair, she says, "So, let me get this straight. You decided to go to a bar?"

"Yes."

She holds up a finger. "When you don't even drink?"

I lift my palms. "Seemed like a great day to start."

Her forehead wrinkles. "Without Zoe or Eve or…ANYONE?!"

I nod slowly.

"On the Seedy Side?" With both hands, she slaps her thighs.

"That's literally everything I just said, yes." My body slumps as my face burns in embarrassment.

"Phoebe, you never go to an unfamiliar place alone! Especially not a bar on the Seedy Side! You could've been hurt. I mean, I'm glad you're okay and you got to know Blake, but what the fuck were you thinking?"

I shift in my seat. Part of me considered this before I went, but I didn't really take the time to process why I decided to go, anyway. It's the same part of me that snuck out and got into Dakota's car at fourteen years old, not knowing where she'd take me. A certain thrill my life of rules and appearances didn't allow. The reckless regard for my safety sprang from not having felt alive since the adventures I shared with Dakota.

When I hopped out of Ethan's car that night after dinner, I felt empty. I felt angry my life was forced into a very specific box with no wiggle room. I longed to be as bold as Blake, wearing men's clothes and not caring if people judged her. She wanted to go to church, and she wasn't going to pretend to be someone she wasn't in order to feel closer to God. She just went.

"You were right, Piper." I stare down at my lap. "One day, I woke up craving the woman I really am. I'm just now starting to figure out who she is."

"Well." She contemplates before letting out a big breath of air. "Did I ever tell you about what made me decide to move to the city?"

"Yeah, it was Mom," I say, walking to the kitchen to refill my glass.

She tsks. "Not completely." Her shoulders slump as she lets out another sigh. "Phoebe, my senior year, I was drinking really heavily. Mom and I had gotten into a fight when she found a bottle of vodka in my room. She said I'd never amount to anything. So, I snuck out, and by the time I found a party, I was bound and determined to prove her right. I got so drunk I blacked out, and when I woke up, I was naked. I didn't know who the guy beside me was or how I'd even gotten to his place.

"I thought I was searching for myself, but that morning, I realized I'd done the complete opposite. I didn't value who I was. Refused to accept her. Most importantly, I was ashamed. I allowed that shame to, yet again, paint me into someone I wasn't. I didn't know who I was, but in that moment, I realized I never would. If I didn't get away from people who told me who to be, I'd never love myself." She meets my gaze, tears forming in her eyes. "The woman you truly are, she's not stupid. So please take care of her, okay? You can't know her if you're dead."

I'm surprised my sister struggled so deeply. I'd heard she'd drink at parties she snuck out to, but I had no idea she was getting plastered and taken advantage of. She'd endured this entire battle of self-discovery I had no idea existed. Outwardly, Piper seemed so self-assured. Always carrying herself as a full display of unwavering confidence.

"Wh-why have you never told me any of this?" My face feels warm from the alcohol.

She wipes her eyes. "Everyone goes through a period of self-discovery, Peep. Yours just happened a little later than everyone else." She waves her hand passively. Her famous lets-change-the-subject gesture. "Okay, so you went to the bar."

She actually snorts when I tell her about Blake driving me home and how our mother had mistaken her for a boy the day we planted the flowers. I can't make sense of why I feel so comfortable. I decide to tell her about the kiss, my climax, and how I pleased Blake on the rug by her fireplace. She sits nondiscriminatory the entire time.

"...which leads us to the best part," I say sardonically as I huff out a breath. "Do you remember Dakota?"

Her head snaps up from the pillow she's been hugging. "The Seedy Sider? The one you snuck out with a few times?"

"Last night, I found out that's Blake." I hang my head.

Her mouth drops open. "What the fuck?"

Pinching the bridge of my nose, I nod. "See my issue?"

"She didn't tell you?"

Falling back on the couch, I groan. "No."

"Why the fuck not?" she shrieks.

"I don't know!"

Piper sits tapping her lip in contemplation for a moment before kicking off her shoes. She rolls up her sleeves as I glare at her. "I'm going to address the elephant in the room first." She raises her finger at me before rising to her feet and grabbing her shoes. "You're cheating on your fiancé?"

I search the white walls of my living room, scrambling to find a good response. "I-I..."

Piper nods slowly, dropping her shoes carelessly in front of my door. "You are. Even if you're not interested in that dicknose, you're still cheating on him. So," she studies her nails, "when's that going to end?"

"I don't know if it ever can," I sigh, running a hand through some tangles in my hair. "I never wanted to say yes to him, to begin with! He did it during church. Everyone was staring at me. If I would've said no, it would've made our family look bad. Airing out our dirty laundry in the middle of Sunday mass. I've tried to tell him I really have!"

My sister waves the air aggressively. "Who gives a fuck?"

Sometimes I wonder if my sister is even capable of considering anyone other than herself. No. She's perfectly fine burning her world to the ground. "Umm, Mom, for starters." She knows how she is. Not all of us have the luxury of abandoning the people who gave us life to gallivant around the city, doing Lord knows what.

Her nose wrinkles. "And?"

"I was so embarrassed, Piper. I know it's stupid." I wipe my unexpectedly leaking eyes. For someone who doesn't cry very often, I sure have made it a hobby these last few weeks. "You have no idea how hard this is for me! I'm not like you."

"I know it's hard, sis, but you need to make this right. This is not you, and it sure as shit isn't who you're becoming. It's just plain reckless." Her head teeters from shoulder to shoulder. "But don't get me wrong, because I really don't like that douchebag."

"There's nothing wrong with him." I put my head in my hands. "It's me."

"Oh, the classic 'it's not you, it's me 'trope. I love that!" She collapses back down beside me on the sofa, practically landing in my lap. "But promise me when you do break up with him—" she pats my back "—because you and I both know you need to—you won't let him down that easy."

"Okay, seriously." I scooch away from her, pushing at her arm. "What is your problem with him?" I can't believe her right now. He hasn't done anything to anyone. He's always respected me and the people around him. Piper doesn't even know him.

"He's a fuckboy, Peep." She tosses one of my throw pillows at me. "Everyone can see it. I'm not sure how you don't. He's disrespectful as shit. Hijacking a church service? You know he didn't even ask Dad for your hand? What kind of bullshit is that?"

"Yeah, I don't get it either." I press the heels of my hands into my eyes before scrubbing at them intensely. "For someone who cares about appearances as much as Mom, it doesn't make sense to me he wouldn't want the movie moment of asking Dad."

"He knew he'd say no, Peep. Dad hates that guy."

My father doesn't hate anyone. I don't understand how she could possibly even know any of this for sure. "How would you know he didn't ask him? You don't talk to our mother, and I doubt our father would've said anything because he doesn't hate anyone."

"Dad *does* hate people, Peep. I've brought a lot of people around, Dad. He has a tell. I saw it when he looked at Ethan during Christmas."

I furrow my brows, contemplating her words. "A tell, really? Like what?" My father has always been a man of few words who tries to stay as subjective as possible for his profession.

She crosses her arms in disbelief. "Seriously?" She imitates our father's facial expressions and mannerisms. "He looks at you, then at the person he doesn't like, then back at you. He won't make eye contact for more than two seconds. Phoebe, he barely *talks* while they're around!"

I reminisce back to dinner the other night. He did every single one of those things. How did I not see it? This only leads me to wonder what he could've been talking to Ethan about when I was helping my mother clean the kitchen.

"Anyway, you need to do what's right, Phoebe. And cheating on him isn't okay, even if I don't like him."

I hear her, I do, but when deciding to do what's right, wouldn't it be to stop what I'm doing with Blake? I mean, even if she were a man, she lied to me—and not "That dress looks good on you" when it doesn't kind of lie. I don't even know her!

"Listen, I don't think it'll be an issue." I shake my head. "I don't even know who Blake is. There won't be any more cheating."

"That's not the point!" Piper leans in and grabs either side of my head. "You're not even into men, Phoebe. You think calling it off with Blake is going to somehow make you want Ethan?" I grab her wrists and force her to release. She crosses her arms in disdainful silence. "It doesn't matter that it's Ethan. It could be any guy," she finally says.

I scowl. "That's not true. I've—I've had boyfriends."

Without uncrossing her arms, my sister's eyebrows shoot upward. "That you didn't even kiss."

"I wasn't ready! I'm not a—" I can't say it. Something about the word as an adjective for me sounds surreal. It sounds disgusting.

"A what, Phoebe? A lesbian?" She blinks at me.

"I'm not." A pit forms in my stomach as tears threaten to fall once more.

She clearly can tell I'm not okay with this accusation, which prompts her to wave off the topic and pivot to another one on a sigh.

"Fine. Let's address the Blake thing now." She rubs her chin and narrows her eyes. Her voice is low and irritated. "She doesn't need fixing, Phoebe. That's very fucked up of you." I squirm on the cushions and smooth out my hair. Blake does seem surer of herself than I am. "It's not wrong that she's gay. Besides, even if Blake and Dakota *were* different people, making amends by saving someone *else's* soul isn't a thing."

"How?!" I slam my quaking hands down at my sides. I need to be moving, so I rise to my feet, pacing back and forth in front of the coffee table, rubbing my forehead. "I feel so stupid, Pipez. How did I not know? She has the same eyes! The same cute little crooked canine. The way she rubs the back of her neck when she's uncomfortable." I mimic the gesture. "Dakota has been on my mind since I met Blake at church that first Sunday. Making amends with her was the reason I decided to help Blake. If I could've spent my time fixing Dakota when I knew her, she wouldn't have been outcast and forced to transfer. And if Blake wasn't gay, she'd be welcomed by the church."

Piper rises to her feet, rounding the small table to pull me into her chest. The soft chenille material of her oversized fuzzy sweater is infused with the scent of burned incense. The same woman whose smokey voice would sing Landslide to me when I was twelve, is comforting me once more. And for some reason, I miss her voice. I miss her guitar. I miss her. When everyone else was busy with their own lives, my sister had always been my comfort. Until one day, she wasn't. "That's exactly what's wrong with that church. They throw stones from glass houses. *Forcing* you to stay away from someone like Dakota? You think their hands are clean? Think they've never sinned?" She runs her hand through my hair.

"Phoebe, there isn't a single saint in EC. They abuse power. Everyone has flaws, even you." She steps back to meet my gaze. "Did you ever stop to consider you weren't really trying to fix Blake, but rather giving yourself an excuse to be near her?"

I hadn't fully thought about it. The magnetism I felt toward her was so strong I couldn't stay away, no matter how hard I tried to resist her. There has to be a reason for that. God always has a plan, right? Maybe I wasn't tempted at all. Maybe God kept sending me a message in the form of Dakota and then again with Blake for me to come to terms with who I really am. But who am I? I'm not a—I can't be.

She notices my epiphany. "There it is!" She snaps her fingers and grabs my arms. "Phoebe, it's not a bad thing! If God did send her to you, I can bet you money it wasn't for *you* to fix *her*. If anything, it was for *her* to fix *you*. I've always known who you were, and it doesn't need fixing. It needs to be accepted."

Who I am? What? I'm not gay!

"And Blake, if God really sent her as you believe, was sent to hold your hand while you meander through your self-discovery. You think from the time Blake was Dakota to this new 'Blake' character she's become, she never discovered who she was? You said you wanted to find yourself, right? I promise you, Blake—or Dakota—or whoever the fuck she is—was sent to be your spirit guide!"

Heat rises to my face. "Then why fucking lie?!" I shout, pushing out of her grasp.

She takes a step back. "You're becoming quite the mouth. Who knew the real you would be part sailor?" she quips.

I'm pacing around so frustrated, the blood beneath my skin boils. How can she think this is funny? "I'm serious, Piper."

She holds her hands up in defense. "I can't answer that…and you know as well as I do the only one who can is Blake." She walks to my kitchen, opens my fridge, and pulls out some grapes. Mouth full, she mutters, "And break up with dicknose. Seriously."

✝

That night, I lay awake staring at my ceiling. Piper and I stayed up talking about everything from our childhood to her new job as an event planner. After realizing it was almost eleven, she made the decision to stay the night. She'd never stayed overnight at my place before, always opting to go home around six. Then again, she never came to Mystic Harbor if it wasn't Thanksgiving or Christmas.

I figured maybe it was easier for her to stay in town when my parents didn't know she was here. I kind of wished she'd do it more often, but three hours is kind of a long trip.

I had decided I would take some vacation time and visit her in a few weeks, when everything settled. I'd never seen her place, and she wanted me to meet her new puppy, Checkers. Visiting her had always been something that would've upset my mother, who was mad Piper had left in the first place. "How am I going to explain this to the congregation?" She'd once said to me after she left. The new me promised Piper I would try harder to separate myself from her expectations and give more energy to figuring out who I was.

But I'm still trying to figure out who that is. A part of me wants to believe it's new. The gravitational pull of Blake is influencing my curious nature. It doesn't define who I am. Yet I felt the same thing twelve years ago toward Dakota. Is it safe to assume this entire thing is all magnetism toward the same person? If they were different people, it'd make sense to say it's not a one time thing. Is it possible to exclusively be attracted to *one* girl? Would it make me—no. I can't say it. I can't bring myself to say the word. Thinking about it makes my stomach turn.

Why can't I switch it off? Stop feeling this way? Why can't I stop thinking about her? I'm mad at her, but when she's not around, I'm still pulled toward her. Desire to be near her. Like something's missing when she isn't with me, like I miss her.

Even in high school, when she was gone, when the pebbles on my window stopped, I felt as though I'd lost the best part of my life.

So…what now?

Chapter 17

Phoebe

I stare at the clock on my dash. 1:53 AM. I've been sitting in the parking lot of Siren's Song for over an hour, debating on whether I should go inside or go home.

But when Piper noticed I was leaving, she all but pushed me out the door of my apartment, saying, "Wear a condom!" to which I verbally protested—I really didn't know if I was ready to face Blake.

So here I sat. For the last hour, trying to figure out what I'd say to her. So many questions I needed answered, but what question should come first? And how would I word any of the questions in a nonconfrontational way? Do I call her Dakota? Do I call her Blake? Probably Blake. Right?

All of my inquisitions come to a halt when she exits the building with a bag of trash in her hand, locking up for the night. Her eyes automatically locking onto my car. I guess I could've decided to park somewhere not directly in front, my headlights casting a spotlight on the front door. "No turning back now," I mutter as I turn off the car and follow her to the back of the building.

She doesn't look at me as she continues walking. Is she expecting me to speak first? To start spouting off questions?

"Okay," I sigh, slapping my hands down on my thighs. "You can talk now." Not the best response, but I'm at a loss for words, and now that I'm seeing her, my cognitive functions have gone completely haywire.

She throws the bag of trash in the dumpster and sits down on a pile of pallets. "What do you want to know?" Is she kidding? *What do I want to know? Seriously?*

"Why me?" I say, as heat simmers underneath my skin. "Why lie? Why EC? Why 'Blake?' What do I even call you now?"

"Blake." She rubs the back of her neck. "You still call me Blake."

"Why?!" I shout, frustration meshing with equal parts hilarity and incredulity as I continue my tirade. "You told me to leave you alone in high school, 'Blake.' Why come back into my life as a completely different person? Why hurt me again over a decade later by assuming a new identity when all I ever wanted was to have

186

you back?" I start crying. I can't help it. I feel so confused. So stupid. So angry. "I-I thought you cared about me! How could you?" I wipe my face with the back of my jacket sleeve. "Why did you lie to me?"

"It wasn't intentional, I—" she starts, but I'm so mad I'm shouting over her.

"Then why did you? Was I just some kind of conquest of your sexual prowess? Bag a good Christian girl so you can tell all your friends about it?"

She's staring down at the ground now. "Delaney only knows you're back in my life. My other friends don't even know that much," she says.

I throw my hand up. "And I'm supposed to believe that?" I don't even know who she is or who she's become in the twelve years of not knowing her and now I'm just supposed to believe her when she says she isn't bragging to her friends about bringing me to orgasm twice? I'm glad she has friends now, but what the hell?

Her eyes water as she pinches the bridge of her nose. She's tapping a foot while her entire body trembles. "Phoebe, I understand you're angry—"

"Oh well, that's an understatement!" I huff. I bet her friends found it so hilarious how Blake turned me into a broken record, begging her not to stop as I rode her thigh on my couch that first night. How easy I came for her.

"Then let me explain!" She raises her voice slightly, annoyance threaded with the words. It's enough to quiet me. I stand, arms crossed, as she takes in a breath.

"Umm...where do I begin?" A roll of thunder goes off in the distance as she searches for the words. "Why EC? I'll start there." She scratches her nose, still thinking. "Life after you knew me was horrible, Phoebe. Jude pushed me to move back in with him." Her eyes twinkle through the tears as her mind reminisces on her late brother. "He said, 'No one else should ever have to go through what you did, Kota. They deserve a place of refuge.' He-He." She puts her face in her palms as the tears fall heedlessly from her eyes, chest heaving. "'First step is exposure!' He figured if we stood strong, people would eventually feel safe. And they do! So many people, Phoebe. You should see this place on Thursday karaoke night or Tuesday trivia!"

Icy wind rips around us aggressively. My skin begins to chill as the lid to the dumpster slams violently into the metal rim. But Blake doesn't even seem to notice. "And—and everyone who visits respects it. It's surreal. He was right. This is exactly what Mystic needs. People actually want to protect the confidentiality of it. After high school, I would've never believed good people existed, but Siren's restored my faith in humanity. Jude was determined to create outreach next. He wanted to educate people and break the cycle of children growing up believing the same thing their parents do."

Droplets of water trickle gently onto our heads, but Blake doesn't seem to care. Lost in thought and sobbing, she continues, "When he died, I was lost. I didn't very much care about going on without him, but he made me promise to keep pushing. For the people."

The rain picks up. "Maybe…" She wipes the side of her face on her shoulder. "Maybe I had a death wish when I chose EC—the most prejudiced church in town—to do outreach first. Maybe I wished someone there would take me out, so I could say I tried, but I—" Her body shakes uncontrollably, barely managing to utter, "—I'd still be doing outreach for Jude."

I sit down next to her on the pallets, wrapping my arms around her as water blends with the tears seeping carelessly down her face. "Blake," I say, grabbing her reddened cheeks into my hands and kissing her softly. "It's raining."

"I don't care." She jerks her head away sharply, wiping her tears. "I don't care if I freeze."

Clearly, she's beyond caring for herself, so I try a new approach. "Take me inside," I beg. "Please…I'm cold."

Her blue eyes seem a shade lighter as they peer into mine. Maybe it's the way the streetlight shines down above the dumpster. Maybe it's the redness from crying. Whatever it is, I can't look away.

She rises to her feet, reaching in her pocket for her keys, unlocking the door, and locking it again behind us. She walks over to the bar and switches on the light, illuminating the quote behind it, and we sit. Like the first day I saw her, but this time she's beside me, my hand on her leg as I ask, "What makes you say EC is the most prejudice?"

She dries her face with a napkin from a container on the counter. "Phoebe, it's famous. Everyone knows this."

"I didn't." I struggle to believe it. "But the pastor—"

She pinches the bridge of her nose. "Is your *dad*, Phoebe."

I stare down at my hands in my lap. "Is he one of the…?"

"No!" she says quickly placing a soothing hand on my thigh. "He's a good guy. I honestly don't understand how he ended up preaching in a church like that."

"Probably my mom." I roll my eyes.

She lifts her shoulders. "I had no idea I'd run into you at EC. You said your dad was a pastor, but it could've been any one of the churches on the Holy Side. You have to believe I had no way of knowing you went there."

I do believe her. I have no explanation as to why I'm convinced she wouldn't intentionally hurt me like she did all those years ago. All of this is a mix-up. Has to be. We both share blame for the past. I was completely shattered when she'd told me to stay away from her. And in turn, I hurt her by not standing up for her that day in the bathroom. It was selfish and petty of me.

"You make it seem as though you didn't want to start over…But you introduced yourself to me as 'Blake' rather than tell me who you were," I press, thinking maybe she used a fake name to start over deeming our past issues as irreparable.

"That's a tough one for me to talk about…" She runs her hand through her hair nervously. "Short version is, after Mystic High, I transferred to Cypress. My stepdad—being a Holy Sider—did *not* enjoy having to transfer me to a new school for being gay. He's a piece of work…After the transfer, he took it out on my entire family until one day he left. Guess he'd had enough of us failing and embarrassing him. Either way, I was relieved. But my mom…couldn't function without a man around, and the kids in Cypress weren't any more accepting than Mystic High. I grew up rough and made more than enough bad choices.

"Junior year, I hated who I was, and I hated I wasn't able to be normal. You see, long before you tried to save me, Phoebe, I'd already failed. Or so I thought. I found God too. The real one. Not the one EC teaches. At least He's real to me."

Blake pressed her thumb to my cheek, causing me to close my eyes and move my head into her palm. "I spent way too much time hating who I'd became. I felt I'd never be able to live in Dakota's shadow. I needed to start over. Dakota was a very bad person, Phoebe. I'm glad you didn't know her. She was hurt and angry and I couldn't move past the things she did.

"When I realized you had no idea who I used to be, honestly, I was relieved. That part of me died years ago, and the past, *my* past, shouldn't keep us from starting over. I'd already been going by Blake for five years at that point, which is my middle name, so…" She leaps up and heads behind the bar. "When I saw you, I knew."

She grabs a glass and starts pouring liquids into a metal cup like on the first day I arrived at this bar.

"Knew what."

She starts shaking, the mixture leaning her elbow over the bar and entering my space. "Twelve years ago, the most beautiful girl I'd ever met told me, 'You belong wherever you'd like,' So, I went where I knew I shouldn't, and when I saw her there, I knew I had to bring her where she belonged." She pours the contents of the metal cup over the ice in the glass and adds a slight amount of grenadine on the top of the drink, causing the blue mixture to turn purple at the top. She then pops a cherry in it, followed by a straw, before handing the drink to me.

✝

The headlights from passing cars create long streaks of light as they rush past us. I'm sitting in the passenger seat of Blake's old Dodge as she drives us back to her place. She insisted on driving, and I agreed, given the number of drinks I've had tonight. I was holding onto her waist as she helped me into my seat. I had made the decision to call out of work in the morning.

I blink repeatedly to focus on the clock on her dash. 2:43. She's singing along to music as I slide my hand to her thigh. The corner of her mouth creeps up as she grabs my hand, rubbing her thumb against the top of my palm, causing a rise in my stomach. I'm not sure why, but the warmth of her palm fills me with a sense of security.

After parking her truck in the drive, she jumps out and runs around to my side, opening the door and helping me brace myself as I exit. I only stumble a little bit as she gently guides my hips up her porch. I plop myself down on one of the rocking chairs, swaying back and forth, peering out at the stars.

"I love your house," I say as she twists the key in the lock, smirking into the door. "I could sit here forever." I can't describe the comfort of being in her space. I've always felt this in her presence, and her home is no exception. Is this what she meant when she said she knew she had to bring me where I "belonged?" Is that place beside her? Sitting next to her on this porch or by the fireplace, curling up with her on the couch watching a movie. Warmth washes over my extremities at the thought of never losing her again. A chance at a real life, where I mow the grass while she fixes my car. Because God knows I won't be able to. "You remember when we sat and watched that meteor shower?"

"Like it was yesterday." Her eyes glimmer in the night.

My mind is pulled back to the afternoon within Stone's Throw Manor. *"Imagine lighting a fire and relaxing in front of this!"* I hum pleasantly because I can actually see myself fitting into this life with her now. The desire causes an overwhelming urge to wrap myself around her and keep her from ever leaving me again. I don't think I can handle her pushing me away twice.

As she's lifting me from the chair, I grab her waist, swaying slightly to regain my footing. "Will you hold me?" I ask.

"I'd hold you forever," she whispers, reveling in my current state.

"No," I whine. "I mean right now." But before she can answer, I fall into her body as she catches me. I tighten my grip and rest my head on her chest. "You're so tall." I can't explain this warmth rushing through me as her arms embrace my middle, wrapping me in and making me stable. "It's nice." I close my eyes and feel her take in air.

"Let's go inside," she whispers. "You need to lie down."

I groan. "Don't tell me what to do," I say playfully.

Before I know it, she's picking me up. My legs instinctually wrap around her waist, burying my face into the crook of her neck, taking in her intoxicating cedar smell.

She pushes into the house and turns on a light which floods the room, causing me to squint. "Too bright!" Why am I so whiney right now?

She smirks as she walks me to her room, gently placing me down on her bed before flipping on the light and walking to her dresser. "Put this on." She hands me one of her large T-shirts and sweatpants.

I sit up so my feet hang off the side of the bed as I pull my shirt over my head. As she's walking past me, I grab her hand and pull her in, parting my legs and placing her body in between them. I reach for the bottom of her shirt and start to pull it up before she stops my hands. "Phoebe, you're drunk."

"Am not," I lie, but I totally know I am.

She blinks slowly, in disbelief, which causes me to pout.

"Please," I beg. "I want to feel your skin on mine."

She mulls it over for a second. "What a cute pout," she says, pulling off her shirt and laying me backward onto the bed, causing my stomach to do cartwheels. She lays down beside me, gently pressing her middle against my ribs, propping herself up on one arm. Her palm is so warm on my belly, and her skin is soft on mine.

I exhale and close my eyes. For the first time since I can remember, I'm at peace. I open them when she runs her hand through my hair. The light reflecting off her pupils is encompassing the admiration she has for me perfectly. "You're so beautiful," she whispers.

And I feel it. The way she's beaming at me makes me believe she truly means it. I can't honestly remember a time in my life where I've ever had someone look at me like she is right now. My cheeks flush as butterflies fill my stomach and heat pools below my belly button. My gaze drops to her mouth. I place my hand on her cheek as my thumb traces a scar on her bottom lip. "How'd you get this?" I whisper.

She lowers her head before rejoining my gaze. "Talking shit." The fact she's trying to make light of it causes me to believe the time of its creation was devoid of any humor. "Some people prefer you to be seen rather than heard."

Like my mom, I think, but decide to remain quiet. I choose instead to keep studying her face. There's another scar above her eyebrow. It's not super visible. You'd have to be seriously searching for it since it runs parallel right above the hair of her brow. I run my hand across it. "This one?" I ask.

"Two by four. It was nothing." She shifts uncomfortably.

It hurts me knowing people hurt her. Did anyone defend her, or did they all walk away like I did the day I saw her in the bathroom? What happened to her after she disappeared? I know it's too late to fix it, but I want to spend the rest of my life trying. I want to say I'm sorry. As if words can fix abandoning her. I know they can't. I should've stayed. I should've told my friends to screw off. I should've held her hand and braved our fellow classmates together, but I couldn't.

Struggling to tell my father and Piper about my feelings toward Blake is realization enough I still can't.

I may not be able to fix what's happened to her. I'm unable to make up for leaving her, but maybe I can still say I'm sorry.

I run my index and middle finger along the side of her neck and watch her eyes close gently. Her lips part as she slowly inhales. My hand continues trailing to her shoulder. She shivers and her arm in my hair pebbles with goosebumps. "Phoebe," she whispers.

"Hmm?" I whisper back as her gaze meets mine.

"You need to stop…" She bites the corner of her lip, letting out a deep sigh.

"Why?" Am I upsetting her by bringing up negative things?

"You have no idea how much you're turning me on."

Oh. My eyes widen as the place between my legs gets incredibly warm. "I'm sorry," I say, dropping my hand to her hip.

Her pupils are dilated and gleaming. Cheeks flushed. She's so beautiful. My stomach sinks. The way she takes in her bottom lip fills me with an uncontrollable desire.

"Actually," I decide. "I'm not." I grab the back of her neck and pull her mouth into mine, opening immediately and finding her tongue. She lets out a quiet moan. But I need more.

I push her to lie flat on the bed as I swing my leg over her middle, straddling her as I take in the view. She watches, her thumbs pressing gently into my hip bones, as I run my fingertips down her collarbone, brushing softly before continuing to her shoulders and down her arms. It's then I notice a scar on the inside of her bicep.

"What's this?" I ask, running my hand along it.

She flinches and frowns. "It's…" she stops herself. "It's nothing."

She turns her head away, but I grab her chin between my index finger and thumb and turn her to meet my eyes. I place one hand on her sternum and the other on her hip. Leaning down, I kiss her. "You can tell me," I whisper.

"It was a long time ago." She seems to think this is going to be enough and I won't press, but the alcohol I've consumed is making it hard for me to hold back my inquisitions like I typically do. I'm invested. I need her to know she can tell me anything.

I place tiny kisses on her cheek until I get to her ear. "What is it?" I whisper. "Please."

She rises until we're both upright with me in her lap, sliding her hands under my butt and squeezing. "No," she says, kissing my neck.

What could it possibly be? "Why won't you tell me?" I say, pulling her mouth away, looking at her. She's always been a person who tells you just enough, and I hate having to assume things by filling in the blanks.

"Because," she wraps her arms around me, resting her head on my shoulder, "it's not important."

Clearly, whatever it is, is starting to break her, given she went from sexual to squeezing me in a beg for me to drop it. So, I do. It's going to bother me, but if she isn't ready to talk to me about it, it's not my place to pry. I decide instead to lift her head and kiss her gently. "Fine."

She lifts me in her lap, turning us around until my back is on the bed. She leaves me on the bed to grab her shirt and tosses it at me. "Shirt," she demands.

"No," I huff, sitting up and pouting at her.

"Phoebe, you're drunk."

"But what if I want you to touch me?" I whimper.

She shakes her head. "I will." She kisses my forehead. "When you're sober."

I fall back onto the bed dramatically. "Lame!"

She beams up at me, pulling on the blanket to cover me up. "You said you wanted me to hold you?"

"Mhmm." I nod.

Then she slides under the blankets on the other side, allowing me to rest my head in the perfect divot of her shoulder, sliding my hand along her stomach. I may or may not have ghosted my fingers into her waistband, causing her to shiver and remind me again nothing is going to happen. I drift off to sleep easily, listening to her heartbeat.

†

The smell of cedar floods my nose as I open my eyes, realizing I'm in Blake's bed, the sun flooding through the open blinds. I'm wearing her shirt and my underwear. Where are my pants?

I scour the rug and floor before lifting her blue/green flannel comforter, investigating below. What happened last night? I lean over the side and find them underneath the bed.

"But what if I want you to touch me?" So stupid. I smack my forehead. Oww! My head is killing me. I turn, taking in the room, and notice a glass of water and ibuprofen on the end table nearest me. I take it, downing almost the entire glass of water. I didn't realize I was so thirsty. My stomach feels empty and mad.

I need food. I should probably go, I think, throwing the blanket off my body and swinging my legs over the bed. Right as I do, Blake pushes open the door, holding a tray, wearing nothing but boxers and a plain black sports bra. The tattoo on her rib steals the air from my lungs. Her eyes pan to my bare legs before closing hers and turning around.

"Sorry!" she says nervously, walking back out. "I'll come back."

I smirk. "You're good."

She doesn't turn around, though. I think I may have broken her because now she's frozen, body rigid, standing under the doorway holding the tray. Where's the reset button?

"When." I clear my throat, sliding back under the comforter. This is so embarrassing. "When did I lose my pants?"

She clears her throat. "You said you were hot and kicked them off quite aggressively around 4:00 AM."

"Did we…?" *Oh my God, I'm turning into Piper.*

"No!" She turns around now and places the tray on my lap. "I promise." My eyes beeline for the steaming hot mug filled with what I can only assume is a flat white.

"Phoebe, you're drunk."

Oh, now I remember.

"Mmm…" I close my eyes, letting the aroma flood my nostrils. Nothing beats the smell of fresh coffee.

Blake walks around to the other side of the bed and slides under the blanket. "I hope you like biscuits and gravy." She's pointing to random items on the tray. "I didn't know how you like your eggs. Wasn't sure about bacon or sausage, so I made you both."

I blush. "You didn't have to do this." She really didn't. No one's ever made me breakfast in bed before. Not even my parents when I was sick.

I remember the rocks she threw at my window so we could sneak out and climb onto the roof of that movie theater. She'd brought blankets. She'd planned a speech to convince me. Which wasn't necessary, but she'd thought of one, anyway. Just in case. She was always sweet like that. How could she say Dakota was a bad person? She was the most amazing person I'd ever met.

Then she met Sam. No more late-night car rides. No more handheld trails or meteor showers. Did she do those things for her?

"Blake?" I grab the fork to the left of my plate before peering at her. She's absolutely radiating as the sun peeking in through the window hits her pale skin. "What happened with Sam?"

Chapter 18
Blake

We were having a good morning. I know it'd just started but why do I feel like I'm cursed and will never have a good moment with Phoebe? Do we really have to bring up exes while eating fuckin' breakfast? It's not how I function in the slightest. I reposition my seat on the mattress, suddenly feeling incredibly uncomfortable. Like my bones aren't sitting right inside my skin. "I didn't…"

Phoebe can tell her question has caused some discomfort. Dropping her fork, she sets the tray down on the nightstand beside her. She entangles her fingers with my sweaty ones laying on top of the covers. "No, Blake." She shakes her head. "I believe you."

She lets go of my hand to grab my body and pull herself into mine. Resting her head on my chest she whispers, "You had a million chances to do something to me. You never did—last night included. I don't get how people could think you did anything to her."

I raise my brows and puff out a breath, "I guess I made her uncomfortable." Even though that's not what happened. For a while there, we were really happy. She made me believe she cared. We'd fall asleep on the phone together, she'd make me mixed tapes with my favorite bands. She'd tell me she loved me…

…Then her mom burst through her bedroom door unexpectedly and I jumped. It's not like we were doing anything inherently sexual. She was sitting with her back against the headboard. I had my head on her lap staring up at her ceiling. That's all it took. Her mom knew everything and there was no convincing her otherwise.

Her mother made me leave after that. No more sleepovers. No more phone calls.

Phoebe uses the flat of her palm on my sternum to push up and glare at me. "Please tell me the truth," she says exasperatedly. She needs this. I can't keep giving her the run around. I told myself I'd give her something. Why not give her this?

I drop my hands and let out a sigh. "It's a tale as old as time, Phoebe. I found out when I got older this happens to so many people, not just me." Which is true. The amount of time I told this story at NA and was met with similar stories, with less fortunate endings, was uncanny. Maybe it's just Mystic, but coming out in this small town isn't for the faint of heart. Sometimes it's easier to deny it, than it is to accept it. Case and point: The woman in my bed who made me come the night before last. "We were together, but coming out is hard. When her mom caught us in her room, she told everyone I took advantage of her. Could've been worse, I guess. I mean, I've seen worse."

Phoebe scowls. "Worse how? They were beating you up! You had to transfer schools."

"Phoebe, that's mild." I say nervously. *God, she is so sheltered.* "Gay people accused of molestation or rape by someone too scared to come out happens every day. I'm just grateful I didn't end up in jail or on the sex offender registry." It's clear she's never read the Mystic paper. I wonder if news is banned within her church. "People have been killed for accusations like mine. I've seen it." *Literally people we went to school with.* But I refuse to be the reason she's too scared to walk the streets of her hometown. "I got lucky."

Foolish Phoebe. The confusion on her face as she tries to understand is downright adorable. "If you've seen so much surrounding your lifestyle, why would you keep choosing it?"

Well...less adorable when she says shit like that. I pinch the bridge of my nose. "You're so cute, Phoebe." But I don't want her to stop asking questions. I know she's inquisitive. If Step Two is outreach, then she has the right to ask in order to learn and I need to be able to be impartial.

"Are-are you mad at me?"

I press my fingers to the corners of my eyes as I exhale. "No...I'm honestly glad you don't understand, but Phoebe, I told you before, I didn't choose this. It's not some kind of rebel move to go against the current. It's something I can't control. I'm not attracted to men." My eyes sink into her soul as I say, "And I think deep down, you know you're not either."

She turns away. "I'm not a..."

"It wouldn't be wrong if you were."

"Yeah, but I...I like guys, too."

I squint at her while nodding slowly. "Okay." I can't tell her who she is. That wouldn't be right. I refuse to force her eyes open and steal her rose colored glasses. Even if she's a born natural with my body. It's as if she was made to please mine.

She sits up and grabs the tray. *Well I guess we're tabling it.*

I watch as she eats. "Is it good?"

"So good." Her eyes roll back as she swallows. When was the last time she ate? And why am I getting aroused listening to her moaning with every bite?

After she finishes and places the tray back on the nightstand, we both sink down into the pillows. Her head is turned facing me. She's so pretty. Butterflies dance around within me at the thought I'm seeing more than eyes. I'm peering directly into her. It's peaceful and kind. It's beautiful. Her finger brushes against mine under the blanket, my flesh cooling as her pinky wraps around mine. Heat warms the back of my eyes at the sight of her flushing cheeks.

"Tell me about the scar," she tries again.

And just like that, my expression changes. "Why can't you let this go?" I plead.

"Because you still haven't told me." She drops her arms exasperatedly onto the bed. "Please?"

I shake my head. She can't know about this. Telling her will only make her think less of me. Another lovely thing Dakota left for me to try and explain.

Her voice raises slightly. "Well, why not?"

I have to change this topic before it leads to me getting even more frustrated, and an argument breaks out. We're having a good morning. She's run from every nice moment we've shared together, and the last thing I want is to ruin things for a third time. I need to keep this sweet. Just for now. Eventually, sure, I'll tell her everything, but I need one solid moment where things don't turn ugly.

The corner of my mouth rises. I've got an idea of how I can change this ridiculous conversation—give her what she wanted last night. I couldn't bring myself to take advantage of her inebriated state then, but she's not drunk anymore.

I throw my arm around her waist and prop myself up on my elbow. "I told you," I say seductively, chartering a path up the base of her neck to her ear with my tongue. "It's not important." My skin chills instantly, needing more of her as I take in the scent of her nape.

"Blake," she whispers, eyes shuttering closed. "D-don't change the subject."

The corner of my mouth quirks up, knowing my behavior is having the desired effect.

She clears her throat. "What if I guess?"

"You can try." My hand dips lower, fingertips barely grazing the soft, inexperienced flesh of her inner thigh.

I find her mouth, but as I'm about to take her bottom lip into mine, she pulls away slightly. Her sultry whisper causes her lips to gently graze mine as she speaks. "And if I guess it," her breathing increases as my hand continues its path upward, "you have to help me make welcome baskets for the new guests."

"Ahh," I murmur. "I love a good wager." Her hips move upward, begging for my hand to inch higher. "But for every wrong answer," I press myself closer to her, "I get to find a new way to distract you."

"Sword fight?" she questions playfully.

I swipe my fingers along her breast, causing it to raise. "Try again."

I watch her pulse thrum in her neck as I cup her breast, gently pinching the nipple through the fabric with my thumb and index finger. "Umm." She presses her thighs together. "Car accident?"

I drop my head to nibble on the raised peak as I shake my head. Her hand finds my neck as I continue making slow circles with my tongue.

"Fell…" she moans, "out-out of a tree?"

My hand dips lower once more as she squirms beneath me. Tracing the waistband of her panties, she tries again. "Building a fence?" I can hear the tension in her body escape her lips in breathy words. She's breathing so heavily I think she may actually hyperventilate as her hand run through the hair on the back of my neck.

"Give up yet?" I'm almost certain she's too distracted to actually guess it. And guessing would completely kill the mood. I can tell her mind is incapable of even fathoming the real answer. The guessing game is invigorating, though, my entire body throbbing with the anticipation to keep exploring. Keep eliciting a response.

"Never," she breathes so gently as her feet rub together. "Building a fence?"

The pads of my middle finger trail over her soaked panties as I stroke up and down over the fabric. "You said that already."

Phoebe grabs my wrist, attempting to stop my ministrations. "Blake…" she whimpers. "You…" I apply pressure and continue rolling my wrist as she tries desperately to ignore the pleasure I'm causing her. "You fell off a roof?" She raises a desperate eyebrow, hoping this is it.

I move her panties to the side and find her clit, continuing to make circles as her hips cause my finger to slide along the saturation of her pussy. "Fuck, you're dripping for me, baby. Give up yet?"

She bites her lip and pinches her brows together. "Freak accident…doing… dishes?"

The scent of her arousal travels upward, hitting my olfactory senses and sparking a primal need within me. I can no longer continue with this game or I may actually lose all control. "Let me make you come," I breathe into her ear and watch as her entire body flushes at my desperate plea for respite.

Her hips push into my hand as a tiny moan escapes her lips, causing me to place kiss after lecherous kiss on her throat. "God." She nods in frustration as I position myself on top of her.

"Your scent is intoxicating, you know?" I whisper in her ear, keyed up and hungry.

"Yeah?" she pants as she hugs my shoulders, bucking her hips and concentrating on the slide of my fingers.

"I want you so fucking bad right now," I growl, rising and positioning myself at the end of the bed, hooking the back of her thighs with my arms and pulling her to the edge, into my pelvis. "You were driving me crazy last night." She arches her back slightly, allowing me to pull off her underwear. I watch as she sits up, wrapping her thighs around me, her face flushed, eyes black.

She's so turned on I don't think she could tell me no if she wanted to. Doesn't matter because neither of us wants this to stop. Our previous encounters have been passionate, but this time is different. It's all fiery and hungry. As I focus on breathing, my hand slides along the extremely soaked area, massaging my tongue against hers, kissing furiously. "That feels so good." She shudders into my mouth.

Her trembling fingers hook into my waistband and slide my boxers down. I kick them off with so much vigor, the want coursing through my veins driving me to become more needy as she throws one arm over my shoulder while the other one braces my hip for leverage as her pussy grinds my pelvis, sliding into my fingers.

"You're so wet," I mutter, my throat so dry I struggle to swallow. I dip my hand lower, ghosting her entrance. I would never push any boundaries she has set for herself. Penetration is seemingly sacred to her, and I've made a mental note to never try convincing her to let me take it from her. We don't need to have a conversation for me to know better.

I listen as the wind escapes her lungs, and she digs her fingers into my shoulders from this brand-new feeling enveloping her senses. Her eyes snap closed as a primal need washes over her. Her hands become frantic as she struggles to pull off my sports bra. It's honestly adorable watching her fumble with my clothes and I can't hold back the smile ceasing our kissing. Backing away slightly, I pull it off the rest of the way for her.

"I had it," she groans, letting me know I need to let her do things for herself from now on.

"Faster if I help," I tease.

"Who said I wanted to go fast?" she fires back, beaming at my body, suddenly realizing she has me completely naked. The sight of her drinking me in has me impossibly even more aroused. I need her in my mouth. Need to taste her as she fucks my face.

I bring my fingers to my lips, sucking the taste of her off of them. "God, you taste so good," I hum. I watch as her eyes grow wide at the sight, but she tastes addictive, and I need more. "I want you in my mouth," I hiss. "Can I?"

Her nervous eyes dart around as she spends an unreasonable amount of time clearly weighing the pros and cons. Or, in her case, probably just the cons. This is new for her and extremely intimate. It'd open her up to an entirely new platform of vulnerability, and I can tell if she's going to allow me to do this, it's going to take some serious build-up to get there. I need to show her she can let down those walls for me.

"I'm sorry," I sigh. "You said you don't want to go fast. I'm getting carried away. How about I slow down a little?"

She nods apprehensively. "Please."

We share a silent agreement before I pull her shirt over her head. This is safe. She let me take her shirt off last time. I graze my hand along her ribs as I slowly kiss her neck. Soon, my fingers are creeping under the seam of her bra. She lets out a tiny moan as my thumb brushes against the sensitive skin of her nipple.

"I need this off," I growl before realizing I need to quell this lasciviousness. "Is that okay?"

She nods again, nerves rushing through her at the realization we'll both be naked. My body ignites at the thought of her full body pressed against mine. I can feel myself dripping. She kisses my neck as I unhook it carefully, my fingertips causing her skin to rise as I trace the straps down her arms before throwing it mindlessly across the room.

Pushing her down, I sink onto her, the warmth of her skin sparking electricity throughout my being before a new wave of moisture settles between my legs. Trying to keep things slow rather than ravishing, I walk kisses down her neck to her collarbone, circling the gap above her clavicle while cupping her breasts. Brushing my thumbs over the very sensitive flesh of her nipple. She squirms beneath me, jerking her hips slightly, missing my touch.

I trail my tongue all the way down to one of her perfect nipples, taking it into my mouth, nibbling and sucking, circumnavigating my tongue over it while my left hand cups and massages the other. I whimper as her thighs clench desperately around my middle.

She wants me to touch her again, but I can't. If I start touching her, I don't think I'll be able to stop myself from taking what I want—which is her in my mouth. If I'm going to be respectful, I need to control the narrative. I flatten my hand on her pelvis and push it down, stopping the bucking.

Her fingers scrape my scalp and curl, gripping my hair firmly and pulling, hard. The pain is intense and causes me to struggle even more to control the situation. She's aroused and frustrated, demanding me to touch her without using words. It's so fucking hot I can't restrain the moan escaping the back of my throat as my nails dig into the sides of her ribs.

After taking a few moments to collect myself, my tongue darts out, continuing its journey across her skin, seeking residence at the bottom of her rib, but I'm no longer able to be gentle. I'm kissing with teeth and sucking bruises into the area. She doesn't seem to have an issue with the tension, slightly flinching but biting her lip, frustratingly running her hands through her own hair now.

"Blake," she whimpers. "Why won't you touch me now?"

"I am touching you," I needle playfully while running my nose down to the groove of her hip before replacing it with a kiss, letting my fingertips ghost the sides of her ribs.

Her voice cracks as she whines. "Not how I want it."

"Oh yeah, baby," I whisper as my tongue circles her skin. "Tell me how you want me."

"M-maybe." She throws an arm over her eyes, neck and cheeks flushed red with nerves. "Maybe we can try your mouth on me," she whispers.

"Thought you wanted it slow?" I jab, simpering as I twirl my fingers down the inside of her thighs, descending lower before stopping abruptly. Her hips jerk into me, but I refuse to budge. Refuse to give her what she's asking for so easily. I need her to be extremely sure.

Her hips dance, desperate for my touch. "Please?" she begs, digging the fingers of her free hand into the sheets.

I can't hold on any longer. I fall to my knees, propping her right leg onto my shoulder. Hooking my arm around her other thigh, I lose control, sucking and sinking my teeth, hungry. I charter a path closer and closer to her center. She jerks and giggles when I kiss the crease where her leg joins her body, but she's still too nervous to look at me. I'm yearning for her taste. I need it.

"I might actually die a painful death if you don't touch me soon," she says, her voice shaky. "Can you imagine the funeral? Here lies Phoebe. Death by edging."

I enjoy the quivering of her body in my hands. "I'm surprised you'd even know that expression."

"Please, baby." Her body writhes in anguish, pleading into my arousal. I raise my eyebrows in satisfaction, letting out a heavy exhale before *finally* taking pity on her saturated heat. Ghosting my tongue over her clit so delicately before sinking lower to her entrance, then all the way back up with more pressure. I'm instantly addicted to her taste, unable to stop myself from taking in more and more of it. I repeat this exasperating motion over and over as her knees begin to shake and buckle. "Fuck," she murmurs as her trembling hand finds my hair. Gripping tightly. The pain sending a bolt of electricity to my toes as more moisture settles between my legs. *Fuck yes.*

I twirl my tongue a few more times before wrapping my lips around her clit, latching on and sucking. I let out a series of unintelligible sounds as her fingers dig into my scalp, slowly controlling the motion of my head as her hips buck up and down. She's watching me now. "God, yes," she groans through gritted teeth, her head falling backward onto the bed, back arching. Her knees shake, fingers grasping the sheets impetuously. "I'm so close, baby."

"Look at me," I say. "I wanna watch you as you come."

Her hooded eyes cling to mine as the tip of my finger ghosts her entrance once more. Hips instinctively try to sink into my touch. For the first time since we started our sexual explorations, I'm uneasy. "That feels so good," she keens.

"I wish you could see how beautiful you look through my eyes," I say, flicking my tongue against her center. "How you taste. It's so," lick, "*so*," suck, "good."

My stomach fizzes with enjoyment, blood running cold as her body coils on a deep moan, abruptly collapsing backward again but not breaking eye contact as I continue to lap up her sweetness. "Fuck," she gasps, resolve slowly chipping away the more I flick and suck on her swollen clit. "Oh, God, baby, yeah!" Her entire body trembles, toes curling.

I'm flooded with more arousal at the sight of her face climaxing for me. She's a complete mess, hair screwed up, eyes blown out, panting. She pops up, grabbing my face and tasting herself on my lips. Rolling her tongue against mine before biting down hard on my bottom lip and pulling, causing a searing pain to run through me and translate to pleasure in the pit of my stomach. "Your turn," she pants.

Now I'm smiling, eyes completely enthralled in her sexually feral conduct, forcefully whipping my body around until the back of my knees hit the mattress before shoving me onto the bed.

My body warms as she presses her breasts to my abdomen, spreading my legs wide before heedlessly sinking two fingers into my completely soaked entrance. She curls them forward once fully submerged.

"Oh fuck," I gasp, really fucking enjoying this version of Phoebe. Like, holy shit, I wasn't expecting this from the sweet, nervous girl I've always known.

"You're dripping," she says, allowing my moisture to drench her palm. "You like teasing me?" she demands, increasing the speed, rigorous and insolent. "Like making me beg?"

"Mhmm," I struggle to say through shuddering breaths as the headboard consecutively slams into my wall as she thrusts inside me up to her knuckles. Biting my lip and smiling from the combination of pleasure and pain, I dig my nails into her back. If teasing her means more of this treatment, I think I should've started doing this sooner. "I'm so close, baby. Make me come," I plead, my body surging with the urgency to combust.

She removes her fingers impetuously. My eyes snap open, dazed, desperate, twine unspooling, chest heaving, and clearly upset as my core throbs with want. My hips twitch on the bed with the need to finish.

The way I see it, this is only fair. I deserve a taste of my own medicine. Her lips gently slide along the shell of my ear as she whispers, "Say please for me," before descending, biting a bruise into my chest.

"Please, Phoebe," I gasp, squirming against her body. Phoebe having this sense of power is intoxicating. Her irritation is kindling the fire of my arousal. I had decided to shift the subject of her inquisitions into this. Made the decision to then torment her until she was writhing and achy. The way I see it, she's simply demanding I reap what I've sown, and I'm *more* than okay with that.

It's so sexy to see this woman who has always been forced to be good to others, regardless of their actions against her—a woman forced to forgive way too easily—who's always meant to sit proper with a painted expression of happiness, unable to act out of turn—constantly respecting those who run all over her, now—possibly for the first time in her life—run her fingertips down my ribs making me quiver—holding all the cards—and I'm letting her.

She tsks. "It's your turn to beg." Then leaning in, she takes the shell of my ear into her mouth as her hand barely cups my wetness. "Do better." And fuck, if it isn't literally the single most hottest thing I've ever experienced in all of my sexual conquests.

"Please, baby, please fuck me," I cry, my pelvis seeking desperately for her fingers to finish what they started. "Make me come, please."

A moan erupts from deep within my throat as Phoebe sinks her fingers back in, slowly at first, before picking up speed. "Is this what you want?"

"Uh-huh," I whimper through shuddering breaths as the headboard bangs against the wall in time with her pumping into me again.

When her fingers curl within me, giving way for a few more thrusts, my back arches off the bed, hands gripping the back of her elbows. "Fuck, Phoebe!" I scream as I twitch and coat her fingers with the new wetness of my release.

✝

"Why won't you tell me?" she asks as we lay naked, bodies pressed together, blanket around our waist. She's resting her head on my shoulder, tracing my tattoo with her finger.

I let out an exasperated sigh, unable to change the topic again. "Jesus, you're persistent."

"I prefer the term 'tenacious.'" Her eyebrows furrow. "Seriously, though." She situates a kiss on my collarbone. "Just explain why you won't tell me, and I'll leave it alone."

"I want to tell you. I do." It's not a lie. I just don't want to talk about the past. I've come a long way, and it'll only kill these amazing moments if forced to talk about my own stupidity. I'm not completely delusional. As much as I disassociated Dakota's actions from my own, I know they were all equally my actions. There was just too much hurt in my past to work through unless I could somehow convince myself those decisions in no way corresponded with me. Hence the rebirth. I know she needs some kind of clarity, though. I'll lose her again if I can't somehow open up to her, so I close my eyes and take a deep breath. "When I was seventeen, my life was pretty worse for wear. Sam had just dumped me."

"Wait." This is exactly why I didn't want to tell her…She's going to judge Dakota's decisions and realize she was a dumb bitch. Only problem is, she sees us as one and the same, so…

…She'll see me as the dumb bitch. "You and Sam kept dating? After she turned the entire school against you, forcing you to transfer?"

For a moment, I almost decide to end the conversation here. It's embarrassing having to express the stupidity of Dakota's youth. We are not the same person. I am no longer that person. "What can I say? Dakota was a stupid romantic." She doesn't seem to find the same humor as I intended, however, so I continue. "So, yeah, needless to say, our relationship was toxic. She was emotionally abusive, and growing up how I did, I thought that's how love went. So, I stayed, like an idiot. Kept trying to make it work. At some point, I genuinely started believing the shitty things she'd say I was, and I tried so desperately to change it. She was cheating on me with boys under the guise of 'looking normal,' but truthfully, she was bisexual and scared to confess her attraction to women. I was jealous of this quality within her. If I had the ability to date men, I could ignore the gay side of me altogether and stop being beat up."

"I thought the bullying would've stopped when you transferred."

"Everyone has their opinions on homosexuality, Phoebe. Not just the Holy Side. It's a hot-button topic everywhere." I rub the back of my neck, trying to remember where I was going with this quite nerve-racking tale of woe. "Anyway, if I could've ignored the gay side, I could've prevented myself from being another hate crime. I really thought being bisexual worked like that. Remember, I told you long before you tried to save me I had already failed?"

She nodded, burying her face into my neck and inhaling my scent, which helped the nerves slightly. I just wished I could stop altogether and not have to keep talking about this. Every string holding my heart together felt like it was tearing inside my chest at the admission.

"I hated being gay, Phoebe. It caused nothing but misery, and I decided if I couldn't fix it, there was no point in going on." I realize my grip around her is tightening as I fight back the burning behind my eyes. "Jude found me. I tried to open my brachial artery. Luckily, I was off by a fraction of an inch. Still required stitches, though."

Phoebe blinks repeatedly as she searches for what to say next. "I...I honestly don't even know what to say." She stares up at me disbelievingly. I wish she wasn't looking at me at all right now. I told her life was rough. Why couldn't she have believed me? Taken my word for it. Let it go and move on.

I can almost feel the moment her body recognizes how hard things must have gotten. "Is this when you started going by your middle name?"

"Oh, no." I rub the back of my neck. "That's only the beginning of the story. My downward spiral to rock bottom had a lot more branches. And I hit every single one on the way down. The decision to shed the skin of Dakota is much darker. I can't stress enough how grateful I am you hadn't seen me back then. I wouldn't have you in my arms now if you did."

"You don't know that."

"Oh, but Phoebe, I do." I make sure her eyes are locked to mine before adding, "Dakota wanted everyone to be as miserable as her. She hated herself and hated knowing she hadn't died that day. So, she decided to single-handedly burn her world to the ground piece by piece. Sex, drugs, anything she could use, she did. She didn't care about anything."

"So," she continues, and I really wish this could be over already. "What changed?"

I shift my body from discomfort, fighting a strong, sudden urge to stop feeling so disgusting. "It wasn't one thing exactly, but Jude was a big supporter when I decided to turn my life around. He let me move in with him. Throwing my passion into Siren's as a way to mend the parts of me left abandoned. I was so angry over being alone.

"Before Jude proposed we open the bar, he introduced me to my church, Guiding Light Ministries. I began to view things differently. I wasn't alone. There're tons of people in this town going through the same thing. I wish I could say he was the reason I found God, but...he's not."

"Church?"

That's what she was clinging to? That I go to church? The tattoo of the big cross on my ribs didn't do it for her? She said the word almost with disdain that a church could house a gay person like me.

"It's all-inclusive, Phoebe. You'd love it," I suggest. They saved me and could help her too if, heaven forbid, she ever let someone other than EC show her their ways. But I already know what she's thinking, so before she can respond, I add, "If you're anything like me, I bet you're wondering what God would think about an all-inclusive church."

She nods, turning it over in her mind.

"I've been trying to explain this since we started our lessons. The things you've been learning at EC are radically skewed." I press her cheek to my forehead. "One day…if you're ever ready—I don't want to push you, but I think you could learn a lot. Being gay and a Christian can go hand in hand, Phoebe. It doesn't have to be either or."

I can't help but worry that maybe twenty-six is too old to rebuild your life. She's been taught a homosexual lifestyle is immoral and sinful for so long. Is it even possible to break her of this self-hatred? I started my journey to acceptance only five years earlier, but my support system was stronger than hers seems to be from the untrained eye. Of course, I know she'd have a few people in her corner, but the question is: would it be enough to help her handle all of the negative reactions surrounding coming out?

"Could." She pauses, almost longing to eat her words before they can spew out of her. "Could we maybe learn about your stuff on Mondays?"

I blink flirtatiously. "Is Phoebe Appleton asking *me* to save her soul?"

"No." She smacks my chest playfully. "Just…for better understanding. I'd like to know how your church could possibly view themselves as anything but blasphemous."

The glee I'm brandishing instantly vanishes. "Should've expected that response," I huff before my mind brings me back to the last hour. A devious grin now encompassing my expression as I whisper seductively into her ear, "In that case, I'd like to know how you can view making me beg for your fingers as *not* blasphemous."

The tips of her ears, as well as her cheeks, flush with heat as she swings her leg over my middle, pressing her weight onto my chest. "Can you name someone more equipped to shine a light on your transgressions?"

She's perfect. God has given me a second chance at having this amazing, funny, slightly bossy, *definitely* stubborn beauty, and I refuse to mess it up again. I'm going to need bigger defenses if I'm going to open up to her. If I can't find a way to answer her questions about Dakota without slipping back into my past completely, I'll lose her again. This is a test, and I'm going to make damn sure I don't fuck it up.

Leaning up, I take her bottom lip between my own, savoring the taste of pure, unadulterated peace.

Chapter 19
Phoebe

"Dude," Eve says exasperatedly the second I open my door. "What are you doing?"

I know this is about mine and Zoe's behavior during today's service. I'd asked Blake to sit with us. By us, I mean Ethan, Zoe, Eve, and me.

"The peace of Christ be with you always," my father had said from the altar.

"And also with you!" the Nave said in unison as I raised my palms, offering him peace.

"Please share Christ's peace with your neighbors."

The crowd began shaking hands and hugging one another. Zoe hugged Eve. Eve hugged me, while Zoe hugged Blake. I hugged Ethan before turning and hugging Blake, whispering, "Peace be with you," in her ear.

"Peace," she'd responded. I glanced over to see a disgusted Eve who was now hugging Ethan, but it wasn't just her. A lot of eyes had fallen onto mine and Zoe's reactions to Blake. My mother even pulled me aside after the service when she saw me talking to my father.

Before I could respond, my father chimed in. "Priscilla, God commands us to love our neighbors as we love ourselves. Zoe and Phoebe are following the Lord's commandment."

My mother glanced around, being sure to keep her voice low. "There's whisperings amongst the flock, Peter."

"If there are whisperings, they can approach me themselves, and I'll be happy to remind them the true path of a righteous Christian," he'd addressed, and I figured it'd be the end of it.

However, after service, the usual people who stop and talk to me didn't. No "When you see your father, tell him I said his sermon was beautiful." Or "Say hi to your mother for me." And the ones who did talk to me didn't ask me how Piper was or any variation of small talk they only had questions about Blake. Wanted to know if she was new in town. If she truly was a homosexual. If she'd be leaving soon.

"So you invited her then?" Elouise Sullivan had asked.

I scanned the vestibule, searching for Blake. "No. She came on her own."

"Oh," she laughed. "But surely you know her? Did you girls go to the same school?"

I wasn't sure I wanted to divulge too much information into Blake's past for fear of the telephone game that always seems to follow this line of questioning. If there's one thing to say about EC, it's that they can be quite the misinformed chatty Kathy's at the best of times.

"I mean maybe." I lifted my shoulders. "We are the same age. I met Blake here." It's not *exactly* a lie so much as an omission of information. I *did* meet Blake here. I met Dakota in high school. And regardless, it's been twelve years and our friendship back then was rather brief. I see Zoe coming out from the bathroom and smile toward her. "I met her here, same as you, Eloise."

"Well," she crossed her arms. "Did she say why she's here?" She curled her lip as she spat out the question which caused my chest to hurt.

"She's on a path to righteousness." I was trying to hide my disbelief and repulsion towards her tone. This was the same woman who did my hair and make up for junior prom. "She asks for your grace and understanding during her hour of repentance." I clipped. That shut her up.

She blinked a few times while plastering on one of the most disingenuous expressions I've ever seen. "Well of course." She scraped out, a smile on her face but a burning intensity in her eyes. It caused my spine to stiffen in discomfort. I figured if we gave them time, they'd come around and learn to accept her. It's what God would want.

Ethan had made his usual remarks about her needing to find another place to worship and seek mercy for her transgressions. "EC has tolerated her enough."

I clenched my fist, struggling not to project it forward into his face. I wanted to tell him if she leaves, I'll go too but decided against it. My family was still here after all, and she wasn't going anywhere. If he had such an issue with her, why didn't he leave? I decided instead on saying, "Well, I'll leave you to your bigotry and shallowness then."

"What?!" he'd shouted as I walked away, refusing to acknowledge his incredulity.

And now Eve is standing at my door.

"Eve, this isn't something noteworthy. She's attending the church," I say, walking to my kitchen, having no doubt she'd follow. "As the pastor's daughter, I refuse to ice people out. She's honestly very nice."

"As the pastor's daughter, you should be keeping up with appearances." She scoffs, shutting the door behind her before joining me.

"And what appearance should that be?" I say through gritted teeth, my back turned to her at the sink washing the glasses Blake and I dirtied this morning after she'd stayed over last night. We'd spent the night cuddling. It was truly amazing to be held and not have someone constantly groping me. Truthfully, we'd woken up late, and I hadn't had time to do my usual checklist before leaving for service.

"The congregation isn't happy, Phoebe. She isn't a part of our church. Your dad is offering her communion when she isn't even a member."

"Christ offered up His blood as the holy covenant in His name so we may all take and eat Eve, and with that meal, He cleansed us all of our sins. He wasn't selective on who was allowed to partake. He even fed Judas, knowing he had betrayed Him." I hand her a glass I'd filled with water from the sink.

"That might be true," she says, sinking into the barstool. "And there are plenty of churches out there that participate in open table. The Evangelical Church Of Mystic Harbor is not one of them, though."

"Well, why can't it be?" I slam my hand on the counter as my blood begins to seethe.

"The people voted, Phoebz!" she defends. "You and your dad are creating quite a stir! Don't get mad at me. I'm just telling you."

She's right. Blake is well aware of the powder keg her presence has within the church. It's the whole point, but I wonder what the match to blow the whole thing up is going to be. I start to think maybe Eve is right. I should distance myself from it because what if the church finds out about our little Bible sessions on Monday nights?

In all fairness, it isn't just Monday nights anymore. I've slept beside her—either at her house or mine—every night this week. Not necessarily sexually, but because I miss her when she isn't around. The warmth of her body makes me sleep better than ever. Kissing her goodbye each morning ties me over throughout the day. Even Dr. Auburn has commented on my overall performance this past week.

I'm happier. Fulfilled. I may not understand what is stirring up inside of me when I'm around Blake, but I know I don't want it to dissipate. I also don't want it to blow up the church, though. Or worse, jeopardize my father's career. That's something Piper might not have an issue with, but I'm not sure I could live with the weight of my recklessness quite like she can.

I tell myself learning more about Blake's lifestyle isn't a bad thing. Who knows? Maybe it'll better serve me in my attempts to bring us both back to His righteous path. I've fallen quite a way down this rabbit hole, but once I've completely purged myself of this longing, which I still don't fully understand, I know I can be forgiven.

"You know I love you, right?" Eve breaks through my contemplation by grabbing my hand and giving it a quick squeeze of reassurance. "I just don't want to see you go down for something she's doing."

"I know." I sigh, allowing her to hug me and truly hugging her back. "I love you too."

I should talk with Blake. Explain my concerns about my family's reputation. She'll find another church to continue her outreach. I know she wouldn't completely destroy my father and me just to spur up controversy. She would never use me and my family as a stepping stone to fulfill her and Jude's master plan. I have no doubt in my mind she cares about me.

✝

"Okay." I hand Blake a tool, leaning on her truck as she works underneath. It's the next day, and I'd slipped inside to grab her Bible, which was now propped on the open hood. "Romans."

She huffs, the sound of the tool clicking as she tightens something. Honestly, I know nothing about cars. I just hand my keys to a guy at the dealership, and he does my oil change. "Did you seriously get off work to come over for this?"

"'For this reason, God gave them over to dishonorable passions,'" I say, ignoring her. Romans had jumped into my brain around midday, and I'd even ran out to my car on lunch to leave a note on my dash to bring it up when I got off. "'Their females exchanged natural intercourse for unnatural, and in the same way also the males, giving up natural intercourse with females, were consumed with their passionate desires for one another. Males committed shameless acts with males and received in their own persons the due penalty for their error.'"

She slides out from under the truck, grabbing the ram bar on the grill to hoist herself up, wiping her hands on an orange towel. She's covered in oil. Even down her sleeveless arms. "Let me see that." She grabs the book from my hands. To be perfectly honest, I'm losing my resolve over her covered in dirt. *Play it cool, Appleton.* I take a sharp breath in.

"'For though they knew God, they did not honor him as God or give thanks to him, but they became futile in their thinking, and their senseless hearts were darkened.' They rejected God." She hands me the book back, walking inside.

I follow, still not finished. "And being gay isn't a way to reject God?" She turns on the kitchen sink and begins washing her hands. "Kind of seems like they're going against the entire reason we were created."

"Phoebe, it doesn't even say homosexuality is the 'unnatural' acts they were talking about. Read it again." Her shoulders slump as I try to find my place again in the book. "And during the Old Testament, multiplying was kind of necessary given the average life expectancy was thirty-five if you were lucky. Most didn't even survive their first year. Humans have billions of purposes now. Not just multiplying."

A moment of silence lingers between us as she raps her fingers on the counter, waiting for me to read the passage again. "I'm not seeing it."

She sighs, grabbing a paper towel off the spool and drying her hands before throwing the napkin in my face and grabbing the book once again. "'And in the same way also the males, giving up natural intercourse with females, were consumed with their passionate desires for one another. Males committed shameless acts with males and received in their own persons the due penalty for their error.' The 'natural' relation with a woman would be marriage and love. They were inflamed in lust, fucking anybody for whatever reason, whether they agreed to sleep with them or not. It doesn't say men fucked men, which is wrong. It also doesn't say women slept with women. It said they did unnatural things. Implying consent and love were not involved. Rape is never a natural or loving act, and women and men are both capable of raping a nonconsenting individual. It then goes on to say men committed shameless acts with other men. It said shameless. Not sexual. Couldn't they be saying they killed their neighbors together? Lied, stole, penetrated them by force. Love isn't mentioned in this passage, Phoebe. Just lust and a lack of shame over hurting people."

"Yeah, but wouldn't not bringing life into this world be classified as having sex just for the sake of climax rather than procreation? Isn't that the sheer definition of lust?"

Blake's expression is full of mischief and desire, taking a step closer. "For some...but I'm no different than you."

"I'm not—"

"I'm not saying you're gay, although recent developments would suggest otherwise." She kisses my neck before stepping back. "But that's your business. I'm saying I go to church. I pray. I don't worship or praise you above Him when I touch you. God will always be first in my heart. I'm not like the Romans. They didn't believe in Him or follow his commandments. We're not the same. Do I treat you like a Roman would?" Her eyebrow quirks in curiosity.

I prop myself up onto her counter, kicking my feet. "You treat me better than anyone." I grab her by the waistband and pull her in to settle between my legs on the counter.

The corner of her mouth rises as she her hands slide up the inside of my thighs. I lean down, kissing her softly.

"So do you." She presses her hand into my center over my pants. My lips part as air escapes past my teeth. "No one is completely black and white, Phoebe." My eyes snap shut as I bite my lip, focusing on the circles of her thumb over my clothes. "We're all shades of gray."

I move my hips in time to her wrist for a few moments before deciding I can't get more from this angle. And regardless of how turned on it makes me to fantasize about Blake making me orgasm right here on the counter, she's dirty. I'm probably covered in the sweat of the day—and people eat here. "Sexy as you are, all covered in oil," I say, allowing her another quick kiss before sliding down her body from the counter, "I need you showered." I grab her hand and guide her to the bathroom.

She seems to enjoy this answer as she follows me down the hall like I'm carrying a treat and she's starving. Or perhaps I'm the treat. Pretty sure it's the latter.

"Are you going to help me?" She practically sings the question as she licks her lips.

I stop her right outside the bathroom door. "You're not the only one who wants a shower."

Pressing her against the wall, I lock her into a kiss so passionate, the air escapes her. I love this version of myself. So comfortable around her, I can ask honest questions and she never seems to get mad or upset. She's enjoying the person coming out of my shell. Just like the day she took me to Stone's Throw Manor, she let me lead. Even knowing this trail well, she still allows me to experience it for myself. Hand in hers, ready to take over whenever I become overwhelmed. Spinning me in dance even when I don't know what I'm doing. She never pushes me into her lifestyle. I'm settling into understanding it gradually. Her face softens in adoration when I question her. So much patience.

"Now get naked." I push her back into the bathroom.

She sinks her teeth into her bottom lip, grabbing my waist as she pulls me into the small room with her. Pushing the door closed behind me she says, "You first."

✝

Thursday, I decide to visit Siren's Song for karaoke night. Blake insisted I see it. I spend entirely too long deciding on a pair of jeans that hug my hips and accentuate my butt. My shirt is slightly low cut, showing a modest amount of cleavage. I'm not sure why. I definitely wasn't trying to get Blake's attention. At least, that's what I told myself when I drove to a store in Cypress to buy it and not be seen by anyone on my side of town. I don't own anything even remotely close to this. I even hesitantly asked an employee their thoughts. The teenage boy appeared dumbstruck, nodding vigorously, so I took it as a good sign.

When I walk in it doesn't smell like the chemical lemon mop water this time. More like sweat and stale liquor. A spotlight shines down on a heavyset woman with pink hair on a riser, singing opera with heavy guitar behind it. Honestly, she's not a good singer in the slightest. Her voice is quite deafening as she stares at the words flashing across a flatscreen mounted from the ceiling, but she is giving it her all while others cheer. When she makes eye contact with me, I smile anyway. So glad she has that kind of courage. I'm not sure I could ever sing in front of people, regardless of the dim lights causing the crowd to be nothing more than faceless, cheering shadows. I'm tone deaf at best, always opting to nod my head rather than learn the words. Yet. I've been finding myself unexpectedly humming in the shower lately.

I'd love to hear Blake sing a song. Scanning the crowd to find her, but not. My chest sinks and I wonder if I should even be here if she isn't. *She said she works tonight. She can't not be here.* I've become entranced by her voice. My favorite thing to do lately is watch her sing along to the radio as we drive to literally wherever she wants to take me.

Our friendship has seriously ignited. There isn't a single place I'd rather be than beside her. When she's not around, I find myself missing her company, her voice, the sound of her breathing.

I sit down at the bar next to a man who smells like stale cigarettes and looks me up and down. I pretend to ignore him, propping my elbows on the rail. I'm greeted by a face that definitely isn't Blake. He rushes up with a certain feminine sway to his step.

"You're her," a short, baby-faced man with shaggy, dirty blond hair says, smiling rather flatly at my existence. His voice is quite feminine for a man. Almost higher pitched, and I wonder if his feminine features suggest he's gay. Not that I'm judging. Am I judging?

"Who?" I ask.

He flashes me some of the whitest teeth I've ever seen, which causes the dimple in his chin to become more prominent. "Phoebe."

How much does he know? Blake told me he knows I'm back in her life. This suggests he knew who I was before I'd even came to Siren's. What would she have told him about our past? Does he know about EC? If I say something unintentionally offensive, would he tell my family I was here? *I should leave,* I think.

He notices my discomfort instantly. "Blake is in the cooler. Can I get you something while you wait?"

"How do you know me?" I decide to ask rather than freak out on assumptions.

"Oh, honey." He chuckles. "I've known of you for years!"

"Y-years?" I stutter.

He leans in. "Between you and me, Blake has been gone on you for practically a millennium. You were stuck like glue on Dakota. Right when Blake stopped mentioning you, here you are." He waves his hand as if he is sprinkling magic dust in the air. His back is arched, his weight distributed to one hip as he asks again, "Drink?"

I learned my lesson from last time. "Just water." I need my car tomorrow and so no alcohol for me.

"Water?" He seems genuinely intrigued by my beverage choice as he scans me from bottom to top.

A new person is now on stage. A super scrawny woman with a men's haircut. "This one's for you, Cindy." She blows a kiss at a woman missing some teeth, now blushing at her—*how cute*—before singing a pop song about how amazing seeing her face is. It makes me wonder how genuine this type of expression with the same gender is. It seems weird to even witness. Almost as if they're playing house. Then again, it doesn't seem like make-believe between Blake and me.

This isn't at all similar to when I was younger with Melissa, rescuing the princess from the burning tree. This emotion seems genuine. I've seen women look at men like they hung the moon exactly how the woman with the missing teeth is beaming at the one singing right now. Completely authentic.

Is it possible to feel the same type of love?

Is it simply a play on the mind?

Crossed wires?

Could my emotions toward Blake actually be what falling in love feels like?

Is it possible to be hurt again by allowing myself to once again feel this strongly for her?

December my freshman year, I saw Dakota in her natural habitat, eating lunch alone. When she saw me approaching, her shoulders slumped. I placed my tray down. "You seem off."

Her short blonde hair cascaded over her face. Refusing to look up, she mumbled, "You should go sit with your friends."

"What?" I squinted at her. She knew there wasn't any place I'd rather be. "I wanna be with you."

Her dark eyebrows raised under the paleness of her blonde. Why wouldn't she look at me?

"Dakota," I said, shaking off the confusion, touching her stretched out wrist on the table, almost in my space. She pulled back, using it to straighten her shirt, shifting slightly.

Finally, her eyes met mine. The blue was as light as the sky, almost gray. "I don't need your pity, Phoebe. I'm not a charity case."

"I'm not—you're not a charity case." I shook my head. "We're not alone, remember?"

"Well." She tilted her head. "Now I'm asking you to fuck off."

My body immediately flooded with embarrassment. My blood ran cold, draining the color from my face. My eyes stung as I glanced around, making sure no one was witnessing this. Why would she ask me not to abandon her? Why would she even tell me she enjoyed my company?

"What did I do?" My bottom lip quivered, and I begged myself not to cry. I was embarrassed enough. I didn't need people seeing me cry over someone they viewed as an outcast.

Her eyes softened as she averted her gaze, setting her jaw. Was she about to cry too? Why was she doing this? "Listen, it was cool, you know?" She nodded, but it appeared as though she was trying to convince herself as she spoke. "But your friends miss you." She stood up, tray in hand, depositing it in the trash before leaving the cafeteria.

I sat there alone for a few more minutes, trying to focus on my breathing. Maybe she was having a bad day. I'd try again tomorrow, but when tomorrow came, she continued to avoid me. The second I sat down, she got up and left.

On the third day, I tried to follow. This seemed to really upset her. "Phoebe!" She whipped around, hands up, stopping me in the desolate hallway. "If you don't stop following me, I'm going to get a monitor involved!" Her voice raised. A monitor was an adult in our school who would de-escalate situations. Fights didn't happen more than once or twice in my school career. If someone was bothering you, you'd tell a monitor, and they'd stop the situation before it turned into a full-fledged altercation.

This planted my feet firmly on the ground, watching in shock as she stomped down the hall before disappearing into a bathroom twenty feet away. She shoved the door open so aggressively, I heard it crack into the wall on the inside. I wiped the tears from my face and decided to respect her wishes and stop trying.

When she became friends with Sam a few weeks later, I was relieved she wasn't sitting by herself anymore. So, when they had their falling out, I couldn't stand it. A few months had gone by and I needed to try again. Had to get her to let me back in. I needed her. I'd been so lonely. If I wouldn't have been stopped by Zoe and Eve, I would've. I would've tried to remind her I was still there. No matter how much she tried to push me away. I was ready for her to yell, to tell me to back off again. I needed her to know I wouldn't go anywhere.

When I found out what had supposedly happened with Sam, I felt I had no choice but to respect her request. *"Now I'm asking you to fuck off."*

Just go, I can't help you.

Yet Dakota never forgot me. Why did she stop our nightly adventures then? She stopped talking to me entirely. It didn't take long before she became friends with Sam and forgot about me. At least, I'd convinced myself she had. The day I met Dakota, she became the blueprint for the life I wanted. When she left, I lost sight of who I could become. I needed to believe I was insignificant or I would've never been able to let go of her like she needed me to.

"Gone on me? What do you mean?" I ask.

"Girl," he puts a hand on his hip and waves me off with the other, "it's such a long story. I could tell you things."

"I'd rather you didn't," Blake interjects, popping up beside him. Her eyes shooting him a warning.

What could he tell me? I wonder. Blake doesn't seem to want to go into very much detail about Dakota, but the vaguer she is, the more curious I get. How could she have kept friends if she used everyone and everything? The holes in her description of her past leave me vexed. I can't ignore the fact she hurt me when she pushed me away. Funny how I always assumed I'd abandoned her, but maybe it was the other way around. Zoe had her studies, and Eve had her boyfriends. When I lost Dakota, my weekends became empty. My life became constructed into what others needed and wanted of me. Maybe if Dakota would've stayed, I'd have found my individuality sooner.

No. I can't blame her for my spinelessness. As strong and brave as I felt when she was around, I should've found my voice on my own. Even now, being around her makes me stronger somehow. It makes me question who I've been molded into.

Maybe Piper was right. Maybe she is my spirit guide. Meant to hold my hand down this road of self-discovery. She's always brought that out of me.

It still begs the question of why God would take her from me when I was young, though. If this journey could've happened sooner, why was I meant to suffer for twelve more lonely years? Twelve years being forged into the perfect daughter. Perfect Christian. Always on my best behavior. Why choose now to bring her back into my life? It still doesn't make sense to me what could've changed. One day she was walking me to fifth period and the next she told me to stay away from her.

"You can't keep her all to yourself, Blake," he teases as I shift my gaze between them. "Eventually, you have to do actual work. Pretty sure Susan's already three sheets to the wind."

She sighs, pouring a brown liquor into a glass of ice before spraying in some dark soda. "I'll take care of it." Her eyes soften as she meets mine. "Don't listen to Delaney. He lives for drama." She winks, and my stomach leaps. Gosh, she's so pretty. It should be a crime. I want to feel her soft lips on mine right now.

"Were you going to sing something?" she asks, putting a lemon in the glass. Not her best attempt to shift the conversation, but I take the bait anyway, a minor buzz of irritation forming in my ears.

"And sing what? Today's top Christian?" I razz. I return my attention to Delaney. "So, you knew her?"

"Oh, yeah!" He pats her head as she tries to move away. "Find me later. I'll tell you about the time she—"

"Take this to Herman!" she interrupts, pointing to the drink she made. "He's been asking about you." She waggles her eyebrows.

Delaney rolls his eyes. "How many times do I have to reject him before he gets it?"

"Seventeenth times the charm?" One corner of her mouth curls upward as she fixes another drink.

"Find me later." He shoots Blake a mischievous glare before grabbing the glass and walking away. A certain dance to his step.

"Don't," she urges.

†

"Girl, Susan's throwing up all over the ladies' room." Delaney sidles up next to Blake, breaking our eye contact—which admittedly was lingering a little longer than it probably should've. "And she may or may not be passed out on the floor in there."

"Fucking aye, Delaney. Why didn't anyone cut her off?"

He throws her a disbelieving glare. "Blame your waitress! I know better."

"I'll be right back," she says, squeezing my hand before heading to the bathrooms. I strangely long to lean over the counter and give her a parting kiss, but refrain. This is starting to become a habit. Instead, I watch the way her skinny jeans hug her hips as they sway in the direction of the bathroom.

"I see you looking," Delaney teases.

"What? No, I'm just—" I sink in the barstool, gluing my eyes to my glass of water.

"She told me you were in denial, but I didn't think it was this painful to watch." He raises an eyebrow and crosses his arms.

"I'm not in denial. I'm not a…"

"A lesbian?" He wrinkles his nose, like he doesn't believe me.

"Why does everyone keep calling me that?" My body flushes with irritation and embarrassment again. Is it true what Eve said back in high school? Just associating with Blake somehow makes me guilty of being like her? Or am I right in believing Blake talked to him about how stupid I probably look when I climax? Because there isn't a single doubt in my mind he knows. "Is it not possible to be Blake's friend without going down with the ship?"

"I love your word choice," he responds smugly. "Going down." He holds my gaze resiliently, noticing immediately when my eyes go wide. "And it's fine. I don't care who's going down on whose ship, but if you don't grant yourself acceptance soon, it's going to destroy whatever ship you think you're on."

"There's no ship." I pick at my nail nervously, trying to hide my shakiness. He tsks, making me crave for this conversation to find safer waters. "Dakota." I clear my throat.

He tilts his head and adorns a mischievous expression. "Go on."

"She…" How do I word this without seeming desperate? I decide there is no right way, so I just come out with it. "What did you mean when you said she was 'gone on me?'"

He squints. "She'd never admit it to you because it'd show weakness, and Blake would never admit that to the common man. Then again…" He shifts his gaze around, making sure she's not approaching before leaning over the bar. I follow until we are practically nose to nose. "You're not the 'common man' now, are you?"

"I'm-I'm not sure," I stammer.

He rests his heavy hand on my shoulder. "You left quite the imprint on Dakota, Phoeb. Try as she might to pry you off her soul, you were like some kind of sticky thing she couldn't detach from. An adhesive."

The loud crack of someone sending a white ball into a bunch of colored balls rings out on the pool table behind us and it takes my brain a second to register it hadn't come from my brain. She was about as sticky as a band aid after swimming the last few months before her transfer. Seems like Blake left that part out. "She told me to leave her alone."

His eyebrows raise in delight at this information. "Can you blame her?"

"Blame her?" I can't decide if I enjoy talking to Delaney or not. He seems friendly yet abrasive all at once. Not to mention disgustingly misinformed. I narrow my eyes. "I've done nothing wrong." It comes out a little bit more defensive than I intend it to, but where does he get off? He doesn't know how abandoned I felt after her. How every now and again I could've sworn I saw her.

How many times in the past twelve years I'd slept in her hoodie just to feel closer to her.

Even after her scent had completely vanished from the woven strands, I still clung to the illusion she was with me and I wasn't alone. Honestly, who abandoned who? The thought circled around and around in my brain like buzzards, buzzed like a swarm of a thousand bees. Pricked my skin and tore apart my flesh until I was completely exposed to this man who knew absolutely nothing of our past. My absence was a direct result of her incessant need to push me away. My actions should be justified given I'd all but respected her wishes to be left alone.

"Phoebe, look at you!" He throws his hands up in disbelief. "You don't think denying your feelings for her doesn't hurt her?"

I drop my shoulders as the music from the jukebox becomes a distorted mesh of dissonant sounds. The room spins as my hands quiver in anger. Words are inconceivable because I'm not denying how I feel about her. I've always cared for Blake. Even when she was Dakota.

She left *me*. Her exact words were to fuck off. I feel like I'm back in high school, glancing around the cafeteria, trying not to cry as she tells me to leave her alone. My face is hot, and I can't even pretend to be okay with the fact that maybe everyone in here notices me with Blake. Like it's the funniest thing in the world to not know who you are. Like they know me better than I know myself.

"Okay." I slam my hand on the counter. Before I can even comprehend how to correctly address this situation, I find myself holding my hands up. Words spewing out of me like vomit. "I don't know what you think, you know, but I've always cared about her." The more I speak, the more tense I become. My palms are starting to sweat. "Dakota called off our friendship, not the other way around.

I even tried to follow her until she threatened to involve a mediator to practically pry me off of her. So, I don't know what she told you, Delaney, but I never left her. She left me!" I wipe at my face, feeling even more stupid for not realizing when the tears had started. "And I was devastated. For twelve years." I rise to my feet. My cheeks burn and I no longer feel welcome in this space. I want to leave. My eyes sting at my refusal to continue being the butt of this sick joke where I'm the enemy of her screwed up past. Whatever may have happened, I guess I'll never get an answer because I'm done. Done feeling stupid. Done being confused. Done being gawked at like I'm some kind of...of...

"And she was the adhesive, Delaney!" He doesn't deserve these tears, and neither does Blake. "There hasn't been a single day since I backed off. I haven't thought about her. What she was doing. Where she was. Why she *fucking left me*."

Why am I shouting? Delaney picking at this scab has me realizing it never properly healed. How could it? She refuses to tell me what happened. But now I know she's painted me as the bad guy. I'm the reason she used people. The reason she did horrible things. It's starting to make sense now why she won't answer a single one of my questions with any semblance of detail. She keeps it vague enough to leave out I'm the monster in her past.

"So don't act like you know me! And don't act like you know us!" With shaking hands, I grab my jacket. "Tell Blake I said goodbye."

Chapter 20

Blake

"Where'd Phoebe go?" I ask Delaney when I return thirty minutes later. Admittedly, it took longer than I'm proud of to get Susan off the floor and into a cab before mopping up all the vomit.

"Beats me." He lifts a shoulder, which lets me know he's directly responsible for her absence.

"What the fuck did you do?" I bark.

He holds up his hands in defense. "Nothing," he hums. "I just gingerly told her she needs to come out of that stuffy church closet and start giving my girl the love and devotion she deserves."

I know him better than that. He has never had a good bedside manner in his life. I have no doubt he told her off, which caused her to spook.

"Bullshit," I say, gritting my teeth and clenching my fists, leashing back the urge to punch him. "What did you say, exactly?"

"That's what I said!" he says, holding up two fingers. "Scout's honor."

"Fuck, Delaney!" I search around as if I'll find my composure sitting somewhere by the jukebox. "You're closing," I say, grabbing my keys from under the bar and storming out.

✝

It's around midnight when I find myself at her doorstep knocking with so much urgency, I think I might pound the door off its hinges. I can't breathe. I want to fucking *kill* Delaney. I was trying desperately to stay near them so he wouldn't be able to do what he just did. It was stupid of me to think Delaney would behave himself when I knew he had issues with Phoebe to begin with. Especially given he has never been known for his ability to hold back his opinions.

The sound of her throwing something soft at the door comes before she screams, "Go away, Blake!" anger thread through her words. "I seriously don't want to see you right now."

"Just let me in," I plead exasperatedly.

Her footsteps stomp across her apartment before the door violently swings open, and she positions herself against the frame.

"Why should I?" she growls. "I'm the asshole, right?"

I step back slightly from the curse word. "Language?" I attempt hoping some lighthearted humor might quell the ferocity of her demeanor slightly. I've never seen her so irate. I honestly didn't think she even had an aggressive bone in her body. The loss of all control.

"Oh, shut up!" she shouts, causing me to step back. "How bad am I in the stories you tell your friends, huh? Because it doesn't seem like anyone knows about the amazing time you told me to—what was the proper verbiage?—'fuck off?'"

I'm shocked she's making such a big scene in this hallway. A lovers' quarrel for all the neighbors to hear. This isn't her at all.

Vexation has taken the wheel while she sits in the backseat, allowing it to call the shots. It's disconcerting to stand here and watch my meticulously put-together Phoebe fall victim to this indignation.

"Delaney doesn't know shit. Just—just let me talk to you." I look around in embarrassment before whispering, "You really want the neighbors to hear this?"

Her eyes dart between mine as she mulls it over before finally conceding. Pushing away from the wall, she opens the door wider for me to come inside.

I stand at the door, watching her stomp to the kitchen, fill a cup at the sink, not even bothering to offer me one.

"Did you tell them I was a…" Her words taper off with such disdain as she grinds her teeth. Her reddening eyes form puddles at the bottom as her chin quivers. Why is she so scared to say it? "They think I'm…" She shakes violently as she stammers. Finally, she collects her thoughts enough to yell, "You told me to leave you alone! What do you tell your friends, Blake? That I ditched you in high school. That it's my fault your life went bad? Because Delaney thinks I'm a piece of shit. *I* hurt *you,* apparently!"

"No, he doesn't." I walk on wobbly legs to the couch, collapsing before resting my head in my hands. *I really am going to kill him.* "He doesn't know I pushed you away." I rub my face. "Only that in doing so, I hurt myself pretty badly."

"Why?!" Phoebe slams her hands down on the counter. "I was nice to you! I was your only friend, Blake. It doesn't make sense. You said I wasn't alone but," she hiccups, pacing now, "no one understood me. Only you did. I was so embarrassed. So hurt. So—"

Before she can finish her thought, I'm rising from my seat, hooking my arm around the small of her back, pulling her body into mine, and stealing a kiss. Her whole body weakens into me as she pulls in a sharp breath.

"I know," I say calmly into her neck. "I'm so sorry. If I could go back, I would do everything completely different."

I tumble around the memories leading to the worst decision of my life as a pit forms in my stomach. A pit longing to be filled with something—anything. A scream coming from the base of my brain, demanding I shut it off. "I had to," I finally admit.

"No, you didn't."

"I would've ruined you." My heavy hands drop to her waist. "Sometimes, I worry even now, resurfacing in your world is only going to get you hurt."

"I can handle myself," she protests. *If only she knew...*

"No, you really can't," I groan, fingers involuntarily pressing into her sides. "You refused to see how people looked at you every time you sat down next to me. A quality I love but..."

"I don't care. Blake, I didn't care—"

"Yes, you do!" I spew out. I'm so tired of her ignorance. She doesn't see it. Refuses to admit it. "You act like you don't, but you definitely do. You care what everyone thinks. Always have. You wouldn't have let me in just now if you didn't."

"That's different!" She pushes off me slightly. She thinks she can choose when conditions work and don't work for her. Turn a blind eye to the way of the world.

"Phoebe, it's not! Would you ever leave Ethan? How many of your friends know about what we've been doing? How you warm your hands between my thighs when we snuggle on the couch watching House? How many times have we been seen out in public? I'm your dirty little secret!"

"People would get the wrong idea."

"The wrong idea?" My chest aches as I cast my eyes away from her incredulously. The way I see it, she just admitted giving this a chance is wrong. Facing the world with me is too embarrassing. "Really? Tell me, Phoebe, what's the 'wrong' idea?" I step back from her, completely pushing out of her embrace.

"That I'm—I-I don't know." She shakes her head violently like her brain is an etch-a-sketch and being a lesbian is a bad drawing she can just get rid of. "You expect us to walk around town holding hands?" she spits out disbelievingly. I'm not sure how she can find comedy in this. As if my feelings aren't valid. Being gay is somehow a joke to her. It's not real and I'm not really falling for her. "Kissing?" Can she seriously convince herself what we have is make-believe? "I can't—" she chokes.

"Forget it!" I shout, turning to leave, my entire body thrumming with at least a dozen undecipherable emotions—maybe even a sprinkle of humiliation—I don't fucking know, but it hurts like a bitch and I need a painkiller to numb this dull ache beginning to manifest in my ribcage.

"What do you want from me, Blake?" she shouts, defeated, standing in place.

"I want you!" I yell, whipping around to face her, dropping my arms at my sides.

Her eyes flood. The words land like a blow, forcing her to stagger back slightly. It hit like a factory reset to her cerebellum.

"Blake," she begins, chest heaving as she hyperventilates, bunching her shirt in her fists. Her eyes scan the room as her brain scrambles to fabricate more excuses to justify her recent actions. She's been running from this for too long, avoiding it. Disassociating and convincing herself fucking me hasn't been her. It was someone else entirely. "What's happening to me?" She sobs uncontrollably as I watch, fighting every urge to wrap her up and tell her to forget it. Let everything go back to the way it was. Fun. Simple. I'd give anything to keep her from experiencing these feelings...

...But she has to feel them—I can't take this from her. It's vital. Enough is enough, and she needs to accept this. It's real. I'm real. Being a lesbian is very, very real. "Why can't I keep myself from you? This isn't who I'm supposed to be. Wh-who am I?"

I walk her to the couch, gently laying her down, pressing my entire body weight onto her chest as I lay on top of her in a swaddled embrace. Trailing my nose up the side of her neck, I take in her passionflower scent before placing a kiss on her jaw. "Say gay, Phoebe," I whisper.

She lets out a heaving breath as her whole body spasms with the next words. "I'm not."

"Please," I soothe. "Please. Not for everyone else. Just once. For yourself. No one has to know. It'll stay here."

"I'm not gay. I'm normal." She turns her head away, squirming underneath me.

"You can be both, baby." I glide my fingers through her hair.

She takes in a deep, sputtering breath, burying her head into my shoulder. Her chest heaves painfully as she sobs into me for minutes. I listen to the sound of her disparaging sobs reverberating off the walls, engulfing our bodies on this couch. I hold her in this as her body sweats and shudders in my encapsulated embrace.

"I like you," she eventually whispers unsteadily. I lift my head to capture her vulnerable expression. "I miss you when you're not here. I can't stop thinking about you." Her lip quivers as her entire body convulses while confessing. "I—I might be gay." She sobs.

I let out a breath of relief. *Finally!*

"I'll take it." I bracket her face in my hands, thumbs stroking the tears from her cheeks. I'm smiling as I try to suppress the elation overwhelming me. "I might be gay, too." And with that, she's laughing through her tears. "Shut up." She smacks my arm, but it's a step. *A step toward keeping her,* I think as I press my lips firmly against hers.

Chapter 21

Phoebe

That night, I watch Blake's sleeping body twitching beside me in my bed. My mind is flooded with so many questions still left to answer. Why can't I seem to stop this?

Her laying beside me feels so natural. *"You can be both, baby."* Can I still be normal if I'm gay?

What's to say Blake won't come into my life, mess with my brain, make me desire the unspeakable, then push me out left questioning everything I've done? My chest hurts as I think about it. Is this infatuation? I can't breathe. I've been avoiding thinking about this, but logistically speaking, it doesn't matter whether it's one girl, one time, or a million girls, a million times. It's still gay.

The thought crashes into me like a tidal wave. What about Ethan? Should I stop the engagement or stop this? Piper said the new me wasn't stupid, but I feel pretty damn stupid right now.

Calling off the engagement will end terribly. I'd still have Piper, but my mother would probably disown me. Would my father? Is admitting my attraction to Blake worth losing my friends? Would Blake and Piper be enough?

We've spoken about different takes of the same Bible and what it says about homosexuality. Would I be forced to go to a church I'm not sure can possibly follow God properly? What if Blake is wrong and EC is right? If I fully and completely give in, what will happen to my soul?

One step at a time, I decide. *"No one has to know,"* she'd said. I hope she means it. I think I'm falling in love with Blake.

Chapter 22

Blake

Me (2:36 PM)
I need help

Dylan (2:37 PM)
First off, are you okay?

Me (2:37 PM)
Yes...

I tap my phone to my face, thinking.

Me (2:37 PM)
No.

That seems slightly overdramatic.

Me (2:37 PM)
Honestly...Idk

Dylan (2:38 PM)
Talk to me

Me (2:38 PM)
Phoebe

My phone vibrates in my hand as I see Dylan's name appear on the screen. "Hello?"

"I'm going to need more than that, Blake. Are you okay? Are you hurt? Are you having a hard time reflecting on the past again? What can I do for you? Do you want me to come over?"

"Slow down, Dyl!" I interject. "Take a breath."

"Sorry," she huffs. "I'm glad you called me. What's going on?"

"I…" How do I word this? I rub the back of my neck. "I was doing some outreach—"

"It's only been three months since Jude died, B. Why are you trying to start that up so soon?" Dylan knows me and I know it's not going to take her long to figure it out. She doesn't pause for more than a second before the answer flies out. "You were trying to pull a kamikaze, weren't you?"

"You know me too well." I run my hand through my hair. Pacing down the hallway to my bathroom. "But that's not the point here. I ran into Phoebe. She didn't know who I was, which I thought was fine."

I hear hammering in the background. "Actually, that's fucked, and you know it, but proceed."

"What are you making?" I say, trying to divert the conversation to safer waters.

"A new bedframe for the Millers, but don't think I can't see what you're doing, Blake."

"Okay, fine, yes. It was a little fucked up. She knows now, though." I stare at myself in the mirror of my bathroom, bracing myself against the counter. "We'd kind of started…" Fucking? Well, she'd only been penetrating me and I'd hate to spread lies about Phoebe's innocence. Sleeping together then? That could work. I tilt my head in the mirror, remembering her face this morning buried in the crook of my neck as she sighed deeply in her sleep. Her leg slung lazily over my body as if possessing every inch of me. Making sure I wouldn't leave again. "Umm…" I've never slept better in my life. I clear my throat. "Getting to know each other, and she found out who I was."

A clatter lets me know she's dropped the hammer. "You've been having sex with her, and she didn't even know who you were?"

I rub my face. "No, well, not exactly. Like…she doesn't know she's gay, so…" It sounds stupid coming out of my own mouth. *We've been messing around, but she has no idea she's gay.* Ugh.

"Blake. Tell me what you did?"

"Nothing!" *Much.* "She's a virgin, but she kind of…maybe—"

"Blakeeeee," she whines. I listen as the door hinges to her old barn squeal open before clattering closed behind her. I guess the content of my confession has caused her to stop her carpentry. "Noooo."

"It'd be better if you'd act more like my fucking sponsor instead of my judge," I growl, turning on my heel, unable to endure my reflection any longer. I'm feeling too much like Dakota to keep up the charade. Dakota was notorious for acting sweet and innocent just to seduce someone like Phoebe. The thought I would do that to her fills me with unexpected anger.

"Right." She takes a deep breath. Her dog Boot whines as she enters her house. He typically follows her all over the property, but I guess since she was using power tools, she'd saved him the trauma. "I'm sorry. Yes. Tell me what's going on."

"I really, really like her, Dyl. Like, *really* like her—"

"Oh, well, good to know that never changed."

"And now that she's found out, she's been asking a lot of questions and, you know, me. This shit is hard to talk about, and I *really* want to use, and she keeps bringing up Dakota, but I know she deserves to know, you know?"

"So, you need me to be there when you explain and answer questions?"

"If you don't mind." I wince. I hate asking people for shit. I know Dylan is different. She loves me and would do anything to keep me sober and doing right for the community, but it still doesn't make being vulnerable enough to admit I need help any easier.

"What time?" she asks without the least bit of imposition in her tone. Dylan has always made me a priority in her life. For whatever reason, she has made it her life's mission to never leave my side. Such should be expected from the person who started the first ever NA group in Mystic Harbor, but for whatever reason, she has always held me and my opiate addiction high above anything and everything else in her life.

"Could you be here at five?"

Flash forward to right now, where I'm sitting on my couch tapping my leg, waiting rather nervously for Phoebe to show up. I don't know why I'm so nervous. I've told this story so many times to a room full of strangers, but this is different. It's Phoebe. What if she sees me differently? What if she hates me? I've never much given a shit if people judged me, but what if Phoebe can't see past it?

I'm not going to go into too much detail. I'm going to tell her the basics and answer questions. I'll start at the beginning and tell her the bare minimum, but slightly more than I've been doing, and Dylan will be there. It'll be okay.

It'll be okay. My new mantra. I hear a knock at my door, springing me to life. It's fine. Everything is fine. I need to get it together and tuck it in because if I don't, I'll lose her.

I open the door only to have the breath stolen from my lungs as I'm met with the most beautiful green eyes I've ever set sight on. The corners of her mouth stretch impossibly big, her entire face exposing the whitest teeth known to man. Wish my mom could've afforded braces like hers had. I especially love the way they light up for me. Even in the cafeteria all those years ago, that specific exuberance has always been mine.

"Hi," she says softly, lowering her head nervously after our gazes linger for slightly too long.

"Hi." I rub my neck. "Ready for tonight?" I ask, leading her inside. If I spend too long thinking about it, I'll change my mind.

"You still haven't told me what we're doing here," she reminds me as I interlace our fingers, stopping right before the couch.

"Does it matter?" I ask, grabbing her waist and stepping closer.

She blinks her long lashes a few times before biting her lip. "I guess not. Can I have a hint, though?" she teases.

I stifle the exuberant admiration of being in her presence. As nervous as I am at the thought of losing her once I admit who Dakota had become after they'd known each other, the hope my confessions will bring us closer together is a greater emotion. I want the ocean with her. The moon and the stars. I know it's lame, but I need her. And if knowing my past is what it takes to keep her, I have to give in. "You wanted to know what happened to Dakota, right?"

She bounces slightly with excitement and fuck if it isn't the cutest thing. "Yes."

"Best way for me to do that is to introduce you to the person who helped me become Blake."

"Oh." She shifts nervously. "Do they know I—we..." her voice tapers off.

I knew she didn't want the Holy Side finding out about what we were doing, but I've always trusted my people. I mean, we practically run an underground homo railroad, for fuck's sake. Confidentiality is kind of our bread and butter. I know the entire point of tonight is about honesty and laying everything out on the table, so I can't start it by lying about this.

I tilt my head from shoulder to shoulder before raising them. "In lesser words, yes. She does."

Phoebe's eyes widen and dart around the room. "Okay," she says, messing with the ends of her hair in a manner I assume is meant to calm her. Calm hasn't exactly been her strength when it comes to her sexuality, however. "Okay, this is fine." She starts pacing, chewing on her lip considerably. "Why did you tell them?" she finally shrieks, spinning to face me, throwing up her hands. "Blake, I'm not—"

"Phoebe, stop," I say, grabbing her wrists to stop her gesticulation. "Relax. My friends wouldn't run over to the Holy Side and gossip. We kind of pride ourselves on our ability to conserve people's privacy." I'm about to move in closer when another knock lands on my door. "That's her."

When I open the door, I'm met with the familiar face and hazel eyes I'd confided in a hundred times during my road to sobriety. Her olive skin and braided black hair had become a comfort while I detoxed.

She ruffles my hair as I smack her hand away. Like an older sister, she always enjoys fucking with me. Then she notices Phoebe hiding nervously behind me. "I'm so sorry!" She gives Phoebe her award-winning, ever-famous, heartwarming grin, exposing every pearly white tooth she possesses. "Where are my manners? I'm Dylan Sorenson. Blake's sponsor." She extends her hand as Phoebe returns the gesture.

"Phoebe," she says, catching the contagion of Dylan's beam, mirroring it back to her. Does Phoebe even know what a sponsor is? It was stupid of me to not fill her in before inviting her over. I've never even mentioned Dylan until now.

Dylan's hand stops shaking as she peers up into her eyes. "The infamous Phoebe." Her eyes dart to mine. "My goodness, Blake wasn't kidding. You're absolutely gorgeous!"

My face flushes crimson. Leave it to Dylan to completely embarrass me by giving away the random nights I spent gushing about how I'd never find a woman as beautiful as Phoebe, so why even try? To which she'd told me I had no way of knowing until I tried. A part of me enjoyed seeing the realization hit Dylan as she laid eyes upon the most perfect specimen of all of God's creations.

"Thank you. It seems I'm quite known," she remarks, her face also pinkening as she fidgets with the hem of her shirt. Maybe this was a bad idea. She's getting overwhelmed, and I haven't even started telling her who I used to be. I should call the whole thing off. Right?

I turn to Dylan, who is urging me not to puss out. "Dylan is my sponsor," I supply again not really knowing what to say next.

"Yeah…she said that." Phoebe shifts between the two of us before adding, "What is that?"

Addiction isn't in her church bubble. Of course she has no fucking clue what a sponsor is.

"She's umm…" I gesture for Dylan to speak. *Help me out here.*

"I'm like a sober buddy," Dylan chimes in, saving me from what I know would've been a terrible explanation. "I help her through the twelve-step program by providing support night or day to ensure she keeps a sober life."

Some of the things I've put Dylan through are downright embarrassing. Needless to say, I'm not trying to dive down that rabbit hole. "She's seen me at my absolute worst. She's fought tooth and nail for my sobriety."

She snorts. "And her nails are deadly."

"How many times do I have to apologize?"

"None." She winks playfully. "That's why I'm your sponsor. I love you unconditionally. In all your forms. Blake, Dakota, Dakota Blake Chapel. You're like a little sister to me at this point."

"I couldn't have done it without you, Dyl. Seriously." Knowing I have her in my corner fills my heart with so much warmth. No matter how this goes, I know I can fall back on Dylan, and she'll hold me up until I can do it for myself again. I can't speak to the dynamic of other people and their sponsors, but Dylan is literally family.

"So," Dylan says, clapping before pushing past me and placing her hand on the small of Phoebe's back. She guides her to my couch while saying, "I heard you have some questions, and I'm sure you have figured out by now Blake here is absolute shit at talking about her past." She gestures with her thumb over her shoulder at me as Phoebe slowly sinks down into the cushions. "When dealing with her history, she unfortunately shuts down and starts fiending. I'm honestly surprised she hasn't dashed to the closest medicine cabinet yet. So, I'm here to facilitate that dialogue and ensure she doesn't skimp on the details you need. Right?" She quirks an eyebrow at me.

"Yeah," I say sheepishly, turning toward Phoebe, who seems to be taking it all in.

Dylan holds up her hand. "I'd also like to express the severity of her addiction, while I'm at it." She shoots me a knowing look before addressing Phoebe once more. "The more you get to know about Blake, the more you'll realize just how fragile her sobriety is." She meets my eyes. "I know you've been sober for five years now, Blake, but your brother just died. So, I'm in full support of what you'd like to do here—I understand how much Phoebe has always meant to you." She places a hand over her chest. "But you need to understand, opening up this can of worms a mere three months after Jude's death is going to stir up some settled dirt within her, if you catch my drift."

Phoebe presses her eyes closed tightly while inhaling sharply through her nose. "Okay." She nods smoothing her hands over her tightly pressed thighs.

"If at any point, you begin to worry about her mental stability, I need you to reach out to me or Delaney. Can you do that?"

"Yes," Phoebe says nodding once more. "I promise."

"Okay." Dylan nods. "Good." She holds her hand out gesturing to me. "Please proceed."

I join Phoebe on the couch, placing my hand over hers on her leg. "I know it may seem weird needing someone here to be able to talk about this with you, Phoebe, and I need you to understand first and foremost why that is."

Dylan walks confidently into my kitchen, making herself at home. Quite frankly, when I'm not sparring with her at her house, she's over here. In the beginning, she'd spent practically all her time here with Jude and me. You don't want to go up against her in Uno. She opens my cabinets and places some cups down on the counter as she listens intently.

"That'd be nice," Phoebe says, sitting with her back straight, her palms now squeezed together in between her tightly closed thighs.

Dylan cracks open a few cans of soda, pouring them into the cups. She rolls her wrist without looking up, urging me to keep going.

"I trust you," I continue. "A-and I really care about you." I inhale deeply before letting it out. "It's just…"

Dylan sets down the cups on the table in front of us as discomfort rips through my train of thought. "Coasters, Dyl," I practically shout it through the anxiety. "Please."

"I know, I know," she groans, grabbing the wooden blocks from their holder. "Don't stop now. You were on a roll."

"Dakota was a really tough period of my life. All of my hurt and pain stem from there. Which, in turn, is where my need to use is rooted. You've been unintentionally unearthing some really hard things. I've, umm." What if this is a bad idea? I worry having another person here might make her feel attacked or outed. I hate this. "I've never really been good at talking about my life."

"Yeah," she sighs. "I know. Even as kids, you'd still tell me just enough, omitting the rest. I never pushed you because I knew how much it hurt you to talk about." Her eyes move to Dylan as she slumps down onto the recliner. Her eyebrows pinch together. "It's just…things are different for me now. I've gotten to uh," she clears her throat and closes her eyes tightly, "gotten to know you a little better—"

Dylan shoots me a glance as if asking if Phoebe is aware Dylan knows about us. I nod in response. She returns the nod in understanding.

"And I feel like maybe I'm entitled to a little bit of clarity on the gap between then and now." Phoebe opens her eyes, peering around the room to monitor any negative reactions. Relief washes over her expression upon not finding any.

I rub my neck. "I know, and you deserve that."

She glances between Dylan and me. "Can I know what you were addicted to exactly?"

I suck in a breath. "Opiates, mostly." I confess. "But in all honesty, if I needed an escape, I'd abuse anything, to avoid being sober."

"There wasn't a single thing that wouldn't lead her straight back down the road to painkillers." Dylan adds. "Relapse number two taught us even alcohol isn't safe."

"But alcohol was always my last choice," I supply. "Which is why it's easy for me to bartend. I hate being drunk."

"That was going to be my next question." She let out a nervous laugh. "Okay, so, can someone tell me how it started? Like, what happened to the sweet Dakota I knew and cared about?"

"Sweet?" Dylan echoes, snorting. "Man, how long ago did you know Dakota?"

I shoot her a dagger-filled glare.

"I-I knew her when we were fourteen. Freshman year." Phoebe's eyebrows pinch together in confusion.

"Aww." Dylan beams. "Baby Dakota. I bet she was fucking cute."

"She was!" Phoebe declares. Her eyes soften as they settle on me. "And sweet. She'd throw stones at my window, build me blanket forts, and sneak me out just to look at the stars!" My stomach flips at her reminiscence of me. "Why does everyone keep acting like she's this terrible person? I can't see it!"

"Damn, Blake." Dylan sneers. "Little softy you."

I punch her arm. "Don't piss me off, Dyl," I say, narrowing my eyes.

"Bring it on, you little sap," she needles back. Dylan is the only person I've ever met who isn't afraid to take me head on. Nothing about me has ever intimidated her. Then again, when you've been doing mixed martial arts practically your entire life, I'm sure a kid with a temper isn't all that scary. She's found hundreds of ways to subdue me without ever throwing a punch.

I sigh, rubbing the back of my neck again. "Where do I start?" Making a mental timeline of where everything started shifting south is more difficult than I thought it would be. "Umm…" I shift my gaze toward Dylan for help.

"Don't look at me, fam. It's your story." She waves me off, taking a sip of her drink.

"When I was ten…" Fuck, I hate this. "I had the best dad. He would play with me and read me bedtime stories." I remember the tickle fights and wrestling matches. Helping me with homework, since Jude got his brains, not me. "One day, he came home from a long day at work, and I wanted him to play with me. I begged him to push me on the swings. He'd put it together the day before. I'd been waiting all day for him to come home so he could do underdogs with me." I sniffle, clearing my throat. "Fuck, this is so much harder than it should be after sixteen years!"

Phoebe puts her hand on my knee.

"H-he had the same condition as Jude. SCD—Sudden Cardiac Death. He umm…"

I search toward Dylan, needing a boost. She gives me a thumbs up. "You got this, bro."

"He died pushing me on the swings." The back of my eyes sting as I swallow past the lump forming in my throat. "My body came back and knocked him down, actually. I held him in my arms, Phoebe."

"Oh my gosh!" She wipes away a stray tear I didn't know had escaped. "Blake, I knew he died. I didn't know you were there. It makes sense why you don't talk about it."

I shake my head defiantly, gently wrapping my fingers around her wrist. "I thought it was my—"

"Stop," Phoebe whispers, shaking her head. "You don't have to tell me anymore. I understand if you—"

"No," I interrupt. "You need to know. You deserve to know." More as a reminder to myself not to back down. To keep going.

She's going to continue asking questions and I can't avoid this forever. If I want to spend the rest of my life with her by my side, she has to know me. Has to know how Blake rose from the ashes she'd once known as Dakota.

"For a long time, I blamed myself. I didn't understand the condition. Didn't know how it worked." I search my mind for the words but all I feel is the hurt as I relive the scene over and over in my mind. "I told myself if I wouldn't have asked him to push me. If I would've let him rest like he'd wanted, maybe…" I drift off, remembering the smell of his cologne when my head would rest on his round, dad belly. The way my head would bounce as he laughed at the TV. "My mom and him constantly argued over how to parent us. See, my mom suffers from severe depression." Heat washes over my shoulders at the shitty way my mother handled our formative years after his death. "I could write an entire autobiography on my relationship with her alone," I shake my head, "but what it really boils down to is, she didn't know how to raise my brother and me after he died. She's a very dependent person, and working was out of the question."

I take a sip of my soda. My mouth is so damn dry. This is going to be such a long story. "So, after my dad's death, two things happened. My mom started drinking even more heavily than she already had been." My nostrils flare as my body grows rigid. "And she would jump from man to man, hoping they could save her from being a single mother." For her to think I'd ever have gone on that trip to Italy with her and Greg, astonishes me. I don't care if she claims to be sober now. "I blamed myself." I continue. "She wouldn't have been struggling to raise us if it wasn't for me. She refused my help at first, but after a while, I don't think she had much of a choice. The men she was bringing around were either not good people or couldn't handle her random bouts of depression."

If Jude were alive, even he wouldn't have been able to convince me to go to Italy with that woman. Deciding to vacation one month after burying your son is a whole other topic that has no place within this conversation, though.

"Then she met Austin. He was a Holy Sider and abusive toward her, but he was a lawyer and had money, which is why she stayed. He's the reason I was forced to go to Mystic rather than Cypress." There. That should sum it up. She witnessed that part. Right? No need for details there. I chew on my cheek, realizing if I don't throw her the missing details, the story will remain convoluted.

It's just…

This is the part I dread most…

"That's when you met me." Phoebe grabs my hand, squeezing tightly.

And what a blessing it was having her during the hell that is this part of the story.

"Yeah. Which was literally the only thing I had going for me. The day I ran into you napping in the park, Austin had literally shoved Jude and me out of the house so he could beat on my mom without us being there." I ground my teeth together, watching Phoebe's eyes grow wide. "I had dropped Jude off at the library when I saw you." My eyes light up at the memory of Phoebe sprawled out under an old elm tree. Her arm slung over her face as the other rested flat on her belly. A jacket balled up beneath her head. One leg tucked under her knee. So beautiful. So calm. Not a care in the world. I wanted that peace, that calm. I wanted to steal it for myself. I needed it more than she did.

"Then…" I wiped another tear that had decided to sneakily roll down my cheek. "Then you told me, 'There will always be room for you in my spaces.' And I just…" I let out a huff. "I needed you. I needed to bring you to all of my spaces. I needed to fill those spaces with memories of you." Stone's Throw had become the place I'd set my problems. The walls and floorboard were like pages of a diary, engraved with my negative thoughts and energy. Adding Phoebe to the architecture was like adding lights and heat.

"I thought I needed you," Phoebe admits, realizing just how lonely Dakota had been.

"I needed you more, Phoebe. When we were dancing that first day in Stone's Throw Manor, I felt you. You remember?"

"The cranberries." She laughs, her eyes beginning to fill. "I…" She hesitates, really contemplating whether she should keep talking. Her head shifts to Dylan before settling back on me. "I felt you, too. I just didn't know what it meant. I still don't really understand it."

My heart swells at the admission. She felt me too. Meaning every moment after that day, I hadn't been alone. We shared in the emotions together. Even if she didn't know what it meant, she's still able to recognize it now. She's not denying it. Not denying me. Maybe opening myself to her really will bring us closer together. Maybe I can keep her this time. For good.

"So, why did you stop talking to me?"

A lump forms in my throat at how quickly she can direct this conversation back from the amazing vacation it had been taking. Leaving me to scramble desperately to produce a proper explanation. Placing blame on any one particular region of this decision seems almost petty. Realistically, the only person I can blame is myself anyway, so I land on that. "I got into my head. Got tired of the intrusive looks and whispers. You're such an amazing person, and after months of fighting it, I was finally convinced I'd ruin your life if I stuck around. People would start to hate you like they'd hated me. I couldn't be the reason your life fell apart."

"No." Of course Phoebe would disagree. "There's no way for you to know that for sure."

"You only saw the tip of the iceberg of what happened to me." I'm starting to shake. My heart is beating in my throat. My eyes sting as I push out the next words. "Please let me tell you what happened. That way, you can see for yourself how hard it was to be gay when we were in school."

Her lips press together before nodding.

I rise to my feet and begin pacing. "This next part is hard for me, so I'm sorry. I'm going to move around if that's okay." I shake out my hands and bounce on my toes as I focus on my breathing.

"Of course." She looks over at Dylan, who's sitting with her legs crossed and her fingers entwined on her lap. Unphased. Because of course. I swear this woman has seen it all after eight years in the Army.

"I started sneaking some of my mom's alcohol after I forced myself to stop talking to you to help me sleep. It wasn't long after that I met Sam." I'm hoping if I speed things up, I can get through this faster. I should've written a script or something because my mind is scattered everywhere now. Things happened in flashes, and I don't remember the timeline completely. "So, we went over Sam. Did you have any questions there?"

She scratches her ear. "You said she was abusive. How?"

Fuck. She's digging up all the dirt.

"Umm…She'd call me stupid and gaslight me after she'd cheat. She hated when I drank and told me it was a good thing I'd killed my dad, so he couldn't see how shitty I'd turned out. Tell me she didn't love me when I'd stand up for myself." I lift my palm up loosely. "Shit like that."

"That's…" she says softly. "That honestly upsets me to hear. I can't believe she would do that to you." Phoebe's face reddens as she clenches her fists together. "If I see her, I swear I'll—"

"You won't." I place my hand on her knee. "And it's okay. I mean, honestly, it wasn't back then, but I'm over it now." I wave it off. "It's over, and I never have to see her again. Last I heard, she moved to Wisconsin or something." I remember the day she'd slid back into my DMs, thinking she could hurt me one last time. It'd been six months since our final break up and she told me she'd met some cow tipping farmer and was marrying him and moving to Wisconsin. She was pissed when I'd left her on read. "So, anyway, when I transferred, Austin got physical with me."

"Physical, how?" Phoebe sits up. Her eyes growing wide. I know she's asking for clarification as to not assume. She wants to believe she's wrong, but we both know she's not.

I look at Dylan, pleading to intervene. "Just breathe, Blake," she says, her tone calm and even as she uncrosses her legs and props her elbows on her knees. "It's over. Okay? I need you to remember this stuff happened. What'd your therapist tell you, huh?"

I squeeze my eyes closed, allowing myself to shake in my seat, focusing on calm, steadying breaths. "It made me stronger."

"Yes. It happened to strengthen you, and now that you're stronger. It's just stuff."

"It's just stuff," I repeat, settling my gaze back on Phoebe. "He'd hit me, mostly. Sometimes, after a few drinks, though, he'd convinced himself he could turn me straight by touching me." The thought of being bent over our coffee table, staring at the water rings as he forced himself inside me, resurfaces in my mind. I quickly replace it with the image of that same table ignited in flames.

Jude and I had set it on fire immediately after I'd moved back in. We gutted the entire house and remodeled it until it was completely unrecognizable, too. This house is no longer a memory of my past trauma. It's completely different now. Jude even turned my parent's room into his office. I still refuse to go in there and Jude's room, though.

The expression on Phoebe's face resembles literal glass breaking. Her eyes well up as a single tear trails down her cheek.

"In combination with Sam's break up and Austin's abuse, I tried to kill myself, which I told you about. Jude found me. I survived." He'd busted down the door. I remember when I'd returned from the hospital, he'd completely cleaned the bathroom. The idea I had tried to end it all was like a fever dream. Sometimes I still can't believe I'd attempted something so selfish. It took that moment to realize people cared, though. Glancing at the scar on the inside of my arm now fills me with a combination of shame due to my own selfishness and the overwhelming love Jude had for me. A love now in a burial plot next to Dakota Blake Chapel at Wilkshire Memorial Cemetery on Ashmore Drive.

"Yes, you did!" Dylan cheers, pulling the metaphorical rope attached to my rapidly descending essence into the quicksand of my thoughts. "Such a fucking miracle to still have you here, Blake."

"Agreed. I got you back." Phoebe's mouth quirks up on one side as she strokes her thumb on my cheek.

My body softens at the warmth of her hand. "I can't explain how happy I am to have you back in my life, Phoebe."

"She wouldn't be telling anyone else this, that's for damn sure," Dylan professes, walking back to the kitchen to help herself to my bag of chips. She takes a bite before realizing we're both staring at her. She stops chewing and tips the bag toward us in offering. How can she eat right now? We both decline.

"Anyway." I shake my head as Dylan plops back down in her seat, now armed with chips. "Umm, that's when my aggression started." *Crunch.* "Uhh…" *Crunch, crunch.* "Austin dislocated Jude's arm one day for hiding in his room…" I roll my eyes, trying to concentrate as the bag crinkles and she takes another bite. "So I broke Austin's nose—DYLAN!" I turn and throw my hands down. "Could you find a quieter snack, please?"

"My bad." She pouts and saunters back to the kitchen as I continue.

"Austin's nose was the first of many…and one cheekbone because I was wearing a signet ring." I sit back down and dig my socked toes into the rug, unable to look at anyone now. "I hated being gay, and after Jude graduated insanely early—my sophomore year—by doing summer classes, I started running away from home. I stayed at Stone's Throw, doing shrooms and convincing myself I was in a palace. I didn't have any friends besides Sam, and she was never around, so I started going to church groups. The parents knew I was gay and would try to fix me by messing with me a little bit sexually. Like, umm…thinking if they could turn me on, I'd be saved or something, I guess. A few dads of the kids in my youth group even tried getting their sons into it."

I start crying unexpectedly, pulling my knees to my chest and burying my face in them. "I felt so powerless. So helpless." I wipe my cheeks on my jeans, huffing out a breath, trying to collect myself as I rock back and forth. Phoebe's hand makes gentle circles on my back. "When I turned eighteen, I was three credits shy of graduating, but decided to live in Stone's Throw full time and drop out of high school altogether."

"But we got you those credits, didn't we?" Dylan says, rejoining the conversation over a mouth full of ice cream. She's always there to remind me to never forget the good that came out of the bad.

"Yes," I say through watery eyes at this woman raiding my fridge. Remembering when I got so mad, I flipped the textbook on the table out of frustration. *That rage making you smarter over there, Popeye?* she'd asked, looking up at me incredulously. "Yes, we did. A diploma. Not a GED. I graduated," I state proudly, pushing my shoulders back. Clearing my throat, I recenter myself and find a renewed strength to continue, knowing full well I never make it through this story completely without breaking down a few times. It's the reason I don't talk about it.

"Anyway, I started doing coke and seeking attention anywhere I could get it. At nineteen, I joined a women's Bible study. Thing is, most of these women were the wives of the men who assaulted me. I exacted my revenge, breaking apart their marriages by sleeping with their wives. The husbands caught wind by the time I turned twenty, raping and beating me to a pulp. I thought I was going to die." I let out a disbelieving laugh. Maybe I've hit insanity. Laughing instead of crying is definitely one of my strongest coping mechanisms. "But I didn't. It did make me scared of women, though."

Phoebe's eyes glass over. "That's why you haven't been with anyone in over six years."

"I hadn't slept with anyone since." I nod. "I guess I had a death wish, though, because I still picked fights with men while simultaneously wishing I could be something they approved of. I even tried getting high as fuck on ecstasy and sleeping with one. Boy, was that a bust. Wound up knocking out his tooth instead."

The sound of Dylan's slurping as she finishes the remnants of the ice cream splits through the awkward silence as I try to formulate the next part of the story. "This went on for a few years before I fully hit rock bottom. I was mixing meth and alcohol. Heroine and coke. One time, I did coke, painkillers, weed, and alcohol all in one sitting. Spent the entire work shift puking in the bathroom. Not fun, but eventually, I was forced to face myself. I was hit with the worst kind of reality check, and finally, I called Jude. He knew Dylan through his job." Her spoon clinks against her bowl as she gives me a reassuring nod before shifting her gaze to Phoebe. "And together, they convinced me to go to the NA meetings at Guiding Light. And the rest is history."

And I'd like to leave it there.

I collapse back against the cushions, exhausted.

Silence settles once more before Dylan claps her hands. "Phoebe, do you have any more questions for Blake?"

Phoebe taps her bottom lip as she scans her brain. Clearing her throat, she says, "Just one." She holds up a finger. "Why did you decide to become Blake rather than work through everything?"

"Because I couldn't." I sit upright, letting my hands fall defeated into my lap. "Kept failing to launch." I gesture to Dylan, who is now washing her bowl in the sink. "The decision to become Blake came after my second relapse five years ago. I had only been clean for about six months at this point. Dylan had pulled a rather aggressive and drugged-up me back to her place. She came up with the idea."

"I was working on trying to find a way to get through to her, but she kept getting hung up on Step Four. Making a moral inventory of ourselves." She cuts off the water and begins wiping her hands with a towel.

"A moral inventory?" Phoebe asks sheepishly.

"Yeah, self-reflection on the good and bad things in our lives," Dylan continues. "See, Dakota's issue was she kept getting hung up on the bad, and every time she'd think too hard about it, she'd *deflect* rather than *reflect*. Turning her attention yet again to drugs every single time to avoid experiencing the hurt all over again. Took two relapses before I realized the bad was entirely too overwhelming for her. Which she's been working on in counseling." She pats my shoulder, and I give her a half-hearted smile in return. "The program worked for her, just not in the conventional order, I guess you could say." She waves her hand passively. "So, after almost getting my face clawed off by this drugged-up little gremlin, I decided to try a new approach. I said, 'Really think about who you'd proudly want to be.'"

"Who did you want to be?" Phoebe asks earnestly, looking between us.

Dylan shifts her gaze to me, raising an eyebrow. "Yeah, Blake?" She won't let me lie through this. I know this already, but her look tells me it regardless.

I rub my mouth, blinking a few times. "I, umm, I wanted to be more like you," I confess, staring down at the ground.

"Me?!" she blinks repeatedly. A nervous chuckle escapes as she asks, "Why?"

"Because…" This is so embarrassing. I hate this so fucking much. Why don't I have any alcohol in this house? Admitting I was fangirling on her has to be a recipe for disaster. "My life had never been better than when you were in it. I seriously thought maybe one day I could fit into your world with you." I hold out my hands. "I hope that's not weird. I'd just spent so much time in high school wishing I could stop being bullied and have friends. No one ever looked at you like filth. No one was ever ashamed to be seen with you. I never felt as beautiful as I had through your eyes."

Phoebe pulls me into her arms then, hugging me so tightly I think I might break a rib. "I'm so sorry you went through all of that. I get why it hurts to talk about it now. I just—I wish I could've been there. I wish I could've helped you."

"You couldn't have, Phoebe. I would've ruined your life. I'm glad I got a second chance, though. God works in mysterious ways. It needed to be now. I'm just glad He let me find you again. After all this time, I'd convinced myself I'd never see you again and worked through the idea that that was okay. It's not what I wanted, but it was what it was."

"He knew we needed each other." Her cheeks flush. "He knew it was time."

But is it? Am I somehow more worthy of being with her now that I've gotten help? What if, by some chance, Dakota finds her way back in? Can Phoebe handle a relapse? There really isn't a way of knowing what God's plan is by bringing us back together, which terrifies me. Could I survive losing her again?

I still want to try, regardless. I still want to believe there's a reason and everything will work out. I never want to lose the chance of seeing her mossy green eyes beaming into mine like this ever again.

"On that note." Dylan stands and straightens herself out before walking to a drawer in my kitchen and pulling out a notepad. "I'm out of here. Will you be okay?" she asks while scribbling something down and tearing the page.

"I think so," I say, losing myself deep within the forest of Phoebe's emerald eyes as we sit unblinkingly on this couch.

"Don't let her out of your sight," she says, squeezing Phoebe's shoulder and handing her the paper. "My number if you need it."

She breaks our gaze to gesture down sweetly at her hand as she shoves the paper in her pocket. "I won't," she says, smiling, finding my eyes again. "Let her out of my sight I mean." She meets Dylan's parental stare. "I promise to call if anything happens." A look of desire paints her expression when she meets my gaze once more. Unblinking. "Thank you." And I'm not sure if she was thanking Dylan or me.

Chapter 23

Phoebe

"Shhh..." I whisper into Blake's ear, who's moaning entirely too loud on my barstool. My hand is up the leg of her basketball shorts. Her legs are hooked to the back of my knees, hands under my waistband, nails digging into my butt as I thrust my fingers into her with great emphasis. "People are going to walk past and hear you from the hall." I chuckle.

It's 4:30 at the latest, and we haven't been able to keep our hands off each other since last night's confessional. I even slipped my hand into her pants while she was driving us back to my place. She almost finished, but I made her wait until we were in my apartment. Admittedly, right in the apartment, I'd bent her over the kitchen counter, and we came together before collapsing onto the floor by the fridge.

I'm not even sure how we got into *this* situation. I briefly remember her saying, "Make me," while I was making eggs because we'd stayed in bed the entire morning and afternoon. And now, that's what I was doing. Making her.

Her nose traces my jawline as she pants deeply. "Make me come, and I'll stop." She giggles.

I cup her mouth with my left hand as I thrust even faster inside her while sinking my teeth into a space directly above her collarbone. This did it. Her body rose as she coated my fingers with her wetness before finally collapsing back into the seat, grasping for my face and desperately pulling me close, sinking her tongue against mine.

"I need you so fucking bad right now," she hisses, fumbling to pull down my sleep pants.

"God, I like you," I murmur, but as my head falls back from the sensation of her fingers sliding along my completely drenched surface, there's a knock on my door.

My head snaps forward as I open my eyes and practically fly across the room. Adrenaline courses through my whole body. Who would possibly disrupt my sacred relax-urday? Everyone knows this is my day to disappear from the general population. If it's a Mormon, I might actually lose it.

They knock again. "One second!" I shout, fixing my pants with shaky fingers, running to a mirror to straighten my hair.

"Were you expecting anyone?" Blake whispers, coming up behind me and kissing my neck.

"You think I'd pound you on my barstool if I did?" I hiss.

She bites her lip, her face flushing, as she steps back, fixing her clothes.

I let out a deep breath before opening the door, poking my head out. It's Zoe and Eve. Well, this is a first.

"Get dressed, loser!" Zoe says, pushing my door open wider. "Impromptu girls' nigh—" She notices Blake, who nervously waves. "Oh, hi, Blake." She's now smiling ear to ear.

Eve, on the other hand, looks like she spotted poop on the floor as she enters. "What's *she* doing here?" she asks, crossing her arms.

Blake doesn't seem upset by this. She even plays into her anonymity. "I'm sorry, I don't think we've 'officially' met yet." She approaches Eve bashfully, extending a hand. "Blake."

"Okay. Doesn't answer my question," she says, arms still crossed, body rigid.

"Eve!" Zoe admonishes before looking back at Blake. "Her name's Eve."

"Charming." Blake exposes her crooked canine, walking over to her shoes. "I gotta get going. Have a great time with girls' night." She stops before the door. "Call me later, Phoebe." Then, gesturing to Zoe, she adds, "It was a pleasure seeing you again." She shoots Eve a piercing look. "Eve." It comes out almost a growl.

When the door clicks behind her, the sudden absence gives me whiplash. I didn't get my usual goodbye kiss or at least a hug given present company. I didn't even have time to respond, and then she was gone.

Now I'm looking at Eve and Zoe, who are having a stare-down. Both pairs of eyes darkened. It reminds me of the start of a boxing match. Right before the bell dings and they start throwing punches.

This is usually when I mediate or divert their attention, but my mind is blank. So much has happened in the last two minutes. I'm overwhelmed.

†

A crash erupts as my bowling ball connects with the pins at the end of the lane. I turn around to see Zoe and Eve burning holes into each other as if having a telepathic argument.

The ride over in Eve's car was rather uncomfortable. I wonder why this is so awkward. Why would they even ask me out if it was going to be like this? They couldn't possibly know what was happening before they knocked, could they? I mean, Blake was being pretty loud, but I covered her mouth in more than enough time before she finished for them not to have heard it. Right?

"Eve." I nudge her after sitting down at the table. "It's your turn."

"Whoopy," she says sarcastically, rolling her eyes before rising to her feet and descending to the lane.

"What's her problem?" I ask Zoe when Eve is out of earshot. Hoping maybe she'll give me a clue as to whether they heard Blake.

"Your guess is as good as mine." *Okay, so they probably didn't hear Blake.* Zoe would be pretty blunt about it. I know her. "But it's pissing me off."

This still begs the question, though. Why is she so upset over discovering Blake at my place? I get not liking her, but she's being downright hostile. I'm slightly embarrassed to associate with her, but I refuse to tell Zoe that. She'd grab it like a baton in a relay race and take off with it.

"Everything has been pissing you off lately," I decide to say instead. Perfect way to attempt to defuse the situation. Focus on each person's ill manner separately. One on one.

"Whoa." She shoots me a surprised look. "Did Miss Appleton just say a swear?"

I sigh. "I was just mimicking your words. Calm down."

She holds her hands up defensively. "That's between you and God, Phoebz." Her face forms into a smirk. "How do we feel about Eve's disposition toward Blake?" Great. She's flipping it right back to dangerous territory.

I hated everything about how she treated her. It was embarrassing. Admitting this would only fuel Zoe's aggression and I learned a long time ago it's best to stay directly in between them rather than sway one way or the other.

"I don't know." I lift my palm. "Typical Eve, I guess."

"What's typical Eve?" Eve asks, approaching. I was only lightening the mood. Didn't mean any offense by it, but you can tell she's ready to fight. "If you have something to say, Phoebe, just say it?"

"Stop being a cunt, Eve. It's fucking girls' night!" Zoe shouts, slamming her hands on the table.

"Oh, *I'm* the cunt?" she shouts back as Zoe rises to her feet.

"Is your attitude *and* your hearing malfunctioning?"

"GUYS!" I shout, pushing to my feet. "Stop."

"How about *you* stop, Phoebe?" Eve shouts, shifting her gaze toward me.

What is she talking about? "Stop what, exactly?" My knees tremble as I sink back down into my chair.

"What the fuck was that back there at your apartment, huh?" Eve points to the exit as if somehow gesturing to where I live.

There's no way she heard Blake. Right? Regardless, I'm too nervous to say anything. I'm not sure I want to know what she's referring to. She can't possibly know what's been going on. Yet, I'm not ready to face this conversation.

"I'm...I'm trying to convert her." It feels stupid saying it out loud. "You know, turn her back to Jesus."

Her eyebrows knit together. "Sure she's not converting you?! You can't fix lesbianism, Phoebe. It's physically impossible."

"So, what if she *can't* fix her?" Zoe interjects. "She can't just be friends with Blake, anyway?" Her edge of irritation has returned. "Because she's a lesbian? Is that what you're trying to say, Eve? Because if it is, say it with your fucking chest!"

"That is what I'm saying, Zoe! I think I've made it pretty clear. Phoebe really thinks her decision to hang out with that dyke carpet-muncher isn't going to affect her and Ethan? Her reputation at the church? Her parents? Honestly, Phoebe, do you ever think about anyone other than your fucking self?"

Anger thrums through my veins as I sink back into my seat and ball my fists under the table. How can she say that? All I ever do is think of others. Which has molded me into this cardboard cutout of what perfection should look like. I've always been too scared to act out of turn. The one time I decide I'm going to let myself have what I want, she acts as though I've always chosen myself.

"Anyone who thinks being gay is sinful enough to act grossly and violently toward their neighbor needs to go back and read the fucking Bible!" Zoe shouts. "I have one in my car if you wanna borrow it." Then she fixes back on me, "Phoebe, don't listen to her."

"Oh, fuck you, Zoe!" Eve shouts, pushing out her chest to assert dominance.

"Fuck *me*?" Zoe matches her alpha stance, placing her hand on her own chest. Face red, eyes black. "No, fuck *you*, you bigoted piece of trash!"

They're shouting back and forth now, but I can't hear them anymore as a sudden ringing in my ears overtakes my surroundings. I can't look up from the table. Tunnel vision has my eyes locked on my balled-up fists in my lap. I'm shaking from the rate at which my blood is circulating through my entire body. My skin feels itchy and icy, and my mouth has gone dry.

How did I get here? I reflect on my actions over the last four weeks. Exactly twenty-one days after Blake's foot brushed mine under the table at Blessed Beans. I'm sitting here watching my two best friends locked in a shouting match in the middle of a bowling alley after making Blake come on my barstool.

I look at my hands, feeling the weight of what they've caused. These hands have replaced natural sexual acts with unnatural ones. These hands have committed adultery.

You need to make this right. This is not you, and it sure as shit isn't who you're becoming. It's just plain reckless.

Piper's right.

"This isn't who I'm supposed to be."
"You can be both."

Yeah, right, Blake. I wish she could see this current situation, which *definitely* proves I cannot be normal. I can't be both gay and expect this not to happen.

"Why do you give a shit about Ethan's reputation?!" Zoe shouts as the ringing subsides.

"I care about Phoebe's reputation, not Ethan's! They're getting married, and she needs to step the fuck up before EC starts whispering she's a carpet-munching adulteress."

"He put her on the spot!" Zoe yells. "She isn't going to marry him, Eve. She just needs to remedy this."

Oh great. I can't imagine this is going to go over well with Eve. She's not like me; she's strong. Eve doesn't do anything she doesn't want to do. I didn't tell her about this because I knew she wouldn't be able to wrap her head around how spineless I am. Why is Zoe talking about this? It's not her business to tell.

"What?!" Eve steps back as if she was hit by something physical rather than verbal. "Phoebe, tell me she's lying."

I look at her before sinking down further into my seat and focusing on my lap.

"Really?" Eve shouts. "You guys truly are fucked up. Ethan is over the moon. Over the fucking moon, and you're stringing him along? Do everyone a favor, Phoebe, and stop dragging your fucking feet. Grow a pair!"

She's right, I have to tell him. He doesn't deserve this; no one does. I started this fight. I'm casting nothing but misery onto everyone. On Blake, who wants me to be with her when I can't possibly fathom being *seen* with her. On Ethan, who wants to marry me, and I can't even get past him touching me. Yet I'm too spineless to call it off. On Zoe, who has to deal with Eve's completely accurate honesty. On Eve, who has to deal with the embarrassment of having a queer friend.

I can't even be a good daughter to my parents. A good Christian for God. I'm a tornado, dismantling everything as I spiral out of control. My soul is circling a drain. Not knowing who I am and never being able to find out. The pressure is too high. The destruction too great.

For the sake of everyone around me, I have to be selfless. I have to distance myself. Emily Dickinson holed herself up in her house once, having said, "It might be lonelier without the loneliness." I remember when I was younger, thinking dying alone wouldn't be too bad if I could express myself the way she did. I need to leave. I need to let Ethan off the hook. Disappear from Mystic Harbor once and for all.

"Hello?" Zoe's hand is waving in my face as I realize where I am. The sound of crashing pins behind me makes me jump. I look around and notice Eve must've left. When? "Are you okay?"

"I have to go." I stand, kicking off the rental shoes, replacing them with my own.

"No, Phoebe, wait," Zoe tries as I'm tying my laces. Little does she know my frontal cortex is no longer registering cognitive functions. "Eve doesn't know shit."

"Sure," I say, shifting in place, wanting to leave. *Just go,* being the only thing echoing around in my skull. She may have been talking as I left, but I'm not sure.

I'm really regretting having driven over in Eve's car. Since she's gone, I resort to walking down the street of this tiny town. It's all the same, I think. The fresh, crisp night air is tolerable and needed. Maybe a walk will help clear my head. Ethan's house is only about a thirty-minute walk from here, anyway.

Chapter 24

Phoebe

It's quiet as I walk through the gate of Ethan's neighborhood. American flags hanging from porches of modern-style houses can be seen everywhere. Freshly mowed lawns with top-notch landscaping. One even has a tree house in an old oak tree. Perfect place to raise a family. A family I'd never have after doing what needs to be done.

Ethan deserves so much better than I can provide. Deserves a family and a loving wife. I'm unable to even fathom it. I can't keep holding on to this idea one day, I'll be the person God meant for me to be. Even if I did go through with marrying him, I wouldn't have the mindset to be a good mother. To even carry it inside of me without a poisonous resentment of being made to do what's normal. Even getting to the point of pregnancy would result in so much disgust I doubt I'd be able to look at myself the same.

The idea of him touching me makes my stomach curl and my blood seethe with discomfort. I desperately desire to follow God's plan for me, but I'm not sure I can continue living with any sense of joy by conducting myself as normal. I'm not normal. I never will be.

I've noticed in big manufacturing companies, they will grind out a million copies of the same thing. Ninety-nine percent of the time, those things come out perfectly. Work properly. I'm the one percent, however. I find myself wishing I could go back to my time of construction and find where everything went wrong. Was something not placed in the right grooves properly, causing things to be slightly off? Was it maybe a lack of product or parts? Like a printer low on ink or a missing bolt meant to hold the whole thing together. Could it possibly even be a lack of power generated through the machine, causing a lag in production as things began to stick?

Whatever the issue, I'm defective. Born a woman yet mentally incapable of performing as designed. Incapable of completing the tasks given to me by God himself. Inept.

So, without further ado, I will part ways with all of the things I make miserable. I will bow my head and find the island of misfit toys referenced in "Rudolf the Red-Nosed Reindeer." I'm sure there are others out there. I'm sure the island was created by a select few who were also tired of letting everyone down. People who let themselves down and want to disappear from the social standard. Misery washed away with complacency.

The sun is setting as I approach Ethan's small two-story glass and wood modern-style house. It's no surprise with the amount of wealth his father contains, his home would be a reflection of that. Daddy always paid for the best for his first and only son. His parents were very conventional as well. His mother didn't work but volunteered in every way imaginable for their church in the city. She cooked, she cleaned. Never once has his father changed a diaper or held a baby. If not his mother, this task was left to Ethan's two little sisters.

The few times I met his parents, it was abundantly clear Ethan idolized his father, aspiring to be just as successful and provide just as much for his future wife. It was kind of sad to see how hard his mother worked, yet never being appreciated. I never understood how she could stick around. Then again, marriage is a very permanent thing not meant to be taken lightly. Clearly, they'd figured out a way to traverse through these issues because they've been married for almost thirty years.

All of the lights are off, causing the house to look empty as I walk up the path to the door. He's always been one to park his vehicle in the two-car garage rather than in the driveway, so this is no surprise to me. The only thing suggesting there's life inside is the music blasting through. Kind of strange because the music is very angry. People choosing to scream rather than sing. I can't even make out the words as I ring the bell. It's funny because I've never heard Ethan listen to this kind of music before. He's more of the Christian Top Ten type. Blasting it in his car whenever we travel anywhere, leaving little to no means of communication.

After a moment of no response, I come to the conclusion the music must be up too loud to even hear the doorbell. Typically, I wouldn't walk right in, but as I'm knocking, the door creaks open. *Who does it hurt if I walk in? Until I break the news to him, we are still betrothed. Doesn't that earn me some sense of passage into his personal space?* I think before pushing myself the rest of the way in.

His place is *filthy!*

Clothes thrown everywhere. Every time I've ever seen it, it's been clean. I'm starting to wonder if this was just to make an impression on me. False advertising, if you will. I also surmise he's not the one to clean it, deciding rather to hire a onetime maid or something before I'm meant to arrive. Come to think of it, the only times I've ever been over were on Thursdays. Could this suggest he has a housekeeper visit every Wednesday? I'm probably getting ahead of myself and judging him based on this mess I'm witnessing. Finding more and more fuel to feed what I'm about to do. What I know I need to do.

"Ethan?" I call out over the music, but it's too loud. Where is it coming from? I need to turn it down. I decide to make this my new mission. Follow the sound of the music while trying not to trip over shoes and clothes.

I soon find myself walking past the kitchen, dirty dishes filling the sink. The counter is full of dirt and grime, stacked high with even more grease-caked pots and pans. "Gross." I try to stifle the sudden upset in my stomach. This isn't a few days' worth of dirt accumulation. I haven't been to his house in weeks, and I can only assume he hasn't cleaned a single thing since. Would I be meant to clean up after this pig? Hell no, I wouldn't.

Honestly, I'm glad I came over. The illusion of Ethan has been shattered for me. The façade he embodies for others is clearly a smoke screen.

Eventually, I find myself tripping over a beer bottle on the floor. "Seriously?" I pick it up and place it on the coffee table, which consequently is also full of more cans and bottles and takeout boxes. This place looks like a frat house!

Every muscle in my body wants me to clean as I talk to him, but that's not why I'm here. Besides, cleaning will only make things more confusing. I can almost hear Ethan say, "So you're breaking up with me, but cleaning my house?"

Just find the volume control, Appleton. Find the volume. I continue to meander down the hallway leading to his bedroom. The noise grows to a deafening roar which soon mimics my internal state as I push open the door. My foot instantly snags on a bra on the floor of the entrance. "What the f—"

I raise my head. There on his bed lays a very naked Ethan on his back, toes pointed toward the headboard. Face buried deep between a naked woman's legs who is seated on his face. I watch him bury two fingers deep inside her as he nuzzles deeper. The woman is positioned the opposite direction. My fiancé's penis jammed deeply down her throat. Her dirty blonde hair falls freely as she pinches her own nipple in delight.

Clearly, they didn't hear me walk in, and for a moment, I have no idea what to do. Do I turn around and leave and forget I saw Jaime Bishop sucking off my fiancé on his bed to terrible music? I want to vomit. I want to hit them. Seems as though I have plenty of time to contemplate, as my eyes well with tears.

My head shoots up to the ceiling as I stand, frozen, panning down and around the room. Framed jerseys hang behind the headboard. A desk to my right is occupied with signed baseballs and footballs on stands next to his laptop. His speakers blare screams, which only ignite the anger welling deep within me, more like fireworks at the base of my skull.

This can't be real. How ironic. He proposed to me, knowing full and well he wouldn't be faithful. Can I even be mad about this? No. That'd be one hell of a double standard, but regardless, a dissonant trill overtakes my auditory ability. I can't hear anything! I turn the knob to the volume calmly, causing Jaime to lift her head, making a popping sound as her lips disconnect from Ethan's member. "Shit," she says, wiping her bottom lip and positioning herself away from Ethan, who now is sitting up and looking at me.

My hands are at my sides, fingers rubbing together, keeping me tethered to reality as I stand there expressionless. An immense weight is pulling on my shoulders, making me very cognizant of the gravity grinding me into the floor. I have no words. I have no thoughts. I'm left instead taking in their reactions as this fucking slut is now trying to cover herself up as if it matters anymore. I've already seen her entire asshole as my fiancé sucked a crater into her vagina.

"Phoebe." I hear the muffled sound of Ethan as he trips over his comforter, trying to approach me.

My head is foggy, brain lagging. He's in slow motion as he pulls his boxers on. My heavy eyes take a second to turn toward his figure, drawing closer. The ringing in my ears turns to a roar as my body erupts. I grab an autographed baseball off his desk and throw it like a professional pitcher past his head into a framed jersey on the wall. I see the glass shatter, but it doesn't make a sound. I notice a porcelain mug filled with pens as my hands grip it. Watching the release of my fingers mid-motion, hurling it into the wall. The mug silently shatters, and pens fly everywhere. I kick a metal wastebasket next to his desk, sending it straight into Jaime's face, who is now standing, pulling her pants up her hips. Life is a television set on mute.

I try with great effort to scream, but it's inaudible. I fling my hand into a couple of hats on a coat rack beside his desk. The rack tumbles to the ground as Ethan ducks to avoid the shrapnel of hats. His mouth is moving inaudibly, as if he's screaming. Who gives a fuck what he's saying? I walk past him, ripping down a Texas Tech flag on the wall beside him. Stomping over, I grab his laptop and begin slamming it violently against the desk until plastic pieces and parts of the LED screen fly in every direction, hitting my cheek, but I can't hear the impact. I grab my ears and begin pulling, taking with it some of my own hair. Why can't I hear anything? Hello?! Testing! Testing!

I'm not safe here.

I need to leave.

I turn and run out, crashing into Eve. What the FUCK is she doing here? Is she in on this, too? She's been touching Ethan in front of me for so long, it shouldn't come as a surprise she was about to join in on this disgusting display. My ears continue to produce a sonorous sound, overpowering anything and everything as I shove past her. My vision tunnels as I stumble through the hallway, completely unaware of the disheveled heaps I'm tripping over until I collapse in his driveway.

Ethan grabs my bicep forcefully, pulling me up and into his bare chest as I struggle to be released. I'm punching and kicking as he's trying to drag me inside, but I refuse to go with him. I want to leave. I have to.

"Get off me!" I try to shout as streaks of light surround my vision. "Get off me! Let go!"

Can no one hear me? The world around me is growing fuzzy. Am I losing my mind?

Chapter 25

Blake

Am I ruining Phoebe's life? I think as I throw my old Dodge in park in my driveway. Staring out at my porch, I try to figure out what the fuck I'm doing. This is not at all how I planned this to go when I'd decided to stir up shit at EC.

Try as I might to leave, Phoebe has always had this effect on me. Even when I was with Sam, I couldn't help but scan the cafeteria for Phoebe sitting with her friends. So beautifully confused trying to blend in. It pissed Sam off. She knew. I'd never even needed to tell her the pedestal Phoebe sat upon. Everyone knew.

Something about Phoebe, though, has always pulled me in, messing with my head. Every moral compass I have bending and gravitating back to her. My true north.

Talking about Phoebe has always been and forever will be something that comes from a place of pure love. And something I know beyond a reasonable doubt is that Phoebe is queer. Denying her sexuality to herself and others is making her miserable. She's just floating through life, afraid to go against the current.

The first time I suspected she wasn't straight was when we were fourteen, and she'd taken my hand after dancing in Stone's Throw Manor. I'd let her lead me through the woods back to the car. She didn't let go. She felt it too. The intense pull to be near each other. It felt so natural. I wanted to hold her hand forever. At that moment, I realized no one's hand would ever fit like hers.

Phoebe is miserably trying to be something she isn't. Her quality of life has always been bullshit, and I've never seen her face light up like when we were together.

I'm going to be forthright as I'm collecting my thoughts and say I've known for a very long time that I'm in love with Phoebe. I loved her so much I couldn't bear to be the cause of her anguish. So, I pushed her away and tried to find a world without her. To fill the hole inside my chest in another way, yet nothing could compare. Boy, let me tell you, I tried everything. Sex, drugs, fighting, no high could ever compare to when I barely touched her hand under the stars. The sound of her name rolling off my lips is enough to send me into a cloud of euphoria.

Clearly, I had no idea she'd be at EC, and when I saw her, the strangest phenomena happened. I can turn down drugs. Even avoid any presence of them. Go to a meeting, take up a hobby, contact my support system, yet when Phoebe asked me to stay after service, I couldn't tell her no. Even after discovering she'd gotten engaged, feeling the slow, anguishing tear of muscle in my chest dividing it in two, I still stood at my truck. Thirty-three minutes after the service, like some bozo puppy, reminding myself this wasn't her. I know this means I should've stayed away. I was finally doing better.

I spent a lot of my life not giving a shit about anyone, building walls and defenses. Not letting anyone in. With Phoebe, there isn't a wall high enough or armor strong enough for her not to pass through it.

It sounds stupid, but when her foot brushed mine in that Blessed Beans creepy Jesus coffee shop, I knew she had a boyfriend. And when she'd placed her hand on my wrist, my entire body ignited anyway and threw all of my convictions straight out the window into a dumpster eight stories down. The same thing happened after she became engaged. I'm not sure why my brain believes her personal life isn't real. When I fought back the urge to kiss her at my house that day, I was convinced showing her where she belonged would help remove the pain she was experiencing. I could fix it. If I could wake her up to her true nature, she'd do the right thing and leave him.

And if that didn't work, I would at least flood her head with so many endorphins it'd alleviate the pressure. I can show her a world of God *and* love, what true happiness looks like.

The sight of Eve darkening her doorstep today really took a turn on my mental health. Up until this point, I had managed to turn the dial inside my head. Lower the volume rather than listen to the things I knew I should be focusing on. She has a reputation to uphold. Her dad is the head of a church that does not condone this lifestyle. She has a fiancé. I'd drowned it all out with feeble attempts to make her feel good.

It's time to get realistic, though. What we're doing isn't fixing the issues she's facing; it's only making it worse. The further down this road we go, the more I'll want her for myself and add to her stress. I'm no longer able to be subjective. Honestly, I'm not sure I ever was.

From ages fourteen to twenty-one, the mere mention of her name would send me into a violent fit of rage. The ones who managed to get close enough knew that Phoebe was the only topic that was taboo. I've always instinctually protected her. Even from myself. Now, however, after granting myself a taste of what life could be like with her, I can't stay away if I try. I know it'll get ugly, but I'm

praying she'll let me stick around for those moments. I'd do anything—
everything—to see her face light up again and again.

So, when my phone vibrated in my pocket, illuminating Zoe's name on the
screen, I answered it immediately.

"Blake?"

"The one and only."

"Girl, you need to pick me up. Now." She sounds overwhelmed.

I sit up in my seat. Already turning my key. "What's going on? Where's
Phoebe?"

"I don't know. Shit went sour, man." The sound of wind scratches through the
receiver. "Eve went off on her. Also, that bitch drove, so Phoebe's walking."

I back out of my driveway so quickly my tires squeal as I shift it into drive.
"Where are you right now?"

"The bowling alley."

I know it. There's only one on the Holy Side. Wouldn't be surprised if it had
some dumb as fuck religious name attached to it.

"Bowler's Haven."

Yup, dumb.

†

"Where would she go?" I ask as Zoe hops in. It took about ten minutes for me to
get over to this side of town, so Phoebe's got a little bit of distance on us. My
truck is our only saving grace.

"Ethan's," she says flatly. "I can bet money on it."

"How do you know?"

"Eve called her selfish for befriending you. Told her she needs to step up
because she and Ethan are getting married." She shakes her head. "I'm going to
punch her one day, Blake. Phoebe doesn't think I will, but every day, it gets a little
bit harder to refrain."

As I begin to drive, I start the much-needed conversation. "What the fuck
happened?"

She throws her hands up before slumping back in the seat. "Sometimes, I
really hate Eve. I can't tell you how many times I've tried to convince Phoebe she
sucks. She's such an attention whore. Always stealing the spotlight from
everyone, especially Phoebz. She's been trampling over her for years, Blake. I
don't know how well you know Phoebe, but she's a pushover."

"I like to think I know her pretty well." I sigh, turning on my signal, stopping
at the light. "I've known her for a really long time."

"Really?" She turns in her seat to face me. "How?"

I meet her gaze briefly before shifting my gaze back to the road. "Where am I going?"

She looks at me as if trying to crack the case. "57 E Merchant." I notice a lightbulb switch on in the back of her mind. "Holy fucking shit!"

I smirk nervously as she looks me over. "Dakota?!" she shouts before punching my arm extremely hard. "Damn, girl! You clean up nice! Honestly, never thought you would."

"It's Blake now," I say, rubbing the back of my neck.

She presses her lips together. "Docs Phoebe know?"

"Yes," I respond hastily. She doesn't need the details, though.

Her eyebrows narrow as I turn onto another street. "Do you remember what I told you that night?"

"Yes, Zoe. How could I forget?" I say exasperatedly.

"Seems like you forgot how I said to find me before you found her." She rolls her eyes. "I'll kill you. I'm not playing. If you hurt her, what I told you back then will seem like a compliment."

"First off, I wasn't looking for her. I didn't know you guys attended EC, and I'm positive she didn't know I owned a bar when she came in by herself."

"She what?" Oops. I guess she hadn't told anyone that.

I try to shift the topic back on track. "And second, I'm not the same person you ran into that night. Believe it or not, I really needed your words."

"Well." She turns back to face the front. "Glad I could help, but don't fucking make me kill you."

✝

"What the actual fuck?" Zoe says as we pull up at Ethan's house. My blood boils as I watch him in his boxers, arms wrapped around a screaming and writhing Phoebe. She's crying and kicking her legs as he's lifting and dragging her up the driveway back into his house.

I don't even fully stop the truck before Zoe jumps out, running up the drive. "Ethan, let her the fuck go!"

I hop out, leaving the engine running, as two sets of angered glares burn in my direction. It's always lovely seeing Eve—wait—what the fuck is Eve doing here?

I'm trying to keep my resolve as the events are developing in front of me. I don't care what they think. All I can see is Phoebe on the ground, crawling away, unable to stand. Broken. I bend down and place my hand on her cheek. It's bleeding.

Did he hit her?

Once she sees me, she wraps her arms around me, sobbing into my chest, her tear-soaked blood getting on my shirt, but I don't care. I have no words as I run my hand through her hair, squeezing her head into my chest tightly.

My gaze meets Ethan's as my eyebrows pinch together. He hurt her. He fucking...

Before I can even think it through, I'm springing to my feet and fast walking up to him. My right fist connects straight with his nose, knocking him back a couple steps as he clutches his face. "What the fuck, you dumb dyke!"

I spit on him. "You hurt her, you piece of shit!" I'm shouting. "What the fuck did you do?"

"Eve?" I hear Zoe a few paces in front of me, approaching her at the door. She's just standing there ogling the events. "Is this where you've been instead of hanging out with your supposed friends? You've been fucking Phoebe's fiancé?"

"Zoe, I—" But Eve's words are quickly cut off by Zoe's backhand across her face. Clean. Eve stands there, tears in her eyes as she clutches her cheek. Funny, I would've never figured Eve for a softy. One bitch slap, and she's a glass-jawed pussy.

"I'm doing these women a favor!" Ethan shouts nasally, blood pouring freely from his nose as he struggles to contain it. Good. I hope I fucking broke it. Add that to my countless list of broken noses in the name of Phoebe.

"A favor?" Zoe shrieks. "Yeah, she looks extremely grateful right now, you douchebag!"

"Without holy matrimony, women cannot be accepted into the highest celestial kingdom of heaven!" he shouts. "I'm bringing us all closer to God!"

This causes me to tackle him to the ground, straddling him as I punch repeatedly. He's blocking, but I still manage to connect a few swings. "I'm going to bring you closer to God right now."

"Blake!" I hear Zoe say, pulling me by my shoulders and dragging me to my feet. "We have to go. Get Phoebe!"

Phoebe.

I have to get her out of here. I haven't been this angry in years. Allowing Dakota out of her box was very ill-mannered. I'd been doing so good to keep that part of me at bay, but seeing him overpowering her made me see red. I was ready to kill him if Zoe wouldn't have brought me back to reality.

I walk over to Phoebe, picking her up and cradling her in my arms, her face burying instantly into my neck. "It's okay, baby," I say calmly. "I got you." I walk her to my truck, placing her down gently on the bench.

"I fucking knew it!" Eve shouts as I walk around the car.

My feet stop at the grill as Ethan shouts, "Your lifestyle goes against the nature of mankind! You faggots will burn in flames for all eternity!" I watch as Zoe climbs in, scooching Phoebe over, and closing the door.

I smirk, fire in my eyes as Dakota comes flying out of my mouth again. "How's Mary?" I growl, which causes him to freeze. He questions how I could possibly even know her name. "Funny, when I was fucking her, she failed to mention her son was exactly like his father!"

And on that note, I hop into the driver's seat, and we drive away.

"Mary?" Zoe asks, arms wrapped around Phoebe, who is resting her head on her shoulder.

"Dakota was not a good person," I respond, unable to meet her gaze as I drive to Zoe's house.

"Yeah." Zoe's shoulders slump as she lets out a sigh of disapproval. "I remember all too well."

I glance as she runs a comforting hand through Phoebe's hair. "I just hope you're not the same person I ran into back then."

It's fair she's concerned. I remember all too well the situation in which she ran into me back then. I was not a shining member of society, to put it lightly. And now that I'm back in Phoebe's life, she has more than enough reason to be protective. Zoe had ran into me at my absolute worst. Saw the floor I couldn't fall below, and gave me the coldest reality I could've gotten. Running into Zoe that night was actually the reason I had decided to call Jude and ask for his help. She was the last nail I needed to make me decide to be sober.

Tonight is a lot to watch your best friend go through. Especially when she's nonverbal and bleeding, asleep, with her head on your shoulder.

"Blake," she huffs. "You know I'm protective over her." She gestures to Phoebe in her arms, whose breathing has stilled and calmed as she sleeps. "And I'm glad you heard what I said back then, but I need you to know, I would do anything for her. I told you to stay away because we both know what would've happened if you hadn't. If you changed your name and hair to sneak in and drag her down, I won't hesitate to respond, and you won't like how I do it."

I admire her protectiveness. We both know beyond a reasonable doubt in an all-out physical altercation, I would win hands down, but it still brings me solace knowing Phoebe has someone in her corner.

More than anything, I want to be that person for her as well, but Zoe's right. Dakota could never have been enough for Phoebe. I needed to change. Without Zoe running into me that night, I wouldn't have chosen to work the steps to become the person Phoebe needs me to be. "I wasn't ready then," I finally say, pulling up to her apartment complex. Making sure to meet her gaze when I say, "But I am now. Dakota is in my past. I'd like to keep her there."

Zoe gently pushes Phoebe's sleeping body into mine as I wrap my arm around her. She's sporting a look of concern with a splash of consideration. "You better." She hesitates before adding, "Whatever you guys had when we were teenagers has had a lasting effect on her. She *needs you* to be good. She's had enough ugly, and we know there's more to come. She doesn't need Dakota. I saw her in your eyes tonight. She needs Blake. Dakota will ruin her."

I let out a leveling breath of shame, rubbing my face. I should've done better to contain my emotions. As much as I care about Phoebe and feel called to protect her, I know Zoe is right. I need to remind myself why I changed. I need to prove to Zoe I'm not the same person. I need to do better if I'm going to be strong enough for Phoebe. Tonight, I was weak. I gave in to weakness by trying to show my strength physically. It's an issue Dakota was famous for. By giving in to this anger, I didn't only disappoint myself. I also let down Jude.

A part of me is glad he wasn't here to witness it, but I'm almost positive he saw it, and I'm one hundred percent positive he expects better of me. "I'm sorry. I'll do better."

"Please do." She reaches for my hand in the seat beside her. "She may not realize it. Maybe you don't, either. When I ran into you that night five years ago," Zoe squeezes my hand in hers, "I realized you mean a lot to each other. And it's not something time apparently can make easier. She needs you, Blake. And you need her."

I nod and watch Zoe hop out of my truck and head into her apartment. I'm not sure I believe her, though. I can't help the lingering suspicion I'm taking advantage of Phoebe because it's impossible to control myself around her. I can't shake the belief I'm making her life worse. I'd like to tell myself Zoe knows her better, but seeing Phoebe suffering like this and knowing I'm responsible for even a fraction of it makes me almost believe her life would be better if she had never met Dakota or me in the first place.

Chapter 26

Phoebe

"Your lifestyle goes against the nature of mankind!" Ethan's words bounce around the empty spaces of my brain as Blake dabs my cheek with a warm washcloth. I guess I cut it open pretty good when I was smashing Ethan's laptop.

We made it back to my apartment and are now sitting in the bathroom. I'm sitting on the closed toilet seat lid; Blake is kneeling on the floor in front of me.

"It's going to be okay," she keeps saying on repeat, and quite frankly, it's annoying me. It isn't going to be okay. How can she possibly think that? She didn't see what I had.

As relieved as I was to see her and Zoe when they pulled up, it made things worse. I'm glad I got out of there—and without them, I wouldn't have—but now they know about us. I can't pretend they didn't hear her call me baby. Can't pretend they didn't see how I reacted, digging my face into her neck—seeking solace in the scent of cedar on her pulse point—as she carried me to the truck.

I haven't spoken since Blake and Zoe wedged me between them in the bench seat of her truck. I'm not even sure what to say, but I can guarantee it wouldn't be very nice. She's doing too much for me right now. I should be appreciative, but is it possible to help and make things worse at the same time? Because that's what I feel like her presence is doing right now.

"Good news is, I don't think it needs stitches," she says, ringing out the washcloth in the sink. "It'd probably do you well to use super glue or something on it." She looks around. "Do you have a first aid kit or anything?"

I point to under the sink. I can't believe she's still here, honestly. I didn't ask her to. I haven't said anything at all, actually. She kind of parked her truck, figuring I was this poor frail creature who couldn't get inside without supervision. Lord forbid a demon snatch me up on the stairs and finish what it started.

More annoying still, she followed me inside. She's smothering and I need her to stop. I can't do this. I can't keep disappointing Blake by not choosing her.

"Do you have any superglue? Or…" She's just digging around under my sink, pushing past my tampons and toilet paper like she lives here. "Liquid bandage? Anything?"

Honestly, I probably do, but I don't want her digging through my drawers in the kitchen, that's for sure. I shake my head.

"No matter. We'll just clean it and get a butterfly bandage on it." She nibbles at her bottom lip. "I should've invested stock in those when I was doctoring myself back in the day."

She kneels back down beside me, opening the kit on the floor next to her. "You don't have to talk about it," she says, tipping a bottle of alcohol onto a cotton swab. "But when you want to—if—you want to." Her expression softens, pressing the alcohol-soaked cotton to my cut. I wince, jerking back, causing her to take the back of my neck into her palm before continuing to dab. "I'm always here. I'm not going anywhere, okay?"

God, I wish she would, though. My eyes begin to water. Why am I acting like this? I search her face for what I'd felt before Eve and Zoe ruined our afternoon with a stupid impromptu girls' night. She was my knight and shining armor, yet I feel absolutely nothing. No flutter. No hot-cold feeling.

She smirks at me nervously before returning her eyes to my cheek.

There's a gaping hole in my heart and peering inside, you'd see nothing but broken glass in there. No fire that once burned at the first signs of her touch. I'm hollow, empty. Life is pointless. She deserves better than me. Better than someone who could only ever have her in secret. A coward.

I used to believe if choosing her always felt good, I'd choose her forever, but the reality of it is, life isn't a fairytale. It isn't sunshine and homosexual rainbows. Life is this. Life is Ethan fucking some random slut while I watch from his bedroom door. Life is burning in hell for choosing Blake. Life is fake friends and feigning happiness.

"Phoebe." She lets out a deep breath, ripping me out of my thoughts. I look up from my floor of contemplation to meet her eyes. So soft and kind. An ocean of endless possibilities, but none I can easily have while still maintaining my relationship with God. She's so beautiful. Why can't I be someone else? Someone who sees the world the same way she does. "I know you've been through a lot recently…"

Understatement, I think as I look away, crossing my arms.

"…But…" She drops her gaze, placing a bandage on my cheek, crumpling up the trash in her hand. "I need you to know—I love you."

My eyes grow wide as my stomach lurches. Surely, she means she cares for me a lot. She can't possibly mean *love,* love…right?

She throws the trash in the can beside the toilet I'm sitting on, taking my hands in hers on my lap. "I knew it when we were kids. It's why I pushed you away. I refused to be the cause of your suffering. I knew this would be hard for you. Knew I'd make your life complicated."

I can't speak. She's joking. It can't be true. She *can't* love me. No. I should've never gotten into this. I should've never given in to these curiosities. If I would've kept trying to convert her, none of this would've happened. We would've been happy and maybe even best friends. I'd have her for normal emotional support now as I'm finding out about Ethan. One day, we'd have both gotten boyfriends, been bridesmaids at each other's weddings.

But no. I wish we could rewind. She didn't say she loves me. Didn't mean it. It's out there now, and I don't know what to do with this information. Blots of water hit our hands in my lap. Great, I'm crying again.

"But it's different now." She licks her bottom lip, forcing my chin up to meet her jovial expression. "I can be here for you. I'm not going anywhere, okay?"

Her palm finds my cheek, wiping the tears with her thumb before placing her lips on mine. My body jerks into her as I cry, sliding off the toilet to my knees, wrapping my arms around her waist. Her kiss warms every part of me. The chills return. My stupid fucking body! It keeps illogically choosing her like a poison running through my veins every time she kisses me. Heck, she doesn't even need to kiss me. Just the warmth of her skin next to me pulls me closer. My life is falling apart the more we touch, yet I can't seem to deny myself this disaster.

I can't love her. So why can't I resist her? I open my mouth, inviting her in.

"I fucking knew it!" I hear Eve say in the corners of my mind as I squeeze my eyes closed.

Blake's lips are so sweet. Her tongue on mine sends signals throughout my entire body, making me both weak and alive. Warming all of the hollow portions of my broken soul.

"It will turn your stomach sour, but in your mouth, it will be as sweet as honey."

I feel sick. I can't be who she needs me to be. I can't keep doing this and expecting a different outcome. I need to let her go. *Arms, take your last embrace,* I think as I will myself to remember this last kiss; remember her just like this.

I place my hands on her chest and push her away. Her eyes search mine, but I'm looking down. I can't look at her when I say this. "I can't do this," I whisper, my voice raspy as I force the words past the lump in my throat. "I'm sorry." I stand and head out of the bathroom as more tears push through me.

"Wait," she says, chasing after me. "You don't have to say it back," she tries to correct. "I just need you to know I'm not going anywhere. I know what you're going through."

"No, Blake!" I stop and turn toward her. "You don't! No one does! I just found some woman sucking off my fiancé! While he ate her out and fingered her to shitty metal music in his disgusting fucking house! I showed up right before my best friend could join their fucking party! She knew the entire time but still had the audacity to call *me* selfish for giving in to *you!* I cheated! I turned from God! Everyone's going to know now! My mom! My-my," I hiccup through the tears. I can't seem to catch my breath. "My dad!"

"First off, Ethan cheated too!"

As if this somehow makes it okay for me to do the things I've been doing. Stringing Blake along, causing her to believe this is something that can keep happening. I know this isn't something I can allow to continue.

The laugh erupting from my chest sounds like a lunatic's. "And that makes it better somehow?"

"No." She rubs the back of her neck. "But it's not any worse."

"Yes, it is!" I say, punching the wall beside me. My knuckles now throb from the impact. "His sexual act was within normal realms. What I've done is downright immoral!"

"Maybe in the Old Testament," she quips.

"Blake! Just stop!" I shout, turning to the front door. "This is too much! I can't do this!" I shake my head, opening it. "I need you to leave."

She stands stock-still in front of me, arms at her sides for a moment in silence, reading my expression for any sort of regret. She won't find it, however. Her face and shoulders drop heavily in defeat and exhaustion. I know she's tired of having this argument. The realization that this is pointless to argue encompasses her face before she hastily saunters out the door. Honestly, at this moment, I don't even care if she's mad or frustrated. I don't care about anything. Eve said I was selfish? Well, right now, I'm being completely altruistic. Sparing Blake the train wreck of me.

The door slams shut, causing me to jump as I walk on shaky legs to my couch. Plopping down, I become cognizant of the heat radiating off my skin. My cheeks and ears burn. My hands and chest are on fire, while the rest of my body is sticky with cold sweat. I try to calm my shuddering breaths as I will my heart to slow. The thump, thump, thump, in my ears is timed perfectly with a sharp pain in the pulse point of my neck. Swallowing around the lump in my throat is painful. I stare at the wall as the weight of the past two hours crashes down onto my shoulders, threatening to flatten me. I'm too exhausted to keep fighting it. My lids are so heavy as I try to make sense of everything.

How long has Ethan been seeing Jaime? I always thought I'd been receiving discounts because my dad was the pastor of EC and her dad was the president of the council. They've been working together forever. I've known her my entire life. I guess assuming we were friends was a bit naïve. I've never really spent anytime outside of EC with her. Were there signs?

I close my eyes and inhale through my nose, taking in the aroma of Mediterranean food bleeding through my walls from another apartment. I listen to the heavy footfalls from the unit above me, using both to center me. Ground me back to reality.

Blake didn't deserve that. I'm mad at Ethan, Eve, and Jaime, not her. If she and Zoe hadn't shown up, I'd probably still be there. She'd scooped me up, driven me home, tended to my stupid self-inflicted cut without any context to how I'd obtained it. Hell, she even offered me support. I should set the record straight that Ethan hadn't caused it.

Maybe it had terrified me when she admitted she loved me. Maybe I don't know how to love her back, but should I have run from it? What if everyone is right and loving Blake doesn't hurt anyone? Maybe it's all in my head. Love isn't exactly an easy word to get out of me, though. It had taken Ethan over a year, even though he'd started saying it around six months in. I needed to be certain the affection I had was concrete, not something that would change over time. And yes, I loved Ethan. Just not in the romantic way a girlfriend should. Enough time with him had caused my body to adapt. Something akin to a member of the family.

This situation is completely different, however. I think I do know I love her. I'm just terrified to admit what those feelings mean. It's not fair to confess these feelings and then continue hiding whatever this is from the world. I'm not in a place to handle the backlash of coming out right now.

Regardless of whether I love her or not, she deserves an apology and a better explanation than yelling at her when she's helping me and then kicking her out.

I push myself off the sofa and head to the shower. Scrubbing in silence, I continue to untangle the Gordian knot my life has become.

Blake shouldn't have to pretend to be a straight person or someone who doesn't love me when we're in public. And picturing my life without her is causing an unbearable pain in my chest. It feels absolutely horrible giving thought to it. So what do I do?

Zoe and Blake are the only ones who have been there to calm my random bouts of panic. Even when I became engaged, they were both there staying beside me, offering an escape, listening, calming my unbidden anxiety without judgment. They reminded me I wasn't alone. I should be grateful God gave me them.

I look at myself in the floor-length mirror of my walk-in closet. Last fall, I'd found this white cotton and lace day dress at a thrift store and hadn't been able to wear it out. But the weather was so nice as I was walking to Ethan's. I hadn't needed a jacket, so when I was stripping the clothes forever linked with today's nightmare, I saw it hanging there. I made the decision to wear it for Blake. If I was going to materialize at her door, why not look good for her?

It's definitely an older dress. I was almost positive it was from the 1950s. When I'd seen it at the thrift store displayed on the mannequin, I knew I had to have it. So, I begged an employee to let me try it on. It fit perfectly! Just covering my shoulders, neckline exposing a small amount of my collarbone. Lace clinging to my upper body before turning to cotton at my waist, flaring out slightly. A white, thin lace ribbon tied at my hips into a small bow in the front dividing the different materials. The dress flowed gracefully down my thighs, ending right below my knees. Such a simple dress, but I felt so beautiful in it. Why not wear it for Blake?

I grab Dakota's black hoodie from my closet as well. It doesn't match the dress, but she'd let me wear it during one of our nights out. I was getting cold, and she'd thrown it around my shoulders without question. Total cliché, now that I think about it, but sweet nonetheless. I'd never given it back and today was finally the day I'd part with it.

I'm sure she doesn't even know I've held onto it all these years, but it was my tether to belonging when the entire world had iced me out for bigger and better things. For months after Dakota told me to fuck off, I wore it to sleep, crying into the torn-up cuffs until my tears ran dry and my body succumbed to slumber. Sometimes, I'd pray not to wake up to another day of loneliness. I prayed not to have to wake to another monotonous day of seeing everyone happy. For years, this hoodie was my support blanket. My only friend.

I don't deserve it anymore. If Blake is over my wishy-washy behavior, she deserves to have it back.

Chapter 27

Blake

"Motherfucker!" I scream, punching the bag hanging from the ceiling in my garage. Watching it swing, chain squealing as it came back for more. Jude had put it up shortly after I'd moved back into our childhood home and was detoxing. He told me our house wasn't going to look like Swiss cheese every time I "threw a tantrum." He always compared my violent outbursts to something akin to childish behavior.

The bag proved to be extremely beneficial as I went through my transitional period of pissed-off Dakota to peaceful Blake. This was also when I got into running whenever a craving would strike. I can't tell you how many days I'd spent running, then punching the bag then running some more. It took a few months of detoxing before I was able to even speak to him. We both knew during the body aches and nausea, I'd definitely have taken it out on him. For this reason, he would always make himself scarce. He'd make breakfast and dinner and leave it on the stove. He'd spend his nights when he wasn't working in his room, waiting for me to come to him.

One snowy December evening, the nausea had finally quelled. The body aches had lessened, and I knocked on his door and asked him to play a board game like we always had when we were kids. He insisted on Magic: The Gathering, which was totally his wheelhouse, but I wasn't a fan. We finally settled on Jenga.

I can't tell you the amount of strength it took to not get mad every time my shaking fingers would knock over the stupidly flimsy tower. We'd play it every night, though. Over and over. He'd sit in silence every time my explosive anger would consume me. I'd curse and scream and fling my hand into the stupid wooden blocks, swearing I wouldn't play it anymore. It was a stupid game. The universe was shaking the table. He blew wind and cheated. His demeanor was always level and calm, raising one eyebrow as a show of my ridiculousness.

Jenga definitely taught me patience. Taught me to slow down and focus on precision. Take my time deciding which block to select and make the right choice before making a bad decision, causing the entire tower to topple over.

I still remember the day, months later, when I'd finally beat him. The grin on his face as I slid the block out with such grace and elegance before placing it at the top. When it was his turn, the block he'd chosen had come out with ease, but upon placing the block at the top of the stack, it had toppled over. His brown eyes met mine from across the coffee table. "I think you're finally ready." His toothy grin radiated such pride in my progress.

"Ready for what?"

"Advocacy."

We'd spent the rest of the night creating our very meticulous Five-Step plan. Bar, outreach, shelter, rehabilitation, employment. Of course, he had to die after only the first step, leaving me alone to figure out the rest. The thought makes my eyes sting, a frustrated heat taking control as I swing one fist after the other into the bag.

Here I am, meant to be saving this town from extinction, but getting hung up on a girl. How had I tricked myself into believing I'd ever mean as much to Phoebe as she so clearly does to me? She'll never love me. We'll never run off into the sunset. The illusion had been shattered forever ago. Yet, I keep believing this time will somehow be different. I've been doing so much better, saving people before they go down a road similar to mine.

Yet, every day with Phoebe, I find myself spiraling back into Dakota. At first it felt good to be umbrella'd in the coolness of her shade. Finally, the person I needed to be to have her. But I'm starting to realize the Blake I aspired so hard to become is slipping further from my grasp, the more I'm rejected by Phoebe.

After mastering the patience required for Jenga, Jude had tasked me a new challenge. The strategy behind 8-Ball. Most people see the ball they want to sink into the pocket, but a professional plays five shots ahead before ever stepping to the table. They don't just see the ball they want to make in, but rather where the cue ball will land after. They set themselves up for their next shot. They play the game in their head first, plan every move, considering all mistakes and strategize how they'll compensate for them.

Before Jude even proposed we open a bar, he'd already mapped out every angle for it to be successful. Through 8-Ball, I was taught how to slow down, eliminate all background noise and focus on the task at hand. Map out a course of action on how to win before ever stepping up to the table.

When he died, I'd went to EC impulsively. No back-up plan. On autopilot shooting shots and hoping I made them.

By doing so, I was blindsided by Phoebe.

When I became clean, I moved into a house filled with nothing but trauma. Jude had bought the house, ensuring I'd never have to deal with any monetary issues in the event of his demise, assuming if he changed the wallpaper, I'd be able to somehow look past it when sitting here alone. I can't go into his room. Can't go into his office, which was once my parents' room. Sitting in the silence of this house, I can still hear the sounds of Austin screaming at my mom through the walls. The alienated sounds of my whimpers when he'd force himself on me.

The house is no longer filled with Jude's goofy, boisterous laugh. Me picking him up, dancing him around until I saw a glimmer enter his eyes. Until he was bigger and stronger than me and the tables had turned. Soon, he was holding me up, forcing me to dance, when all I wanted to do was cry. He was the only person who could really put up with me. And he did. Every day. When I was lost, he searched for me. He never gave up or pushed me aside. Even when people would try to convince him I was a lost cause. He always found a way to bring me back. To make me whole again.

Jude knew me better than anyone. He knew when to wait out my stubbornness. Knew when to interject with his opinions. The best part about him was he knew exactly what to say and how to say it when he did interject.

He was the only person I'd turn to with questions. When I say he was a genius, I mean, he was eleven months younger than me but still managed to graduate at fourteen. He got a Ph.D. in psychology. Eventually earning a bachelor's in business, wrote lengthy papers on his participation in studies focusing on human sexuality and its impact on early childhood development. He bought the bar outright with his life savings. He made his life's work helping children and teens who came from similar backgrounds to ours.

His heart was so big, and his sudden death destroyed more than his family. It affected the community as well. His list of life goals was definitely longer than his lifespan. Ever since I was a kid, I knew I could never amount to him. Yet, every day since his death, I've tried, but the number of lives he's touched is insurmountable.

I need to stop this stupid obsession with Phoebe. I owe him that much, but days like today are entirely too overwhelming. His shoes are too big to be filled by a screw up like me. It's impossible to do this without him, but the community we've created needs me now more than ever. All I can hear is the pounding in my ears as the panic sets in while everyone is lying in wait for me to figure out what to do now. And my first line of business as the solitary face of this movement is to fuck everything up by going to EC impulsively without a plan. Chase around a girl I can't have. I'm going to ruin all of our hard work. Show the people who've been abandoned all their lives, everyone is the same. People who we'd, together, convinced could trust us when they had no one.

I screw off the lid on the bottle of whiskey I'd picked up on my way home, fully prepared to spend the night in deep contemplation, revisiting our long-sought-after plan. I miss this smell. Whiskey had always been Dakota's go-to, but as if a sign from God, the doorbell rings before I'm fully able to let go of my convictions. I'm not sure I can handle visitors right now, but what if it's someone needing our help?

When we created Siren's, we prided ourselves on an open-door policy for anyone who visited. They were given mine and Jude's numbers, and after knowing them for a while, we'd allow them 24/7 assistance and a place to stay. One day Jude was hoping to buy a hotel or something for teens left homeless upon coming out. We'd assist them in finding work and prep them with college arrangements or trade opportunities, including access to different scholarships to apply for. But that was a long time coming.

For now, I just answered the door when someone knocked and provided a room for the kids who needed a place to stay. So, I went to my room and stashed the bottle in the back of my closet in the pocket of a long robe I never wore before heading to answer the door.

I seriously wish I wouldn't have, though, because the person behind it was none other than Phoebe fucking Appleton herself. The cause of all my distress. *Great,* I think, body slumping as I notice her wardrobe. My old high school hoodie and a dress that made me want to make her my housewife. Conventional sexiness personified.

I try to stave off the sudden flutter in my chest at the sight of her because, unlike the other people who knock on this door, she doesn't need help. Not from me.

I stand staring, unable to speak, holding her gaze for what seems like an eternity. I focus on my breathing, which abruptly falls short as my heart warms at the black hoodie torn at the cuffs. I thought I'd lost it years ago.

What could she possibly want? I have nothing left to say. I'm done making an ass out of myself. Can't she just stop tormenting me? I have too much on my plate already.

"I'm sorry," she mumbles, looking down at the ground while fiddling with the cross necklace around her neck. Her dress is stunning. I'm embarrassed to say, my breath caught when I realized it was her standing at my door adorning my old black hoodie, unzipped, exposing the lace of that conservatively sexy white dress and portions of her collarbone. I have to stave off the urge to place my fingers there and trace the outline of the fabric.

"I was upset," she continues, stepping closer. "You didn't deserve that. You've been nothing but amazing to me. Nothing but patient and understanding." She takes a deep breath, advancing another step closer, causing me to move back. Too close. I can't fall into the same patterns I always do at the sound of her voice.

She frowns at my resistance. "I shouldn't have rejected your help. Shouldn't have rejected you." A few strands of her hair fall into her face as she shakes her head, speaking slowly. Or has time slowed down? Either way, I have to squeeze the door tightly to resist moving the stray strands out of her face.

I can do this—have to do this. I need to deny these feelings. I *need* to fight them. For Jude. For the work.

My brain is running rapidly. *Why the fuck does she have to look so damn irresistible, though? I'm supposed to be mad, dammit. I have to tell her to leave. Slam the door in her face. I can't take any more. I sure as shit don't deserve to put up with this. It's too hard, too much on my wellbeing. It's causing me to come apart. All my hard work over the last four years is proving to have done nothing to equip me for her.*

Given I have no strength to respond without saying something stupid and counterproductive, like, '*It's all good,*' or, '*Don't worry about it,*' I decide saying nothing is my best approach.

"Can I come in?" she questions after a moment of silence. "Please?" she says, worrying her bottom lip, and fuck if it doesn't make my stomach fizz. *Shit,* I think as I clench my jaw and push the door open, allowing her to walk past me. *Why am I so shitty at telling her no? Fuck, I hate this.*

She makes her way into my kitchen, grabbing two cups out of the cabinet before filling them at the fridge. I watch in astonishment as she makes herself at home. It makes my mind wonder what it would look like if she lived here. No. It's these thoughts that keep me coming back to her, keep breaking my heart.

She sets the cups down on coasters on the coffee table before smoothing her dress, sitting down, meeting my gaze, gesturing with her eyes for me to join her.

When I do, she puts her hand on my thigh, caressing softly with her thumb, causing my heart to thrum instinctually at her touch on the bare skin under my basketball shorts. It reminds me of earlier when she made me come on her barstool.

I have to remind myself to stay strong. If I show my hand right now, she'll only continue making me want her. She'll crank up the enticing gestures until I crack. She may not *act* like she knows what she's doing, but somewhere deep down inside of her, we both know she does. And she does it naturally. The dress? I see right through it. *Play innocent all you want, Phoebe, but I've always been able to see you for who you truly are.*

"Say something," she exasperatedly pleads. Her voice is slightly above a whisper, sending shivers down my spine. I place my hand on her wrist, stopping her movements, and moving her hand away.

"Stop," I say divisively.

"Stop?" she asks, bewildered. "Stop what?"

"This." I wave my hand over her outline. "You may act like you don't know what you're doing, but I'm not dumb."

"I-I never said you were dumb." She pulls her body back slightly to look at me. "Wait…What am I doing?"

I roll my eyes at the ridiculousness of her behavior. She truly is one in a million. "The hoodie?" I challenge, raising one eyebrow, determined to win this proverbial game of chess.

"I needed to give it back," she combats, sliding it off her shoulders before balling it up and handing it to me. "I meant to when we were in high school, but you ditched me before I could, and then I just held on to it. As a way to be near you."

Her contrition is flattering. What's wrong with me? "Are you trying to make me feel guilty?" I question, grabbing the hoodie. "Because we both know it was better I had left."

"You…You can't possibly mean that." She fumbles her words, but I regret nothing.

"Maybe I do." I place the hoodie on the table before crossing my arms. "You've always been unavailable, but my mind keeps believing I have a chance."

"You do," she breathes. "Blake…" The way my name sounds rolling off her lips always sends a chill down the back of my neck. "Please don't give up on me."

Check, I think as our little game of chess intensifies, but this isn't like when I would play with Jude. I know my odds are better against Phoebe. Right? Her plead, like literal glass shattering in my heart as my eyes search hers. They're so wide and pitiful, tears threatening to fall as she struggles to show some shred of vulnerability, but it's too late, dammit. I refuse to accept, out of nowhere, she actually has feelings for me.

Regardless of how my thoughts are trying to protect me, the idea I may actually have a future with her still circles around the walls of my skull as I visualize it. We're walking through the grocery store like we did when we were kids on my side of town, picking out furniture, but this time, I'm holding her hand down the aisles, kissing her in the parking lot after loading the groceries in the trunk. I'm lying on top of her on our new couch. I'm coming home to her after a hard day.

No. Just because she says she's ready to try doesn't mean she actually will. We're a long way from happily ever after, and it'll never be that simple.

"I don't want to give up on you," I finally mumble. "I just don't think I'm helping you."

"But you are," she whines, holding the last word out slightly. "Listen, I'm not sure how all of this was for you—"

"Not good," I stipulate.

"I can imagine," she replies somberly. "I wasn't raised like this. My sister spent all of her time making waves and they still look at her like she's their biggest regret. She's one disappointment after another." She gathers her words. "I never wanted them to look at me like that. They need me to show the world our family isn't completely messed up. Telling them I'm..."

Again, she searches for the right words to express her recent actions and somehow excuse the way she treats me, but it's not going to work, and she's noticing.

"Look, I don't even fully understand myself. This isn't easy. It's not like I can show you every thought inside my head as they come. If I could, I swear I would. It's like, one second, I'm enjoying the feel of you. I'm intoxicated by your touch. Engulfed by something as simple as your smell." She grabs my arm and squeezes. "And then a dark cloud comes in. Tells me my family will regret they ever had me. God's not listening anymore. The deeper I fall for you, the further I am from Him. The thoughts are so crippling." She rubs her face.

"And I keep telling you, you're not alone." I turn my head in frustration. "Ever since you resurfaced, I've questioned every move we've made together. I've been struggling with the idea my existence is ruining both our lives." I find her eyes, which soften mine. "I was convinced for years we were meant to be, but as each day passes, shit becomes progressively more questionable." I was warned this would happen. Hence why I pushed her away in the first place.

I should be focusing on the next steps to rebuilding Mystic Harbor, yet I can't seem to walk away from what we're creating when we're together. When she'd hurt me a few hours ago by telling me to leave her place, I longed for her embrace, and I'm most definitely not a hugger.

I take a breath and rub my eyes. "I have nothing left," I finally manage. "I can't help you anymore."

"I don't need you to help me, Blake. I never needed you to help me. I'm not some project," she protests, scanning my face for a reaction before finally adding, "I just need you with me while I figure it out. Need you to hold me when I'm losing everything."

"And what if I can't?" I admit, rupturing our lingering gaze, choosing to look past her instead as heat floods my face. "I can't keep being your secret, Phoebe."

Check.

"I'm not asking you to stay a secret forever, Blake..." Her voice is just above a whisper as she drops to her knees in front of me on the floor. "I-I just need more time to prepare myself emotionally. I'm not ready."

"You actually have to make attempts to try, though, and you're not." I huff in frustration. "I have too much on my plate to dedicate all of my time to you. Too many people depend on me. I-I have too much to accomplish. I'm only one person." I slam my hands on my lap.

Her fingers gently push my chin up. "That's too much to take on by yourself."

Check. Shit.

"I-I have Dylan. And Delaney," I say. She doesn't need to know they know even less than me about Jude's plans for Mystic.

I'm now realizing just how close her face has gotten as her emerald eyes bore into my core, filling my body with heat. My cheeks flush as I attempt desperately to hold on to the last bit of my convictions that haven't broken off yet.

She sighs, her breath hitting my face, causing my fingers and toes to burn as an excessive amount of blood pumps to my extremities. Her eyes scan my lap. "Could I..." She tapers off, turning her head to shake off whatever hair-brained thought has filled her consciousness. One corner of her mouth lifts slightly.

"Could you what?" I'm hanging onto her soft words, realizing I'm beyond any form of rationality. It's not like she could even begin to understand the overwhelming issue I've been struggling with since Jude passed away. The impossible weight of this movement I'm forced to carry without him.

I've always prided myself on knowing Phoebe down to her core, but is it possible she somehow knows me as well? I spent our childhood not giving any details, yet when I told her everything the other night, she mentioned she never pushed me to talk because she knew how much I was hurting. Is it possible, without knowing the details, Phoebe still understands me enough to somehow see into me in the same way I see into her?

"It's stupid." She titters nervously under her breath, her face flushes at whatever it is. "I love what you're doing, okay? I think it's extremely necessary for the people of Mystic to have access to this. I love the idea you created some sort of outreach for lost people. I know I'm nowhere near ready to talk to people while I'm still sorting through what this is, but when I'm with you, it feels right. Craving you doesn't seem wrong. And one day…" She takes a deep breath, returning her heavy-lidded eyes to mine. "I want to be able to do this *with* you."

> *"You're not alone."*
> *"Neither are you. I promise."*

Checkmate.

Ever since Jude died unexpectedly, I've felt utterly overwhelmed standing on the precipice of this beautiful idea—already in motion—with no one around to guide me. He'd given me the outline. He'd mapped out the course. Gave me every single bullet point for how to make it successful. I could turn my head when I wasn't sure which avenue to venture toward, and there he'd be. Always. Pointing me in a direction and telling me to walk. He may have been younger, but the mind he embodied was older and wiser, and I need him. I can't do this without him, can't do it alone.

Phoebe may still be figuring out her sexuality, but she is extremely well-versed in counseling people through the various charities at EC. Is it too much of a stretch to assume after she accepts her sexuality and finds resolve, maybe she could help others like herself? Not everyone's story is like mine. Oftentimes, people are stuck in a family of expectation. A family with unreachable standards leaves a child desperate to please everyone. We could work together to build a safe and diverse city people would be proud to live in and then nestle into each other after a long day and decompress.

"Don't give up on me," Phoebe whispers, sending a shiver down my spine as heat coils in my belly.

My mouth runs dry as I try to swallow over the lump forming in my throat. I watch her beautiful verdant irises dip to my lips before joining mine once again. She bites her lip as she exhales through her nose.

My hands find themselves involuntarily sliding behind her neck as they pull her mouth into mine. The kiss is soft and slow, carrying more emotion than I want because I need her. She's right. I can't do this alone.

My breath hitches as she takes my bottom lip between her teeth before sucking and licking it tenderly. I pull away gently to peer into the mossy forest of her soul, allowing it to calm all of my chaotic thoughts. "I-I can try…" I whisper.

I can't guarantee this journey will be easy. I can't even be sure I'm strong enough to hold her together as she falls apart in my arms. Life has taught me there are no promises and to enjoy things as they funnel in because you never know when they'll vanish. This blistering love I have for Phoebe has branded me. It's left its mark upon my soul, and there's no guarantee I'll ever be able to recover from it when it's gone. Loving Phoebe feels like cheating death over and over, and I'm an adrenaline junkie constantly searching for my next fix. I'll never be able to rid myself of the high, even with the knowledge it could kill me. I know too much now. Being the cause of her glistening gaze, even if only for a split second, has me hopelessly habituated and craving more, regardless of the cost.

I've never felt so deeply for someone. I've only ever loved Sam, or so I'd thought. But loving her never felt like this. Sam never made my heart beat in my ears like it does with Phoebe. It never clouded my judgment on what was right and wrong. Loving Sam only hurt. It never felt like tiny firecrackers exploding from a simple touch.

"I will too. You deserve that." Phoebe's fingers trail underneath my shirt, gently strumming along the skin of my hips. She leans in and kisses my cheek. My entire body flushes. "So try hard," she teases. I love her bossiness more than I love air.

If you had told me Phoebe Appleton was naturally officious once you got her out of her shell, I wouldn't have believed you. I'm not sure anybody would have. She spends so much of her energy sacrificing her own wants and needs to satisfy others, she presents to the outside world as a doormat. Yet, once you see the real her, get her comfortable enough to let down her walls and trust you with her deepest desires. She's demanding as hell. I'm not sure how anyone can tell her no. It's such a sight to see. Equal parts adorable and sexy. Simply magnificent. This is a side of her worth showing to the world. And it's a damn shame she doesn't show them.

My mouth finds hers again, unable to be apart for any longer. Her fingers tighten as our kiss grows hungrier, and God, she's intoxicating. Sweet. She smells of fresh flowers and a scent only describable as her own. I've never been able to place it. Like a garden after a fresh rainfall. Like spring personified. I'm convinced flowers bloom for her. My chest swells at her touch on my hips as she hooks the bottom hem of my shirt and pulls it over my head, discarding it on the floor behind me on the couch.

Her cheeks pinken when her sight beelines back to my mouth, going slightly cross-eyed. She's unable to take her eyes off my lips, closing them just before our mouths meet again. Her fingers apply slight pressure as she massages my ribcage, flexing before relaxing her palms over and over. My breathing picks up speed as want enraptures my senses, craving to pull her even closer.

Her thumbs slide underneath my sports bra and find their way to both nipples, brushing the backs of them against my already sensitive peaks. My body twitches from the sensation, causing us to separate as I gasp. "I need this off," she demands in the gentlest way imaginable.

How can I refuse?

My hands reflexively do as told for her. Crossing my arms to grip the bottom and pull it off my chest, I throw it behind me on the couch to join my shirt on the floor. Now topless, I fall onto the back cushions, allowing her mouth to explore every inch of my torso. Electricity shoots throughout my entire body as I grow wetter with every press of her kiss on my skin.

When her lips finally wrap around one of my nipples, my legs tighten around her waist. I watch in amusement as her tongue works over my flesh. Using my fingers to move her hair from where it falls over her shoulders, I trail a path along the seam to her clavicle. She really does look fucking amazing in this dress. It suits her so well. It's as if it was made specifically for her, complimenting the sharp angles of her collarbone and shoulder blades. My hands barely apply pressure as I trace the fabric, watching my fingers slope across the curves of the sharp angles. Goosebumps pebble the back of her neck as I do.

I'll never grow tired of watching her body respond to me. The way it reacts to my every touch. "God, this dress is so..." The words catch in my throat as I struggle to catch my breath as her teeth nip slightly before her tongue circles my nipple.

"So what?" she asks in between kisses, but I can feel the warmth settling in her cheeks.

"Beautiful." I exhale in relief, trying and failing to contain my composure.

"*You're* beautiful," she whispers while her hands slide my shorts and boxers down my legs. "And," I lift, allowing her access, "I want to show you how much." Now completely naked, I watch her mouth venture lower. Butterflies do fucking backflips in my chest.

I've honestly never felt comfortable enough to allow someone to do something as intimate as go down on me. It leaves me with an uncomfortable sense of vulnerability. Touching is hard enough for me. I've never allowed sex to become personal, and oral is about as personal as I think you can get.

But this isn't just anyone, I try to remind myself. This is Phoebe. Sweet, curious, not-so-innocent Phoebe kissing my hip bones. "I believe you," I croak. "You really don't have to...to..." My words catch again as her finger slides up my insanely damp center.

"Shh..." she whispers, kissing the crease between my leg and body, her tongue doing circles as she inserts her finger slowly. Her eyes look up at me, locking on as she removes it, only slightly, before slowly reinserting herself inside me. Relishing my reaction, her cheeks redden. "Let me."

Fuck, it's so insanely hot. Her eyes are so dark, lids so heavy, cheeks so flushed. I'm a goner. I can't say no. How could anyone tell those big doughy eyes no? For a second, I wonder if maybe I've died. Is this what heaven looks like?

No. No, this is real fucking life, and Phoebe fucking Appleton is about to boldly go where I've never allowed anyone else to go. She's practically fucking trailblazing me like a Jeep or Ford commercial. Why am I thinking about car commercials right now?

"Can I?" she pleads as I try not to hyperventilate.

I can't…words. If I do, I know it'll come out scratchy, so I make do with a nod and "Mhmm" barely managing to scrape past my vocal cords. Embarrassed at the noise, I try to clear my throat as quietly as possible. What if she doesn't like it? It could scare her off of women forever. Is that possible?

All of my insecurities quickly die when her tongue slides along my clit simultaneously as her finger penetrates me deeper this time. My eyes instantly snap shut. *Fuck! How is she actually good at this on her first try? Is she a quick study? Did I somehow teach her this through all the different times I've done it to her?* It's like when she first fucked me; she found my G-spot faster than the average person ever has on their first time. A goddamn savant in the bedroom. Someone attuned to your every mannerism—regardless of how minuscule you may think they are—and then repeating the actions, producing the best results until you're crying out her name in ecstasy. I can't help but think maybe it's a quality she obtained by spending a lifetime constantly reading people to please them. It would only make sense to spill over into the bedroom, as well.

And fuck, now *I'm* spilling over. My legs have gone weak from her tongue trailing over my pussy in perfectly precise circles before she inserts a second finger to her first. "Fuck," I choke out, causing her to let out a moan into me. My hands grab her hair, tightening as I watch her devour me.

It's only then she opens her eyes and watches my reaction as she latches onto my clit, tongue completing a full circle with every thrust into me. "Oh my God," I whimper as my body quakes, legs tensing around her head. "You're doing such a good job, baby," I choke. "Oh…*fuck,* Don't stop. *Uh*…yeah. I'm gonna, oh God, I'm gonna…"

My head falls back against the couch as I come harder than I think I ever have. She doesn't stop, though. She continues groaning into me, her face riding the waves of my orgasm, sure not to lose the spot she's latched onto, fingers pumping in tandem with her tongue until I come a second time.

I lift my head from the back of the couch as I feel the press of Phoebe's body sliding up mine. Stopping at my neck to plant a kiss before journeying the rest of the way back to my mouth. My hands rest shakily on her hips as I taste myself on her mouth, kissing me passionately. "You taste good." She blushes.

"Were you worried I wouldn't?" I say, hoping she'll read it more as ego rather than the insecurity it so obviously is.

"No." She licks her bottom lip. "I just…" She looks down to my chin and then back up. "It's different from me. Like," she ponders, "almost like nothing. You don't really have a taste." She shrugs.

I don't think she even realizes the relief she's given me with her words. I've allowed myself to be weak in front of her, and she's nurturing it. She isn't taking my emotions and stomping all over them like Sam and other women have in the past. It's taking everything I have to fight off this incessant urge to say I love her right now. I can't scare her off again, not after this. I need her more than I care to admit right now.

I scrape my nails gently up the sides of her thighs, hiking up her dress instead of saying anything. After a moment, she's standing, locking onto me, looking unreasonably nervous, contemplating something. The look only lasts a second, though, before she lifts her dress to slide down her panties.

The gesture causes me to lift in my seat, licking my bottom lip as her knees cradle me, sitting down on my lap. Her hands find my shoulders as mine venture past her short curls to the wetness between her legs. She's soaked, so it's safe to say she wasn't turned off by me coming in her mouth—twice. Good to know.

Her tongue hits my neck leaving heavy, passionate kisses there while I massage and stroke her clit. Her hips move into my fingers, so demanding I probably could just sit here and let her take what she needs, but I'm a hands-on kind of girl. Where would the fun in that be? I've never had her in this position before, and it's so fucking sexy to feel her power on top of me as she dissolves slowly into my touch.

The sound of her panting in my ear is the prettiest noise you can ever imagine. Hearing her breath shudder as her hips twitch into me is something otherworldly, and I don't think anything will ever be able to top it. It's a sound with the ability to send both flutters to my chest and tingles to my center at the same time.

"I want to feel you," she whispers shakily into my ear, her voice so quiet I almost don't hear it. She lets out a huff as her hips rock against my finger. The warm air from her mouth causes the hairs on my neck to stand before she buries her face into the crook of my neck shyly.

"You are," I breathe back, running my free hand up her bicep, admiring the pebbling of her skin to my touch. It's soft as silk.

"I-inside me," she stammers, her voice barely even audible. "I…want to feel your fingers inside me."

Ice runs from my head all the way down to my toes. It's in this moment I decide I need to make some revisions to my previous statement. Nothing will ever be able to top *this*. The sound of her breathing into me as her hips work my hand before somehow deciding she trusts me enough. She's stated her indignation toward penetration so passionately I figured until she was married, it'd never happen—and given she isn't actually attracted to men and can't seem to grasp the idea of ever marrying a woman, she'd die on the hill of virginity. So, I'd refused to ever push the clear boundary she had set for any and all romantic partners she'd ever possess.

Could the fact I didn't push be the reason why she wants it to be me now? Regardless of the reason, I'm not sure I can do it. Anxiety washes over me as my eyes widen, stopping all movement my hand has been making between her thighs.

This truly is a night of firsts from Phoebe. I would've never assumed she'd want to go down on me, but never in a million years would I have expected this. My heart races as she stops her movements and lifts her head from my neck, face flushed with nerves, taking in my expression, trying to assess why I'm suddenly frozen. I'm sure her assessment is giving a clear representation of sheer panic.

"You—" I begin before my tongue falls short. Let me try this again. "I couldn—" Nope, those aren't the right words either. "I—"

She bites her lip. "I know," she grunts in frustration. "But I want it to be you." Her fingers encase my wrist in between her legs before her finger ghosts over my middle one. Her thumb hooks around the top of my palm, gently pushing my finger slowly into her. Our eyes search each other's as the tightness of her body encloses around half my finger. Sending even more wetness to collect between my own legs. Her eyelashes flutter, her hand losing its grip around mine as I slide back out, contemplating if I should really do this.

"You're sure?" I ask, voice shaking. Hell, my whole body is shaking. I only sank halfway into her before retreating. But *fuck*, it felt good. Her expression was exhilarating.

"Mhmm," she mumbles, biting her lip again. "I can't imagine it being with anyone else."

Something almost primal takes over my other senses and before I can think it through, I'm slowly sinking back in, slightly deeper, but still not to the knuckle. Watching to ensure she hasn't changed her mind.

Her eyes grow darker, boring into my soul as her eyebrows furrow, the green of her pupils almost nonexistent slivers under their heavy lids. I'm enthralled by her beauty, intently studying the way her lips part, panting in short bursts as I slide in again, this time as deep as it'll go. She moans as I descend again and again, picking up the pace slightly. A puddle has officially formed between my thighs, and my face burns as I watch her, eyes rolling back as her eyelashes flutter with each gentle exhale, responding to every inward slide of my finger.

"Is this okay?" my shaky voice whispers, unable to stop my own insecurities. As addicted as I am to this new experience, if she told me to stop, I would. In the past, I never cared enough to worry, but this is Phoebe. She will never be like anyone else. I never want to hurt her.

"Yeah," she breathes weakly, her forehead pressing against mine. The warm moisture of her breath against my face as she struggles to keep it steady is making it hard to focus. "So good." It comes out so tenderly as her hips start moving again, keeping time with my slow and steady ministrations while looking into my eyes.

I'm hooked, unable to look away as she rides my hand. "More," she pleads. Completely entranced, I add a second to my first. Phoebe gasps as her face falls into my neck. My free hand wraps around the small of her back, pulling her closer to me. I'm panting, swallowing hard, my mouth consequently dry. "You feel…so…*good*," she whimpers between gasps.

I can't believe this is real, I think working my fingers into her. This has to be a dream, right? Tomorrow, I'll wake up and realize life is still shitty. I drank myself into a coma or something, choked on my puke after passing out on my floor. She didn't really come over to my house to apologize. People never really apologize. This is seriously too good to be true. It's not really happening, right?

I'm careful not to hurt her. I can't recall my first time very well—given the amount of alcohol I had consumed—but I have it on good authority from others that sometimes, it hurts. I've also been told my fingers are quite long compared to the average person, which used to be a compliment until now. So, it stands to reason the slightest misstep of my fingers could possibly ruin this for her. If I'm going to take Phoebe Appleton's virginity, I'm sure as fuck going to make it as magical as humanly possible, goddammit.

She may have boldly gone where no one has gone before when she went down on me, but I'm boldly going—

"Deeper," she groans, her voice needy and guttural. One hand digs into my hair while the other's nails claw at my ribs. I'm panting heavily, trying to keep my composure over how beautiful she looks. Her face and chest flush as I use my free hand to cup her breast, making short work of finding her already-raised nipple through the fabric of her dress, pinching it between my fingers as I slide deeper into her.

"Does this feel good?" I ask teasingly, allowing a smirk to form at the corner of my mouth. I can tell it does; I just like hearing her say it.

"Oh…*yeah*," she moans low and shuddered. Hearing the words makes me ache. I'm so wet, I think I might come again, just watching her glow as she takes my fingers.

"You look so good fucking my hand," I hiss as she pushes away from me, allowing her hips to rotate more freely. She bites down on her lip and runs a hand through her own hair. I wish I was a painter right now so I could capture this look: her body in my lap, biting her lip to stave off the way her mouth wants to hang open in pleasure. The rock of her hips, dancing in perfect step with my hand between her legs. I pick up the pace. "You take my fingers so well." I curl them inside of her with the next thrust and watch her come undone.

An indescribable, feral feeling becomes me. I need to have her. Need to hear her say it. "Tell me you're mine," I growl, stopping to work a circle inside of her. "No one else's."

Her mouth falls open, eyes meeting mine, passionate and pleading as I press in again. And again. Bracing herself on my shoulder with one hand for support, tensing, nails digging into my skin. Her hips twitch in rapture.

"God, baby," she whimpers, a pout of arousal forming as she shouts, "I never want to be anyone else's."

I lift her with one arm and lay her on her back on the couch, getting on top. I pump into her, her head lowering, mouth agape, watching my fingers disappear and reappear. "Faster," she pleads, eyes shooting up to meet mine. "Fuck me faster," she moans between gasps.

I comply. Like I said, it's damn near impossible for me to tell Phoebe no. Not when I have her, not when she's mine. Especially not while her gaze is bouncing from my eyes to my hand. Clearly enthralled by what I'm doing to her, how I'm making her come apart.

Her breathing labors as I increase the speed, curling upward with every press in. My hand lifts her dress higher to stroke my thumb over her belly button as I bury my face in her neck, leaving passionate kisses on her collarbone, trailing all the way up her neck before nibbling on the bottom of her earlobe. "All mine," I hiss, completely consumed. *She's mine. She's finally mine.* I press my forehead back to hers, continuing my rhythm within her.

Phoebe's nails scratch deeply down the back of my ribcage as she begins to tighten and close around my fingers. "Are you going to come for me?" I whisper, sending a shiver throughout her body as she twitches and shakes.

"Yeah...mmm Blake...oh God, yeah, make me come for you," Phoebe mewls, her eyebrows tensing. Within seconds, her center is closing so tightly around my fingers I struggle to continue moving within her, but if it was hurting her, she doesn't give any sign of it.

Our eyes connect again as she comes, and it's as if we're connecting in so much more than a visual sense. We are becoming entangled within each other. One being. I feel an intense emotion, and I know she's feeling it too. Fireworks ignite within my chest, synchronizing with her spasms. It almost sounds stupid explaining it, but I could see into her soul, and she's peering into mine. The world around us ceases to exist, and all our senses become engulfed in nothing but each other.

This indescribable connection doesn't subside right away, either. It doesn't stop when I gently slide my hand out from within her, causing a slight twitch of her hips from the sensitivity. It doesn't even stop as we continue to look at each other as she tastes herself on my fingers. I run my other hand through her hair while continuing to lie on top of her. I kiss her cheek, a cold chill still washing over every inch of my skin. The flutters in my stomach go haywire as I find her still staring when I pull away from her.

She braces my face in her hands, pulling me down into yet another mind-numbing, mountain-moving kiss. I miss her mouth the second we part. We meet again, leaving something unspoken between us, but both of us in a silent understanding of what it is. Oftentimes, I find it hard to meet people's gaze, but this time, I can't seem to look *away.* I see my future there. I see the person I've worked so hard to become. The person deserving of her.

"I love you so much."

WHY DO I KEEP DOING THAT?!

It's impossible to hold it in now. *Stupid, stupid!* The electricity between us has been charging it up since we started. Intensifying with every moment. I feel stupid as I wait for what seems like forever for a response. It may have only been a second, but my heart is pounding so violently in my ears, I begin to panic.

Right as I decide to apologize, two things happen simultaneously: she opens her mouth to speak, and my phone rings on the coffee table. Our heads swivel to it in unison. "Doe-Boy."

Saved by the bell, I think, letting out a sigh of relief, moving my body to sit beside her on the couch, trying my best to remain calm and not leap for the phone. Her legs stretch out over my lap as I reach for it.

I have to break this spell I'm under. Damn those gorgeous emeralds and phenomenally beautiful soul. It obviously makes me do stupid, unsolicited shit. Shit like spouting out I love you's, regardless of how many times I tell myself to hold it in.

"Hang on," I mime, swiping my thumb over the screen to answer. Delaney never calls me this late.

Chapter 28

Phoebe

"Why?" Blake asks into the phone. I'm not sure who "Doe-Boy" is, but anger soon floods her face at his response.

"What?!" she shouts in disbelief, her spine ramrod straight before standing completely, pushing my legs off of her lap and collecting her clothes. "No," Blake gasps, her eyes flooding as she paces around. "No!" A pause lingers between us as she grabs her shorts and boxers off the floor, sliding them onto her hips. "I'll be right there. No. Delan—stop! I'll meet you there. I'm going."

Her glare burns with intense anger in my direction as she ends the call. "You need to leave," she says quietly through gritted teeth as she tosses me my underwear. I can see her trying to keep her resolve but fighting back an intense urge to explode.

"What happened?" I ask, inserting my suddenly cold legs into my underwear, while still seated on her couch.

"You happened," she mumbles through her gritted teeth. My stomach sinks. "I knew I shouldn't have done this." She wanders behind the couch to grab her shirt and bra.

"What?" I say disbelievingly, now feeling incredibly exposed. "Done what?" Surely, she doesn't mean…

"Phoebe, we can't be together." Her spirit sounds broken, all anger seemingly replaced with disappointment and sadness. My heart pounds in my neck leaving behind an ache.

"Why not? I'm—" *in love with you.* I try to swallow the lump in my throat, not having any luck. I have no fucking idea what Delaney said on that phone call, but I'm quickly regretting my choices within the last few hours. I should've stayed home. Shouldn't have come here.

No. I regret nothing because I know she felt it, too. None of this makes any sense. What happened during that phone call? What did Delaney tell her?

"You're what?" she snaps. "Sorry?" The scoff escaping her throat is making it hard to breathe, crushing my insides. I just gave myself to her.

"No." I clear my throat. I can't apologize without first knowing what I've done. She interrupts before I can say that thought.

"Figures," she bites out. "Just give it up! You can't even accept yourself. Can't accept me enough to love me! You can't help me. Every time you're around, you make things worse! All you ever do is make things worse!"

I wince. Ouch. I have no idea what's going on. What the fuck? Panic runs like ice through my veins as her shouting rips through the quiet, intense cloud of magic we'd shared only moments prior. She feels it, too. I know she does. She loves me…so why is she saying all of this now?

"And now your presence has impacted Jude! What he worked for!" Jude? What did I do to Jude? "I should've listened to Eve!"

"Eve?" At this point, I'm shaking and so utterly confused, I'm not sure she's even listening. Her emotions are clearly strong-arming any rational faculties.

"Funny," she continues, her words frosted, sending a shiver down my spine as they land. "She thought I'd fuck *you* up back in high school. But all her fucking threats never accounted for what *you'd* do to *me!* What you'd do to Jude!" Her eyes water. "I'm leaving. You need to go home."

"No!" I shout, struggling to make my brain comprehend more than the lace fabric of my dress between my fingers. "I'd never hurt Jude—what did Eve—I…" I have no idea where to start. So much new information just barreled out of Blake's mouth, and now I'm struggling to articulate an appropriate response. We can work through this. I'll just go with her. We can figure this out together, and she can explain what Eve did on the way to wherever we're going. She'll tell me what she thinks I did to Jude. "I wanna go with you." My eyes sting. I can feel my lip quivering. "Let me go with you," I beg as I watch her put on her shoes. I sound so desperate. God, I am desperate. She can't leave it like this. I'm not entirely sure why she's attacking me. It makes no sense. Everything that just happened was so amazing. Why did she have to pick up the phone? What did I do?

It takes me a second to collect the events and realize Eve had to have been behind me losing Dakota all those years ago. A burning sensation horrendously explodes in my chest. A pit forms in my stomach as I stand shaking. Why hadn't she said that sooner? Even if fear had driven her to stay quiet all those years ago, she could've told me now. Could've told me anytime within the almost four weeks she's been back in my life. If I would've known, maybe I could've spoken to Eve.

No. We both know she wouldn't have listened, and even more issues would've erupted from it. The sheer mention of Blake had caused a violent distaste on Eve's tongue during bowling, so to confront her about Dakota or even explain Blake and

Dakota were one and the same would've resulted in nothing but disaster. I can see that now.

"Go home, Phoebe!" she asserts, unable to look at me as she opens the door. Her eyes soften. "This isn't going to work out between us."

I immediately understand how she must've felt earlier when I'd demanded she leave my apartment. She was only trying to care for me, and I was unreachable. Now that the tables have turned, I feel so stupid. Heat and embarrassment creep up my face and ears as I stand there, trying to find the perfect words to change her mind.

Now it's my turn to know there aren't any. Her mind is made up, and there's no convincing her otherwise right now. Because this isn't like the last time she'd told me to leave her house. The look in her eye in this moment is a warning that if I so much as try to invade her personal space or refuse to leave, she'll hurt me. It's almost pleading to not try. She's desperately trying to hold it together but it's a battle we can both see she's losing. Whatever Blake is convinced I did is overshadowing any and all ability she has at listening to reason right now.

And what if she's right? What if we do bring out the worst in each other? What if all we are capable of is bringing the other pain and misery? I sure am pretty damn miserable right now. I gave myself to her. The soreness between my legs continues to remind me of the evident mistakes I've just made.

She *is* right. I need to stop making her miserable. Need to leave her alone. In this moment, however, I refuse to let her see me cry. I feel stupid enough. So, with a dry mouth and a broken heart, I slip on my sandals and leave as quickly as I came, stopping only once to take a final glimpse over the house I'll never feel safe in again. One last look at the woman I know I'm in love with. She doesn't think I ever could, but I'm realizing now it was impossible not to.

Maybe it's best if I let her continue believing that.

Chapter 29
Blake

I screech to a halt, throwing my truck into park before jumping out. The windows to Siren's Song are shattered as I walk up to Delaney standing outside the door.

"Do we know who did it?" I demand of one of the police officers inside as the blue and red lights blink through the broken panes.

He lifts his shoulders, not seeming to care much about a dyke and her bar. They don't give a shit. Why would they? They've been trying to shut this place down for two years now. It's probably a relief to them. I'm sure if they do figure out who did it, they'll give them a pat on the back, congratulating them on a job well done.

I hope they know if they leave the detective work to me, I'll go to prison with a smile on my face after I find the culprits who destroyed my brother's fuckin' bar. I'll make it slow. The police will have to stop me because I'll torture them for weeks until they find me.

The bar is fuckin' wrecked!

My body vibrates as I step over the wet, broken glass of shattered bottles. I notice the sign behind the counter torn off the wall, laying crooked on the floor. My eyes sting as heat rises to my ears. Everything is hazy, like a bad dream. I struggle coming to terms with this being my actual reality. Some of the tables are completely destroyed. Nothing more than piles of wood scattered everywhere around me. In combination with the shattered liquor spewed all across the back wall and behind the counter, they could've lit a match on their way out. They even slashed the expensive felt cloth we'd chosen for the pool tables.

I trace the word "Carpet Muncher" etched into the bar top with my finger as tears of anger fill my eyes. A pestering hum forms at the base of my skull, growing louder as the world around me falls away. I close my eyes, trying to block out the useless blue and red lights flashing through the broken glass of the front windows, no doubt the intruders' point of entrance.

"Blake," Delaney says placing a soothing hand on my shoulder behind me. I swing my arms violently as he holds up his hands, shielding his face. "Stop! We all lost something here," he pleads through his desperate sobs. "You think Siren's isn't Jude for me too?" He wipes his tear-soaked cheeks with the backs of his palms.

"Just back the fuck off, Delaney," I bark. "It's not the fucking same." I imagine the look of disappointment on Jude's face, if he were alive right now to see this.

"Blake!" Dylan's voice booms through the tension. "This isn't anyone's fault."

"That's fucking bullshit!" I slam my hand on the bar. "Right, Delaney?" I set my jaw, grinding my back molars as my eyes burn through him. I throw a hand up. "Say I fucked it all up like you knew I would. Say it's my fucking fault I went to EC. I poked the beehive." I realize how sweaty I've become when I grab a fistful of my hair, looking around at the wreckage. "I was looking for a fucking fight, and I found one!" I kick a broken chair in front of me before stomping back to where he's standing next to Dylan. "I ruined the last thing I had of my brother because I couldn't stay away from Phoebe." I ball my fists into his shirt, pulling him nose to nose. "Fucking say it!"

"That's enough!" Dylan wedges her arm between us, trying to get me to release the death grip I have on his expensive pink Psycho Bunny polo. Delaney stares at me through tear-soaked eyes. His jaw is clenched, his body rigid, refusing to move or make a sound. He knows if he says anything, I'll knock his ass out. "Think about what you're doing, Blake." Dylan levels her tone as she places her palm in the middle of my chest. "Fucking use your brain." I shift my narrowed eyes, meeting hers. "You're not mad at Delaney. This isn't his fault. Think about who you're becoming because you're going to have to live with what you do next."

I look into Delaney's eyes once more, the muscles in my jaw flexing. Dylan is right. Dakota would have beaten Delaney to a pulp. Would've convinced herself all of his comments were a self-fulfilling prophecy, and if he had kept his mouth shut, we wouldn't be here right now. She would've shut his mouth for him. Dakota wouldn't have accepted her fault in all of this. There was always someone else to blame.

I release my grip around his shirt and exhale, collapsing to my knees. Dylan joins me, rubbing my shoulders as I shake, trying to catch my breath. "Good choice. Now." She looks around. "Who could've done this?"

"Ethan Fenech," I rasp out, wiping my nose. "He was hurting Phoebe, so I..." I'm so embarrassed. "It's all my fault. Jude would be so pissed. I'm such a fuck-up."

"You're not." Delaney sighs, meeting Dylan and me on the floor now. "I mean, he'd probably be a little mad, but I have no doubt in my mind he expected this to happen when you went to Step Two. He even told me that."

I squint and turn to him. "You didn't think to tell me that after you found out I went to EC?"

He cocks his head. "Well, I don't think anyone expected you to choose EC as your first fucking outreach attempt. I think I speak for everyone when I say we were more worried about your wellbeing."

Dylan nods in agreement. "We didn't even know you were starting outreach, Blake. Jude just died. We figured there'd be more conversation on next steps before you made a move."

"I have no idea what I'm doing," I confess. "And not telling me he'd had conversations with you guys isn't helping."

"Just before he died," Delaney says. "I asked him why we were dragging our feet."

I wipe the tears from my neck and cheeks, swallowing hard. "What'd he say?"

Delaney lifts my chin. "That he was almost done setting up insurance. That was two months before he died."

Dylan's eyes widen. "Did he tell you any insurance stuff?"

I think about it for a minute. Jude kept everything pretty close to the chest until it was meant for me to know. If he didn't tell me he was setting something up, it meant it wasn't set in stone yet. "The night he died, he'd asked me to come home early. Said he had something he wanted to talk to me about. He was in such a good mood." My bottom lip quivers at the memory of him dancing around like an idiot. "He was dancing. Pulled me in to join him, 'I have the best news,' he said…but then he collapsed. He-he died. Could that have been the insurance?" I bury my face in my knees and begin rocking.

"It was," a low voice behind us booms through the bar. Standing at the door is Conroy Adams, mayor of Mystic Harbor. "Sorry it took me so long to get here. Turns out most of the police don't view this as a high priority." He rotates his palms upward, looking around, eyebrows pinched into a "V" as he flips over a chair that had managed to survive this tornado of destruction. "Rest assured, the station will be retrained on what priorities take precedence, but for now," he raises his voice, allowing it to reverberate through the entire bar, "you guys are good." He motions to the police. "Pack up and go home."

After they're gone, Conroy approaches us once more. "I need to see your back room."

"Back room?" Delaney echoes.

I rise, leading Conroy to the kitchen, and watch as he peers around the room, shifting his gaze to the walls. "This is going to seem a little strange, but did you walk the building before it opened?"

"I saw the blueprint, but no. Jude already knew he'd wanted this place before he'd even told me his plans for it."

"You wouldn't happen to know where that blueprint is, would you?"

I chew the inside of my cheek, sinking my gaze to the floor. "No."

"Hmm, no matter, I suppose," he huffs. "We need to find a supply closet."

"It's over here." Delaney points to the other side of the room.

"No." Conroy tsks. "Not that one. Did your brother do any reorganizing of this kitchen in the time before his death?" He's now feeling the walls and glancing behind shelves.

"I mean." I shuffle through my memories of the layout. "No. He did decide to add paneling to this wall because he said the wall looked ugly being just white. He did it after hours, so we didn't have to shut down."

"Perfect!" He walks over to the wall and points to the tall cabinets. "We need to move these."

Delaney and I move one while Dylan and Conroy move the other, and we watch as he runs his hand along the wall.

"Blake," he asks, "do you trust these people?" He bounces his head from Dylan to Delaney.

"With my life," I assure him.

"Okay, good. I'd advised Jude to keep this one close to him. We didn't fully know who to trust, so I can guarantee he didn't mention this until it was done because he didn't want this falling into the wrong hands."

"Didn't want what falling into the wrong hands?" I ask.

"This." Conroy twists a light bulb inside the sconce on the wall, and the whole thing opens like a door. "This used to be a supply closet. When you guys signed the lease, we juggled around the idea of a hidden surveillance room. I guess he chose this, barricading it off when you guys first started moving things in."

"Why wouldn't he have told me?" I step inside and view the ten monitors wrapped around the tiny room.

"When Jude brought me the idea for this movement, I cautioned him people would pretend to be a part of the mission just to infiltrate it from the inside. This isn't the first time we've tried to set something like this up in Mystic Harbor. I hate to say it, but EC is very resourceful, and anything threatening their political standings doesn't last very long." He begins typing on the keyboard. "He ensured me he'd keep Siren's above board with health codes and vet people during the hiring process, but people still manage to slip through the cracks. So, after two years, I was shocked you guys were still standing. That's when I gave him the go-ahead to begin outreach." He stops typing and turns to me. "On one condition."

Why does all of this sound like some fucking covert mission shit? "Was Jude a fucking secret agent or something? What the fuck is happening right now?" I can't believe this. How did I not know this shit would be so convoluted?

"I have a feeling he didn't tell you everything because he knew it'd discourage you, Blake. The idea he had was brilliant, but he'd been keeping a close eye on it for years. He really was a smart one. He knew it would take more than a bar to go against a church that controls more than half of Mystic Harbor. I told him he needed to have security set up before you moved forward because their pastor is good, but even Peter Appleton hasn't been able to reign in his flock. Even he tried to rally for change, and in the almost three decades he's been working for EC, he's only ever managed to get them to expand the size of their Nave." He tsks. "Been working with him too. It's tragic, really. He's just a face. He has no real power. The council have voted against him at every turn. I bet you didn't even hear about when he took the idea of making EC all-inclusive to the board fifteen years ago. His career almost didn't make it. It was worse than the time he suggested an open table congregation."

He hits the enter key. "Gotcha," he says, swiveling around to face me in his chair. I watch on the screen as Ethan and some woman grab liquor bottles, smashing them on the ground. Upon moving closer, I know exactly who it is. "Jaime?" The barista from that creepy Jesus coffee shop? "What the fuck?"

"You know her?" he asks, but I can tell he does too.

"I know both of them. That's Ethan Fenech and Jaime…honestly, I don't know her last name. She works at Blessed Beans near EC."

Conroy nods. "Bishop. Her parents own it. They're lifetime members. Her parents, parents, *parents* all attend or have attended, womb-to-tomb. I wish Jude would've explained some of this to you before you started the outreach phase. We've been working with Peter for over a year now. Pretty sure he expected you."

I look at the screen, watching Ethan mounting Jaime on the bar top. My lip curls. "I'm going to need to bleach that counter now."

"Really?" Delaney huffs. "Were you planning on keeping the 'carpet muncher' inscription?"

"Won't have to." Conroy's booming guffaw seems slightly over-extravagant as he adds, "Jude has this place insured better than Fort Knox."

✝

"I don't need a fucking chaperone," I grumble. It's 5:00 in the morning and Delaney followed me to my house like I'm some kind of child who can't be trusted.

In all honesty, I probably shouldn't be alone, but I hate it nonetheless. All I want to do is curl up with the bottle of whiskey I stashed away when Phoebe knocked on my door earlier. There's a strong urge in the pit of my stomach to feel the burn. I can taste it on my tongue.

"We both know that's not true. Dylan agrees we need to take turns."

"I'm heading to the bathroom," I say sardonically. "You wanna follow me while I piss too?"

"Come on, B." He groans. "Stop acting like this. It's good to have friends."

A normal person wouldn't have friends crawling up their ass, but because I'm a recovering addict, I have to have a babysitter. Instead of sorting through my emotions alone, someone has to hold my hand and tell me how to feel. "It's good to have space, too."

"That's bullshit." Delaney lets out an exhausted sigh. "The night Jude died, you begged for this. And don't think I didn't find out about you needing Dylan when you talked to Phoebe—"

"Fuck, can anything at all be confidential?!" I shout.

"Don't get mad at her, B. You need—*WE* need each other." *Nice save, dickhead.* "We're a team. If any of us fall, this whole thing goes tits up, and we need you most. You and Jude mapped everything out—"

"He didn't tell me shit, Delaney! You guys probably know more than I do. He didn't tell me about working with Pastor Pete. He didn't tell me about the cameras. I'm stupid, and he knew I'd fuck it up! Why can't you guys see that, too?" The room spins from the amount of anger seething through my veins. If I don't figure out a way to calm down, I think I might actually hit him. Maybe Dylan would've been a better person to stay tonight. At least she knows how to box. Why couldn't I be left alone? *The bag,* I think and head to the garage. Delaney follows, not letting up.

"We got those fuckers, Blake. In a few hours, everything will be taken care of. Insurance will cover the damages, and we'll be smooth sailing. They just paid for a massive upgrade. Jude probably knew they'd be playing into our hands and helping us by doing this."

I start throwing punches blindly at the bag while Delaney continues. "He was going to tell you."

I stop and look at him, fire burning the back of my eyes.

"He was! What do you think the good news was?"

"I don't fucking know! He died, Doe-Boy! He never got to tell me, and now he's dead." I start swinging violently again. "He knew I couldn't do this shit. He knew it was too much for me. Hell, even Conroy fucking Adams thinks it's too much for me!"

"That's not what he said," Delaney says, holding the bag. "Can you just stop for a second?"

I throw my hands up before grabbing at my hair, trying to calm my thundering heart by counting to ten. I turn around, unable to face Delaney in fear I'll hit him next.

"I can't believe you think you don't have it in you," he says, slightly softer. "Because everyone who cares about you does. Especially Jude, and him not telling you wasn't his fault. He wanted to tell you everything."

"What makes you think that?" I say through gritted teeth. "You contact him from the grave? He visit you in a dream? Tell me, Madame Delaney, are you a ghost whisperer now?" I walk over and plop down on a folding lawn chair in the middle of the room, taking in the scent of motor oil and gasoline as I continue to catch my breath.

"I don't need to be, Blake. He didn't come up with this shit *because* of you."

"He literally told me he did!" I lean forward, resting my head in my hands.

"I don't think you understood him correctly, then," he says, sitting down in the chair next to me. "Do you know what he was doing the night you called him and said you needed help—that you were done fighting and wanted to be sober?"

I don't reply.

"He was doing research into ways to reach you. He'd been searching for months. One day, he found Guiding Light while looking for an all-inclusive church because he knew you. He knew you still believed."

"How the fuck would he have known that?" I blink rapidly.

"You spent all of your time in high school at youth groups. You went to Bible studies when you were nineteen. Sure, you started fucking the wives, but Jude wasn't convinced the reason you went was for revenge. It didn't matter how many times you told him, either. He knew you went there looking for a safe space to find God, Blake. Jude didn't even *believe* in God, but he believed in you. When he learned they were trying to start an NA program, he went looking for someone to help him reach you. That's where he met Dylan."

"I thought he met Dylan through his work?"

"Not exactly...He knew you wouldn't take the news he'd been trying to find a way to help you very well. So, he decided a visit to Guiding Light might be more receptive if he told you a lesbian he worked with suggested you guys visit." He swallows.

"How the fuck do you know all of this?" I laugh as tears form in my vision. I can't believe Jude went through all of that trouble for me. He was always so busy with college and the research he did, I had a hard time believing he had any spare time to worry about me.

"So." He clears his throat. "When you dropped out of school, I couldn't find you anywhere, and I sure as shit wasn't about to go looking in the places I feared you were. I was scared you'd died." He pins me with a look. "You really dove off the deep end, man." *Yeah, yeah. So they've told me.* "So, I asked Jude if he'd heard from you. We'd talk all the time after that. He told me you called him every day. He'd fill me in when you were sober, when you weren't, how bad it was getting…He convinced me not to give up on you after I'd given you that five hundred dollars. New car, my ass. I knew you spent it on meth or pills, but whatever. He even paid me back."

"*I* was going to pay you back," I grumble, knowing he was right.

"Yeah, sure, bitch." He squeezes my arm. "Blake, that's not the point. You know I have the money. What's important here is this: He told me you were lost. You'd been through so much and were drowning trying to find a way through it. Said deep down, he knew you wanted to help people. You just didn't know how to help yourself. Jude told me about how you helped him through so many bad times when you guys were kids. How you'd bought him the Adele CD and got him headphones to drown out the noise when your mom was being abused. You broke your stepdad's nose for him."

He gets up and gestures for us to walk into the kitchen. I follow and watch as he cracks open a soda for me. "He said he needed to repay you for convincing your mom to let him go to college at fourteen. He owed you everything."

"He didn't owe me anything," I say, sinking down in a chair at my dining table.

Delaney stands on the other side but doesn't sit down. "That's what I said— granted, I was still mad about the car thing, but whatever." He waves off the comment before bracing himself with one hand on the table. "Obviously, he didn't like my answer. He said no money or material possession would ever be enough to make up for what you did for him.

"So, he started coming up with the plan for Siren's Song. He talked to Dylan, the mayor, and even me. Dylan told him not to mess with your sobriety unless he could provide stability to it first. We all knew this was going to be rough and didn't want it triggering a relapse."

I took a sip of my drink, wishing it was something stronger. My chest hurts at the thought of people talking about me as if I'm some kind of delicate flower. Fearful a gentle breeze could ruin all their hard work.

"I guess he visited EC, too," Delaney continues, finally sitting down. "I'm still surprised how far he went to make all of this a reality for you. Jude would always tell Dylan and me he wanted to give you the power back you'd lost as a kid." His expression softens as he covers my hand with both of his. The warmth from his palms makes me realize just how cold I am. "Everything he created, he created for you. We only kept things from you because he wanted to give you the ability to save people without getting overwhelmed."

Little good that did. He died before he could even fill me in. I blink repeatedly, fighting back the unexpected tears now blurring my vision. If everyone would've kept me in the loop from the start, maybe I wouldn't be drowning while I try to keep up with all the secrets.

Sensing my indignation, Delaney shakes his head. "Blake, you heard Conroy. EC is a clusterfuck of power, and one wrong move would've torn down everything he was building for you. I can guarantee he was going to tell you everything the night he died. Everything was finally in place to start Step Two."

Delaney's words hit hard as I walk over to the mantel, picking up the picture of Jude and me, cutting the ribbon. I can still remember the moment vividly. I can even smell his Irish Spring body wash when he'd pulled my face into his chest. I'll never feel the soft padding of his body again.

"It's not a dream," he'd said, my ear pressed tightly to his ribcage. I could hear his lungs take in air. "It's really yours." At the time, I'd figured he was saying it to reassure me this was really happening. This place was really ours.

But that night, as we drank our sparkling cider in celebration, He'd said more:

"The further down this road we go, the more things you're going to discover that will make you question the decision to continue. You'll find out things that'll make you want to turn back to your old life, but the people you meet, they'll need Blake Chapel."

Did Jude know I'd meet Phoebe at EC? Did he know Peter was her dad? Most importantly, if he were the one sitting adjacent from me, my hand swallowed up by his much larger ones, how would he be handling my recent decisions?

Chapter 30

Phoebe

I push past Blake, struggling to keep my balance over the thundering vibration under my feet. I have to get out of here, *I think as I try to escape a crumbling EC. Flinging the heavy door open, I notice the ground around the church has cracked and started splintering off from the yard, circling a whirlpool in a despairing storm on the ocean. The storm threatening to suck up the small chapel in its entirety.* How do I get out of here?

A whisper unexpectedly manifests behind me, causing the hairs on the back of my neck to rise. It's Blake. "Then the angel I had seen standing on the sea and on the land raised his right hand to heaven."

"Blake?" I shout, searching, yet finding no one anywhere.

"Then the angel whom I saw standing on the sea and the land raised his right hand to heaven and swore by him who lives forever and ever, who created heaven and what is in it, the Earth and what is in it, and the sea and what is in it: "There will be no more delay!"

Where is she? *I think, still searching, finding nothing apart from lightning striking the bell on top of my church, causing a boisterous ring.*

The sound of chains clinking together takes form behind me. It takes a moment for me to realize they are attached to my back, trying to pull my body higher into the clouds. A flood of panic washes over me. I have no idea where I'll go and can't surmise which is worse: this literal hell I am experiencing or the hell awaiting me once I allow my feet to part with the ground.

I've known EC all my life. Can I trust these chains won't pull my form higher, only to drop me directly into the eye of the vortex?

"The second woe has passed. The third woe is coming very soon," Blake whispers. "Come up here."

Up where? Can I trust her? Where do these chains lead? Is "up there" even safe?

"Let me go!" I shout, trying to keep my feet on the shaky, crumbling ground, gripping the railing to the steps of EC.

"Phoebe," she whispers into my ear calmly. "Come up here. Let go,"
reverberates in my ears. "Come up here..."

I shoot out from under my blankets, terrified of my bed. I'm sweating and panting. My face hurts, reminding me of the gash from last night. A quick glance at my alarm clock reminds me it's time for church.

"You faggots will burn in flames for all eternity!" Ethan. I'm going to have to see him today. Ugh and Eve. I'm not ready to face this, but what am I supposed to do, not go to church? I have to. With any luck, they won't be there. It is my father's church, after all. Maybe they'll assume he knows and won't have the stones to face him after what they've done to me.

I wince as I lift myself out of bed. My knuckles are bruised from punching the wall last night when I told Blake to leave. My whole *body* is sore. *Motrin is going to be my best friend today,* I think as I head to the medicine cabinet above the bathroom sink.

My phone vibrates in my bag as I'm locking my door. I dig it out with my opposite hand to see a new message.

Zo (7:43 AM)
I'm outside.

Great.

When I make it outside the building, I decide to drive. No way I'm having another recurrence of last night when I was left stranded at the bowling alley without my car. Walking might not ensure enough time to grab coffee before the service, and gosh, do I need coffee. And a lobotomy, honestly, but coffee will have to do for now.

Zoe is leaning against my car when I make it to the parking lot. *Ugh,* I think. *It's practically impossible to avoid these people.*

"I'm driving," I say before she can say anything.

"I'm not going to stop you, Phoebz." The corner of her mouth rises slightly. Does everyone think I'm too frail to conduct myself? She's giving me the most sympathetic look. Like a wounded puppy. "How's your cheek?" She lifts her arm, about to touch my face. I jerk back. I'm over people touching me for the next million years.

"Fuck, Zoe!" I snap, causing her to startle. "It's fine. I'm fine." I unlock my car before sliding in.

"Okay." She holds her hands up defensively. "I won't say anything."

"You don't have to," I grumble. She slips into the seat next to me. "Your face says it all."

This clearly has her looking even more miserable. "*I'm* not going to say anything because *you* need to talk about this, Phoebe, not me," she corrects.

"No. I don't." I grip the wheel tightly, sending a searing pain to my knuckles. "I need to go to church. I need everything to be normal. *I* need to be normal."

"You are normal."

I pinch my lips together, shaking my head. "Yeah, okay."

"You are, though!" She raises her voice slightly.

"Can we just forget about it?!" I shout, lifting a hand to cut her off.

"Fine," she sighs. "Let's go to church."

"Thank you," I huff, starting the car and heading to EC.

"I'm here, okay?" Zoe says as we sit in the parking lot, gently placing a hand on my shoulder, which I quickly shrug out of. *Stop touching me!* I want to shout but stop myself, deciding to gather my strength to face the hell I figure is ahead of me. No way everyone's heard yet, right?

When we walk up, the air feels different. Eyes are lingering on me for longer than they should. No one greets me, either. Do they know? How could they? It's as if I have something other than a bandage on my face. Like I have a brand on my forehead. A big "L" for lesbo. I love this.

Groups quiet to a whisper as we pass until I finally notice Ethan and Jaime standing together to the left of the steps leading into the church.

Ethan's nose is definitely broken with a butterfly bandage on the bridge. Dark pink and purple bruising circle his eyes like a raccoon. The look adorning his face is similar to a smug trash panda.

We walk past Eve standing by herself under a tree. She has two parallel bruises on her cheekbone from where Zoe had slapped her. This didn't stop her from shooting a nervous grin in our direction, however. It amazed me last night she hadn't fought back. That definitely wasn't the Eve I knew at all.

Then again, the Eve I thought I knew wouldn't have slept with someone's fiancé and Jaime. She wouldn't have betrayed her best friend, either. She was loyal. She was fierce. I honestly don't think I ever really knew her at all.

Zoe grabs my bicep to pull me into the church, which causes me to wince. I'm now realizing Ethan must've bruised my arm as he was ripping me up from the asphalt of his driveway last night.

The heavy door slams behind us once we enter the narthex. The boom reverberates off the entire room. My mother's shoes clack up to us quickly. "What is going on?" She's flustered. Of course she is. Normally, she'd be outside talking to everyone, being the center of attention. Is she hiding in here? "What happened to your face?"

Does my mother suddenly care about me? I toss around the idea. "It's nothing."

"Phoebe, don't," Zoe says, holding up her hand. "You tell her, or I do, but you're not going to lie about this."

I sigh as a billow of cold air carrying the faint smell of varnish ripples over the exposed skin on the back of my neck, causing my flesh to pebble. "Last night, I found Ethan in bed with another woman."

"Another woman?" My mother's gaze bounces between Zoe and me a few times. "Who?"

I look down at the floor, coiling my arms around my middle. "Jaime," I mumble.

My mother's hand clutches her chest as she gasps. "Did you hit them?" Her eyebrows knit together tight enough to be mistaken as one. "Because Ethan looks terrible!"

I step back and present my palms. "No!"

"Eve's face has my name written all over it," Zoe preens, pushing her shoulders back, sticking her nose proudly in the air. She's inhaling the dust glittering in the beams of light in this stuffy church.

My mother crosses her arms and shifts her weight to one leg. "Eve? I thought you said it was Jaime."

"Ethan was sleeping with Jaime," I huff. "But Eve was there."

"What?" She squints. "Why?"

Canting my head, I raise an eyebrow. "Take a guess, Mom."

She scrambles for words. "Eve wouldn't do that, she…" Her thoughts taper before she continues moving away from the topic of Eve. "So, if you didn't hit them, what happened to Ethan's nose? He looks like he got in a car accident!" Her questions are starting to make me wonder if she feels sorry for them more than her own daughter. Of course, she doesn't care about me over her image.

Regardless of her opinions, she deserves to hear this from me first. I'm sure by now Ethan and Jaime have told their own versions of the story to the entire congregation, so it's only a matter of time before it gets back to her. I need to be the one to clear the air before it becomes too convoluted to explain or believe.

I drop my hands to my sides. "Blake happened."

"Blake? Wha—" Before she can finish her thought, people start to pile in.

"We'll talk later, Mrs. A." Zoe hooks her arm in mine and pulls me to my seat in the center near the aisle.

Once we're seated, she whispers to me, "It's going to be okay."

I roll my eyes, tapping my leg in the seat, hands in my lap. "Really wish everyone would stop saying that."

"It's true, Phoebz."

"Whatever."

✝

"Today's reading." My father stands at the altar looking kind of nervous as he peers amongst the congregation. I can tell he knows something bad is going on. I wish I could fix this. "Is from the book of Matthew, Chapter 27, Verses 32-44. 'As they were going out, they met a man from Cyrene, named Simon, and they forced him to carry the cross. They came to a place called Golgotha. There they offered Jesus wine to drink, mixed with gall; but after tasting it, he refused to drink it. When they had crucified him, they divided up his clothes by casting lots. And sitting down, they kept watch over him there.

"Above his head, they placed the written charge against him: THIS IS JESUS, THE KING OF THE JEWS. Two rebels were crucified with him, one on his right and one on his left. Those who passed by hurled insults at him, shaking their heads and saying, "You who are going to destroy the temple and build it in three days, save yourself! Come down from the cross, if you are the Son of God!" In the same way the chief priests, the teachers of the law and the elders mocked him. 'He saved others,' they said, 'but he can't save himself! He's the king of Israel! Let him come down now from the cross, and we will believe in him. He trusts in God. Let God rescue him now if he wants him, for he said, 'I am the Son of God.' In the same way the rebels who were crucified with him also heaped insults on him.'"

He steps out from behind the pulpit, walking into the center of the Nave. "Ridicule." My father searches the crowd.

I bite my nails as I listen to his calm, steadying voice. Low and soothing. Just like when I was a child. I wish I was a kid again. A time when things were simpler. No cheating partners and sinful shame. People looked at you with patience and kindness as you figured out the world. One day, you wake up and are expected to somehow know everything. Know how to muddle through the world correctly. Know yourself with confidence and strength. Even now, I still feel like a confused, scared child struggling to differentiate right from wrong.

I'm twenty-six years old, and no one is looking at me with patience anymore. Not a single face within this crowd has kindness woven into it. I should know better by now. *Do* better. *Be* better.

"God called upon Jesus to unify mankind. Yet, he was made a mockery of and later crucified as reward for His efforts at peace."

Even Jesus was given a purpose. Purpose must be what gives people the confidence to proceed. If you truly know within your heart who you are and what you're meant for, doing right probably comes easy. Living every moment with spirit and strength to go on. When you're mocked or ridiculed, it'd still be simple to press on because you know what's right, and you know what needs to happen. Let them talk; let them cast you aside because deep within. You know what you're doing is right.

But what if you're convinced what you're doing is wrong, and you decide to continue doing it, anyway? Over and over. What if it doesn't feel wrong until you're met with the hateful stares of the ones who raised you and the friends you grew up with? Stares reminding you you're nothing but a terrible person who gave in to something you can't even comprehend is in you in the first place.

Why can't I get rid of this? Normal people don't seem to have this issue. I understand we all have internalized struggles, but replaying the events, I still don't see how it would've even been possible to deny them. I struggled with this my entire life and only grew emptier and more confused, losing interest in the textbook definition of love and attraction. I craved that spark, but never found it with any boy I pursued. Bottling the curiosity only built up the pressure. My thoughts were no longer a quiet whisper, but rather a boisterous roar. By the time Blake resurfaced in my life, I was already a shaken two liter of diet soda, and she was the mentos. A simple game of footsie under a table at Blessed Beans woke up the inactive volcano lying dormant under my skin.

Out of the corner of my eye, I see Ethan stand, straightening out his Armani suit vest before raising his hand in proclamation. *Great.* He has chosen to sit near the aisle—Jaime beside him—probably for this exact reason. The whole church turns their heads to face him. My father seems to shrink as he lets out a disappointed sigh. My poor dad. It's almost as if he expected it to be Ethan, though, to make a scene. I'm sure he hoped he would be wrong, though. I feel sick.

My father steels himself as he raises both palms in unison. "Yes, Ethan." He knows giving him the floor isn't good, but he braves it anyway. Faces it head-on. I wish I had half his courage. Instead, I sit here picking at my nails.

"The words you speak continuously make a mockery out of our Lord," he says, rolling up the sleeves of his black dress shirt as Jaime smirks next to him in the pew. An unwarranted warmth of rage ignites in my chest. I want to hurt them. Interrupting church yet again to be the center of attention. Disrespecting my father. I push down my intrusive thoughts and try to compose myself, shifting in my seat before reminding myself to remain still. I know better than to make a scene. My parents raised me better than him.

"And how is that?" my father asks, clearing his throat and joining his hands together in front of him. He's exuding confidence with his legs shoulder's width apart.

"The Bible has a firm structure on many of the things you have grossly misconstrued to this lovely congregation." He guides his hand across the crowd. "And from what I've discovered, you have been trying for decades to turn this church away from the sanctity of our Lord."

"And again, Ethan," my father blinks slowly, "I implore you to tell me how?" My father now walks back to the altar to look upon everyone equally. "How is spreading the word of God as love and light steering *you* away from Him?"

Ethan tilts his head and crosses his arms as he locks eyes with me from across the room. I turn my attention back to my father. My pulse pounds in my neck as I stare at my lap. "The transgressions of your daughter, for starters." His tone suggests my father should already know everything. Smug bastard. The congregation whispers, causing me to sink in my seat as the chairs creak. All eyes now fall on me. My blood runs cold as the color leaves my face. I try to focus on breathing as I shake, fingers fidgeting with the bottom hem of my shirt.

"Transgressions? I must not be following Ethan." My father pushes his eyebrows together. "My daughter is nothing but a beautiful spirit who has warmed the hearts of all these people. Some actually aiding in her growth."

I look up at my father, eyes pleading, stinging.

"The first Corinthians verses 9 and 10 clearly address that homosexuals will not be welcomed into the kingdom of God. Homosexuality is an abomination, and all those in support of her unnatural and immoral acts shall go down along with her." The crowd gasps as I sink into the booth.

I cover my face as my skin clams up. My brimming tears threaten to fall at any second.

Don't cry, don't cry, don't cry. Not here. Not now.

"You're right." My father sighs. "But only to a certain degree, Ethan. The letters Paul wrote to the church in Corinth were in fact to address the issues within their community. A lot of terrible things were taking place there."

Ethan nods raising the pretentious big head resting atop his smug, egotistical shoulders.

"Depending on which translation of the historic text you read, it does say man lying with man is a sin." Pastor Pete's words wipe Ethan's Cheshire-like grin right off his stupid face. "However," he continues, "Paul was the only apostle to have never met Jesus during his life before crucifixion. Many of the other apostles would argue that an innumerable amount of his methods and practices were actually not of the teachings Jesus encapsulated during his life. Simon Peter, one of Christ's closest disciples, bumped heads with Paul quite frequently, disagreeing with many of his practices." My father tsks, shaking his head at Ethan. "Paul's heart for the Lord and Christianity were in the right place but Paul himself confessed to having various imperfections and issues and through his acceptance of being a flawed individual, he believed it made him strong. His arrogance was unprecedented, and the Bible describes it at great length." My father opens his sermon book once more to return to today's service. "Corinthians in and of itself is full of contradictions, showcasing just how imperfect Paul was. We must appreciate Paul for his contributions to the infancy of the New Testament. However, we must also understand, he himself was a flawed human. Just like everyone before you today."

For a moment, the nave is silent. A low hum rumbles in my eardrums as I pray my father's words are enough to stop Ethan's tirade dead in its tracks. Yet, Ethan, once more, interrupts just as my father is about to open his mouth.

"While lying with me, Phoebe Appleton has been consorting with a woman." Ethan searches the faces of the crowd for validation, ignoring my father completely. *I never "lied" with him!* Yet he proceeds. "She has broken the ninth commandment while you sit and condone her behavior. In turn, you *also* bear false witness to her falsified normalcy!" He points a stern, accusatory finger at my father as the crowd whispers amongst themselves.

"Phoebe has done no such thing!" he booms, clearly triggered by Ethan's repulsive accusations. I actually wish the ground would swallow me whole. Tears brim, threatening to fall at the slightest provocation, but I refuse to let these people see me cry. I feel so helpless as Zoe grabs my hand, squeezing tightly, her knuckles turning white. Her eyes blacken as she bites the inside of her cheek. She isn't saying it, but I know she's pleading for me to hold on and make it through this. I need it to be over. I need to disappear. Emily Dickinson was right. It's lonelier without loneliness.

"Oh, yeah?" He grimaces. I finger the ends of hair resting at my collarbone, taking long, steadying breaths. "Ask her. Ask her how I broke my nose, Pastor Pete. If she says anything other than her female consort came to my house and attacked me and Jaime last night, she is lying." The breathing isn't helping. I might actually faint as I try to cross my legs, hoping movement might coerce my blood, which has seemingly turned to sludge, to pump more freely throughout my body. He gestures to Jaime's face, who is now putting on a pitying frown. The crowd is eating it up, growing more upset the more lies Ethan spouts.

My leg falls asleep, which leads me to believe my heart has frozen up, and with it, my blood has become solid ice. I shake violently in my seat. I flatten my feet on the ground, tapping my foot in time with my finger on my lap. I fight the urge to vomit as I force myself to sit and witness this. I've embarrassed my father, and I have no idea how to help him now. My mind is blank. I've succumbed to this fear and embarrassment. I did this. I deserve to face it.

Ethan is now walking up the center aisle and looking more toward everyone else rather than my father, eating up all of the sudden attention he's getting. When he reaches the front, he puts his hand on his hips and lifts his chin in the air. "She agreed to marry me as a ruse to continue her depraved lifestyle behind everyone's back. Disguising herself as a woman of God while choosing to give in to the immoral temptations of another woman's flesh in private." He's in the perfect stare down with my father now.

I didn't choose this. It's who I am. I wasn't made. I was born. Blake's voice rattles around my brain. Is it possible to be born to hurt others? To destroy those around you? If it isn't a choice, if I truly was born like this, it almost seems unreasonable to go on. I can't continue to hurt the ones I love because I was destined to be this way. But I *am* this way.

How does anyone choose to go on knowing this?

Do they ignore the impact their actions have on others?

Are they selfish? Do they even care?

By loving Blake, am I being inconsiderate of those around me and ignoring the damage I cause?

No, it doesn't matter because after last night, I know, now more than ever, I need to do what's right. I can no longer choose her. No longer decide these transgressions are somehow excusable. This situation is proof enough: Blake's lifestyle only leads to disaster and misery. To hurting my family. To hurting *her*.

Ethan grabs a Bible Jaime is handing him that's already propped open. It's clear they spent all of last night preparing for this speech. "Ephesians 5:6-13, 'Let no one deceive you with empty words, for because of such things God's wrath comes on those who are disobedient. Therefore do not be partners with them. For you were once darkness, but now you are light in the Lord. Live as children of light (for the fruit of the light consists in all goodness, righteousness and truth) and find out what pleases the Lord. Have nothing to do with the fruitless deeds of darkness, but rather expose them. It is shameful even to mention what the disobedient do in secret. But everything exposed by the light becomes visible—and everything that is illuminated becomes a light.'"

My fingers freeze as I tuck my hair behind one ear. Ethan continues flipping to another bookmarked section. "In Romans 1:32, it is said, 'Although they know God's righteous decree that those who do such things deserve death, they not only continue to do these very things but also approve of those who practice them.' Your sermons every week are tailor made to shift this congregation into the arms of this gross transgression, and so I stand before you to rebuke you for your corrupt wrongdoings and implore you cast out this devil from our place of worship!"

My mother clutches her chest and gasps beside me. I need this to be over. I pray God will make it end, but why would He show me any mercy after what I've done to my family?

"My child is no devil!" my father shouts. "If casting her out is what you wish, then by all means, my family will part ways with this church. However," he points his finger at Ethan sternly before waggling it around the room at the various churchgoers, "I must remind each and every one of you to look inside your own homes. Aren't we all made of imperfections? Yet, do we not all share the same love within ourselves by prioritizing His love above others? The love my daughter has toward every single one of you is not a sin. Homosexuality is also not a sin!"

"So, do you deny these accusations against your daughter?" Ethan rebuttals, shaking his head in disapproval.

"John 7:51," my father continues, "'Does our law condemn a man without first hearing him to find out what he has been doing?' I have no way of knowing this for certain without first consulting the accuser head-on, Ethan. Yet, I refuse to allow such whisperings to waver this church. Regardless of these accusations against my daughter, homosexuality is not a sin. As long as she is willing to put her love for our creator above the love of her neighbor, which she so clearly does, she is not doing anything wrong." My father props his elbows onto the pulpit. "This belief you have been taught is simply a fear due to misunderstanding and not reading the subtext around the passages you've chosen." He tsks. "It's as if you googled 'what the Bible says about homosexuality' rather than read the Bible for yourself. Man has been manipulating people through fear and misconception since the dawn of time! The truly misguided even crucified Jesus after he'd created a covenant in his blood for us. John 4:18 'There is no fear in love. But perfect love drives out fear, because fear has to do with punishment. The one who fears is not made perfect in love—'"

Ethan claps his hands, interrupting my father. He turns to rouse the crowd. "He refuses to acknowledge, let alone seek repentance for, his transgressions against this congregation!" He extends his hand behind him, gesturing toward my father. "Still choosing to poison all of you with his deceptions." His dark eyes return to my father as he growls to the people behind him. "I implore we remove him from his seat within this church!"

The crowd roars to life as I swallow past the bolder in my throat with saliva I don't have.

"That's ridiculous, Ethan!" Zoe tries to shout over the boisterous room, rising to her feet.

My father shouts over everyone, "In Luke 23:34, we learn even in death, Jesus's most despairing hour, he still was filled with love for mankind!" The crowd begins to settle, listening more intently to his words. "They placed a crown on his head. They made a joke out of him. Embarrassing him and abusing him. Yet he still called out to God to forgive them, 'for they do not know what they are doing.' So, I stand before God and this church today and ask He forgive you and your peers, Ethan. May God have mercy on your souls. A mercy you were unable to show my family."

And on that note, my father walks down the aisle in silence as the people turn their heads to follow his movements. He heads to his office, gently closing the door behind him as the crowd whispers among themselves.

I watch as Ethan and Jaime share a snarky glimpse of accomplishment. My body and brain misfire as confusion settles within me. Unable to process any singular emotion. I rise and try to ignore the whispers and lingering stares as I walk, like the coward I am, out of the Nave, not stopping at the narthex.

Chapter 31

Phoebe

I push the front door open, which seems even heavier than normal, given my arms and legs are now jelly. The adrenaline of the last five minutes causes me to stumble going down the steps.

I'm weak. I'm nauseous. The sound of my breath is too loud. Too rapid. I can't believe this is happening. I collapse to the ground. Zoe falls to her knees beside me, bracing my shoulders. I had no idea she was following me. "We need to go, Phoebe." Her voice is quiet. The words fighting for dominance over the hammering of my heart.

"No! I deserve this," I cry. "I need to get my dad." My mind tumbles despairingly into my nightmares. *Dad, we have to go! The building is collapsing!* Chained to the pulpit. Well, he isn't anymore. "H-he doesn't deserve this." Blades of grass dig into my palms, causing a burning, itchy sensation. "Deserves so much better than me," I shriek through my bated breath.

"Phoebe," she says softly. "This isn't your fault."

"It is. It's all my fault." I'm on my knees, but my body jerks forward until I'm sobbing into my palms on the grass.

"What did you do?!" I hear my mother's voice blast from the top of the steps, the heavy door slamming behind her. I lift my head and turn in time to watch her storm over. She grabs my arm the same way Ethan had, ripping me up off the ground. My bicep burns and stings from the freshly irritated bruise as I let out an uncontrollable whimper.

"Priscilla, stop!" Zoe shouts, trying to pull her off of me. This causes my mother to squeeze the bruising tighter. My eyes water as I wince. "It's not her fault."

"Are you serious? It's completely her fault!" she screams at Zoe disbelievingly before returning to me. "And you will fix it! Tell them it's not true."

She's shouting in my face, but the ringing has returned. I can't seem to focus on any one thing as spit flies from her mouth onto me. Her face is red, eyes bulging. Beads of sweat are collecting on her forehead. I've never seen her this mad. Even when I embarrassed her in kindergarten with my stage fright, her shouting all of my failures and imperfections, it never reached this level of frustration. Pretty positive even Piper, try as she might to get a rise out of my mother, never managed to make the artery in her neck protrude quite like this. I'm sure she would've loved to witness it, though. She'll be sad she missed the show.

I glance over my mother's shoulder to see the people finally pouring out of the church to watch the performance. At least they aren't missing it, I guess. What a great day to come to worship.

"And you're not going to see that Blake character anymore," she shouts.

A flash of Dakota surfaces in my mind. She's dancing like an idiot on a rock, her arms outstretched, body facing the water, presenting it to me. She looked back to where I was standing, her one crooked canine prominent as she bared her teeth in glee. Another beautiful weekend adventure.

My soul radiates as elation covers me like a warm blanket.

> "I know it might be embarrassing being seen with me, but…could you…If people gave you shit, would you leave me alone?"
> "No? How about I promise if I ever glance over and see no one sitting beside you, I'll sit next to you?"

"THAT'S ENOUGH!" I shout, releasing my arm from her death grip and stumbling backward. Pins and needles replace the searing pain in my bicep and I can't tell if it's fallen asleep from lack of circulation or worsening damage to the already tender muscle.

My mother steps back as well. I've never talked to her this way, but enough is enough. "I'm done! I'm done walking around like a fucking doll, boosting your reputation. I WILL be seeing Blake. It's my life. I'm an adult! You've stifled my growth long enough. You've kept me down for so long, making me walk and talk and act like some perfect Christian princess. I don't even know who I am!"

Seriously, how do I have so many tears? I'm surprised I haven't shriveled up by now.

"I'm not a toy. And I'm not YOU! And you know what?" I look at the congregation. No more fear. No longer feeling the need to please everyone. It doesn't matter anymore. "I love a woman." I drop my hands to my sides in defeat. "I've denied myself this simple happiness for my entire life, too busy bending over backward for all of you. Twenty-six years of misery and self-hatred."

I run my fingers through my hair before looking at Ethan.

"I'm fucking gay. Okay? And if that's what you think is the worst thing about me, I'm fine with it. Because I love with more heart than all of you combined!"

I turn to Jaime. "You're the real liar." I point. "You masqueraded as my friend while *fucking* my fiancé. A relationship I chose over finding true happiness to spare myself this truly vile moment!" I zero in on Ethan once more. "Did you tell them about your polygamy? How you wanted Jaime *and* me as wives? Did you tell them I caught you fornicating out of wedlock? Or is jamming Ethan's dick down your throat while he fingers you not fornicating?" I spit out, completely hysterical now.

"Phoebe." Zoe grabs my good arm, but I fly out of her grasp and continue walking toward Ethan.

"So yeah, Blake beat the shit out of you. Should I show them the bruise you left on my arm from pulling me around like I'm some malleable thing you and my mom can mold into whatever you think my life should be? A perfect girl to have on your arm. Just keep her in a box, kicking her back down if she tries to come up for air. You guys decide how much wiggle room I have in there. How much air I'm allotted. Between the two of you, there isn't any room for me!"

"Should I show them my laptop? How's your cheek, by the way?" Ethan feigns concern. I wonder if the crowd actually believes he's the victim.

"It's better than your nose after I found you with Jaime!"

My mother inexplicably appears between us. My nose and face suddenly burn, a sharp stinging radiates from the cut on my cheek as I stagger back. I watch Zoe pull my mother away by her arm. It takes a second to even register she'd slapped me.

"That's enough!" My mother stumbles backward into Zoe's tugging restraint as I clutch my face. "You've said enough!"

I start to laugh and cry at the same time. "Shame on you!" I shriek. "All of you! The judgment you pass over me is no better than the ones who sentenced Jesus to death on that cross. SHAME ON ALL OF YOU!"

My feet skid against the wet grass as I realize Zoe's now dragging me to my car as I continue to shout, "When you stand before your maker and are judged for your sins, remember the judgment you passed on your neighbor. Remember the lack of compassion you held for those different than you. The mercy you didn't have!"

Chapter 32

Phoebe

They know.

They *all* know.

My hands are shaking as I stare at the death grip my fingers are making around a mug of hot coffee. Zoe had given it to me as I sat on her couch. I can't believe what happened. My life is officially a nightmare. A nightmare I'm sure will replay over and over in my mind until I am pulled asunder in embarrassment and grief. I caused this. I ruined everything. And to think it started with an actual nightmare this morning.

"Your cheek is bleeding again," Zoe says, handing me a paper towel from her kitchen. Less than twenty-four hours ago, I was performing unspeakable acts to someone I just admitted to myself I love. In front of God and the entire congregation. Yet today, I've lost my church, my God, my father and mother, the person I was supposed to marry, Blake, and one of my best friends. The warmth of my former life now cold, empty, and desolate. I need to leave. Now more than ever, I know I can't please anyone.

Zoe breaks the silence. "Your car drives nice." She'd always wanted to drive it and after today's events, I couldn't. She did well not to fawn too hard over it. I know she's trying to cheer me up, but I'm not really in a joking mood. I'm incapable of elation. Incapable of anything. I choose instead to dab my cheek with the towel. "Listen," she sighs. "Your mom will come around."

I shake my head, setting the mug down on her coffee table. "No, she won't."

"I know you're processing a lot right now, but you took big strides today. You finally gave in to your true self. It's a good step."

Chester, her large black and white cat jumps onto my lap, immediately purring and rubbing against me. "Yeah." I nod absentmindedly sinking my fingers gently into his fur. "Good. Sure." Although, I'm not sure 'good' is the word I would use to describe this despair welling deep within me.

"Chess, get down." Zoe tries to shoo him away. He ignores her and continues to purr and demand my attention. He's always been the man of the house ever since she found him as a kitten under a dumpster a few months before we graduated high school. The rest of his litter didn't make it. He was so malnourished she thought he wouldn't either. He's the reason she decided to become a vet. "Phoebe, we've always known. Okay?"

"What? Who?"

"Your dad, Piper, me. Even Eve and Priscilla. They just refuse to accept it like we do. Thinking it's a problem. Something they could fix." She sighs. "It's not a fixable issue. It's not an issue that even needs to *be* fixed."

Sure. It doesn't need to be fixed. Look at my life. I definitely disagree. This is horrible. I've embarrassed my mother, my dad lost his job, and I gave myself to Blake, only to have my heart completely shattered. "How long?" I ask, wondering why they hadn't told me sooner so I could've fixed the issue before it transpired to today's events.

Before she can answer, there's a knock on the door.

"I can't speak for everyone else," she answers, rising to her feet. "But I've known my entire life." I watch her face light at the mystery guest at the door. "Hey, Pastor Pete."

I turn and watch as my dad walks in. His face is pale with a look of pure misery.

"I never really thought there was an issue with it because I've always known and loved you as you are," she continues. "I guess I never thought it was a problem because there isn't anything wrong with you. You're such a beautiful person."

"The only problems have been with that church. Since the start, Peep," my father finishes, knowing exactly where Zoe's going with it. No time for small talk or introductions, I see. I lost him his job, but I guess finishing her sentence is more important. I'm relieved he's here. Ready for him to tell me off. He should. I deserve it. "Can you give us a minute?" he asks, gesturing to Zoe.

"Of course," she says, walking to her room and closing the door.

"When did you know?" I ask him as he sits down on Zoe's couch right next to me.

"Before I start this discussion." He exhales sharply. "How are you?"

That's a loaded question, and he knows it.

I lift my hand lamely. "I'm still alive."

"And thank God for that." He wraps me into his strong embrace. How can he be so loving after being completely humiliated by my ridiculous transgressions during today's service? He should be mad. Upset. My mother's reaction was more on point to normal human response than his.

"I'm so sorry, Dad," I say into his chest. "That was horrible. Humiliating."

"Peep." He pulls away, sadness in his eyes. "It's fine, but I do have to ask. Is it true?"

I look down, unable to meet his eyes anymore. I know he's trying to comfort me by saying it's fine, but today was beyond words. I can't even imagine a daughter who has done such a horrific thing to their parents. This is inexcusable.

His sigh is full of relief. He pulls me in again. "I'm so glad you finally did it."

Why is he being so nonchalant about it? I get my father's more understanding than most, but he was made a mockery by someone I was going to marry. Someone he didn't allow to marry his daughter in the first place, but still. Ethan cost him his job. No. *I* cost him his job because I couldn't fight my feelings toward Blake.

He sighs. "Did you know when you were little, I tried to change EC?"

"No?" I question, shaking my head in confusion. "What kind of change?"

My father's entire body slumps on a heavy sigh. "I tried to make it all-inclusive."

Blake had mentioned her church being this way. Why would he want that for EC?

"That's what Ethan was referring to today when he said I've been trying for decades to corrupt the church." He places my hands in his. "It's harder than it seems. There's so much that goes into it before it's taken to a vote. The council turned it down. I've known for so long this church was horrible."

"Why would you do it then?" I sniffle.

"When you were five, your mother told me about a time when you pretended two Barbies were a boy and a girl. You saw no issue in them making each other happy. This made me wonder if maybe you were gay."

"God created men and women so they could find each other. We are all puzzles, looking for our missing pieces. He wants girls to make babies one day. You can't make babies if you kiss girls. Do you see what I'm saying, Peep?"

"It makes God mad if we don't make babies someday?"

"It upsets Him. And without God's protection, you'll be left with only the Devil who'll hurt you. Do you want to be hurt?"

"No. I love God," I declared. "I love Him very much."

"He loves you too, baby, and wants to see you by His side in heaven one day. Do you want to meet Him someday?"

"I'd love to meet Him!" I clapped, bouncing on my knees.

"Good!" My mother beamed. "If you want to meet God someday, you have to make Him happy every single day. Can you do that?"

"How do I make Him happy, Mommy?" I had asked. I thought I had been doing everything right. It was a hard reality to learn I was still messing up.

"Well, for starters, you don't kiss girls. You don't make your dolls kiss girls either, okay? Now, God is merciful to children, Peep, but one day, you'll grow up and find your missing piece, and I know you'll make God so happy! Together, you and your husband will make a baby. You'll start a family, and God will be so, so proud of you."

"Then," my father continues, "when I found out you were beat up at the start of sixth grade…"

My head shot up to meet his gaze. He knew about that? How?

"The nurse called me. I never told you because I wanted you to come to me about it when you were ready. She said some girl accused you of being gay and threw sand in your face. This made me push for a safe place for you to worship. I didn't know about men, but if loving a woman was something you'd have to tackle emotionally, I needed you to know it was okay. Your mother refuses to accept it. I've been trying to convince her. She's always cared about our image first and everything else second. So, I figured if I could change the church, she'd come around."

"Why does she care so much?" I ask.

He searches my eyes, his are full of sorrow. "You need to talk to her, Peep. It's not my story to tell."

"Why not just change churches?" I ask, pushing his hands away. I hate that he never tells me things. It's a respectable quality, sure, but the last person my mother wants to see right now is me.

"Well, it started out as needing to carry out my contract. But as you got older, you started dating boys. I didn't want to assume something that may or may not actually be true, and I didn't want to have to explain my suspicions to you. If I were wrong, it'd only hurt you that I would think you were someone you weren't, and I definitely didn't want to force you to talk about it if you weren't ready. It's wrong to tell people how to live. Case and point."

"Great. Just let everyone else do it." I scoff.

"Why do you think I've always kept my sermons positive and inviting toward all types of people? I tried to combat every negative thing people had to say. Tried to drown out the negative things being thrown into your head with counteractive points." He rubs my back as he speaks. "I tried with your mom as well. She really did a number on you and Pip. I'm so sorry for what happened today, sweetie. Your mom definitely got a rude awakening this morning and we're going to have a talk when I get home about how she handled things with you. That wasn't right or fair to you at all."

"Don't," I say hesitantly. "I don't want you and Mom to fight over something I knew was wrong."

"Certain parts of what you did were wrong, yes, but you are only human. Denying yourself happiness for so long will only cause you to act on impulse, given the opportunity."

It's silent for a moment before my father finally speaks again. "I have to tell you what I spoke to Ethan about the night you guys came over for dinner after your engagement."

I blink. "I figured you were upset with him for not asking for my hand."

"You're absolutely right!" My father growls, crinkling his nose. "But the fact of the matter is, I knew why he'd done it."

"I'm guessing it's because he knew you'd say no."

"Absolutely, but not for what you may think."

"Piper filled me in that you didn't like him...I just don't fully understand why."

"The second Ethan started visiting the church. I could tell he was a man of selfish intent. Maybe you didn't notice this, maybe you did, but he had visited EC before you met him."

"What?" I squint. "No, that's not right. He met me at the skating rink. He wanted to pick me up, but I refused. Then he started going to EC to try and 'woo' me. I guess he figured if he could show me he was a good Christian, I might like him better."

My father presses his lips together, tapping his chin. "No, Peep. He had been to service two weeks prior to meeting you. After the second time seeing him, I actually approached him. He seemed very egotistical. He asked if EC was exclusively for the righteous. How we go about ensuring no sinners are welcome. I knew then he wasn't a good person. He didn't seem to like my answers about loving those who sin against us and showing mercy to all of God's children, regardless of their sins. He respectfully disagreed."

I held my head in my hands. "Why didn't you tell me?"

"It wasn't my place," my father admits. "A part of me was hoping once you two got together, he would've learned a thing or two about being respectful. I know you. There wasn't a doubt in my mind you wouldn't play into his ridiculous ideations. So, when I approached him in my office, I informed him I didn't appreciate his behavior during service. He responded with arrogance. Stated it wouldn't matter soon, because he'd ensure I was no longer a part of EC. Said my actions over the last thirty years were sinful, and it was only a matter of time before the entire congregation knew. He threatened to keep you from me when he married you. Quoted Genesis 2:23-24."

He pulls out his phone and searches for the quote. "The man said, 'This is now bone of my bones and flesh of my flesh; she shall be called 'woman,' for she was taken out of man.' It's why a man leaves his father and mother and is united to his wife, and they become one flesh.' Before I could say anything, you were calling for him to leave. I was worried for you, and honestly, when I found you praying in the pews a few days later, I thought you had learned about Ethan. I knew my actions weren't right when I urged you closer to Blake. I messed up too. I didn't know how to tell you, Peep. I didn't want to create issues."

My father grabs both of my hands in his much larger ones. Warmth radiated from his touch, calming me. "I need you to understand God's not punishing you for your love of another woman. I love you so much, Peep. You'll always be my baby, no matter who you fall in love with."

I don't believe him. It's hard to see past all of the recent events and believe I'm not being punished for my time with Blake.

"I'm more concerned about what you're going to do now."

"Did you call Blake?" Zoe asks, poking her head out of her bedroom. "Sorry, I'm not trying to eavesdrop. It's just a small apartment, and the walls are thin."

"That's okay." He gestures for her to join us.

"Blake? Wait, what?" I look between the two of them. Is it possible I ruined my father's chances after she told me to stay out of her life last night? "Why Blake?"

My father pulls out his phone. "No, I haven't, but we all knew this day would come." *Oh no,* I think, *I just can't stop screwing up their lives.* He scrolls through his contacts. "Siren's Song was vandalized last night."

"What happened at Siren's?"

"Talk to Blake, Peep. I only know it happened. I can't honestly tell you why." Great. Another thing I caused. I'm batting a thousand today!

I see "Chapel" on his screen as he stands. I'm about to stop him when he begins again. "And to answer your question about Blake: when we were planting the flowers, she told me they were looking for another pastor at her church, but do you think she even knows about Jude's plan for me at Guiding Light Ministries?" Zoe walks back into the living room. "I was already planning on leaving when my contract expired next month, but I guess we'll have to see if they'll still have me."

"I'm sure they will, Pastor Pete," Zoe says as my father stands, giving her a hug. "I have every faith," she mumbles into his chest.

He kisses her forehead as I remain seated, trying to process what the heck is happening right now. Can you imagine how much worse this would be if I ruined his chances at another church? No. I don't even want to think about it. I want to tell them what I did. I want to warn my father before he tries to call her, but a new wave of embarrassment is already building within me. I need to disappear.

"Yeah, I mean, we record all of the services. So, hopefully, they can see what happened and realize I'm truly not guilty of the charges they have placed upon me. They'll also be able to see how inappropriately this rebuke was handled." He puts the phone to his ear, dialing her number. Maybe I can text her and tell her I won't be around anymore. Not to punish my father for whatever I did to upset her last night. My heart pounds in my chest, knowing she'll be on the other end. If she answers him at all. Would she even tell him about last night if she does answer?

Worst of all, I miss her. I want to fix this. Not only for me, but also for my father. He doesn't deserve to be punished for my stupid choices. It hasn't even been that long since I last saw her. She looked so upset when she told me to stay away from her before telling me to leave.

"I'm glad I made copies for my own personal records in the event they try to remove the recordings," he adds.

"Hello?" My stomach flips at the sound of her voice.

"Excuse me," he whispers, bending down to kiss my forehead. "I love you, honey. I'm not upset about you offering me a new beginning." And on that note, he's gone.

I hope he gets the job. He deserves to continue preaching. Just wish I could be around to see it. Wish I could see Blake one more time. She doesn't want to see me, though, which makes my decision to vanish slightly easier.

"I have to go too," I say, rising and giving Zoe a hug. "I love you, Zo. You're the most amazing sister from another mister a lesbian could have."

She squeezes me tightly. "I love you too. See you at work tomorrow?"

"Yeah," I lie. I can't bring myself to tell her I'm going to be taking some time off.

Chapter 33

Blake

The tenebrous night air is brisk as I sit in the bed of my truck, staring at the bottle of whiskey. Dylan is asleep on my couch, and I snuck out of my window like a fucking child to look at the stars. The house was stuffy, and even though I had no intention of leaving, I needed air. Worse yet, I've been wanting this drink. NA has taught me to take it one day at a time or even one minute at a time if I need to, but for the past twenty-four hours, my mind hasn't wavered on the desire to take this drink. To just stop these pestering thoughts. Numb the hurt.

I miss Jude. I miss Phoebe. I miss the person I was before I decided to rely so heavily on anything and everything that would pull me out of my thoughts because right now, I'm drowning in them, and nothing I do is helping. I ran over five miles today in total, spent three hours punching the bag. I haven't been hungry, but I tried that too, just to keep myself fixated on anything other than the whiskey stashed away in my closet.

All day, I could see it in my mind's eye like an astral projection gliding down the hallway, opening the closet door, flowing along like a breeze through the articles of clothing before settling on the pocket to the robe in the back where the bottle was nestled like a baby comfortably within the layers of fabric. Random undertones of the sweet caramel and smoky, full-bodied vanilla hit the back of my throat every time I swallow.

> "If you don't shut that disrespectful mouth of yours, I'll hit that stupid shit right out of your empty fucking skull." Austin's words reverberated in my head as I walked along the shore below the pier. I had to get out of there. I couldn't take another minute of being reminded I was worthless. It was too early to go to Phoebe's and my mother had the car taking Jude to his Scholar's Bowl meet.

I thought the noise coming off of the boardwalk would be enough to clear my head, but it wasn't working. Even the sounds of the attractions above me couldn't stop the boisterous noise rattling around in my "empty fucking skull."

He's right, I thought. *I'm so stupid I can't even keep my mouth shut. I can't stop arguing.* No one should have to put up with everything that comes with me.

I sat down under the pier and trailed my fingers through the sand. The graininess of the tiny rocks scratching my palms, made me wonder what it'd be like to dissolve myself into microscopic pieces. Disintegrate into nothing and blend completely into my surroundings. If only I could be left permanently alone.

A voice of pure disgust sliced through the tranquility of the waves and seagulls. "What are you doing down here?"

I peered up to see Eve standing only ten feet from me with some douchey guy. No doubt they came down here to make out, only to find something repulsive lying beneath the wooden pillars of the attractions up above. Like birth control, I was doing the Lord's work by stopping shitty people from procreating.

"Oh, what a pleasant surprise," I groaned. Of course it'd be her. Why wouldn't it be? It's totally God's kind of funny to kick me while I was down.

"Give us a minute?" Eve asked, gesturing to her fuck toy.

"You sure you wanna do that?" he asked, looking at me with an expression that could only be described as incredulous disapproval.

"You'll get your nut in a second, Brad, I'm sure," I teased, rising to my feet. "Can't imagine it'll take you more than a second anyway," I mumbled under my breath.

"My name's not Brad." Oh, good. He was smart too.

Eve rolled her eyes as she walked toward me. "Call me when you're done." He kissed her cheek before turning and walking back up to probably join their friends on the boardwalk.

"What's your fucking problem?" she asked, sitting down in the sand beside my standing figure.

"What's yours?" I shot back, refusing to join her. "You've never enjoyed my existence, anyway. Should I reward you with kindness for some reason I'm missing?"

Eve mulled it over in her mind before hissing, "Maybe if you weren't so fucking disgusting, people would like you more."

"Maybe I don't need snobby bitches liking me." I sneered.

"Maybe you should. A simple shower and wardrobe change could save your reputation in Mystic High."

"A simple personality transplant could help you too."

"Jesus!" she shouted. "I seriously don't understand why Phoebe fucking likes you!"

"Yeah?" I squared my shoulders and joined her on the ground, staring into her shitty blue eyes. "I don't see why she'd like you. You're perfectly horrible."

"I'm only trying to protect her, Dakota," Eve spat back. "Phoebe's always finding herself in trouble." Her scrunched-up face meets mine. "I mean, she found you." A malevolent grin spread across her features. "I mean, you honestly expect me to believe you've never considered that associating with a shitkicker emo dyke from the Seedy Side, wouldn't ruin her reputation? It won't be long before the entire school starts to talk."

"Talk about what, exactly? How she's a good person and loves everyone?"

Eve's eyes twinkled mischievously. "No—that's cute though." She pointed at me. "More like about how you turned the sweet, innocent Phoebe Appleton into a fucking carpet muncher." She brought her knees to her chest and rested her head in her hands. Shaking her head while staring out at the waves crashing on the shore, she said, "I've already had to rescue her from it once."

"Bullshit," I snapped. "That didn't happen. You didn't—"

"—Oh, but I did," she interrupted. Her eyes widening as she placed her hand on my shoulder.

I shrugged it off. "Don't fucking touch me."

Her eyebrows pinched together as her nose wrinkled in disgust. "Let's face it, the way you are right now, doesn't belong in our school and the longer you go down this road with Phoebe, the harder her life will get. And she'll let you do it too. Phoebe is too sweet to turn her back on anyone. She cares too much to walk away. That's where Zoe and I come in. We're here to keep her safe. Do you even care about her?"

I couldn't even believe she was asking me that. Of course I did. With the exception of Jude, she was the only thing I cared about, honestly. "You have to know I do, Eve. I would do anything for her." Maybe saying that was too far. She already thought I was gay, and now I all but confessed my appreciation for Phoebe to the one person who shouldn't know a modicum about my life.

"Then if you're not willing to change for her, Dakota, you have to let her go. She'll never stop clinging to you, and the more she does, the further you'll take her down with you. She doesn't know how badly she needs to walk away from this 'friendship' you guys have going on, but you do."

"No, I don't." I shook my head violently, trying to ward off the stinging in my eyes. I couldn't let her go. I couldn't walk away from the only good thing I had. I needed her.

"Seriously?" She furrowed her brow. "Okay, fine, let's play this out." She shifted her body to face me, sand clinging to her thigh before quickly brushing it off. "You guys keep hanging out."

"We will," I snapped.

"I know, and the light, gentle touches starting between you guys in the lunchroom are more obvious because, let's face it, the hugging is getting out of hand. You're sitting on the same side of the fucking table now with your shoulders brushing, Dakota!"

"Something you and I have in common. You're also a tactile person. You touch her all the time, too, Eve."

"Yeah, but I'm not a Seedy Sider who looks like she's going to perform a seance every single time I come to school! See, that's the difference between you and me. I can blend into a crowd, whereas you," she gestured to my outline, "stick out like a sore thumb. I can afford to be tactile because I have a boyfriend. Phoebe doesn't. She won't. You know as well as I do she probably never will. She can hide behind her religion all she wants, but deep down, we both know something isn't right. Soon, we won't be the only ones who see it either. She'll go down as being just as disgusting as people view you."

"I'm not fucking disgusting!" I flew to my feet. "I fucking shower! I can't help that my parents smoke in our house. I brush my hair and my teeth every single day. So, what if I can't afford new clothes or shoes? I'm just like everyone else!"

"You're not though." She rose to her feet brushing off sand from her legs. "That's the problem. You'll never be able to protect Phoebe because you'll never be able to change the way people look at you, while looking like this." She waved a hand up my figure. "It's only a matter of time before people start looking at Phoebe the same way. You're ruining her, Dakota. If you fucking cared about her at all, you'd tell her to come back to Zoe and me. If you refuse to fit in, you'd tell her to fuck off. You'd make it hurt! Make her want to stay away from you."

Tears welled as I fell back down onto the earth. She was right. As much as I wanted to be like them, I'd never be able to change the way people looked at me. I cared way too much to see Phoebe go down the same path I'd been stuck walking since birth.

"Hey," Eve said softly, kneeling, placing a hand on my shoulder. "I know she means a lot to you. It's obvious. Maybe one day, the world will be different."

A tear fell down my face as I met her eyes. Her sincerity was genuine. Or perhaps she was really good at conning people into believing she cared, because why else would she do this? If she knew how much Phoebe meant to me, how could she possibly have asked me to walk away?

"But the world is ugly," Eve continued, now rubbing circles on my back. "I know you know that. Don't put Phoebe through it, too. She isn't strong enough to handle a life like yours."

"You don't think I'm strong." I swallowed past the lump in my throat.

"Debatable." Her fingers tensed on my shoulder. "You're either really brave or really stupid to keep going against the current of Mystic High like you do. You're good at being alone. You don't even try to make friends."

"No one wants to be my friend."

Eve huffed. "People are scared to associate with you, dude."

"Then why does Phoebe do it?" I mean, Phoebe wasn't stupid, and she definitely wasn't blind. Why, then, had she continued to choose my time over everyone else's?

"Because Phoebe is a fixer." Eve sighed. "She sees someone hurting and makes it her own personal mission to make it better. The world needs more of that beauty." Eve stood and brushed off the sand from her legs. "If you continue to make her fix you, you'll snuff out that light inside of her. Soon, she'll be just as miserable as you. She won't see the beauty this world has to offer anymore. She'll start to see the ugliness you face every day when you wake up. Just think about it, okay?"

Without another word, Eve turned and headed back up to the pier to join her friends, leaving me crying in

the sand as the shore crashed into the pillars in front of
me.

"Maybe one day, the world will be different," I say taking a giant swig of the
whiskey I hadn't even realized I'd opened.

Chapter 34

Phoebe

My suitcase is full to the brim and loaded into the car. I've never really left this town before, and I can't think of a better reason to.

Being frugal is seriously paying off right now. I have enough money saved up that I could probably move into the mountains. Get a tiny home. Live off the grid. The idea of making anyone else miserable won't be possible if I'm alone. I can finally escape the embarrassment and live my life like Emily Dickinson.

I ignore the phone vibrating in my pocket as I close the trunk of my car. There's only one more stop I need to make before I can disappear entirely.

✝

Piper lives in a basement apartment of an elderly woman's house. She had explained to me during her most recent visit the entrance is around the back through the backyard. It's extremely awkward walking through someone's back gate in the dark. I had to use the flashlight on my phone to unhook the latch to the fence.

I knock on the back door and immediately hear her new puppy, Checkers. It takes a moment before she finally answers, choosing to tell him to be quiet before opening the door. She's definitely surprised to see me. I guess I could've called. Honestly, I wasn't really in the mood to talk to anyone. I'd ignored three calls and probably half a dozen or more texts on the way up here.

Shutting myself in and refusing to take calls in combination with driving three hours helped center some of my restless thoughts, though. Now that I'm standing at her door, I'm more like a shell. Devoid of emotion. I don't want to cry. I'm not angry or upset. I just am. Like I'm on autopilot, my body and mind are only partaking in involuntary functions necessary for survival. Lungs moving, heart beating, blood pumping.

Checkers bursts through the door, sniffing my feet first. I curve the corner of my mouth habitually. Like it always does when I see an animal or a child. "What's going on?" she asks, pushing the three-month-old chocolate lab back into the house and body blocking the door. His paws—too big for his little body—still swipe between Piper and the door, trying to coax her to move so he can greet me. His nose is going wild, trying to gather my scent. "Check, go lay down." She points. Normally, I'd frown and demand to give him love. I'd spend all of my time in Piper's presence with Checkers in my arms or lap. Normally, I'd even relish playing with him, but my heart doesn't even delight in an animal's presence like it usually would.

Her house contains a thick aroma of something spicy she'd made for dinner. I wonder if I interrupted her. I feel like a burden, and I can't explain why. If I had a nickel for every time she's said I was welcome over "anytime," well, I'd probably be able to pay for research into fixing my disposition.

"Dad didn't tell you?" Her eyes dart around in confusion, weighing over something in her mind. She knows everything when it comes to me. I refuse to believe she hasn't somehow found out about this already. So why does her face look surprised? If my dad didn't tell her, Zoe would've.

She's playing stupid. Which is annoying. If she knows me as well as she always says she does, she knows there's no way I want to dredge up the last twenty-four hours again.

"Of course he did," she says affectionately, but her tone has a hint of consternation to it. She pulls me into her arms, regardless, squeezing tightly. I really want her to let go. Why is everyone so intent on touching me? I'm growing tired of everyone's affection. I don't deserve it, and quite frankly, after allowing Blake to touch me, I never want to be touched again. I feel dirty. Unworthy of everyone's affection since touching me is like being marked by the devil. One touch, and I'll ruin your life.

After a moment of hugging me, to which I didn't really react—knowing it only leads to arguing, and I don't have it in me—she finally pulls me inside. "I just made dinner."

"Not hungry." I sink my hands into my pockets as I follow her down the stairs.

"I don't care," she fires back. "You're eating."

I roll my eyes and sit down at the table at the bottom of the steps in a room directly to the right. This clearly used to be a regular room of some sort where someone took the door off the hinges and added counters, a sink, and appliances. She's trying her best to make this humid, dingy basement feel like home, but it's hard to imagine it as more than what it is.

> *I used to envision myself fixing this place up. Look at this kitchen! Breakfast nook! I could see a bench table here! Just imagine it, Phoebe!"*

I shake off the memory. I'm trying to leave, not get hung up on thoughts of Blake. It's going to be a long road to recovery if I can't fend off these thoughts.

Piper places the food down in front of me before sliding into her own seat. She takes a bite of her own, holding the bowl in her hand. It's hamburger helper, but it smells delicious. Then again, Piper has never been one to follow instructions, choosing rather to spice things up, add her own flair to it. I'm guessing this is the best hamburger helper a person can ask for on a budget.

"Eat," she commands through a mouth full of food after a moment of watching me stare at it.

"I'm really not hungry," I sigh. I know I should eat. Checkers laps at my jeans, looking like he wants it more, and I debate feeding it to him. I know table scraps are bad for dogs due to all the seasonings, but how can anyone tell those cute little eyes no?

"When was the last time you ate?" she presses.

My eyes snap closed.

"Make me come, and I'll stop."

Oh, that's right.

The sex on Saturday had started because Blake was flirting with me. We had just finished breakfast—more like a late brunch, given it was already 2:00. She kept hurling compliments at me.

I'm not sure why I always find her praise so arousing. "Stop," I'd snickered.

"Make me," she'd hissed, raising one eyebrow.

And so I'd walked around to the barstool she was sitting on and did.

"Why are you smiling?" Piper asks, swallowing another bite. "I just asked when the last time you ate was. Are you okay?"

"Yesterday afternoon," I respond while consciously willing my face to fall. "I'm fine." Under my breath, I grumble, "I really wish people would stop asking me that."

Guess she heard me. Pointing her fork at me, she says, "We're worried about you. There's nothing wrong with talking about it."

"Yeah?" I scowl. "Great, but what exactly does talking about it do? Dad is still unemployed. Humiliated in front of everyone."

Piper raises her eyebrows. I swear I hear her gasp before she looks away. The reaction is so quick I would've missed it if I blinked. Just as fast, she clears her throat and her expression levels back out. "Phoebe, he's been preparing for this moment for almost two decades," she sighs, getting up, placing her bowl on the counter before pulling out her phone to text. After a moment, she puts her phone back in her pocket and refills her dish.

"Somehow, everyone knew before I did I wasn't normal. Yet none of you guys wanted to help."

"Oh, come on," she says exhaustedly, slouching back down in her chair and kicking her legs out. "Would you have even let us in?"

She has a point. Up until this morning, I have been refusing to fully accept I'm gay, and since they have a messed-up way of thinking all of this is somehow normal, I doubt I'd have taken any advice from them. So, I haven't been asking for it. Through everything with Blake, I've been telling myself it is exclusively shame keeping me from talking about it. Yet even knowing I have people who support this lifestyle, I still don't want to talk to them because I don't agree with what they have to say.

"Letting in this immoral transgression was what caused all of this. You think I'm going to ask you or Zoe or even Dad about it?" I blink repeatedly while crossing my arms. "You all keep saying it's going to be fine. But it's not going to be fine."

"Time heals all things, Peep." I lick my lips as I watch her eat before shaking my head.

"Not this! I'm not healing. I'm getting worse. With every day, I want Blake more and have God less." *Now I have her less too.* "The proof is there! Regardless of what you guys say, that's a fact."

"Let me ask you." She sits up, propping her elbows on the table. "If the roles were reversed. If men *had* to be with men and women with women, do you think these people could make *themselves* be attracted to the same gender?"

"They don't have to because that's not normal." I cross my arms. "It's not how the world works."

"Fuck, you're so damn literal. Sometimes I forget you can't imagine anything." She shakes her head.

"What? Yes, I can!" The smell of the food is making my stomach rumble. Maybe I am hungry after all.

"Really?" She doesn't believe me in the slightest. "What do you think of my house?"

"What do you mean?" I scan the room. "I mean, it's nice…for a basement."

"See! That!" She stands up and points at me. "You don't see things the way others do. Life is black and white. Mom had the hardest time with your imagination when we were little! Climbing trees. Being Tarzan! Somewhere along the way, you became this literal black-and-white cardboard cutout of Christian values. You stopped thinking 'what if' and started living in 'what should.' You've convinced yourself your beliefs are surrounded in proof—"

"In fact," I grumble, "I live in facts. If today isn't a perfect indication, proof will always shine through the fairytale."

"You live in fact?" Her forehead creases. "You and Blake did those little Bible lesson bullshits, right?"

"Your point?" I finally take a bite of my food. *Sorry, Checkers.*

"What did she say about your little 'God burns down all queers' spiel?"

"She read the verses around it and further explained what her perception of the passages were." Gosh, I'm so hungry. I shovel another large amount onto my fork before jamming it into my mouth. I ignore her accomplished smirk upon realizing her plan to feed me is working.

It amazes me how she manages to transform a simple dish into a gourmet feast. Or am I just that hungry? Could I eat anything right now, and it'd still be delicious?

"Okay, and why would someone reading you a single line from a book be more factual than reading the subtext and finding a broader, more definitive explanation of the same passage?"

I set down my fork, swallowing hard. There has to be a reason. I pride myself on forming logical conclusions by analyzing every angle. Why, then, am I being so close-minded about this?

"What if all of you are wrong? What if when I die, I don't get to meet Him? All because I believed everyone telling me being gay isn't wrong. What if I give in completely and continue not to feel God's hand guiding me? Since I started all of this with Blake, my life has gotten significantly more difficult. God is silent! Something you guys have said should make me happy has only ever made me miserable."

"I think you're being subjective. You're not seeing the full picture here, sis. You've convinced yourself you're surrounded in proof and fact when, in reality, you refuse to listen to any evidence disproving what you've been *told* is how you *should* live."

"I see the full picture!" My fork clangs loudly in the bowl as my palms hit the table a little more aggressively than I want them to. "I'm seeing it! Dad's embarrassingly unemployed. Ethan and Jaime turned the whole church against our family. My fiancé was cheating on me. Mom hates me. What could I possibly be missing? My life was better before Blake showed up at EC." It's definitely better Blake abandoned me before I could tell her I loved her back. It was so stupid of me to give up such an important part of myself, only to be accused of ruining her life and hurting her deceased brother somehow. The fact is, we were better without each other. A resonating fact, regardless of whether I tell Piper everything.

She leads me to the living room, an open space at the end of the hall where a three-seat couch faces a TV on a desk against a painted concrete wall. Maybe the lack of windows makes me struggle to see it as a home. That and the humidity sticking to my skin combined with the fact I can tell Piper uses air fresheners, but it still has a hint of cave smell to it.

"Dakota," she says, causing my heart to break as a flash of white blonde hair fell in Dakota's face as she held my right hand on the steering wheel of her mom's car. She'd taught me to drive in an abandoned parking lot on the Seedy Side one night after I'd told her I was too terrified to learn. My family was shocked at how "naturally" I'd taken to being behind the wheel when I'd finally turned sixteen.

Why has it taken me this long to realize her compliments have always made me believe I'm a better person than I am? They made me confident enough to both drive a car for the first time and believe I was good enough to make her come on my barstool. To want her to be the one to take my virginity because I thought she loved me.

"Don't tell me reuniting with Dakota didn't make you happy," Piper pushes. "And Blake's touch hadn't ignited something you didn't even know could be ignited."

My mind shoots back to when she nearly kissed me on her couch. "Isn't all temptation enjoyable until it ruins your life?" And boy, did loving her ruin mine. She said she'd *try* not to give up on me. She never said she wouldn't.

Piper began hitting her head repeatedly on the coffee table in front of us. "She's not ruining your life…Everyone keeping you down is!" If only she knew.

She stands up and walks to the other side of the room, disappearing through a door. When she returns, she throws me blankets and a pair of jammies. "You're staying until tomorrow."

"No, I really have to—"

"Phoebe," she shouts, holding up her hand to stop me. "I didn't ask. Call work or whatever you need to do."

"Why?" I demand. "What's so important about tomorrow?"

"There's someone I need you to meet. It gets really cold in here at night, so if you need another blanket, just ask."

I decide it doesn't really matter when I disappear. Spending some much-needed time with my sister might be a good thing. I'll miss her when I'm gone. What's another day, anyway?

"Fine," I groan. "But I brought my own clothes."

Chapter 35

Phoebe

I lay awake on Piper's couch, staring at the gigantic water spot on her ceiling before finally deciding to check my phone. I'm shocked. Fourteen messages and three missed calls. The messages are from the typical people you'd expect. Zoe, my father...then there's the few I wouldn't have expected. Disappointment washes over me when I realize the one person I'd hoped to hear from isn't on the list. I just wish I knew what I'd done to make her decide we shouldn't be together.

"You gonna call her?" Piper had asked earlier when we were talking about being kids and all our random teenage adventures. Our parents definitely would've grounded us for life if they'd known half of it. Obviously, all of my stories included Dakota. I mean, they were my best memories.

I shake my head. "I'm hanging out with you."

She saw right through it but didn't press. Just shook her head. I'm fairly confident she knows I'm avoiding Blake. She may not understand why, but I'm sure the way I buried my face in my hands before smoothing back my hair told her it's bad and to leave it alone.

What could I say about Blake, anyway? It was stupid to think giving myself to her would somehow show her I loved her, and honestly, I'm not ready to listen to anyone's opinions on it. I made a choice. Which happened to be the wrong one. I'm the one who has to live with it. I honestly can't decide what hurts worse. Feeling so vulnerable only to have the one I care so deeply for, destroy me, or being embarrassed so badly by the people I've known all my life. Both are equally mortifying. Things were so much easier when people were telling me who to be and how to feel.

Even so, I want to thank Blake for helping my father.

A few hours after I'd arrived, Piper had received a text my father would have an interview tomorrow at Guiding Light Ministries. Blake had actually managed to make it happen for him. She'd lifted a very heavy weight off my shoulders. I figure I should avoid speaking to Blake altogether, though. It's what she wants.

Speaking to her will only hurt, anyway. Besides, if I did, I wouldn't be able to trust myself not to tell her how much I miss her right now. How much I need her arms around me. I'd even apologize for whatever I did and beg her to take me back. I'd only be saying things that made it more convoluted when I never come back to Mystic. Or maybe I'd be so desperate to have her I'd decide to stay. I'd keep making everyone miserable while also remaining miserable myself. I can't face those people. Blake said it herself: I can't accept myself enough to accept her. It isn't fair for me to continue hurting her by not being able to give her what she wants. Me. Even now, it's impossible to see a world where we can be together and not make everyone miserable.

"Every time you're around, you make things worse!"

I take a deep breath as I open the message from Zoe first.

Zo (1:14 PM)

If you need me to come by, just say the word, ok? I know all of this probably seems horrible right now, but I'm not going anywhere.

Yeah, I have every faith she'll be by my side through all of this, but I can't do it. I can't allow her to carry this burden with me. It's mine and mine alone. I have to leave. The thought of spending another second in Mystic is unbearable. Regardless of how nice it is knowing Zoe is in my corner, I refuse to take her down with me. She's trying to build a reputation for herself before opening her own affordable vet clinic in Mystic. That kind of dream doesn't support screw-ups like me.

I decide to leave her on read and continue scrolling. Next message is from my mother.

Mother (3:43 PM)

I know you and your father aren't too happy with me right now and I apologize for my actions outside of the church today. I shouldn't have hit you, but you know your behavior was downright hysterical and someone needed to bring you back to reality. Pip told us you're with her. When you get home, we need to talk. I love you so much sweetie.

Yup. Not touching that conversation with a ten-foot pole. This message gives me more reason to never come back. NEXT.

My eyes water as I read over a few messages from people in the congregation apologizing for how today went. Expressing they had no idea how ugly EC truly was and they'd be searching for a new place of worship. They told me to let them know when my father finds a new church because they love his sermons and wholeheartedly agreed with his proclamation today. I message them all back with a group text.

Me (11:22 PM)
Thank you for all the kindness and consideration during this extremely hard time for my family and me, but if you have any messages, please contact my father directly.

Then I send them his number, refusing to ever place myself in between my father and his profession—or, to put it simply, his happiness—ever again. My father has very little surrounding his life that isn't his love for God. All of his advice comes straight from the good book itself. He'd pray for you or help you give your struggles to God. Which is a beautiful thing, but some struggles you can't give to God. Like mine. Pretty sure I'm beyond his advice at this point. If others enjoy his guidance and Blake gets him in with her church after all, I'll never get in the way of that again.

I then make the very healthy decision to block Jaime and Ethan on all social media. I even go as far as blocking their numbers. This wound will never close if I give them a window to slip back in.

I kick my feet out from under the blankets, staring at Blake's name on my phone. I want to message her. I sigh a deep, contemplative breath as I hover my thumb over her name. *No*, I think. *She told you to leave her alone, and you need to respect that.* And so, I close out of her name and lock my screen.

Regardless of how tempted I am, I'm going to leave her alone, and she'll never see me again. I can't…because I meant what I said outside the church. I do love her. I know I do. I've never met someone with such a lasting effect on me. Never felt butterflies from the sound of their voice on the other end of someone else's phone. I've never longed for a specific person to hold me while I was struggling.

It's deeper than that, though. I've never known someone who could build me up and challenge me to be brave the way Blake does. Someone who believes I'm stronger than who I see in the mirror. I felt so beautiful in her eyes. She was showing me how to love myself. It's more than her touch. More than the smell of cedar and the way she lives rent-free in my head 24/7. I love her because of the way she convinced me I could be better. And for a second, I truly did believe I had the strength to be that person. I genuinely believed it wasn't wrong to want her.

When I was a kid and she took me on my first adventure through the woods, my life had no purpose. All my friends were normal. Falling for guys, dating. I've always felt alone, but with her, I knew I never was. She may have been sitting alone in the lunchroom, but I was sitting alone in a group of people. Maybe that's why I sat with her, introduced myself. "Hi, I'm lonely. Want to be lonely together?" I'll never be like my friends. It's impossible to relate to them.

For a brief moment, I was whole. I finally knew what it felt like for one shred of a second to not have to wear a mask and blend in. So, after Eve somehow convinced Dakota to stay away, I felt even more solitary than before. Going without her once I'd learned what it felt like to have her was agonizing. Reflecting on the last day and a half, I've really started to notice that pattern. Only now, my life has been completely obliterated into a fine powder. Everything I had is now gone. There was so much more between Blake and me now, which means so much more was lost. Now I'm lost.

With Blake, I never had to blend. She made me feel like I belonged without trying. The scariest part I'm now realizing is what belonging to her meant. And I can't handle it. I'm more alone now than I ever was before. No one can possibly understand this feeling.

She was always guiding me. Teaching me to journey even if I didn't know where I was going. Teaching me to live outside of the lines, sneaking out, breaking rules. How to see the stars or an old run-down house in a way I'd never thought to see them before. She taught me to drive in her mom's old car. Taught me how and what to drink—and I still suck at that. The most important part about this is for every one of those things. She was there. She never left, never let me get as lost as I so obviously am now. Yet, there will always be one thing, try as she might, she can't help me with: loving her. Because loving her is selfish. I can't be with her the way she needs me to. I'll never be able to brave the glares and the comments. The whispers and the disgust.

"How many times have we been seen out in public? I'm
your dirty little secret!"
"What do you want from me, Blake?"
"I want you!"

I shake off the memory. She needs someone else. It was selfish of me to string her along when I can't give her that. I'm too embarrassed to ever show my face in Mystic again. As much as I care for her, I have to let her go. I have no strength left to fight.

After a while, I'm sure she'll move on and find someone who isn't ashamed to be seen out in public with her. Someone who doesn't care when people judge them for holding hands or kissing. As much as the idea of someone else giving her those things hurts me, I know it's what she deserves.

I'll be okay, and she'll find someone better.

Chapter 36

Blake

Delaney's boisterous voice snaps me awake. "Girl, wake up."

I grumble, head pounding.

"The bar isn't going to clean itself."

"What time is it?" I groan desperately, craving water for my dry, sticky mouth. I haven't felt this shitty in over five years, and honestly, I'm not missing it. I polished off the entire bottle last night while looking at the stars in the bed of my truck. Not sure how I made it back inside, especially without Dylan hearing me, since I'm going to assume it wasn't gracefully.

The bottle. Where the fuck did I put the bottle? If Dylan or Delaney find it before I do, they'll know what I've done, and I'm not sure I can face any reprimand right now. I feel shitty enough.

The bed sinks as Delaney sits down beside me. "Are you okay? I know the last few days have been insane for you, and I need you to know we're here."

"I'm good," I say, voice scratchy as I try to clear it. "Just give me a minute to get dressed. I'll be out there." I'm still slightly dizzy as I sit up. I reach for my phone but can't find it. "Have—have you seen my phone?"

"No." He squints curiously. "Wait, are you?" I can feel his judgement as he pans out to scan my body. "Blake, are you fucking hungover?"

Panic washes over me as he leans in closer to smell my breath. I shove him away and quickly stand, which causes my stomach to turn. "No, I—" but then, the room spins violently and I know I'm going to puke. I run to the bathroom, and as I'm kneeling, praying to the porcelain gods, I hear Delaney yelling at Dylan in the living room.

"Where the fuck were you, Dylan?!" he shouts.

"What? I've been here! What the fuck?"

"Yeah? Well, she's in the bathroom throwing up with liquor on her breath, so why the fuck weren't you watching her?"

"Shit," she scratches out as my body upheaves violently for a second time. "When would she even have been able to get a bottle?"

Footsteps approach the bathroom as I spit into the bowl.

"Blake," Dylan says, pushing the door open and sitting down next to me. She places her hand on my back as I groan.

"Don't touch me, Dyl," I say, shifting my body away from her, exhaling. "I'm fine, I just—I just need some fuckin' space." The smothering is making me even more nauseous. I can't fuckin' breathe! Maybe if they'd have left me alone like I asked for on Saturday night, I wouldn't have felt suffocated. None of this is making me want to stay clean. I feel like a fuckin' child.

Her hand falls to her side. "Okay, then."

The room is silent as I spew my guts out yet again. My stomach is upset. I think I might have alcohol poisoning because, with every regurgitation, I'm dizzy. I absolutely hate alcohol. Everything wants to evacuate from everywhere, and I want her to leave me alone in this fuckin' bathroom so I can shower and try to regulate my body temperature. Every room I walk into feels stuffy. I want my house back. I'm tired of being reminded my life is a piece of shit. Forever alone. The ones I want around me aren't, and the ones I need to step the fuck back won't go away.

"When was the last time you talked to your therapist?" she asks softly.

"Dyl!" I shout, holding my hands out in frustration. I'm not about to admit it's been a while. I had a session scheduled for a week after Jude died, but between the funeral preparations and figuring out how to divide up all of his assets, I missed it. If I'm being completely honest, I don't want to talk about his death, anyway. Admitting he's gone is one thing. Admitting my emotions about it is another. "I need a fuckin' shower. I need some fuckin' space. I need everyone to back the fuck off and leave me alone! I need you guys to get the fuck out of my house!" I throw my fist forward with so much aggression it creates a crater in the wall behind the toilet. "Leave me alone!" I scream. "Leave me the fuck alone!"

Out of the corner of my eye, I see Dylan lift herself off the floor. I refuse to look at her, choosing rather to slow my breathing. She stands there for only a second before closing the bathroom door. From the hallway, her voice breaks slightly, "We're going to give you some space, Blake. We'll be at Siren's. I expect a text by two. If I don't hear anything, I'm going to come back here. Is that clear?"

I groan in frustration over needing to check-in. I'm not a baby. I've been good for five years! It's bullshit one night of letting off steam after five years of being clean somehow constitutes them needing to chaperone me again. "Crystal fuckin' clear," I grit out, wiping my mouth and turning on the shower before stripping off my clothes.

As the water traces the outline of my face, I sit crouched, holding on to the faucet for balance. I throw up a few more times before the water runs cold, and I need to get out. I push the fog off the mirror out of habit, before deciding to avoid my reflection. I know what I look like. I know who I am.

I hear Phoebe's voice before rubbing my tired, blurry eyes.

Don't give up on me.

You'll never be able to protect Phoebe because you'll never be able to change the way people look at you!

Eve's right. I'm disgusting. I spent all this time getting clean, making a change, and yet, she can still see me for who I truly am. The only person I've never been able to fool is Eve. I have to hand it to Phoebe; a quality like that is good to keep around. Finally, it all makes sense. You shouldn't throw a friendship like that away.

I walk out to my kitchen to finally grab some water and Motrin for this killer headache and am pleasantly surprised to see it already sitting out on my counter with food and a note beside it. "**2PM.**"

"Oh, fuck this," I grumble, wadding up the note and throwing it across the room. I can't help other people. I can't carry out this mission. Jude gifted it to me? Well, he's wrong. This isn't a gift. It's a burden, and I'm done being a part of it. I'm treated like a child, and no one should entrust a child with a movement as big as this one. I'll let the grown-ups handle it. Thinking I could change my name and reinvent myself was stupid because no one will ever be able to see me as anyone other than Dakota, anyway.

So, I ask myself: What Would Dakota Do?

Anything but this.

I grab my keys and leave this stuffy house where the ghost of Jude lurks around every corner, judging my every move. This was never my house, anyway. Never my mission.

Never my life.

Chapter 37

Phoebe

It doesn't seem to matter what I'm doing at this point. I can't do it without thinking about Blake. Her crooked canine, the smell of cedar wafting past my nose as I'm brushing my hair. The sound of my name rolling off her tongue. Her moans in my ear. Everything. I'm not safe anywhere. Even in a place I don't know, memories of Blake still haunt me. When I close my eyes, I see her. When I open them, I'm devastated she isn't here.

Is this what detoxing feels like? Does it ever get easier? I could've sworn I felt her twitching body beside me when I woke up this morning, but when my vision came into focus, I realized I was on the couch in my sister's basement home. She isn't here, and she never will be.

Piper had been keeping me extremely busy this morning before leaving to check out the venue for a party she was planning. Yet it didn't matter how overloaded my mind had been. I still craved to be near Blake. I miss her voice and continue to battle the urge to call her. Any free moment I get, I find myself looking at my phone and wishing there would be a text from her. There never is, which makes my chest hurt. I almost messaged her a few times but fought back the urge reminding myself it won't help anything. She doesn't want to talk to me anymore.

It's almost noon as I stand peering at myself in Piper's mirror. I look different. I can't fully place how, though. It's like my soul has left my body. My spirit has died. My face is pale. My eyes aren't as vibrant. I've lost a certain glow I'm used to seeing when I look into my reflection. Maybe it's the permanent frown blended into the expressionless visage currently inhabiting every fiber of my reflection.

My sister had sent me an address and told me to meet her there at two. After looking it up, I learn it's a coffee shop. Thank God. I'm in desperate need of coffee. Then again, when haven't I needed coffee? Let's be honest, even Phoebe 2.0 can't quit caffeine.

As I thread my hand through my hair, wishing I could find my straightener, I'm hit with an unexpected recollection.

I just hope you're not the same person I ran into back then.

It was Zoe in Blake's truck after they'd found me at Ethan's. She was stroking my head as I began to doze off.

Why hadn't I remembered this sooner? Zoe had run into Dakota and she failed to tell me? Even after learning I'd missed her every single day since I'd lost her? I lunge for my phone so quickly, scrolling to her number and dialing it. Heat sparks below my ribs, rising to my face as it rings. I'm supposed to be letting this go, supposed to be putting my past aside, starting new, yet here I am, falling right back into it.

The mystery behind Dakota has been haunting me for the past twelve years, and if Zoe has answers, I have the right to know before I close this chapter of my life completely.

"Hey, you aren't at work. Everything o—"

"How long did you know Blake was Dakota?" I interrupt.

Zoe pauses before finally deciding on a response. "Not long…Saturday. She came and picked me up—"

"That's another thing!" I'm not even fully comprehending her answers before spouting off more questions. "How long have you guys been friends? Was this some kind of plan? She told me *you* gave her my number after I got engaged! What the fuck, Zoe?! How did she even have your number?"

"Fuck, calm down, and let me explain since it's apparent you weren't actually asleep," she grumbles.

"Obviously." I focus on my breathing as silence floods the line. She remains this way for so long I have to actually look at my screen because if she hangs up on me, I may actually lose my mind.

Lucky for her, she's still there. Finally sighing, "Okay, remember when we were, what, maybe twenty-one years old, and I broke up with Marcus after that party?"

How could I forget? She'd invited me, but I was relieved I declined after I'd found out they'd broken up. He treated her like trash. Always drinking and putting her in bad situations. Honestly, Marcus was an idiot. Always doing dumb wild stuff, and if he invited you to a party, it'd almost always end with the police being called. That night was no different.

"Yeah, didn't you tell me the cops were called?" I can't express how happy I'd been to hear she'd finally dumped him. Sad for her, of course, but I was still relieved she was okay after she'd told me an ambulance and police had broken up the party. Her leaving him was a long time coming. I'd never really asked her what had happened because she had been so devastated over the breakup.

She let out a deep breath. "That's the one. Well, that night, I ran into your girl—"

"Okay, don't call her that," I snap. Now more than ever, I have no possession over Blake and I'd rather people stopped thinking that. Blake deserves someone more available than me.

"Feisty," she teases. When I don't join her in jest, however, she continues. "Fine, I ran into Dakota. Girl, let me tell you, she had *changed.* She wasn't the adorable little weird kid you'd grown to admire. She was *scary.*"

"Scary, how?" I want to know. *Need* to know. She needs to tell me. "Like, violent? What?"

"Phoebe, it's probably best you don't know."

"Zoe, I swear to God!" I shout, pacing around the room. "Tell me. I have a right to know."

"She doesn't appear to be the same person in the slightest, Phoebz. That's why I didn't even recognize her. It shouldn't matter."

"Shouldn't matter?" My brows furrow. "How do I know I can even be safe around her if I don't know what she's capable of?"

Zoe ponders this for a moment before finally saying, "Fair point." Another long pause lingers on the line. "Okay, *fine,*" she finally concedes. "I was hanging out watching Marcus be Marcus." I can practically hear her eyes roll through the phone. "Getting drunk and being dumb when Dakota stumbled in. Loud, clearly already drunk, shouting 'who wants coke?' waving around a baggy. Marcus fucking flew over there so quick."

"Wait." I pause, trying to wrap my head around what I'm hearing. My feet move involuntarily, chartering a path around the entirety of Piper's basement apartment. "Like cocaine?"

"Well, it wasn't Pepsi, princess," she sighs. "I really shouldn't be telling you this. This isn't who she is anymore, Phoebe."

I run my finger along the dusty desk in my sister's living room area. "Tell me," I demand, rubbing the velvety mess in between my fingers.

"So, Marcus went over there, causing me to follow—"

My heart drops into my stomach. "You did coke?!"

"What the fuck, Phoebe? NO! I was stopping him." I mean, I wouldn't judge her if she did. It just never made sense to me why she would date such a troublemaker like Marcus. I'm relieved to know she never stooped to his level, but why entertain that type of company in the first place? I know this is a question I'll never get an answer to. She'll do anything and everything to shift the focus off herself.

"Oh," I breathe. My chest hurts. Maybe I should tell her to stop. Knowing Dakota abused drugs is one thing, but am I truly ready to handle the reality of it by hearing a full-blown example?

Yes.

I have to be.

Because even though she hates me and will likely never want to see me again, time has taught me one inalienable truth. I will never stop loving this woman. She can change her name. She can vanish from my life completely. But I will never be able to scrub her off my skin. Remove her from my DNA. She's a part of me, bound and determined to stick around for a lifetime. And, unfortunately, we can't change the past and hers led her to addiction. Recovering or not, it'll always be a part of her and I need to understand it.

"Anyway, turns out I didn't have to stop him because Dakota was on a mission. And it wasn't with guys. She pushed everyone away who wasn't a woman. She was degrading them. Demanding to do lines off their necks and cleavage, slapping their asses, but they kept coming back for more."

My legs grow weak as I sit down on the couch, my reflection heavy in the small TV screen piecing the puzzle together in my mind. After the husbands had hurt her in her childhood, her mind had decided to sleep with their wives. A vindication after being made to feel powerless.

Is it a stretch to believe maybe she didn't think she could end her own life after her failed attempt and was finally done losing, done feeling weak? So, she went to this party, with a death wish, trying to start a fight.

"The boyfriends started getting pissed," Zoe continues. "Which seemed to only entice her more. Dakota egged the guys on, begging them to do something, hit her. Calling them bitches and pussies. When Dakota started making out with some guy's really inebriated girlfriend, he lost it. Snatched her up by the hair and threw her across the kitchen. Her face crashed into a chair and blood was pouring out of her mouth like a faucet."

The scar on her lip, I think. She'd said she'd gotten it for "talking shit." I ghost my finger across my own mouth as I visualize how bad the damage must have been if blood was gushing out. Did it require stitches? Honestly, I doubt she even had it looked at by a doctor.

After a moment, Zoe's voice begins again. "When she got up, she was *pissed*, swinging on him, knocking him out cold with the first blow, but then she got on top of him, still swinging at his limp body. She was going to kill him if she didn't stop, but I was too scared to grab her, pull her off, you know?"

I throw myself backward on the couch and scrub my face with my hands. Luckily, Zoe's voice is boisterous enough to be heard from my chest because I forgot to put her on speaker.

"Finally, I'd seen enough and realized if no one else was going to do something, I had to. I shouted, 'COPS!' That got her to jump up and bolt out, kicking the screen door off its hinges as she left."

Closing my eyes, I try to imagine a bleeding, scared—albeit angry—Dakota running off into the night. Nowhere to go. No one to call. Alone and hurt. A burning forms around my lids.

"I chased her down the street before she cut through a playground a few blocks away from the party. When I shouted her name, she stopped and turned. Her eyes were black with the tiniest sliver of blue. They were sunken in. She looked like a meth head, Phoebe. She was grinding her teeth and itching the sores on her arms and face. This didn't look like the result of coke. Not to mention, she was skinnier than she is now, which is saying something because that girl's a fucking twig! She got impossibly more pissed when she realized who I was.

"Her voice wasn't her own Phoebe. It was terrifying. Which only amplified when she said she hated all your friends. All of us were pieces of shit. Wreckers of joy. Bigots. She wanted us all dead."

Eyes still closed, my nose takes in the incents and mildew scent of Piper's humble abode. A scent that will forever be tied to images of my beautiful, sweet Dakota, bleeding, angry, feral. Lost and aching, battered and broken.

"She asked if I'd still love you if you were gay." This gets my attention, causing me to put my phone back up to my ear and sit bolt upright. "So I asked her what the fuck I did to make her think I'd be against gay people. She didn't know anything about me. She ignored the question and started blaming us for her being a drug addict. She was straight up sobbing, so I held her. Got blood and tears all over my shirt, Phoebz. Then she said she loved you."

A painful knot forms in my throat as I remember her confessing her love, only to have me reject her. I deserved the way she treated me when I'd shown back up at her house. I didn't deserve forgiveness for my apologies. Blake knew she loved me all this time, yet she never sought me out. I would've been more than happy to see her again. To be with her one more time. It didn't make sense why she stayed away if she knew.

Why did she travel down such a dark path when she could've just thrown a rock at my window? I honestly couldn't tell you how many times after she'd left that I'd prayed for her to show back up. Longed to hear that little "clink" on my windowpane. If she had told me back then Eve was behind it, I could've done something. I could've stopped being her friend sooner.

It all began to make sense when Zoe continued, however. "I had to break it to her. I had to be honest. She needed to hear it. I told her she couldn't come anywhere near you, or I'd make the shitty little life she had look like paradise compared to the hell I'd rain down on her.

"I told her you remembered her a certain way, and it'd kill you to see her like that. 'Phoebe doesn't need *this* Dakota. She needs the old one. Find her, and we'll talk,' I said. Then I hugged her and went back to the party. I honestly never saw her again after that. Wasn't sure if she'd died or went to jail."

Hearing she'd told her to stay away from me caused a sinking in my gut. Why did all of my friends keep her from me? It isn't their place to decide my life for me. What if I could've helped Dakota? What if she would've died?

There is no point focusing on 'what ifs,' though. If I had experienced a life with Dakota sooner, I wouldn't have been able to help her. We'd still be in the same situation we are in right now. I mean, it may not have panned out quite as dreadfully given I would've never met Ethan, but I would still be struggling. Blake would've still left me after I gave myself to her. Who knows? I might've made it worse.

Maybe it was a good thing Zoe told her to stay away. Maybe she needed to be as strong as she is now in order to be able to get the closure she needed back then. Maybe the reason God brought us back into each other's lives was to close the door once and for all, so at least one of us could finally be happy. Judging by this story, I think she deserves happiness. She wasn't ready for the devastation of my present existence back then, and when she finally was ready, God sent her to me.

"I didn't realize Blake was Dakota until we came to pick you up from Ethan's," Zoe continues. "She'd made a comment in her truck about having known you for a really long time, and it all kind of clicked together. I punched her and reminded her of our talk. And when she beat up Ethan on the ground, I saw Dakota at that party and felt I needed to warn her not to slip again."

My mind struggles desperately to process Dakota painted in such a terrible light. The sweet girl who taught me to drive. How could she have fallen so far? I'd learned how difficult her life had become after she'd been forced out. I just hadn't understood it could've gotten so bad she'd become violent. A hairpin trigger of emotions she could no longer keep in the chamber. She'd always seemed so resilient. So brave. Even now, she was so patient with me. Brave enough to wander over to EC by herself, knowing how terrible a place it is.

"Did you try to set us up?" It was the only question I had left to ask her. "You gave her my number. Why?"

"Phoebe," she groans. "You've been drowning. When you started dating Ethan, it became more and more obvious how hard you were struggling to mesh. How unhappy it made you. I couldn't see you so unfulfilled anymore. You deserve a happy ending. You deserve love. Every time I saw you with Blake, I could tell there was something there. For the first time in over a decade, you looked happy."

Her tone becomes frazzled as she rambles out the next bit so fast I struggle to keep up. "After the flowerbeds, we'd started helping create outreach because

Pastor Pete and I were instantly in love with Blake and her idea. She informed your dad he might potentially have job security through her church for helping. We exchanged numbers and started secretly referring people who were curious about her to Guiding Light Ministries." She finally pauses for a second to take in a breath. "She's an amazing woman." Her nervousness grows more apparent, as if she's begging me not to be mad while at the same time standing her ground on the matter. "Again, I had no idea she and Dakota were one and the same. Her movement was beautiful, and if anyone was going to be able to help you accept yourself, who better than the one trying to create outreach?"

Right when I think she's done, she continues. "Honestly, your dad, Piper, and I hit a brick wall trying to show you it was okay. So yes…I gave her your number when she asked." The awkwardness in her tone is interesting. She's trying to be firm while still struggling to come up with the right words to add.

"Not to necessarily play matchmaker," she adds. "But to send you a gift-wrapped version of what life could be like if you accepted yourself. Show you it isn't a death sentence."

"You sent me a letter bomb, Zo. My entire life has exploded. So, thanks. It's greatly appreciated." My hand is vibrating as I hold the phone. Blake's life and mine are ruined. Her bar is destroyed, her mission is in shambles. My family's namesake is obliterated. What if, by trying to bring us closer together, Blake relapses back into Dakota? The blood would be on all of our hands.

"I regret nothing," she insists. "You guys need each other, Phoebe. Don't push her out because you're convinced the ones who kept you down for so long are right." If only she knew I hadn't pushed her out. She pushed me out. She told me to stay away from her.

"Whatever," I say exasperatedly, not wanting to divulge what really happened. There seemingly is no getting through to anyone, anyway.

"Just think about it," Zoe pleads, but I think we both know I've been thinking on it long enough.

"There's nothing to think about, Zo. She doesn't want anything to do with me," I say.

"What? No way." I can practically see her shaking her head disbelievingly through the phone.

"Well start believing it because her bar was the only connection she still had to her late brother and thanks to me, it's ruined. She's over me." My eyes burn and I'm so sick of crying, so before Zoe has permission to talk, I keep going. "We'll talk later. Piper wants me to meet her for coffee."

I end the call before she can say anything else.

Chapter 38

Phoebe

Equinox Coffee is deep in the heart of downtown. Finding a parking space takes a second since there really isn't much need to parallel park in the tiny town of Mystic Harbor. I remember getting my license was relatively easy since they didn't test for it. So, I'd never really learned how. Never figured I'd need to, since I assumed I'd never leave.

The test has changed since I'd gotten my license ten years ago, though. Last Sunday, I'd overheard someone at church talking about their son getting his license, and they were scrambling to find a place to teach him how to do it. There really isn't a single parallel parking space; it's all slanted spaces or parking lots. Up until this moment, I had been relieved I'd never had to learn it.

I finally found a parking garage two blocks down. So, what if I had to walk a little further? I wasn't about to put a dent in my baby trying to learn today.

Throwing the ticket onto my dash, I check my bag for my pepper spray before hopping out. It's the middle of the day, but in a big city, you never know when crime will strike. At least, that's what my mother always told me. They worry about Piper every day. My father calls her once a week to check in and make sure she hasn't been mugged or raped. Doesn't mean she always answers, though.

The wind is blowing through my dress as a light breeze whirls through the trees. Newspaper and plastic bottles tumble along the pavement until finally landing in the gutters. The sidewalks sparkle with a type of rock I'm not familiar with, similar to granite or maybe marble. The sound of cars whooshing past me makes me wonder if this is the reason Piper likes it here. This area of town truly is a sight, with colorful banners hanging from streetlights occasionally tethered across the street connecting to a light on the opposite side saying things like "Affirm Your Pride!" and "Live Loud, Live Proud!" with a bunch of different patterns of color behind it.

Equinox's front window has rainbows painted in window chalk on it. Rainbow banners hang on either side of the front door as well. I know instantly what Piper is trying to do, but I'm seriously hoping maybe I'll get lucky and find a pot of gold inside. Maybe a few leprechauns. Surely, she wouldn't have brought me to a gay coffee shop in a gay neighborhood to meet someone.

But I know Piper too well to stay ignorant of her intentions. I let out a deep breath as I push open the door to be flooded with even more flags of various different colors. Not sure what they all mean, though. I figured the rainbow kind of summed it up for everyone. Turns out I'm wrong, like usual. They all need their own flag, I guess.

I see Piper sitting in a chair, talking to a stout, blonde-haired woman whose back is turned toward me. When she sees me approaching, Piper's face warms, rising to greet me.

"I already got your flat white." She gestures at the to-go cup on the table. Great, now I don't even have an excuse to walk away from whatever Piper's plan is. I do appreciate that it's in a to-go cup, suggesting I can leave at any time during the conversation, though. "Phoebe, this is Lisa." She points to her friend. "Lisa, this is my sister, Phoebe." The exuberance on Piper's face looks uncomfortable, but it's genuine. I'm not sure I've seen her this happy since we were kids. I shake the blonde woman's hand. Her ice-blue eyes are so soft and caring as Piper gestures for me to sit in her seat.

"Nice to meet you, Phoebe." Perfectly rounded circles present themselves high on Lisa's cheeks with the upward curve of her mouth. She appears to be about our parents' age, which makes me wonder if maybe Piper has replaced them with this woman.

"Nice to meet you too," I say politely, even though I no longer want to be here, and I have no clue why Piper is doing this to me. I shoot her an inquisitive look because our table is only made for two. Where exactly is Piper going to sit since I'm in her chair?

After a moment of awkwardly standing there, silence dwindling between us while I shift my gaze between the two of them, Piper finally claps her hands together and says, "Well, I have to get back to work. I'll let you guys get to it."

I grab her sleeve and pull her down. "What are you doing?" I whisper, panic on my breath.

"Stay and listen," she murmurs nervously. "If you pay attention, you might actually learn something." She raises a challenging eyebrow at me before kissing my cheek and straightening out.

I roll my eyes, quite frankly irritated she's leaving me alone in this neighborhood with a stranger, but the stuff I had packed the night before is already loaded up in the car, just waiting for me to be done here so I can venture to new lands. If this turns out to be anything I deem unfavorable, I can just high-tail it out of town and never look back.

I watch Piper's gait as she sways confidently away, a bounce in her step, waving to a man behind the counter before disappearing out the door as it closes behind her.

"Your sister tells me you're having a hard time," Lisa begins, grabbing her mug and taking a sip before holding it chest level in her hands. Straight to the point. I almost admire it. No need to beat around the bush with a forced version of small talk. We both know why we're here.

I turn back toward Lisa, remembering I also have a coffee. When the hot, lovely liquid hits the back of my throat, my tension loosens slightly. The warmth of the coffee embraces my spine until settling deep within my belly. Who knew coffee could warm the soul as much as it does? Me. That's why I love it. In all of my many forms, coffee will always be my sole constant. "I'm sorry," I begin. "But who exactly are you?"

I don't mean to be rude, but clearly, there's a reason why Piper wants me to meet this person here, and before I say anything at all on the subject of my life to a random stranger, I have the right to know what her purpose is.

She beams before repeating, "I'm Lisa."

"I gathered that much." I fight back the completely rude impulse to roll my eyes, choosing rather to drop my gaze to my lap, where I rub my finger over my thumb. When she doesn't say more, I try a different approach. "What is it you do, Lisa?"

"I'm a pastor."

"Great," I mumble under my breath.

"Your sister figured you'd want to talk to someone who may be able to help you from a religious standpoint on your struggles," she adds.

"No offense, Lisa. But I'd rather not talk to you about this," I say, rising to my feet. I can't stay here. Quite frankly, one of two things is going to happen: she'll tell me this is normal, I'm not going to hell—which I've already heard. Or she'll tell me what I already know is true. I'm damned. I need saving. I have money on the former option, though, because it doesn't make sense to me Piper would introduce me to someone who would ever agree with me. Either way, it doesn't matter. I don't need to hear what I've already heard a million times before. It's over between Blake and me. I'm never going to see her again. The damage is already done, and my foot is already out the door.

"You think you can do this without faith?" she says as I turn to leave. Her eyes are still fixed on her coffee. This causes my feet to stop on a dime. I turn my head to look at her. She raises her eyebrows, pressing the rim of her cup to her bottom lip. "Or are you planning on letting the guilt consume you until you die old and miserable?" She slurps her drink before finally looking up at me. Her light, steely blue eyes soften as they meet mine.

When she realizes I'm still glued between leaving and staying, she pats the table closest to where I was sitting. "Just...Please sit down and hear me out."

I glance from her to the seat a few times in contemplation. What do I have to lose? She's right. Either way, I'll be miserable. Even if I don't have Blake or any other woman, I still have to live with all of the things I've already done with her. Still have to deal with God's silence on the matter. I doubt she'll have anything new to add to what's been said by everyone else, but what's the harm in humoring her while I drink my coffee? After this coffee though, I'm gone.

I sink back down in the seat, placing my hands flat on my thighs, waiting for her to speak.

"I was where you were once."

I doubt that.

"And I know you probably doubt it, but at least hear my story before you make any assumptions about who I am."

Is my face really *that* readable? Or is she that good? I nod for her to proceed while I mull it over.

"When I was about six or seven, I started to wonder if I was different. Started fixating on the older women on TV. I'd tell myself it was the female empowerment I found intriguing. My family is womb-to-tomb devout Catholics. Misery and sadness are kind of their thing. I figured if I wasn't in a constant state of regret, I wasn't loving God correctly. We're all sinners, and we must always remember the guilt of being imperfect. When I felt happiness, I was made to feel bad about it. Pride is a horrible thing. It's important to stay humble and atone until we're accepted into His good graces." Lisa repositions, wrapping her leg around the other under the table.

"When I was around thirteen, I started to notice inappropriate things about my female friends. Enough was enough. I'm a person of God and through Him, I'd find strength to resist."

I can definitely relate, but I'm still not sure where her point is in saying all of this.

"I told myself it was a lack of exposure, so I began to see men. The more I pushed away these desires—ones I was convinced were delivered from the devil himself—I could carry forth what was normal and right. In doing this, I'd more than likely grow accustomed. You've felt this too, haven't you?"

I look down at my nails, picking at them with my other hand before nodding.

"Did you notice the more you stifled it, the more the wanting grew?" Her eyebrows raise as she asks, but I can tell by her eyes she already knows my answer.

Rather than respond outright, I decide to meet her with the biggest question plaguing my mind. "Why was it put into me in the first place? Everyone says it's 'okay,' it's 'normal.' So, to humor you guys for a minute by assuming it actually is, why not put this into everyone? I've always been faithful. Always tried my hardest to do what was right for my family. Always fulfilling my duties to God. How could He decide to curse me with such a horrible disease?"

She sits up further in her seat, smiling. "Honey, I know you've heard this from everyone who loves you, and I know you won't listen to a stranger saying it now, but it's not a disease. It's love. So let me break it down more rationally for you. Because you strike me as a very analytical person."

She's really good at reading people, I think. *Either that or Piper has already given her the cliff notes on her queer sister.* I decide it's the latter. Doesn't matter though. Until she upsets me or I'm out of coffee, I have nowhere better to be. Figure I might as well hear her out.

"Science has been trying to solve the quagmire of homosexuality for quite some time now. Some have found it to be trauma-based, yet there are plenty of people out there who have no definitive sexual trauma to associate this with. Others believe the issue is genetic." She cocks her head to one side. "Science has yet to find substantial evidence of this."

She waves her hand passively before reaching again for her cup. Taking a sip, she says, "There's also evidence suggesting a mother releases certain chemicals in the womb to prevent from having the same gender twice in a row. All we know is that everything—ranging from dark studies on mental illness to fascinating research on randomized childhood fixations—continues to vex us.

"However, science has definitely concluded it isn't a choice someone makes. That's an outdated argument used to create self-hatred. Hoping you'll 'make the right decision' and put homosexuality behind you is ridiculous." She rolls her eyes. "However, homosexuality—which can lead to violent crimes such as immoral, nonconsenting, sexual behavior—oftentimes doesn't. The violent homosexual crimes often referenced are done by people unable to accept this part of themselves. They're raised to believe homosexuality is a bad thing. Remember how I stated the more you stifle these urges, the more the want grows?"

I nod again.

"Denial only leads to resentment. Anger. A sense of selfishness. An insatiable desire to do immoral things because you view *yourself* as unacceptable. Denying love in any form will turn you against God. Whether the decision to hurt others stems from feeling unworthy or spiteful, the end result is the same. You'll resent your neighbors. They were made right, and you were made wrong. Deny the attraction or accept it. It's your choice. But before you do, I need you to understand one thing."

She pauses to garner my full attention.

"God gave us all love. Sure, your romantic side presents itself as same-gendered, but this isn't a tribulation for you to do evil. Evil is determined by how you manifest the love you've been given. If you choose denial, you'll find resentment. God made us all in His image. God is love. Therefore, we all gravitate toward wanting love and to be loved. Being a lesbian is *still* love. God didn't specify what love is because it isn't specific. God asked we respect and care for our neighbors and to keep Him in our hearts.

"Each passage used against homosexuality in the Bible was woven into a lack of respect for your neighbor. Greed, power, anger caused their actions. They did not love their neighbors when they overpowered them. The message of these passages was *never* love. God is. The people who manipulate the message are blinded by their own selfishness. It keeps us fighting and hurting each other."

I can hear the creaking of a proverbial door slowly opening in my brain as my perspective begins to shift. A million more questions come rushing in.

"Then why am I suffering now? If accepting this *love* within myself is what He wants, why did it cause my dad to lose the job he was called to do? Why was I made a fool in front of everyone? Why am I emptier? Why did the woman I love leave after I gave her my heart?" I protest.

Her eyes grow wide. "Throughout the Bible, we see many passages of others who endured tests of strength, countless hardships in the name of the Lord. The road to His everlasting light has never been without its challenges. After all, the Lord always meets us at our deepest. Can you name one who didn't struggle?"

She makes a good point. Not only did Jesus suffer mockery, deceit, famine, poverty, and more. Job, Moses, Joseph, Paul, even women such as Ruth, spring to mind; they all suffered. The greatest stories in the Bible were filled with events so devastating, it's hard to even fathom striving to continue having faith. Yet, each one persevered. Each one stood unwavering beside God and allowed Him to carry them through it. And for that, they were rewarded. Perhaps not in life, but always in death.

"But God stopped listening, stopped sending me messages." My eyes burn as I admit my shame. "Ever since I kissed her, I've been flooded with nightmares of revelations and the three woes. I see my father chained to the pulpit of our former church that's crumbling to ruins. Chains in my back, pulling me away from him. From my church."

Her eyebrows press together, pained, as she taps her lip in contemplation, leaning back in her chair. "Three woes, huh?" Her eyes search the inner depths of her mind.

"Yes." I continue to explain the first dream with my father preaching and his chains as I tried to take him with me but couldn't. I ended it with, "The last one was the night before my father's exit from the church. Literally predicting it before it happened. The third 'woe.'"

She sits up in her seat slowly. "How so?"

"The church was crumbling, as it had in the last dream. I pushed past—er, Blake, the woman who awakened these desires before leaving me. Her name's Blake…" I hesitate, trying to read her face for any discomfort over my confession, but finding none. Yet, I'm still uncomfortable talking to a paster about my transgressions. Saying Blake's name makes the guilt more real somehow. She nods, blinking slowly, listening as if unphased by my admission of attraction to a woman. I shake off the shame and continue. "Anyway, I pushed past her and out the door to see the world had dissipated around the church and was being sucked into a whirlpool."

"Truly terrifying ordeal." She nods, genuinely concerned, expression sympathetic.

"Right?" I lift my hands in exasperation. "Then I heard Blake behind me saying to let go three times. There were these chains hooked into my back, pulling me while I held onto the railing of the steps. I couldn't see Blake anywhere; I only heard her behind me."

"That's interesting," she states, tapping her lip again. "You don't believe God is talking to you?" One corner of her mouth creeps upward.

"I know He *is*, but only to tell me He's mad."

"I think," she raises one eyebrow as she searches my face, "your shame and anxiety are causing you to misinterpret His message."

I think she wasn't there. How could she possibly know? I don't say it though. I figure the more polite way is, "What makes you think that?"

"Imagine for a moment, your church is destroying itself with hatred and judgment. They've turned from righteousness, choosing aggression over love. Couldn't your dream be a representation of this? Your father was chained to the pulpit?"

I bob my head up and down.

"He seems to be stuck in a place he can't even desire to leave. Trapped. Going down with the proverbial ship as it gets sucked into the nether of anguish and despair. In this first dream, you said he was preaching. Spouting off revelations?"

"Yes, talk about foreshadowing." I roll my eyes.

"Uhh, yes, but not in the way you're thinking," she insists. "Many people believe revelations to be a tale predicting the exact end of times." She takes another sip of her coffee. "I might need to get another one of these. You need one?" I look down at my cup. How had I somehow finished it without realizing?

"Why not?" I say, staring intently at my mug as she continues.

"The real significance behind revelations was a warning. God sent John a message to warn the people of what *could* happen if they didn't shy away from the wrongdoings inhabiting the world at the time. To warn the people of Satan and his manipulations. Many speculate it wasn't meant to be taken as literal text. 'God wanted me to warn you of what could happen. Wouldn't it be terrible? Let's avoid any possibility of this by staying true to Him.' The ones who followed it followed it too well, which is great! The message was heard loud and clear. To this day, however, people utilize it as a map, not a warning. To me, it seems your dad was trying to warn the church and even you of their wrongdoings. Stuck, but still preaching, fixing, saving, until the very end. Hazelnut flat white? Extra shot?" After I tell her yes, she says, "Hang on, I'll be right back."

She orders us two more while I sit, contemplating her words. I grew up thinking homosexuality was a choice. When I stood at the crossroads between denying or giving into my urges with Blake, I had given in completely. Yet, if I had ignored it, would it have been any easier the second Bible lesson, or even the third? Was it my destiny to give myself to her? Regardless of the avenue I chose to take, would I have still ended up in this chair talking to Lisa?

Ignoring any thoughts of my sexuality in general, Ethan was still cheating on me with Jaime. If it weren't for Blake in my life, I wouldn't have gotten into a fight with Eve at the bowling alley, which wouldn't have led me to his house to catch him in the throes of passion. I would've married him and given he knew I didn't believe in divorce, would I have eventually allowed Jaime into our marriage? He'd have pulled me away from my family, and I would've watched from a distance as he rebuked my father on the stand. I wonder if Ethan didn't tell me about Jaime or try to work it into a conversation because he knew how I'd react. Once I was trapped, so to speak, I would've had no choice but to go along with it. Did Blake's existence do more for me than I'd thought?

This entire time, I've been so mad at myself for loving Blake, that I refused to realize the good her presence had created in my life. Without her, my father would still be preaching at the most prejudiced church in Mystic Harbor. I'd still be with Ethan, stuck in a polyamorous relationship. I bet I'd have even lost my family in the process. Refusing to embarrass myself with divorce. I'd have become resentful and angry at myself, too, thinking something was wrong with me.

Blake has also taught me so much more about the Bible than I thought I already knew. The way the church has been misinterpreting scripture in attempts to keep indifferent people out. I'm not sure why I'd never considered the church would use the Bible to generate discrimination.

I watch as Lisa returns, placing a mug and a chocolate chip muffin in front of me. I notice this coffee isn't in a to-go cup. I think we've both surmised I'm comfortable enough to stay at this point.

"So, what happened?" I begin as she slides back into her seat, pushing it closer to the table.

She blinks rapidly. "What happened, when?"

"To you." I take the first sip of the fresh coffee, feeling it burn and warm the inside of my chest before pooling in my stomach. "You said you tried to see men."

She nods. "Well, I was miserable and angry for a long time. When my family found out I had a girlfriend, they sent me to a conversion camp. Which was extremely counterintuitive." She closes her eyes tightly, shaking her head.

"Conversion?" I have never heard of this kind of camp before. Is there seriously a camp to turn you straight? Maybe I should sign up.

"Yes. Many naïve people believe you can 'fix' the issue. Some camps are more dangerous than others. Using chemicals and electroshock therapy. Luckily, the one I was sent to was only physically abusive." Never mind. I don't want to be abused or worse. I'm still vexed by how people can think others abusing them is luck, though.

Blake had said the same thing. She was 'lucky' when our school beat her up, threatening her every day. In my world, luck doesn't live in these places. It's horrible, no matter how you try to spin it.

"None of them work," Lisa continues. "They only increase depression and, unfortunately, suicide rates in young adults."

"Did you?" I ask. "Try?"

Blake had admitted she'd tried to take her life, and even I had started to question whether life was worth living after being forced out. Not that I would. I know that's the worst thing you can do in the eyes of the Lord. I've let Him down enough. Hence why I've made the decision to disappear after this conversation.

"No, I did question why I was here, though," she admits. "As many so often do. I struggled with what the nature of being a woman is. Having children couldn't be all we were meant to do in today's age. There's no longer a scarcity within the population. People don't die as frequently in infancy anymore. Honestly, I couldn't bring myself to believe there wasn't something more I was meant for." Her fingers tap the side of her mug as a smile peeks up one corner of her mouth. "And I found it. The first few years were worse than the next: losing my family, finding myself. But after a while, it became easier. I am who I am, and I found my purpose."

Something we differ on. I've lost my purpose. It's always been to please others and lately, I've been failing at my only reason for existing.

"And what was it?" I hold my mug to my mouth, the hot steam dampening my nose, taking in the aroma as I close my eyes. "Your purpose, I mean."

She pulls out her Bible and reads, "1 Corinthians 12:4-7 says, 'There are different kinds of gifts, but the same Spirit distributes them. There are different kinds of service, but the same Lord. There are different kinds of working, but in all of them and in everyone it is the same God at work. Now to each one, the manifestation of the Spirit is given for the common good.' God gave us all a gift to help others. That's the *true* nature of mankind. Not to have children or be subservient. It's to help each other by sharing our gifts." She tilts her head. "I became a pastor to educate those losing their way from God. To help shine a light on homosexuality for all of those who already have faith. My gift," her smirk intensifies to full elation, "is being a lesbian. God made me this way to help others. And I do. Every day. No matter what."

Is that how Blake feels? Why she accepted my little Bible study in the first place? She'd asked if I was sure I wanted to debate scripture. Was I somehow giving her purpose by believing I was saving her? It seemed as though her initial goal wasn't to educate me. Wasn't to use me as part of her outreach. It was as if I asked without realizing it.

No. God sent me to save her. Not the other way around.

"I'm still confused." My eyebrows scrunch together as I try to comprehend this version of destiny. It's backward. It's *wrong*. "God sent Blake to me on three separate occasions. Each time reminding me of injustice due to being a homosexual. He wanted me to save her."

She almost spits out her drink. "Save her? From what?"

"From living a life of sin." I nod with a slight twinge of frustration because I refuse to feel ashamed for trying to help someone. "First time we met was at my church. God sent her to *my* church. She even said after she'd lost her brother, she couldn't figure out how to move on, but her feet led her to EC.

"Then, even though I don't drink, I was moved to find her bar. Made no sense in the moment, but I did. I didn't even know how to order. I had no idea she owned it, yet when I pulled up the nearest bars in my area, it was the first location, even though I passed three others on my way to hers. The third time was again at a church function I was forced to be a part of. She just showed up. Early. We got coffee beforehand. No one other than who I deemed family even volunteered. Not even my boyfriend at the time showed up. Three times."

"That's beautiful." Lisa places her hand over her heart, her eyes softening. The wooden chair squeaks as she leans back. "Truly romantic."

"Not romantic," I correct, tasting the dissolving sweetness of chocolate from the muffin rolling over my tongue. "I answered His call. He wanted me to save her. And now she's not even a part of my life. She told me to leave her alone. God stopped speaking to me, and I don't even have her now."

"Honey." Her hand slides over mine, offering comfort to her words. They're incredibly warm in contrast to the cold marble tabletop my free hand is resting on. "This is destiny. I can promise you this isn't over. You said God hasn't been sending you messages?"

This stops my chewing as my vision moves slowly over the room. A woman is staring at her laptop. A textbook open on the table in front of her. I shake my head, returning my focus to Lisa's rotund cheekbones. "Not since I kissed her, no." Finally, my throat decides to work again, allowing me to swallow. When I deviated from saving Blake, He seemingly stopped speaking to me. I can't feel Him anymore. "And it's over. She doesn't want to see me."

"Are you familiar with numerology?" she asks, pulling her phone out of her pocket and swiping up on the screen with her thumb to unlock it.

"Like the study of numbers?"

"Yes...and their underlying message within text." Her hand slides from my wrist to tuck her hair behind her ear before using both hands to type on the keypad. "Biblical numerology is a study used to show meaning beyond a numerical value. It's a way of saying something using numbers rather than words. You said she was brought to you on three separate instances before you orchestrated your own meeting?"

"Yeah, and?" It's quiet for a moment as she skims the screen. The Lofi music over the speakers change their melody with the changing of the song. The new track has the sound of gentle rain playing behind a guitar.

Lisa lifts her gaze, glaring at me inquisitively from under her lashes. "And earlier, you said Blake came to you in a dream telling you to let go three times?"

She returns to the screen, continuing to scroll as I sit in confusion. Didn't she hear me? Neither God nor Blake are speaking to me now. I nod anyway, though. *Get to the point.*

"Any other instances?"

Brows furrowing, I say, "I mean, maybe? I'm not sure. It's just a number, Lisa." My fingers unconsciously tap on the table to the low beating of the music.

"Yes, but the fact continuation of it's manifestation is curious." Her face lights as she sets her phone face down on the marble surface between us. "I think God's been speaking to you for a while. I think He has been trying to get you to leave that church. Trying to get you to follow Blake. Blake is more significant in your life than you know. God has been giving you signs for a while, but you've been too wrapped up in worrying what you were doing was wrong to notice the subtle details right in front of you." She spins the device and slides it closer to me with her finger.

"How can you possibly think that based off a stupid number?" I sneer. It's honestly so stupid to think she's cracked the case formally known as my life, simply by deducing it to a number.

"Now take this as you will. It's just an observation. You can choose to think a number is just a number. But if you dare to dream in what if's...Have you ever thought you might need to fight for Blake? That God has been telling you to stand your ground. Maybe the true testament to your love would be to stand up and *show* her you love her. Show her you won't be pushed away."

I gasp as I read. My brain completely explodes as I'm hit by this far from black-and-white explanation. My throat is dry as I struggle to swallow around the lump beginning to form.

"Personally, God doesn't speak to me in numerology. However, I know he speaks to all of us differently. Whether through butterflies or feelings within us…or numbers."

I blink repeatedly, eyes still wide as I read the lines a few times over to make sure I'm not reading it wrong. Not misunderstanding because what Lisa's phone says is, *"Three is represented in the Bible in various ways, the Holy Trinity (The Father, the Son, and the Holy Spirit) being the most prominent. Also, oftentimes we notice things being repeated three times throughout scripture. Three is interpreted as God trying to speak to us. If we see something mentioned thrice in scripture, He is either pointing to something with great emphasis or trying to express the completeness of it."*

My mind scrambles at the possibility. Could the reality of numerology be me desperately grasping at straws? I want to be convinced my life can't possibly have become as horrible as it is, but up until this moment, I had nothing to make me believe I'd be okay. And I need it to be okay. Am I using this as a coping mechanism? Regardless of the culprit in my mind, Lisa's words are warming me enough to want to reach for a way to finally accept who I am. My soul has been struggling to create an explanation for all of this. Struggling to find a "why" for Blake resurfacing in my orbit again after twelve years. Maybe I'll never find an answer, and the number three means absolutely nothing. But maybe, just maybe, it could mean everything.

Doesn't matter, because, in this moment, it's exactly what I need.

Piper was right to introduce me to Lisa because right now, I'm holding fast and desperate to her words. Using them to soothe me in a way no one else was able to. Try as they might, I think I needed to hear it from a perfect stranger who believed as strongly as I do. Someone older who has been in this tunnel, clinging unwaveringly to the idea of a light at the end of it.

Regardless of the reality, I can finally breathe again as relief washes over my every extremity. All the pieces finally seem to fall into place, and it's as if I'm seeing the bigger picture as her screen goes black in my hands.

I'm now left peering into my own reflection on the screen rather than the Google search. The weight pressing on my chest, suffocating me for the last few days, is finally gone.

"Don't run from this," she pleads, which makes me wonder if we truly are more similar than I'd initially thought. How else could she know I'd been planning to disappear? No way Piper could've seen that coming and prompted her I was fully and completely packed. "It's terrifying, believe me, I know. But I need you to understand you're right to feel like a part of you is dying…because it is. You've built this wall around yourself. Armor you plastered on to create a barrier between the person you truly are and the person you needed people to see.

"Right now, in this specific place in your life, you're losing that façade. It's scary. You've been hiding behind it for so long because it felt warm. Comfortable even. Now you're vulnerable. People are finally seeing you. Moreover, *you're* seeing you. You feel cold, weak, *exposed* even. You're standing there looking around at the rubble of your past self and panicking, realizing there is no way to piece it back together. There's no going back now. It's no surprise you're terrified. No surprise why you'd want to disappear. But don't."

My eyes sting as a droplet of water hits her phone, landing directly on the image of my face on the blackened screen. It makes me look distorted before my vision blurs completely, and more tears threaten to fall.

I wipe off her phone, apologizing, before handing it back to her and wiping my face. "Thank you." I clear my throat and sniffle.

She stands, walking to my side of the table, pulling my hand to stand before wrapping her arms around me tightly. "I know it might be weird hugging a stranger, but I can tell you need it."

I let out a shuddering breath and nod into her shoulder, squeezing her tightly as I cry into her. "Thank you," I say again.

"Don't be too hard on your new self, okay?" she whispers calmly. "It's not her fault. She's been through enough. It might feel like you're dying, but I assure you it isn't a bad thing. It's beautiful. You're being reborn. Like a child in the womb, the pain was excruciating. But, I promise, one day, you're going to curl up beside your lover, no longer ashamed. You'll pan out and finally see the bigger picture God's been trying to show you. And in this moment, entrenched in the new warmth of genuine security, you'll realize this pain was completely trivial. It's nothing compared to the happiness of having the freedom to be yourself. To open your heart completely to God *and* to people. You'll never dream of going back to the person you were before all of this."

As I leave to head back to Piper's, the last resounding words Lisa had said to me continue to ring in my head. "Fight for the new you, Phoebe. Fight for what you want."

I want to be happy. I want Blake. I want us.

Chapter 39

Phoebe

Before I go home, I have to thank Piper. I need to apologize for my ignorance. Lisa really opened my eyes by somehow putting things into perspective in a way my stubborn brain could finally comprehend.

I park my car outside her house and make my way around the back where I find Checkers running around the backyard first. I hear Piper before I see her, but as I round the corner, I hear a very familiar laugh that isn't hers.

"He's so cute, Pipez," Eve says, stopping my feet in their tracks. My heart sinks.

"I know! He's such a goofball. He definitely gave my life purpose. I've been so lonely since—Phoebz! Your friend is here," Piper says when she notices I'm frozen. "Are you okay? How'd it go? Did Lisa help you?" As she approaches me for a hug, she realizes I'm not okay. "What's wrong? Did she say something? I thought she'd be able to—"

"What's she doing here?" I gesture to Eve, who is picking herself up off the ground where she is crouched, petting Piper's puppy.

"What? She said she's here for you." Piper looks confused, which I guess is fair, seeing as how I hadn't gotten around to telling her anything about the situation.

Fire burns intensely in my eyes as I continue staring at Eve. "It went really good. I wanted to thank you before I leave. Now that I have, I'm going to head back home."

"Phoebe, wait." Eve sighs taking a step toward me. "Just let me talk to you."

"There's nothing to say," I say flatly stepping back. "I think you've done enough talking."

Piper looks between us before scooping Checkers up off the ground. "We're gonna go inside." She turns to me and huffs. "Just talk to her. Whatever this is, I'm sure you guys will work through it. You always do."

I bite the inside of my cheek. "Not this time, Piper."

"I don't want to know," she groans, clutching a squirming, whining Checkers to her chest. "I'm going inside." She gives me a hug and safe travels back to Mystic before turning on her heel and disappearing back inside. Who is this person, and what have they done with my sister? Usually, she lives for drama and chaos. The air changes at the sound of her screen door swinging shut. The yard now blanketed in an eerie silence where dogs aren't barking, birds aren't chirping. Not even the sound of cars can be heard through the tension.

I start to head back to my car when Eve calls out, "Phoebe, please."

"Seriously?" I turn on a dime. "You have some nerve coming here after everything you've done."

"What exactly do you think I've done?" she asks, dropping her hands to her side. "I know I'm not the best person, but I need to set the record straight before you go on hating me for some shit I *didn't* do."

"That's so typical of you." I shift from foot to foot, crossing my arms. "No accountability for anything! You don't care about anyone but yourself."

"What?!" she shouts. "I care so much, it's ridiculous. I've been trailing behind you, cleaning up your messes since the sixth grade!"

"You have to be joking."

She points at the ground. "Oh, but I'm not!" She steps into my space once more and again I step back, avoiding the urge to shove her. "You—"

"Why are you here?" I interrupt, not really wanting to continue this back and forth. The sooner she tells me, the sooner I can get back to the people who really care about me. "Why are you bringing our dirty laundry to my sister's house, three hours away from Mystic? How'd you even know I was here? Are you following me so you can mess up even more of my life?"

"Mess up your life?" Eve places a hand on her chest, clearly shaken that I could be accusing her of something so on brand for her. "What the fuck are you talking about? I wanted to tell you right after you left EC, the police showed up and arrested Jaime and Ethan. Something about vandalizing some gay bar called Siren's Song." Her expression is unconcerned at the mention of 'some gay bar'.

"And you didn't think that could wait until I got home?" I cross my arms and raise an eyebrow. "You expect me to believe you came all the way down here to tell me that?"

She combs her fingers through the ends of her hair. A nervous tick she's had since we met. She wraps it around her fingers when she's extremely on edge. "You won't answer my calls. You leave me on read. What was I supposed to do?"

"Maybe take a hint," I scold. "Obviously, I'm done talking to you. You can't accept me for who I am, anyway."

"I-I never said that. Phoebe, just hear me out, man." Her eyes are bloodshot as she pushes her auburn hair out of her face. "Catching me at Ethan's was a misunderstanding. I just—I—words can't describe how sorry I am for what happened, but you have to believe me when I tell you I had nothing to do with whatever the hell went on in his house the other night."

"Then what were you doing? Why were you there? Were you sleeping with my fiancé? Is that why you talked down to me and then decided to ditch us without a car? To go to his place?"

"Absolutely not! Eww," she yells, wrinkling her nose, sitting down on Piper's doorstep. She gathers her breath before letting it out. "I made a mistake. Actually, I realized that night I've made this mistake a lot. Ever since we were kids, I've been looking out for you—a little too close, honestly. I've known you were into women since the day I met you. You—" Her gunmetal blue eyes look up at me as I walk over to her on the step. "You are…right? I'm done assuming shit. I need to hear you say it."

"Yes," I groan, rubbing my forehead to stave off the burning heat of sudden embarrassment. "I'm finally done denying it. I'm a lesbian." The word stings as I let it fall from my lips.

"H—" She clears her throat. "How long?"

"How long what? How long have I known, or how long have I thought I was?"

"I mean, I guess both."

"I guess everyone knew before I did." I scoff. "I think I kind of suspected it when I was little, but I didn't actively give in to the idea that I might be until I met Blake."

She lifts her head, stopping the work her fingers are doing to her ends. "You mean Dakota?"

My brows knit together. "You knew?"

"You didn't?" She raises one eyebrow. "How? She dyes her hair, and we're just supposed to believe she's a totally different person? Wait," her eyes widen as she pieces it all together, "is that why you think I can't accept you? You think I hate Blake because she's gay?"

"Hmm." I tap my chin sarcastically. "I'm going to go with the obvious answer here: yes, because you've always hated gay people."

Eve cocks her head to the side. "I mean, I don't enjoy most people, you know that, but being gay has never been a deciding factor in it." She lets out a light laugh as she returns to running her fingers through her locks. "My issue with her is solely rooted in the fact she was pretending to be someone else. Walking into EC being all ignorant. She knew they were a closed-table church, and she just goes up for communion, anyway." Her face scrunches. "She gets close to you and Zoe while pretending to be someone else?" Eve is now shaking her head and extending her palm. "Hell, when we showed up for girls' night, she acted like I didn't know who the fuck she was. You have to see why I'd have an issue with that." She drops her head into her hands. "If she cared about you at all, she wouldn't have put your entire family's reputation at risk."

She does have a point. I'd never thought about it, and by my own rule, I hadn't learned both sides before I'd formed my opinion, and in this instance, I hadn't even thought to talk to Eve because I'd assumed I already knew the answer.

"Phoebe," she raises her head and grabs my hand, "when I saw you getting beat up in the sixth grade, I was pissed they were gay bashing you. I had no idea if you actually were, but I stuck up for you, anyway." Applying gentle pressure to my hand she continues. "When I got to know you, I learned how much not disappointing your family meant to you. I could relate. Sure, your family didn't beat the shit out of you when you messed up like mine did, but other than that," she waves off being abused as if it's a small insignificant thing, "I understood you. So, I tried everything I could to make sure your life didn't go up in flames. You saw what happened to Dakota."

"So, you what?" The familiar feeling of irritation pricks at the base of my spine once more. Blake told me she'd made her back off. She was the reason we lost twelve years together. "Threatened her to stay away from me?"

"I didn't threaten her." She groans, rolling her eyes. "I told her she'd get you in a lot of trouble if she didn't blend in. That's what I do." Eve gestures her hands from the top of her head to her feet. "I blend." She grabs both sides of my face, looking me right in the eyes. With all of the seriousness she can muster in those gray/blue eyes she says, "I have no issue with you being a lesbian. I've known since the sixth grade. I love you."

She rises to her feet then, hands threading through her hair once more. "The world is an ugly place, Phoebe. You saw what happened when she came out. The world attacked her. When I ran into her under the pier, I wanted to talk to her alone. I wanted to help her fit in, but fucking aye, she's stubborn! Everything I was suggesting, she took offensively." She grabs my hand and pulls us both down to sit on the step. "And I've never been good at keeping a level head. I found myself matching her energy. Eventually, I realized there was no getting through to her. If she wasn't going to at least change her wardrobe, she'd destroy your reputation. I could tell her upbringing wasn't much different than mine, but she didn't have money like my family, and to her, money meant everything. If she would've been willing, I would've lent her clothes, but she didn't want to hear me out."

"She shouldn't have to change, Eve," I growl.

"Listen, I know it was wrong of me to try, but I saw how happy she made you. I knew she was going to go through a hell of a time at Mystic High, and I couldn't let you go down the same path. It was the only solution I could think of if she was going to stick around. I couldn't see you get hurt or beat up." Eve rests her head on my shoulder.

"The first day I saw you sit down at her table instead of ours, it freaked me out. It wasn't safe, and I had to do something. Some of the people we went to school with are sitting in jail for hate crimes now. Talking to you was pointless, though. I tried to explain the way the school viewed her. You didn't see it. You always choose to see the beauty in everyone, and I love you for it. I'd die to protect that part of you. I never wanted you to get hurt, and yeah, I was a little pissed off when she kept putting you at risk rather than change her fucking clothes. And then she ditched you, which was my second option, not my first. She never even tried to be mine and Zoe's friend."

She places her freckled hand on my arm and squeezes. "Zoe and I both try to protect you. We just can't seem to agree on which way is best. She grew up believing we should nurture the gay side of you, and reflecting on it, I should've too. But I grew up seeing how dangerous that lifestyle can be, and I didn't want you to be another statistic. You're too beautiful of a person to be that girl in a murder documentary where everyone talks about how her face lit up a room, and she was a saint but then was killed in the most heinous way imaginable.

"But I messed up. I realized it after Ethan's. So, rewinding a little. I was pissed Dakota was at your house when we showed up to take you bowling."

"Blake," I deadpan.

Eve pinches the bridge of her nose. "You'll have to explain that to me in a second, but I really need to get this out."

"Okay." I nod.

"So, I was pissed because she was at your house. She tried to pass herself off as Blake and I knew she was Dakota, and I hated seeing you guys together when she was so clearly lying to you."

"I actually knew at this point."

Eve's shoulders deflate. "Well, thanks for filling me in because I thought she was tricking you, and doing the same shit at EC she'd done in high school. She's gay—and I know, I know, so are you—but the more time you spent with her, the more EC asked questions. Dangerous questions. Your mom was scared. I was scared. It was a lot. And then, when she tried to introduce herself to me all smug, I wasn't about to play into it. It was like she totally ignored my warning from high school, but we aren't kids anymore." She's talking so fast, I'm struggling to keep up.

"Your impression at EC affected more than just you, you know? It affected all of us. Especially, the parsonage that was given to your dad when he signed his contract with EC. Sleeping over practically every day in middle school practically saved me from becoming something terrible like my brothers."

I gulp remembering that. I hadn't even considered the fact that my parents would now be looking for a new home. All my childhood memories are buried deep within those walls.

"You and Zoe are my world," Eve continues, "so, when you said, 'typical Eve,' I felt so estranged. Zoe was mad at me, and I figured you guys were phasing me out of the circle. I don't feel like I belong anymore. I know I'm abrasive. That's why I've been staying away since she came back from school. It hurts." She rubs her eyes and lets out a breath.

"That's never been the case, Eve." I hate that she thinks it is. "I always figured you were too busy pulling doubles at the diner." I rub circles on her shoulders. "I think, maybe, we need to work on communicating with each other better because, honestly, everything you're telling me is not how it's been coming across. We've missed you, and the more you explain, the more I realize I've been the issue."

"No, you haven't," she groans. "It's been me."

"No, seriously, I've always stood in between you and Zoe, playing peacekeeper. I didn't realize until now my inability to accept myself was creating this gigantic rift between the two of you. Both of you want to help me with the things you each deem important. You've always tried to save me from getting hurt, and Zoe wants what's best for me in the long run. You both did what you thought necessary to preserve my happiness, but neither one of you can agree on what happiness should look like."

Eve put her hand on mine in my lap. "That could definitely have contributed." The look in her eye lets me know she'd never thought this before. "Thank you for saying that." She pulls me into her embrace. After a moment she pulls apart, her hands still on my shoulders. "But now that you're out, and EC is out of the picture, maybe me and Zoe can work on actually agreeing. I don't hate gay people, Phoebe." She shakes her head. "When Zoe called me a bigot, I realized she didn't understand the point I was trying to make. I just, I didn't want to see you embarrassed or hurt. Seeing what happened on Sunday was crushing. I've never seen you lose it like that. I've never seen Priscilla pull a card out of my mother's playbook. I figured if I ever did, it'd be Piper to bring that side out of her," she admits nervously.

"Oh, believe me." I laugh. "She's came pretty close." I try to steer the conversation back on track. "So why were you at Ethan's?"

"Right, yes." She clears her throat. "So, after I'd left, I sat in my car crying. I know. I'm not a crier; I'm a hitter, but I thought I'd lost you guys. Neither of you really understand me. I get so angry, and my tone says way more than it should when I feel attacked, which doesn't take much. I knew my words would lead you to Ethan's, and I wanted to apologize and try again. Offer support. I pulled up right as you were going in. I had my window down and turned off the engine, waiting. I was literally ready to wait all night if I had to for you to come out. I heard that disgusting music blasting in his house. I got bad vibes.

"When the music cut off, I heard screaming and ran in after you. No way would I let that sack of shit hurt you for not wanting to be with him. You pushed past me, and then so did Ethan in his boxers. To say I was astonished is an understatement. I didn't put the pieces together until I saw Jaime and turned around to go after Ethan, but by the time I got out there, Zoe and Blake had already pulled up, and Zoe figured I was the reason Ethan was in his boxers. When she slapped me, I realized I probably shouldn't have come. They handled it, and I was the reason you fell apart. So, I decided to stay away the next day at church. Sat in the back, watching the drama unfold. Saw Ethan wreak havoc, yet again, tearing apart your family at the seams. After you left, I watched as the police cuffed Jaime and Ethan. I needed to tell you. Needed to explain everything, but you've been ignoring my calls and texts. So, I asked your parents where you were. They gave me Piper's address. I've been waiting for the last two hours."

"You're lucky." I chuckle. "I wasn't planning on coming back here. I was planning on leaving after I met up with Piper's friend. Turns out, Piper has been going to a church."

"Piper?!" Eve huffs out in amusement. "Is anyone who you think they are?" she screeches.

"Apparently not." I crinkle my nose. "And Blake *was* Dakota, but I guess after everything happened, her life spiraled out of control, and she decided she needed a change. She's been going by 'Blake' for the last five years. She came to EC to do outreach for a movement she and her brother started before he died."

"She lost her brother?" Her eyes fill with concern. "I imagine she actually liked hers, if she started a movement with him. I personally wish I could lose some of mine."

I slap her arm. "No, you don't."

She flattens her lips. Definitely not joking. Given how brutal her brothers are, I believe it.

"Still barely keeping in touch with them?"

"Only one Sunday a month when my mom forces us all to get together. It's easier that way." She waves me off. "At least I get to see Declan, even if my brother is totally screwing him up. What's the movement?"

"It's a refuge for people who grew up like Dakota. You'd have to talk to Blake about it. Honestly, I don't want to mess up the details."

She shakes her head, looking down. "I'm the last person she'd want to talk to."

"I'll try to talk to her. And Zoe. As mad as I am about the things you've said, I think we need to square all of this away." I push to my feet and offer her my hand to stand as well. "After all, there's always two sides to every story. It's time everyone heard yours."

✝

Part of showing Blake I'm ready to love her the way she deserves is coming out to my mother properly. She may not enjoy it. She'll definitely disagree, and when she does, I'll have to accept it, and she'll have to accept my absence. There's no way I'll be staying away from Blake, and if my mother doesn't want to see it, I won't make her. I can't very well show Blake I'm "all in" while still hiding her in the shadows, even if it's from my mother. It wouldn't be fair to either one of them. I have to be my true self and face whatever consequences lie ahead.

Ethan has already greased the wheels for this conversation, so I know she's expecting it. It wouldn't be right to avoid the conversation altogether, bring Blake around my mother, and wait for a reaction, either. She deserves to hear it from her own daughter first. I need to have this conversation with her in order to clear the air as well. This isn't church gossip. Her baby girl is, in fact, a lesbian. A lesbian who loves Blake.

When I arrive at the small craftsman I had grown up in all my life, it's almost 5:00 at night. I made it just in time for dinner and I'd told my father to expect me. So, obviously, he'd have told my mother, and she'd already be expecting me inside.

The sun is peeking through the leaves of the old oak tree, creating a glimmery image on the lawn. The old rope swing my father had tied to the tree when I was in kindergarten sways elegantly in the breeze. I remember spending hours with Zoe on that swing growing up. Swinging, climbing, pretending to be Tarzan. Then I remember using it to climb the tree and read a book in the branches when I was a lonely teenager. Dakota would climb it to sneak into my room from time to time too. It's been years since anyone's used it and weather has caused it to tatter and fray slightly. I'm not sure I'd trust it to bear my weight anymore. So many memories lay on the front porch, too—and the roof! I sat with Zoe and Eve as preteens there, listening to them talk about boys.

I let out a sigh as my heart picks up at the idea of admitting to my mother I'm a lesbian. How will she react? Will she hit me again knowing I cost them their house? What if she refuses to even look at me? Will she make me leave? *I won't know standing out here.*

I cram down all of my intrusive thoughts with as much vigor as I can muster before pushing the front door open. The familiar smell of fresh laundry, pears, and gardenias hit my olfactory senses immediately. The hall is lined in boxes, some half full, others not even taped together yet. My stomach sinks.

"Mom?" I call out, hands trembling as I try to steady them.

"I'm in here," she calls from her bedroom. When I find her, she's leaning over her bed, folding laundry before placing them neatly in a box. "Did you hear? Your father got the job. He'll be starting at Guiding Light this Sunday." She says it so casually. As if this is a typical Monday and I didn't just uproot the last two decades of their lives within a matter of minutes yesterday.

"Is he here?" I scrape out before clearing my throat. I have a sneaking suspicion my mother is trying to pretend our little spat outside of EC didn't happen. Typical Priscilla Appleton. Avoid and ignore. I decide I need to ease into this conversation. If I approach it incorrectly, I have absolutely no doubt this will lead to a shouting match, resulting in my swift exit. I grab a shirt out of the hamper and begin helping her fold.

"No," she sighs, placing a pair of jeans into the box. "This morning, he was at Guiding Light, getting a feel for the place. Around noon, he left to go to a bar called Siren's Song and help them with some cleanup since it'd been vandalized. I guess they help out the church a lot, and now Guiding Light is returning the favor. He should be home soon."

"Mom?" I begin. This may be the only opportunity I get, so I have to try. "Do you know who owns that bar?"

She stops folding and looks at me, tears brimming in the bottom of her eyes. "Yes," my mother whispers, her voice scratchy.

"Who?"

"Blake and Jude Chapel." Her body trembles as a single tear escapes her lid, rolling down her cheek. She grabs a shirt and tries to push away her sudden despondency. It doesn't work. Soon she's sitting on the bed, using the shirt to dab at her face as more fall.

I sit beside her and place my hand on her back as her chest heaves, sobbing into the shirt she's now holding with both hands. This isn't the first time I've seen my mother fall apart. The last time had been when I was fifteen, and she'd found out my sister was moving. Piper has caused my mother to weep several times throughout the course of our lives. I don't think I'll ever get used to it being me who's the culprit. This feeling is devastating.

We remain in silence, the sound of her sniffles and whimpers filling the space for minutes before she's finally able to find her voice once more. It's shaky and filled with so much defeat, my chest tightens. "You know I love you, right?"

"I know," I say. My lids sting from her admission. "I love you too."

"It's true, isn't it? You're into—" she chokes before finishing, "women?"

"Yes." I lower my head and look at my feet. "I am."

"Just women?" She dabs at her eyes. "Did you ever love Ethan?"

"I-I mean…" This is such a confusing subject, and I worry she may not understand. I know I need to at least try, though. "I cared for him deeply. I really tried to like him how I was supposed to. I just..." I rub my face, "I never felt attracted to him in the ways I knew I was supposed to. I never should've said yes when he asked for my hand. I just didn't know what to do. The whole congregation was watching. I didn't want to upset you or him or Dad. Then, when it was all over with, I couldn't find a way to tell you. I didn't even know how to tell him. I drove myself so crazy trying to be normal."

Her lip quivers. "I hate that I put you in a position in which you'd ever feel you weren't normal because you are, and I love you so much. It pains me to hear you felt you didn't have a choice. So, you're not bisexual?" she asks, her voice ragged.

I nod. "I'm pretty sure I'm a lesbian," I whisper. Will it ever get easier saying it? It still feels foreign on my tongue. Not wrong, necessarily. It's just a new word I've always avoided saying. Growing up, it was always used in a derogatory sense. It's taking some getting used to expressing it as a positive descriptor of myself or others rather than a discriminatory term.

"I'm just scared," she whimpers.

"Me too," I admit.

"I've lived in Mystic Harbor all my life, and it has never been a safe place to raise a homosexual child. I just—I—" She hugs me so tight I think I may actually suffocate. "I never wanted you to turn out like Jasmine."

My brows raise in piqued interest as I squirm slightly for release. "Jasmine? Zoe's aunt?" I ask.

"Yes." She wipes at her face, trying to regain her composure. "Jeremy was my childhood best friend. We were born around the same time, like you and Zoe. The tradition of having kids that grew up together started with Zoe's grandmother and my mom. Anyway, when we hit fifteen, he confessed to me he liked boys. After a while, he confessed to me he didn't identify as male. The signs were always there. He would beg me to do his makeup. He would sometimes borrow my clothes. He loved Barbies and the color pink." The realization of what she's saying seems to hit her all at once. "Honey, I know this stuff doesn't inherently mean you'll be trans or do drag, but there was always something very feminine about him, and so when he'd admitted to me he felt more like a woman than a man, I wasn't surprised. I loved her anyway. She looked better in a pair of heels and a pencil skirt than I ever could.

"Around the time we graduated, she started really embracing her feminine side. That was when she began transitioning into Jasmine. She was beautiful, Phoebe. A spitting image of Zoe. I can't even describe to you how much happier she was because, throughout school, she was getting bullied. I stepped in when I could, but the boys in our school were the worst."

"What happened to her?" I ask, folding a few more shirts.

"One night around eleven, I'd gotten a call from her mother. Jasmine was hit by a car walking her Pomeranian, Wiggles. Someone just..." my mother struggles to contain her sob as she pushes out the next words, "...popped the curb and ran them both down. The driver was never caught."

She lets out a steadying breath as she stands and moves a pile she'd been folding to another box across the room. "Sweetie, she died, and whoever murdered her got away with it. They could, very well, still be walking around Mystic. When your dad and I got the call from your school that someone had thrown sand in your face. I was worried you'd turn out like Jasmine. So, I started really doubling up on yours and Pip's appearances around Mystic. EC isn't a good place, and we knew that. While your father tried to make a change, I tried to make sure you girls were safe. Pip never understood it, and I know it wasn't fair to you guys. I let my own fear keep my daughters from being who they deserved to be. I kept both of you from being happy."

"Honey, I'm home." My father's voice chuckles his little dad joke down the hall. "Are you in the room?"

"Yeah, I'll have dinner ready in just a second," she responds.

"Is Peep here yet?"

"Yeah, Dad. I'm here," I answer.

"Oh, well, I'll let you two keep talking," he says.

"I shouldn't have put so much pressure on you girls growing up. By trying to help, I made things worse, and now Pip won't even speak to me. I hurt you— embarrassed you. I made everything worse for you yesterday. All eyes were on our family, and I couldn't stop thinking about Jasmine's family at her funeral. People actually showed up to protest, and a bunch of us had to form a circle around her parents as they walked to their car. It was a nightmare. They were throwing stuff and screaming out the wildest insults at us as we fought through the crowd. I haven't seen a single trans person since, but even the homosexuals in your school suffered similar fates until they were forced to move.

"I've been keeping up with the news, and you know that kid Justin from your class? He's in jail for trying to set a kid on fire who was complimenting his shirt. The worst part is his sentence was shortened because his lawyer used a thing called the gay panic defense. They can actually do that. They can say, 'I killed him because I panicked when I discovered he was gay,' and get away with hurting someone. I worry every day about Pip in the city, and I didn't want to have to worry about you, too. I'm so sorry for the things I did. By making sure no one hurt my children, I did it for them. I hurt you guys worse."

I throw myself into my mother's chest and hug her while she sobs. "I never meant to hurt you. I want to start over. I want to make it right for you and Pip. You deserve a better mother."

"Mom," I murmur as tears stream down my own face. "You're an amazing mother. No one is perfect, and if there's one thing I've learned in the past month, it's that everyone is working through their own trauma. We can only see the world in the way it's presented itself to us. I understand now why you did what you did. I think you need to tell Piper this. You raised an amazing woman. She just isn't here for you to see it."

"Hey." My father pokes his head into the room. "I'm sorry to interrupt. I'm just really hungry. Is the food in the oven? I can start setting it up."

"Yes." My mother wipes her eyes, taking a step back. "Yes, let's eat. You must be hungry, too."

"You have no idea," I admit.

We head to the kitchen and set up the table before joining hands to say a prayer.

"Phoebe, would you like to lead us in Grace?" my father asks.

"Of course." We bow our heads. "Lord, we thank you for this beautiful meal and for opening up new opportunities for our family. For loving me as I am. In you, I've found the blessing of direction. I am filled with a profound gratitude for you, oh Lord. You've bestowed upon me the most amazing gift of family and friends, new and old, who have aided in my journey to enlightenment. We ask you fill our home with joy and strength as we continue to walk beside you. Amen."

As we eat, I tell them about my time with Pastor Lisa and the lessons I've learned. My father tells us about Guiding Light.

"You know this means you're going to have to start coming around to a more inclusive way of thinking," my father directs toward my mother.

"Yes," she sighs. "I'm going to try."

"Time to mend some of those bridges." He nods.

We talk of Piper and the new revelation that she's been attending church. My parents are completely taken aback by this.

"I thought for sure she wouldn't ever step foot in another church after EC," my mother says. "She was miserable there."

"I think she's found the perfect pastor." I smirk. "I mean, she's not Dad, but she's amazing. Maybe we can go down there and visit one Sunday."

My mother's expression softens at the thought. "That'd be amazing. You think she'd have us?"

We discuss my mother's apology and opening herself up to the idea of letting us live our own lives. "Can I call her off your phone after dinner, Pete?" Piper hasn't answered a call from my mother in years, preferring only to speak with my father.

Times are changing in our family, and there's nowhere it can go but up. I know it won't change overnight, but God has finally given us the tools to function better as a family.

"So, as awkward as this is to bring up," my mother says as we're clearing the table. "I kind of booked you and Ethan for a couple's massage next month."

My stomach drops as I remember the canceled wedding for the first time since Saturday. "I know you really liked Ethan," I say.

She winces slightly before closing my palm around both of hers. I hadn't noticed until now that we have the same hands. "No, Peep, it wasn't that. Ever since you and Pip were little girls, I've been dreaming of the day one of you would finally be able to share a love like the one your dad and I have. I got carried away. I shouldn't have started planning it without you. I'd hope one day if you ever do find the person you want to spend forever with, I could share in at least a little of the planning with you."

I set the plates from the table in the sink, brace myself against the counter, and close my eyes. An image of Blake projects itself against the back of my eyelids as I think of what it'd be like to see her standing at the end of the aisle in a nice, fitted suit. Handsome. Not the wedding my mother would've imagined. I'm not even sure if *Blake* could imagine ever getting married, but I can. There isn't a single doubt in my mind she's the person I want to spend the rest of my life with. On the good days and the bad. No more running unless we're doing it together.

"I-I think I've found her," I manage to muster through a shaky breath.

My mind returns to when I was younger. "*We are all puzzles, looking for our missing pieces.*"

I turn and face my mom, who stops wiping down the table when she notices I am chewing on a proverbial ball of nerves. "I think I've found my missing piece."

"It's that Blake Chapel girl, isn't it?" she asks, straightening herself.

I bob my head nervously. "I never knew I was missing something until I met her. Whenever I'm without her, I'm emptier than before." As if on autopilot, I've been going through the motions because it never feels as good as it does to have her. "I know it may sound crazy because you've always known her as Blake." I shake off the realization my mother has no idea when it really began. "You think we met a month ago? It's a little bit more complicated than that, though. You see, when I was a freshman, I met this amazing girl named Dakota…"

Then I proceed to tell her about the day I met my soulmate. I spew it all. I'm done keeping secrets. I tell her about the sneaking out, the blanket forts, the time she taught me how to drive. I don't even worry about whether she'll be mad. It happened. We were kids. We turned out fine.

"I have to get her back, Mom. I have to show her I'm done hiding. I'm ready to be with her, no matter what that means."

My mother walks silently to the hall closet and tosses me my jacket. "I'll finish up here. Stop wasting time and go find her."

Chapter 40

Phoebe

When I arrive at Siren's Song, it's 7:45 at night. My heart hurts at the way this place looks. The windows have boards over them as I walk to the door, pushing it open. Inside, I find Dylan and Delaney trying to hang the heavy quote behind the bar.

I rush over, lifting the middle. "Let me help."

We all step back once it's attached to the wall. Delaney rolls his eyes. "She's not here."

"Where is she?" I ask, looking around like an idiot.

He frowns. "This place is all she had left of Jude."

"I know," I sigh. "Is she okay?"

"No." His tone is abrasive. I'm not sure why I expect anything less at this point. It's pretty obvious he doesn't like me, and I still have no idea why. "She found out Jude hadn't told her everything about the plan and these new developments seemingly dove her off the deep end."

My blood chills as I very respectfully think the worst. "Delaney," I begin, trying to keep my tone level, but inside I'm screaming. "Is she at her house?"

"Nope."

"Honestly, I'm getting pretty sick of the riddles. Where the fuck is she?" I shout. "I have no idea why you don't like me, but I have to find her."

"You won't like what you find," he says, his tone completely obnoxiously. "Blake's gone."

My belly hollows out as panic floods my system. "Gone where? Is she hurt?"

Dylan places her hand on my shoulder. "He means she relapsed, Phoebe. Blake isn't the person you'll find if you go looking."

"I don't care." I throw my hands up. "Even if I find Dakota, I knew her too. Where is she?"

"Well, I can tell you where she's *not*," Delaney interjects before Dylan can speak. "Her fucking house. We told her to message us by 2:00. When she didn't,

I went there. We should've known she'd run off. This is why we were keeping a close eye on her. Ethan destroying the fucking bar was too much for her. Jude knew it would happen."

"No," Dylan argues. "She's coming apart at the seams because Jude wasn't here when it happened. She decided to rush into outreach only two months after he died."

"Yeah, and everyone—Jude included—knew EC would retaliate like the Homo KKK. You can't tell me Blake didn't see this coming." Delaney hops up to sit on the bar. The words "carpet muncher" scratched into the granite.

"I have no idea," Dylan admits. "Honestly, I think it's more than that. She said she needed space, so we gave it to her. Looking back on it, I honestly think she's self-sabotaging."

I nod. "Pushing herself away from everyone because she thinks she's fucking up Jude's plan." Obviously, I can relate. After my little "incident" at EC on Sunday, I was going to run away. I felt as though I was making everyone miserable, and I can almost guarantee that's what Blake is doing now. "Last time I saw her, she told me she should've stayed away from me. Being with her impacted Jude. I had no idea this was what she was talking about."

I tell them about the fight at Ethan's. "Dakota had taken over her emotions. She was turning back to her old ways. My friend Zoe had to stop her from killing Ethan."

"Then the bar got destroyed," Dylan says, realizing everything.

"Mmm," Delaney groans, his voice drenched with irritation. "Back in Dakota's day, nothing set her off more than someone mentioning Phoebe in any fashion. If she so much as thought anyone hurt her, Blake would've murdered them." He crosses his arms, speaking to Dylan, not me. "This is exactly why I lost it when I found out she was talking to Phoebe again."

"I'm right here!" I snap. "And I'm going to continue to be here, so I'm going to go find her."

"You have a death wish?" He shakes his head dismissively.

"No!" I steady my shoulders. "She'd hurt anyone to protect me. She'd never hurt me."

"She also told your dumbass to stay away," he shouts. "The one thing Dakota hated most was feeling like she wasn't being heard."

"Like when she told us to back off," Dylan groans, rubbing her eyes. "Shit. We drove her over the edge. She said she needed space."

"Space to fucking relapse, obviously!"

"Delaney!" she shouts. "I get you're pissed, but if you don't learn how to fucking put a lid on it, you're going to drive her further down the rabbit hole than she already is!" She shoves him. "She already feels like she's screwing up all of

Jude's hard work. If you can't find a way to be more understanding, she's going to keep using!"

Quite frankly, I'm getting sick of Delaney. I want to say something, but I know it's not my place. Luckily, Dylan takes the statement right out of my mouth. "She just lost Jude. Outreach was going to cause this, but since she's the one who initiated it, she's blaming herself. This place has been her home, the only thing she had left of her brother. Try to put yourself in her shoes."

"I'm going to find her." I'm done talking. The more time we waste, the more of a chance she has to overdose. I can't lose her again. I don't care if she hurts me. I don't care if she's Dakota or Blake when I find her. She may not even listen to me. Still, I have to talk to her. Have to be there for her in ways I wasn't in high school. I refuse to let history repeat itself.

Dylan grabs my arm as I storm out to my car. "I'm going with you."

✝

Stone's Throw is quiet and destitute when we arrive. I parked my car a distance away, avoiding raising awareness to my arrival with my headlights.

"Wait here," I tell Dylan as I walk up the old gravel driveway. It doesn't even seem as though anyone is here. The only indicator is the sound of The Cranberries playing softly through one of the broken windows. She's in the living room, seemingly reliving the moment we were dancing back in high school.

I peek inside to confirm my suspicions. Three flashlights are propped in various corners of the room, illuminating the space as she takes a swig off a big bottle of whisky. Not for long. I'm taking that shit from her.

Anger tinged with nervousness surges through my joints as I quietly walk into the front entrance devoid of a door...

Chapter 41

Blake

"Dakota!" I heard a shout coming from behind me as I cut through Thompson Park. I stopped on my heel, spitting out a mouthful of blood, only confirming I'd busted my lip on the chair that fucker threw me into. His girlfriend had obviously realized he wasn't shit, but I can't be held responsible for the effect I have on women. Even his.

When I turned, I automatically craved any substance I could get my hands on, but of course, I'd left my blow at the party. I had it on good authority there was still some Oxy left in my coat pocket, in the closet at Stone's Throw, though. I knew what I was doing when I got back to my drafty little haven.

But would the pill even do anything to take the edge off of the sting of getting my lip split open?

Ice has a way of overpowering literally every other substance. Talk about a waste of someone else's money. The liquor and blow from the party had done absolutely nothing to quell the vibration under my skin from the residual effects of the meth. I'd smoked the ice when the sun had come up. It was night now, so I was sure it'd be fine to do a painkiller. Dying from mixing highs and lows didn't matter, anyway. Who would even give a fuck?

I spat out another round of blood, trying to rub off the hair on my arm even though I knew there wasn't anything there. My skin just itched and crawled, as it always did when I did crystal. It always came after the intense painkiller feeling. It was like hair or a bug was crawling around on my skin. Not really an itch as much as an annoyance needing to be staved off.

"I know you," I seethed. Zoe fucking Weatherly. Best friend of Phoebe "wish-you-were-out" Appleton.

Pieces of shit, I thought. If she were anything like Eve McAllis, I could bet I had an earful coming to me. I was sure she was only inches away from calling the fucking cops to have me removed from the general population quicker than I could do a hot rail.

"Yeah…"

I recalled her pulling Phoebe back down at their lunch table before that small-dicked jock had dumped his food on me back in high school. She'd kept her from me. She and that bitch Eve just loved to remind me how I wasn't good enough to breathe the same air as Phoebe. I get it! You made your point already! I didn't need another reminder to stay away from their precious little angel, pure as driven snow. I was nothing more than shit on a shoe. I heard them loud and clear. I was staying away. What more could they want?

"Yeah!" I shake my finger and nod my head. "You're Phoebe's friend, right?"

"Since birth," she said almost smugly. Or was it maybe fear? Did Zoe Weatherly actually fear me? Who the fuck cared, honestly? Either way, it was the perfect kindling for the effervescent boil growing deep within my bowels.

"I fucking hate all of you. Why she still keeps you guys around is beyond me." I spat out another round of blood at her feet. I finally touched my middle and index finger to the gash on my bottom lip, instantly coating them in blood. It was definitely gonna scar, but would I bleed out here in this park? Prolly not. Here's wishing though. "Pure fucking wreckers of joy!" I throw my hands in the air carelessly.

"You don't know anything about me," Zoe grit out.

"Oh, yeah?" I scoff. "You all walk around with rose-colored fucking glasses. You probably think

Phoebe's straight, huh? Hate to break it to you, sweetie, but she's a dyke like me. Snuffing it out is only ruining her chance at happiness, you know? Would you still love her if she was?"

"I don't think it's anyone's place to assume they know her, Dakota," she defended. "If you do, you're no better than the ones telling her who not to be!"

"So, you're in denial!" I threw my hands up in disbelief.

"I know she's gay!" she screamed, dropping her arms at her sides. "Dakota, I've always known!" She let out a large breath as she continued. "I love her more than life itself and, unlike everyone else, I'm waiting until she can accept it and is able to tell me for herself."

"Well, if you fucking know, then why aren't you *helping* her accept it? She's going to drown, Zoe! She's living this plastic fairytale life, surrounded by plastic fake ass people. Her quality of life dwindles while you ignore it's happening."

"Don't act like you know anything about me," she protested. "It's not anyone's place to tell her who to fucking be, but I'm always offering a shoulder, always combatting Eve's stupid fucking bigotry!"

"Yet, you abandoned her!" The disbelief welling inside me was boiling over. "You all do! How can you possibly believe you're there for her? She's always alone while you guys are out, slutting it up?!"

"Slutting it up?! Seriously? You don't know me at all! I'm always going against the current of Eve and Priscilla."

"I don't know who the fuck that even is," I argued.

"And you think you know Phoebe?" She tsked. "Priscilla is her mom, Dakota, and it's very admirable of you to think I'm anything like either one of them. I'm constantly dropping hints being gay isn't an issue."

Before I could even think, tears erupted from deep within me. Tears I'd pushed down for seven fucking years as visions of Phoebe came flying back into my memory. "You and Eve created me! You took away the only good thing I had. If I could've stayed with her, I wouldn't need to drown out the pain of not having her!"

"What?!"

I collapsed onto the merry-go-round, chest heaving. She let out a deep sigh and sat down next to me. Her voice softened. "Come here," she said, tugging my shirt until I found myself buried in her shoulder balling. Her hand rubbed my back and...I let her soothe me.

"I love her, Zoe. I've always loved her. I know we can't be together. I know it's not possible. I'm scum. I'm nothing."

"Hey!" she cut me off, irritation on her breath. "Stop."

"I know...I'm pathetic."

"Right now?" A quick deliberation took place within Zoe's mind before she selected her next words. "Yes. It's pathetic. You're not the Dakota Phoebe deserves. Hell, you're not even the one she remembers. Seeing you like this would ruin her." Here we go again, being told my existence will ruin her. She pulled away from me to meet my gaze. Blood and spit and tears now covered the front of her shirt, but she didn't seem to care. "You need to promise me you won't go looking for her, Dakota." Her eyes were stern. "She can't see you like this. She's too fragile and even I'm having a hard time seeing this version of you."

"I know." I wiped my eyes—probably spreading everything around worse—before steadying my breath because she was right. If my presence wouldn't have ruined her before, it definitely would've now. How had I fallen this far? Was it even possible to fix this now, or was I nothing more than a lost cause? "I know..."

"If I find out you do..." She didn't seem to want to finish her sentence. This side of her was what I could only surmise she deemed necessary for Phoebe, and I had to admire it. "I will make this shitty little hell you're living look like paradise."

She knew I could overpower her, which is why she added, "Don't think I won't. You may have strength, but it doesn't always take muscle to have power. You'd do well to learn that. All the anger—it's getting you nowhere. You're still weak. Deep down, I can tell you know that.

"Phoebe deserves the girl she sat down next to in the lunchroom when she saw you all alone. The one that made her whole when she knew you were both empty. Find that girl again, Dakota." She rose to her feet, grabbing my hand, a gesture she tied to the seriousness in her tone, "And then find me, and I'll bring you back to Phoebe myself. You have no idea how much she still needs you." She squeezed my hand before dropping it at her sides. "But if you find her before then, I'll kill you. I don't know how, but I will rain down hell if you do anything to destroy the beauty within that girl. There aren't many people left in the world like her, as I'm sure you know. If you love her, like you claim, you won't take that from her."

And on that note, she left. I sat for a few minutes longer, gaining my composure before making my way back to Stone's Throw on foot.

Before I decided to doctor my lip, I headed to the closet in the bedroom I was sleeping in. After tripping on the blanket I'd been calling my bed for months, I finally reached into the jacket pocket to find my Oxy wasn't there. No way I'd done them all. I could've sworn I had two left.

Then, the memory came back to me. Last night, I had told myself to save two, but after a few hours, I hadn't fallen asleep. The pills were wearing off, and I'd convinced myself I'd get more tomorrow. When I'd woken up, I had decided to spend the $40 I'd stolen on blow instead. Figured I could convince Jacob to front me some but never got around to asking. So, I pulled out my phone and called him. He didn't answer.

"Fuck, come on, Jacob," I grumbled, deciding maybe a text would work.

Me (12:27 AM)

Hey man. So I busted my lip pretty bad. Think you could front me some till I can pay you back?

He responded almost immediately. Oh, thank God.

Jacob (12:27 AM)

You still owe me $120 from last time.

Jacob (12:27 AM)

Thought you were selling them? Shouldn't you have some cash from that?

Jacob (12:27 AM)

Bro the answers no.

Unfortunately, all of the pills had gone up my nose. I couldn't exactly tell him that, though. Especially since I'd used the forty I'd stolen on the blow for the party instead of paying him back.

Me (12:27 AM)

I was robbed bro.

Me (12:28 AM)

But my lip is really fucked.

Me (12:28 AM)

Could you please just lend me two or three? I can get the money back by Thursday.

He didn't respond. Annoyance began to creep up the base of my spine. I needed this.

Me (12:29 AM)

Come on man, you know I got you. My lip is killing me.

Nothing...

"Fuck!" I shouted, throwing my phone at the blanket on the floor.

It was in this moment, as Zoe's words echoed around my thoughts, I'd realized I needed to change. I was numbing out all the pain, refusing to sit with it. Always laughing. Always high, but eventually, the joking stopped. The friends were gone, the party ended, and I was sitting alone in Stone's Throw Manor. My connects wouldn't be answering. I'd officially taken out my last front. I didn't have any money for booze, either.

I was forced to sit in this broken-down house that would never be my mansion. I couldn't take another second of self-reflection. I needed to get clean. I walked over to my phone, dialing the number. Placing it to my ear, as I wiped away a tear. I cleared my throat as his familiar baritone voice wrapped me up like a warm blanket on a cold and drafty night.

"I need your help." I buried my head in my hand. I hated this. I hated admitting defeat, accepting I had no idea who I was or where I was going or how to get myself out of this hole I'd buried myself alive in. Admitting I'd lost all control. "Fuck." I sniffled. "I'm sorry. I-I'm done fighting, Jude. I need to get sober."

"Love what you've done with the place," Phoebe says, walking in slowly.

"Bess, I could do," I slur, shoving down the vulnerability of her eyes roaming over the space. I take another swig of the now half-empty bottle of whiskey I'd bought on my way over here. "Want some?" How cliché of me to be offering the love of my life a bit of my relapse while being confronted in the place I'd run to while escaping my responsibilities.

"Give me the bottle, Blake."

"Didn't you hear? It's Dakota again. It was always Dakota, ak-chully. She's what you wanted, right?" She sits down next to me on the torn-up couch. Where it all started. How fitting. "Surprise, I'm here." My body sways slightly while I tilt my head back to take another drink.

She lets out a heavy sigh. "I never wanted that. I've never cared what name you went by—"

"—'Cause you never cared about me in the firs place."

Her tone is soft as she says, "You have no idea how much I care about you. I couldn't stop thinking about you. Wishing you were with me."

"In secret." I chuckle. "Heaven forbid someone ak-chully saw us together outside of your apartment."

"Blake, I—"

"Save it, Phoebe!" I stand but immediately fall to the ground. "Whoops." I giggle. At least I didn't spill my drink. I should be embarrassed. At least the alcohol is doing something right. I'm feeling no pain. And fuck have I been hurting.

"No, *you* save it!" she says, yanking the bottle out of my hand.

I stand, struggling to gain my composure. "Phoebe, I'm only going to aks you once: give me the bottle."

"Blake, I'm only going to tell you once." She crosses her arms and raises a challenging brow. "No."

I grab her and tackle her to the ground. My body now pressed on top of her. I bring my face an inch from hers, shouting, "Don't act like you fucking care!"

"Fuck, your breath is straight alcohol!" She shifts her head from side to side, trying to avoid the smell.

I ignore her and continue. "We all have shit we're ashamed of, Phoebe. Mine's Dakota, and yours is fuckin' me!" My lip quivers at the words. I'm worthless. An embarrassment.

She flips me over so fast my head spins violently. "I'm not ashamed of you! I thought I was, but I've learned so much in these past few days, and by the end of it, I realized if everything else in my life falls apart, it'll be worth it if it means I have you."

"Bullshit!" I shout before she presses a kiss to my lips.

"I love you," she whispers, moving a strand of my hair out of my face. My entire body fills with a warmth, booze will never be able to mimic. My eyes sting, my heart pounds. "I love you so much. I don't care about the stares or the whispering anymore. Having you at the end of each and every day is worth more than worrying about terrible people's misinformed opinions. But it's completely justifiable as to why you'd want to numb the pain of everything you've been facing. I can't stop you, Blake—or Dakota—or whatever the fuck you want me to call you now." She sniffles. "Because I'll love you in all your forms."

She climbs to her feet while continuing. "I had a hard time accepting who I really am, too." Phoebe stomps toward the door, being sure to take the bottle with her. I try to stop my head from spiraling as I grasp for her leg and miss. When she reaches the archway, she turns. "Just remember. Life also gave you, Dylan. And Delaney. He hates me, but he loves you." She titters slightly. "God brought us back together." She shakes her head disbelievingly. "Just so you could walk out on everyone all over again."

"No, Phoebe." My mind pivots back to being alone in this house five years ago with no one but my strung-out self. I sob. "Please."

I try to stand but topple over, bumping my head on the couch. I can't tell if it's hard, though. I can't feel it. "Don't go, help me."

She stops dead in her tracks and looks behind her shoulder at me on the floor. "Please," I mouth, my voice catching in my throat. "Don't leave me because I'm a fuck-up. I-I..." I rest my forehead on the floor as tears and snot form a puddle below me. "I can't lose you too. I can't do this on my own."

"Help me get her up," I hear her say to someone before my world goes completely black.

✝

The sun is shining through the window when I wake up in my bed. My head is pounding as I squint, panning around the room. A chair has been moved into a corner, where I find Dylan crashed out.

> *"I love you so much. I don't care about the stares or the whispering anymore. Having you at the end of each and every day is worth more than worrying about terrible people's misinformed opinions."*

It was a dream. Had to be, I think as I sit up.

The stirring causes Dylan to wake. "Morning." She yawns, rubbing her eyes. "How you feeling?"

"Like I need water," I reply, my mouth sticky as my stomach turns.

"Right there," she says, pointing to a glass of water on my nightstand, sitting next to some Motrin and a multivitamin. "Take it all."

"What happened?" I ask, trying to put together the filtering events of last night, resurfacing foggily in bits and pieces.

"Found you at Stone's Throw." Dylan stands up and stretches. "You were passed out, so I picked you up and brought you back here."

This is when I notice I'm in boxers and nothing else. "Why am I naked?" Shame consumes me as cold air wafts across my exposed nipples, causing me to clutch the blanket and cover up.

"You threw up all over yourself on the ride home. We threw you in the shower and hosed you down—not my idea!" She adds the last part once she sees my face. It's not the first time Dylan has seen me naked. She's not one to grow nervous around nudity in any fashion. Her favorite phrase is, "A body is just a body. It's nothing to get excited about unless you're allowed to touch."

"We?" Obviously, she wasn't alone, and I need to know who else saw me naked. "Delaney?" I sigh.

"Phoebe, actually," Dylan says, interlacing her fingers before bending them backward, popping her knuckles. "She took you to the shower and stripped you down. Even washed you and got you dressed, but you passed out again before she could put your top on. So, I helped her carry you to the bed."

Dylan tosses me a shirt. I slide it over my head.

"Where is she?"

"She went home. Made me promise I wouldn't leave your side."

I hang my head as a new wave of nausea settles in my stomach. Was it a dream? The idea she would actually say she wasn't ashamed of me sounds too good to be true.

"Phoebe wants you to meet her at Siren's later. When you're feeling better." She walks out of the room and yells from the hall. "If you want to. She said to tell you it's your choice."

"Wait. Where are you going?" I push myself off the bed and follow her.

"Bed, Blake." She snaps her finger and her cattle dog, Boot, rushes to her side. "I realized treating you like a child who needs a babysitter will never keep you sober." She drops her hands to her side without turning around. "If you don't want to be, that's your decision. Smothering you when you were asking for space was wrong." She then turns and gives me a hug. "We love you, and if you don't want to continue the mission, we understand. It'll always be a lot."

She kisses my forehead and heads out the door. Boot hops in the second she opens her door. "If you decide you're still interested," she calls from her open window while looking for the time on the dash. "Phoebe will be at Siren's until six."

I watch her silver Jeep back out of my driveway and disappear. For once in my life, I'm completely alone. I'm left to my own devices, and I don't know what I want to do.

Correction. I know what I want to do. I head back inside and throw some leftovers in the microwave. While it's heating, I decide I need another shower. Even though Phoebe had tried her best to clean me up last night, I can still smell the mildew from the couch I'd been splayed out on for most of the night. My scalp itches like I ran through cobwebs and tiny spiders are still crawling around in my hair. I can't imagine washing a limp, useless body would be easy. It was probably a chore just keeping me upright while I was sick. I turn on the water and stand under the spray taking deep, collective breaths before scrubbing last night's ick off my skin.

✝

It takes a few hours for me to feel slightly back to normal with the help of meds and Gatorade. The multivitamin really came in clutch as well.

When I'm finally restored, it's 5:15. Phoebe will be leaving soon. Do I face her? I'm sure I made an ass out of myself last night. What if she wants to go off on me? Can I handle the aftermath of my shitty decisions? Do I even want to continue Jude's mission? *Our* mission?

Chapter 42

Phoebe

I hear the sound of tires crunching on the gravel behind me. My stomach leaps as I consider who it may be. Unfortunately, I'm holding a heavy board over one of the broken front windows of Siren's Song while my father screws it to the window frame, so I can't turn to see who it is.

I told her I loved her. As all of her pain came flooding out, I saw the girl I'd known twelve years ago. All the hurt, the fear of being abandoned. It'd make sense why someone with so much baggage would choose to run from it. She'd been braving the storms resiliently as wave after wave crashed into her boat until it'd finally capsized.

I'd been part of that storm when I'd convinced her she was something to be ashamed of. She'd spent twelve years aspiring to be something worthy of my love. Whether we ever came back together, her soul longed to live on the tranquil shores of an ocean similar to mine. A shore where seagulls were the biggest nuisance. But upon dipping her toes in my sand, I made her believe she was garbage. Polluting me with her presence. She could not be seen on my beach.

I feel horrible and the second she shows up, I will apologize for everything. I'll draw a heart in my sand and stand in the middle. I'll wrap my arms around her and remind her every single day she's worthy. I'm the one who's not. I don't deserve her. She's the first Corinthians. Patient and kind. Never boastful or arrogant. She's never insisted on her own way. Rejoicing in truths.

When I have her in my arms, I will endure all things for her. I know the road back to sobriety won't be an easy one now that she's been reminded of how good it is to not feel the death of her brother, the stress of the movement, the shame of existing.

"She's awake," Dylan says, closing the door to her Jeep. "And she's okay." A Black and white speckled dog trails behind her as she approaches.

I'm a little disappointed she isn't Blake, but knowing she's okay will have to be enough until she gets here. "Did you tell her I'd be here?" I ask, grabbing the next board and moving to the other window.

"Till six." She runs over and holds one corner of the board while I take the other side.

The sound of birdsong is interrupted by my father's drill.

"Do you think I should bring her something? Is she hungry?" I ask.

My father pulls the last screw from his mouth. "Give her space, Peep. I'm sure she needs time to process last night."

Dylan places a reassuring hand on my shoulder. "She's incredibly embarrassed."

We head inside and I grab the broom next to the front door, sweeping up the broken glass from the freshly boarded windows.

Dylan continues, lifting the rug off the floor of the entrance, shaking it out. "Not to mention, this is the first time since she decided to get clean she's been given the freedom to choose."

"Choose what?"

"Everything. The movement, the bar," she drops the rug and looks at me, "you."

My father materializes with a red bucket of sanitizer. A few towels are already submerged within the contents. I sweep the remaining glass into a dustpan as Dylan wrings out one of the towels. For a moment, I worry for her dog but he is so impressively off leash trained that he's clinging to her hip. It's incredible to watch.

"You're not worried it might be too much for her?" my father asks, wiping off a table that managed to survive the destruction.

Dylan lifts her shoulders. "Could be." My eyes widen at the realization this may not be over. "But she has to choose this for herself. Smothering her hasn't ever helped. I'm calling it The Jude Method." She lifts her chin proudly, staring at the ceiling as if communicating with the heavens.

"I'm going to need more than that, Dylan." I bump her shoulder as I walk past her to the trash.

"When Dakota started using, Jude would check in on her every few days but kept his distance. He paid for her phone and, by leaving her alone, he realized she would always reach out to him. She'd visit him when she found a way to get to him. When she'd come to visit, he'd ask her reflective, non-threatening questions about her decisions. Things to make her think without ever imposing his opinions or suggesting she stop." Dylan stops to blow at a strand of hair getting in her face. "One day, she called him. Asked for help getting sober." She drops the towel on the table, wiping her brow. "I have no idea what made her decide it was time. And with Jude being gone, who knows what will happen this time around—"

An image of Blake's lifeless body lying on her living room rug enters my mind. "What if she overdoses?!" I snap. "Dylan, you just said she doesn't have Jude to fall back on this time. What if she decides to fucking join him?"

"Language, Peep!" My father's booming yell is terrifying, even as an adult. My ears push back as I cower slightly. "There is no reason to use that kind of talk."

I hang my head. "I'm sorry, but," I gather myself, "I don't know if I can do this."

"I agree with Dylan," my father sighs. "As terrifying as it is, this can only come from her."

✝

I stare at the clock on my phone as I sit on the curb outside of Siren's Song. 7:48. A million thoughts tumble around like rocks in my brain.

She was supposed to be here.

I should've stayed with her last night.

Is she using?

What if she choked on her own vomit?

Is it something more than alcohol?

I should go to her house. Pound on her door and demand she explain herself. I should smash the bottle. Flush the pills? Wipe off the mirror? Break the… goddamn joint or whatever. I should stop this. I need to—have to—stop her.

She just needs a reminder. I need to remind her.

I look back down at my phone to make sure she hasn't texted. She hasn't. Why not? Don't I deserve an apology? Explanation? Something?!

A tear rolls down my face as I inhale the smell of barbeque in the cool night air. Good to know other people are meeting up with their loved ones, sharing a positive moment.

Me (7:49 PM)
I can't believe you did this.

I wipe my face with the back of my palm. Sniffling and clearing my throat. My phone buzzes. I look down.

Dylan (7:49 PM)
Give it time, Phoebe.

I relax my palms as I realize I'm gripping my phone entirely too aggressively.

Dylan (7:50 PM)
Have faith she'll find the strength to ask for help when the time is right.

Chapter 43

My lids are heavy as the lines on my coffee table shift in and out of focus. My thumb and index finger twitch as they struggle to hold the small purple straw. I swallow, tasting the drain in the back of my throat from the lines of pill I'd already done.

If only Jude could see me now. Such an upstanding member of society. Making glorious new memories on our replacement coffee table.

"Better than water rings," I joke to myself because who else would bear witness to my upstanding achievements? Dylan has checked in a few times but doesn't really seem to care. I'm sure her and Delaney are too busy sourcing any and all able hands to fix up Siren's. Nurturing my brother's achievements, ignoring his sister's disappointments. "It's for the best," I tell Jude's dorky argyle sweater vest thrown over the seat. "Once they clean up all my stupidity, your mission will run smoother than ever." I point at him with the straw, causing it to fly out of my hand. "You have some really smart friends, Jude Bug. Oops." I search the floor around my crossed legs.

This is my last pill and then I'm getting sober. I told Jacob to tell me no if I ask again. Which coincidentally I remember telling him yesterday, but I guess I can be quite persuasive since he'd let me buy ten more.

He's a really good guy. Turns out, he was only mad I owed him money. When I turned up at his door with the money I owed him—plus interest—we were all good again. He's a businessman, like me. Owning a bar has definitely taught me the seriousness of turning profit. I wonder how Siren's is doing without me.

No. Showing up there would only fuck up Jude's mission even more. I have to stay away.

I think the hardest part so far has been pretending I don't miss her...

Every night when I'm lying in bed, I catch a whiff of her passionflower shampoo. I should wash the sheets but I can't bring myself to do it. Can't bring myself to wash her off of me. I refuse to process why, resorting instead to sniffing another pill. Last night, I actually passed out sitting up on the couch. The same couch where'd we'd made love before I shouted at her and forced her to leave.

The couch where I had blamed her for ruining Jude's bar…

I hurt her. Not Dakota.

"Where the fuck is my goddamn straw, Jude?" I look over at the blue and green diamond shapes of the fabric. I can't think about Phoebe anymore. This self-reflection is self-destructive.

> *"It's completely justifiable as to why you'd want to numb the pain of everything you've been facing. I can't stop you, Blake—or Dakota—or whatever the fuck you want me to call you now. Because I'll love you in all your forms."*

She'd seen me at my worst. I attacked her. Yet she chose that moment to admit she loved me. She'd entrusted me with something as vulnerable as her body, yet she still searched for me after I pushed her away.

I rest my elbows on the coffee table on either side of the lines as I run my fingers through my hair until I'm holding the weight of my head in my hands.

> *"I realized treating you like a child who needs a babysitter will never keep you sober. If you don't want to be, that's your decision."*

"I'm not a child," I murmur, rocking back and forth. The lines under me blur as I work my jaw, biting back the forming tears.

> *"I'll be damned if our house looks like swiss cheese every time you throw a tantrum."*

"Fuck you, Jude." I hit the side of my head, trying to stop the intrusive voices from spilling out.

> *"If you don't shut that disrespectful mouth of yours, I'll hit that stupid shit right out of your empty fucking skull."*

Tears fall onto the table, mixing with the powder in front of me. "Where are you, Jude Bug?" I crawl over to the sweater vest and press the bunched-up fabric into my tear-soaked face. It still harbors the faintest scent of him. Or is my mind playing tricks on me? "Without you, I have nothing."

> "...*she knew you were both empty. Find that girl again, Dakota. And then find me, and I'll bring you back to Phoebe myself. You have no idea how much she still needs you.*"

✝

It's 5:35 when I make it on foot to Siren's Song. Delaney is outside, hitting his vape in the parking lot.

Time to face the music. I take in a deep, steadying breath.

"Blake?" He approaches me slowly. Before I can say anything, he begins first, "You're alive!"

He clobbers me with a hug. I'm taken aback. "Doe-Boy," I grunt, but don't move away as his embrace squeezes the air from my lungs. "You're touching me." I laugh.

"You bet your ass I am." I stare at him in confusion as he steps back, holding my shoulders, looking me over. "How you feeling?"

"Who are you, and what have you done with Delaney?" Am I hallucinating or something?

"He's seen the error of his ways, my dear Blake friend." The happiness drains as his playfulness dissipates. "Listen, Dylan and Phoebe had a talk with me. Really shined a light on my 'judginess,' and it made me realize I haven't been being a very good friend. You've been going through a lot. Trying to find some form of comfort during all of this, and I've been too abrasive. So, after I apologized to Phoebe—"

"You what?" The idea of him apologizing to anyone is about as common as snow in the Bahamas. To hear he actually apologized to Phoebe...? I wonder when my unicorn will come in the mail.

"I've been being a dick." He sits down on the curb outside the front door. "I had my mind made up about her because from where I was sitting, she hurt you, and that was enough for me to decide you need to stay away from her." He takes another long drag off his vape and, through smoky words, continues speaking. "But it's not my life, is it?"

I shake my head. "You need to know her to understand."

"I know, and like I said, after I apologized, I've spent the last few days really getting to know her and her family. She's got it bad for you, Blake. I'd be an asshole to try to take that from you."

"Is she in there?" I ask.

"She is." He looks up at me through his perfectly sculpted brows. "Her mom is…" he scratches his nose as he weighs out his next sentence. "…interesting."

I lift an inquisitive brow.

"Mainly," he sighs, "you can just tell she's trying to be okay with this whole 'my daughter's a lesbo' thing. But her comments are just very…off."

I suck in a breath and nod. "I'm honestly surprised she's even trying."

"Trying," he tsks, "we'll go with that."

I steel myself, batting off a few intrusive thoughts beginning to grind away at the base of my skull. Thoughts telling me to turn around. Walk away and hit up Jacob. "I'm going in," I say, letting out a deep breath.

"You should." His eyebrows raise in delight.

I push open the door. What I see makes me think I'm still dreaming. This can't be real. Eve and Zoe are sitting on the floor in one corner, joking. Priscilla and Phoebe's sister are in another corner, hugging. There's a sense of peace and warmth wrapping me up and pulling me into the center of this room. Pastor Pete is playing pool at one of the tables with some heavy-set woman around his age. They don't even seem to care their shots are off due to the torn up felt.

The only person I don't see is Phoebe.

Eve and Zoe climb to their feet. I watch as Zoe joyfully approaches the woman and Pastor Pete. My heart drops as Eve follows a different path—toward me.

"Can we talk?" she asks, shoulders slumping.

"Do we have to?" I raise one eyebrow, rubbing the back of my neck. I came to apologize to the ones who care about me, not to be ridiculed for relapsing by Phoebe's most obnoxious body guard.

"That's up to you." She crosses her arms and waits for my response.

If there's one thing I remember from the first time Dylan helped me sober up, it was facing the uncomfortable things. Accept responsibility for my role in people's lives. What better way to break into sober living? I nod.

"I've known since the first day you showed up at EC who you were. When you introduced yourself as this 'Blake' character," she wrinkles her nose, "I didn't handle it well. I'm sorry. For then and also high school."

"Did Phoebe force you to come over here and apologize to me?" I say, scanning the open area. Still no sign of her.

"No," she says hastily, her steely blue eyes search mine. She drops her shoulders on an exhale. "Okay, a little."

"I knew it," I tease, narrowing my eyes.

"Can you just stop for a second and let me explain? I'm trying here." Eve lets out a breath of frustration and I realize we both are.

"I love Phoebe with every fiber of my being," she begins. "When I saw her trying to befriend you in high school, I got scared. I was more concerned about fitting in than I was about being a good person. I was a bitch. I was more concerned about our reputations than Phoebe's happiness. When I tried to talk to you, I was trying to get you to blend. Which was shitty, and you had every right to take offense. You shouldn't have to change." Eve put her hand on my cheek. "I shouldn't have asked that of you. It's just." My face softens as Eve wipes away a single tear trickling down her cheek. Never took her for the crying type. "Associating with a person who looked like you could've gotten her hurt. Did Phoebe ever tell you how we met?"

I shake my head, looking away, hoping if I pretend I can't see her crying, she'll be less embarrassed about sharing her emotions.

"In middle school, some bitchy upperclassman attacked her for being gay. Threw sand in her face. Could've blinded her. Phoebe hadn't even seen it coming. She can't fight, and no one was stepping in. I should've stood up for you too, but I'd convinced myself you didn't want help," she says. "I'm not asking you to forgive me. I'm struggling to forgive myself, actually." She fidgets with the ends of her braided hair. "I should've invited you into our friend group. I worried more about how we looked rather than standing up for injustice, and I have no idea when I lost that part of myself. In middle school, I broke a bitch's nose for Phoebe. Yet in high school, I was too far gone to care about you."

I can feel a knot forming in my throat. I refuse to show Eve weakness, though. I shake my head. "It's whatever, Eve. It was twelve years ago." My chest burns. Never in a million years did I expect to get an explanation out of the one and only Evangeline McAllis, let alone an actual heartfelt apology.

"It's not 'whatever,' Blake. I need you to know I don't have an issue with you being with Phoebe. You guys have seriously always made sense." She holds my hand in both of hers. "I want us to try again. I think you'll learn, our childhoods weren't as different as you think. No pressure. I won't be going anywhere, though, so if you plan on being with Phoebe, you'll be seeing a lot more of me. I am one of her closest friends, and if you try to keep us apart, I'll beat your ass." Her eyes suggest she's joking, but I know there's some truth etched into her playfulness.

A smile creeps up one side of my mouth as I pull her in for a hug.

"If you hurt her," she adds into my ear. "Same thing."

"Wait, Eve?" I say, grabbing her arm as she starts her retreat. "I'm sorry, too. That night, under the pier, I was going through some stuff. My brain was spiraling into a pit of survival, and by the time I saw you, I was already emotionally unreachable. I'm hot-headed, too."

She blinks sardonically. "No shit."

Through tightened lips, I add, "I'd love to try again…for Phoebe."

That's when I feel it. Soothing hands slide against my waist from behind as a warm, gentle exhale falls onto my neck. "I knew you'd come," she whispers into my shoulder blades. My entire body shivers as I glance at Priscilla, who is now staring.

Phoebe's chest is pressed into my back so tightly when I try to push away, I can't. "Phoebe, your mom," I whisper.

Fuck, Priscilla's walking over now. I'm not ready. This has to be a dream—or a nightmare—ask me again in fifteen seconds.

"Get a room, you too," she giggles awkwardly upon her approach, not even trying to mask how disingenuous her smile is. She looks deeply uncomfortable before sliding back into the cold, steely woman I've grown accustomed to. "It's about time, though." Priscilla crosses her arms. "We've been waiting for you." She purses her lips tightly.

"Mother!" Phoebe releases her grip around my waist, and I turn to face her.

I open my mouth to apologize, but before I can Phoebe closes her eyes and blurts, "Can I take you out on a date?" before I can say anything.

Any rational thought I had has officially left my brain. I nod as my eyes sting. "People will see," my voice manages to scrape out.

"Let them look," she says, kissing me in front of God, Eve, and her mother.

I push away from her lips. "This is weird. What is actually happening?"

"I'll explain over dinner." Those eyes. It's as if no one else in the room exists. "Are you hungry?"

Chapter 44

Blake

Less than an hour later, Phoebe is driving us to a floating restaurant near the Double H resort. She's a much better driver than when I taught her at fourteen. On the way, she explains that her sister and mother are finally talking about their issues. She goes into full detail about Priscilla's fears and childhood friend Jasmine. I've heard so many stories similar to this. Yet, knowing her mom figured teaching her child to fear homosexuality was safer than protecting her from the world is still heartbreaking. Makes sense, though. No one ever tried to protect me. Honestly, I can't decide which is worse.

When we arrive at the dimly lit restaurant, the hostess sees us to a table overlooking the tranquil water outside. I can tell the woman is trying to read the situation, but when I look over at Phoebe, she doesn't seem to notice. Or maybe she doesn't care. Who is this person? Did I drink myself into a coma last night? Phoebe doesn't seem to care about anyone's opinions, even holding her hand palm up on the table, gesturing for me to place mine in hers.

After we order our drinks—two waters, to kick start my sobriety—I begin. "What's going on with you?"

"What do you mean?" She bites her lip, blinking nervously.

"You don't even seem to care the hostess and half the people in this restaurant are staring at us."

"I'm terrified." Phoebe laughs, shaking her head as we receive our drinks with lemon wedges spiraled into a twist with a toothpick. *Fancy.* Really wish they had coasters; I resort to placing a napkin underneath our cups instead. Her eyes soften at my gesture. "But I know I need to get used to saying it out loud." Her leg brushes mine under the table. "You deserve to be flaunted. I've been so selfish, and it hasn't been fair to you. I'm a lesbian." She rubs one of the silky rose petals they'd sprinkled onto our table between her fingers. "I've always been a lesbian. I'm done pretending because I'm done hiding you."

I squint. "What made you finally decide this?"

She steadies herself before speaking. "I was outed at EC."

My eyes grow wide, and I squeeze her hand. Gritting my teeth I say, "Ethan?"

She nods, looking down at our hands before clearing her throat. "I thought I was making everyone around me miserable. I was ready to leave. I thought I'd lost you, my parents, my friends."

"I'm sorry I pushed you away. I—"

Phoebe waves me off. "You blamed me for the bar getting ruined, and so did I. I figured it'd be better for everyone if I disappeared." She shifts in her seat. "I packed up my stuff and headed to say goodbye to Piper in the city. I didn't know where I was going. I just knew I couldn't bear being in Mystic anymore."

"What can I get you guys to eat?" the waiter interrupts.

After we order, Phoebe continues. "Piper introduced me to Lisa."

"The woman playing pool with your dad?"

She nods. "I felt like God had stopped talking to me. He was disgusted. He was punishing me for choosing you. It took a while for me to realize if He *was* punishing me, it was for what I did to Ethan. Whether he deserved his own punishments is beside the point. No one gets off scot-free. I did the crime. I just refused to realize what those crimes were. Loving you was never the issue."

I choke on my water. "L-loving me?"

Phoebe peers deep into my gaze and nods. "Blake," she breathes. "I love you."

My body flushes, and my knees grow weak. *It wasn't a dream. She loves me.* "I—" I shake my head, trying to comprehend what's happening.

"Turns out God has been trying to help me from the start. He's been in my dreams, in my prayers. Everywhere. My dad once told me my thoughts were too loud to hear Him, and he was right. He sent me you, to help me move past this shame. He sent me my dad when I was being rattled around in my own turbulence. He sent Zoe when I was panicking. He even tried to shed light on how horrible EC was and how badly my father was stuck in my dreams. Blake?" She grabs my chin, gently peering into my eyes. "You were there."

The waiter returns, destroying the moment by depositing our food onto the table. *There goes his tip.* I grab a fork. "I was where?"

"In my dream. You were trying to pull me away from EC. You tried to pull me up into the clouds with you. EC was falling apart, and I was sure to die if I stayed there. I was so scared, I was willing to go down with it rather than risk the unknown. I need you. I want you. When you walked out of my life twelve years ago, I held on to the hope that you'd be back. I never went looking, but I'd sleep in your hoodie. Before I knew who you were at EC, I approached you, secretly wishing you could lead me back to Dakota. I never stopped hoping. I was scared to accept who I was when I introduced myself outside EC, and I don't know why.

When we were kids, I trusted you to keep me safe on the Seedy Side. I trusted an unlicensed fourteen-year-old behind the wheel." We delight in the memory.

"I told you, I'd been driving for years," I admit again.

"I know," she smiles. "It didn't make sense. I was going through so much that scared me. I wasn't ready to accept any more changes, even if it meant my life would've been better."

I look down at the table remembering my decision to push her away. "Was it better?"

She looks out at the purples, pinks, and reddish oranges of the setting sun over the water. "For a little while." Her eyes were brimming with tears when she finally met my gaze once more. "After you left, I would fall asleep in your hoodie, slip out my window to look at the night sky. Anything to take off the mask and escape into the only happiness I'd ever known. Our time together might have been brief, but it was always enough." Phoebe leaned in closer waiting for me to do the same. "I know you have a hard time understanding your worth, Blake, but my life has never felt as good as when you were at the center of it. You've always been my happiness. My safe space, my home." Her thumb gently brushes over my eyebrow. "Without you to guide me, I was lost. I just didn't understand it fully until you showed up at EC. It may have taken my brain a second to realize who you were, but my heart knew right away that I'd found my way home."

✝

After dinner, we walk the quiet streets of the Holy Side hand-in-hand. The silence is comfortable.

"I don't want this night to end," I admit, pulling on her hand to stop her.

"Me neither." She wraps her arms around my waist.

"I'm scared if I go to sleep, I'll wake up to find this was all a dream," I snort.

She pulls me in until our bodies are pressed together under the streetlight. Our lips meet for a slow, lingering kiss as heat settles below my belly, forcing me to break away. "If we don't stop, I might take you right here," I confess playfully.

"Later." She giggles. "I have one more thing."

"Oh, you do?" I grin flirtatiously. "What's that?"

She turns her head and beams over at a pool hall. "Teach me how to play? Delaney and Dylan told me you used to be in a league or whatever."

"You don't know how to play pool?"

"Never been able to be seen in a place like this." She blushes.

I grab her hand and take her inside. "You should've said something on karaoke night. I would've taught you then."

I open a tab for the table and walk her over, placing our balls in the rack. This table isn't as good as our Diamonds, but I'm not sure what I could expect. The cloth is slow, and the balls are worn. I have no doubt the rails are shot, and the house cues are bent, but I'm not here to compete, so I grab two random cues with decent ferrules.

"What are you looking at?" Phoebe asks as I run the pad of my index finger over the tip of the cue.

"The tip," I explain shyly. "It needs to be roughed in for the chalk to stick properly."

"Chalk?" She tilts her head.

"Yeah." I laugh. "The chalk gives you better grip when you make contact with the cue ball. It's—" This is a lot harder to explain than to show. "I'll show you."

When we get to the table, I show her how to hold the cue, which looks foreign in her hands. "You put this hand down on the table," I say, stepping behind her and grabbing her hand. "It's your bridge hand, which means the cue will rest on it." She lays the cue on top of her hand, and I put her thumb and index finger together, tip to tip, and slide the ferrule through the hole. "That's your support. The better the bridge, the more accurate the shot. Now bend at your hips."

I hear her breath catch as she bends over. "The more level your stick is, the better the shot." I kick apart her legs. "Point your left toes toward the shot. It should be parallel with your stick and your back leg should be facing perpendicular behind your front."

"How the heck is this so complicated?" she asks, straightening back out inches from my face.

"You said you wanted to learn, right?" I bite back seductively. "You're a clean slate." I gesture to another group of people playing pool a distance away. "See that guy taking his shot?" I whisper in her ear from behind her. His form is truly horrendous, and I hope she can see what I see, knowing she won't. Not right away. Hopefully, if she keeps letting me teach her, she'll be running circles around me soon enough. A worthy adversary. "He looks like an Aztec wall painting. He's going to miss the shot, and it's simple. It'd be harder to train him, though. He's probably been playing that way for ages."

"How long have you been playing?" she asks.

"Five years. Pool taught me a lot about patience. Planning your shot, taking your time, and not rushing into it. That guy." I point as we both watch him miss a straight-in shot, the ball bouncing between the rails before popping back out of the pocket. He slams his cue against the table in frustration. "He's cocky. The humbler you are, the more likely you are to slow down and really think about what you're doing. Let the room fall away until there's nothing but you and the problem—er—your shot. He thought he'd make it, so he didn't even consider how hard he was hitting it. The harder you hit, the more inaccurate you'll be."

"Is this how you managed your anger?" she asks.

"Yes." I chuckle at my own admission. "I would get so mad. Try to force the ball to do what I wanted. It took a minute for me to really slow down and use my brain instead of my strength."

We play for an hour as I watch her form get better and better. She's still missing shots, but if we practice often, I'm certain I can have her on my team next season. Not as a sandbagger, but a genuine threat in my league.

"So," she says, fixing her gaze on me when we make it back to her place. "Pool is fun. I'll have to practice more, though. Can we play again?" She unlocks the door and turns, her beautiful mossy green eyes lock onto mine.

"I'd love that," I say, my body filling with so much warmth, I think I might explode.

Her hands wrap around my waist as she pulls me in for a scorching kiss. My body ignites under her touch. My heart rate quickens as I become very aware of the moisture settling between my legs. "Will you stay with me tonight?" she whispers on my lips.

"I love you!" I blurt out. I didn't even realize my mind was going there.

Her elation radiates against my mouth. "I love you too. Will you hold me while I sleep?"

I kiss her softly, opening her door. "Do we have to sleep right away?"

"No." She chuckles, kissing me again. "I need you to teach me more about pool." Another kiss. "How it taught you nothing is a sure thing until you see every angle first."

"I can do that." I guide her backward through the door, kissing her neck as she lets out a slight moan. "I can even show you how to be patient and go slow."

Her hands lift my shirt before resting her fingertips on my ribs. "What if I don't want to go slow?" She grins.

"Well, then." I shut her door. "We can learn more about pool another time."

Epilogue

Blake

Three Years Later

"I'm sorry, Ashton," I say to the newest addition to our group. Ashton's dad was retired military and moved them to the quiet town of Mystic Harbor as a means to keep him out of trouble.

Ashton struggled with bullies all his life, which only worsened after coming out. No surprise there. When his dad found out he'd been seeing a boy named Henry, he'd kicked him out.

"Talk to Phoebe, okay? She's really good at creating dialogue." I grab his hand, which causes him to stop and turn toward me. "Just promise me you'll let her help you before you go in, guns blazing." He nods before walking back up the steps into Stone's Throw Manor.

It took over a year, but we'd managed to fix it up completely. There were a few side steps along the way: foundation issues, infestations, and a few people bound and determined to level the place completely before we could finalize Step Three: Shelter.

The cameras helped with that. There were even a few months when Dylan, Delaney, Phoebe, and I all took turns taking post to ensure the safety of the new development.

Such a large space has allowed us to fit two bunk beds into each room, giving way for thirty-six visitors at a time. We help them rehabilitate into society with scholarships, jobs, and a new sense of direction Mystic refuses to offer them. They're all assigned house chores and a curfew to create some much-needed accountability as well. The house is always full and bustling with disgruntled teens.

Times are changing in Mystic Harbor, and the Evangelical Church of Mystic Harbor hated every moment of it. Guess that's why they lost their flock. Most of them are facing charges for trespassing. A few were jailed for trying to touch Stone's Throw and even Siren's Song. When they became desperate, they even tried to attack us outright. Like rubber and glue, though, everything bounced off of us and stuck to them.

The renovations Pastor Pete had made to EC were a moot point after his rebuke. Most of the members hadn't taken too kindly to how Ethan Fenech had tried to destroy the Appletons' namesake with his homophobic rhetoric. Most of the congregation now attend Guiding Light Ministries.

EC thought they had all of the power within their congregation when, in reality, Pastor Pete's sermons are what brought people in. His words had staying power, and Guiding Light is more than happy to house his beautiful sermons for years to come. Honestly, I'm sure the feeling is mutual.

As I walk into the office, I'm met with Peter's busied expression. "What about this one?" he asks, walking around his desk, pointing to a printout for a hotel for lease.

"Good idea." I grin. "That'd house a good fifty adults going through recovery."

"And the kids aging out of here," he adds.

"Talk to Dylan to make the arrangements." I close the door behind me, checking the hall to make sure no one is around. When I know the coast is clear, I sit in the chair in front of his desk as he slumps back into his rolling chair. He picks up the phone to make the call before realizing I haven't left.

"Did you need something?"

My face immediately flushes as I try to gather my nerves and figure out how to articulate my next sentences. "Um, yes."

He stares at me intently, placing the phone back on the receiver. "Is everything okay?" he asks, a look of concern weighing heavy on his face. "You and Phoebe okay?"

"That's what I came to talk to you about." I swallow, clearing my throat.

Phoebe

"Just remember, Ashton," I say, checking the clock on the stove. Blake should be home soon.

We've had our ups and downs with her sobriety. Blake had contacted her therapist the morning after our date and set up weekly appointments for the first few months to finally talk about the impact of losing her brother. She'd requested to not be left alone during her detox and so Dylan, Delaney, and I had taken shifts. The first week was met with body aches and restless nights. I'd rub her back or draw her baths. Her impetuous mood swings were not for the faint of heart. On the third night, she'd spit the vilest venom through her teeth, officially breaking me completely. I called Dylan to switch me and told Blake I was done. She'd spent every day making me feel worse and worse for sticking around and finally convinced me I needed to leave.

Something changed in her that night when she'd shown up at my house at 2:00 AM crying. She admitted she didn't value herself and this caused her to inadvertently self-sabotage every chance of happiness. She started telling me her every thought. Admittedly, not all of them were needed. Like her restroom experiences. But I valued them none-the-less. I guess since she'd only been using for a week, her detox was a lot easier than they had been previously. She was nauseous, but still able to eat. She admitted the discomfort was what made her testy and unable to sleep. Every night after, when we'd lay down for bed, Blake would curl her body up into mine in a firm embrace with her head on my chest. I'd run my hand through her hair as she held on to me for dear life. A silent plea for me not to wonder off while she slept.

Four months into dating, I moved in. I was right in saying when you know, you know. I've known I wanted to be beside Blake since we were fourteen years old, and we still have never really separated for more than a few hours since the night at the pool hall three years ago. The idea of sleeping alone is uncomfortable. I still never want to be apart from her like I was forced to for twelve years before we reunited. I even miss her when we're working. I know she misses me too because sometimes she shows up at my work just to bring me lunch. On weekends, I'll help out around the bar, too. The insurance check came in, and they were able to reopen two months after Ethan and Jaime had destroyed the place.

The decision to move into her house was a no-brainer anyway, given my apartment was small and didn't have a yard for our dogs to run in—or tear up is more like it. That's right, I finally got dogs. Not one either. Obviously, he'd get lonely. As they say, two is better than one. We're still working on building a run for them to destroy so we can get our yard back. We've just been extremely busy with Steps Three and Four of Blake and Jude's plan for saving Mystic.

Honestly, I didn't even notice it had been three years until my phone went off around 10:00 AM, reminding me about our anniversary tonight. Blake requested we stay in, so I asked Zoe if she'd let me off early to prepare a proper meal and scramble around for a gift.

Right, Zoe.

A year ago, she made it official and opened up her own practice. She hired a few of the newly eighteen-year-olds from Stone's Throw to help around the facility and trained them to become vet and kennel techs. Dr. Auburn required a degree to work at our old vet clinic, which is the only reason I joined Zoe in college classes. Turns out, you don't need college to be a vet tech. You can be trained on-site, which is what Zoe is doing to help guide our freshly adult clients into the real world. Give them a trade.

After some incessant begging from Eve, Zoe finally agreed to let me off early. Eve picked me up, and we went shopping. It's still not often I get to see her, but not because she's staying away anymore.

A few months after Siren's reopened, she'd started dating Colton over in Cypress. Three months into their relationship, things became pretty serious (like we knew they would), which led her to move in with him. Even living only a town over, Zoe and I don't see her very often unless it's between her deliveries for DoorDash. It's bittersweet. We're getting older and settling down, which leaves little room outside of work and relationships for your friends. Even Blake and I prefer staying in after a hard day's work. There isn't a single day I don't miss Eve, though.

I had decided on a new pool cue for Blake. She'd been talking about one in particular and luckily, the Billiard store in Cypress managed to have it! It was a miracle! I was beginning to worry I'd have to tell Blake her gift was in the mail when she sat down for dinner tonight.

"Remember what?" Ashton prompts, bumping my shoulder with his, pulling me out of my embarrassingly deep moment of self-reflection.

Ever since the reminder this morning about our anniversary, I've been thinking about how fulfilled my life truly has become. No more masks, no more people pleasing. I don't even overthink that often anymore. I'm comfortable in my own skin. "Sorry, just remember not to give in or break down. They might try to make you feel worthless or selfish, but your happiness matters. Stick to your convictions, okay? And follow your heart. If it's telling you to leave, get up and walk out. Don't allow yourself to boil over." I glare at him. "Because I know your temper. It's like Blake's."

I poke his chest playfully. Soliciting a shy simper from the teen.

"Silence is the best comeback." I check the clock again.

"It's your anniversary tonight, isn't it?" he asks.

"Yeah. I'm sorry if I seem distracted." I shake off the thought I'm being insensitive.

"No worries." He glances behind his shoulder at the clock. "I have to meet Henry, anyway. Can we talk more on Monday?"

Such a sweet boy. I seriously have no idea how his family could've tossed him out. One thing I've learned in the three years I've been helping Blake is we may not have wanted to have our own children, but we still find ourselves being parents to these kids, which is more than rewarding for both of us. It's an amazing feeling and provides us countless hours of dedication and so many sleepless nights to be here for them in ways no one else would. It's more than either one of us could've asked for.

I throw on Blake's black hoodie before walking Ashton to the door. Seeing he makes it safely to his van. I sit down on the rocking chair on the porch, looking out at the life Lisa promised me I'd have once I learned to accept myself. It's even better than she ever could've described it. I'm happy. I'm fulfilled. I no longer wish I was someone else, and I thank God every day for His patience. For not giving up on me when I was too stubborn to listen. "Thank you," I whisper to myself, unable to contain my happiness.

✝

Blake's 1987 Dodge Dakota—I'm learning so much about cars it's insane—pulls in fifteen minutes later as I watch the tires crunch on the gravel of the driveway. She hops out with so much exuberance, it's practically dripping out of her ears.

"You pull that hoodie off better than I ever did." She grabs my waist firmly, pulling me in for a passionate kiss. "I missed you so much."

"You must've had a good day." I chuckle.

"The best!" She's gleaming. "Happy three years, baby."

Even after three years, my face still flushes when she calls me baby.

"I have something for you!" I say, pulling her by the hand into the house. I rush off into the room, leaving her standing in the middle of our living room.

When I return, I'm holding her gift. It's kind of obvious what it is, but she pretends anyway. Blake walks over, placing it on the kitchen table, smiling ear to ear as she unveils the new pool cue. "They had it custom weighted, like your last one. Weighs exactly the same, so you won't have to adjust to it."

I can't tell which is better, the tightness of her embrace or the Earth-shattering kiss she gives me as she picks me up. I wrap my legs around her as she puts me on the table. "I love it." She kisses me again. "I love *you*." Another kiss. "Will you play with me?"

"Right now?" I joke. "On the table?"

Blake flashes me a toothy grin, exposing that incredibly unique crooked canine before saying. "Just one game? And then you can have me however you want."

"I want you fed," I admit. "I made your favorite. Chicken enchiladas."

"Fuck, when will this fairytale end?" She blinks slowly. "I fucking love you."

"I 'fucking' love you too." I chuckle as she grabs my hand and leads me to the garage where our pool table is. She'd added it last year after reaching the conclusion we liked playing too much to stop. We'd stay at Siren's for hours after closing time just to run drills. Turns out, I'm really good at English and she's really good at banking. We each bring our own strengths and weaknesses to the table. We balance each other out so wondrously I couldn't ask for a better place in life.

"You wanna break?" she asks me while racking.

"Sure," I say, grabbing the break cue. I've been getting better at it. Learned a closed bridge hand works better for me, even if it kills some of the action during the break. I'm still able to hit the yellow "1" ball accurately and full-on, typically sinking at least two. "Power isn't everything." Blake always reassures me.

She places the triangle rack on the hook, joining me on the other side of the table, critiquing my form as I bend. "That's it, Phoebe," she whispers into my ear as I'm trying to concentrate. The sound causes my entire body to thrum.

"Excuse me." I clear my throat, not standing up but turning my head to look at her smirking figure beside me. "I'm trying to focus."

"Sorry." She waves her hand while taking one step back. Before she can decide again to throw off my game, I take the shot, pushing my cue with so much force the balls scatter all over the table.

"Best break ev—" I turn to find Blake kneeling beside me at the table, holding an open jewelry box. The prettiest ring I've ever seen inside.

"Phoebe Appleton," she begins as my eyes instantly well with tears. "Our story started out rough. Hell, even the middle was kind of a nightmare, but if you'll let me, I want to make every chapter after this one better than the last. Will you marry me?"

I pull her to her feet, trailing kisses along every scar on her face. I kiss her neck, her forehead, before finally planting the most passionate kiss on her lips. "Yes." I half laugh, half cry out my response. "Yes! Yes!" This was the proposal I should've had with the person who should've done it.

She's crying slightly as she pulls the ring from the box. "Did I do good?" she asks sliding the ring on my slender finger.

"Of course you did." I nudge her, still looking at the pear-shaped diamond on my hand. "I just have one question." I avert my gaze from the ring for a moment to smirk deviously at my new fiancé. "What's your dress going to look like?"

Blake's face goes pale as she staggers to find a friendly way to refuse.

"Just kidding," I tease, kissing her with every bit of my soul. Giving her everything I have from now until we meet again.

As I've learned, a life without Dakota Blake Chapel isn't really a life at all.

Acknowledgments

I want to start by thanking my wife. For over two months, I was searching for a sapphic romance where a closeted Christian woman discovers she's a lesbian but doesn't renounce her faith. When I couldn't find it, you suggested I write it. Having no idea whether I could string more than a few sentences together, you urged me to begin this journey. What's more, you listened to each chapter right when I finished them. Even if it was the middle of the night. Anytime a change was made, you'd listen to that too. You've been my number one cheerleader. My biggest fan. Even if you didn't have the words to express how the chapters made you feel, beyond "It was good" or "I liked it," you were still there to listen and offer suggestions. Secondly, I have to thank my son for his patience and understanding while I wrote. There were many moments when he'd give me the space needed to work to get it done. When I was finally finished, he was the first to celebrate with me. Without my small family, I would've never published. This story started out as a way for me to process the trauma of my youth and it took quite a few people to finally convince me there are others out there that may need this story just as much as I did.

A big thank you to my father for his need to learn everything. You're the smartest man I know and without your historical insight and knowledge surrounding scripture, I wouldn't have had much back and forth between Phoebe and the other characters. It wouldn't have been nearly as amazing either.

I also want to thank my friends: Shane, Casey, Bri, Krista, Kate, Eric, and anyone else who shared their personal journeys. On top of these people, I have to add my coworkers for putting up with the excessive hyper fixated ramblings about this "novel I decided to write." Even before I knew I was going to publish, my boss would have to wake up every morning and listen to my newest ideas…and she's not a morning person. I seriously appreciate all of you! Not only for putting up with me but also for urging me to publish it.

Michelle Schuler. My first beta reader! I had no idea a person could read so fast! You read the book a fair few times and even sections before and after revisions. I can't forget the other betas as well! Michelle Gilbey-Mills, Stephanie

Capo, Jessica Lower, Kristin, Jade and Victoria MackAnders, and Tyson Chambliss for answering any and all questions and boosting my self-esteem when I was overloaded with doubts. Having a people who didn't know me very well or even at all, read my work was much needed and I thank all of you for your time and devotion to the project.

Maryssa, my editor. I was going to try my best to do my own editing due to a lack of funds but I am SO glad I didn't. The Book of Phoebe was a good book before I found an editor but looking back on the first draft is extremely cringy. I learned so much through the editing process, and I truly believe a book is only as good as your editor to a certain respect. I'd never written a book or even taken classes. I knew nothing going in. Getting my manuscript back was like going through literary boot camp but at the end of the day, gave me the ability to see the story in a whole new light. You've made me a better writer. Thank you so much for reading the story a billion times through fevers and health issues and still dedicating your everything to the work.

Pastor Lori for sitting down next to an extremely nervous soft butch lesbian and starting a conversation of the true meaning of Evangelical. For making my little family feel welcomed at church. I'll never forget the day I went to receive the ashen cross upon my head and you said, "What is your name?" I really thought you were going to tell me I wasn't welcome and needed to leave. I stammered out my name in a whisper and you repeated it. "___, remember that you are dust and to dust you shall return." Later you said my name again during communion. And every Sunday after that when I'd returned. On the second visit, you sat beside me before service when you saw me sitting alone. You invited my family for coffee and dove deep into the historical time periods within the bible. You'd even answer all of my questions, regardless of how silly or offensive they may have been. Your sermons meshing science and scripture were amazing and spoke to me in a way no one has ever been able to. You implored me to do my own research and spurred me on a much-needed journey to healing. Words cannot express how impactful you were in my world and I will never forget you or your sermons. My experience with you may have been short, but when I heard about your diagnosis, it broke me. I hope you understand how great an impact you've made in this world.

Pastor Edwin. Having been raised in the Midwest, I look to you as one of the bravest men I've ever met. Being an openly gay pastor with an agnostic husband is absolutely beautiful and I admire your strength. Where I was taught to hide and cower, you stand tall and proud. I'll never forget our talk over coffee when I had completely written myself into a hole. I'm not sure if you had realized it, but you helped me realize, I'd never be able to give Blake and Phoebe the happy ending they deserved until I healed myself. Your suggestion to add a character was exactly what was needed. Thank you so much for helping me find the strength within me.

Thank you so much Jae for answering a billion questions from a first-time author and for pointing me in Lee Winter's direction for help with my blurb. Thank you both for all of the advice.

I guess I should also thank my cat, Echo, for keeping my lap warm while I created. Even if I'm convinced she's going to unalive me in my sleep one day. The best dog in the world, Quinzel, for giving me space but also reminding me on occasion to peel myself from my chair and do basic things like sleep, eat, use the restroom, and also tend for them as well.

There were many nights when I'd only sleep for a few hours, and when I slept, I'd dream about Phoebe, Dakota, Blake, and Mystic Harbor. So, for every single person who funded this project, I love you! Thank you so much!

And lastly, thank you! Yeah, you. Thank you for being a reader. Thank you for opening your mind and giving this book a chance. Thank you for waking up this morning and braving another day. Most importantly, thank you for being you. I hope you enjoyed Phoebe and Blake's story and found a little bit of yourself within their journey.

Can't get enough?

Continue on for:

The Book of Phoebe Playlist

Bonus Material

AND

A chapter from the second book

in the

Mystic Harbor Series:

The Construct of Eve

Playlist

(In No Official Order)

Dirty Thoughts – Chloe Adams
Beautiful Things – Benson Boone
Colorblind – Counting Crows
Reptilia – The Strokes
The Night We Met – Lord Huron
Human – Civil Twilight
Sextape – Deftones
Way Down We Go – KALEO
Yellow – Xana
A Message – Coldplay
Dreams – The Cranberries
What Was I Made For? – Billie Eilish
Taste Of You – Rez ft Cameron Dove
New Constellations – Ryn Weaver
High Enough – K. Flay
I Can't Walk Away – Cold War Kids
Kitchen Light – Xana
Green Eyes – Coldplay
Kaleidoscope – Chappell Roan
Hymn For Her – Ames
I Could Love You – Phoebe Green
Spiracle – Flower Face
Daylight – David Kushner
Oh GOD – Orla Gartland
Stare At The Sun – Thrice
Light On – Maggie Rogers
Fully Alive – Flyleaf
MakeDamnSure – Taking Back Sunday
Holy – King Princess
Sidelines – Phoebe Bridgers
Freak Like Me – Transviolet
Shameless – Camila Cabello
Lose Someone Like Me – Tones and I

Bonus Scene

Eve

"You seriously want to keep these shoes?" Zoe asks Phoebe incredulously, gesturing toward the old torn-up Converse stuffed in the back of her closet. "You've had them since junior year, Phoebz."

We're currently all sitting on the floor in Phoebe's now disheveled walk-in closet, the last place that needs to be boxed up before we start loading everything we can into my and her car. I was actually surprised to learn Phoebe was still paying rent on her place since she and Blake hadn't spent a single moment apart— besides work—since their first official date four months ago.

The drama surrounding her coming out had sparked a ton of much-needed conversations between us, though. We ultimately came to a unanimous agreement to spend more time as a group, mending the miscommunications that had been drawing a wedge between us since puberty. I've been coming around more, trying to convince myself I'm not the odd man out. After the disaster that led to quite possibly the worst fight we've ever had in our little friend group, we agreed to never attempt another impromptu girls' night.

"Yes!" she shrieks, walking on her knees across the closet to grab the sour-smelling footwear out of Zoe's hands. "They have sentimental value."

Zoe raises an inquisitive brow. "Phoebe, they have holes."

She rests her back on the white wall beside me. "So?"

"You're never going to wear them again," I chime in wishing she'd move back to the other side of the closet so I don't have to smell them anymore. "What sentimental value could these smelly things possibly even have?"

She beams at them nervously, running her fingers along a crusty old gray lace. "Before Zoe left for med school in the city to do her clinicals, her debit card fell through the crack on the pier. I ran down there, remember?"

"I remember. You came back up soaked head to toe." Zoe laughs, poking Phoebe with a black plastic hanger.

"Well, obviously!" Her shoulders slump. "The tide almost got it! I had to jump in the water with my clothes on."

Zoe crosses her arms and purses her lips. "I could've canceled the card. Which I told you before you went all Indiana Jones on us."

"You could just be grateful and say thank you," Phoebe mumbles.

"Which I did after it happened." Zoe lets out another giggle. She leans forward to place a reassuring palm on Phoebe's bicep. "But now it's time to throw the shoes away."

"The toes are curling up, and I'm pretty sure Blake doesn't want them stinking up her closet," I add after catching another whiff of the sour material. I seriously can't get past the smell. It's horrendous.

"Yeah," Zoe teases. "She'll be thanking us for intervening, Phoebz."

"Fine," she grumbles, depositing the shoes into my hands. I discard them in the trash bag we've been dragging around the apartment along with a donate box. "But I'm not getting rid of this hoodie!" She yanks Dakota's old, ripped-up jacket off the hanger, nuzzling it against her cheek. How cheesy. At what point am I allowed to comment on the level of codependency within their relationship?

"We know," I say, rolling my eyes. "It's not yours to throw away, anyway."

"Yes, it is! It's mine now."

"Lesbians," Zoe needles, shouldering me.

"I know, right?" I scrunch my nose. Their relationship is something out of a sappy chick flick, and I find it hard not to be repulsed most of the time. "Gross."

"Stop making fun of me," Phoebe huffs. "One day, I won't be the only one in love here."

"You can keep that shit over there." Zoe holds up an indignant palm metaphorically big facing the statement.

"Agreed." I sigh. It's not that I don't want to find love. I'm just starting to think I never will, and I'm tired of the sappy shit constantly being thrust into my periphery.

"Mmm, I don't know, Eve, you'll probably be the next one," Phoebe sings playfully.

"Not a chance." I scoff, shaking my head in defiance.

Zoe tsks. "Whatever, Eve. Who's the man of the hour this week?"

Admittedly, I have been on entirely too many dates to keep track of in the past four months. To my dismay, the various dating apps have been keeping me quite busy with train wreck after devastating train wreck. And if I have to hear my mother prattle on one more time about how I'm "not getting any younger" and "needing to settle down," I may actually lose my collective shit. Pretty sure the exact verbiage was, "Find a man before your ovaries shrivel up." Sheila McAllis is apparently in desperate need of a second grandchild. It doesn't bother me, though. Honestly, I've always wanted to have children, if only finding a prospective partner to procreate with wasn't part of it. That's the part that I can't seem to nail down.

Hell, becoming head cheerleader my senior year was easier. And I completely fucking hated it. I couldn't tell my mom that, though. Instead, I just used it to my advantage, saying we had practice every day when, in reality, it was every other day. It just got me out of the house.

"I'm fucking serious," I protest.

"Language," we all say in unison before breaking out in a boisterous laugh.

"You don't have to believe me," I continue, wiping a tear from the corner of my eye. "I'm done dating. Why are men such assholes?" I slump, throwing a folded pair of socks into a box labeled "Home."

I'm pretty sure the only men I'm going to find on dating apps are just jerks looking for a good time. Lately, every man I've met is seemingly only interested in one thing.

"Pretty sure the people on those apps aren't looking for more than what they can see in your profile picture, Eve," Zoe states as she folds a pair of pants.

"How would you even know?" I fire back, knowing she's right. "You probably have cobwebs down there from how long it's been since you've let a man touch you."

"Man?" Zoe's eyebrow shoots up, her gaze fixed to the half-folded pants in her hands. She cocks her head, grimacing. "Yeah…it's been a minute."

Phoebe's jaw drops. "Zoe Weatherly, are you saying what I think you're saying?"

My forehead crinkles as I observe their interaction curiously.

Zoe shrugs, dimples becoming more prominent in her pinkening cheeks. "College was an enlightening experience. For many reasons."

Phoebe gasps. "Do tell."

I'm honestly surprised Phoebe doesn't know about this already. I kind of figured it was common knowledge that Zoe is pansexual. They've known each other since birth, given a tradition that started with Phoebe and Zoe's grandmothers. So, if you ask them, they're sisters through and through.

The families later had a falling out over core values. Spoiler alert: It had to do with sexuality. Zoe's family nurtured it, while Phoebe's family—similar to mine—thought they could "cure" the disposition by instilling the fear of God into her.

"Nope. No!" Zoe stands up, pulling more clothes off hangers, letting them fall into a pile on the floor to be folded. "We're not doing this." She smiles a devilish grin before casting her gaze back to me. "Not when Eve is so clearly about to meet the love of her life and shit out a billion babies."

Ah, Zoe's classic trademark. Deflection.

Zoe is the opposite of us. Extremely selfless with absolutely no desire to talk about herself. She always finds reasons to shift the focus anywhere else. Her life is a massive mystery, which only worsened when she left for clinicals in the city.

Regardless of her aversion to talking about herself, she is the biggest advocate for her friends. Phone conversations back then were more to keep tabs on Phoebe and me, and the second questions shifted to what she was doing in the big city— or even how school was going—she'd suddenly have to go to bed or do homework. Whatever excuse she could pull out of her ass to get off the phone, immediately.

I spent a great deal of my early twenties pissed off by how selfless and accepting she is. It took longer than I'm proud of to realize I was only jealous because acceptance was a beautiful quality I knew nothing about.

Apparently, my brain doesn't understand healthy relationships. Zoe comes from positive family values. Meanwhile, my brothers would use me as a punching bag, cock battling each other for the alpha title after my dad died in high school.

I always thought Phoebe and I were similar in the ways we were raised. Definitely not. Phoebe's family is at least *trying* to accept her sexuality. Given my family has never tried to keep an open mind about anything—ever—I doubt they'd understand my vivid imagination toward women. I have no idea what my family would've done if the entire town had found out I was cheating on my fiancé with a woman either. I wouldn't put it past them to have actually beaten me to death. My mother would've gotten her licks in, but it would've been my three brothers that finished the job.

Which is why I've never talked to them about my attraction to women. Honestly, I've only ever considered talking to Phoebe about it. If anyone would understand, I think it'd be her.

That is, if I ever work up the nerve to mention it.

"Fuck you, Zoe," I groan, throwing a sock at her as she returns to her spot on the floor beside me. "Also, why do you have so many socks? I swear this is like the thirtieth pair I've folded."

"No one in the history of living has ever sworn off dating and then *not* immediately met their soulmate." Zoe shrugs, ignoring my own attempt at deflection. She's clearly better at it than I'll ever be. "It just doesn't happen."

"Pretty sure you're not going to meet him on any of those dating apps, though," Phoebe inserts. "And maybe," she scratches her nose in contemplation, "donate the knee highs. I never wear them anyway."

I can't imagine her wearing these checkered monstrosities. I can't even fathom what kind of outfit they'd match with, anyway. I toss a good twelve pairs from the home box into the donate box sitting in the middle of her white carpeted closet.

"I'm thinking some crazy meet-cute!" Zoe continues, extending a hand, painting the scene. "Maybe the tire on your Beetle pops in the middle of an intersection, and some hottie helps you push it off the road."

"OOO!" Phoebe literally bounces in glee. "How about a date stands her up, and the sexy waiter slips her their number instead of the check?"

I bite my cheek. "You guys can stop at any time." I point at Phoebe. "Especially you, because who would stand me up?" I run arrogant fingers through my soft auburn strands before inspecting my nails. "Get real."

Zoe nudges me with her shoulder. "Doesn't matter how it happens, Eve. The point is, it's *going* to happen. The only real question is, do we start the poll now or when you officially meet up with him?"

I push the heels of my palms into my eyes, inhaling a deep breath of the lavender scent of her room. "Do I even want to ask?"

We look at Zoe inquisitively, but she doesn't continue her ramble, choosing rather to stare at me intently until I finally concede and ask.

Letting out a sigh, I say. "What poll, Zoe?"

"Will you be U-hauling faster than the lesbian of this group?"

"We—we've been over this, Zoe!" Phoebe stammers. "The time I knew Dakota should count toward the time we've been together!"

"It doesn't," Zoe and I reply in unison.

"It totally does!" She holds up her hand, counting on her fingers. "Four months since our first date added to the two months of talking before said date. That—that's half a year, right there." And now she adds her other hand. "A-and then there's the roughly eight months of high school before she transferred. That's like…" she counts in her head, "almost a year and a half!"

"Wow." I tsk glancing over at Zoe, concealing my elation.

"Right? Never seen someone grasp so hard at straws," Zoe needles, shaking her head.

"I'm not grasping, dammit! It's at least over a year!" she protests before finally submitting. "Whatever." Her nostrils flare in frustration. "It doesn't matter. When you know, you know." She lifts to her knees and pulls a pile of underwear out of the dresser, throwing it in the same box I'm chucking socks into.

"I've known I loved Blake since we were in high school," Phoebe continues. "Doesn't matter where I live or what anyone else thinks. I'm the only one who can understand the way I feel." A smile breaks across her lips as she—I'm assuming—fantasizes about her long-lost lover. "This is forever." She nods triumphantly before returning her attention back to the closet we're sitting in.

For an awkward moment, the room is silent. Besides the second hand tick, ticking on the analogue clock in her bedroom.

"I hope you're not contagious," Zoe finally deadpans.

"Seriously," I second, scrunching my face. "You're gross."

"Speaking of where you live," Zoe continues. "How'd your family trip to visit Piper go?"

"Went about as good as it could, I guess," she responds with a shrug. "Literally took everything within my mother not to have an entire aneurysm when she saw Piper's basement apartment." She tries to conceal her giggle. "Best form of entertainment ever. She forced a smile and complimented the space. It looked so painful." Phoebe lifts her nose in the air. Giving her best impression of her mom, she says, "'You've done such a good job making a home for yourself, Pip.' And you could tell Piper was miserable but keeping the peace. I think she knew her mother was trying. Checkers was all over my mother, though."

"Oh, I bet your mom loved that." I snort.

Anyone who knows even the slightest bit about Priscilla Appleton knows she is *not* an animal person. Especially animals that shed.

"She spent most of the time standing because Checkers is allowed on the furniture. When we left, she made my dad take us to the closest grocery store for a lint roller."

"She didn't expect Piper to have animals?" Zoe asks. "Pretty sure if she would've let you guys have pets growing up, you wouldn't have shifted so far into the animal world for a career choice. We were always fixing up the hurt birds as kids."

"I'm still hung up on why you didn't think to warn your mom that Piper had a dog," I admit as she helps Zoe fold shirts.

"What fun would that have been?" Phoebe grimaces.

"You're terrible." Zoe chuckles as she throws the final article into the box and closes it up.

"No," Phoebe says, picking up a box and bringing it to the empty living room as Zoe and I follow with the other two boxes. "What's terrible is the fact that Piper didn't even tell us she had a boyfriend until he randomly showed up."

"What?" Zoe double-takes. I fight the urge to shake my head. She thinks I haven't noticed her childhood crush on her best friend's sister. Realistically, I'd be the last person Zoe would talk to, which is why I haven't brought it up. "She has a boyfriend now?"

"Apparently. One she didn't want our parents to meet so quickly."

"Yeah, well." Zoe scoffs. "She's never been the best at letting people in, especially after they've hurt her."

"Agreed." Phoebe chortles. "Guess he was just as surprised as we were. Piper told him he should've called. I guess he texted, but you know how my sister is at checking texts."

"Don't I ever." Zoe rolls her eyes, laughing under her breath. I honestly don't know how this crush has lasted so long. More often than not, Piper is kind of an asshole.

We make a plan to regroup at Phoebe's new place. Zoe left to check on the animals staying overnight at the clinic but promised she'd swing by after.

After the final boxes are brought in from our vehicles, Phoebe offers me some water. I glance around her new residence before letting out a small laugh.

"What's so funny?" Phoebe asks.

"Nothing." The corner of my mouth twitches slightly. "Just wondering if you had the right idea in dating a woman." I wave off the thought, attempting to downplay my nervousness. What if Phoebe isn't the best person to admit this to after all? She hasn't been out for very long and before that, she was trying to save her now girlfriend from eternal damnation.

"It's not much different than I assume being with a guy would be." She shrugs, eyebrows pinching together as if trying to gauge why I'd be mentioning her sexuality. "The other day, Blake got upset because I've been forgetting to put a new bag in the trash after I take it out. I guess she went to throw some tuna away, and there were still some bits left in the can. Got all over, and she had to wipe it down."

I wrinkle my nose. "Such a petty thing to choose to be upset about."

"Yeah? You want to know petty? Ever since, she's been leaving little notes everywhere." Phoebe gestures to the trash can. 'Replace the bag.' Then to the shoe rack. 'Shoes go here.' "Being with a woman isn't any different than being with a man. Who would've thought *I'd* be the messy one in the relationship?"

"Yeah, I would've lost money betting on that horse," I admit. "But seriously." I fidget with the hem of the cloth placemat nervously. "How did you know you were into women?"

Phoebe shakes her head in bewilderment. I'm sure she never expected this question out of a woman she'd assumed was homophobic only five months prior to us sitting at this table. "Is this why you gave me such a hard time over Blake?"

I swear it's like I can explain myself until I'm blue in the face and people still don't see me beyond the image they've painted. "We've been over this." I scrub my face and sigh. "I knew who she was. She was putting my chosen family at risk."

"I know," she holds her hands up in defense, "I know."

"If you guys would've kept me in the loop—"

She waves me off. "You're right. I'm sorry." After shaking her head, she decides to answer the question. "Honestly, I think I've always been attracted to women. Is that how you feel?"

After a long pause, my heart pounding in my neck, I break the silence. "I mean, I've always found girls attractive," I admit. "I've even thought about what it'd be like to kiss one. More than kiss, actually." My cheeks burn at my truth. "But women scare me."

I let out a deep sigh, feeling an intense weight being lifted from my shoulders. "Scare you how?" Phoebe presses, interested to learn more.

"Because, you know..." I taper off, scraping around inside my brain, struggling to come up with the proper words. "Men don't know women as well as another woman would. We have the same parts, so I should know how a woman wants to be kissed and touched. What if I don't? What if I happen to be bad at it?"

"Has a guy ever told you that you were bad at it?"

"Well, no." I look at her, embarrassed, which, honestly, is a first. I've always been a confident woman. I'm attractive enough and not afraid to tell it like it is. "But honestly, the guys I've been with wouldn't exactly turn you away for being bad at anything. They could practically finish without me."

She scrunches her nose in disgust. *Right, I forgot I was talking to innocent Phoebe.*

"Too much?"

She holds her thumb and index finger just a fraction apart. "But I get what you're saying. The men you've been with haven't exactly been ones who are interested in anything other than who you are physically, though. There's so much more underneath the surface."

"Well, how am I supposed to know that going in?" I sink down into my chair. "Things would be so much easier if you could just ask people their intentions upfront. You can't just ask a man if he's only interested in your looks. If he's going to ghost you in the morning. Even women are tricky. How do I know I'm not reading into a kind gesture? Like, if she jokes with me or grabs my arm when we're talking, how do I know she's interested and not just being friendly? What if I'm just reading too much into it?"

"It's hard to explain." Phoebe lets out a small laugh. "With Blake, there were a lot of instances that led to me knowing the attraction was mutual. Leg brushes under the table. Slightly positioning yourself in their space and seeing if they do the same or create distance. Sometimes, you just have to take the leap and pray that they reciprocate. All the while expecting rejection, if that makes sense."

"It does." I smile slightly. "Maybe I should try dating a woman."

We share a giggle. "In all seriousness, Eve. I'll support you no matter what, okay? I know how hard it is figuring yourself out, and if you want to spend some of your energy understanding if this is for you, regardless of who disagrees, you know you'll always have me and Zoe."

I rise to my feet, pulling my best friend's body into the tightest embrace I can muster. Because this nervousness, this gut-wrenching fear taking place within me, she knows it all too well.

ა

2 Months Later

Colton (8:47 AM)
Hey

Eve (10:16 AM)
Hey yourself.

Colton (9:22 PM)
Sorry about messaging you so early. I didn't know you slept in so late.

Eve (9:22 PM)
Only when I work nights. Which unfortunately is practically every night.

Colton (9:24 PM)
Oh really? What is it that you do?

Eve (9:25 PM)
Jewel thief.

Colton (9:25 PM)
Oh good. I was worried my job would be the deal breaker.

Eve (9:27 PM)
Which is?

Colton (9:27 PM)
Bank robber.

Eve (9:28 PM)
Hmm...Sounds like a day job. When would we ever see each other?

Colton (9:35 PM)
Well, I was hoping maybe this Saturday? If it doesn't interfere with any heists you have planned.

Eve (9:36 PM)
I'm heist free after 6. Does that work?

Colton (9:37 PM)
I may have to rush through my last job.

Colton (9:37 PM)
But I think I can make it work.

Eve (9:38 PM)
It's a date then ;)

"You should've said no, Eve," Zoe sighs as she pauses the movie we're watching at my apartment.

"Seconded," Phoebe says, rubbing her face.

"What?" I scoff in disbelief. "Clearly, you guys aren't understanding me here."

"We understand just fine," Phoebe says softly, grabbing my wrist. "But—"

"—We also remember *last* week, when your bitch ass said you were done dating," Zoe interrupts her. Everyone who knows us knows Phoebe's bedside manner does absolutely nothing for me.

"I know what I said," I growl, unlocking my phone to show them a picture of Colton. "But look at him!"

Zoe staggers to her feet. "I'm getting another drink. Anyone need one?" She pulls down her camisole to cover the exposed bronze skin of her belly.

"He's very handsome, Eve." Phoebe smiles, cheeks already pinkening from her first hard seltzer. "I'll take another one."

"Sure you'll be able to drive?" I ask.

"Blake's going to pick me up," she huffs, "so I can be as fun as I want to be."

"We love Fun Phoebe!" I clap excitedly before declaring, "Tonight, we party!"

Phoebe is an extreme lightweight when it comes to alcohol. Which has led to some rather funny stories since she started drinking less than six months ago.

Zoe returns from the kitchen, handing us our drinks. "I'm going to have to pass, guys," she says, sighing.

"What?" Phoebe asks incredulously.

"No." I stand. "You always do this, Zo. You always dip out just when things get interesting."

"I do not!" Zoe practically shrieks. "A few weeks ago, we closed down The Side Pocket together!"

"That was almost six months ago, Zo," I challenge, rising to my feet, heading to my bedroom, shouting my next words. "And you only did that to celebrate Phoebe finally coming out." I return, setting a full bottle of tequila on the coffee table in front of us before grabbing three shot glasses out of a cabinet in my kitchen. "It's Friday night. The clinic doesn't open until noon tomorrow." I set them down on the table and begin pouring the tequila. "Blake will be here to drive you guys home at midnight, and I'm fucking lonely."

I plop down on the couch between Zoe and Phoebe.

"Lonely?" Zoe scoffs as tequila spills over the rim of the shot I'm attempting to hand her.

"Yes," I groan, slumping my shoulders, looking between her and Phoebe. "I'll be twenty-eight next month. I'm almost thirty, and a fucking waitress at a shitty small-town diner. The most entertaining part of my day is when I get to go to bed. I didn't go to college, and I'm not a kept woman—"

"—That's your mother talking," Phoebe supplies, grabbing her shot off the table. "Nothing about you has ever suggested you'd allow someone to care for you."

"Shit." I laugh, gesturing again for Zoe to take her shot, which she finally does. "I'd settle for anything at this point if it meant finally having a baby." My throat tightens as I continue. "I'm starting to worry I'll never be a mother."

"Would it be the worst thing?" Zoe asks, wiping at the spilled liquor on the coffee table with her palm before wiping it on her sleep pants. She's never been much for children. She's good with them, and I know she and Phoebe would both make great chosen aunts for my little ones, but they've never been able to understand the desire I have to bring life into this world and break the cycles of my own family. To see myself reflected in those small eyes and preserve the innocence my parents didn't.

"Yes," I admit through gritted teeth, digging my bare toes into the ugly brown carpet that covers practically my entire apartment. "I'm not asking you guys to get pregnant with me." I tilt my head, weighing the idea that we could somehow keep up the tradition Phoebe and Zoe's grandmothers had started when they'd chosen to raise children together. It'd make me so happy knowing my child would have someone they've known since birth. A second family. A different atmosphere from their own. "What if I never find someone? What if the only future I've ever wanted for myself doesn't happen and I'm alone on my deathbed with no one to care for me? No family of my own."

"You'll always have us," Phoebe chirps, a bit of the tequila spilling onto her fingers before dripping on the floor. *There goes my deposit.* "You'd never be alone."

I ask as I pour myself a shot, "Who will take care of us when we can't care for ourselves though? You guys never worry about that?"

"I mean." Zoe shrugs. "Pretty sure even if I did have kids—which is a long shot because I love my body too much to ever carry one—they'd just ship me off to a nursing home, anyway."

"I wouldn't want to pressure my children to watch me die," Phoebe supplies. "Not sure I'm even prepared to do that for mine."

"You would," Zoe and I say in unison.

"Yeah," Phoebe admits, shoulders slumping slightly. "I guess I couldn't just abandon them. They never abandoned me when I was weak and vulnerable. Lord knows Piper won't."

"I hate this topic," Zoe says, setting down the shot she's been holding for entirely too long before walking to the kitchen. "If I'm going to get drunk, I refuse to spend the night crying and hugging." She opens my fridge. "I know you have limes."

I get up and shove past her playfully. "I'll have to cut them."

I turn to find Phoebe already rummaging through a drawer for a cutting board.

And this is a pivotal moment in my life. The first stone within the pathway to being understood. To finally being heard. Support I'd need—from the ones I love most—three years from now when my life completely falls apart. That kind of love and support is the true definition of family. It's stronger than metal. Softer than a whisper. And thicker than blood.

Keep reading for an excerpt from

The

CONSTRUCT

of

EVE

The second novel in the Mystic Harbor Series by J. Fez

Dylan

"Remember," I remind the group, eyes shifting to the squeaking door opening at the back of the room. An underweight kid enters with bruises on his arms and black under his eyes. He's been booting up and doesn't look a day over sixteen. I push back the pain in my chest at the sight of his shifty demeanor. Eyes darting around to the other members as if ashamed to be here. Hoping no one in this small town recognizes him. "What's broken *can* be mended once we understand what needs fixing."

I have about sixty seconds before this kid collapses into his own internal guilt, convinces himself it was a stupid idea to come, and leaves hoping no one even noticed he'd slipped in. If this happens, I won't be able to sleep tonight. I can't in good conscience allow this person to go back to the drug house he came from and use again, knowing I didn't at least try to change his perspective.

Without appearing too interested or desperate, I gesture to a chair. "Welcome. Have a seat anywhere you'd like." I give him my most genuine smile. The one no one can resist. The one that's talked even the most aggressive people down from their ledge of self-destruction. "We were just discussing our toolboxes. Do you have one?"

The boy sinks into the chair to my right, rubbing the bruises on his inner elbow, shaking his head in ashamed confusion. No words. Which is good. Reticence means he's still on the fence. I'll take that over someone forced to be here any day of the week.

You can lead a horse to water, but you can never make it drink. You can take away their kids, their house, their pride, and none of it will stop them from using. Showing them it's hurting *you* or trying to force them to sober isn't an effective way to elicit change—it's an effective way to make them need an escape. To understand an addict, you have to first understand that until they decide to become sober, they will never be able to fight off the urges. Because every person's story is different, but I can tell you one thing is always inherently the same: nothing is stronger than the bond between a person and their addiction.

Unfortunately, not all people have the opportunity to want better for themselves before it's too late. Hosting Narcotics Anonymous meetings is a hard line to toe. You have to know when to let go and allow them to fight through the waters that are drowning them. You toss them the life jacket, but it's up to them to figure out how to get to it and put it on. You can't kick their legs and expect them to figure out how to swim. And this is why I'll keep saying it until I'm blue in the face; sobriety *needs* to come from the addict.

"Can anyone give an example of what I mean by understanding what needs fixing?" I look amongst the crowd.

After a moment's pause, a man in his mid-fifties raises his hand.

I nod. "Go ahead, Paul."

He clears his throat before allowing the low timber of his voice to do its usual introduction. "My name's Paul, and I'm an addict."

"Hi, Paul," the group says in unison.

He's confident as he speaks, given he's been an active member of Narcotics Anonymous for years now. "My ex-wife had gotten my rights taken away when my daughter was still pretty young." Paul has been clean for over fifteen years now and expressing this part of his life is second nature to him at this point, so he doesn't give any visible indication to the pain he once felt as this part of his life was crumbling. "When I got clean, I tried to make amends and see my daughter, but she was twenty at this point and had a lifetime of hating me. Hell, I'm not mad at her. I should've been a better man to her mother and a better father to her, but when I was using, it's like I had blinders on. I didn't believe using hurt them as much as *not* using hurt me."

I nod. It's unfortunate how common this is. Addicts who delude themselves into believing the dangerous situations they put themselves in to find their next fix will never affect their loved ones as much as not having their next fix will hurt them.

"Anyway, when Siraya finally agreed to meet with me, she already had another family. A stepdad, her mom, she even had a son of her own. I couldn't seem to figure out where I fit in this equation. That thought made me want to use because I was trying to fix what I'd done to her when she was still a little girl. It took a minute of digging around in my toolbox to find a way to center myself and realize: That shit happened years ago. I'm not the same person I was back then, and neither is Siraya. If we're going to have a relationship, it needs to be one based on who we are now. Not who we aren't anymore."

"Beautifully said, Paul." I clap and allow everyone else to join in. "A Sobriety Toolbox is a collection of tools we can use to keep ourselves sober. Meditation, sponsors, hobbies, anything we can use to get our minds off of the negative feelings that make us want to hide from the problem. Tools to keep us on the sober path we want to be on. When life is raining down on us pretty hard, it's easy to fall back into the comforts of a high to avoid doing the work to mend what's broken. What isn't easy is facing the issue head-on, tools in hand, refusing to hide behind disassociation."

My eyes fall on the kid, now leaning forward in his seat with his elbows propped on his knees. He's messing with the frayed edges of his torn jeans, refusing to look at anyone. "If anyone would like to discuss a plan for making a toolbox after the meeting, I'd love to help in any way I can." I toss out the proverbial life jacket. Question is: is he willing to swim?

ۃ

After the meeting, it looks as though he's going to talk to me. He shakes his head, however, as if giving in to some intrusive thought, then walks out the door instead.

I hope I'll see more of him. Hope he'll change his mind. Like I said, you can lead a horse to water, but only he can decide to drink.

"He'll be back," Blake says, noticing my consternation as I'm folding chairs in the now empty room of Guiding Light Ministries' basement. She steps closer, taking the chairs from me and stacking them against the wall. "He's come into Siren's a few times now. How old you think he is?"

"I wouldn't think he'd be a day over seventeen." I shrug. "Surprised you guys would let him in."

"Believe it or not, he's nineteen. I guess Delaney went to school with his older brother. His name's Brandon Elliot. Word on the street is that he started using junior year but didn't get on the heavier shit until recently. His brother noticed the track marks a couple months ago." Blake flips off the coffee machine and opens the lid on the top.

"It's a damn shame. Hate it when it's kids." I grab a cookie from the pack on the same table before closing it up, setting it on top of my pack on the floor.

"Isn't it always?" Blake shrugs, pulling out the filter full of soggy coffee grounds. The smell of stale coffee mixing with the chewed-up chocolate chip cookie in my mouth. Not sure why store-bought cookies always taste so stale in comparison to scratch-made ones. She tosses it in the trash beside the table. "I started around his age too."

Grabbing a napkin, I begin wiping off the table. "Yeah, but you didn't shoot it."

"Lord knows where I'd be now." She laughs nervously, disappearing to the restroom down the hall to pour out the coffeepot.

"You'd be right here, Blake." I shout down the hall. Upon her return, I pat her back firmly. "Because it's where you were always meant to be."

Drying the inside of the now rinsed—but forever stained—glass coffee pot with a paper towel, she sucks in her teeth. "I don't know, Dyl. If you weren't around, life would've played out completely different."

I nod, refusing to speak my mind.

Because it doesn't matter. Life *didn't* play out differently. Had it played out differently, I wouldn't have been selfish. I'd have left the Army instead of re-enlisting for a second term. I'd be living in Colorado Springs, still be married. By now, we'd have the two kids we always said we'd have, and I'd only be visiting Mystic Harbor three times a year. I wouldn't be living alone, twenty-five minutes outside of town, with only my dog and chickens for company at thirty-two years old.

I know I need to be thankful for the things I do have, though. If I were religious, I'd be thanking God for the struggle, too. I'd be grateful that His lessons taught me to slow down and consider other people for once. I heard that lesson loud and clear. So much so that there isn't a single selfish bone in my body anymore.

You see, seventeen-year-old me disregarded every plea from my family not to enlist. Hell, even my dad, who served over twenty years, advised me not to join up. But, like I said, I was selfish and, above all, stubborn. Enlisting made me an adult. Not some small-town girl who would never see the world. It was structured, regimented too. I was born to build muscle and fight. I was born to be an American soldier.

Fighting is my own personal therapy. A way to clear my head and let off steam. Turns out, I'm not the only one. When I first met Blake, she was strung out and angry and thought she could blindly swing her fists around to keep people at arm's length. No one ever took the time to block her shots and pin down that molten anger that was destroying her from the inside out. I planted the seed within her, and have watched it grow over the last five years.

And for that I *am* thankful for the lessons that taught me to consider others. I just wish I could've learned them sooner.

I fold up the table and rest it against the wall before glancing down at my watch. 8:43 PM. "Is everything okay? You're never late for a meeting."

She follows me out, coffee machine in hand. "You think I forgot what time meetings are on Friday nights?" she jokes, waiting for me to lock the door before following me out to the parking lot. "I was about to call you when I got off but realized you'd be in a meeting. Since Siren's is just down the street, I figured I'd just swing by. Catch you as you were leaving."

"So what's up?"

Things have been seemingly going well for Blake within the last four months. She's reunited with the love of her life, Phoebe Appleton; she's expanded her and her late brother, Jude's, mission to create a voice for the queer community within Mystic Harbor. Siren's Song, a bar Blake and Jude opened together, was finally reopened to the public after some vandals tried to destroy it. A bar that's very well known throughout Mystic Harbor as an advocate for the LGBTQ+ community.

With everything going so well for her, the pessimist in me can't help but expect the worst. In my life at least, things never seem to stay good for long.

One of the most sensitive portions of Blake's history was the existence of Phoebe, so a part of me will always worry that when they have their first nasty fight, the addict in Blake will try to wriggle its way back into the life she's worked so hard to create. A life I know Jude dreamed she'd have.

"Phoebe's having a little get-together with her friends, and there's booze," Blake says, rubbing the back of her neck—a dead giveaway she's uncomfortable. Blake doesn't like asking anyone for anything and, honestly, I don't think she's comfortable asking anyone for help.

"Do you need me to talk to her about drinking in front of you? Is it bothering you?"

"No!" she answers hastily. "I work at a bar, for fuck's sake. I love drunk Phoebe. Can't think of anyone who doesn't." She laughs. And she's right. Everyone—excluding probably her parents—loves drunk Phoebe. The normally shy, reserved woman always keeping up impressions for her family, becomes goofy and honest. Downright bossy at times. It's the most adorable sight to see. You just want to wrap her up and keep her safe. "No, she just sent me a text."

Blake hands me her phone.

Baby Peep (7:38 PM)
Wold you stil ned coaster f Dylan mad a tble fomm I?

"Wow." I laugh. "That's more than three sheets to the wind, Blake. That's twenty-seven at least."

"Suffice it to say," Blake sighs, letting a small smirk creep up one corner of her mouth, "I may need reinforcements."

"What time?" I chuckle.

"I told her I'd pick her up at midnight. Phoebe told me Zoe will need a ride home too."

"Bet." I unlock my Jeep Wrangler. "We sparring or running drills till then?"

"We could do a little of both at my house." She shrugs.

"Sweet, hop in," I say, climbing in and twisting the key in the ignition. "Cool if we swing by and grab Boot? I haven't been home all day."

Blake smiles. "Of course."

೧೩

The hallway to this apartment isn't the worst, but it also isn't the nicest-seeming joint on the Holy Side of Mystic Harbor. Granted, I can't imagine any apartment on the Holy Side being unsafe. I'm just surprised that a place like this could exist over here.

What I'm not surprised about, however, is never having met this other friend of Phoebe's. Since I've met Phoebe, I've been introduced to her entire circle in one way or another. Obviously, I've met her dad, Peter, given he's one of the pastors at the same church I host my NA meetings out of. I've met her mother, Priscilla, through the few Sunday services I've actually woken up early enough to attend. I've met her sister Piper once when she visited from the city. I then learned that Piper had a no-contact situation with their mom due to some issues growing up but is now bridging the gap and trying again.

I've even met Phoebe's best friend Zoe, who is a veterinarian. When I found this out, I immediately made her Boot's regular vet. She's planning on eventually opening up her own clinic, and I can guarantee Boot will be her first patient. He loves her. His last vet made him shake, but when he sees Zoe, he lights up and starts dancing around. He's a smart guy, Boot. I swear he can understand me, maybe even read my thoughts.

However, the friend who lives in this apartment, I can honestly say, I've never met. I've heard mentions of her from Blake, but not exactly the best mentions if we're being completely honest. She and Blake are apparently working through their differences from high school. Differences apparently involving this woman having issues with gay people.

Given one of her best friends is gay, I figure she's working through it. To be even more honest, though, I'm not sure I'm ready to meet her.

Blake knocks on the door. A rumble of giggles can be heard on the other side.

"I got it!" I hear Phoebe say before a crash and an *oof.*

"Lock," someone gasps through hysterical laughter.

I smirk and nudge Blake. "Oh, this is going to be fun." I'm excited to see the mess that awaits us behind this door, and that's not even sarcasm. Drunk people are one of my favorite forms of entertainment when they're all smiles and clumsiness.

Blake sighs.

A banging sound followed by a snort and even more hysterical laughter come next.

"Blake, I'm not even sure they can make it to the door." I chuckle. "This might be like trying to get a baby to unlock a car after they've locked themselves in type situation."

"Shut up," Blake grumbles, but I can see she's trying to stifle a laugh.

"I'm coming," a voice chimes in before we hear the sound of something rolling toward the door.

"Can none of them stand?" Blake questions, running a hand through her hair in concern.

"I'm going to pee my pants," I hear Zoe practically whine.

I elbow Blake. "That vet degree's coming in clutch right now, huh?"

Blake sucks in a breath.

We listen as the lock finally flips. Blake grabs the knob, readying herself for the disaster that lies beyond. I'm so excited I'm about to push it open myself.

"Maybe Blake can bring a spare change of pants for you, Zo," Phoebe calls out to Zoe, whom I hope made it to the bathroom because neither of us expected it would be this bad when we arrived. "Where's my phone? I'll text her."

"Even if you did manage to find your phone," Blake says, causing Phoebe and a woman with red hair to both look in our general direction. "It probably wouldn't make any more sense than the last one you sent me. Hence why I brought Dylan."

I make my grand entrance into the apartment only to be stopped instantly by a redhead laughing hysterically, rolling her head over onto my shoe. She squints, her blue eyes like a nebula struggling to stay in focus as she scans up the length of my body, searching desperately for my face.

This must be Eve, I think as I try to make it easier for her by crouching down to her level. The second I do meet her inebriated gaze, however, it's like someone took the wind out of me. It's impossible to hide my smile at how cute this woman is drunk off her ass. Literally. *What a first impression.*

"Well, hello. Can I help you up?"

I watch as the smile leaves her face. She almost looks as if she's in trouble and needs to sober up as she nods.

I give her my hand, and when she wraps her thumb around mine, I refuse to take any chances. Using both hands, I grab either side of her soft, delicate palm and pull her to her feet. What I didn't calculate was the strength of my pull and how little the smaller woman weighs. My strength in combination with her inebriation causes her to lose balance and continue forward until her face crashes into my chest.

"Whoa." I chuckle, wrapping my arms around her tiny frame. *So dainty.* From this angle, I can smell her tea tree shampoo and a hint of tequila. I could probably pick her up and—nope. She's drunk, and I know myself well enough to know where my thoughts will go if I continue on this train, so I—very respectfully— decide to sidle us to the couch. I need to remove my hands from her body as quickly as possible and get as far away from this woman as I can. "Cool if I grab you some water?"

She nods again, and I'm starting to wonder why she's suddenly mute. While I head to the kitchen, I debate asking her whether my presence makes her uncomfortable. I am a stranger in her home after all. It's the only logical conclusion I can come up with as to why she isn't speaking.

"Where's Zoe?" I hear Blake ask as she lets go of Phoebe, who immediately plops down on the couch, almost landing on Eve.

"Bathroom." She giggles and points to the hallway. Then I watch from the kitchen as her body turns to complete jelly, sinking until her head is in Eve's lap. "I love you, Evie."

"I love you too, Phoebz." Eve sighs contentedly as a small smile creeps up one corner of her mouth. She runs her hand gently through Phoebe's hair as she closes her eyes in bliss before hiccupping with her entire body.

I quirk a smile as I watch this heartfelt moment unravel. I'm not quite sure how Blake can view this person as horrible. The love between these two friends is something completely indescribable. Something immovable. Regardless of whatever squabble these two may have experienced, this friendship isn't going anywhere. And I can't see how this woman could possibly be mistaken as homophobic. Phoebe's arm is between her legs, constricting her thigh, and this woman doesn't seem the least bit concerned. Maybe drunk Eve is completely different from sober Eve?

I almost don't hear Phoebe's gentle whisper of reassurance to her best friend. "You'll find it, you know."

"Find what?" Eve asks.

"'The One.'" Phoebe bends her fingers into quotations.

"I don't know, Phoebz." Eve practically snorts. "I'm starting to think my soulmate died in the womb or something." Her eyes begin to glisten as my chest aches. The familiar loneliness living rent-free within my gut bubbles up like it always does around this subject. Seeing her reaction to it is something I understand all too well.

"No," Phoebe breathes. "God had a plan for them that didn't involve a soulmate. That's why He called them home so soon."

Is that what He does? All-seeing Phoebe, do tell me more about the inner workings of God. Explain to me why He would make addicts and why—shut up, Dyl. Shut up.

"If not in the womb, maybe they died years ago, and I'm too late." I watch as a single tear escapes Eve's eye, trailing slowly down her freckled cheek, and I can't take it. I can't listen to any more of this. Seeing that tear fall errantly from the lid she's struggling to keep it in makes me want to walk over, set the cup down, and wrap her in my arms. Blanket her in the embrace of my own loneliness and hope that it could be enough to remove this shitty feeling from existence.

Instead, I walk over and hand her the glass. "Here you go." She wipes at her cheek quickly, as if embarrassed to have emotions, hoping I didn't see it.

"Thank you." She smiles, but her eyes are filled with so much pain, it's hard for me to look away. I know that pain. I know that feeling. I feel it every single day. A pain you mask with a smile. Fill with distractions. It's not the blue/gray rings shifting in and out of focus that I see as I peer into her eyes; it's me. It's my pain. It's the lies I tell myself in order to fake it for everyone around me. I see it, and I know it's not a projection. Is it?

"Dylan, I'munna need your help in here," Blake calls from the bathroom.

"Gotcha," I say, ripping our souls apart like a band-aid from skin to bolt off to find Blake.

"Not dead," I hear Phoebe groan as I walk down the hallway to the bathroom. "Just not ready for you yet."

Meet The Author

J. Fez is an award winning poet and lesbian romance author known for her raw, intense emotional depth and character development. She strives to enlighten readers with deep inner monologues meant to elicit questions about other ways of life. Born into a military family, she moved around quite frequently before finally settling into a house in the middle of nowhere thirty minutes from anything but corn in Kansas for most of her formative years. She lives with her wife, son and miniature zoo comprised of two completely opposite dogs, a cat secretly plotting her demise, a bearded dragon always side eyeing and judging her, and one fish that is just happy to be in a big tank instead of a cup.

When she isn't writing spicy, thought-provoking characters, J. Fez can be found trying to make people smile with her bad dad jokes or sweeping for the hundredth time this week because her dogs never stop shedding but still somehow have fur.

www.ingramcontent.com/pod-product-compliance
Lightning Source LLC
Chambersburg PA
CBHW010651100726
47901CB00012B/2512